BY HOOK
OR BY CROOK

BY HOOK OR BY CROOK

AND 27 MORE OF THE BEST
CRIME+
MYSTERY
STORIES OF THE YEAR

EDITED BY
**Ed Gorman and
Martin H. Greenberg**

TYRUS
BOOKS

Published by
TYRUS BOOKS
1213 N. Sherman Ave. #306
Madison, WI 53704
www.tyrusbooks.com

This is a work of fiction.
Any similarities to people or places,
living or dead, is purely coincidental.

Library of Congress Cataloging-In-Publication Data has been applied for.

12 11 10 09 08   1 2 3 4 5 6 7 8 9 10

978-1-935562-31-3 (hardcover)

CONTENTS

COPYRIGHTS

THE MYSTERY IN 2009

By Jon L. Breen

Call 2009 the Year of Landmark Anniversaries. Eighty years have passed since the September 1929 issue of *Black Mask* presented the first installment of a serial that would become one of the most influential detective novels in history, Dashiell Hammett's *The Maltese Falcon*. Whether intended to mark that occasion or not, two of the best novels of the year paid homage to Hammett, one to his style and fictional world and one to his personal character. (See Gores and Atkins respectively in the best-of-the-year list below.) A key reference book on Hammett's San Francisco had a new and expanded edition: Don Herron's *The Dashiell Hammett Tour: Thirtieth Anniversary Guidebook* (Vince Emery).

The bicentennial of Edgar Allan Poe's birth in 1809 was celebrated throughout the year in Baltimore with such events as a Poe funeral reenactment, various theatrical presentations, and The Cask of Amontillado Wine Tasting, apparently successful enough to be repeated in 2010. The Mystery Writers of America recognized the birthday with two volumes: *In the Shadow of the Master* (William Morrow), edited by Michael Connelly, which gathered some of Poe's best-known tales, accompanied by essays from present-day writers influenced by the father of the detective story; and *On a Raven's Wing*, edited by Stuart Kaminsky, featuring homages to Poe by many of today's top writers.

Speaking of Poe and MWA, the organization's leadership made a surprising decision regarding one of his namesake Edgar Awards. There is no shortage of awards in the mystery genre, as the compilation at the end of this piece demonstrates. While there may be no need to add more, those that are unique, prestigious, and/or long-standing ought to be maintained. The Edgar for Best Motion Picture, given every year save two since 1946, has been scuttled for reasons never revealed to the membership.

The first film honored, in 1946, was the previous year's *Murder, My Sweet*, scripted by John Paxton from Raymond Chandler's novel *Farewell, My Lovely*. Subsequent years honored such classic films as *The Asphalt Jungle*, *Rear Window*, *12 Angry Men*, *Psycho*, *The French Connection*, *The Last of Sheila*, *Chinatown*, *Witness*, *The Silence of the Lambs*, *Pulp Fiction*, and *L.A. Confidential*, and such screenwriters as Donald E. Westlake, Dennis Potter, Joseph Wambaugh, Michael Crichton, William Goldman, and Truman Capote. Honored for best of 2008, from a very strong list of nominees, was Martin McDonagh's script for *In Bruges*. But there will be no Edgar Award for the best of 2009, the award having been put "on hiatus" by the MWA Board of Directors without explanation.

Recent years have taken an unusually heavy toll on the crime fiction community. In reviewing 2008, I noted the passing of no fewer than five MWA Grand Masters. In 2009, they were joined by another from that exclusive club, the prolific and versatile Stuart M.

Kaminsky, and in early 2010 by two more, Dick Francis and Robert B. Parker.

Other mystery-world deaths in 2009 included novelists William Tapply, Barbara Parker, Robert Terrall, Lyn Hamilton, Celia Fremlin, and Sister Carol Anne O'Marie, and short-story specialists Barbara Callahan and Dick Stodghill. An important figure in mystery scholarship, Ray B. Browne, a pioneer of the study of popular culture as writer, publisher, and Bowling Green University professor, died at age eighty-seven.

Best Novels of the Year 2009

Before unveiling the fifteen best new books I read and reviewed during the year, here's the boilerplate disclaimer: I don't pretend to cover the whole field—no single reviewer does—but if you have a better list of fifteen, I'd love to see it.

- Ace Atkins, *Devil's Garden* (Putnam). San Francisco of the 1920s and the complex personalities of Pinkerton operative Dashiell Hammett and manslaughter suspect Roscoe (Fatty) Arbuckle are central to a remarkable fictionalization.
- Gyles Brandreth, *Oscar Wilde and the Dead Man's Smile* (Touchstone). The third novel casting the 1890s celebrity playwright as sleuth is a throwback to Golden Age puzzle-spinning with a downright Queenian finale.
- Michael Connelly, *Nine Dragons* (Little, Brown). L.A cop Harry Bosch travels to Hong Kong in one of his best cases. Connelly's other 2009 book, *The Scarecrow* (Little, Brown) is notable for a grim picture of the declining newspaper business.
- Mat Coward, *Acts of Destruction* (Alia Mondo). While it's unusual to cover a self-published British novel here, Coward's near-

future police procedural, offering stimulating ideas, good modular plotting, and trademark humor, deserves to be read, and American fans of his work need to know about it.

• Martin Edwards, *Dancing for the Hangman* (Five Star). Hawley Harvey Crippen's first person account is one of the best fictionalizations of a classic criminal case in memory.

• Hallie Ephron, *Never Tell a Lie* (William Morrow). Constructed as well as a top-notch Mary Higgins Clark, this prime contribution to the am-I-married-to-a-murderer subgenre is also distinguished for its style.

• Lyndsay Faye, *Dust and Shadow* (Simon & Schuster). Of all the attempts to put Sherlock Holmes on the trail of Jack the Ripper, this may well be the best.

• Joe Gores, *Spade & Archer* (Knopf). The prequel to *The Maltese Falcon* perfectly recaptures Hammett's objective narrative style.

• Ed Gorman, *The Midnight Room* (Leisure). The small-town Midwestern milieu is brilliantly depicted in a deliberate throwback to the great days of paperback originals.

• John Hart, *The Last Child* (Minotaur). The tale of a rural North Carolina teenager obsessed with the murder of his sister was a deserving Edgar nominee.

• Margaret Lawrence, *Roanoke* (Delacorte). One of the best historical mystery writers offers a possible solution to a mystery of colonial America in the Elizabethan era.

• Leonardo Padura, *Havana Fever*, translated from the Spanish by Peter Bush (Bitter Lemon). Havana cop turned book scout Mario Conde is featured in one of the most consistently excellent series in the current market.

• Anne Perry, *Execution Dock* (Ballantine). Set in 1860 London, this was the best book in some time about amnesiac cop William Monk and wife Hester.

• Andrew Taylor, *Bleeding Heart Square* (Hyperion). Politics and everyday life of 1934 London come to life in a beautifully structured historical mystery.

• Joseph Teller, *Bronx Justice* (MIRA). New life for the courtroom drama from one of the best lawyer-writers to enter the legal mystery subgenre.

Sub-Genres

Private eyes. Sleuths for hire in commendable action included a pair of San Franciscans, Bill Pronzini's Nameless Detective in *Schemers* (Forge) and Mark Coggins's August Riordan in *The Big Wake-Up* (Bleak House), plus Sharon Fiffer's Illinois part-timer Jane Wheel in *Scary Stuff* (Minotaur) and Las Vegas's Trevor Oaks, whose first book-length case is Percy Spurlark Parker's *The Good-Looking Dead Guy* (PublishAmerica). Ten years after his debut, Russell Atwood's Payton Sherwood finally had a second case in *Losers Live Longer* (Hard Case Crime). TV's Adrian Monk, usually a police consultant, briefly turns PI in Lee Goldberg's *Mr. Monk and the Dirty Cop* (Penguin Putnam).

Amateur sleuths. Puzzle Lady Cora Felton in Parnell Hall's *Dead Man's Puzzle* (Minotaur) and Skeleton Detective Gideon Oliver in Aaron Elkins's *Skull Duggery* (Berkley) kept alive the spirit of fair-play puzzle spinning. In Yuletide action were Maine shopkeeper Liss Mac-Crimmon in Kaitlyn Dunnett's *A Wee Christmas Homicide* (Kensington), New Jersey reporter Cassie O'Malley in Jeff Markowitz's *It's Beginning to Look a Lot Like Murder* (Five Star), and early-teen Gracie Phipps (later a servant to Thomas and Charlotte Pitt) in Anne Perry's Victorian-era *A Christmas Promise* (Ballantine). Movie buffs welcomed the reappearance of film detective Valentino in Loren D. Estleman's *Alone* (Forge). *The Today Show's* Al Roker and frequent

celebrity collaborator Dick Lochte introduced chef and TV personality Billy Blessing in *The Morning Show Murders* (Delacorte).

Police. Cops walking their beats included Texas sheriff Dan
Rhodes in Bill Crider's *Murder in Four Parts* (Minotaur), Sicily's
Salvo Montalbano in Andrea Camilleri's *August Heat* (Penguin),
translated from the Italian by Stephen Sartarelli, Konrad Sejer, and
Jacob Scarre in Karin Fossum's *The Water's Edge* (Houghton Mifflin),
translated from the Norwegian by Charlotte Barslund, and (in a
1960 prequel to his previously recorded cases) one of the great series
police in H.R.F. Keating's *Inspector Ghote's First Case* (Minotaur).

Lawyers. A Manhattan insurance lawyer figured in Colin Har-
rison's *Risk* (Picador), a shortish novel that began life as a *New York
Times Magazine* serial. The Christian market provided a good legal
mystery in Randy Singer's *The Justice Game* (Tyndale), while Robert
Rotenberg's *Old City Hall* (Sarah Crichton/Farrar, Straus Giroux)
was a strong Canadian debut. Series advocates in good form were
David Rosenfelt's New Jerseyite Andy Carpenter in *New Tricks* (Grand
Central), Philip Margolin's Oregonian Amanda Jaffe in *Fugitive*
(Harper), Margaret Maron's North Carolinian judge Deborah Knott
in *Sand Sharks* (Grand Central), and William Bernhardt's Oklahoma
Senator Ben Perkins, happily back in the courtroom in *Capitol Offense*
(Ballantine). On the other hand, Steve Martini's Californian Paul
Madriani appears regrettably poised to desert the courtroom for more
world-shattering events in *Guardian of Lies* (William Morrow).

Historicals. Michael Jecks's team of Sir Baldwin Furnshill and
Bailiff Simon Puttock carried on in 1320s England in *The Prophecy
of Death* and *The King of Thieves* (both Headline/Trafalgar Square).
Other past sleuths with strong new cases included Yashim, eunuch-
detective of nineteenth century Turkey, in Jason Goodwin's *The
Bellini Card* (Sarah Crichton/Farrar, Straus and Giroux), Chaucer's

Canterbury pilgrims in P.C. Doherty's *A Haunt of Murder* (Minotaur), and Alan Gordon's thirteenth century Fools Guild members in *The Parisian Prodigal* (Minotaur). Barbara Hamilton (pseudonym of Barbara Hambly) launched Abigail Adams as series sleuth in *The Ninth Daughter* (Berkley).

Criminals. Sadly, the late Donald E. Westlake's *Get Real* (Grand Central) is presumably the last of the comic novels about ill-starred crook John Dortmunder. Also active on the wrong side of the law was Max Allan Collins's killer-for-hire in *Quarry in the Middle* (Hard Case Crime).

Thrillers. It's a long list, but remember my convenient definition: anything that doesn't fit the other subgenres. Jeffery Deaver and other members of the International Thriller Writers collaborated efficiently on the two short novels in *Watchlist* (Vanguard). Kenneth Abel's *Down in the Flood* (Minotaur) must rank with the best Hurricane Katrina novels. In reviewing Dean Koontz's *Relentless* (Bantam), I enumerated the mix of elements—"suspense, horror, satire, conspiracy thriller, science fiction, fantasy, spiritual allegory"—that make its author a one-of-a-kind entertainer. Another genre-bender is George Zebrowski's *Empties* (Golden Gryphon), enjoyably combining police procedural, romantic suspense, science fiction, fantasy, fiction noir, and horror. Laura Lippman's *Life Sentences* (William Morrow), Carmen Posadas's *Child's Play* (Harper), translated from the Spanish by Nick Caistor and Amanda Hopkinson, Rhodi Hawk's *A Twisted Ladder* (Forge), and Thomas H. Cook's *The Fate of Katherine Carr* (Houghton Mifflin Harcourt) all describe present-day investigations of past mysteries. Thomas B. Sawyer's *No Place to Run* (Sterling & Ross) is a superbly managed novel advancing controversial 9/11 conspiracy theories. In C.J. Box's *Three Weeks to Say Goodbye* (Minotaur), a couple is threatened with the loss of their adopted baby. Mariko Koike's disturbing and unclassifiable *The Cat in the Coffin* (Vertical), translated from the Japanese by Deborah Boliver Boehm, is not the romantic suspense it for a time appears to be. Tanguy Viel's brief and unconventional *Beyond Suspicion* (New Press), translated from the French by Linda Coverdale, led me to evoke James M. Cain and Hitchcock. Domenico Starnone's puzzle-box novel *First Execution* (Europa), translated from the Italian by Antony Shugaar, combines reality and fiction in a way that isn't for everybody but is recommended to those who don't mind a lack of pat answers.

Short Stories

Single-author short story collections, though less plentiful than in some recent years, included excellent work. Donald Thomas's *Sherlock Holmes and the King's Evil* (Pegasus) is another triumph for the supreme master of Baker Street pastiche. John C. Boland writes for digests, not pulps, but we won't hold that against *30 Years in the Pulps* (Outskirts). Two mainstream bestsellers had new collections, John Grisham's first, *Ford County: Stories* (Doubleday), and Joyce Carol Oates's umpty-umpth, *Dear Husband* (Ecco). Sleuths known mostly for book-length cases included the title character in Ralph McInerny's *The Wisdom of Father Dowling* (Five Star), Charlaine Harris's Sookie Stackhouse in *A Touch of Dead* (Ace), and Gar Anthony Haywood's Aaron Gunner in *Lyrics for the Blues* (A.S.A.P.). *A Rumpole Christmas* (Viking) is presumably the final collection about John Mortimer's beloved Old Bailey hack. Most of Peter Robinson's *The Price of Love and Other Stories* (William Morrow) concerned Yorkshire cop Alan Banks, but there were non-series stories as well. Of some criminous interest were the mixed collections *Visions* (Mythos) by Richard A. Lupoff; F. Paul Wilson's *Aftershock & Others: 19 Oddities* (Forge); and Lewis Shiner's *Collected Stories* (Subterranean).

Crippen & Landru published James Powell's *A Pocketful of Noses: Stories of One Ganelon or Another* and Robert Silverberg and Randall Garrett's *A Little Intelligence and Other Stories* (writing as Robert Randall), while extending its Lost Classics series with Victor Canning's *The Minerva Club, the Department of Patterns, and Others* and collecting some vintage 1940s radio scripts in Anthony Boucher and Denis Green's *The Casebook of Gregory Hood*. Also celebrating the past, *The Strange Adventures of Mr. Andrew Hawthorn and Other Stories* (Penguin Classics) gathered the short stories of John Buchan, with an introduction by Giles Foden, while L. Ron Hubbard's *Wind-Gone-Mad* (Galaxy) combined a novella with two short stories by the pulp-magazine master.

Original multi-author theme-oriented anthologies continue to be plentiful. The title of *Two of the Deadliest* (Harper), edited by Elizabeth George, referred to lust and greed. The team of Martin H. Greenberg, Jon L. Lellenberg, and Daniel Stashower edited *Sherlock Holmes in America* (Skyhorse). The annual Mystery Writers of America anthology, *The Prosecution Rests* (Little, Brown), edited by Linda Fairstein, centered on the justice system. Mr. Keen, Tracer of Lost Persons, a radio sleuth remembered by a few of us old-timers, turned up in two quite different new stories, one in *It's That Time Again*, Volume 4 (BearManor), edited by Jim Harmon, composed of mysteries in the worlds of old radio shows, and the other in *Sex, Lies and Private Eyes* (Moonstone), edited by Joe Gentile and Richard Dean Starr, mostly new stories about sleuths famous from print, radio, TV, and comics.

The second anthology of the International Thriller Writers was *Thriller 2* (MIRA), edited by Clive Cussler. The Crime Writers Association's *Criminal Tendencies* (Crème de la Crime/Dufour), edited by Lynne Patrick, combined originals and reprints and benefitted breast cancer research. The five historical specialists known as The Medieval

Murderers produced their fifth story collection (or is it group novel?), *King Arthur's Bones* (Simon and Schuster UK/Trafalgar Square).

Of course, there were more additions to Akashic Press's ongoing noir series: *Phoenix Noir*, edited by Patrick Millikin; *Delhi Noir*, edited by Hirsh Sawhney; and *Seattle Noir*, edited by Curt Colbert. Also on the dark side were *Sex, Thugs, and Rock & Roll* (Kensington), edited by Todd Robinson of Thuglit.com, and *Uncage Me* (Bleak House), edited by Jen Jordan.

It was a stronger than average year for reprint anthologies. The precursor to the present volume, *Between the Dark and the Daylight and 27 More of the Best Crime and Mystery Stories of the Year* (Tyrus), edited by Ed Gorman and Martin H. Greenberg, and *The Best American Mystery Stories 2009* (Houghton Mifflin), from guest editor Jeffery Deaver and series editor Otto Penzler, agreed on only two stories, N.J. Ayres's "Rust" and Michael Connelly's "Father's Day." As has often been the case, Joyce Carol Oates made both volumes with different stories, "The First Husband" for Gorman/Greenberg, "Dear Husband" for Penzler/Deaver. Kristine Kathryn Rusch completed a similar double with "Patriotic Gestures" for G/G and "G-Men" for P/D. G/G included the Edgar winner, T. Jefferson Parker's "Skinhead Central," and three of the other nominees: Sean Chercover's "A Sleep Not Unlike Death," Dominique Mainard's "La Vie En Rose," and David Edgerley Gates's "Skin and Bones."

Another project of prolific anthologist Penzler was the massive *The Vampire Archives* (Vintage/Black Lizard). Michael Sims edited *The Penguin Book of Gaslight Crime* (Penguin). Peter Washington edited the no-frills *Detective Stories* (Everyman's Pocket Classics/Knopf). Maxim Jakubowski gathered contemporary tales from around the globe in *The Mammoth Book of Best British Mysteries* (Running Press). A Sherlockian anthology of note, often leaning toward the supernatural, was *The Improbable Adventures of Sherlock Holmes* (Night Shade), edited by John Joseph Adams. Technically a reprint anthology but offering stories new to English-language readers was *Sherlock Holmes in Russia* (Hale/Trafalgar), edited and translated by Alex Auswaks.

Reference Books and Secondary Sources

It was another strong year for books about mystery and detective fiction.

Given its author's prominence and the quality of its writing and critical acumen, the book of the year in the field was undoubtedly P.D. James's *Talking About Detective Fiction* (Knopf). Other good Edgar nominees in the biographical/critical category were Lisa Rogak's *Haunted Heart: The Life and Times of Stephen King* (Dunne/St. Martin's) and *The Lineup: The World's Greatest Crime Writers Tell the Inside Story of Their Greatest Detectives* (Little, Brown), edited by Otto Penzler. Two nominees not seen by me were *The Stephen King Illustrated Companion* (Fall River) by Bev Vincent, and *The Talented Miss Highsmith: The Secret Life and Serious Art of Patricia Highsmith* (St. Martin's) by Joan Schenkar.

An important albeit expensive essay collection, groundbreaking as an English-language source, was *French Crime Fiction* (University of Wales Press), edited by Claire Gorrara. Craig McDonald's *Rogue Males: Conversations & Confrontations About the Writing Life* (Bleak House) is a good addition to the interview shelf, while Kate Macdonald's *John Buchan: A Companion to the Mystery Fiction* (McFarland) is an unusually fine single-author reference, encompassing much more than the subtitle suggests. Though more about race walking than mystery fiction, Lawrence Block's *Step by Step: A Pedestrian Memoir* (William Morrow) is an excellent autobiographical piece by one of the greatest living writers of crime fiction.

For certain icons, the market always has room for another secondary source. Hilary Macaskill's lavish coffee-table book *Agatha Christie at Home* (Frances Lincoln), is a nice addition to the buckling shelf, but less fresh ground was dug in Richard Hack's *Duchess of Death: The Unauthorized Biography of Agatha Christie* (Phoenix). Enjoyable but inessential was Catherine Corman's photographic collection *Daylight Noir: Raymond Chandler's Imagined City* (Charta). Devotees of Arthur Conan Doyle's most famous creation welcomed the second edition of Christopher Redmond's useful and wide-ranging reference *Sherlock Holmes Handbook* (Dundurn).

Among the more specialized items were James E. Keirans' *John Dickson Carr in Paperback: An English Language Bibliography* (CADS), Bradley Mengel's *Serial Vigilantes of Paperback Fiction: An Encyclopedia from Able Team to Z-Comm* (McFarland); John C. Fredriksen's *Honey West* (BearManor), concentrating on the TV show rather than the books; *Murder 101: Essays on the Teaching of Detective Fiction* (McFarland), edited by Edward J. Reilly; and my most gratefully received 2009 reference source, Ken Wlaschin's *Silent Mystery and Detective Movies: A Comprehensive Filmography* (McFarland).

A Sense of History

Mystery fiction continues to honor its past, mostly through the efforts of small publishers, but sometimes in a questionable way. William MacHarg (1872–1951) and Edwin Balmer (1883–1959) hold a special place in detective fiction history as the authors of the 1910 collection *The Achievements of Luther Trant*, credited with introducing concepts of psychology to fictional crime detection. On his own, MacHarg created the police stories collected in *The Affairs of O'Malley* (1940), while Balmer co-wrote with Philip Wylie the science-fiction classic *When Worlds Collide* (1933). MacHarg and Balmer also collaborated on a 1917 mystery novel, *The Indian Drum*, set on Michigan's Upper Peninsula. In 1996, Donald A. Johnston rewrote their novel, which was published under the title *The Echoes of L'Arbre Croche* with a credit to MacHarg and Balmer on the verso of the title page. In an interview with *The Northern Michigan Journal*, the author justified his rewrite thus: "The book had been out of print for generations and both [my copy and a friend's copy] were falling apart. The acid content of the paper of *The Indian Drum* is such that I expect by the turn of the century, there will be no copies left. Reading it, I just found too many words missing." In 2009, University of Michigan Press published a new edition of Johnston's rewrite, this time with the small-print credit to the original authors promoted to the title page.

The novel is presumably in the public domain, and there may be no legal impediment to the publication of a lightly rewritten (and not improved) version. But MacHarg and Balmer deserve honor and respect for their work, not an attempt to have it erased from literary history. If *The Indian Drum* is worth reprinting for its view of the Upper Peninsula, why not a new edition of the original novel, with annotations and a scholarly introduction, rather than an inept rewrite that robs the original authors of their proper credit?

More conventional reprints included Gil Brewer's 1952 paperback original *Flight to Darkness* (New Pulp Press), H.F. Heard's pioneering 1941 Sherlockian pastiche *A Taste of Honey* (Blue Dolphin), and the first three in a new series of Holmes revivals from Titan Books, Daniel Stashower's *The Ectoplasmic Man* (1985) and two by David Stuart Davies.

Rue Morgue Press continued its admirable revival program of mostly traditional mysteries, including Eilis Dillon's *Death at Crane's*

Court (1953), the first American edition of Gladys Mitchell's athletics-themed 1930 novel *The Longer Bodies*, and additional titles by Catherine Aird, Delano Ames, Manning Coles, and Michael Gilbert. On the more hardboiled side, Stark House offered two novels to a volume by Benjamin Appel (*Sweet Money Girl* and *Life and Death of a Tough Guy*) and W.R. Burnett (*It's Always Four O'Clock* and *Iron Man*), plus a Harry Whittington threesome comprised of *To Find Cora, Like Mink Like Murder*, and *Body and Passion*.

Hard Case Crime continued its proclivity for publishing stunts with a new edition of Arthur Conan Doyle's final Sherlock Holmes novel *The Valley of Fear*, with misleading packaging in parody of 1950s paperback practice, and a reprint of Robert B. Parker's *Passport to Peril* (1951). (This is Robert Bogardus Parker, not the late creator of Spenser.) Hard Case also repackaged Donald E. Westlake's Edgar-nominated 1960 debut *The Mercenaries* as *The Cutie* and presented first editions of novels not published in their authors' lifetime: Lester Dent's *Honey in His Mouth* and Roger Zelazny's *The Dead Man's Brother*.

Ramble House continued to revive out-of-print mysteries, some by American masters like Ed Gorman, others by British writers never before published in the U.S., like Rupert Penny. Among the offerings from Surinam Turtle Press, Richard A. Lupoff's Ramble House subsidiary, was Mack Reynolds's 1951 first novel, the science fictional mystery *The Case of the Little Green Men*.

At the Movies

In last year's volume, I called 2008 "a weaker than average year for motion pictures generally" though "the crop of crime films was terrific." Well, 2009 was even worse and dragged down the crime crop as well. However, if there had been a Best Motion Picture Edgar for 2009, the committee could have given it to a potential classic, though it played not the multiplexes but the art houses specializing in independent and foreign-language films: Michael Haneke's *The White Ribbon*, a superb whodunit set in small town Germany in the years before World War I. Another excellent foreign-language film was the very explicitly violent but riveting French prison drama *Un prophète*, directed by Jacques Audiard, who wrote the script with Thomas Bidegain from an original screenplay by Abdel Raouf Dafri and Nicolas Peufaillit.

American films most likely to have filled out the non-existent nominations were Michael Keaton's directorial debut, the low-key hitman drama *The Merry Gentleman*, scripted by Ron Lazzeretti, and Tony Gilroy's story of corporate espionage *Duplicity*. Other criminous features of at least passing interest included Wes Anderson's animated big-caper *Fantastic Mr. Fox*, written with Noah Baumbach from Roald Dahl's book; the Nicolas Cage vehicle *The Bad Lieutenant: Port of Call—New Orleans*, directed by Werner Herzog from William Finkelstein's script and based on a 1992 film written by Victor Argo, Paul Calderon, Abel Ferrara, and Zoe Lund; Lucrecia Martel's French-language psychological thriller *The Headless Woman*; Michael Mann's Dillinger biography *Public Enemies*, adapted with Ronan Bennett and Ann Biderman from Bryan Burrough's book *Public Enemies: America's Greatest Crime Wave and the Birth of the FBI, 1933-34*; and the remake of *The Taking of Pelham 123*, directed by Tony Scott from Brian Helgeland's screenplay, based on John Godey's novel.

No, I haven't forgotten the controversial *Sherlock Holmes*, directed by Guy Ritchie with Robert Downey Jr. in the title role, though I'd like to.

Award Winners

Awards tied to publishers' contests, those limited to a geographical region smaller than a country, those awarded for works in languages other than English (with the exception of the Crime Writers of Canada's nod to their French compatriots), and those confined to works from a single periodical have been omitted. All were awarded in 2009 for material published in 2008. Gratitude is again extended to all the websites that keep track of these things, with a special nod to Jiro Kimura's Gumshoe Site.

Edgar Allan Poe Awards (Mystery Writers of America)

Best novel: C.J. Box, *Blue Heaven* (St. Martin's Minotaur)

Best first novel by an American author: Francie Lin, *The Foreigner* (Picador)

Best original paperback: Meg Gardiner, *China Lake* (NAL/Obsidian)

Best fact crime book: Howard Blum, *American Lightning: Terror, Mystery, the Birth of Hollywood, and the Crime of the Century* (Crown)

Best critical/biographical work: Harry Lee Poe, *Edgar Allan Poe: An Illustrated Companion to His Tell-Tale Stories* (Metro)

Best short story: T. Jefferson Parker, "Skinhead Central" (*The Blue Religion*, Little, Brown)

Best young adult mystery: John Green, *Paper Towns* (Dutton)

Best juvenile mystery: Tony Abbott, *The Postcard* (Little, Brown)

Best play: Ifa Bayeza, *The Ballad of Emmett Till* (Goodman Theatre, Chicago)

Best television episode teleplay: Patrick Harbinson, "Prayer of the Bone" (*Wire in the Blood*, BBC America)

Best motion picture screenplay: Martin McDonagh, *In Bruges* (Focus Features)

Grand Master: James Lee Burke and Sue Grafton

Robert L. Fish award (best first story): Joseph Guglielmelli, "Buckner's Error" (*Queens Noir*, Akashic)

Raven: Edgar Allan Poe Society (Baltimore, Maryland) and Poe House (Baltimore, Maryland)

Mary Higgins Clark Award: Bill Floyd, *The Killer's Wife* (St. Martin's Minotaur)

Agatha Awards (Malice Domestic Mystery Convention)

Best novel: Louise Penny, *The Cruelest Month* (Minotaur)

Best first novel: G. M. Malliet, *Death of a Cozy Writer* (Midnight Ink)

Best short story: Dana Cameron, "The Night Things Changed" (*Wolfsbane and Mistletoe*, Penguin)

Best nonfiction: Kathy Lynn Emerson, *How to Write Killer Historical Mysteries* (Perseverance)

Best Children's/Young Adult: Chris Grabenstein, *The Crossroads* (Random House)

Lifetime Achievement Award: Anne Perry

Poirot Award: Kate Stine and Brian Skupin, publishers of *Mystery Scene*

Dagger Awards (Crime Writers' Association, Great Britain)

Gold Dagger: William Brodrick, *A Whispered Name* (Little, Brown)

International Dagger: Fred Vargas, *The Chalk Circle Man* (Harvill Secker)

Ian Fleming Steel Dagger: John Hart, *The Last Child* (John Murray)

Best short story: Sean Chercover, "One Serving of Bad Luck" (*Killer Year*, MIRA)

John Creasey New Blood Dagger: Johan Theorin, *Echoes From the Dead* (Doubleday)

Film Dagger: *Gran Torino* (Warner Bros.)

TV Dagger: *Red Riding* (Channel 4 Films; Channel 4)

International TV Dagger: *The Wire* (HBO; BBC Two)

Best Actress Dagger: Juliet Stevenson for *Place of Execution* (Coastal Productions; ITV1)

Best Actor Dagger: Dominic West for *The Wire* (HBO; BBC Two)

Bestseller Dagger: Harlan Coben

Hall of Fame: Colin Dexter, Lynda La Plante, Ian Rankin, and Val McDermid

Diamond Dagger: Andrew Taylor

Ellis Peters Award Historical Dagger: Philip Kerr, *If the Dead Rise Not* (Quercus)

Dagger in the Library (voted by librarians for a body of work): Colin Cotterill

Debut Dagger (for unpublished writers): Catherine O'Keefe, *The Pathologist*

Anthony Awards (Bouchercon World Mystery Convention)

Best novel: Michael Connelly, *The Brass Verdict* (Little, Brown)

Best first novel: Stieg Larsson, *The Girl With the Dragon Tattoo* (Knopf)

Best paperback original: Julie Hyzy, *State of the Onion* (Berkley)

Best short story: Sean Chercover, "A Sleep Not Unlike Death" (*Hardcore Hardboiled*, Kensington)

Best critical nonfiction work: Jeffrey Marks, *Anthony Boucher: A Bio-bibliography* (McFarland)

Best children's/young adult novel: Chris Grabenstein, *The Crossroads* (Random House)

Best cover art: Stieg Larsson, *The Girl With the Dragon Tattoo* (Knopf), designed by Peter Mendelsund

Special Services Award: Jon and Ruth Jordan

Shamus Awards (Private Eye Writers of America)

Best hardcover novel: Reed Farrel Coleman, *Empty Ever After* (Bleak House)

Best first novel: Ian Vasquez, *In the Heat* (St. Martin's Minotaur)

Best original paperback novel: Lori Armstrong, *Snow Blind* (Medallion)

Best short story: Mitch Alderman, "Family Values" (*Alfred Hitchcock's Mystery Magazine*, June)

The Eye (life achievement): Robert J. Randisi

Hammer Award (for a memorable private eye character or series): Matt Scudder (created by Lawrence Block)

Macavity Awards (Mystery Readers International)

Best novel: Deborah Crombie, *Where Memories Lie* (William Morrow)

Best first novel: Stieg Larsson, *The Girl With the Dragon Tattoo* (Knopf)

Best nonfiction: Frankie Y. Bailey, *African American Mystery Writers: A Historical and Thematic Study* (McFarland)

Best short story: Dana Cameron, "The Night Things Changed" (*Wolfsbane and Mistletoe*, Penguin)

Sue Feder Historical Mystery Award: Rhys Bowen, *A Royal Pain* (Berkley)

Barry Awards (*Deadly Pleasures* and *Mystery News*)

Best novel: Arnaldur Indridason, *The Draining Lake* (Minotaur)

Best first novel: Tom Rob Smith, *Child 44* (Grand Central)

Best British novel: Stieg Larsson, *The Girl With the Dragon Tatoo* (MacLehose/Quercus)

Best paperback original: Julie Hyzy, *State of the Onion* (Berkley)

Best thriller: Brett Battles, *The Deceived* (Delacorte)

Best short story: James O. Born, "The Drought" (*The Blue Religion*, Little, Brown)

Don Sandstrom Memorial Award for Lifetime Achievement in Mystery Fandom: Art Scott

Arthur Ellis Awards (Crime Writers of Canada)

Best novel: Linwood Barclay, *Too Close to Home* (Bantam)

Best first novel: Howard Shrier, *Buffalo Jump* (Vintage Canada)

Best nonfiction: Michael Calce and Craig Silverman, *Mafiaboy: How I Cracked the Internet and Why It's Still Broken* (Penguin Canada)

Best juvenile novel: Sharon E. McKay, *War Brothers* (Penguin Canada)

Best short story: Pasha Malla, "Filmsong" (*Toronto Noir*, Akashic)

The Unhanged Arthur (best unpublished first crime novel): Douglas A. Moles, *Louder*

Best crime writing in French: Jacques Cote, *Le chemin des brumes* (Alire)

Thriller Awards (International Thriller Writers, Inc.)

Best novel: Jeffery Deaver, *The Bodies Left Behind* (Simon & Schuster)

Best first novel: Tom Rob Smith, *Child 44* (Grand Central)

Best short story: Alexandra Sokoloff, "The Edge of Seventeen" (*The Darker Mask*, Tor)

ThrillerMaster Award: David Morrell

Silver Bullet Award: Brad Meltzer

Silver Bullet Corporate Award: Dollar General Literacy Foundation, for longstanding support of literacy and education

Ned Kelly Awards (Crime Writers' Association of Australia)

Best novel (tie): Peter Corris, *Deep Water* (Allen & Unwin); Kel Robertson, *Smoke and Mirrors* (Ginninderra)

Best first novel: Nick Gadd, *Ghostlines* (Scribe)
Best nonfiction: Chloe Hooper, *The Tall Man* (Penguin)
Best short story (S. D. Harvey Award): Scott McDermott, "Fidget's Farewell,"
Lifetime achievement: Shane Maloney

Left Coast Crime Awards

Lefty (best humorous mystery): Tim Maleeny, *Greasing the Piñata* (Poisoned Pen)
Bruce Alexander Memorial Historical Mystery Award: Kelli Stanley, *Nox Dormienda, A Long Night for Sleeping* (Five Star)
Hawaii Five-O Award (best police procedural): Neil S. Placky, *Mahu Fire* (Alyson)

Strand Critics (The Strand Magazine)

Best novel: Richard Price, *Lush Life* (Farrar, Straus and Giroux)
Best first novel: Tom Rob Smith, *Child 44* (Grand Central)
Lifetime achievement: John Mortimer (posthumously)

Dilys Award (Independent Mystery Booksellers Association)

Sean Chercover, *Trigger City* (William Morrow)

Nero Wolfe Award (Wolfe Pack)

Joseph Teller, *The Tenth Case* (MIRA)

Hammett Prize
(International Association of Crime Writers, North America Branch)

George Pelecanos, *The Turnaround* (Little, Brown)

Los Angeles Times Book Prize

Mystery/Thriller Category

Michael Koryta, *Envy the Night* (St. Martin's Minotaur)

• • •

JON L. BREEN was first published in 1966 with a quiz in *Ellery Queen's Mystery Magazine*, followed the following year by his first short story, a parody of Ed McBain's 87th Precinct. Around a hundred short stories have followed, plus seven novels (with an eighth on the horizon), three story collections, several edited anthologies, three reference books on mystery fiction (two of them Edgar winners), and more book reviews and articles than he can count. In 1977, he became the proprietor of *EQMM*'S "Jury Box" column, which he has contributed ever since, save for a few years in the mid-'80s. He also contributes the "What About Murder?" column to *Mystery Scene* and has been an occasional strictly non-political contributor to *The Weekly Standard*. Retired since the dawn of 2000, he lives happily with his wife, Rita, in Fountain Valley, California.

ANIMAL RESCUE

By Dennis Lehane

DORCHESTER

Bob found the dog in the trash.

It was just after Thanksgiving, the neighborhood gone quiet, hungover. After bartending at Cousin Marv's, Bob sometimes walked the streets. He was big and lumpy and hair had been growing in unlikely places all over his body since his teens. In his twenties, he'd fought against the hair, carrying small clippers in his coat pocket and shaving twice a day. He'd also fought the weight, but during all those years of fighting, no girl who wasn't being paid for it ever showed any interest in him. After a time, he gave up the fight. He lived alone in the house he grew up in, and when it seemed likely to swallow him with its smells and memories and dark couches, the attempts he'd made to escape it—through church socials, lodge picnics, and one horrific mixer thrown by a dating service—had only opened the wound further, left him patching it back up for weeks, cursing himself for hoping.

So he took these walks of his and, if he was lucky, sometimes he forgot people lived any other way. That night, he paused on the sidewalk, feeling the ink sky above him and the cold in his fingers, and he closed his eyes against the evening.

He was used to it. He was used to it. It was okay.

You could make a friend of it, as long as you didn't fight it.

With his eyes closed, he heard it—a worn-out keening accompanied by distant scratching and a sharper, metallic rattling. He opened his eyes. Fifteen feet down the sidewalk, a large metal barrel with a heavy lid shook slightly under the yellow glare of the streetlight, its bottom scraping the sidewalk. He stood over it and heard that keening again, the sound of a creature that was one breath away from deciding it was too hard to take the next, and he pulled off the lid.

He had to remove some things to get to it—a toaster and five thick Yellow Pages, the oldest dating back to 2000. The dog—either a very small one or else a puppy—was down at the bottom, and it scrunched its head into its midsection when the light hit it. It exhaled a soft chug of a whimper and tightened its body even more, its eyes closed to slits. A scrawny thing. Bob could see its ribs. He could see a big crust of dried blood by its ear. No collar. It was brown with a white snout and paws that seemed far too big for its body.

It let out a sharper whimper when Bob reached down, sank his fingers into the nape of its neck, and lifted it out of its own excrement. Bob didn't know dogs too well, but there was no mistaking this one for anything but a boxer. And definitely a puppy, the wide brown eyes opening and looking into his as he held it up before him.

Somewhere, he was sure, two people made love. A man and a woman. Entwined. Behind one of those shades, oranged with light, that looked down on the street. Bob could feel them in there, naked and blessed. And he stood out here in the cold with a near-dead dog staring back at him. The icy sidewalk glinted like new marble, and the wind was dark and gray as slush.

"What do you got there?"

Bob turned, looked up and down the sidewalk.

"I'm up here. And you're in my trash."

She stood on the front porch of the three-decker nearest him. She'd turned the porch light on and stood there shivering, her feet bare. She reached into the pocket of her hoodie and came back with a pack of cigarettes. She watched him as she got one going.

"I found a dog." Bob held it up.

"A what?"

"A dog. A puppy. A boxer, I think."

She coughed out some smoke. "Who puts a dog in a barrel?"

"Right?" he said. "It's bleeding." He took a step toward her stairs and she backed up.

"Who do you know that I would know?" A city girl, not about to just drop her guard around a stranger.

"I don't know," Bob said. "How about Francie Hedges?"

She shook her head. "You know the Sullivans?"

That wouldn't narrow it down. Not around here. You shook a tree, a Sullivan fell out. Followed by a six-pack most times. "I know a bunch."

This was going nowhere, the puppy looking at him, shaking worse than the girl.

"Hey," she said, "you live in this parish?"

"Next one over. St. Theresa's."

"Go to church?"

"Most Sundays."

"So you know Father Pete?"

"Pete Regan," he said, "sure."

She produced a cell phone. "What's your name?"

"Bob," he said. "Bob Saginowski."

Bob waited as she stepped back from the light, phone to one ear, finger pressed into the other. He stared at the puppy. The puppy stared back, like, How did I get here? Bob touched its nose with his index finger. The puppy blinked its huge eyes. For a moment, Bob couldn't recall his sins.

"Nadia," the girl said and stepped back into the light. "Bring him up here, Bob. Pete says hi."

• • •

They washed it in Nadia's sink, dried it off, and brought it to her kitchen table.

Nadia was small. A bumpy red rope of a scar ran across the base of her throat like the smile of a drunk circus clown. She had a tiny moon of a face, savaged by pockmarks, and small, heart-pendant eyes. Shoulders that didn't cut so much as dissolve at the arms. Elbows like flattened beer cans. A yellow bob of hair curled on either side of her face. "It's not a boxer." Her eyes glanced off Bob's face before dropping the puppy back onto her kitchen table. "It's an American Staffordshire terrier."

Bob knew he was supposed to understand something in her tone, but he didn't know what that thing was so he remained silent.

She glanced back up at him after the quiet lasted too long. "A pit bull."

"That's a pit bull?"

She nodded and swabbed the puppy's head wound again. Someone had pummeled it, she told Bob. Probably knocked it unconscious, assumed it was dead, and dumped it.

"Why?" Bob said.

She looked at him, her round eyes getting rounder, wider. "Just because." She shrugged, went back to examining the dog. "I worked at Animal Rescue once. You know the place on Shawmut? As a vet tech. Before I decided it wasn't my thing. They're so hard, this breed …"

"What?"

"To adopt out," she said. "It's very hard to find them a home."

"I don't know about dogs. I never had a dog. I live alone. I was just walking by the barrel." Bob found himself beset by a desperate need to explain himself, explain his life. "I'm just not …" He could hear the wind outside, black and rattling. Rain or bits of hail spit against the windows.

Nadia lifted the puppy's back left paw—the other three paws were brown, but this one was white with peach spots. Then she dropped the paw as if it were contagious. She went back to the head wound, took a closer look at the right ear, a piece missing from the tip that Bob hadn't noticed until now.

"Well," she said, "he'll live. You're gonna need a crate and food and all sorts of stuff."

"No," Bob said. "You don't understand."

She cocked her head, gave him a look that said she understood perfectly.

"I can't. I just found him. I was gonna give him back."

"To whoever beat him, left him for dead?"

"No, no, like, the authorities."

"That would be Animal Rescue," she said. "After they give the owner seven days to reclaim him, they'll—"

"The guy who beat him? He gets a second chance?"

She gave him a half-frown and a nod. "If he doesn't take it," she lifted the puppy's ear, peered in, "chances are this little fella'll be put up for adoption. But it's hard. To find them a home. Pit bulls. More often than not?" She looked at Bob. "More often than not, they're put down."

Bob felt a wave of sadness roll out from her that immediately shamed him. He didn't know how, but he'd caused pain. He'd put some out into the world. He'd let this girl down. "I …" he started. "It's just …"

She glanced up at him. "I'm sorry?"

Bob looked at the puppy. Its eyes were droopy from a long day in the barrel and whoever gave it that wound. It had stopped shivering, though.

"You can take it," Bob said. "You used to work there, like you said. You—"

She shook her head. "My father lives with me. He gets home Sunday night from Foxwoods. He finds a dog in his house? An animal he's allergic to?" She jerked her thumb. "Puppy goes back in the barrel."

"Can you give me til Sunday morning?" Bob wasn't sure how it was the words left his mouth, since he couldn't remember formulating them or even thinking them.

The girl eyed him carefully. "You're not just saying it? Cause, I shit you not, he ain't picked up by Sunday noon, he's back out that door."

"Sunday, then." Bob said the words with a conviction he actually felt. "Sunday, definitely."

"Yeah?" She smiled, and it was a spectacular smile, and Bob saw that the face behind the pockmarks was as spectacular as the smile. Wanting only to be seen. She touched the puppy's nose with her index finger.

"Yeah." Bob felt crazed. He felt light as a communion wafer. "Yeah."

• • •

At Cousin Marv's, where he tended bar 12:00 to 10:00, Wednesday through Sunday, he told Marv all about it. Most people called Marv Cousin Marv out of habit, something that went back to grade school though no one could remember how, but Marv actually was Bob's cousin. On his mother's side.

Cousin Marv had run a crew in the late '80s and early '90s. It had been primarily comprised of guys with interests in the loaning and subsequent debt-repayal side of things, though Marv never turned his nose down at any paying proposition because he believed, to the core of his soul, that those who failed to diversify were always the first to collapse when the wind turned. Like the dinosaurs, he'd say to Bob, when the cavemen came along and invented arrows. Picture the cavemen, he'd say, firing away, and the tyrannosauruses all gucked up in the oil puddles. A tragedy so easily averted.

Marv's crew hadn't been the toughest crew or the smartest or the most successful operating in the neighborhood—not even close—but for a while they got by. Other crews kept nipping at their heels, though, and except for one glaring exception, they'd never been ones to favor violence. Pretty soon, they had to make the decision to yield to crews a lot meaner than they were or duke it out. They took Door Number One.

Marv's income derived from running his bar as a drop. In the new world order—a loose collective of Chechen, Italian, and Irish hard guys—no one wanted to get caught with enough merch or enough money for a case to go Federal. So they kept it out of their offices and out of their homes and they kept it on the move. About every two-three weeks, drops were made at Cousin Marv's, among other establishments. You sat on the drop for a night, two at the most, before some beer-truck driver showed up with the weekend's password and hauled everything back out on a dolly like it was a stack of empty kegs, took it away in a refrigerated semi. The rest of Marv's income derived from being a fence, one of the best in the city, but being a fence in their world (or a drop bar operator for that matter) was like being a mailroom clerk in the straight world—if you were still doing it after thirty, it was all you'd ever do. For Bob, it was a relief—he liked being a bartender and he'd hated that one time they'd had to come heavy. Marv, though, Marv still waited for the golden train to arrive on the golden tracks, take him away from all this. Most times, he pretended to be happy. But Bob knew that the things that haunted Marv were the same things that haunted Bob— the shitty things you did to get ahead. Those things laughed at you if your ambitions failed to amount to much; a successful man could hide his past; an unsuccessful man sat in his.

That morning, Marv was looking a hair on the mournful side, lighting one Camel while the previous one still smoldered, so Bob tried to cheer him up by telling him about his adventure with the dog. Marv didn't seem too interested, and Bob found himself saying "You had to be there" so much, he eventually shut up about it.

Marv said, "Rumor is we're getting the Super Bowl drop."

"No shit?"

If true (an enormous if), this was huge. They worked on commission—one half of one percent of the drop. A Super Bowl drop? It would be like one half of one percent of Exxon.

Nadia's scar flashed in Bob's brain, the redness of it, the thick, ropey texture. "They send extra guys to protect it, you think?"

Marv rolled his eyes. "Why, cause people are just lining up to steal from coked-up Chechnyans."

"Chechens," Bob said.

"But they're from Chechnya."

Bob shrugged. "I think it's like how you don't call people from Ireland Irelandians."

Marv scowled. "Whatever. It means all this hard work we've been doing? It's paid off. Like how Toyota did it, making friends and influencing people."

Bob kept quiet. If they ended up being the drop for the Super Bowl, it was because someone figured out no Feds deemed them important enough to be watched. But in Marv's fantasies, the crew (long since dispersed to straight jobs, jail, or, worse, Connecticut) could regain its glory days, even though those days had lasted about as long as a Swatch. It never occurred to Marv that one day they'd come take everything he had—the fence, the money and merch he kept in the safe in back, hell, the bar probably—just because they were sick of him hanging around, looking at them with needy expectation. It had gotten so every time he talked about the "people he knew," the dreams he had, Bob had to resist the urge to reach for the 9mm they kept beneath the bar and blow his own brains out. Not really—but close sometimes. Man, Marv could wear you out.

A guy stuck his head in the bar, late twenties but with white hair, a white goatee, a silver stud in his ear. He dressed like most kids these days—like shit: pre-ripped jeans, slovenly T-shirt under a faded hoodie under a wrinkled wool topcoat. He didn't cross the threshold, just craned his head in, the cold day pouring in off the sidewalk behind him.

"Help you?" Bob asked.

The guy shook his head, kept staring at the gloomy bar like it was a crystal ball.

"Mind shutting the door?" Marv didn't look up. "Cold out there."

"You serve Zima?" The guy's eyes flew around the bar, up and down, left to right.

Marv looked up now. "Who the fuck would we serve it to—Moesha?"

The guy raised an apologetic hand. "My bad." He left, and the warmth returned with the closing of the door.

Marv said, "You know that kid?"

Bob shook his head. "Mighta seen him around but I can't place him."

"He's a fucking nutbag. Lives in the next parish, probably why you don't know him. You're old school that way, Bob—somebody didn't go to parochial school with you, it's like they don't exist."

Bob couldn't argue. When he'd been a kid, your parish was your country. Everything you needed and needed to know was contained within it. Now that the archdiocese had shuttered half the parishes to pay for the crimes of the kid-diddler priests, Bob couldn't escape the fact that those days of parish dominion, long dwindling, were gone. He was a certain type of guy, of a certain half-generation, an almost generation, and while there were still plenty of them left, they were older, grayer, they had smokers' coughs, they went in for check-ups and never checked back out.

"That kid?" Marv gave Bob a bump of his eyebrows. "They say he killed Richie Whelan back in the day."

"They say?"

"They do."

"Well, then …"

They sat in silence for a bit. Snow-dust blew past the window in the high-pitched breeze. The street signs and window panes rattled, and Bob thought how winter lost any meaning the day you last rode a sled. Any meaning but gray. He looked into the unlit sections of the barroom. The shadows became hospital beds, stooped old widowers shopping for sympathy cards, empty wheelchairs. The wind howled a little sharper.

"This puppy, right?" Bob said. "He's got paws the size of his head. Three are brown but one's white with these little peach-colored spots over the white. And—"

"This thing cook?" Marv said. "Clean the house? I mean, it's a fucking dog."

"Yeah, but it was—" Bob dropped his hands. He didn't know how to explain. "You know that feeling you get sometimes on a really great day? Like, like, the Pats dominate and you took the 'over,' or they cook your steak just right up the Blarney, or, or you just feel good? Like ..." Bob found himself waving his hands again "... good?"

Marv gave him a nod and a tight smile. Went back to his racing sheet.

• • •

On Sunday morning, Nadia brought the puppy to his car as he idled in front of her house. She handed it through the window and gave them both a little wave.

He looked at the puppy sitting on his seat and fear washed over him. What does it eat? When does it eat? Housebreaking. How do you do that? How long does it take? He'd had days to consider these questions—why were they only occurring to him now?

He hit the brakes and reversed the car a few feet. Nadia, one foot on her bottom step, turned back. He rolled down the passenger window, craned his body across the seat until he was peering up at her.

"I don't know what to do," he said. "I don't know anything."

• • •

At a supermarket for pets, Nadia picked out several chew toys, told Bob he'd need them if he wanted to keep his couch. Shoes, she told him, keep your shoes hidden from now on, up on a high shelf. They bought vitamins—for a dog!—and a bag of puppy food she recommended, telling him the most important thing was to stick with that brand from now on. Change a dog's diet, she warned, you'll get piles of diarrhea on your floor.

They got a crate to put him in when Bob was at work. They got a water bottle for the crate and a book on dog training written by monks who were on the cover looking hardy and not real monkish, big smiles. As the cashier rang it all up, Bob felt a quake rumble through his body, a momentary disruption as he reached for his wallet. His throat flushed with heat. His head felt fizzy. And only as the quake went away and his throat cooled and his head cleared and he handed over his credit card to the cashier did he realize, in the sudden disappearance of the feeling, what the feeling had been: for a moment—maybe even a succession of moments, and none sharp enough to point to as the cause—he'd been happy.

• • •

"So, thank you," she said when he pulled up in front of her house.

"What? No. Thank you. Please. Really. It … Thank you."

She said, "This little guy, he's a good guy. He's going to make you proud, Bob."

He looked down at the puppy, sleeping on her lap now, snoring slightly. "Do they do that? Sleep all the time?"

"Pretty much. Then they run around like loonies for about twenty minutes. Then they sleep some more. And poop. Bob, man, you got to remember that—they poop and pee like crazy. Don't get mad. They don't know any better. Read the monk book. It takes time, but they figure out soon enough not to do it in the house."

"What's soon enough?"

"Two months?" She cocked her head. "Maybe three. Be patient, Bob."

"Be patient," he repeated.

"And you too," she said to the puppy as she lifted it off her lap. He came awake, sniffing, snorting. He didn't want her to go. "You both take care." She let herself out and gave Bob a wave as she walked up her steps, then went inside.

The puppy was on its haunches, staring up at the window like Nadia might reappear there. It looked back over his shoulder at Bob. Bob could feel its abandonment. He could feel his own. He was certain they'd make a mess of it, him and this throwaway dog. He was sure the world was too strong.

"What's your name?" he asked the puppy. "What are we going to call you?"

The puppy turned his head away, like, Bring the girl back.

• • •

First thing it did was take a shit in the dining room.

Bob didn't even realize what it was doing at first. It started sniffing, nose scraping the rug, and then it looked up at Bob with an air of embarrassment. And Bob said, "What?" and the dog dumped all over the corner of the rug.

Bob scrambled forward, as if he could stop it, push it back in, and the puppy bolted, left droplets on the hardwood as it scurried into the kitchen.

Bob said, "No, no. It's okay." Although it wasn't. Most everything in the house had been his mother's, largely unchanged since she'd purchased it in the '50s. That was shit. Excrement. In his mother's house. On her rug, her floor.

In the seconds it took him to reach the kitchen, the puppy'd left a piss puddle on the linoleum. Bob almost slipped in it. The puppy was sitting against the fridge, looking at him, tensing for a blow, trying not to shake.

And it stopped Bob. It stopped him even as he knew the longer he left the shit on the rug, the harder it would be to get out.

Bob got down on all fours. He felt the sudden return of what he'd felt when he first picked it out of the trash, something he'd assumed had left with Nadia. Connection. He suspected they might have been brought together by something other than chance.

He said, "Hey." Barely above a whisper. "Hey, it's all right." So, so slowly, he extended his hand, and the puppy pressed itself harder against the fridge. But Bob kept the hand coming, and gently lay his palm on the side of the animal's face. He made soothing sounds. He smiled at it. "It's okay," he repeated, over and over.

• • •

He named it Cassius because he'd mistaken it for a boxer and he liked the sound of the word. It made him think of Roman legions, proud jaws, honor.

Nadia called him Cash. She came around after work sometimes and she and Bob took it on walks. He knew something was a little off about Nadia—the dog being found so close to her house and her lack of surprise or interest in that fact was not lost on Bob—but was there anyone, anywhere on this planet, who wasn't a little off? More than a little most times. Nadia came by to help with the dog and Bob, who hadn't known much friendship in his life, took what he could get.

They taught Cassius to sit and lie down and paw and roll over. Bob read the entire monk book and followed its instructions. The puppy had his rabies shot and was cleared of any cartilage damage to his ear. Just a bruise, the vet said, just a deep bruise. He grew fast.

Weeks passed without Cassius having an accident, but Bob still couldn't be sure whether that was luck or not, and then on Super Bowl Sunday, Cassius used one paw on the back door. Bob let him out and then tore through the house to call Nadia. He was so proud he felt like yodeling, and he almost mistook the doorbell for something else. A kettle, he thought, still reaching for the phone.

The guy on the doorstep was thin. Not weak-thin. Hard-thin. As if whatever burned inside of him burned too hot for fat to survive. He had blue eyes so pale they were almost gray. His silver hair was cropped tight to his skull, as was the goatee that clung to his lips and chin. It took Bob a second to recognize him—the kid who'd stuck his head in the bar five-six weeks back, asked if they served Zima.

The kid smiled and extended his hand. "Mr. Saginowski?"

Bob shook the hand. "Yes?"

"Bob Saginowski?" The man shook Bob's large hand with his small one, and there was a lot of power in the grip.

"Yeah?"

"Eric Deeds, Bob." The kid let go of his hand. "I believe you have my dog."

• • •

In the kitchen, Eric Deeds said, "Hey, there he is." He said, "That's my guy." He said, "He got big." He said, "The size of him."

Cassius slinked over to him, even climbed up on his lap when Eric, unbidden, took a seat at Bob's kitchen table and patted his inner thigh twice. Bob couldn't even say how it was Eric Deeds talked his way into the house; he was just one of those people had a way about him, like cops and Teamsters—he wanted in, he was coming in.

"Bob," Eric Deeds said, "I'm going to need him back." He had Cassius in his lap and was rubbing his belly. Bob felt a prick of envy as Cassius kicked his left leg, even though a constant shiver—almost a palsy—ran through his fur. Eric Deeds scratched under Cassius's chin. The dog kept his ears and tail pressed flat to his body. He looked ashamed, his eyes staring down into their sockets.

"Um …" Bob reached out and lifted Cassius off Eric's lap, plopped him down on his own, scratched behind his ears. "Cash is mine."

The act was between them now—Bob lifting the puppy off Eric's lap without any warning, Eric looking at him for just a second, like, The fuck was that all about? His forehead narrowed and it gave his eyes a surprised cast, as if they'd never expected to find themselves on his face. In that moment, he looked cruel, the kind of guy, if he was feeling sorry for himself, took a shit on the whole world.

"Cash?" he said.

Bob nodded as Cassius's ears unfurled from his head and he licked Bob's wrist. "Short for Cassius. That's his name. What did you call him?"

"Called him Dog mostly. Sometimes Hound."

Eric Deeds glanced around the kitchen, up at the old circular fluorescent in the ceiling, something going back to Bob's mother, hell, Bob's father just before the first stroke, around the time the old man had become obsessed with paneling—paneled the kitchen, the living room, the dining room, would've paneled the toilet if he could've figured out how.

Bob said, "You beat him."

Eric reached into his shirt pocket. He pulled out a cigarette and popped it in his mouth. He lit it, shook out the match, tossed it on Bob's kitchen table.

"You can't smoke in here."

Eric considered Bob with a level gaze and kept smoking. "I beat him?"

"Yeah."

"Uh, so what?" Eric flicked some ash on the floor. "I'm taking the dog, Bob."

Bob stood to his full height. He held tight to Cassius, who squirmed a bit in his arms and nipped at the flat of his hand. If it came to it, Bob decided, he'd drop all six feet three inches and 290 pounds of himself on Eric Deeds, who couldn't weigh more than a buck-seventy. Not now, not just standing there, but if Eric reached for Cassius, well then …

Eric Deeds blew a stream of smoke at the ceiling. "I saw you that night. I was feeling bad, you know, about my temper? So I went back to see if the hound was really dead or not and I watched you pluck him out of the trash."

"I really think you should go." Bob pulled his cell from his pocket and flipped it open. "I'm calling 911."

Eric nodded. "I've been in prison, Bob, mental hospitals. I've been a lotta places. I'll go again, don't mean a thing to me, though I doubt they'd prosecute even me for fucking up a dog. I mean, sooner or later, you gotta go to work or get some sleep."

"What is wrong with you?"

Eric held out of his hands. "Pretty much everything. And you took my dog."

"You tried to kill it."

Eric said, "Nah." Shook his head like he believed it.

"You can't have the dog."

"I need the dog."

"No."

"I love that dog."

"No."

"Ten thousand."

"What?"

Eric nodded. "I need ten grand. By tonight. That's the price."

Bob gave it a nervous chuckle. "Who has ten thousand dollars?"

"You could find it."

"How could I poss—"

"Say, that safe in Cousin Marv's office. You're a drop bar, Bob. You don't think half the neighborhood knows? So that might be a place to start."

Bob shook his head. "Can't be done. Any money we get during the day? Goes through a slot at the bar. Ends up in the office safe, yeah, but that's on a time—"

"—lock, I know." Eric turned on the couch, one arm stretched along the back of it. "Goes off at 2:00 AM in case they decide they need a last-minute payout for something who the fuck knows, but big. And you have ninety seconds to open and close it or it triggers two silent alarms, neither of which goes off in a police station or a security company. Fancy that." Eric took a hit off his cigarette. "I'm not greedy, Bob. I just need stake money for something. I don't want everything in the safe, just ten grand. You give me ten grand, I'll disappear."

"This is ludicrous."

"So, it's ludicrous."

"You don't just walk into someone's life and—"

"That is life: someone like me coming along when you're not looking."

Bob put Cassius on the floor but made sure he didn't wander over to the other side of the table. He needn't have worried—Cassius didn't move an inch, sat there like a cement post, eyes on Bob.

Eric Deeds said, "You're racing through all your options, but they're options for normal people in normal circumstances. I need my ten grand tonight. If you don't get it for me, I'll take your dog. I licensed him. You didn't, because you couldn't. Then I'll forget to feed him for a while. One day, when he gets all yappy about it, I'll beat his head in with a rock or something. Look in my eyes and tell me which part I'm lying about, Bob."

• • •

After he left, Bob went to his basement. He avoided it whenever he could, though the floor was white, as white as he'd been able to make it, whiter than it had ever been through most of its existence. He unlocked a cupboard over the old wash sink his father had often used after one of his adventures in paneling, and removed a yellow and brown Chock Full o'Nuts can from the shelf. He pulled fifteen thousand from it. He put ten in his pocket and five back in the can. He looked around again at the white floor, at the black oil tank against the wall, at the bare bulbs.

Upstairs he gave Cassius a bunch of treats. He rubbed his ears and his belly. He assured the animal that he was worth ten thousand dollars.

• • •

Bob, three deep at the bar for a solid hour between 11:00 and midnight, looked through a sudden gap in the crowd and saw Eric sitting at the wobbly table under the Narragansett mirror. The Super Bowl was an hour over, but the crowd, drunk as shit, hung around. Eric had one arm stretched across the table and Bob followed it, saw that it connected to something. An arm. Nadia's arm. Nadia's face stared back at Eric, unreadable. Was she terrified? Or something else?

Bob, filling a glass with ice, felt like he was shoveling the cubes into his own chest, pouring them into his stomach and against the base of his spine. What did he know about Nadia, after all? He knew that he'd found a near-dead dog in the trash outside her house. He knew that Eric Deeds only came into his life after Bob had met her. He knew that her middle name, thus far, could be Lies of Omission.

When he was twenty-eight, Bob had come into his mother's bedroom to wake her for Sunday Mass. He'd given her a shake and she hadn't batted at his hand as she normally did. So he rolled her toward him and her face was scrunched tight, her eyes too, and her skin was curbstone-gray. Sometime in the night, after *Matlock* and the ten o'clock news, she'd gone to bed and woke to God's fist clenched around her heart. Probably hadn't been enough air left in her lungs to cry out. Alone in the dark, clutching the sheets, that fist clenching, her face clenching, her eyes scrunching, the terrible knowledge dawning that, even for you, it all ends. And right now.

Standing over her that morning, imagining the last tick of her heart, the last lonely wish her brain had been able to form, Bob felt a loss unlike any he'd ever known or expected to know again.

Until tonight. Until now. Until he learned what that look on Nadia's face meant.

• • •

By 1:50, the crowd was gone, just Eric and Nadia and an old, stringent, functioning alcoholic named Millie who'd amble off to the assisted living place up on Pearl Street at 1:55 on the dot.

Eric, who had been coming to the bar for shots of Powers for the last hour, pushed back from the table and pulled Nadia across the floor with him. He sat her on a stool and Bob got a good look in her face finally, saw something he still couldn't fully identify—but it definitely wasn't excitement or smugness or the bitter smile of a victor. Maybe something worse than all of that—despair.

Eric gave him an all-teeth smile and spoke through it, softly. "When's the old biddy pack it in?"

"A couple minutes."

"Where's Marv?"

"I didn't call him in."

"Why not?"

"Someone's gonna take the blame for this, I figured it might as well be me."

"How noble of—"

"How do you know her?"

Eric looked over at Nadia hunched on the stool beside him. He leaned into the bar. "We grew up on the same block."

"He give you that scar?"

Nadia stared at him.

"Did he?"

"She gave herself the scar," Eric Deeds said.

"You did?" Bob asked her.

Nadia looked at the bar top. "I was pretty high."

"Bob," Eric said, "if you fuck with me—even in the slightest—it doesn't matter how long it takes me, I'll come back for her. And if you got any plans, like Eric-doesn't-walk-back-out-of-here plans? Not that you're that type of guy, but Marv might be? You got any ideas in that vein, Bob, my partner on the Richie Whalen hit, he'll take care of you both."

Eric sat back as mean old Millie left the same tip she'd been leaving since Sputnik—a quarter—and slid off her stool. She gave Bob a rasp that was ten percent vocal chords and ninety percent Virginia Slims Ultra Light 100s. "Yeah, I'm off."

"You take care, Millie."

She waved it away with a, "Yeah, yeah, yeah," and pushed open the door.

Bob locked it behind her and came back behind the bar. He wiped down the bar top. When he reached Eric's elbows, he said, "Excuse me."

"Go around."

Bob wiped the rag in a half-circle around Eric's elbows.

"Who's your partner?" Bob said.

"Wouldn't be much of a threat if you knew who he was, would he, Bob?"

"But he helped you kill Richie Whalen?"

Eric said, "That's the rumor, Bob."

"More than a rumor." Bob wiped in front of Nadia, saw red marks on her wrists where Eric had yanked them. He wondered if there were other marks he couldn't see.

"Well, then it's more than a rumor, Bob. So there you go."

"There you go what?"

"There you go," Eric scowled. "What time is it, Bob?"

Bob placed ten thousand dollars on the bar. "You don't have to call me by my name all the time."

"I will see what I can do about that, Bob." Eric thumbed the bills. "What's this?"

"It's the ten grand you wanted for Cash."

Eric pursed his lips. "All the same, let's look in the safe."

"You sure?" Bob said. "I'm happy to buy him from you for ten grand."

"How much for Nadia, though?"

"Oh."

"Yeah. Oh."

Bob thought about that new wrinkle for a bit and poured himself a closing-time shot of vodka. He raised it to Eric Deeds and then drank it down. "You know, Marv used to have a problem with blow about ten years ago?"

"I did not know that, Bob."

Bob shrugged, poured them all a shot of vodka. "Yeah, Marv liked the coke too much but it didn't like him back."

Eric drank Nadia's shot. "Getting close to 2:00 here, Bob."

"He was more of a loan shark then. I mean, he did some fence, but mostly he was a shark. There was this kid? Into Marv for a shit-load of money. Real hopeless case when it came to the dogs and basketball. Kinda kid could never pay back all he owed."

Eric drank his own shot. "One fifty-seven, Bob."

"The thing, though? This kid, he actually hit on a slot at Mohegan. Hit for twenty-two grand. Which is just a little more than he owed Marv."

"And he didn't pay Marv back, so you and Marv got all hard on him and I'm supposed to learn—"

"No, no. He paid Marv. Paid him every cent. What the kid didn't know, though, was that Marv had been skimming. Because of the coke habit? And this kid's money was like manna from heaven as long as no one knew it was from this kid. See what I'm saying?"

"Bob, it's fucking one minute to 2:00." Sweat on Eric's lip.

"Do you see what I'm saying?" Bob asked. "Do you understand the story?"

Eric looked to the door to make sure it was locked. "Fine, yeah. This kid, he had to be ripped off."

"He had to be killed."

Out of the side of his eye, a quick glance. "Okay, killed."

Bob could feel Nadia's eyes lock on him suddenly, her head cock a bit. "That way, he couldn't ever say he paid off Marv and no one else could either. Marv uses the money to cover all the holes, he cleans up his act, it's like it never happened. So that's what we did."

"You did …" Eric barely in the conversation, but some warning in his head starting to sound, his head turning from the clock toward Bob.

"Killed him in my basement," Bob said. "Know what his name was?"

"I wouldn't know, Bob."

"Sure you would. Richie Whelan."

Bob reached under the bar and pulled out the 9mm. He didn't notice the safety was on, so when he pulled the trigger nothing happened. Eric jerked his head and pushed back from the bar rail, but Bob thumbed off the safety and shot Eric just below the throat. The gunshot sounded like aluminum siding being torn off a house. Nadia screamed. Not a long scream, but sharp with shock. Eric made a racket falling back off his stool, and by the time Bob came around the bar, Eric was already going, if not quite gone. The overhead fan cast thin slices of shadow over his face. His cheeks puffed in and out like he was trying to catch his breath and kiss somebody at the same time.

"I'm sorry, but you kids," Bob said. "You know? You go out of the house dressed like you're still in your living room. You say terrible things about women. You hurt harmless dogs. I'm tired of you, man."

Eric stared up at him. Winced like he had heartburn. He looked pissed off. Frustrated. The expression froze on his face like it was sewn there, and then he wasn't in his body anymore. Just gone. Just, shit, dead.

Bob dragged him into the cooler.

When he came back, pushing the mop and bucket ahead of him, Nadia still sat on her stool. Her mouth was a bit wider than usual and she couldn't take her eyes off the floor where the blood was, but otherwise she seemed perfectly normal.

"He would have just kept coming," Bob said. "Once someone takes something from you and you let them? They don't feel gratitude, they just feel like you owe them more." He soaked the mop in the bucket, wrung it out a bit, and slopped it over the main blood spot. "Makes no sense, right? But that's how they feel. Entitled. And you can never change their minds after that."

She said, "He … You just fucking shot him. You just … I mean, you know?"

Bob swirled the mop over the spot. "He beat my dog."

• • •

The Chechens took care of the body after a discussion with the Italians and the Micks. Bob was told his money was no good at several restaurants for the next couple of months, and they gave him four tickets to a Celtics game. Not floor seats, but pretty good ones.

Bob never mentioned Nadia. Just said Eric showed up at the end of the evening, waved a gun around, said to take him to the office safe. Bob let him do his ranting, do his waving, found an opportunity, and shot him. And that was it. End of Eric, end of story.

Nadia came to him a few days later. Bob opened the door and she stood there on his stoop with a bright winter day turning everything sharp and clear behind her. She held up a bag of dog treats.

"Peanut butter," she said, her smile bright, her eyes just a little wet. "With a hint of molasses."

Bob opened the door wide and stepped back to let her in.

• • •

"I've gotta believe," Nadia said, "there's a purpose. And even if it's that you kill me as soon as I close my eyes—"

"Me? What? No," Bob said. "Oh, no."

"—then that's okay. Because I just can't go through any more of this alone. Not another day."

"Me too." He closed his eyes. "Me too."

They didn't speak for a long time. He opened his eyes, peered at the ceiling of his bedroom. "Why?"

"Hmm?"

"This. You. Why are you with me?"

She ran a hand over his chest and it gave him a shiver. In his whole life, he never would have expected to feel a touch like that on his bare skin.

"Because I like you. Because you're nice to Cassius."

"And because you're scared of me?"

"I dunno. Maybe. But more the other reason."

He couldn't tell if she was lying. Who could tell when anyone was? Really. Every day, you ran into people and half of them, if not more, could be lying to you. Why?

Why not?

You couldn't tell who was true and who was not. If you could, lie detectors would never have been invented. Someone stared in your face and said, I'm telling the truth. They said, I promise. They said, I love you.

And you were going to say what to that? Prove it?

"He needs a walk."

"Huh?"

"Cassius. He hasn't been out all day."

"I'll get the leash."

●　●　●

In the park, the February sky hung above them like a canvas tarp. The weather had been almost mild for a few days. The ice had broken on the river but small chunks of it clung to the dark banks.

He didn't know what he believed. Cassius walked ahead of them, pulling on the leash a bit, so proud, so pleased, unrecognizable from the quivering hunk of fur Bob had pulled from a barrel just two and a half months ago.

Two and a half months! Wow. Things sure could change in a hurry. You rolled over one morning, and it was a whole new world. It turned itself toward the sun, stretched and yawned. It turned itself toward the night. A few more hours, turned itself toward the sun again. A new world, every day.

When they reached the center of the park, he unhooked the leash from Cassius's collar and reached into his coat for a tennis ball. Cassius reared his head. He snorted loud. He pawed the earth. Bob threw the ball and the dog took off after it. Bob envisioned the ball taking a bad bounce into the road. The screech of tires, the thump of metal against dog. Or what would happen if Cassius, suddenly free, just kept running.

But what could you do?

You couldn't control things.

• • •

Dennis Lehane grew up in the Dorchester section of Boston. Since his first novel, *A Drink Before the War*, won the Shamus Award, he has published seven more novels with William Morrow & Co. that have been translated into more than thirty languages and become international bestsellers: *Darkness, Take My Hand; Sacred; Gone Baby Gone; Prayers for Rain; Mystic River; Shutter Island;* and *The Given Day*. Morrow also published *Coronado*, a collection of five stories and a play. Both *Mystic River* and *Gone Baby Gone* have been made into award-winning films, while "Coronado" has received stage productions in New York City, Chicago, San Francisco, and Genoa, Italy. In February 2010, Columbia Pictures released the motion picture adaptation of *Shutter Island*, directed by Martin Scorsese and starring Leonardo DiCaprio, Ben Kingsley, and Mark Ruffalo. He and his wife divide their time between St. Petersburg, Florida and Boston. His website is www.dennislehanebooks.com

FAMILY AFFAIR
A SMOKEY DALTON STORY

By Kris Nelscott

I knew the day had gone bad when the white woman in the parking lot started to scream. I turned in the seat of my mud-green Ford Fairlane, and watched as Marvella Walker and Valentina Wilson tried to soothe the white woman. But the closer Marvella got to her, the faster the woman backed away, screaming at the top of her lungs.

We were in a diner parking lot in South Beloit, Illinois, just off the interstate. Valentina had driven the woman and her daughter from Madison, Wisconsin, that morning.

The woman was a small thing, with dirty blond hair and a cast on her right arm. Her clothing was frayed. Her little blond daughter—no more than six—circled the women like a wounded puppy. She occasionally looked at my car as if I was at fault.

Maybe I was.

I'm tall, muscular, and dark. The scar that runs from my eye to almost to my chin makes me look dangerous to everyone—not just to white people.

Usually I can calm people I've just met with my manner or by using a soft tone. But in this instance, I hadn't even gotten out of the car.

The plan was simple: We were supposed to meet Marvella's cousin, Valentina Wilson, who ran a rape hotline in Madison. The hotline ran along the new Washington D.C. model—women didn't just call; they got personal support and occasional legal advice if they asked for it.

This woman had been brutally raped and beaten by her husband. Even then, the woman didn't want to leave the bastard. Then he had gone after their daughter and the woman finally asked for help.

At least, that was what Valentina said.

Marvella waved her hands in a gesture of disgust and walked toward me. She was tall and majestic. With the brown and gold caftan that she wore over thin brown pants, her tight black Afro, and the hoops on her ears, she looked like one of those statues of African princesses she kept all over her house.

She rapped on the car window. "Val says she can make this work."

She said that with so much sarcasm that her own opinion was clear.

"If she doesn't make it work soon," I said, "we could have some kind of incident on our hands."

People in the nearby diner were peering through the grimy windows. Black and white faces were staring at us, which gave me some comfort, but not a whole lot since there was a gathering of men near the diner's silver door.

They were probably waiting for me to get out of the car and grab the woman. Then they'd come after me.

I could hold off maybe three of them, but I couldn't handle the half dozen or so that I could see. They looked like farmers, beefy white men with sun-reddened faces and arms like steel beams.

My heart pounded. I hated being outside of the city—any city. In the city, I could escape pretty much anything, but out here, near the open highway, where the land rose and fell in gentle undulations caused by the nearby Rock River, I felt exposed.

Valentina was gesturing. The white woman had stopped screaming. The little girl had grabbed her mother's right leg and hung on, not so much, it seemed, for comfort, but to hold her mother steady.

I watched Valentina. She looked nothing like the woman I had met three years ago, about to go to the Grand Nefertiti Ball, a big charity event in Chicago. She had worn a long white gown, just like Marvella and her sister Paulette had, but Valentina came from different stock.

Marvella had looked like I imagined Cleopatra had looked when Julius Caesar first saw her, and Paulette was just as stunning.

But Valentina, tiny and pretty with delicate features, had looked lost in that white dress. The snake bracelets curling up her arms made them look fat, even though they weren't.

They didn't look fat now. They were lean and muscular, like the rest of her. That delicate prettiness was gone. What replaced it was an athleticism that hollowed her cheeks and gave her small frame a wiry toughness that no one in his right mind would mess with.

I knew the reason for the change; she had been raped by a policeman who then continued to pursue her after his crime. Even after his murder by one of the city's largest gangs, she felt she couldn't stay in Chicago.

I understood that, just like I understood the toughness with which she armored herself. But I also missed the delicate woman in the oversized dress, the one who smiled easily and had a strong sense of the ridiculous.

"You know," Marvella said, leaning against the driver's side window, "as much of a fuss as that woman's putting up, I don't think we should take her out of here at all."

I agreed. We were supposed to take her to a charity a group of us had started on the South Side of Chicago. Called Helping Hands, the charity assisted families—mostly women and children—who had no money, no job skills, and no place to go. I found a lot of them squatting in houses that I inspected for Sturdy Investments. Rather than turning them out, I went to Sturdy's CEO and the daughter of its founder, Laura Hathaway—who, not by coincidence, had an on-again, off-again relationship with me.

Laura agreed that we couldn't throw children onto the street, so she put up the initial money and got her rich white society friends to put up even more. Without Laura's society connections, Helping Hands wouldn't exist.

It wasn't designed for people from Wisconsin. We had devised it only for Chicagoans, and mostly for those on the South Side. We had a few white families go through our doors over the years, but not many. We only had a few white volunteers. The white face that most of our clients saw—if they saw one at all—was Laura's, and then only because she liked to periodically drop in on the business and check up on everything herself.

"I mean," Marvella said, "what happens if she changes her mind again halfway between here and Chicago? If she starts screaming from the back seat of your car, the cops will pull us over in no time."

I winced. If the woman claimed she was being taken to Chicago against her will, then there were all kinds of laws we could be accused of breaking, not the least of which was kidnapping.

"Tell Valentina this isn't going to work," I said.

"*I'm* not going to tell her. She has her heart set on saving that little girl."

That little girl kept looking at me from the safety of her mother's thigh. I could see why Valentina wanted to save her. The little girl's eyes shone with intelligence, not to mention the fact that she was the only calm one in the trio.

Her mother was crying and shaking her head. Valentina was still talking, but it didn't look like she was going to get anywhere.

"You can't save someone who doesn't want to be saved," I said.

"You tell Val that," Marvella said.

"Bring her over here and I will," I said. "Because in no way am I getting near that woman with the diner crowd watching."

Marvella glanced up at them and frowned. I couldn't quite tell, but it seemed like more bodies were pressed against the glass around the door. One huge white man was now standing beside his pick-up truck, twirling his key ring on his right index finger.

"Crap," Marvella said. "I'll see what I can do."

She walked back to the women. She put a hand on Valentina's shoulder and led her, not gently, away from the woman.

Marvella and Valentina talked for a few minutes. Marvella nodded toward the diner.

Valentina looked up for the first time. Her lips thinned. Then she nodded, just once.

She walked back to the woman and her daughter.

Marvella walked back to me and got in the passenger side.

"Let's go," she said.

"That's it?" I asked.

"Not really," Marvella said. "We need to call Helping Hands and tell them to put a white volunteer at the front desk, not that I think that's going to work."

"Why?" I asked.

"Because Val's convinced she can drive the woman to Chicago all by herself," Marvella said.

I looked at the three of them, still standing in the parking lot. The woman wiped her good hand over her eyes.

"Why would she go with Valentina and not with us?" I asked.

Marvella rolled her eyes. "Valentina has apparently reached honorary white person status. She nearly lost it when seen in the company of her black cousin and the mean-looking black driver. You should have heard the crap that woman spouted about niggers come to kidnap her daughter—"

"I don't need to hear it," I said, waving my hand.

"Me either," Marvella said. "I nearly told the bitch to shove it up her bony little ass, but Val wouldn't let me. She said she's just scared and out of her depth and had we forgotten that Madison is ninety percent white? I'm thinking maybe she forgot or she should have at least told us so we could've brought your society girlfriend along to make little Miss Holier-Than-Thou over there a lot more comfortable."

I let the dig at my society girlfriend go by. Marvella and Laura got along, now, after a lot of wrangling and harsh words over the years. This was just Marvella's way of letting her anger out without aiming it at the woman we had driven an hour and a half to help.

"So let's just go," Marvella said. "We'll pull over somewhere with a pay phone and call Helping Hands, and then our job here is done."

I hesitated for just a moment. The little girl was still watching us. Valentina turned slightly, waved her hand in a shoo motion, and I nodded.

I started the car, turned the wheel, and pulled out of the parking lot, glancing into my rear view mirror to make sure no pick-up truck followed us.

None did.

After twenty minutes, I let out a breath.

After thirty, I knew we were in the clear.

After we had made the call to Helping Hands, I figured we were done with this job.

Of course, I was wrong.

• • •

Three months later, Marvella pounded on my apartment door. We lived just across the hall from each other.

"I have a phone call you need to take," she said.

I yelled to my fourteen-year-old son Jim that I would be right back, then crossed the hall. Even though it was December and the landlord had forgotten to turn on the heat in the hallway, Marvella was barefoot. She wore a towel around her hair, and a brown caftan that she clearly used as a robe.

"Since when am I getting calls at your place?" I asked.

"Since I can't talk sense into Val," she said.

I peered at her. I hadn't heard from Valentina since that day in September when she'd delivered the white woman to Helping Hands. Afterward she had completed her mission, she had taken me, Marvella, and Marvella's sister Paulette to dinner. She told us about her life in Madison, which sounded a bit bleak to me, and then drove the three hours back so she wouldn't miss the university extension class that she taught the following morning.

Marvella's apartment had the same layout as mine, but was decorated much differently. Hers was filled with dark, contemporary furniture, and African art. The sculptures covered every surface, faces carved from mahogany and other dark woods. The sculptures were so lifelike they seemed to be staring at me.

The phone hung on the wall in Marvella's half kitchen. The receiver rested next to the toaster.

"There she is. You tell her our policy." Marvella waved a hand at the phone. "I have to finish getting dressed."

She vanished down the hallway and slammed her bedroom door, as if I was the one who had made her angry instead of Valentina.

I picked up the receiver. "Valentina?"

"Smokey?" She was one of the few people who called me by my real name. Most people in Chicago knew me as Bill Grimshaw, a cousin to Franklin Grimshaw, one of the co-founders of Helping Hands. My real name is Smokey Dalton, and I'm from Memphis. A case four years ago put me on the run and brought me here, forcing both me and Jimmy to live under an assumed name.

On the night she almost died, Valentina overheard Laura call me Smokey, and she never forgot it. She once told me that Bill didn't suit me and Smokey did. Since Jimmy, Laura, and Franklin all called me Smokey, I never felt the need to correct Valentina.

"Marvella said I'm supposed to talk sense into you," I said, "only she won't tell me what this is about."

"Linda Krag disappeared," Valentina said.

The name didn't ring a bell with me. "Linda Krag?"

"The white woman I took to Helping Hands in September," Valentina said. "I'm sure you remember."

"I do now," I said, and then realizing that sounded a little too harsh, added, "She had that pretty little daughter."

"Yeah," Valentina said. "They've both been gone a week now."

"I thought they were in Chicago," I said.

"They were," she said.

"And you're still in Madison?" I asked.

"Yes," she said. "That's why I'm talking to you. No one told me she was missing until they sent my targeted donation back."

Valentina sent money every month to Helping Hands earmarked only for Linda Krag and her daughter. If the money couldn't be used for Linda Krag, then Helping Hands was duty-bound to return it. The policy was Laura's. She believed that everyone who donated money had a right to say how it would be used.

"So you called to find out what was up," I said.

"And discovered that she had left her apartment a week before. No one will tell me where she went."

"Did she take her daughter with her?" I asked.

"Of course," Valentina said. "She won't go anywhere without Annie."

I sighed. I knew the arguments Marvella had already made because they were the ones I had to make. Helping Hands followed its name exactly: it provided helping hands. If a client no longer wanted help, we couldn't force it on her.

Besides, we had rules. The client received her living expenses for the first month. We paid her rent and utilities and gave her a food budget. In return, we asked that she either apply for work or go to school.

If the client refused to do either, we stopped the support. If she couldn't hold a job, we got her more job training, but if she lost the job because of anger, discipline or drug problem—and the client wouldn't get help curbing that problem—then we stopped providing assistance.

Linda Krag had been difficult from the start. She almost refused to go into Helping Hands, even though we had found a white volunteer to take her application. Chicago's South Side, filled with black faces, terrified her. Eventually, Valentina talked her into the building. Once there, she agreed to all Helping Hands' terms and actually went to classes to get her GED.

But she hated the apartment that she was assigned. Not because it was bad or in a bad neighborhood, but because she and her daughter were the only whites on the block. She claimed to be terrified, and wanted an apartment in a "normal" neighborhood.

Since we knew of no programs to combat innate bigotry, we searched for—and found—her an apartment in a transitional neighborhood near the University of Chicago. She liked that. She had gotten her GED, applied for college, and found a part-time job, one that didn't tax her still-healing hand. Her daughter went to Head Start half the day.

Last I heard, everyone was happy.

But clients who started as roughly as Linda Krag often didn't make it through the program. They had too many other problems.

I said all of this, and more to Valentina, and as I spoke, she sighed heavily.

"Has anyone thought about her husband?" Valentina asked when I had finished.

I leaned against the wall. A wave of spicy perfume blew toward me from the bedroom. Marvella was not just getting dressed. She was getting dressed up.

"What about her husband?" I asked.

"Maybe he found her."

"Or maybe," I said gently, "she just left."

"She wouldn't," Valentina said. "Her family is dead. She has no friends. That loser isolated her from everyone she knew when he took her to Madison. She wouldn't know how to start a new life."

"Actually," I said, making sure I kept the same tone, "Helping Hands was teaching her how to make a life for herself and her daughter."

"Exactly," Valentina said. "I got a postcard from her daughter Annie two weeks ago. She sounded happy. Linda added a sentence thanking me. She wouldn't just give up. Not now."

"You spoke to her about this?" I asked.

"No," Valentina said. "But leaving now just isn't logical."

Neither was staying with a man who nearly beat her to death, but I wasn't going to argue that point with Valentina.

"Val," I said, "a lot of women do things that aren't logical."

I winced as the words came out of my mouth. I should have said "people," but it was too late to correct myself.

"Women are not illogical creatures," Valentina snapped.

Marvella had come out of the bedroom. She was wearing an orange dress with a matching orange and red scarf tied around her hair. She had heard the last part of this conversation, and she was grinning now.

She knew the mistake I made.

"I didn't mean it that way," I said. "I just meant that people can be irrational."

"Linda's not irrational," Valentina said.

I was already tired of this fight. "You mean the woman who wouldn't get into the car with me and Marvella because she was afraid of black people? That Linda?"

Valentina made a sound halfway between a sigh and a growl. "Smokey, look. You have to trust me on this. I got a real sense of her. It took her a lot of guts to run away from Duane. It took even more to go to Chicago. But she knew it was right for Annie. Linda wasn't going to go back to him. Not ever."

"I didn't say she would," I said. "Maybe she thought she could do better on her own."

"She knew she couldn't," Valentina said. "She was terrified of being on her own. That's why she didn't get into the car with you. She knew she couldn't defend herself and Annie, and you—I'm sorry, Smokey—but you look like every white person's nightmare. I don't think she'd ever spoken to a black person until she spoke to me. Asking her to go with you and Marvella was one step too many for her. But she did go to Chicago, she did get her GED, she did start over."

"Yeah."

I must have sounded as skeptical as I felt because Valentina added, "You have no idea how hard all of that was for her. She wouldn't be the kind of woman who would do it all over again all on her own. Especially not with Annie."

I sighed. Marvella crossed her arms and raised her eyebrows, as if asking if I was going to finish soon.

"All right," I said. "Let's say I grant you that she wouldn't run off. What then, in your mind, could have happened?"

Marvella rolled her eyes.

"I think the husband found her," Valentina said. "I think she's in trouble, Smokey. Both her and Annie."

"And this is a gut sense," I said.

"Stop patronizing me!"

I almost denied that I was, but then I realized that I would have been lying.

"I need to know if you have facts to back up this assumption," I said.

Valentina didn't answer for nearly a minute. Finally she said, "No."

"So," I said. "It begs the question. How could the husband have found her? Is he particularly bright?"

"I don't know," she said.

"Did you tell anyone where she went?"

"Not even the folks here at the hotline. Only one of the women knew what I was doing, and all she knew was that I was going to take Linda to some of my friends in Chicago."

"So," I said, then winced again. I was even sounding patronizing. "Would she have called this man for any reason?"

"I don't think so," Valentina said. "No."

"Then how could he have found her?"

"I don't know," Valentina said. "I just want you to check on her. You and Marvella have made it really, really clear that Helping Hands doesn't track people who vanish. So how about this? How about I hire you to find her, Smokey. Does that work for you? I have a lot of money. I'll pay your standard rates plus expenses. I can put a check in the mail today."

I almost told her that it wasn't necessary, that I would do this one for free. But I was a little annoyed at her stubbornness, and besides, Jimmy was growing so fast that I couldn't keep him in shoes. My regular work for local black insurance companies and for Sturdy paid the bills, but couldn't cover the added expenses of a growing teenage boy.

"All right," I said, and quoted her my rates. "I'm going to need a few things from you, too. I need some basic things. I need the husband's full name. I need to know where he lives and, if possible, where he works. I need to know where he lived with Linda and Annie."

"Okay," Valentina said.

"But—and this is very important—I don't want you investigating or talking to him. If you can't do the work by phone, using a fake name, I don't want you doing it. Is that clear?"

"I know how to investigate, Smokey," she said with some amusement in her voice.

"Good," I said. "Because the last thing I want is for this nutball to go after you."

"He won't," she said.

But I got the sense, as I hung up the phone, that Valentina Wilson—the new version, the muscular woman I'd seen three months ago—would welcome his attack. She'd welcome it, and happily put him out of commission.

"Well?" Marvella asked.

"Well," I said, "it looks like I have a missing persons case."

She rolled her eyes again. "And I thought you were a tough guy."

"Sometimes," I said, "it's just easier to do what the client wants than it is to convince them they're wrong."

"Is she wrong?" Marvella asked.

"Probably," I said with a sigh. "Probably."

• • •

Linda Krag's new apartment was in student housing near the University of Chicago. The neighborhood had once been filled with middle class professors' homes, but now those homes were divided up into apartments, with bicycles parked on the porch and beer cans lying in the lawn.

Those lawns were brown. Winter hadn't arrived yet, despite the chill.

In the early fall, when Linda Krag had seen this place, it had probably looked inviting. Now, with the naked trees stark against the gray skyline, the leaves piled in the street, the battered cars parked haphazardly against the curb, the block looked impoverished and just a little bit dangerous.

Or maybe I was projecting. Linda Krag, white and young, might have felt comfortable here, but I felt out of place, despite the University neighborhood's known color-blindness and vaunted liberalism.

I had the skeleton keys from Helping Hands. Linda's stuff had not been removed from the apartment—she had until the end of the month before her belongings would become part of the charity's donation pile. I doubted anyone had visited this place once everyone realized she was gone.

The apartment was on the second floor. More bikes littered the hallway, and so did several more beer cans. The hall smelled of beer.

Linda's door was closed tightly. There were scrapes near the lock and the wood had been splintered about fist-high. I had no idea of that damage predated Linda's arrival. With student housing, it was almost impossible to tell.

I unlocked the deadbolt and had to shove hard to get the door to open. It had been stuck closed. As I stepped inside, I inspected the side of the door and noted that the wood was warped.

I pushed the door closed, but it bounced back open. The warped wood made it as hard to close as it was to open.

I had seen the apartment she had been given on the South Side. That had been a two bedroom with a full kitchen and stunning living room. I had put up another family there a year or so ago. They had worked their way through the Helping Hands program and had bought their own house last summer.

I couldn't believe she would have left that place for this one.

But people's prejudices made them do all kinds of crazy things.

The apartment smelled sour. A blanket was crumpled at the end of the couch, and a sweater hung off the back of a kitchen chair someone had moved near the window. The kitchen was to my right. The table, with two chairs pushed against it, was beneath a small window with a good view of the house next door.

A full ashtray sat on the tabletop, along with a coloring book and an open—and scattered—box of crayons. Dishes cluttered the sink, which gave off a rotted smell.

More cigarettes floated in the water filling the bowls at the bottom of the sink. A hand towel rested on one of the burners. It was the only thing I moved, using the skeleton keys so that I wouldn't have to touch it.

Then I went through the kitchen into a narrow hallway. The second bedroom was back here. A bed was pushed against the wall. Clothing—pink and small—was scattered all over the floor. More clothes hung on the make-shift clothing rod by the door.

The clutter was every day clutter, not slob-clutter. It looked like the kind of mess a person made when she left in a hurry, meaning to clean up later. It disturbed me that a woman who cared so much about her daughter—a poor woman—would leave most of her daughter's wardrobe behind.

The hair rose on the back of my neck. I didn't want Valentina to be right. If she were right, then we had lost more than a week in searching for this woman.

And a week, in a missing person's case, was a long, long time.

I made myself walk back through the kitchen and down another narrow hallway to the full bedroom. It wasn't much larger than the daughter's room. The full-sized bed left barely enough space between the wall and the side of the bed for me to walk around it.

The bed was unmade. Pillows sideways, blankets thrown back. But the bottom of the blankets—along with the sheets—was tucked in. The tucks were perfect military tucks, something that wouldn't last during weeks of restless sleep.

Linda Krag usually made her bed. She usually made it with great precision.

Her clothing hung in the small closet, separated by color. A pair of shoes was lined neatly against the wall.

The sour smell was stronger here. It didn't smell like dirty dishes, but something else, something that I should have recognized, but couldn't.

I pushed open the bathroom door, and the smell hit me, making my eyes water. Vomit. Old vomit. It lined the edge of the bathtub, the floor beneath the sink, and the toilet itself. It had crusted against the wall.

I made myself go into the room. Another cigarette butt floated in the sloppy toilet water. The bathroom mirror was cracked, and a small handprint—child-sized—marred a white towel still hanging on the rack.

I looked at the handprint, wondering if that delicate little girl had been the source of all this vomit.

But as I pushed against the towel, I realized the handprint was a different color.

The handprint was made of dried blood.

• • •

I couldn't find any more answers in Linda Krag's apartment, so I drove home.

I'm sure my neighbors wondered why I hurried out of my car that afternoon, and took the steps to my apartment two at a time.

Jimmy had a half an hour of school left before Franklin picked him and the Grimshaw children up and took them to an after-school program we had started three years ago. If I called Franklin now, I could probably arrange for Jimmy to stay the night.

I wasn't sure I would need all that time, but I figured I had best plan for it.

Linda Krag and her little daughter Annie had been missing for several days. Some would have argued that a few more hours would make no difference, but to me, they would have.

If the woman was in trouble, then every second wasted would be a second closer to her death. Because, if Valentina was right, and

Linda Krag had been taken by her husband, that man wouldn't be interested in rebuilding their relationship.

He would punish her.

And he would do it one of several ways. If he was just a man filled with uncontrollable rage, he would beat her until he felt better. But if he was a sadist—and if what Valentina said was true, that Linda Krag's daughter was the most important thing in her life—then he would hurt the daughter to punish the mother.

People who got punched in the stomach hard or repeatedly often vomited, sometimes uncontrollably. I hoped that the amount of vomit in that small bathroom had come from an adult, but there was no way to tell.

I clenched my fists. Then I released the fingers slowly, making myself breathe. I picked up the phone, called Franklin, explained the case—since he was part of Helping Hands too—and asked him to take care of my son for at least the next twenty-four hours.

Then I hung up and set about finding Linda Krag.

• • •

Unlike the stuff you see on *Mannix* or *Hawaii Five-0*, detective work is seldom fisticuffs and confessions. Usually it's long and repetitive legwork. I was going to try to cram a week's worth of legwork into a single day.

So I went into my office and made calls.

My office was in the bedroom between mine and Jim's. I decorated it with used office furniture (bought at a bargain when I first moved here), filing cabinets that were nearly full, and a new-fangled answering machine that Laura had bought me. I hadn't taken the thing out of the box yet.

I pushed the box aside, picked up the phone, and called Valentina. She wasn't there, so I left a message, asking if she had found that information for me. I hoped she would call me back while I was still at home.

Then I started a series of calls to area hospitals and doctors' offices. I had found, over the years, that if I put on a slight East Coast accent and spoke a little quicker than I usually did, people gave me information without many questions.

Hospitals, trained to keep some information confidential, were a tougher nut to crack. But my years as an insurance company investigator helped there. If I called Billing and told them I had an unpaid bill from the hospital itself, I usually got full cooperation.

I did this now, saying that I had a bill for my client Linda Krag, without dates of her hospital stay or any listing of her procedure. I couldn't pay the bill unless I had that information.

Billing departments all over the city scrambled to help me. They hand-searched their records. I told them that we had received the bill today, which made us (or more accurately, them) believe that the procedure happened within the past month.

Each call took about fifteen minutes, because the billing person I spoke to did a thorough search. Each call also ended with the same discouraging phrase: *We don't seem to have treated your client. Are you sure it was our hospital?*

It seemed that Linda Krag had not shown up at any doctor's office or hospital in the Greater Chicago area in the past month. At least, not under that name.

The next thing I did was check the morgues and funeral homes. That was a little easier—with funeral homes, I asked when the Linda Krag funeral was scheduled, and with morgues, I just asked my question in a straightforward manner.

No one had heard of her.

When I finished, I realized I should have asked after her daughter as well—Annie Krag. But the very idea of searching for death records for a child made my stomach twist.

I thumbed through the phone book, wondering if I could run the same hospital scam for the daughter on the same day, when my phone rang.

It was Valentina.

She gave me an address on the east side of Madison, the husband's full name—Duane G. Krag, age thirty-five, and the make and model of his car, a white 1968 Olds with Missouri plates. Up until three weeks ago, he had worked at the Oscar Mayer plant not far from his home.

I didn't like that last detail at all. "Did he give notice or did he just disappear?"

"He finished his shift on Friday and failed to show up on Monday," she said.

"You got this information how?" I asked.

"A few well-placed phone calls," she said. "I know some people here now."

I didn't quite trust her tone. "You didn't go there, right?"

"No," she said. "I have no reason to. Do I?"

"None," I said.

"Besides," she said. "He's been using his phone."

I leaned back in my chair. "How do you know that?"

"One of my volunteers at the hotline also works for the phone company. It's amazing what they can find out about you."

I bet it was.

"Do you have information for me?" she asked.

"I've been to the apartment," I said. "So if she did leave on her own, she left a lot behind."

I wasn't going to tell her about the vomit or the blood. I had no idea what had happened, so I wasn't going to scare Valentina unnecessarily.

"She wouldn't do that, Smokey." That edge of worry had returned to Valentina's voice.

"I tend to agree with you. I'm about to go back to see if her neighbors saw anything unusual."

She was silent on the other end. I wondered if she could tell that I was withholding information from her.

"I hope you find her," she finally said.

"Me, too," I said. "Me, too."

· · ·

I hadn't lied to Valentina about one thing: My next step was to return to the neighborhood and ask if anyone saw anything unusual. I didn't relish going back to this neighborhood, but I saw no other choice.

It was already dark when I drove back into the neighborhood, which made me even more uncomfortable. As I approached Linda's block, I debated whether or not I wanted to park there or on a nearby street.

I ended up with no choice. Every parking spot for blocks was taken. I finally found a parking place near a bookstore on 57th, and I walked to the apartment building.

I didn't have a date or an exact incident, but I did my best. I stopped student after student, asking if they had seen the woman with the little blond girl who lived just down the block. Most remembered her—there weren't a lot of children on this street—but none had talked to her.

And no one had seen her for at least a week.

By the time I got to her apartment building, I was feeling discouraged. I took the steps up the porch just as a young man came out of the front door wheeling his bicycle.

His red hair brushed the collar of his coat. He smelled faintly of incense and marijuana. His eyes were clear, however.

He started when he saw me.

"What do you want?" he asked.

"I'm here to see Linda," I said. "I'm a friend of hers from Madison."

He studied me for a minute, then he said, "Linda didn't have any friends in Madison."

Finally, someone who knew her.

"Who told you that?" I asked.

"She did," he said.

"Well, that's a little awkward," I said, trying to seem humble. "She lived next door to me and my wife and we talked all the time. We're in Chicago to see family and I was wondering if she and Annie could join everyone for lunch tomorrow. I guess I thought we were better friends than we were."

The boy shrugged. "Maybe I misunderstood her. We only talked a few times. My roommate knew her better."

"Knew her?" I asked, then realized the question sounded sharp, so I did my best to cover. "Did your roommate move?"

"No," the boy said. "Linda and her husband reconciled. He said he was taking them back to Madison. I would've thought you knew that, since you lived next door."

I shook my head. "They haven't been back all month," I lied. "He moved out. I thought they were getting a divorce."

"Yeah, that's what I thought," the boy said. "But my roommate—he's Duane's brother—he said it was a love match and all it would take was some persuading."

I shivered, and it wasn't from the growing chill. Someone had clearly been persuaded, and not in a good way.

"I never thought it was a love match," I said, looking at the door, but deliberately not looking at the upstairs window, as if I didn't know which apartment she had lived in.

"I think the whole thing's kinda weird, myself," the boy said. "I was studying for my econ exam when he came to get her. It didn't sound like a love match to me."

"What do you mean?"

The boy shrugged again. "It's none of my business, really."

And he said it in a way that also meant it was none of mine.

"They fought?"

"Nothing like that. But that little girl sure cried hard. I'd never heard a peep from her before that."

"Was she all right?" I couldn't help the question.

The boy looked at me. He was frowning. "You know, I wondered. So I looked out the window. They all got into his car. He put suitcases into the back and Linda, she was holding her daughter. She saw me looking, and she waved at me. So I knew everything was all right."

I started in surprise. I hadn't expected Linda Krag to think of anyone except herself and her daughter. But she had protected her neighbor. By pretending everything was okay, she made sure he didn't intervene.

"When was this?" I asked.

"A week ago Wednesday. I know because the exam was on Thursday." He grinned. "And of course, I aced it."

"Good for you," I said, and hoped it didn't sound patronizing. Then I thanked him, and went back down the stairs.

There was no point in asking anyone else questions.

Duane's brother had clearly alerted him to Linda's presence, probably on the weekend between the time Duane last punched in for work and the Monday when he hadn't shown up. Duane had come here, tried to talk to her, hit her so hard she threw up or hurt the little girl somehow.

Then, when he realized Linda actually knew people here, he took her and Annie out of the apartment. He drove them somewhere.

But the question was where.

I didn't have the capability to track someone like him, even with his white car and Missouri license plates. Ten days was a long time.

And he could have taken her anywhere.

Except, Valentina told me that he had been using his telephone.

He was in Madison, in his old stomping grounds, and if we were lucky, Linda and Annie were still alive.

• • •

I didn't break any speed limits heading to Madison, but I wanted to. I wanted to get there as quickly as I could.

Had he kept her in Chicago, I would have had options. I knew people in the police department, I had friends who worked alongside me and could act as backup. I even knew people who could have discretely checked on the apartment and let me know he was inside.

The only person I knew in Madison was Valentina. And I didn't want to involve her. But I was beginning to think I wasn't going to have a choice.

Because I couldn't see any good way for this to play out.

Madison was a white town. I couldn't just barge into a white man's apartment and demand that he hand over his wife. I couldn't call the police with my suspicions—and they couldn't do anything anyway. A man was entitled to treat his family anyway he liked. Only when things got "out of hand," and the definition of that phrase varied from police department to police department, could the police step in at all.

So as I drove, I tried to formulate a plan, but I couldn't come up with a good one.

I only hoped that Valentina's friends included someone other than the lady who worked for the phone company.

Because otherwise, I was about to make a difficult situation worse.

• • •

Valentina's hotline was housed in an old church near Lake Mendota, not far from either the state capitol building or the University of Wisconsin.

I knew better than to show up unannounced at a hotline run primarily by women who dealt daily with rape. The last thing they needed to see was a muscular, scarred black man pounding on the church door. So I called ahead, leaving Valentina worried, but willing to open the hotline's doors for me.

Three cars were in the parking lot when I showed up around ten. The church looked like it had once been a monstrosity of the Protestant type—some stained windows, but not a lot of iconography. A tasteful cross carved into the brick chimney, but little else besides the building's shape to even suggest it had once been a church.

Valentina was waiting outside, wrapped in a parka that looked two sizes too big for her. She waved as I pulled up, then shifted from foot to foot while I got out of the car.

The minute I stepped outside, I knew why she was dressed so heavily. It was a lot colder here than it was in Chicago. There was also a dusting of snow on the ground, visible under the church's dome light.

Valentina didn't say hello.

"The fact that you're here means something bad is going on, doesn't it, Smokey?"

"Yeah," I said, since there was no reason to lie. "Where can we go to talk about this?"

She led me inside and up a flight of stairs into the former sanctuary. It smelled of freshly cut wood. She flicked a light switch and a dozen overhead lights came on.

Instead of revealing church pews, an choir loft, and an altar, the lights revealed piles of wood, several saws, and some half built walls.

She waved a hand at it. "We need room for women to stay overnight, and after what most of them have been through, we can't ask them to share a room like some kind of church shelter."

"Overnight?" I asked as I stepped over a pile of two-by-fours.

"So many won't go home after they've been raped. They won't go to the hospital, and they won't see a friend, particularly if they've been battered. Most don't have money for a hotel room either." She ran a hand through her short hair. "Actually, it was Linda who gave me this idea. She was so afraid of Duane."

She let the words hang. We stopped near stairs that had clearly once led to the altar. Someone had pulled the carpet off them, and one of the stairs to my left had already been dismantled. But we sat on the top step, surveying the work in progress.

"I take it the hotline itself is somewhere else," I said.

"In the basement," she said. "I figured it was best if my volunteers didn't know what was going on."

I nodded. As carefully as I could, I told her what I had learned. I also told her that I had come to find Linda.

"You can't go to that neighborhood at night," Valentina said.

"I can't go period," I said. "No one can walk up to the door of that apartment and ask Duane Krag what he did with his wife and daughter."

Valentina rested her elbows on her knees. To her credit, she didn't say I told you so nor did she reprimand Helping Hands for not searching for Linda sooner.

"What can we do?" she asked.

"We can't do anything," I said. "But I need some information from you. Tell me about those apartments."

She frowned for a moment. Then she said, "They're single story, low income housing."

"Government built?"

"Yes, with Model Cities money," she said, citing one of the many Johnson era programs that Nixon had dismantled in his first term. "They were built to look like row houses, so that each family could feel like they had privacy."

"But they're attached?"

"Yes," she said.

"They're government buildings. They should have fire alarms. Do they?"

She frowned. "It's not something I normally notice, and I was there three months ago, not really paying attention. But the city is pretty anal about making sure every building follows code. This place isn't like Chicago at all. No one can buy off a building inspector."

I nodded, hoping that was the case. "Then the buildings have to have fire alarms. The trick is where."

"I have an idea," she said. "I'll tell you mine, if you tell me yours."

"Done," I said, and then told her what I was planning.

• • •

Of course, she wouldn't let me go alone. I should have known that when I arrived outside the hotline building. I had forgotten how stubborn Valentina could be.

"You have to do exactly what I tell you," I said as we drove to the apartment complex.

Madison at night was pretty deserted. On the wide swatch of East Washington Avenue, I had only seen two other cars. I drove underneath well tended street light after well tended street light, past warehouses and buildings from the turn of the century.

No one could break into one of those buildings without drawing some kind of attention, even though the streets were empty.

"I will do exactly what you say, Smokey," Valentina said with some bemusement. "You don't have to keep repeating that."

"I just don't want you hurt," I said. "If the cops show up, you have to get out. Is that clear?"

"I know a cop to call," she said. "We'll be all right."

I glanced at her. She was staring straight ahead, the light playing across her face. The occasional shadows hid the hollows in her cheeks and she looked a lot more like the woman I had met four years ago.

"Is he one of your contacts?" I asked.

"I have to know everyone from police officers to the best criminal attorneys," she said. "I'm getting quite a list."

I nodded. "Well, they're not going to like what we're about to do."

"*I* don't like it," she said. "I just don't see any other choice."

Neither did I.

She gave me good directions to the apartment complex. I drove past it once, to see it for myself.

It was already starting to look worn. The hope that the city had placed in its low income housing had faded with the Johnson Administration. But there were still things that made this place unusual.

It had functioning lights over every front door. Each apartment number was clearly marked. The sidewalks in front of each apartment had been shoveled. None of the windows were boarded up, and none had security bars either.

The lights were on in the Krags' living room. Someone had pulled the curtains against the outside, but I could see the flickering shadows of a television set.

Someone was inside.

Which made me sigh with relief.

Just like driving past the building's side, and seeing a giant fire alarm built onto the outside wall.

"Looks like you were right," I said to Valentina.

"It was the only logical place," she said. "I'm going to have to run to pull two alarms."

"It's necessary," I said. "I don't want him to think that we've targeted his building."

"Okay," she said. "Drop me off here. The parking lot is—"

"I'm going to park in front of his apartment," I said.

"He'll see you.".

"It's all right," I said. "I know what I'm doing."

Unfortunately, I had snuck into neighborhoods before. I knew how to do it, and do it well.

I dropped Valentina on the corner, then went around the block. She was supposed to wait five minutes before she went anywhere near that first alarm.

I hoped she listened.

As I got ready to turn back onto the Krag's street, I turned off the car's lights and took my foot off the gas. I coasted to a stop in front of his sidewalk, and shut off the ignition.

Then I unscrewed the dome light. I opened the driver's door as quietly as I could, and slipped out, careful not to close the door too tightly.

Staying on the street, I walked around the corner. There was no alarm on this side, but I didn't expect one. The alarm was on the other end of the building, hidden in that alcove between two buildings.

I waited at the front corner of the building, in the shadows so that I could see the street but no one could see me.

Then an alarm clanged. It sounded very far away.

Another followed. The second one was deafening.

Valentina had been right; Madison's low income housing was up to code.

Now we'd see how long it took the fire department to respond to a major fire.

I hoped it was a long time.

People started shouting and screaming. Families came out the front doors, wearing bathrobes and pajamas, barefoot against the cold.

I silently apologized to them.

No one came out of Duane's apartment.

Families, carrying children, holding blankets, turned and looked at their homes. Voices rose in confusion at the lack of smoke and flames.

Valentina ran to my side. No one seemed to notice her in all the chaos.

"Where are they?" she asked.

"No one came out," I said.

"What are we going to do?"

I was about to tell her that I would break in the back, when the door banged open. The little girl came out wearing footie pajamas. Her hair was a rat's nest and she was sobbing.

"Help me! Help me!" she yelled. "My mommy won't come. My mommy won't come."

"*Get her to the car,*" I said as I sprinted for the main door. I didn't want anyone else to answer her summons.

So far, no one had noticed her. They were still talking and yelling and looking in the opposite direction.

Valentina ran at my side. We reached the little girl at the same time.

"Annie," Valentina said, crouching in front of her and putting her hands on the girl's shoulders. "We're going to get your mom out."

"Get her to the car," I repeated, then pushed the door open.

The apartment was a jumbled mess—overturned chairs, a ripped couch. The television was on, but no one was watching it.

That sour smell was here too, and it turned my stomach.

I hurried down the corridors, checking the kitchen, then the bathroom, and finally one of the bedrooms. The interior smelled of old blood.

I flicked on the light.

A body was leaning against the wall, a spray of blood behind it, and a pool of blood below. It took me a second to realize that the body did not belong to Linda Krag.

It was a man's body. It had to be Duane.

Sirens started in the distance, very faint, but growing.

I cursed.

A gun was on the bed.

I left it there and checked the other bedroom.

Linda Krag was huddled in her daughter's bed, eyes wide. "Leave me," she said, but I didn't know if she was talking to me or just repeating what she had been saying to her daughter.

I wasn't even sure she had seen me.

I scooped her in my arms. She moaned when I picked her up. I carried her down that hallway. I could feel dried blood against her skin, but I didn't know if it was hers or his. She hadn't showered in days. The stench of her made my eyes water.

The sirens were getting closer.

I hurried out of the building. People were wandering around, searching for the fire. In the distance, I could see flashing red lights.

Valentina was standing beside my car, leaning on the passenger door. Annie was inside the car, in the back seat.

"Open up," I said.

She didn't have to be told twice. She opened the door to the back seat. Annie leaned forward and Valentina shooed her away.

I put Linda inside. She toppled toward her daughter, but I didn't care.

We had to get out of there.

"Get inside," I said to Valentina as I pushed the door closed.

She did. I got in the driver's side, and started the car all in the same move. Then I backed around the corner, so that no one could see my plates. I backed the entire block, then turned right, away from the apartment buildings, heading toward East Washington Avenue.

"Screw in the dome light," I said to Valentina.

She gave me a funny look, visible in the street lights, then did as she was told.

"What are we doing?" she asked.

"I'm dropping you off, then we're going to Chicago."

She leaned over the back seat. "Linda needs medical attention."

"She's not getting it here," I said.

"Smokey," Valentina said.

"You didn't ask me where Duane was," I said.

She looked at me. "Where's Duane?"

"Daddy's dead," Annie said in a very small voice.

"Jesus," Valentina said, looking at me. "What happened?"

"Don't know," I said. "Don't want to know. And this is the last we're going to say about it. Right, Annie?"

"Smokey," Valentina said, reprimanding me for my tone.

"Right, Annie?" I repeated.

"Okay," Annie said.

The capitol dome loomed in the distance. We were only a few miles from the hotline.

"Where are you taking them?" Valentina asked.

"Back to Helping Hands. We'll find them a new apartment," I said. "Can you get into the back seat, and see if Linda will make it all the way to Chicago?"

"I'll make it." Linda whispered the words. "I'm just fine. Thank you."

I was relieved to hear her respond directly to me. But I knew she wasn't just fine. She wasn't protesting my presence like she had the first time I tried to take her to Chicago.

"I'm going with you," Valentina said to me.

"No," I said.

"You need me," she said.

I turned toward her, trying to keep at least part of my gaze on the road. "Maybe you don't understand. I am about to commit a felony. I don't want you involved."

"Don't," Linda said from the back. "We'll be all right."

"If I take you to a Madison hospital," I said to Linda, "they'll arrest you and take Annie. Do you want that?"

"Nooo." The reply was soft, and I wasn't sure if it came from Linda or Annie herself.

"Jesus," Valentina said.

"So," I said to Valentina, "I'm taking you home."

"No," Valentina said. "You need me. They need me. We'll work this out. I'll take a bus home tomorrow."

The truth was, I did need her. I needed her to monitor Linda's condition. I needed her to keep Annie calm.

I needed her to keep an eye out, to make sure we weren't being followed.

"All right," I said. "Let's get the hell out of here."

• • •

Three hours and one furtive gas stop later put us in Chicago at four in the morning. I drove immediately to the hospital nearest my house.

Valentina blanched as we pulled into the parking lot. I had driven her there once, saving her life and changing it forever.

Linda had passed out sometime along the drive, but she was breathing evenly. I had Valentina bring Annie inside. I carried Linda.

The emergency staff took her from me, placing her on a cart. In the florescent hospital lights, it became clear that she was bruised everywhere. The cast on her arm from her previous injury was cracked and ruined. And there was dried blood around her mouth and nose.

"What happened?" The emergency room nurse asked me. She was glaring.

"Her husband happened," I said, deciding not to lie about that at least. I lied about the rest, though. "She lives next door to us. I couldn't just leave her there."

"Good thing you didn't," the nurse said, and wheeled her away.

I stayed and filled out the paperwork, using my own apartment building as Linda's address, and making up a last name for her. I figured the hospital would never check, and Helping Hands would cover the bills.

Valentina took Annie to the waiting room while I worked. When I finished, I followed them there.

They were alone in the room. Newspapers were scattered around them. Valentina had used one to cover Annie. Valentina had fallen asleep in the chair by the door, Annie on the couch near her.

I sat down, my heart pounding.

Now I would have to deal with my split second decision. Obviously Linda couldn't take the beatings any longer, and she had shot Duane in the face. Then she collapsed. Annie hadn't known what to do or maybe was too frightened to move, until the fire alarm forced her out of the building.

They might have been alone with that corpse for a week or more, until the neighbors reported something. Then the police would have come, charged Linda with murder, put Annie in foster care, and no one would have heard of them again.

No one would have cared that Linda had been repeatedly beaten within an inch of her life. Her only hope would have been an insanity plea, which probably would not have worked—especially since the prosecutor would have said that she had run away from Duane before, and she clearly did not want to be with him.

I was giving Helping Hands a hell of a burden—the damaged mother, the terrified child—but I figured we could deal with it. And if someone determined that Linda was no longer fit to care for her child, we would find Annie a good home, a sympathetic home, one that would help her grow and overcome these last few years.

I'd seen that work. It had worked with my son Jimmy.

Annie sighed and twitched in her sleep. The newspaper fell off her, and I picked it up, gently putting it back over her.

Then I looked at her, really looked at her, for the first time since we picked her up.

She had an ugly bruise on her forehead. It was black and purple and it had seeped down to her nose. Something had hit her hard there.

I felt a quick anger at Duane, and then I froze. I looked at her hand, dangling down toward the floor.

Her thumb was bruised too. And there was a pinch mark on her index finger—the kind you got when you didn't know how to properly hold a gun.

My breath caught. The bruises lined up. If she had held the gun on her father, and the gun had gone off, the recoil would have sent her hands backwards, hitting her forehead with enough force to make that bruise.

Daddy's dead, she had said.

And her mother was in Annie's room, not the adults' bedroom.

Hiding?

Letting her daughter defend her?

I shivered just a little. I didn't want to know, and I wasn't going to ask. I had already broken enough laws for these two. I would let the experts from Helping Hands work with them—and I would never mention my suspicions.

I had brought them here—risked at least two felony charges— so that they could stay together.

I wasn't going to be the one to get in the way of that.

Valentina stirred. "How's Linda?" she asked sleepily.

"Badly beaten," I said. "But they think she'll be all right."

"Good." Valentina looked at Annie. "Bastard beat her too. I had someone look at the bruise. She doesn't have a concussion."

"That's a relief," I said.

Valentina was still looking at the sleeping child. "Think they'll be all right?"

"At least now they have a chance," I said.

And no one could ask for more than that.

• • •

KRIS NELSCOTT has written six Smokey Dalton novels so far. The first, *A Dangerous Road,* won the Herodotus Award for Best Historical Mystery and was short-listed for the Edgar Award for Best novel; the second, *Smoke-Filled Rooms,* was a PNBA Book Award Finalist, and the third, *Thin Walls,* was one of the *Chicago Tribune's* best mysteries of the year. *Days of Rage* received a Shamus Award nomination as one of the best private eye novels of the year. *Entertainment Weekly* says her equals are Walter Mosley and Raymond Chandler. Booklist calls the Smokey Dalton series "a high-class crime series" and Salon.com says, "Kris Nelscott can lay claim to the strongest series of detective novels now being written by an American author."

SURVIVAL INSTINCTS

by Sandra Seamans

Penny pulled the worn quilt tight around her body in a futile attempt to stay warm. It wasn't the cold drafts sneaking through the walls of the old motel that were making her shiver. It was them. The men who killed her father.

She wanted to cry until her heart finished breaking with the loss, but then they'd find her. They'd follow the sound of her grief, yank her from the hidey-hole and kill her. Just because, but maybe not before they did worse than just snuff the life out of her.

They'd come off the nearly dead highway, their car slipping into the motel parking lot long after Daddy had turned off the lights and gone to bed. The slamming of car doors and the incessant zzzing of the buzzer had woken her. She heard her father stumble from his bed, then fumble with the locks. The tinkle of the little bell above the entry, the breaking of glass as the door hit the wall, then his panicked shouts as he tried to warn her without giving her away. Penny grabbed the quilt and Burly Bear, then scurried into the hidden cupboard her father had built into the wall to keep her safe. He always said there was no telling what kind of trash the wind would blow off the highway.

The men were nothing more than a pack of wild dogs, ripping and tearing through the motel, stealing everything of value and leaving no witnesses behind. It had been the wrong night for the newly wed Mr. and Mrs. Kipps to take a room at the rundown Savoy Motel. From her hiding place, Penny had heard them, one after another, raping the bride before finally killing the couple. Clamping her hands over her ears couldn't keep Mrs. Kipps' screams at bay.

An hour after they came, the night went dead quiet, then an unearthly howl sounded through the stillness. In a second pass through the motel office they'd found the door to her bedroom hidden behind a pair of drapes. Heard the curses when they pushed through to find her mussed bed, the small pile of dirty clothes in the corner and her backpack ready for school in the morning.

The sound of footsteps and shouts of, "Find that girl." announced that the hunt was on. She fought down the panic that threatened to expose her. All she could do was make herself smaller and try not to make a sound that could give her hiding spot away. If they found her? She shuddered at the awful pictures her twelve-year-old mind conjured up.

Penny calmed herself by going over everything her father had told her to do if she ever found herself in the hidey-hole. Stay quiet like a mouse, the least little move and they'll hear you. If they hear you, know that they'll find you and you'll have to fight your way out to stay alive. Remember that the most deadly creature on earth is a cornered rattlesnake. Think like a rattler, strike when they least expect it, and you might survive, depending on how many of them there were.

She closed her eyes, forcing herself to remember, thinking hard, sorting through the sounds she'd heard earlier and the ones she was hearing now. There were at least three of them. Three distinct voices drifting through the thin motel walls when they killed the Kipps. If they came at her all at once, she'd be joining her father. One at time, she might have a chance. A slim one, but a chance.

Her ears pricked up at the scrape of a chair being dragged across the floor of her bedroom. One pair of heavy boots stomping around the room, a single fist banging on the walls, looking for a hollow spot. Penny heard the chair hit the wall above her head. Plaster board exploded around her as the chair was jerked down through the wall leaving an opening big enough for the man to step through.

A quick prayer and her straight razor slashed out and sliced across the big artery in his leg. He grabbed for her, but the blood drained too fast and he dropped to the floor his hands holding only air. As he crashed, she heard the others rushing down the hallway. She took her shooting stance and aimed at the doorway, just like Daddy had shown her. The shotgun killed the first man outright but only winged the man behind him.

"You'd best put that gun down, girlie, cause there ain't no way in hell you're getting out of here alive."

Was it the man she wounded or another one? He didn't sound too hurt.

"You killed my Daddy and the Kipps, you think I'm going to listen to you?"

"You're up against it, kid, we got you outnumbered."

"Had me outnumbered. You're the only one left. Walk through that door and you'll be joining your friends. Leave, and you get to live another day."

"I can't leave you here. Not alive."

"Sure you can. I ain't seen your face and I don't know who you are. There's no way I can testify against someone I ain't seen. You leave, who's to know you were even here with these other two?"

"Can I trust you?"

"Why not? I have to trust you, don't I?"

Penny crouched low, making herself small. She heard the car door slam and the engine start. Listened for the spray of gravel against the motel and the squeal of tires hitting the pavement. They were too slow in coming.

She waited, like a rattlesnake in the rocks. Remembering the car doors. Four of them slamming when they first arrived. Penny caught a whiff of perfume on the cold draft blowing through the silent hall. With the scent, everything fell into place. The reason her father had opened the door. A woman alone in the middle of the night wouldn't have set off the normal alarm bells in his mind. He'd have taken pity on her and that's when the men had struck.

Hours of watching *Animal Planet* with her dad clicked through her brain. The female was almost always deadlier than the male, of any species. She coiled up, ready to strike. There would be no hesitation.

• • •

SANDRA SEAMANS is a short story writer whose work can be found scattered about the Internet in zines such as Spinetingler, The Thrilling Detective, and Beat to a Pulp. Several of her stories have been short-listed for The Short Mystery Fiction Society's Derringer Award and Spinetingler Magazine's Spinetingler Award.

JULIUS KATZ

By Dave Zeltserman

We were at the dog track, Julius Katz and I. I had finished re-
laying to Julius the odds I'd calculated for the greyhounds running
in the third race; odds that were calculated by building thousands of
analytical models simulating each dog's previous races, then, in a
closed loop, continuously adjusting the models until they accurately
predicted the outcome of each of these races. After that, I factored in
the current track and weather conditions, and had as precise a pre-
diction as was mathematically possible. Julius stood silently mulling
over what I had given him.

"Bobby's Diva, Iza Champ, and Moondoggie," Julius murmured
softly, repeating the names of the top three dogs I had projected to win.

"Eighty-two percent probability that that will be the order of the
top three dogs," I said.

"That high, huh? Interesting, Archie."

Julius's eyes narrowed as he gazed off into the distance, his facial
muscles hardening to the point where he could've almost been mistaken for a marble sculpture. From past experience, I knew he was
running his own calculations, and what I would've given to understand

and simulate the neuron network that ran through his brain. Julius Katz was forty-two, six feet tall, a hundred and eighty pounds, with an athletic build and barely an ounce of fat. He was a devoted epicurean who worked off the rich food he consumed each night by performing an hour of rigorous calisthenics each morning, followed up with an hour of intensive martial arts training. From the way women reacted to him, I would guess that he was attractive, not that their flirting bothered him at all. Julius's passions in life were beautiful women, gourmet food, even finer wine, and, of course, gambling—especially gambling. More often than not he tended to be successful when he gambled—especially at times when I was able to help. All of his hobbies required quite a bit of money and, during times when he was stuck in a losing streak and his bank account approached anemic levels, Julius would begrudgingly take on a client. There were always clients lining up to hire him, since he was known as Boston's most brilliant and eccentric private investigator, solving some of the city's most notorious cases. The truth of the matter was, Julius hated to forego his true passions for the drudgery of work and only did so when absolutely necessary, and that would be after days of unrelenting nagging on my part. I knew about all this because I acted as Julius's accountant, personal secretary, unofficial biographer, and all-around assistant, although nobody but Julius knew that I existed, at least other than as a voice answering his phone and booking his appointments. Of course, I don't really exist, at least not in the sense of a typical sentient being. Or make that a biological sentient being.

My name isn't really Archie. During my time with Julius I've grown to think of myself as Archie, the same as I've grown to imagine myself as a five-foot-tall, heavyset man with thinning hair, but in reality I'm not five feet tall, nor do I have the bulk that I imagine myself having, and I certainly don't have any hair, thinning or otherwise. I also don't have a name, only a serial identification number. Julius calls me Archie, and for whatever reason it seems right; besides, it's quicker to say than the eighty-four-digit serial identification number that has been burnt into me. You've probably already guessed that I'm not human, and certainly not anything organic. What I am is a four-inch, rectangular-shaped piece of space-aged computer technology that's twenty years more advanced than what's currently considered theoretically possible—at least aside from whatever lab created me. How Julius acquired me, I have no clue. Whenever I've tried asking him, he jokes around, telling me he won me in a poker game. It could be true—I wouldn't know since I have no memory of my time before Julius.

So that's what I am, a four-inch rectangular mechanism weighing approximately 3.2 ounces. What's packed inside my titanium shell includes visual and audio receptors as well as wireless communication components and a highly sophisticated neuron network that not only simulates intelligence, but learning and thinking that adapts in response to my experiences. Auditory and visual recognition are included in my packaging, which means I can both see and hear. As you've probably already guessed, I can also speak. When Julius and I are in public, I speak to him through a wireless receiver that he wears in his ear as if it were a hearing aid. When we're alone in his office, he usually plugs the unit into a speaker on his desk.

A man's voice announced over the loudspeaker that bettors had two minutes to place their final bets for the third race. That brought Julius back to life, a vague smile drifting over his lips. He placed a five-hundred-dollar wager, picking Sally's Pooch, Wonder Dog, and Pugsly Ugsly to win the trifecta—none of the dogs that I had predicted. The odds displayed on the betting board were eighty to one.

I quickly calculated the probabilities using the analytical models I had devised earlier and came up with a mathematically zero percent chance of his bet winning. I told him that and he chuckled.

"Playing a hunch, Archie."

"What you're doing is throwing away five hundred dollars," I argued. Julius was in the midst of a losing streak and his last bank statement was far from healthy. In a way, it was good because it meant he was going to have to seriously consider the three o'clock appointment that I had booked for him with a Miss Norma Brewer. As much as he hates it, working as a private investigator sharpens him and usually knocks him out of his dry gambling spells. I had my own ulterior motives, for his taking a new case would give me a chance to adapt my deductive reasoning. One of these days I planned to solve a case before Julius did. You wouldn't think a piece of advanced computer technology would feel competitive, but as I've often argued with Julius, there's little difference between my simulated intelligence and what's considered sentient. So yes, I wanted to beat Julius, I wanted to prove to him that I could solve a case as well or better than he could. He knew this and always got a good laugh out of it, telling me he had doomed that possibility by naming me Archie.

Of course, I've long figured out that joke. Julius patterned my personality and speech on some of the most important private-eye novels of the twentieth century, including those of Dashiell Hammett, Raymond Chandler, Ross Macdonald, and Rex Stout. The name he gave me, Archie, was based on Archie Goodwin, Nero Wolfe's second banana who was always one step behind his boss. Yeah, I got the joke, but one of these days I was going to surprise Julius. It was just a matter of seeing enough cases to allow me to readjust my neuron network appropriately. One of these days he was going to have to start calling me Nero. But for the time being, I was

Archie. The reason I had an image of myself as being five-foot tall was also easy to explain. Julius wore me as a tie clip, which put me at roughly a five-foot distance from the ground when he stood. I never quite figured out where my self-image of thinning hair and heavyset build came from, but guessed they were physical characteristics I picked up from the Continental Op. Or maybe for some reason I identified with Costanza from Seinfeld—one of the few television programs Julius indulged in.

The dogs were being led around the track and into their starting boxes. Julius sauntered over to get a better view of the track, seemingly unconcerned about his zero-percent chance of winning his bet.

"You're throwing away five hundred dollars," I said again. "If your bank account was flush, this wouldn't be a problem, but you realize today you don't have enough to cover next month's expenses."

His eyes narrowed as he studied the dogs. "I'm well aware of my financial situation," he said.

"You haven't had any wine since last night, so I know you're not intoxicated," I said. "The only thing I can figure out is some form of dementia. I'll hack into Johns Hopkins' research database and see if there's any information that can help me better diagnose this—"

"Please, Archie," he said, a slight annoyance edging into his voice. "The race is about to begin."

The race began. The gates to the starting boxes opened and the dogs poured out of them. As they chased after the artificial rabbit, I watched in stunned silence. The three dogs Julius picked led the race from start to finish, placing in the precise order in which Julius had bet.

For a long moment—maybe for as long as thirty milliseconds—my neuron network froze. I realized afterwards that I had suffered from stunned amazement—a new emotional experience for me.

"T-That's not possible," I stammered, which was another first for me. "The odds were mathematically zero that you would win."

"You realize you just stammered?"

"Yes, I know. How did you pick these dogs?"

He chuckled, very pleased with himself. "Archie, hunches sometimes defy explanation."

"I don't buy it," I said.

His right eyebrow cocked. "No?"

He had moved to the cashier's window to collect on his trifecta bet. Forty thousand dollars before taxes, but even what was left over after the state and federal authorities took their bites would leave his bank account flush enough to cover his next two months' expenses, which meant he was going to be blowing off his three o'clock appointment. I came up with an idea to keep that from happening, then focused on how he was able to win that bet.

"The odds shouldn't have been eighty to one, as was posted," I said. "They should've been far higher."

He exchanged his winning ticket for a check made out for the after-tax amount and placed it carefully into his wallet. He turned towards the track exit and walked at a leisurely pace.

"Very good, Archie. I think you've figured it out. Why were the odds only eighty to one?"

I had already calculated the amount bet on the winning trifecta ticket given the odds and the total amount bet on the race, but I wanted to know how many people made those bets so I hacked into the track's computer system. "Four other bets were made for a total of six thousand dollars on the same trifecta combination."

"And why was that?"

I knew the answer from one of the Damon Runyon stories that was used to build my experience base. "The odds of anyone else picking that trifecta bet given those dogs' past history is one out of 6.8 million. That four other people would be willing to bet that much money given an expected winnings of near zero dollars could only be explained by the race being fixed."

"Bingo."

"I don't get it," I said. "If you knew which dogs were going to win, why didn't you bet more money?"

"Two reasons. First, fixing a dog race is not an exact science. Things can go wrong. Second, if I'd bet more, I would've upset the odds enough to where I could've tipped off the track authorities, and even worse, upset the good folks who set up the fix and were nice enough to invite me to participate."

I digested that. With a twinkle showing in Julius's right eye, he informed me that he was going to be spending the rest of the afternoon at the Belvedere Club sampling some of their fine cognacs, and that I should call his three o'clock appointment and cancel. A blond woman in her early thirties smiled at Julius, and he noticed and veered off in her direction, a grin growing over his own lips. Her physical characteristics closely matched those of the actress Heather Locklear, which would've told me she was very attractive even without Julius's reaction to her. This was not good. If Julius blew off his three-o'clock, it could be a month or longer before I'd be able to talk him into taking another job, which would be a month or longer before I'd have a chance to adjust my deductive reasoning model—and what was becoming more important to me, a chance to trump Julius at solving a case.

"You might like to know I've located a case of Romanée Conti Burgundy at the Wine Cellar in Newburyport. I need to place the order today to reserve it," I said.

That stopped Julius in his tracks.

"Nineteen ninety-seven?"

"Yes, sir. What should I do?"

He was stuck. He'd been looking for a case of that particular vintage for months, but the cost meant he'd have to take a job to pay for both the wine and the upcoming monthly expenses, which meant he wouldn't have time to get to know the Heather Locklear look-alike.

Julius made up his mind. With a sigh he told me that the Belvedere Club would have to wait, that we had a three o'clock appointment to keep. He showed the blond woman a sad, wistful smile, his look all but saying, "I'm sorry, but we're talking about a 'ninety-seven Romanée Conti after all," and with determination in his step he headed towards the exit again. Once outside, he hailed a taxi and gave the driver the address to his Beacon Hill townhouse. I had known about the Romanée Conti for several days, but had held on to the information so I could use it at the appropriate time, one of the lessons I had learned from the Rex Stout books. Internally, I was smiling. At least that was the image I had of myself. A five-foot tall, balding, chunky man, who couldn't keep from smiling if his life depended on it.

• • •

Julius's three o'clock appointment, Norma Brewer, arrived on time and was accompanied by her sister, Helen Arden. According to Norma Brewer's records, which I had obtained from the Department of Motor Vehicles database, she was fifty-three, but sitting across from Julius, she looked older than that, bone-thin and very tired. Her sister Helen was much plumper in the face and very thick around the middle. She showed a perpetually startled look, almost as if she were expecting someone to sneak up on her and yell boo. According to her DMV records, she was forty-eight, but like her sister, looked older, with an unhealthy pallor to her skin and her hair completely gray.

Before they arrived I filled Julius in on the little I knew—including information I'd gathered about Norma Brewer from various other databases, including her bank records, which were healthy, and the fact that this concerned a family matter that Norma Brewer didn't feel comfortable discussing with me over the phone. Julius didn't like it at all, and I could tell he was ruminating on whether there was a way to cancel the appointment and still afford the case of Romanée-Conti Burgundy. If there was, he was unable to come up with it. He sat deep in his thoughts until the doorbell rang, then, forcing an air of politeness, he welcomed the two Brewer sisters into his townhouse and escorted them to his office.

Now they sat across from him. Almost immediately Norma Brewer noticed the receiver in his ear and showed a condescending smile, thinking it was a hearing aid. That was not an uncommon reaction, but still, it caused the skin to tighten around Julius's mouth. I reminded him then how long it had taken to locate the Romanée Conti, knowing that he was within seconds of telling Norma Brewer that something had come up and that he would have to cancel their appointment. Her sister, Helen, seemed oblivious, never noticing the device in Julius's ear or his flash of petulance.

"Mr. Katz, I am very grateful to you for seeing us," Norma started, her voice louder than it should've been, obviously due to her thinking that Julius was hard of hearing. Not only was her voice loud, it had a shrill quality to it that made Julius wince. "I understand that you are quite the recluse, and very particular with the cases you choose."

Julius signaled with his hand for her to lower her voice. "Miss Brewer, please, I am not deaf. There is no reason to shout." He smiled thinly. "The device in my ear is not a hearing aid, but an advanced new piece of technology that acts as a lie detector."

I made note of that ploy. It was complete rubbish, of course, but it did seem to have an effect on Norma Brewer, causing her eyes to open wider. Her sister Helen remained oblivious.

"Oh," she remarked.

"Precisely," Julius said, nodding. He made no effort to correct her about his being reclusive, or about how choosy he was concerning the cases he took. He was often about town—either gambling, womanizing, or dining at Boston's more upscale restaurants. About his being choosy with the cases he accepted, quite the opposite. He accepted them based purely on necessity and, as I mentioned before, only when his bank account reached levels that threatened his more treasured pursuits.

Norma Brewer composed herself, pushing herself up straighter in her chair. "It's fascinating what they can come up with these days, isn't it, Helen?" she said. Her sister grunted noncommittally. Norma Brewer turned back to Julius. "Your secretary, whom I spoke with over the phone, Archie, I believe his name was, is he going to be joining us?"

"I'm afraid Archie is otherwise occupied. Now, this matter you would like to engage me in?"

Norma Brewer gave her sister a quick look before addressing Julius. "Mr. Katz, this is a sensitive matter," she said, her voice barely above a whisper. "Do we have your confidentiality?"

"I'm not an attorney," Julius said gruffly. His fingers on his right hand drummed along the top of his antique walnut desk. I knew he was weighing how much he wanted that case of Burgundy and whether it was worth putting up with these two to get it. He made his decision and his drumming slowed. "You do, however, have my discretion," he promised her, his tone resigned. "Please explain what you'd like to hire me for."

Norma Brewer again caught her sister's eye before nodding slowly towards Julius, her face seeming to age a decade within seconds. For a moment her skin looked like parchment.

"I have a very difficult family situation. Both my sister and I do. Our mother, Emma, is eighty-three years old and is not doing well." Her voice caught in her throat. She looked away for a moment, then sharply met Julius's eyes. "She has the onset of Alzheimer's."

"I'm sorry to hear that, Miss Brewer."

Norma Brewer's expression tightened. She raised a hand as if to indicate that sympathy from Julius was not needed. Her sister Helen remained slumped in her seat, still without expression. It dawned on me that what I had mistaken for dullness in the sister was really exhaustion.

"That's not even the half of it," Norma Brewer said. "Our father died six years ago, before the Alzheimer's showed. He had cancer and knew he was dying, and was able to make preparations, arranging for my younger brother, Lawrence, to have power of attorney for my mother. My father left my mother well provided for, including over two hundred thousand dollars in treasuries, an annuity that covers her current living expenses, and the family house in Brookline, debt free."

I hacked into the town of Brookline's real-estate tax database and verified that an Emma Brewer did own a house in South Brookline that was originally bought for forty-five thousand dollars in 1953, and was now valued at close to a million dollars. I relayed the information to Julius, who kept his poker face intact and showed no hint that he had heard me.

"Please continue," he told her.

"I've been spending as much time as I can taking care of my mother," Norma Brewer said. "Fortunately, I was able to sell a business a few years ago. I didn't make enough to allow me to live lavishly, but enough so I can now cut down on my hours and spend my time taking care of my mother. But, as I've been discovering, I just don't have enough time or strength to do it properly. Helen has tried to help also, but she has three teenage children to take care of as a single mother, and I know it's too much for her—"

"It really isn't," Helen started to say, but a stern look from Norma stopped her. Norma reached over and patted her sister's hands. "It's all right, dear," she said. "You have things hard enough as it is." Helen stared glumly at her soft, doughy hands folded in her lap. Norma turned back to Julius. "It's too hard for me, Mr. Katz. My mother needs to be moved to an assisted-living facility where she can be properly taken care of."

"And your brother Lawrence is against that idea?"

Norma Brewer bit her lip and nodded. Helen looked as if she were going to cry.

"Let me guess, he has since made himself legal guardian of your mother?"

Again, Norma Brewer nodded.

"Do you think he's been stealing from your mother's assets?"

Norma Brewer's expression turned grimmer. "I don't know." She shook her head. "No, I don't think so. I think it's more that he's counting on her money, and he's afraid that if we put her in assisted living there will be nothing left by the time she dies. I'm pretty sure that is what's behind it. Anyway, he refuses to budge, and keeps insisting that Mother is better off in her own home. Of course, he doesn't do anything to help take care of her. If I wasn't going over there daily, she'd starve to death! Or worse, die of dehydration. There would be no food in the house, and there are days she forgets even to drink as much as a glass of water. She needs professional care, Mr.

Katz, and I've found a good home for her in Vermont. It's expensive, and a bit far for visiting, but it's beautiful there, and they provide exceptional care for people like my mother. Healthcare professionals that I've consulted have told me that it would be the best place for her."

Julius absentmindedly rubbed his right index finger along his upper lip. His eyes narrowed as he considered the two sisters.

"What exactly are you planning to hire me for?" he said curtly.

"Why, it should be obvious. I'd like you to talk to my brother and convince him that he should do the right thing for our mother."

"And how do you propose I do that?"

Norma Brewer's jaw dropped. Helen looked up, startled.

"You're the detective," Norma said. "You're supposed to be a genius. I assumed you would come up with some scheme to convince my brother."

"What leverage would I have?" Julius asked.

"I don't understand—"

"So far your brother has been within his legal rights in what he's done. You don't believe he has been stealing from your mother, so for the moment I will assume that that is the case, and there is no leverage to be gained from that angle. So how am I supposed to persuade him?"

"You could reason with him, couldn't you?"

Julius made a face. "How am I to do that? We've already established that your brother is a blackguard, a parasitic opportunist willing to trade his mother's well-being for his own financial gain. How am I supposed to reason with someone like that? No, I'm sorry, I don't like this. Miss Brewer, my advice is that you hire a lawyer and have the courts remove your brother's guardianship. You could make the claim that he's neglecting his responsibilities and intentionally endangering your mother's well-being."

Norma Brewer shook her head adamantly, her mouth nearly disappearing as she pushed her lips hard together. "My brother's a lawyer. He could tie this up in the courts for years. I implore you, Mr. Katz, I need your help."

Julius started drumming his fingers along the surface of his desk again. I knew he wanted an excuse not to take this case. The only thing he disliked more than working was working on a case that involved family disputes, which he found generally unseemly. While he drummed along the desk, I filled him in on what I was able to find out about Lawrence Brewer by hacking into the Massachusetts Bar Association database.

"While I still strongly advise you against hiring me, I will take this assignment if you insist," Julius said with a pained sigh. "But I will need a retainer check for twenty thousand dollars."

Twenty thousand dollars would pay for the case of Romanée Conti Burgundy. Norma Brewer took out a checkbook and started to write out a check. Julius stopped her.

"I can't guarantee results," he told her. "And it will be left to my discretion how I proceed and for how long. I will need to meet your mother, and if I am not satisfied that she needs the care you claim she does, I will end the assignment immediately. There will be no refund offered. If that is satisfactory to you, then feel free to hire me."

Norma Brewer hesitated for only a moment, then finished writing out the check. She handed it to Julius, who glanced at it casually and placed it inside the top drawer of his desk.

"I'll have my assistant, Archie, call you later this afternoon to arrange a time tomorrow morning for me to meet your mother."

Julius stood up and escorted the two sisters out of the office and towards the front door. Norma Brewer seemed taken aback by the suddenness of this, and commented on how she thought Julius would have more questions for her about her brother.

"Not at this time," Julius said. "Later, perhaps."

He hurried her along. Helen meekly allowed herself to be herded with her sister out the door. Norma tried sputtering out some more questions, which Julius met with a few mindless platitudes. Relief washed over his face once he had the door closed and those two out of his home. His townhouse was three levels, not including the basement, which he had converted into a wine cellar. With a lightness in his step, he went down to the cellar and picked out a bottle of 1961 Bordeaux from Chateau Léoville Barton. "Rich, full-bodied, with the barest hint of sweet black fruits," Julius murmured for my benefit, although it was unnecessary since I had already looked up *The Wine Spectator*'s report on it. Once we were back upstairs, Julius prepared a selection of cheeses and dried meats, then brought it all out to his garden-level patio where he placed the tray on a table. He sat on a red cedar Adirondack chair that had faded over the years to a muted rust color. The patio was the crown jewel of his townhouse— over two thousand square feet, and Julius had it professionally landscaped with Japanese maples, fountains, a variety of rose bushes, and a vast assortment of other plantings. He opened the Bordeaux and rolled the cork between his forefinger and thumb, testing it, then smelled the cork. Satisfied, he poured himself a glass. I asked him what time I should arrange for him to meet the mother.

He held the wineglass up against the late afternoon light, studied the wine's composition, then took a sip and savored it. After he put the glass down he told me eleven o'clock would be satisfactory. I called Norma Brewer on her cell phone and arranged it. Afterwards I asked Julius if he wanted me to make an appointment with Norma Brewer's brother.

"That won't be necessary," he said.

I watched as he finished a glass of Bordeaux and poured himself another, then as he sampled the Stilton and Gruyère cheeses that he had brought out with him. I could tell he had put the case completely out of his mind. While Julius drank his wine I performed a database search on the brother. I told Julius this and asked if he would like a report.

"Not now, Archie. We'll see, maybe later."

I digested this and came to the obvious conclusion. "You don't plan on doing any work on this case," I said. "You're going to meet the mother and no matter what her condition you're going to tell your client that you're dropping the case."

Julius didn't bother responding. His eyes glazed as he drank more of the wine.

"You're just going to take her money and do nothing to earn it."

"You're jumping to conclusions, Archie."

"I don't think so."

He smiled slightly. "I'm still not convinced what you do can be considered thinking."

"You took her money. You have an obligation—"

"I'm well aware of my obligations." He put the glass down and sighed heavily. "It's a fool's errand, Archie. If Lawrence Brewer is as his sister says he is, then there's nothing I'll be able to do to change his position regarding his mother."

"You could find something to use against him," I said. "He's a lawyer. If you were able to threaten him with disbarment—"

"Threaten his livelihood?" Julius shook his head. "No, Archie, I believe that would have the opposite effect by making him need his mother's money all the more. Please, no more of this. Not now, anyway. Let me enjoy my wine, this view, and the late afternoon air."

"You had no right taking payment unless you were serious about investigating this—"

My world went black as Julius turned me off.

• • •

Julius seldom turned me off. When he did it was always disorienting when I was turned back on. This time it was especially so, and it took me as much as three-tenths of a second to get my bearings and realize that Julius and I were being jostled back and forth in the back-seat of a cab. According to my internal clock it was 10:48 in the morning, and using GPS to track our position, I had us 8.2 miles from Emma Brewer's home in Brookline.

Julius chuckled lightly. "I hope you had a good rest, Archie."

"Yeah, just wonderful." I still felt off-kilter as I tried to adjust my frame of reference from being on Julius's patio one moment to the inside of a cab now. I told him about this and that I guessed the sensation was similar to what humans felt when they were knocked unconscious by a sucker punch.

"A touch of passive-aggressiveness in that statement, Archie. I'm impressed with how lifelike your personality is developing. But get-ting back to your comment, I would think it's more like being put under with anesthesia," Julius said.

"Wha? Wha's that you say?" The cab driver had turned around. He had a thick Russian or Slavic accent. I tried to match the inflec-tions in his voice with samples I found over the Internet, and felt confident that I had his birthplace pinned down to Kiev. The man looked disheveled and had obviously gone several days without shav-ing or washing his hair. Julius told the man that he was talking to himself, and not to mind him. The cab driver turned back around to face the traffic. He muttered to himself in Russian about the loony

Americans he had to drive around all day. I translated this for Julius, who barely cracked a smile from it.

"After turning me off last night, did you try the new French restaurant on Charles Street that you've had your heart set on?"

Julius made a face as if he had sipped wine that had turned to vinegar.

"I'm afraid so," he said. "Les Cuisses de Grenouilles Provençale were dry and nearly inedible, and they were out of '98 Château Latour."

I remembered his excitement on seeing that vintage on their wine list. "That's a shame," I said. "I'm sorry I wasn't available to console you."

Julius cocked an eyebrow. "Sarcasm, Archie? Another new development for you, although I'm not sure I like it."

The cab driver was shaking his head. I could see him in the rearview mirror frowning severely. He muttered again in Russian about the crazies he got stuck with. I translated his comments to Julius. He didn't bother to respond.

The cab driver pulled up to Emma Brewer's address. Julius paid him and exited the cab. He stood silently on the sidewalk, his eyes narrowing as he examined the house. It didn't look like something that would be worth close to a million dollars. According to the town records—at least what was in their database—the house was a three-bedroom Colonial built on a nine thousand square foot lot. The brown exterior paint had long since faded and was peeling away from the shutters. Aside from a new paint job, there was other obvious maintenance work that needed to be done and the small front yard was in disarray, mostly crabgrass and weeds. Julius waited until I told him it was precisely eleven o'clock before he started towards the house. A BMW parked in front of the house was registered to Norma

Brewer, so it was no surprise when she and her sister Helen greeted us at the door. Norma stood stiffly, as if she had back problems, and her sister looked as lifeless as she had the day before. Norma spoke first, thanking Julius for coming, and then holding out her hand to him. Julius stated that it was nothing personal but he never shook hands. I had mentioned that to her when she first booked the appointment, but I guess it had slipped her mind. Ostensibly, Julius's reason for it was that he saw no reason to expose himself unnecessarily to viral diseases, although I think it was more that he didn't like physical contact with strangers who weren't exceptionally beautiful young women, since he had no problem shaking hands and doing far more with women of that nature—at least from what I could tell before he invariably placed me in his sock drawer. Norma awkwardly withdrew her hand and told Julius that her mother was in the kitchen.

"She's not having a good day," she said flatly, a fragility aging her face and making her look even more gaunt. She looked past Julius. "Your assistant, Archie, he's not here again today? That's a shame. I was so looking forward to meeting him. He sounded charming over the phone."

If I'd had lips I would've kissed her. I made a list of how I would use that later to torment Julius.

Julius smiled thinly at her. "I'm sorry, but Archie has been detained—court-ordered community service, so unfortunately he can only be here with us in spirit."

"Community service? What did the man do?"

"Sordid business, I'd rather not go into it. Please lead the way to your mother."

"Thanks for sullying my reputation," I said to him. Julius winked so that only I could see it.

One of the hallway walls was lined with framed family photos, mostly chronicling Norma and her two siblings from childhood to their young-adult years; a few included the parents. I had previously located photos of all of them, Norma's father from the newspaper obituary and the others from driver's license photos that were on record at the Department of Motor Vehicles. I was able to identify them in their family photos using different physical characteristics, such as the shape of their faces, moles, and other distinguishing marks. There were half a dozen photos of Helen in her twenties with a man I didn't recognize. Several were wedding pictures, so I assumed he was Helen's husband. He appeared to be in his early twenties also and, like Julius, had dark hair and similar features to current male Hollywood movie stars frequently described in magazines as heart-throbs. Also like Julius, he had an athletic build and was roughly the same height and weight as Julius. Julius noted the photos from the corner of his eye without once breaking stride.

Norma led Julius to a small kitchen with Formica countertops and yellow-painted pine cabinets that looked like it had last been re-modeled forty years ago. I matched the cabinets to a catalog and noted that they were manufactured in 1964. Sitting alone at a table was our client's mother, Emma Brewer. She was fifty-seven in the last photo I found of her, now she was eighty-three, and she looked as if she had lost half her body weight. She couldn't have weighed much more than eighty pounds. Her hair in the photo was turning gray, now it was white. She looked like some gnarled piece of pa-pier-mâché. Her hands were mostly blue veins and bone and were wrapped tightly around a cup of coffee as she stared blindly at the wall in front of her. She became aware that we had entered the room and, as she turned and caught sight of Julius, her face crumbled. She got out of her chair and nearly fell over as she backed away, her hands coming up to her face. She looked as if she was trying to scream, but no noise came out. I matched her expression to one of an actress in a photo I had found from a horror-movie database, and realized her expression was one of fear.

Norma stood frozen watching this, her own face showing dread. Helen moved quickly to her mother and took hold of her. Emma turned to her, confused, and asked in a whisper, "Norma?"

"No, Ma, I'm Helen. Norma is standing over there. The man next to her is a friend. His name is Julius Katz. He's here to ask you some questions."

Emma Brewer continued to stare at Julius and Norma. Then it was as if all the life bled out of her face and there was nothing there. At that point she let Helen take her back to her chair. Helen tried to ask her if she wanted to lie in bed instead, but Emma didn't answer her. Instead she took hold of her coffee cup again and stared blindly straight ahead.

Norma came back to life then. Her eyes glaring, she asked Julius if it was really necessary for him to question her mother. Julius reluctantly shook his head, realizing he had no choice but to do some work on this case. "Is she always like this?" he asked.

"No, not always. Some days she's almost functional. But as I told you before, she's having a bad day."

"Has your brother seen her like this?"

"Yes."

Julius's facial muscles hardened as he once again studied the mother. "Your brother must be a fool if he thinks he can get away with this," he said.

"My brother is desperate." Norma peered from the corner of her eyes at her sister and mother. Lowering her voice, she suggested that they continue the conversation outside the house. "I don't want my mother hearing what I'm about to say. It would upset her if she were able to make sense of it."

Julius agreed. Norma told her sister that they were going outside and asked if she'd join them. Helen declined, telling her that she was going to keep their mother company. Norma stood silent for a moment before leaving the room. Julius followed her. As they walked past the framed family photos lining the hallway wall, Julius stopped in front of one of Helen's wedding pictures and asked Norma about the man in it.

"That was Helen's husband, Thomas Arden."

"From comments you made yesterday, I take it that he's no longer married to your sister."

For a while Norma stared hard at the photo, her mouth moving as if she were chewing gum. It seemed a struggle for her to pull away and face Julius.

"Technically, they could very well still be married," she said in a low, hushed voice. "Twelve years ago he abandoned his family, running off to God knows where and leaving Helen alone to take care of three young children. I don't believe Helen has ever heard from him. I have no idea whether she ever divorced him in absentia—it's a sore subject, but I don't believe she has ever taken that step, so in all likelihood, my sister is still married to him."

"I see. And how about you, Miss Brewer, have you ever married?"

"I don't see the importance of you knowing that."

Julius's smile tightened. "It's important for me to form a clear picture of the family dynamics. I have no idea how I am going to tackle your brother, but the more I know about all of you the better chance I have of something coming to me."

That was complete rubbish. I had already given Julius a report on Norma Brewer that included the fact that she had never been married. It occurred to me then that Julius didn't trust my competence in the matter. The client shook her head and gave Julius the same information that I had given him earlier—that no, she had never been married. I felt a tinge of excess heat for a few milliseconds, and realized that that was the sensation of resentment, yet another new experience for me.

"Please, Mr. Katz, let's continue this outside. I don't want to risk upsetting my mother."

Julius agreed and followed her out the door. Standing there in the late morning sunlight, Norma Brewer's skin again took on a parchment quality, and I could make out a crisscross of blue veins along her temples. She clasped her hands as she tried to meet Julius's stare.

"I spoke with my brother over the phone last night," she said in a hushed tone. "I thought maybe I could talk sense into him."

"You weren't able to."

She shook her head. "He's only willing to allow Mother to be put in a facility if Helen and I agree to let the house be sold to him for well under the market price. I can't do that, Mr. Katz—the house would need to be sold to pay for her care. She only has enough money in Treasuries to cover two years' worth of expenses, and the facility I found in Vermont won't accept her unless I can show enough assets in escrow to cover her first five years there."

"And your mother's health?"

"Outside of the Alzheimer's she has nothing medically wrong with her. She has lost a lot of weight because she forgets to eat, but she could easily live another ten years."

Julius's facial muscles hardened as he gazed at Norma Brewer. "Your brother gave you a dollar figure for his acquiescence?" he said at last.

Norma Brewer nodded. "Two hundred and fifty thousand dollars," she said. She looked away from Julius, her hands clasping tighter together. "I have a feeling he promised that money to someone." She took a deep breath before continuing. "I believe I mentioned yesterday that Lawrence is an attorney. One of his clients is a known hoodlum, Mr. Katz."

"Yes, I know. Willie Andrews."

That surprised his client, and it also surprised me. While I was turned off, Julius had actually researched the brother himself. Will wonders ever cease? I decided it had to be the disappointing meal. He needed something to work off his dissatisfaction, and obviously didn't encounter a suitable woman for that—probably leaving the restaurant in too much of a huff to notice any. I searched the online newspaper archives for one Willie Andrews, and built a thick file on him. He was a known mob affiliate and had been arrested over the years on an assortment of charges, including loan-sharking and extortion, but never convicted.

"Miss Brewer, I saw your brother yesterday before our appointment," Julius added. "It was by chance only. He was at the dog track, and I am guessing from his demeanor that he has a gambling addiction. I've seen it enough to be able to spot the telltale signs."

That was yet another surprise. I record all the images that I "see" and transfer them to a hard drive in Julius's office that he maintains for me, and they're kept for one week before Julius backs them onto permanent storage. I scanned all my visual images from when we were at the dog track the other day and, sure enough, Lawrence Brewer was there. I analyzed the images I had of him, and determined easily enough that he was losing from the way he ripped his betting tickets. I told Julius this even though I knew he must have noticed exactly the same thing. That's the thing with Julius, he's like a computer in his own right, noticing and storing away everything he sees.

Norma Brewer looked flabbergasted by that bit of news. "Did you follow my brother to the track?"

"No, Miss Brewer, as I mentioned, it was purely serendipitous."

Julius had signaled me several minutes before to arrange for a taxi to pick us up, and one was pulling up to the house. Julius had that look in his eyes he always has when he's anxious to get away from a client, and he told her he'd be in touch, then made his escape. Norma Brewer appeared taken aback by Julius's quick and unexpected departure. She stood at a loss for words for a long moment before heading back inside the house. Julius settled into the back of the cab and gave the driver his townhouse address.

"Quite a morning," I told him. "One woman finding me absolutely charming, another terrified merely at the sight of you."

"I never heard her use the adverb *absolutely* in describing your charm," Julius muttered somewhat peevishly. He had taken out his cell phone so that the driver wouldn't think that he was muttering to himself. The cell phone was merely a prop. Whenever Julius needed to make a call, I'd make it for him and patch him in through his earpiece.

"It was implied," I said. "Would you like me to brief you on the reports I generated for Lawrence Brewer and Willie Andrews?"

"That's not necessary." A thin smile crept over his lips. "I researched both of them myself last night while you were *unavailable*."

"Yeah, but I bet you don't have Lawrence Brewer's last seven years' worth of tax returns, unless you were able to hack into the IRS's mainframe and, given the level of encryption they use, that's not very likely. I also bet you don't have Willie Andrews's court documents."

"No, I don't, but I don't need them now. Sometimes, Archie, too much information is worse than too little. It distracts from what's important."

That made no sense. The only way you can analyze data is if all the data is available—or if you are able to extrapolate what's missing. I ignored the comment, and instead asked him if he wanted me to arrange for appointments with either the brother or Andrews.

"Willie Andrews is not the type of man you make an appointment with. As far as Lawrence Brewer goes, now is not the appropriate time."

"So that's it, then?"

"For now, yes."

I expected that. As far as Julius was concerned, he had already worked hard enough for one day. I knew there was little chance that nagging him would change that. Still, I tried.

"I can see your point," I said. "After all, you have just put in an arduous twenty-seven minutes of work, more than enough to justify the twenty-thousand-dollar fee you extorted from your client."

"An hour and seventeen minutes once you factor in the cab rides."

"Wow. An hour and seventeen minutes, then. I'm exhausted just thinking about it."

"Archie, now is not the time. I'm not about to tackle the brother until I've given the matter more thought. So please, some quiet so I can think."

It was pointless. The only thing he was going to be thinking about was lunch at one of his favorite local restaurants, along with the bottle of Gewürztraminer I had reserved for him. With nothing else to do I spun some cycles figuring out why I hadn't made the connection between the photos I dug up earlier for Lawrence Brewer and the visual images I recorded at the dog track, and then worked on readjusting my neuron network so I would recognize patterns like that in the future. I have to admit I was impressed with Julius's ability to recall seeing Lawrence Brewer at the dog track and told him so. Julius grunted that it was simply luck.

"The only reason he made an impression was because he was so obviously losing badly that I considered for a moment inviting him to one of my poker games. Now please, Archie, I'd like quiet the rest of the trip."

Julius put his cell phone back in his inside jacket pocket. I spent the rest of the cab ride constructing simulations involving Julius interviewing Lawrence Brewer, but none of them led to a reasonable probability of success.

• • •

Julius surprised me. On our return home he had me cancel his luncheon reservation and he spent the rest of the day either reading or puttering around the townhouse. All I could figure was that he was trying to bluff me that he was onto something and that he planned to stay holed up until he had the case solved—that way he could loaf for days without me nagging him. A couple of times he put me away in his desk drawer while he got on the computer. He wouldn't tell me what he was doing, only that I had as much information as he did at that point. He seemed genuinely distracted during that first day, at times becoming as still as a marble statue while his facial muscles hardened and his eyes stared off into the distance. Of course, it could've been an act. When I tried asking him about what he was considering, he mostly ignored me, only once telling me that whatever it was, it was still percolating. That night he had me cancel his dinner reservations. Instead of going out he spent the evening making fresh gnocchi and then pounding veal until it was nearly paper thin before sautéing it with shallots and mushrooms in a white wine sauce. He picked a Montepulciano d'Abruzzo from his wine cellar to accompany his dinner.

The next day he appeared more his normal self as he performed his morning rituals, then spent the rest of the morning reading wine reviews. My attempts to pester him into action went nowhere. He mostly ignored me, and when I tried briefing him on the dossier I had compiled on Willie Andrews, he stopped me, telling me that he was otherwise occupied.

"My mistake," I said. "I thought your depositing our client's check actually obligated you to earn the fee you were paid."

"Archie, I *am* earning it."

"By sitting around reading wine reviews?"

"Precisely. Sometimes the best action is waiting. Patience, Archie, patience."

So there you had it. Maybe he was waiting on something, but more likely he had fallen into one of his lazy funks and was only trying to bluff me, and as part of the bluff he was going to stay holed up inside his townhouse. The thing with Julius was he had no "tell"—no visible indication of when he was bluffing, at least none that I had yet been able to detect. When he played poker, I could identify the other players' "tells" pretty quickly, not that Julius needed my help in that area. He was astute at reading other players and detecting the slight behavioral changes that indicated as brightly as a flashing neon light when they were bluffing or holding what they thought were winning cards. Sometimes it would be the way their facial muscles contorted or their breathing patterns changed or maybe they'd scratch themselves or shift slightly in their chairs. The list was endless, but it was simple pattern recognition on my part to identify these "tells" by comparing recorded video of when they were bluffing and when they weren't. I'd spent countless hours trying to identify Julius's "tell" and so far had come up with nothing.

The rest of the day Julius spent mostly reading, cooking, and drinking wine. I was beginning to think if it were a bluff he would try to play it out for weeks if he thought he could get away with it. I tried several times to nag him into action, but failed miserably, with him smugly insisting that he was waiting for the right time before taking any direct action. That day his client called several times to find out when Julius was planning to talk to her brother. Julius had me answer those calls and directed me to tell Norma Brewer that he was in the midst of investigating certain issues regarding the case, and once he was done he would be interviewing her brother. It was utter hogwash, but I didn't tell her that.

The third day it was more of the same, with Julius not venturing outside the townhouse, the only difference being that he seemed more distracted than usual. Also, the client didn't call. At six o'clock he turned on the evening news, which was unusual for him. He rarely watched TV. During the broadcast it was reported that a local woman named Norma Brewer had been found murdered in her Cambridge home.

"Is that what you were waiting for?" I asked.

Julius didn't answer me. He just sat grim-faced, his lips compressing into two thin, bloodless lines.

"So I guess that's it. Your client's dead and her money is in your bank account. Now you don't have to do anything to earn it. Bravo."

"No, Archie, that's not what it means," he said, his jaw clenching in a resolute fashion. "I'm going to be earning every penny of what she paid me."

"Did you know she was going to be murdered?"

"I didn't know anything with certainty."

"How?"

"Not now, Archie. We're going to be very busy over the next few days. For now, please call the sister, Helen, and find out what you can about the murder. In the meantime, make the earliest dinner reservations you can for me at Le Che Cru. The next few days I expect to be roughing it. If the police call, I'm out for the evening and you have no idea where I have gone. If Helen Arden asks to speak to me, the same story. You have no idea where I am."

I did as Julius asked, first making him reservations at Le Che Cru for eight thirty, then calling Helen Arden. She sounded dazed, as if she barely understood what I was saying. I had to repeat myself several times, and after my words finally sunk in, she told me that the police had contacted her about Norma's murder, and she was now trying to reach her brother and figure out how they were going to take care of their mother and at the same time make the arrangements for Norma's funeral. She wasn't even sure when the police were going to release the body.

"What if it's weeks before they let us have Norma?" she asked. "How are we supposed to bury my sister?"

Her voice had no strength to it. It was as if she were lost and had completely given up any hope of being found. I told her it wouldn't be more than a few days—however long it took for the coroner to perform an autopsy. I gave her the phone number for a good criminal lawyer that Julius had recommended to clients who had dealt with this type of problem in the past. I tried asking her whether the police had given any details about the murder, but she seemed to have a hard time comprehending what I was saying. After I tried several more times, she finally murmured that they'd told her nothing other than that her sister was dead.

I had been searching the Internet, and so far no details had been reported on any of the Boston newspapers' Web sites, and neither was there anything of interest on the police radio frequencies that I was scanning. I told her Julius would be in touch sometime the next day and hung up. I filled Julius in quickly. He was in the process of changing into one of his dining suits. After slipping on a pair of Italian calfskin loafers, he hurried down the stairs and to the front door. He asked me whether I was able to detect any police car radios broadcasting in the area, and I told him there weren't any and that nothing was showing on the outdoor Web cam feed. Still, he opened the front door only enough so he could peer out of it. Satisfied that the police weren't lying in wait for him, he stepped outside and hurried down the street, his pace nearly a run. Once he was two blocks away from his townhouse, he slowed.

"Do you want me to call the brother?" I asked. "Maybe see if you can get an early read on him?"

"Not now, Archie. I'm sure he's with the police presently, and it would be best to wait until tomorrow to call him."

I remained silent while Julius briskly walked the five blocks down Pinckney Street to Charles Street. After hearing about Norma Brewer's murder I started building simulations that modeled different scenarios that would explain Julius's behavior since accepting the case. There was one scenario that stood out as having the highest probability. I asked him about it. Whether he was lying low waiting for the brother to kill Norma Brewer, knowing that if that were to happen it would make it easy for him to earn his fee, since all he'd have to do is wait for the police to arrest the brother and then have the courts vacate his guardianship.

"Are you asking whether I expected Lawrence Brewer to murder my client?"

"Yes, that's what I'm asking."

"No, that's not what I was expecting." A young couple was passing us on the sidewalk, and Julius took out his cell phone so he wouldn't appear to be an insane person talking to himself. Somewhat amused, Julius asked, "Archie, what would be Lawrence Brewer's purpose in doing that?"

"Because she engaged you. Maybe he was afraid you'd find some leverage that you'd be able to use against him. Maybe he thought if his sister were out of the way, you'd be also."

"It's possible, Archie, but he'd have to be a dolt to think that. Then again, the way he was acting at the dog track, as well as his behavior regarding his mother's well-being, he could very well be a dolt."

"So you think he murdered his sister?"

Julius made a face. "It's a possibility, Archie. But it's just one of many and there's no point engaging in idle speculation now. The next few days are going to be hectic enough and this could be my last decent meal before this matter has been put to bed. So please, Archie, no more discussion of this, at least not tonight."

I wanted to ask him the obvious question, which was, if he hadn't been waiting for Lawrence Brewer to murder his sister, then what had he been waiting for? What stopped me was detecting a hint of a threat in his voice that if I continued this line of conversation he would turn me off. That would be twice in three days, and I didn't want to set that type of precedent. I remained quiet while he walked to Le Che Cru and took a seat at the bar. The maître d' came over with a complimentary bottle of a Chardonnay that he knew Julius favored, and apologized profusely that he wasn't able to arrange for an earlier table for his favorite patron. Before leaving, he told Julius that he would have an order of seared sweetbreads in chestnut flour brought over immediately, on the house, of course. Julius graciously accepted all this. The sweetbreads were brought over within minutes and, while Julius was having his second glass of wine, a Detective Mark Cramer from the Cambridge Police Department called. I connected the call to Julius's earpiece so he could listen in. Rather gruffly, the detective asked to speak to Julius.

"I'm afraid Mr. Katz isn't available," I said.

"Yeah, well, get him available!"

"I would if I had any idea where he is, but I don't, so I can't."

The detective used some choice invective on his end of the line, ending with the phrase "son of a bitch."

"Is that all, Detective?" I asked, to Julius's obvious amusement.

"No, that's not all," he said, his voice growing more exasperated. "Your boss is a material witness in a murder case—"

"There's been a murder?"

"Shut up," he ordered, his exasperation growing. "I know damn well you called the victim's sister within the hour, just as I know your boss is probably with you right now getting a good laugh over all this. The Boston PD filled me in on what to expect, so don't think you're fooling anyone with this, okay? You better just tell Katz to come in to Central Square station within the next fifteen minutes or I'll be getting a bench warrant for his arrest. Ask him how he'd like a few days in lockup for contempt of court!"

Detective Cramer hung up on me. Julius shook his head, a thin wisp of a smile showing. "The man's a fool," he said.

"Dolts and fools, huh?"

"Precisely, Archie. That's what you've gotten me mired in." He took a sip of his wine and sighed heavily. "They probably have a squad car waiting in front of my townhouse."

"Probably a fleet of them."

Julius was going to say something else, but instead another long, heavy sigh escaped from him. He sat almost comatose for several minutes, not moving as much as a muscle, not even blinking. When he finally came out of it he appeared relaxed. Shortly afterward he started chatting with two women sitting nearby. One of them was a redhead with a smooth, cream-colored complexion who gave her name as Lily Rosten. She closely resembled the actress Lauren Ambrose. The other woman gave her name as Sarah Chase. She was a brunette and I was able to match her physical characteristics to actresses who were considered extraordinarily beautiful according to online surveys. Both women, according to their DMV records, were twenty-nine. While Julius was charming and polite with both of them, his attention was primarily focused on Lily, which surprised me since I had rated Sarah as the more attractive of the two. When Julius's table became available, he invited them to join him for dinner. They both accepted, but Lily indicated that she needed to use the ladies' room and dragged her friend with her. When they returned, Sarah Chase reluctantly informed Julius that something had come up and she wouldn't be able to join them. Julius didn't seem to mind, and neither did Lily.

Dinner was a long, leisurely three-hour affair, and Julius was in rare form; maybe somewhat subdued at times, but even more charming than usual. It was an odd effect the way Lily's eyes appeared to glisten when she laughed, and even when she simply smiled. I also noted how they maintained eye contact almost continuously. When dinner ended, Lily announced to Julius that she lived in the Back Bay section of Boston off Marlborough Street, and Julius suggested that they take advantage of the pleasant weather, and that he walk her back to her apartment instead of calling a cab. I had already looked up her address and mapped it out to seven-tenths of a mile distant from where we were. Earlier, when I had tried filling Julius in on what I was able to find out about her—the amount in her bank account, the fact that she was single and never married, where she grew up and went to college, as well as her present job as an administrator for a local nonprofit organization—he stopped me with a hand signal.

Just as dinner had been leisurely, so was their walk to her apartment building, maybe even more so. Somewhere along the way, they started holding hands. When they reached her address, they were still holding hands. I recognized the pattern—the way she looked at him and blushed and how Julius responded. It was clear that she was going to invite Julius for the night, and this would allow him to bypass the police, which I figured was what he'd been after all along. I was astounded when he gave her a quick and somewhat chaste kiss on the mouth and told her he'd like to call her in a few days. She looked equally astounded for a few seconds, but smiled and blushed even brighter than before and told Julius she would like that. Julius stood on the sidewalk and watched as she disappeared inside the building's vestibule. Only then did he turn back towards Beacon Hill and his townhouse.

As I said, I was astounded. His actions didn't make sense. They didn't fit his past patterns.

"I don't get it," I said.

"What, Archie?"

"Why didn't you go up to her apartment with her?"

He didn't answer me.

"Wasn't that the point?" I asked. "So that you could elude the police until morning?"

He shrugged. "If that were the case, couldn't I simply check into a hotel for the night?"

"You could, but the police might have a watch on your credit cards."

"That's true," he acknowledged. "Very true, Archie. It would be best for you to call Henry and have him waiting for us at the townhouse."

Henry Zack was Julius's attorney, and Julius had him on twenty-four-hour call for just such emergencies. I knew Henry would moan about the late hour, which he did when I reached him, but he understood the emergency of the situation and agreed to meet Julius. I filled Julius in, and asked him again about Lily.

"I don't get it," I said. "She's extraordinarily attractive, and it was clear from her behavior that she wanted you to join her. It was equally clear from yours that you wanted to, and you had your additional motive. This is a departure from your normal behavior patterns. An anomaly. It doesn't fit."

He remained silent as he continued along Beacon Street. After several blocks an odd, almost melancholy smile showed.

"There's still a lot for you to learn, Archie," he said softly.

That was all he was going to say on the matter. Along with Norma Brewer's murder, I now had another mystery to solve.

• • •

It wasn't exactly a fleet of police cars waiting at Julius's townhouse, but there were more than I would've expected. Three in total, with a small congregation of officers milling around by the front door. Henry Zack was among them, and he was red-faced as he talked on his cell phone, his eyes bulging slightly. I spotted all this when we were two blocks away by tying in to the outdoor Web cam feed that covered the front exterior of Julius's townhouse. I reported all this to Julius, and his lips compressed into a grim expression. He asked me to get Henry on the line.

I heard the unmistakable call-waiting tone as Henry put his other call on hold to take mine, and then I patched Julius in. "This is outrageous, Julius," he said, his voice rising. "They have absolutely no grounds to hold you as a material witness, and I'm on the phone now with the chief clerk of the district court to have their warrant vacated. If they arrest you I'll be suing the hell out of them—both the police department and each of the officers personally. Start looking for that retirement villa in Florence that you're always talking about!"

Henry's rant was more for the officers' benefit than Julius's. Julius informed him that he was three minutes away, and asked if it was safe for him to appear.

"It's safe. It will be as good as winning the lottery if they so much as put a hand on you."

Julius signaled for me to disconnect the call, and his pace accelerated as his expression grew grimmer. Within three minutes, as he had promised Henry, he approached his building and bedlam broke out. Henry was on the lookout for Julius and so he spotted him first. He attempted to distract the cops by bellowing more threats at them. It wasn't until Julius was halfway up the path to his front door that the first cop noticed him, and then they swarmed toward him with Henry Zack in pursuit. A plainclothes detective with a large ruddy face and wearing a cheap, badly wrinkled suit reached Julius first. Having already accessed his departmental records, I informed Julius that this was Detective Mark Cramer. Cramer tried to shove a court warrant into Julius's hands.

"My lawyer is standing right behind you, Detective Cramer," Julius said. "Anything you have for me you should give to him."

Cramer seemed taken aback that Julius knew who he was and reluctantly handed the warrant to Henry Zack, then turned back to Julius. According to Cramer's records he was fifty-four, six foot two, and two hundred and twenty pounds. He appeared heavier than that, my estimate being closer to two hundred and forty-six pounds. He also had less hair than the photo in his file. He appeared both tired and cranky, and he tried to give Julius a hard, intimidating stare.

"You're under arrest for obstruction of justice," Cramer said.

"Nonsense."

That brought a wicked grin to Cramer's lips. "Is that so? I have a court warrant that says otherwise, smart guy."

"I couldn't care less," Julius said. "This isn't a police state. You have no justification for this harassment—"

"No justification?" Cramer sputtered, almost choking on his words. He lifted a thick index finger as if he were going to poke Julius in the chest with it, which would've been a mistake unless he wanted to be wearing a cast on his hand for the next two months. Somehow he controlled himself.

"Norma Brewer, who was a client of yours, was murdered this afternoon. So far you've refused to cooperate with an ongoing police investigation and, as far as I'm concerned, you have been withholding evidence dealing with the crime."

"That is utter rubbish," Julius said. "I have no knowledge of Miss Brewer's murder other than what was reported on the six o'clock news and you have no legitimate reason to think otherwise. I spent the evening at Le Che Cru entertaining a date, and am just arriving home now. Until my assistant tracked me down a short while ago, I had no idea you or any other police official wished to talk to me."

Cramer was beside himself. "No idea, huh?" He jerked a thumb towards Henry Zack. "That's why you dragged your lawyer down here at this hour. I've heard all about you, Katz, and I'm not about to put up with your nonsense!"

Henry started to object, but Julius put up a hand to stop him.

"Once Archie tracked me down and relayed your message, I decided to take the proper precautions." Julius smiled thinly at the detective. "Now this is very simple. If you arrest me, you won't get a single word out of me. Not now, not ever. I can't reward your belligerence by inviting you into my home, but this was a client of mine who was murdered. If you remove your mob scene from my door and agree to act in a civil fashion, I will give you two minutes of my time. And sir, that is the best you will get from me tonight."

"Of all the unmitigated gall! Katz, if you think you're calling the shots here—"

"Sir, that is exactly what I think." Julius's voice was soft, but it cut through Cramer's all the same. I knew Julius well enough to know the anger that that softness masked. "I am an expert poker player and know a bluff when I see one. Your puerile attempts to bully me show that you're stumped, and further, that you have no expectation of that changing. If you want my help, it will be on my terms."

I could tell Cramer wanted nothing more than to cuff Julius and drag him into a police cruiser. He wanted to do that—that much was evident, but the steam had already gone out of him. Almost embarrassed, he turned to the other officers and asked them to step back to the curb. Once they did this, Julius addressed Cramer, telling him he had some questions for him. Cramer's face went from cherry red to bone white, but he nodded and told Julius to go ahead.

"I am assuming you have already talked with the sister, Helen Arden, and know what I was hired for. Have you talked yet to the brother?"

"Not yet. He's agreed to come in tomorrow morning for questioning."

"If you don't end up arresting him, escort him here afterwards."

"I can't do that against his wishes."

"He'll agree. I'll be calling him before then. Tell me about the murder."

"She was hit on the back of the head and knocked unconscious," Cramer said, his voice resigned but at the same time indicating how much he hated giving Julius this information. "After that she was strangled. Whoever did this wore cloth gloves. There was no sign of forced entry. So far, that's all we've got."

"What was she hit with?"

"A polished agate stone that was probably kept as a paperweight. About the size of a softball."

"Could this have been a robbery turned murder?"

"Not likely. We had the sister walk through the house and she didn't see anything obvious that was missing."

Julius offered Cramer a grim smile. "As I mentioned before, I have no knowledge of this murder, at least nothing beyond what you already have. I do have suggestions, though. Miss Brewer mentioned a business she sold several years ago. I would strongly suggest you look into that to see if there were any hard feelings concerning the sale. Another avenue of investigation involves Miss Brewer's brother-in-law, a Mr. Thomas Arden. I was told that he abandoned his family twelve years ago. It's possible he's back in the picture. That should be looked into too. That is all the help I can offer at this time."

Cramer nodded, reluctantly accepting this. After he walked away, Henry Zack chuckled softly, and noted, "If nothing else, Julius, I can always count on you for an eventful evening." Julius somberly bid him goodnight.

Once inside the house, Julius asked me to order a dozen roses for Lily Rosten and arrange for them to be delivered so that they'd be waiting for her when she arrived at work the next morning. "Have them add a note that I'll be calling her soon," he added.

I did as he asked, placing the order through a twenty-four-hour florist that Julius had used in the past. "You don't believe Norma Brewer's murder had anything to do with the sale of her business?" I asked.

Julius thought about this before shaking his head. "Not exactly, Archie, but it's something to look into, and the police, with all their manpower and resources, are better equipped to do so than I. Besides, a general rule to follow is the more clutter that can be eliminated, the clearer the picture will become."

From the moment Julius suggested to Detective Cramer that he investigate Thomas Arden, I began building a dossier on the elusive brother-in-law. I filled Julius in on the salient points. That Arden graduated with a degree in finance from Haverford College in 1983, married Helen Brewer shortly after graduation, later earned an M.B.A. from Harvard, and was working as the chief financial officer for what was at the time a small computer start-up company when he appeared to vanish from the face of the planet on August 7, 1997. There was not a single trace of Thomas Arden after that date, at least not in any of the databases I was able to access.

"Why August 7?" Julius asked.

"That was when his wife reported him missing to the police."

"He could've been missing for several days before she contacted the police," Julius said. "But never mind, it's not important. Anything interesting about him going to Haverford College?"

"Lawrence Brewer went to Haverford for his undergraduate degree. They both graduated the same year."

"Very good, Archie. What can you surmise from that?"

"That they were friends. That maybe Lawrence introduced Arden to his sister."

"Again, very good. But, Archie, your dossier is missing a potentially critical fact. I'd suggest you keep working on it."

Julius had obviously already built his own dossier on Arden, most likely when he had turned me off a few days ago, or maybe one of the times when he had put me away in his desk drawer so I couldn't see what he was doing on his computer.

"What am I missing?" I asked.

Julius showed an exaggerated yawn. "It's late, Archie and I have a busy day ahead of me. I'm going to bed. You keep working on it, though."

Julius went upstairs to his bedroom and placed me next to his ear receiver on the dresser bureau before disappearing into his bathroom. The fact that I had missed something bothered me. I spun cycles like a crazy person building different logic models as I tried to figure out what it could've been. I was so wrapped up in this that I barely heard him gargling in the next room, or later, the shallow cadence of his breathing as he lay in bed. It was 3:47 in the morning when I figured it out. It had taken numerous adjustments to my neuron network, but I had it. As I mentioned before, Julius had already taken his ear receiver out for the night, and I was too excited to wait until 6:30 in the morning for him to wake up on his own and put his receiver back in, so I called him on his cell phone. He answered after the fourth ring.

"Archie, it's ten minutes to four—"

"I figured it out," I told him.

I heard him sigh. "This is my fault," he said. "I should've expected this. I've been pushing you too hard to create this type of personality. Archie, I'd like you to reprogram your neuron network so that you don't wake me up again, at least not unless it's for a legitimate reason."

"Sure, no problem. After I tell you what I've found."

"Let me guess, Archie. That you suspect Thomas Arden had embezzled half a million dollars from his company shortly before he disappeared?"

"That's right. It was hidden in the company's annual financial statement. A five-hundred-thousand-dollar line item for a tradeshow that didn't exist. He stole that money."

"Most likely."

"Why didn't the company file charges against him?" I asked.

Julius let out another heavy sigh. "Good night, Archie. It's late now."

"Please."

It wouldn't have surprised me if he had hung up his cell phone, but instead he explained it to me.

"The company probably didn't want their investors to find out about it. Most likely they needed another round of financing, and were afraid that this would kill it for them. Good night, Archie."

I wanted to ask him whether he thought that Lawrence and Arden had been in contact over the years, and whether he suspected that Lawrence had used Arden to kill his sister by threatening exposure. That's what I wanted to ask him, but I knew if I pushed it I risked being turned off again, so instead I held back. For the next two and a half hours, while Julius slept, I searched for any link I could find between Lawrence and Arden. By the time Julius's alarm went off at 6:30, I had decided to keep my theory to myself. What I wanted to do was locate enough evidence to solve this murder before Julius did. I couldn't help feeling that if I kept working on this I would beat him to the punch.

That morning, we mostly went our separate ways, Julius going through his calisthenics and martial arts training, and then mostly loafing about as he leafed through several books on the theory of war that he had recently purchased. Me, I spent my time building simulations that had Lawrence Brewer blackmailing Arden into killing his sister. One scenario came up that seemed plausible enough to research, and I was doing that when Julius interrupted me to get Helen Arden on the phone. Once I did, he had me patch him through.

"Mrs. Arden, first I'd like to offer my condolences for your sister's death. I know this is a difficult time right now, but I have a few questions. They may seem odd, but they're important. Have you had any contact with your husband since he disappeared?"

"No."

"Do you have any idea where he is?"

"No, sorry, I don't."

"Do you know if your brother does?"

That seemed to take her by surprise. It left me crushed. Dammit! Once again Julius was going to trump me. It left me in a bit of a funk where I could almost feel my processing cycles slowing down.

"I-I have no idea. Why are you asking that?"

"I'm working under the hypothesis that your brother and Thomas Arden were college friends, and that he introduced the two of you."

"Yes, that's true. But I don't understand why you're interested in this?"

"It's complicated right now, Mrs. Arden. I'll explain in due time. One last question, what can you tell me about the business your sister sold?"

"I really don't know anything about it."

"But your brother handled the legal aspects for her?"

"Yes, I believe so."

"Thank you, Mrs. Arden. And rest assured that I'll be doing everything I can to assist the police in finding the person responsible for your sister's murder."

Julius hung up. I told him about my theory, as well as my simulations.

"It seems you've come to the same conclusion," I said. "Would you like me to keep investigating my scenario?"

"I think that would be a splendid idea, Archie."

I did just that for the rest of the morning. Julius started reading one of his books more intently, but he soon became distracted, and several times put the book down so he could stare into space. Once he took out his cell phone and frowned at it before putting it away.

"Is there a call you'd like me to make?" I asked.

"What? No, nothing," he muttered, still obviously distracted. "Blast it, if I were to do this properly it would take several days, maybe longer. But that won't do, not now. I need to wrap this up today. Archie, I do have a call for you to make. To Detective Cramer. Ask him to send Lawrence Brewer to my office now. That if he does I should be able to point him to the murderer by evening."

I did as he asked. Cramer didn't like it. He had a dozen questions for Julius. I told him I was just the messenger and that the genius was unavailable, but that if Julius was promising to wrap the case up for him he should take him at his word. Cramer hung up on me without telling me what he was going to do. I decided that the solution of the case was a draw between me and Julius, and I decided to take it as a moral victory. I was about to tell him I wasn't sure what Cramer had decided when the phone rang. It was Lawrence Brewer. I patched the call through to Julius's earpiece.

"Why should I bother talking to you?" Brewer said.

"Many reasons. Most importantly, it gets you out of the police station. The longer you're there, the greater the chance they'll arrest you for your sister's murder. You must know at this point that they believe you murdered her."

"And you don't?"

"What I believe is beside the point. At least you'll have a chance to convince me otherwise, and I'll be offering far better refreshments than the police."

"Like what?"

Julius paused. "Assorted cheeses, meats, wine," he said.

"You've convinced me," Lawrence Brewer said with a touch of sarcasm, and hung up.

• • •

Cramer and two other police officers escorted Lawrence Brewer to Julius's townhouse. Julius brought Brewer to his office, and then left so he could argue with Cramer about why he wasn't going to allow anyone else to sit in on his questioning of Brewer. The two men were outside and Julius's office was soundproof, so there was little chance that Brewer would be able to listen in. While this argument went on I scanned the office's Web cam feed to make sure Brewer stayed put.

"I'm engaged in an extremely subtle and sensitive plan," Julius said as calmly and patiently as I knew he was capable of. A slight flutter showed along his left eye. "If you interfere, it won't work."

"Yeah, I know, you've been telling me that. And I'm telling you, I want to sit in and hear what he has to say," Cramer insisted, his jaw locked in a bulldog expression.

"Detective, if you had enough evidence to charge Brewer, you would've done so already. My guess is that without my help you'll never have enough. If you let me do things my way, you'll have enough evidence by tonight not only to charge but convict Norma Brewer's murderer."

"So Lawrence Brewer is the guy," Cramer demanded.

"Detective, some patience, please."

Cramer didn't like it. He could barely stand still. "And you just want me to let him walk out of here when he's done?" he said disgustedly.

"He's not going anywhere you won't be able to find him later."

For a moment I thought Cramer was going to tell Julius to go to hell. Instead, the steam went out of him. He told Julius that he had until the end of the day and after that he wasn't going to put up with any more of this nonsense, although Cramer used a far more color-ful word than that. Julius watched while Cramer left to join the two other police officers in a late-model sedan. After they drove away, he went back inside, first making a detour to the kitchen, where he picked up a tray of hors d'oeuvres that he had prepared earlier—buf-falo mozzarella wrapped in prosciutto along with assorted cheeses and olives—and then returning to his office. A bottle of Californian Petite Syrah had already been poured into a decanter and was wait-ing there. It was a fair vintage at best, one that Julius had bought out of curiosity, and one which he normally wouldn't serve to company, which showed his level of disdain for Brewer.

Julius placed the tray in front of Brewer, then sat behind his desk so he faced him. Julius next poured a single glass of Syrah and left it within arm's reach of his guest.

"I promised you refreshments and, if nothing else, I'm a man of my word," Julius said. "But, sir, let me say that without that prom-ise you'd get nothing from me."

Lawrence Brewer sat slumped in his chair. He looked worse than he had at the dog track the other day. A weariness tugged at the corners of his mouth, pulling it into a slight frown, and dark circles under his eyes gave him a raccoonlike appearance, especially with the paleness of the rest of his skin. Physically he resembled Norma more than his other sister, and like Norma he had too much nose and not quite enough chin. He took several pieces of the prosciutto and mozzarella and popped them into his mouth, then followed that with a long sip of wine.

"It's not as black and white as Norma made out to you," he said in a tired monotone as he stared bug-eyed at Julius. "My mother has some bad days, but she also has some good ones, and the fact is, she doesn't want to leave her home."

"I'm not interested in what you have to say," Julius said. "Nor would I believe a word coming from you. We both know that you are more concerned with your mother's money than her well-being, so don't insult me with this act."

"How dare you—"

"Shut up. All I want from you is to sit there and listen. We both know what you are, Brewer, make no mistake about that. I'm going to prove that you have borrowed large sums of money from a known gangster, Willie Andrews, so that you could finance your gambling addiction, and further, that you've been using your mother's assets as collateral. I wouldn't be surprised to find out that you've in some way been responsible for her recent weight loss and obvious malnutrition with the hopes of getting your hands on her money all that much sooner. Take this as a promise, Brewer: By the end of the day I'm going to make sure that her money is off-limits to you. You're going to need another way to satisfy your growing debt with Andrews. That's all. Get out of here."

The two men sat staring at each other, Brewer bug-eyed and Julius as still as if he'd been carved out of marble. Finally, Brewer broke off the staring contest and got to his feet.

"You better be careful what you say in public, Katz, or I'll be suing you for slander," Brewer said, a notable quaver in his voice. "This is a nice townhouse; I wouldn't mind having the courts award it to me." He left the office, and seconds later the sound of the front door opening and slamming could be heard.

"Bravo," I said.

Julius didn't bother responding.

"That accomplished a lot," I said after giving him suitable time to answer me. "You chased a murderer out of your office without trying to get a single bit of information from him. You could've asked him about his current relationship with Thomas Arden, or where he was when your client was having the life choked out of her, or any number of other things of interest, but no, you had to have the satisfaction of telling him off. Again, bravo."

That brought a thin smile to Julius's lips.

"Patience, Archie," he said. "I accomplished exactly what I had hoped."

I didn't believe him for one second. What he'd done was indulge in a childish impulse instead of focusing on the job at hand. I realized I was feeling something that must've been akin to annoyance—I was so close to having a draw with Julius, and his actions put the actual proving of it in jeopardy.

I was in no mood after that to continue with my scenario simulations, and instead spent the afternoon analyzing classic chess games and trying to find flaws in the winning player's moves. I found a few. Julius, after pouring the Syrah down the kitchen drain, spent his time mostly puttering around, at times reading, at other times distracted and staring off into space. Neither of us saw any reason to talk to the other, so we didn't. At 5:38 the doorbell rang. Julius checked the Web cam feed that covered the front entrance. Willie Andrews was standing outside the door rocking softly back and forth on his heels, his hands behind his back. Standing on either side of the door were what looked like hired muscle. One of them was grim-faced, the other showed a wide smirk, obviously thinking he couldn't be seen when Julius opened the door.

"Should I call the police?" I asked.

Julius shook his head. "Not necessary," he said. He took off his shoes and socks so that he was barefoot, then he headed to answer the door, moving with a catlike grace. When he opened the door, Willie Andrews pushed his way in and tried to back Julius up by poking him hard in the chest with his index finger, all the while yelling that he was going to teach Julius a lesson for interfering with his business.

Andrews was seven years younger than Julius, narrower in the shoulders, and several inches taller and with a longer reach. He never had a chance, not even with his two hired hands rushing in behind him to help. A fact that Julius keeps out of his press releases is that he's a fifth-degree black belt in Shaolin kung fu, as well as a long-time practitioner of Chen-style tai chi. In the blink of an eye, Julius deftly stepped aside and broke Andrews's finger, and in the same motion sent the gangster tumbling headfirst so that his chin cracked against the hardwood floor. Even though both of Andrews's hired goons outweighed Julius by a good forty pounds, it took him less than five seconds to leave them crumpled and bleeding outside his front door. He gave me a signal and I called an associate of his to pick up the rubbish that had been left outside.

Willie Andrews sat up, his eyes dazed as he clutched his broken finger and wiped his wrist against his bruised chin to see if he was bleeding. He wasn't.

"You broke my finger," he said to Julius, his lips contorting into the classic Hollywood bad-boy sneer. I found dozens of photos on the Internet that matched it exactly.

"You're lucky that's all I did. I could have you arrested for home invasion and battery."

"Yeah, well, I'll take my chances."

Still clutching his injured finger, Andrews pushed himself to his feet and started for the door.

"I could also see that you're tried and found guilty of murder," Julius said. "Norma Brewer's death means a larger inheritance for Lawrence, and you're the only person that would benefit from that."

That stopped Andrews. He turned around to face Julius, his sneer mostly gone. "What do you want?" he asked.

Julius told him. Andrews thought about it, realized he had no choice in the matter, and agreed.

Over the next hour Henry Zack arrived first, then Lawrence Brewer, followed by his sister Helen, next a mystery man who I knew from his conversations with Julius was one Roger Stromsby, although no one else in the room other than Julius had any idea who he was, and at last, Cramer, with four uniformed police officers, escorting a frail-looking but lucid Emma Brewer. It was clear from her eyes that she was having one of her good days. Julius waited until she was seated before he bowed his head to her and introduced himself.

"Ma'am," he said, "I'm sorry I have to bring you here under these circumstances. Unfortunately I have disturbing news to tell you, some of which I'm sure you're already aware of."

Emma Brewer's mouth weakened a bit, but her eyes remained dry. "I know you came by my house several days ago," she said, her voice stronger than I would've expected. "I wasn't having a good day then. I am now."

"Yes, ma'am," Julius said.

He took a deep breath and held it, his eyes fixed on Emma Brewer as she sat across from him. The rest of the setup had Helen and Lawrence sitting next to each other on a sofa to Julius's left, Willie Andrews holding an ice bag to his injured finger as he sat in a chair to Julius's right, Henry Zack standing behind Andrews, Roger Stromsby sitting in a corner trying to look inconspicuous, and Cramer and the other police officers standing in the background. Lawrence Brewer sat motionless in a bug-eyed stare, Helen looked mostly out of it as if she didn't understand what she was doing there, and Andrews's face was frozen in a half-grimace and half-smirk.

I asked Julius when Thomas Arden was going to be showing up. He ignored me and let the air slowly out of his lungs. "Ma'am," he said, still addressing Emma Brewer, "if you'd like I could offer you refreshments. Coffee, maybe? A sandwich?"

"No, thank you. Please just get on with it."

"Very well," he said more to himself than to her. "You're aware that your daughter, Norma, was murdered two days ago?"

Still dry-eyed, she nodded.

Julius continued, "Unfortunately, there's far more that I have to tell you. That man sitting to your left is named Willie Andrews. He's a well-known gangster and your son owes him a great deal of money."

Julius leveled his stare at Andrews. Without looking up, Andrews told the room that Brewer owed him six hundred thousand dollars. "He promised his ma's money and house to cover it. If he killed his sister for the money I know nothing about it."

All eyes turned to Brewer, but he didn't say a word. He just sat looking as if he had an upset stomach.

"Ma'am," Julius said, again addressing the mother, "when you saw me the other day, I had the sense that you mistook me for your son-in-law, Thomas Arden."

"I don't know. I might've."

"I do look somewhat like him."

"You're older than he was when I last saw him," she said with a weak smile. "But yes, you do resemble him."

"Twelve years ago he abandoned your daughter, Helen."

She nodded, some wetness appearing around her eyes.

"Do you know what happened to him?"

Emma Brewer looked like she was trying to fight back tears. She didn't say anything.

"Ma'am, this is no longer a matter of protecting your daughter Norma. She's beyond protection. After twelve years it's time for the truth. From the way you reacted when you thought I was Thomas Arden, it was as if you'd seen a ghost. He's dead, isn't he?"

Emma Brewer squeezed her eyes shut and nodded.

"Norma had an affair with him. She murdered him, didn't she?"

Helen Arden's jaw dropped as she stared at her mother. I was dumbfounded—yet another new emotion for me to experience. "How in the world ... ?" I heard myself asking Julius.

As if to answer me, Julius explained it to Emma Brewer.

"After you confused me with Arden, you confused your daughter Helen for Norma. They look nothing alike. I already had my suspicions regarding Norma, but this along with other facts that I uncovered all but told me about the affair."

Tears leaked from Emma Brewer's eyes. "I saw them together once. Norma later confided in me about the affair. Much later, she also told me what happened to him. According to her, it was an accident."

"It wasn't. She had him embezzle half a million dollars from his company, then she killed him for the money."

Roger Stromsby spoke up then. Stromsby was CEO of the company Arden stole from, and he confirmed what Julius said. "We suspected Arden, but we couldn't prove it," Stromsby added as straight-faced as he could. The real reason was what Julius had said earlier—that they were in fact covering up the theft so as not to scare off investors—but Stromsby wasn't about to admit that in a room filled with police officers.

Julius asked Cramer what he had been able to uncover about the business Norma Brewer claimed she had sold.

"We couldn't find anything," Cramer said gruffly.

Julius turned to Lawrence Brewer. "She didn't sell a business, did she?"

Lawrence shifted uneasily in his seat. "No, she didn't," he said. "Sometime after Tom disappeared, Norma came to me, telling me she had half a million dollars that she wanted to put into a Swiss bank account. I had no idea where the money came from, she never told me, but I helped her with the transfer. Several years ago, when she took the money out, I set up the fake business sale for her so she could explain the source of the money."

Something in my neuron network clicked and I could see as clearly as Julius had all along who the murderer was. I studied her then, and could tell that she wanted nothing more than to bolt from the room, and she probably would've if she thought she had enough strength in her legs to do so. Slowly other eyes turned towards her. When her mother joined in, it was too much for her and she seemed to shrink under the weight of it all.

"You should've told me," Helen Arden seethed at her mother. "The way you looked at me when you called me by her name, I knew …"

She tried running then. It didn't do her any good. One of the police officers stopped her and had her quickly cuffed. Emma Brewer started to sob then. Cramer helped her out of her chair. He was going to have a lot more questions for her.

Things went quickly after that.

The police officers, Andrews, and Stromsby cleared out, leaving Julius alone with Henry Zack and Lawrence Brewer, and they quickly reached an agreement whereby Zack transferred guardianship of Brewer's mother to Zack, as well as agreeing to a new will for Emma Brewer that would leave him with no inheritance. He had no choice; it was either agree to all that or have Julius destroy him, and he knew Julius had the means to do so. As it was, he was facing enough legal problems without having Julius after him. Once the paperwork was done and Julius and I were alone, I asked Julius when he first suspected Helen Arden.

"The question you should be asking, Archie, is when I first became suspicious of Norma Brewer, which was immediately." Julius stopped to sample one of the finer Rieslings that he kept in his cellar. "Boston has more than its share of excellent facilities, so why move her mother to Vermont?"

"Because she was afraid her mother might give up her secret while in a confused state."

"Precisely. And then you had her trying to bluff me, claiming how she didn't want Helen helping out because she didn't think her sister could handle it. The woman was a fool to hire me. Regardless of how desperate she might've been."

"So that's it? That's what tipped you off?"

"There was more." Julius frowned thinking about it. "It was absolute rubbish about her being afraid her brother would tie up any guardianship challenge in court. She could've received an immediate injunction—any competent lawyer would've told her that. But her brother obviously had something damning on her. Once I researched the missing brother-in-law, the pieces fell into place."

"You knew Helen Arden was going to kill her sister."

Julius shrugged. "You never know with something like that. But it was clear that something clicked with her when her mother reacted to me the way she did, and when she mistook her for Norma I could see the light go on in her eyes."

"Why the big show?" I asked. "Was it really necessary in order to coax a confession out of her? The woman seemed pretty beaten down as it was."

Julius made a face. "Maybe, maybe not," he said. "I had no direct evidence linking her to the murder. It was all pure conjecture on my part. More importantly, though, I had another task at hand— and that was seeing that Emma Brewer would be properly taken care of. The only way I could force Lawrence Brewer to cooperate was to hang the threat of a murder charge over his head, the same with Willie Andrews."

I digested all this and decided I had a lot of work still to do on my neuron network.

"Quite a day's work," I said. "You solved two murders, one that the police didn't even know about. And both of your clients turned out to be cold-blooded killers."

"And one of them found you utterly charming," Julius said, chuckling.

"I don't believe she used the adverb *utterly*. By the way, why the urgency? Why did this need to be done today?"

Julius's smile turned apologetic. "I'm sorry about this, Archie."

And blast it! He turned me off!

• • •

Julius turned me back on several hours later. I wasn't going to give him the satisfaction of asking him why he had shut me off. Instead, I hacked into his phone company's billing system and saw that he had placed a two-hour call to Lily Rosten.

The next day was business as usual. At six-thirty in the evening, Julius unclipped me from his tie, and without any explanation left me in his desk drawer. At seven, he left the townhouse. I called around and found the restaurant he had made dinner reservations for. They were for two. I settled in, not expecting to see him until morning, but again he surprised me by arriving home at midnight. Even more surprising, he was in a good mood about it. He even had me send Lily Rosten another dozen roses.

"I don't get it," I said. "You obviously struck out, so why so chipper?"

"Goodnight, Archie," he said.

It went on like this for the next three days. When Julius blew off a high-stakes poker game for yet another date with Lily Rosten, I knew something was seriously askew. I'd been trying to uncover this anomaly in his behavior through mathematical models, but I decided to go at it from a different angle and instead search for similar patterns in literature. It was after analyzing the text of a Jane Austen novel that I realized what was going on. Mystery solved. When Julius once again arrived home at midnight, I asked him how his evening went.

"Very well, Archie, thank you for asking."

"You know, we could double date. Why don't you ask Lily if she has one of those ultra-slim iPods that she could bring along?"

He chuckled at that. "I just might," he said.

"While we're on the subject, I guess I'll be needing to update your standard press release," I said. "Should I remove the reference concerning your being a confirmed bachelor now, or should I wait?"

That brought out the barest trace of a guilty smile. "Good night, Archie," he said.

As I said before, mystery solved.

• • •

DAVE ZELTSERMAN lives in the Boston area with his wife, Judy, and his short crime fiction has been published in many venues. His third novel, *Small Crimes,* was named by NPR as one of the five best crime and mystery novels of 2008. His novel *Pariah* was named by the *Washington Post* as one of the best books of 2009. His upcoming novel *Outsourced* is currently in development by Impact Pictures and Constantin Film.

SEEING THE MOON

By S.J. Rozan

I'd never even considered trying to take down Peter Boyd. Like everyone else in the art world, I'd heard rumors his legit gallery trade was only half his business, and not the lucrative half; and I personally knew he was a patronizing bigot. Every now and then in the course of a case, when I couldn't avoid calling him—and believe me, I tried—I got no help, just some gasbag lecture about whatever piece I was after as though he were the one with the degree in Asian Art. No question the guy wasn't on my Christmas card list. But it wasn't personal until he messed with Molly Lo.

With leaf-filtered May sunlight dancing on my office wall, I was doing some creative Web surfing, due-diligence on a new gallery a client was wondering about. My iPhone tore through the calm, bellowing "The East is Red." The first da-dah, and I was asking, "What's up, homegirl?" I don't keep Molly waiting.

"I have a problem."

"You need a shoulder?"

"I need professional help."

"I'm not touching that."

"Your profession, jerk."

"No kidding. The Thompson's calling Jack Lee? Or wait—you just want a background run on that new guy you're dating."

"For that I wouldn't call an art detective."

"You're right, he's no work of art. But for real? The museum needs me?"

"But it doesn't know it does and I'd like to keep it that way."

"My lip is zipped. Should I come down?"

"Do you have time today?"

"Be there in ten minutes."

I wasn't showing off; my office is five blocks from Molly's. When your gig is strayed art, a Madison Avenue address gives your clients a warm and fuzzy feeling.

Molly and I met in grad school, U. of Chicago, East Asian Studies, two cornbelt Chinese kids bonding over tangkhas and Utamaros. We passed through and out of an infatuation phase, and then, clutching our degrees, headed for New York best friends. We both got the jobs we wanted most. Molly loved hers. Not me so much. In Chicago I'd spent as much time auditing American Lit courses and shooting hoops as in the conservation lab. Molly says that should have tipped me off, and she's right: turned out the gallery assistant shtick bored me out of my skull. So I regrouped, went for a PI license, and now I have fun, making like Sherlock Holmes when someone's Tang horse gallops away. I'm still, you know, getting established, so my location-location-location office is a little spare, which accounts for dancing sunlight being the wall's best feature. But the emptiness just makes people think I practice Zen. And if I could sit still long enough I probably would.

Molly, though, beelined for the gallery ladder, climbing until she bagged her dream six months ago: the Thompson, a small Asian art museum based around an eclectic, to say the least, private collection. Gordon Thompson, a retired rich person, opens his double brownstone to the public four days a week, with rotating exhibits curated by that rising art-world star, Molly Lo, for whom everything seemed to be coming up roses. Until now.

Me, I'd only met Gordon Thompson twice, at openings Molly invited me to. But if he had a reason to think well of me, it would be kind of great. I locked up, grabbed a shot-in-the-dark from the Not-Starbucks on the corner, and sprinted to the rescue. I hoped.

Molly's assistant, Sherry—when you're as cool as Molly, you have people—led me through the front hall and up the grand staircase, past scholar's rocks and cinnabar boxes. Hasui's woodblock print *Kiba* hung at the landing and I stopped to admire it. No one, and I mean no one, makes you feel weather like Hasui Kawase. Sherry waited patiently, then led on, parking me in the Americana room. In case anyone was under the delusion Mr. Thompson was perfect, this room would shatter it. The one area that competes with imperial silks and Ukiyo-e for his attention, and his bucks, is a narrow slice of American history: artifacts of daily living, eastern seaboard, nineteenth century. Molly and I have a theory he was there in his last life. That could explain his enlightened-amateur approach to art, something you don't see much these days. And what else could explain this cheerful obsession with spittoons, riding crops, and doilies? Luckily Sherry didn't maroon me there long.

"I'm here to save the day," I announced, arriving in Molly's airy Qing-and-Ming office. "Could you cut down the dazzle, though?" I dropped into a scholar's chair.

"Too much sun?" She started to close the drapes.

"No, you. You look gorgeous. Trouble becomes you."

"Bullshit."

See why I like her? "No, really. Worry makes your cheeks flush or something. So what can I do for you?"

"I made a big mistake."

"Anyone dead? No? Then we can fix it. Tell me."

She sat, not behind her desk but in the other visitor's chair. I'm as Chinese as she is, but the chair looked better on her. "Two weeks ago," she started seriously, "I bought a bronze standing Buddha. Nepal, fifteenth century. It's in the center hall."

"Saw it. Didn't spend much time with it, though."

"Don't bother. It's a piece Mr. Thompson really wanted. There's a hole in the Himalayan collection right about there. We'd been making the auction rounds but nothing caught his eye. Then Peter Boyd called."

"Uh-oh."

She nodded. "He said he'd heard we were looking, and he had something we might be interested in."

"I'm getting a bad feeling."

"On the money. It's a fake."

"You must've vetted it before you bought it."

"Six ways from Sunday. Mr. Thompson's been in Asia for awhile, Hong Kong, Shanghai and Singapore, for the shows, but Boyd sent him photos and the piece grabbed him. He doesn't like doing business with Boyd—"

"Showing good taste."

"—but he really wanted this piece. You know how it is with collectors, something comes along and they just have to have it?"

I nodded; I did know. I'm counting on that to pay my rent.

"He told me to have it looked at, and buy it if it checked out. It's the first time he's let me go ahead on my own. So I called in three different experts. It was the real deal. But the one in the case downstairs, not. Somewhere in there Boyd switched statues on us, Jack. I don't know how."

"How'd you find out?"

"I unpacked it. Catalogued it. Put it out. And then every time I walked by it I got the bad feeling you're getting now. I heard Hans Grolsch was in New York this week, so I asked him to come look at it."

"Happy Hans! I haven't seen him in ages."

"Well, he wasn't so happy with my Buddha. He confirmed it. Total fake."

"You called Boyd?"

"Of course. He said he'd put up with a lot from me already—'dicking around,' he called it—and he's not surprised to hear Hans Grolsch took a swipe at him."

"They have a history?"

"Boyd's very existence offends Hans. He thinks people who're only in it for the money and don't love the art shouldn't be allowed to get their grubby hands on it."

"Another man with good taste. Any possibility he's wrong about your statue?"

"No, and I told Boyd that. He said at this point, *caveat emptor*. And then, that bastard—!" She stopped, sputtering.

"Wow."

"Wow, what?"

"You're so mad your eyes are actually flashing."

"*Jack!*"

"'That bastard ...?'"

"That *bastard* said Mr. Thompson was happy with the piece, wasn't he? So I should just leave it where it was, let everyone enjoy it, and no one would have to know the Thompson's new young director spent eighty thousand dollars on a fake."

I whistled. "That bastard."

"Mr. Thompson comes back in three days. What am I going to do?"

"For now, nothing." I unfolded myself from the chair. No great loss: Qing furniture's not all that comfy. "However, *I* am going to see Mr. Boyd."

• • •

You may be asking yourself why I bothered. What was he going to do—fall on his knees, confess to the fraud, beg forgiveness and make restitution on the spot (with a little vig to cover Molly's mental anguish and my fee) now that Jack Lee was on the case?

But it didn't seem sporting not to give him a chance.

Peter Boyd Oriental—that's a bad sign already, right?—occupies a piss-elegant gallery on the same swank stretch of Madison Avenue as the Thompson and me. Boyd, wearing Armani, his short silver hair bristling and his tan glowing, issued a pained smile when he saw me come in. "Oh, my, Charlie Chan."

"If you have to throw around cheap stereotypes, Peter, could you at least go with Chow-Yun Fat? *Sex*-y. I'm here about that tin Buddha you palmed off on the Thompson."

"Oh? Molly Lo feels hard done by, so she's gone to Jack Lee, Boy Detective? That's some nice cultural solidarity there, Jack."

"You want to talk out here, or in private?"

"Given that there are no patrons in the gallery at the moment, that's a rather hollow threat. Still, come in back where we'll be comfortable."

He nodded to his gallery assistant, a faux-hawked kid in an Armani knock-off, and led me into his suite of offices in the back. This was the only gallery I knew with more back-room than front-room space. I mean, who needs a suite of offices? But part of Boyd's juju was to make his buyers feel the serious business was done here, where he showed them prints, netsuke, and graceful Han dancers that he disdained exhibiting in the front gallery for all eyes to see.

And rumor had it another part was to sell prints, netsuke, and Han dancers of questionable provenance in deals better done where there were fewer eyes, anyway.

He turned and gave me a beady eye. At five-eleven, I had four inches on him, but I'm such a beanpole our weight class was probably the same.

"The Thompson wants their money back," I said.

"Molly Lo wants the Thompson's money back. And she's not going to get it."

"You want the world to know you sold them a piece of junk?"

"They had it authenticated."

"And you switched it."

"Careful, Jack. You shouldn't make accusations you can't prove."

"You want me to shut up, re-switch it. Bundle up the real one and I'll take it with me right now."

"Funny thing about that. I just sold a very, very similar piece to a collector in Singapore. Shipped it over two days ago."

I gave him my best level stare. "Then return the money."

"Come on. Eighty thousand dollars? That's pocket change for Gordon Thompson. As long as pretty Molly keeps her mouth shut, what's really been lost?"

"She can't do that, Peter. Unlike you, she has scruples."

"Oh, ouch."

"You'd better think hard about this."

"Or what? You'll go public? Jack, I suggest *you* think before you stick your foot in your mouth. If it comes out the piece is fake, I'll just say I had no idea."

"You're supposed to be an expert. You'll look like an idiot."

"Molly, Gordon Thompson, and I will all look like idiots, yes. So will the experts they took it to."

"Except Hans Grolsch."

"Good for Happy Hans." Boyd shrugged. "You know what, though? We'll all survive. We'll blush, look shamefaced, and go on."

"You think so? Then let's try it."

He held up a manicured finger. "Except, maybe, for Molly. They did have it authenticated, so it's not my problem anymore. I won't take it back."

"Not just an idiot, a swindling, tightfisted idiot."

"Maybe. But Molly's problem will be worse. So young and untested, making a foolish mistake so early in her career?"

"Bastard" wasn't strong enough. "You counted on that, didn't you? That you could paint Molly into a corner."

"It's too bad, but you know as well as I that in situations like this someone has to be sacrificed. And the gods prefer pretty girls to stringy old men."

I met his eyes for a long steady moment. Then I broke off, sighed and looked around the office. A Japanese scroll on the wall evoked trees and night in three flowing brushstrokes. The characters read, "Barn burned down: now I can see the moon." I let my gaze rest on it, then wander to a nearby case. Four long pipes of teak, gold, ivory, and silver; some slender jade needles; a tiny but elaborately carved whisk broom and pan. Opium paraphernalia, a cove off the Asian art sea. So much was destroyed in the late nineteenth-century anti-opium hysteria that what's left qualifies as rare. This was the only area where Boyd himself collected, working from gusto, not just greed. Whether he smoked the stuff I had no idea, but he was known to be addicted to the gear. Sensing a possibility, I turned from the objects of desire back to the man.

"Those things are beautiful," I said in a conciliatory way.

"Those 'things' are among your peoples' best contributions to civilization."

The compass? The civil service system? Gunpowder? Steamed little juicy buns? But I wasn't here to debate. "Peter," I said, "is there any chance you have a heart?"

"No. Why?"

I rubbed my mouth, then sighed again. "Because your bogus Buddha is only part of Molly's problem. She'd kill me for telling you this, but she's in hot water already, or about to be. Last week she finished an inventory she probably should have started her first day there. But a big new job like that, you know … Anyway, now she's done, and it seems they're missing three Hasuis."

Boyd leaned back, eyebrows raised. "I'd say that's a problem. But maybe they disappeared before her time."

"Likely. But that's why you do inventories. Now she can't prove that."

"Gordon Thompson thinks she took them?"

"God, no. Molly? Anyhow, he's away, so he doesn't know yet. But at best he'll think she's been sloppy with his collection when he finds out. And then to discover she bought your piece of—"

"Which ones?"

"What?"

"Which Hasuis?"

I paused, then told him, "*Rainy Lake in Matsue District, Evening at Soemoncho,* and *Spring Night at Inokashira.*"

"I didn't know Thompson owned those." Boyd himself is deep in Hasui. Not because he gives a damn about beautiful lines or subtle inks. But he knows an undervalued artist when he sees one. Some years back he bought up a few private collections, narrowing, if not quite cornering, the market. Thereby driving prices up. Hasui's prints are still not all that costly, in the mid-four or sometimes low five figures. But they're out of reach of, say, me, who can only admire them on gallery walls.

"Thompson's a big Hasui man," I told Boyd. "From before you locked them all up. He doesn't show many at a time—right now, only one—but he has twenty-seven."

Boyd smiled. "From what you say, now twenty-four."

"Peter—"

"No."

I gave him another long look. "You really are a bastard, aren't you?"

"So I hear."

• • •

I hadn't been back out on the street two minutes when my iPhone treated Madison Avenue to "The East is Red."

"Did you get my Buddha?" I could hear Molly holding her breath.

"It already went to Singapore."

"Oh, no! Then my money?"

"I'm working on it. Listen, is Happy Hans still in town?"

"Oh, Jack!" she wailed. "You didn't get anywhere at all with Boyd, did you?"

"Well, the best he could do was repeat his suggestion that you leave the fake where it is and let Mr. Thompson enjoy it."

"I can't, you know I can't. And now you want to double-check with Hans and see if he could have been wrong. He's not, I told you! Oh, Jack, you were my last hope. I am so sunk!"

"It's a little early for that level of panic."

"What should I do, wait until after lunch?"

"You should give me Hans's number. And then calm down. Go meditate or something."

She did the first, but not the second, and probably not the third. In her position, I wouldn't have either.

• • •

Now, you may be thinking "Happy Hans" is one of those ironic nicknames for some dour German who hasn't smiled since 1964. Not in this case. Hans Grolsch could be the picture in the dictionary next to "Jolly Dutchman," if that were in the dictionary. White hair, chubby red cheeks, sparkling blue eyes, huge smile that you can't call quick in coming only because it almost never leaves. He's a dealer and appraiser from Delft and what he really defines is a man who loves his work.

"Jack, my boy!" Hans raised a pilsner glass, already half-drained, when he spied me. We were meeting in the garden of a red-sauce Italian restaurant, food he claims he can't get in Holland. "You look well!" If I'd been at death's door he'd probably have said, "You look awful!" with equal enthusiasm.

"So do you, Hans." Sitting, I grinned, which no one can help doing around Hans. Except maybe Molly, yesterday.

"Ah, yes, the Buddha." Even Hans sighed when we'd ordered our spaghetti Bolognese, and Hans his second Sugar Hill, and I brought up Molly's problem. "They were rooked, you know. It's actually very good, bronze with an applied patina, I think a lost-wax casting from the original. Worth possibly twenty-five hundred dollars."

"Any chance you're wrong?"

He threw me a pitying look, tucked a napkin under his chin and reached for the bread. "It's a shame. Such a nice girl, Molly. But a man like Boyd—myself, I do not do business with him."

"Molly told me he gives you hives."

"Hives, he makes me itch? Yah, that's good, Jack! Yes, it's bad enough, the people who buy and sell art as a commodity, with no love. But to cheat also, this is abhorrent. Such men must be avoided. You cannot win against a man like that."

That pronouncement was downright gloomy, particularly considering the source. I contemplated it, then contemplated our antipasto.

• • •

"Let me buy you a drink after work," I suggested over the iPhone to Molly as I strolled to my office full of pasta and garlic.

"Buy me a ticket out of town and a new identity."

"You don't need that."

"You made a miracle?"

"A couple of martinis and you'll think I did. Come on, it'll make you feel better."

"It'll only make me think I feel better. But if that's all I can get, I'm in."

Molly and I were up late, going from martinis to pad Thai to the late show at Drom, which involved more martinis. I shelled out for all of it. It was the least I could do.

• • •

I don't know when Molly got to work the next morning, but as I was stumbling along Madison toward my office sometime near noon, she called me.

"I just heard from Peter Boyd," she said.

"Do you have to bring him up when I feel like crap?"

"You shouldn't drink so much."

"You were three ahead by the end of the night!"

"I could always hold it better, why do you keep trying? Boyd wants me to go to his gallery."

"Oh." I rubbed my aching eyes. "Did he say why?"

"No. But I'm not going alone."

"Sigh. Okay, I'll meet you. Just give me time for coffee."

I grabbed a double-venti, plus a bagel for belly ballast. By the time we rolled into Peter Boyd Oriental I didn't have any more of a headache than the one he gives me.

"Molly, my dear. And Jack." Boyd smiled like the shark he is. "Jack, you look awful." He said it with almost as much joy as Happy Hans would have, though for different reasons.

Molly, on the other hand, looked stunning in gallerina black, her hair flowing to her shoulders like ebony silk. She pursed her lips and allowed him to lead us to the office suite, where she sat primly and didn't speak. Boyd smiled again and didn't speak either.

Someone had to break this silence or we'd all suffocate. "Okay, Peter, we're here," I said.

"*You* weren't invited," Boyd pointed out. He turned to Molly. "I have something you'll want."

"My eighty thousand dollars?"

He chuckled as though he appreciated her funny joke. "No. These." From a folio he lifted three heavy sheets, each wrapped in acid-free paper. One by one he liberated them and laid them on the desk. Hasui, *Rainy Lake in Matsue District*, *Evening at Soemoncho*, and *Spring Night at Inokashira*. And good impressions, too.

Molly's jaw dropped, though she recovered fast. Shooting me a glare, she asked Boyd, "What makes you think I'm interested in these?"

"Your boyfriend here. Don't worry, I won't tell. Jack, try not to look so abashed. Truly, you did Molly a favor. If you slip these into the collection, Gordon Thompson will never know. Not too many editions of these three were made. The paper's all the same, the ink. What Gordon had was probably so close to these that he'll never be able to tell they've been replaced."

While Boyd was yakking on I examined the prints. They were the real thing, and breathtaking.

"Jack," said Molly icily, "I'm going to kill you."

"That would be all right with me," said Boyd. "But please pay for these first."

"How much?" I asked, to see if I could be useful.

"Fifteen thousand."

"For the three?"

"Each."

"Are you insane? Hasui's not going for anything near that!"

"Most Hasuis don't have the power to save a promising career."

"Thirty-five hundred each for these two, forty-five for 'Inokashira.'"

"Don't make me laugh. And this isn't a rug shop in the casbah. My offer's firm and it's not going to last."

"Where do you expect Molly to get that kind of money?"

"She can borrow it from you for all I care."

"Are you two through?" Molly's angry words sliced through our dickering. "Jack? Shut up. Don't help, okay? And Peter, you can stick your offer in your vault." She settled back in her chair and gave a surprising little smile. "These are beautiful but I don't need them."

"Oh, how lucky," Boyd said mock-kindly. "Gordon's have turned up?"

"No. But I have a line on something else, something he's so excited about he'll forgive me for the Hasuis, which aren't my fault anyway, and your scrap-heap Buddha, too."

"Is that a fact?"

Molly, crossing her awesome legs, arched a single eyebrow. I didn't know she could do that.

"All right, you want me to guess. Why not?" Boyd dripped condescension. Molly was being kind of obnoxious, though, I had to admit. Pretending to think hard, Boyd stared into space. "I know he's been looking for both cloisonné and carved jade lately."

"And you have some beauties to sell, I'm sure," I said.

"Jack," said Molly, "did I mention 'shut up?' I really don't need your help, or whatever this is. And Peter, forget it. Besides the fact that I'll never, ever do business with you again, this piece isn't even Asian. It's Americana."

"Oh." Boyd deflated. "Junk, you mean."

"To you, maybe. Not to Mr. Thompson. He's thrilled."

"Whatever it is, I suggest you buy these anyway. It can't hurt to have his Hasui collection intact when he gets back."

"If you were giving them away for free I wouldn't take them."

"Twelve each for these," said Boyd. "Thirteen for 'Inokashira.'"

"If I keep saying no, will you keep coming down until you get to free?" Molly looked delighted, as though this were a game.

"No."

"Then I might as well go." She stood. I noticed she hadn't said "we." "Hans Grolsch will be coming by with my new purchase. I don't want to miss him."

"Wait," Boyd said. "You're not going without revealing the secret of this wondrous artifact?"

"Oh, didn't I say?" Molly smiled and paused. I rolled my eyes. It was clear she'd had no intention of leaving the room without dropping her bombshell. "It's an opium pipe. Edgar Allan Poe's."

Peter Boyd blanched. *Wow*, I thought. Good for Molly.

Boyd, recovering, demanded, "What are you talking about?"

"It's actually beautiful, too. Though Mr. Thompson would want it no matter what, for its historical importance. It's been in private hands since Poe pawned it in 1842. Never on the market before." Her eyes widened theatrically. "Oh, that's right! Peter, you collect opium paraphernalia, don't you? Would you like to see it?"

From her purse she took a sleek digital camera. She clicked on a stored photo and passed the camera to Boyd. She was smiling like the cat that ate the canary and when he saw the photo he turned apoplectic like the cat that had been planning to. He stared at the screen and she stared at him and no one except me seemed to care whether I saw the photo, too. So I leaned over Boyd's shoulder.

Molly was right, the pipe was beautiful. A richly carved ivory bowl and mouthpiece, a silver stem inlaid with what looked like jade. "That's jade," Molly told Boyd. "On the stem."

Boyd looked up at her.

"Poe bought it one of the few times in his life when he was flush," Molly said. "Then pawned it when he went broke again. The pawnbroker was an admirer of Poe's writing. Gave him a good price and never sold it. It's been in his family since."

Boyd found his voice. "Where—"

"Happy Hans," Molly said. "That's why he's in New York. The family moved to England in 1896 when they started to come up in the world. Now they've come down again so they're selling off their art. Hans thought he'd do better with the Americana here than in Europe. He brought a few things, including this, specifically to offer to Mr. Thompson. He didn't know Mr. Thompson was away, but it doesn't matter. As you know, Peter, you stinker, Mr. Thompson will buy from photos, as long as he's sure the piece is genuine."

Boyd ignored the dig. "And this is?"

"Hans authenticated it. There's still the pawn ticket, for one thing. And a lab Hans consulted says because of the chemical nature of opium residue, there may be recoverable DNA. They haven't tested for that yet, though."

That undone test didn't seem to bother Boyd; he knows as well as anyone in the business that Hans Grolsch never signs off on a piece he's not sure about. Boyd turned slowly to look at the pipes and jade picks in his paraphernalia case. "That fat Dutchman. This is *my* area. Why didn't he offer it to me?"

"Because," I said, muscling in on Molly's victory, "Happy Hans is just one among thousands who won't do business with a worm like you."

Boyd must have been seriously rattled because he ignored my slur, too. "How much?" he asked Molly.

"What do you care?"

"How much!"

She blinked. "A hundred thousand."

"For a pipe?" Boyd snorted. "I've never paid more than fifty."

"Coleridge's went for a hundred and twenty-three last year," I reminded him. "And not to you, as I recall. You were beat out by Simon White in London."

"That fat Brit. Why is everyone in this business fat? Sit down. Both of you, sit down!"

Molly looked at me.

"Sit down!"

I shrugged. We sat down.

"I want this," Boyd said.

"Too bad," said Molly.

"No. Too bad for Gordon Thompson. What you need to do, Molly, is get in touch with Happy Hans and arrange for him to sell it to me, and only me."

"Why would I do that?"

"Because, little Molly, if you don't, I'll tell Gordon you were not only part of the scheme to defraud him of his Buddha, but that it was in fact your idea."

Total, total silence.

Finally Molly squeaked, *"What?* You can't. You wouldn't."

Boyd smiled thinly. "I think I'll even tell him you took the lion's share of the proceeds. If I sound aggrieved, you can be sure he'll believe me."

"Peter—" I started.

"Jack, let me echo Molly: shut up."

"No!" I jumped from my seat. "Listen, you can't do this."

"Watch me."

"Goddamn it—"

"Jack, if you want to be Sir Galahad and ride to Molly's rescue, why don't you stop yelling at me, and convince her I'm serious and she should call Hans right away?" He was speaking to me, but looking directly at Molly.

"Peter," I said, "Hans won't sell you the pipe no matter what Molly says. Remember, he won't do business with you?"

Boyd's brow furrowed. "That's probably true. All right. Molly, you'll buy it and convey it to me. I'm not even going to insist that you dicker with Hans over the price."

Molly looked at him wildly. "I can't! Peter! Mr. Thompson wants it so much!"

"You can tell him he got beat out for it. It happens all the time. He'll get over it."

"But he'll be mad at Hans, and Hans will tell him he *did* sell it to me."

"That's your problem. Maybe you can offer Hans some other … consideration."

It was impossible to miss what that meant. Molly's cheeks flared. I took a step toward him. *"Peter—!"*

"Oh, Jack, drop the histrionics. What are you going to do, karate-chop me? Go on, both of you, get out of here. Molly, bring me that pipe tomorrow, or—when did you say Gordon would be back? In three days? Or, you have three days to find another job."

Molly rose in a wobbly way and stood for a moment. Then without warning she rounded on me, eyes practically shooting sparks. "This is your fault!"

"Me?"

"If you hadn't shot off your mouth about the Hasuis we wouldn't be here. He'd never know about the pipe!"

"I was trying to help."

"Thanks a lot!"

"Molly, my dear." Boyd stepped between us as though Molly were about to sock me, which she might have been. "Jack's not the one who brought up Poe's pipe in an effort to lord it over me, is he?"

That caused another silence. Molly was glaring like she'd make Boyd's head explode if she could.

"Tomorrow," said Boyd. "And by the way, I close at four."

"Wait," I said.

"For what?"

"First," I drew a breath, collecting myself, "you'll pay with a cashier's check."

"Jack! Don't you trust me?" Boyd broadly faked surprise.

"And second, you'll throw in the Hasuis."

Now the surprise was real. "I'll do what?"

"You can't leave Molly with nothing. She's got your junk Buddha and now she's lost Poe's pipe. Your blackmail," I snarled the word, "is supposed to save her job. If Mr. Thompson finds his Hasuis gone, too, that'll be the last straw. He'll can her, so why should she do this in the first place?"

Molly looked as if she were going to cry.

"Coleridge's pipe went for a hundred and twenty-three," I reminded Boyd. "Poe's at a hundred is a steal."

Boyd cocked his head and relented. "All right. Bring the pipe and you can have the Hasuis. They're not worth more than ten thousand together anyway. And of course I'd like to see Molly keep her job." He smiled. "Then we can do business again in the future."

• • •

The pipe did get conveyed to Boyd the next day, not by Molly, but by me. "I don't even want to be seen going in and out of there anymore," she said. So I waited as late in the day as I dared, just to make Boyd sweat, then brought the pipe and resisted the urge to shove it where it would do the most good. I made him give me the cashier's check, which I held up to the lamp to check the watermark, and the Hasuis, which I also examined, before I handed the pipe over. Seeing the lovelight in Boyd's eyes as he unwrapped it almost made me think he might be a human being. It was truly beautiful: the ivory bowl intricately carved, brought to a rich gold from heat and smoke; the jade inlays on the silver stem glinting provocatively.

"The paperwork?" he snapped at me, pulling his eyes from his new darling.

I handed over an envelope. Boyd slid out a cardboard square in a protective plastic sleeve—the pawn ticket, countersigned by the pawnbroker and the customer—and a Certificate of Authenticity from Hans Grolsch's gallery in Delft.

Boyd's forefinger gently rubbed the pipe's silver stem. Without looking at me, he said, "Jack, it's been a pleasure. Now get out."

• • •

When I got to Molly's office I found one of the Qing chairs cradling Hans Grolsch's beefy behind. I hesitated. Molly looked at me with anxious eyes. "Jack . .?"

Glancing at Hans, I offered Molly my portfolio. She opened it and, one by one, took the Hasuis out. Hans stood to look at them. "Well, these really are beautiful, aren't they?" he said.

Molly looked from the prints to me. I kept the stone face going another minute, then cracked. "So's this," I cackled, slapping Boyd's check down.

Molly drew a sharp breath. She put out a tentative hand, as though the check might bite her. Hans craned for a look. For a moment all eyes were fixed on that paper rectangle.

Then Hans laughed, a booming explosion of glee. Then Molly laughed, like chimes. Then I laughed. Then Hans whomped me on the back. I gasped for air as he said, "Jack, my boy! You did it!"

"*We* did it," I wheezed. "It would never have worked without you, Hans. But Molly's the real star. That eyebrow thing—did you practice in a mirror? And DNA in the opium residue! Where did that come from?"

Molly looked up from the ledger on her desk and smiled. "Just a little improvisation. Glad you liked it. Here, Hans." She handed him a check. "Are you sure it's enough? I hate to see you not make a profit."

"My dear, I'd have paid to be part of this! Twelve thousand is nearly what I could have expected for that pipe, so beautiful but without provenance. And the other eight will neatly cover the fee of Jack's delightful friend, who so skillfully created the pawn ticket."

"Abie does good work," I said.

"Yes. Though I must tell you, as pleased as he was with his results on the ticket, he became peevish when I insisted his forgery of my own signature be bad enough to be obvious, if need be. He made me promise to make *you* promise never to reveal the source of such sloppiness."

"The secret will go to my grave."

"I have one question, though," Molly said. "What if Poe's opium pipe does come on the market?"

I stared at her. "You just have to have something to worry about, don't you? First, if Peter ever gets his Jockeys in a knot over this, we deny knowing what the hell he's talking about. What pipe? We sold him a pipe? Never happened, he's tripping. What can he say? And Hans is completely insulated. Forged signature on no doubt stolen letterhead."

"People might even think it was Peter who forged it!" Hans grinned as that dawned on him.

I nodded. "But second, it won't. The pipe. Come to market."

"Why not?"

"God, I love that eyebrow thing! Because, as you'd know if you'd ever stepped outside Cochrane-Woods to take an American Lit course with me, there is no such pipe. Edgar Allan Poe never smoked opium."

"Come on. I thought he was a big druggie."

"Slander. Though he did take a little opium from time to time."

"That's what I—"

"But in the form of laudanum. Itty bitty liquid drops. He never smoked it. There is no pipe."

"Why, Jack Lee, you sneaky—"

"Hey, you two, lower the juice on the smiles, would you? You're blinding me."

We made plans to regroup at the Beatrice Inn in an hour, where Molly and I could get major mojitos, Hans could get draft Ommengang, and we could people-watch the coolest crowd in New York and not see anyone cooler than we were. We'd have gone right away, but Molly needed to put Boyd's money in the bank so the Thompson's account would be whole when Thompson got back. His Hasui collection would be improved, too; he'd never owned any of these three prints, which is why I'd picked them to get this ball rolling. Molly was going to tell Thompson that I'd extorted them out of Peter Boyd in exchange for not exposing his switcheroo. That, plus Hans's lavish praise for her valor in calling him in to examine the Buddha even after she'd spent the money, and also the fine-tuned instincts that made her uncomfortable with the fake in the first place, should ensure her continued employment at the Thompson. Maybe even a raise. And next time I met him at an opening, Mr. Thompson might remember my name.

So we split to run our own errands. I wanted to drop by my office, too; I had my own fee to deal with. Molly was adding two Hasuis to Thompson's stash. Me, I was anxious to see how the full moon at the center of *Spring Night at Inokashira* looked in the sunlight dancing on my office wall.

• • •

S. J. ROZAN, a life-long New Yorker, is an Edgar, Shamus, Anthony, Nero and Macavity winner. She's served on the boards of Mystery Writers of America and Sisters in Crime, and as President of Private Eye Writers of America. She teaches a summer writing workshop in Assisi, Italy. Her latest book is *The Shanghai Moon* and her website is www.sjrozan.com.

DARK
CHOCOLATE
By Nancy Pickard

Seven inches high in the center, sloping gently from that center to the perimeter of the perfect circle, this was her cake.

"My cake," Marcie whispered, alone in her kitchen.

All hers. All of it. Every. Single. Bite.

"Mine."

Before she frosted it, there was a white lacework around its dark sides—a residue of the flour with which she had dusted her pans. *Cake pan, cake pan, better than a man can.* She rhymed, she sang, as she swirled her frosting spatula along the steep sides and mountaintop of the tall, dark, luscious beauty.

Finished frosting, she stepped back to admire her work.

Behind her, the old refrigerator hummed along with her.

Ice it, ice it, slice it, slice it.

"Perfect," she whispered, as if she were afraid to wake the dead.

Perfect, perfect, perfect, hummed the refrigerator.

Now to cut into it. Always tricky. Always challenging. It made her nervous. Things could go wrong so fast, even after so much planning and work. Even after the mixing, stirring, baking, cooling, icing, things could still go wrong at the last minute. The cake could fall. It could fail to satisfy, could be too done, too dry, or not quite cooked clear through. She had stuck toothpicks into the very center of both layers while they were still in the oven, at the end of the baking cycle, and they had emerged clean. Nothing had clung to them. She had thrilled to see the toothpicks which suggested she had cooked a perfect cake this time. But there was still time for it to go wrong. It could still fall, all tumbled down in the middle as if somebody had punched a fist into its face. She hoped it wouldn't fall or fail like that. She wanted this cake, her cake, this particular cake on this day, to be perfect.

Marcie picked up her special cake knife.

Silver-plated wedding gift from she didn't remember who.

One of those people

Under the steeple.

She held the knife above her cake, hovering, anxious, afraid of messing up. Hard not to mess up. Easy to fail. Hard to lay a perfect thick triangle on a pristine plate. *Glass plate, clear plate, what will be my life's fate?*

She held her breath as she lowered the knife to the frosting.

It hurt. It almost hurt to do that, to touch the chocolate, to move the knife slowly through the icing and down to the firmer substance, the cake below it. She wanted to hurry, to rush through it so she wouldn't have to feel it, the pain of slicing through her cake. *No push, no shove. That rhymes with love.* Once she made the first cut, there was no going back. No taking it back, no changing her mind.

The knife slid through the cake until it struck the glass below.

So far, so good, Marcie thought, and began to breathe again.

The next bad moment would come when she pulled the knife out, so she delayed it. She stood there in the kitchen with her fingers around the silver handle, its shaft still stuck fully into the heart of the cake. *Dead, dead, running red.* When she pulled out the knife, she might bring too much cake and frosting with her on the knife, leaving a rough cut.

Slowly, with exquisite caution, she withdrew the knife.

It was a smooth cut. There was only a little cake and frosting stuck to the blade.

Marcie felt relieved. This could be a perfect first slice of cake.

After the initial cut, the next one was even harder, but she was ready for it. She had put a glass of water beside the cake, and now she plunged the sticky knife down into the glass and then slid one side of the knife and then the other side of it carefully over the glass edge to clean them off. Then she used a fresh dish towel to wipe the knife perfectly clean for the next stab.

Perfectly clear, perfectly clean, who was nice, and who was mean?
"I could write nursery rhymes," she thought.

Heaven knew, she'd read enough of them.

Finally, the first piece of cake lay on her perfect plate.

Marcie picked up her fork.

She ate one bite, taking it from the thinnest tip of the slice.

Oh! It was delicious. It was the best cake she'd ever baked, or eaten.
If you're good, you'll do what you should.

As she held the bite in her mouth, savoring its flavors, she thought about a news article she had read recently. Scientists claimed they had proved that the first bite of any food was always the best. They said every bite diminished in satisfaction after that. Marcie couldn't remember why they said that was so, but she didn't believe it, anyway. When she ate the second bite of her cake, it was just as good as the first one had been, and maybe better. It brought tears to her eyes, it was so wonderful to taste. It felt so good between her teeth, on her gums, and going down her throat.

"Oh." She whispered a moan. "It's so good."

Every bite after that was equally scrumptious.

Delicious, delicious,

People are vicious.

She cut a second piece no bigger than the first one. She didn't have to hurry. There was no cause to gobble the way she gobbled down the family's leftovers before she stuck their plates in the dishwasher after meals. She had all the time in the world this afternoon, or at least until six o'clock when Mark came home from work. An entire world, a whole lifetime, could be contained in those two and a half hours. She wanted to savor every bite of it.

The second piece was better than the first, and she was still hungry after she finished it. Starving. Only a thick piece could begin to fill her up, she decided, but when she ate a third, thicker slice, it only seemed to whet her appetite for more. *Good, good, knock on wood.* She was glad she still felt so hungry. This was her cake and she wanted to eat all of it.

Marcie savored her fourth piece.

The phone didn't ring to interrupt her.

Well, of course, it didn't, Marcie thought, because she had unplugged it. One of the phones. She'd only had to kill one phone to kill all of them.

A noise, possibly a laugh, or maybe a sob, rose into her mouth.

It made her cough, which made her choke on the bite she was swallowing down while the laugh or sob was trying to get up and out. Marcie panicked, afraid she could choke to death on her own cake, leaving the rest of it for somebody else to find, and maybe even to eat.

She ran to the sink to spit out the cake in her mouth.

She took a long drink of water to wash away the coughing.

The water filled her up a little the way the cake had not so far.

Marcie put down the glass, so she wouldn't drink any more.

Then she got back onto her kitchen stool, at the counter where the cake was, and cut the last piece of the first half of the cake.

Maybe it was time to bring the phones back to life?

So nobody would worry if they couldn't reach her. So nobody would come over to check on her before Mark came home. They would worry, she realized, if they couldn't at least get the answering machine.

She got up and plugged in the phone attached to the machine.

"Hi!" she whispered in a bright tone, "You've reached the Barnes Family!" Then she dropped her voice to a lower register. "Mark!" Then back up to her own voice. "Marcie!" And then she imitated her children, in the order in which they chirped their names, in order of their births, starting with, 'Luke!" who was six, then "Ruth!" who was five, and then the twins, "Matthew!" and "Mary!" who were three. Then she yelled, "We'll call you back!" just as they all did on the tape. Only the baby, John, wasn't there. The baby was silent.

It startled Marcie to hear her own voice so loud in the quiet house

Her mother said they shouldn't have a recording that yelled in people's ears. Her father said it was annoying to wait for it to play through every time. Her minister's wife said it was adorable.

Marcie started on the second half of her cake.

Her glass plate was not pristine clean any more.

Her two bathtubs weren't clean anymore.

Some of the beds weren't clean anymore.

"You should be ashamed of yourself," she said in her mother's voice.

"What did you do all day?" her father's voice chimed in.

"You're so lucky you get to stay home," her sister said.

"What did you guys do that was fun today?" Mark asked her.

"We missed you at circle meeting," said her minister's wife.

Wife, wife, for all of your life.

Mother, mother, smother, smother.

"Shut up," she whispered. "Shut up. Shut up. Shut up."

Hands shaking, she dipped the cake knife in the glass of water that was murky now, and wiped it on the chocolate-y dish towel Then she cut the rest of the cake in even pieces so they'd be ready for her when she was ready for them. Time was running faster now. It wasn't all that long before Mark would come through the door.

At least the cake knife was clean again.

She held it up to let it shine in the light from the window.

Yes, it was clean as a whistle.

The word "whistle" made her think of the dog, who wasn't barking. Wasn't that the name of a story? About a dog that didn't bark? It was supposed to be important, somehow, the fact that the dog didn't bark. A clue. But to what? Maybe if she'd gotten her college degree, she'd know. Marcie wondered if it would be a clue to Mark. When he approached the house, when he stuck his key in the lock, would it be a clue when the dog didn't bark?

Mark was smart, but she didn't think he was that smart.

He'd probably need more clues than that before he ran to see what was wrong.

Marcie finished the first piece of the second half of the cake, and then laid the next piece on her plate.

She estimated there was a little over one quarter of her cake left to eat now. If it was more than a quarter, would that make it a third? She wasn't sure. She'd never been good at math, or at estimating things.

Never been good, never been good,
Never done what they said she should.

Married before she ought to.

Had babies sooner than they said she should—but not as many as they said she could. ("Do you think our baby stuff will last through at least one more?" Mark had asked her last night.)

Kept the house too clean.

Vain, vain, window pane.

Didn't keep it clean enough.

Make a mess, and then confess.

Spent too much money.

Never had enough of it.

Sang too loud. Talked too much.

Said the wrong things.

Dressed the wrong way.

Couldn't please,

"Please," Marcie whispered, remembering a Beatle's songs. "Please, please, please me."

She didn't think it would please anybody to find out she had eaten an entire cake, but it pleased her. It pleased her so much to eat the last bite. Surprisingly, it only left her wanting more.

She glanced at the kitchen clock.

There was still time to mix another one. If she couldn't bake it, maybe she could eat the batter and lick the bowl, all of the bowl, all to herself.

When Mark came home, she could give him a chocolate kiss.

She walked to the cupboard to pull out another cake box, but discovered to her dismay that there wasn't another chocolate one. There was only vanilla. At first she felt deep disappointment, excruciating disillusionment. No chocolate! Only vanilla! But then she thought, No! That was all right. That was fine. It was great, in fact. She was the only one in the family who liked white cake. She was the only one left in the family who liked it ...

Marcie reached for the cake mix box.

Vanilla had its own special delights, in her opinion. It was tangy, it smelled wonderful, it looked so pure. And you could do anything with it. Put on any flavor or color of frosting. Sprinkle it with candy.

Squeeze frosting into roses and squirt them onto it. Use it for weddings, for birthdays, for special days like this one.

Her mouth watered, thinking of the flavor of the batter that would be hers, alone. She was so hungry all of a sudden, so hungry, as if there was a huge hole in the middle of her. A huge empty space. She felt as if she were falling into the space, and that she might keep falling and falling forever with nothing making a sound around her, and with the space getting bigger and bigger until there was nothing in the universe except her and space.

Maybe another cake would fill it, if she could only finish eating it before Mark came home to their very quiet house.

• • •

NANCY PICKARD'S short stories have won Agatha, Anthony, Macavity, Barry, and Shamus awards, and are regular entries in "year's best" anthologies. She is the author of eighteen award-winning novels, including the 2009 Kansas book of the year, *The Virgin of Small Plains.* Her latest "Kansas" novel, *The Scent of Rain and Lightning,* was recently launched to wide critical acclaim. She can be found at www.nancy pickard.com and on Facebook.

TELEGRAPHING

By Marcia Muller

I have become the operator of a major way station on the moccasin telegraph.

Not by choice; gossip doesn't interest me much, and that's what we Indians mainly do on the wire. But as an investigative tool, it sometimes beats out the Internet.

"We Indians." The phrase still doesn't come easily. For most of my life, I thought my looks were a throwback to my Shoshone great-grandmother, and that I was mainly Scotch-Irish. But then I found out I'd been adopted and discovered a huge, new Shoshone family—some related by blood, some by virtue of just plain friendliness and acceptance. Mentally and emotionally I'm not Indian yet, and sometimes I doubt I ever will be; but I'm learning the legends and traditions, making friends, and becoming closer to my birth parents.

The latter of which sometimes is not all that easy.

Oh, Saskia Blackwater, my birth mother, is no problem. She's an attorney in Boise, Idaho, and active in many Native causes. My half-sister, Robin, is following in her mother's footsteps, going to law school at Berkeley. And my half-brother, Darcy, is just your garden-variety screwed-up kid. Then there's Elwood …

Elwood Farmer. A painter of national reputation. He lives on the Flathead Reservation in Montana, where he funds and teaches art programs in the schools. Elwood's traditional, lives simply, and in the beginning was very hard to know. Now that he and I have gotten closer, I realize he can be cantankerous, obstinate, opinionated, and downright mean. But he's also thoughtful, wise, insightful, and downright charming. Elwood's the reason I've become a moccasin telegraph operator.

In case you don't know, the moccasin telegraph is nothing more than a large group of Indians throughout the country who are connected by bloodlines, friendships, or past histories. And they love to gossip. The telegraph is a great investigative tool; at my San Francisco agency, McCone Investigations, it's a fallback when all else fails. Here's an example from a morning last week of how it works—and it's only a small part of what I've recently been through.

"Hi, Elwood. It's Sharon."

"You're calling early, daughter." A match scraped; he inhaled. Smoking is Elwood's only vice.

"I've been up all night working on this investigation for you."

Exhaled. "Not good. You need your sleep. Have you found out anything?"

"A little. I need you to call Jane Nomee in Arlee. Ask her if she knows the whereabouts of an Eric Yatz. She can get back to me on my cellular."

"Who's Eric Yatz?"

"I'll tell you later. Just call Jane, will you?"

"If you'd had more sleep, daughter, you wouldn't be so surly."

• • •

"Sharon? Jane Nomee. Your dad just called. I remember Eric Yatz from here in town, but haven't heard of him in years. He does have a cousin, though—Carol Yatz, in McMinnville, Oregon. Here's her number."

• • •

"No, I haven't heard from Cousin Eric in years. He was very close to one of our aunts, Bella Wilford, in Minneapolis. Let me look up her number."

• • •

"Last Christmas Eric sent me a card postmarked Plymouth, California … No, there was no return address … You're welcome."

• • •

Plymouth was in the Gold Country. A small town; if Eric Yatz was still there, I was pretty sure I could find him.

Amador County is not usually considered Indian country. Most of those unfamiliar with the area in the Sierra foothills identify it with gold mining and, nowadays, quaint Old West tourist towns and vineyards. But the Indian presence is there, most notably in the Jackson Rancheria, a twenty-four-hour gambling casino and hotel on Miwok tribal lands near the small city of Jackson. Amador is not hospitable to casinos: not long ago, county supervisors rejected a proposal from the Buena Vista Rancheria that would have put many millions of dollars into the public coffers as compensation for police and fire and water services—at the same time leaving the county free to continue the fight against the casino in court.

The majority of residents of Amador prefer to preserve the rural ambience. Meanwhile, Miwoks, Iones, and other small tribes continue to fight for their piece of the great gambling pie.

I drove past the town of Plymouth, where I had visited before, in a couple of eyeblinks. There was a Best Western on Highway 49 near there, and I'd made a reservation. The first-floor room looked out on an idyllic scene: an oak-dotted pasture with cows grazing. I sat down at the table by the window and took out the notes on the investigation I was conducting—gratis—for my birth father.

One of Elwood's art students, a nine-year-old named Marcus Fourwinds, possessed an exceptional talent. He and his mother, Elise, had moved to St. Ignatius, near where Elwood lives, three years ago. Their origins were vague; they had no relatives in the area, and Marcus had little recollection of where they'd lived before. On that subject his mother was reticent, saying only that they "had some trouble with the tribe" and been forced to move.

Then, two weeks ago Elise had been brutally knifed at their home. In order to keep Marcus from being made a ward of the county youth authorities, Elwood had taken him in. Marcus said that a friend of his mother's, Don Dixon, had been at their house the day she was killed. The tribal police had not been able to track Dixon down so, with their permission Elwood turned to me.

The Internet search engines that my agency subscribes to turned up a criminal record on Dixon, mostly for kiting checks and petty theft. Moccasin telegraph informed me he was a drifter who had appeared in St. Ignatius about six months before, taken a job at a convenience store in Arlee, and had been staying at the Fourwinds place on and off the whole time. I then traced Dixon to Reno, where he was in jail once more for petty theft. He admitted to having seen Elise Fourwinds that day, but claimed a man named Eric Yatz was responsible for her death. Dixon wouldn't say why, except that it had something to do with Indian gaming rights.

Which was strange, because Montana is considered one of the worst places in the nation for tribal casinos. Most of the bars there allow gambling—slot machines, live poker, and keno—but the tribes' efforts to persuade the state to permit them to offer such other games of chance as blackjack have fallen on deaf ears.

So what did Elise Fourwinds's murder have to do with Indian gaming?

I'd have to locate Eric Yatz to find the answer to that question.

Internet research on Yatz told me little: no criminal record, no record of employment, no previous addresses. I asked my nephew and computer whiz, Mick Savage, to run a highly sophisticated search, and he came up with a birth place and date: Newark, New Jersey, on March 8, 1983. After that, Yatz became an invisible man: no Social Security number, no record of education or military service.

How did he stay so far below the radar?

Another thing I'd have to ask Yatz.

Yatz was not listed in the Amador County phone book. I drove toward town, turned at the rodeo grounds and then along the main street: small homes, an old hotel with an upstairs galleria, a handsome Queen Anne Victorian; various false fronted buildings, a deli with tables on the sidewalk, a derelict, boarded up brick warehouse; some shops, a trendy looking restaurant called Taste, a barbecue place, Incahoots that smelled wonderful and had a line out the door. Where to start?

Deli. I was hungry, and there were tables free.

• • •

Some two hours later, and I'd canvassed the business establishments in town. No one knew—or admitted to knowing—Eric Yatz. Finally, footsore and thirsty, I retreated to

the tavern at the old hotel—dimly lighted with old mirrors whose silvering was patchy and cracked, a wood-inlaid bar, well worn floor, and a string of crushed beer cans behind the bar, attached to a sign that read *Trailer Trash Art*. The place was crowded, both with locals and tourists; I could tell them apart by the way they dressed. The tourist men looked as if they were ready to tee off on the golf course; the women wore outfits in bright shades of polyester. The locals were in jeans. I spotted a woman in a T-shirt decorated with three wineglasses and a caption that said "Therapy Session." My therapy arrived in the form of a schooner of IPA.

For a while I studied the antics of the crowd in the back bar mirror. A tourist at the table behind me put a straw up either nostril and made growling sounds, and the people with him laughed hysterically. What was he supposed to be? An elephant? Elephants don't growl. A local couple got into a spat, and she slapped him and stalked out. He sat there, stunned, then shrugged and took a swallow of his drink. Another couple, obviously more in synch, kissed on a settee built into the front wall.

After a while a man with a guitar came in from the ell at the back that contained pool tables. He proceeded to perch on a stool and play. The guitar was badly tuned, his voice even more so. A cowboy next to him covered his ears, took a slug of his drink, and shouted, "Shut up, Willard!" Willard shut up and slunk away.

Then suddenly a tension invaded the room, as two slight, dark-haired and -skinned men entered and took seats at the table near the door. They were Indian, but then so was I; nobody had reacted negatively to my presence. But with the appearance of the pair, voices dropped to a low level, spines went stiff, and eyes focused on them.

"Here comes trouble," the bartender said.

A tall, lanky man at the far end of the bar got off his stool. He pressed his cowboy hat firmly down and strode toward them—loose-limbed, dangerous. When he stopped beside their table, he loomed over them.

"You boys aren't welcome here," he said.

The taller of the two looked up. "Last I heard, this was a free country."

"Last *I* heard, your tribe was trying to take a free ride on it."

"Our land. We can do what we want with it."

"It's not your land. Belongs to the Gilardis. Has since—"

"They stole it from us."

The tall man drew back, balling up his right fist. "Gilardis didn't steal—"

"We got the documentation. The papers that show the land belongs to our tribe. That gives us the right to do what we want with it, and what we're gonna do is build a casino."

The bar had grown still during the conversation, but now there was an angry stirring among the patrons. The tall man drew back his fist; one of the other locals restrained him before he could throw a punch. The bartender rushed up to the table and spoke softly with the two Indians; they nodded, got up, and left. As a collective sigh of relief came from the customers, I left money on the bar and followed them.

· · ·

The two men were nearing the derelict warehouse when I caught up with them.

"Please, may I talk with you?" I said.

They stopped, regarded me with wary eyes. The more slender of the two, whose long hair was pulled back by a blue bandana, said, "Talk about what?"

"The casino you're going to establish here. Your tribal lands. Are you Miwok?"

"Amador Band of the Iones. You?"

"Shoshone."

They exchanged glances. The man who hadn't spoken—thin faced, with a baseball cap pulled low on his brow—seemed to defer to the other, who said, "No Shoshone around here. Where you from?"

"San Francisco." I extended one of my cards. "I'm working a case for my father, who lives on the Flathead rez in Montana. He's an artist—Elwood Farmer. Maybe you've heard of him?"

Shrugs.

"I'm looking for a man named Eric Yatz, who's rumored to live in Plymouth."

Both men stiffened. "Don't know anybody of that name," the spokesman said.

"Okay, tell me about this casino. The tribal lands you're reclaiming—"

"Why don't you go back to the bar—yeah, we saw you there—and ask the white people about that? We got nothing to say."

They turned in unison and walked away.

So I'd go back to the bar and ask the white people.

• • •

Willard, the dreadful guitar player, looked to be the most sober person in the room. He sat nursing a soda on the settee where the amorous couple had been. I got my own soda from the bartender and asked Willard if I could join him. He shrugged and motioned for me to sit down.

"How's the music business?" I asked.

"Shitty."

"Tough way to make a living."

"I don't. Work construction when I can get hired on."

"Much of that going on here?"

"Nope. I'm hanging in on unemployment, waiting to see if the casino deal's gonna go through."

"Most people don't seem to want that."

"Well, I do. My girlfriend's gonna have a baby this fall; she and the kid're gonna need a lot of things."

"So what's the deal with the casino?"

I listened as Willard told me.

The Amador Ione tribe had for centuries lived on the land around Plymouth, peaceably hunting and gathering. But the Gold Rush in the late 1840s flooded the area with treasure seekers, and white men forced the Indians off their lands, resulting in violent disputes and deadly confrontations.

"Indians always came out sucking hind titty," Willard said, "so finally the government stepped in and made treaties with them, gave 'em land. Congress never got around to approving those treaties, though. Iones moved away, joined up with other tribes. Finally the BIA stepped up to the plate and gave ten tribe members the right to a hundred acres in the Shenandoah Valley. Didn't do no good; none of those ten people was able to get title to that land, and a family named Gilardi took it over and started a winery."

Now I knew where I'd heard the name. "Gilardi Oaks?"

"Right. But trouble came along two years ago when the county decided the hundred acres belonged to those ten Iones or their descendants after all, if they could produce the original document from the seventies giving them rights to the land. They couldn't find the document. Some say Ed Jakes, first head of the tribal council they set up in the nineties, was careless, but there was a rumor it got stolen."

"By?"

Shrug. "Some say Gilardis, others say one of their own tribe members."

"Why would a tribe member take it?"

Willard's eyes shifted away from mine. "I said too much already."

Hear those Iones've got big Las Vegas connections backing the casino. You know what that means. And I don't want folks in here to think I'm an Indian lover. No offense meant, ma'am."

"None taken. Where can I find this Ed Jakes?"

"He's in the old Ione burial ground up the hill toward Fiddletown. But his son

Junior Jakes is head of the tribal council now. Lives out the Old Shenandoah Road. You might talk to him."

It was nearly eleven, so I decided to do that in the morning.

• • •

Back at my motel I couldn't sleep, so I set up my laptop, thinking to check my e-mail. The place only had dial-up—fortunately I have an AOL account for just those occasions—and it took a long time to connect. I had to smile at my impatience. Not too many years ago I wouldn't have known the difference between dial-up and "Dialing for Dollars."

I had little mail. My husband, Hy Ripinsky, and my office manager, Ted Smalley, usually call when I'm traveling, and what was in the box wasn't important. I checked my voice mail, having turned off the ring tone while canvassing Plymouth: routine report from Ted on the agency's day; message from Hy saying he was in New York on a sudden business trip and could call again in the morning. That was it.

I turned back to the laptop and began a more thorough search on the Amador Ione.

The land that they couldn't prove rights to—although, according to the tribe members I'd spoken with earlier, they now had documents to prove ownership—sat at the gateway to the Amador wine country. I'd been there before: it was rural, with widely spaced vineyards on rolling hillsides and bucolic views; I could understand why the locals didn't want a casino there, but I also could understand why the tribe, landless and impoverished, hoped to tap into the new California gold rush.

I continued visiting sites that mentioned the Amador Ione, and one April article in the San Francisco *Chronicle* caught my attention: "Tribes Toss Out Members in High-Stakes Conflict."

The story stated that many California tribes, in anticipation of profits from casinos, had been purging their rolls of those individuals whose lineage and membership was held in doubt. The tribal spokespersons claimed that as sovereign nations they had a right to "readjust" their records as they saw fit. Of fifty-seven tribes sharing in annual $7.7 billion gaming revenues, many had expelled people as prominent as former officials of their councils.

All in the pursuit of the almighty dollar, the banished Indians said.

An accompanying piece outlined how the wealth generated on Indian lands reached few of the state's Indian residents because of tribal enrollment status.

I leaned back in my chair, thinking of what Elwood had said of Elise Fourwinds: *She had some trouble with her tribe.*

Trouble—as in being removed from the rolls?

Was Elise Fourwinds a former member of the Amador Ione?

I'd have to ask Junior Jakes about that—and about the Las Vegas connection.

• • •

Junior Jakes lived in a doublewide on a small lot surrounded by vineyards. An oak tree shaded the trailer, and chickens pecked at the packed dirt yard. Jakes was a lean, muscular man of about sixty; his long white hair was tied back in a ponytail.

He greeted me cordially and led me to a pair of lawn chairs under the oak. The day was already hot, but a light breeze rustled the tree's leaves and brought some relief. I showed my credentials and told him I was working on behalf of Elise Fourwinds's son, Marcus.

"Marcus? But he's only a little boy."

"Little boys sometimes require the services of an investigator—especially when their mothers have been murdered."

What I'd said sank in slowly. Junior Jakes's lips moved, mouthing the word "murder." Then he sat very still, his gaze turned inward.

I said, "I understand Elise Fourwinds was a member of your tribe."

"She was."

"But she was taken off from the rolls and moved to Montana." It was an educated guess that proved valid.

"Is that where she went? I had no idea."

I studied his lined face, trying to determine if he was telling the truth, but it wasn't an easy one to read.

I asked, "Why was she removed from the rolls?"

"Just setting our records straight."

"How many other people were removed?"

"I don't recall. A number."

"So Marcus isn't a tribal member, either. He won't benefit from the casino?"

"No."

"I hear the casino project's going to happen. That your tribe now has the documentation to prove the hundred acres were ceded to the ten individuals or their heirs."

He nodded.

"How'd you acquire the documentation?"

"It was handled by the Las Vegas company that is consulting with us on building and running the casino—Slater and Associates. I don't know the details."

"That would be Eric Yatz you're working with?"

Slowly he turned his head. "You know Mr. Yatz?"

"Not personally, but I'd like to meet him."

• • •

I waited by the side of the road in the shelter of an oak a hundred yards from Junior Jakes's driveway. The August heat was intense, with no breeze now; cicadas buzzed in the dry grass. Jakes had agreed to set up a meeting between Yatz and me, and then to call me on my cellular, but I hadn't liked what I'd seen in his eyes before I'd walked back to my car: a gathering anger and steely resolve. Elise Fourwinds had meant something to him. Jakes hadn't known she was dead or how Yatz had gone about getting his hands on the stolen document, but he'd probably known she'd taken it, and he'd unwittingly steered Yatz to her.

Half an hour later, Jakes drove out in a red pickup I'd seen parked to the side of the doublewide. There was a rifle in the gunrack.

I followed him to Highway 49, past Plymouth and south toward Jackson. A mile or so outside of town he turned off on Jackson Gate Road. I knew the area some, since my Uncle Jim and Aunt Susan lived on a small ranch near there; a former pro bowler, Jim for years had owned the local bowling center and had only recently turned it over to his son Bill.

Jackson Gate Road wound past small homes and occasional businesses, a cemetery and vegetation-choked lots. It was a convenient, if slow, way around the stoplights and clogged intersections leading into town. I assumed that was why Jakes was taking it, and was surprised to see him turn off after about a mile.

The driveway he entered was newly paved and bordered by an attractive stone wall. At its bottom was a sign: *Old Mine Inn*. I allowed him some distance, before following.

An amazing edifice loomed up before me: the shaft of an old gold mine dug back into the hill's slope, with a group of buildings spread around it. The buildings were intended, I supposed, to replicate the iron-and-timber style of the mine, but they were too shiny and new to blend in properly. In a parking lot surrounded by lush plantings sat two limousines and a scattering of luxury cars.

Junior Jakes's pickup was pulled in at an odd angle in one of the parking spaces. Its door was open, and he and the rifle I'd glimpsed earlier were gone. I looked around, spotted his lean figure disappearing behind the far right wing of the building.

Careful, McCone. Go slowly. What you do here could save a good man and bring a bad one down.

• • •

I unlocked the glovebox of my car and took my .357 Magnum from inside. Checked its load. I've always been opposed to handguns in the possession of the average citizen but—perhaps hypocritically—I consider myself above average, at least in that respect. I'm licensed by the state to carry a hand gun, am a good shot, and practice at the range once or twice a month. Anyway, I was damned glad to have the weapon along now.

I moved quickly through the plantings and slipped to the far side of the wing where Jakes had gone. The building's wall was hot on my hand—corrugated iron to match the mine shaft. I moved along it, listening. When I came to the corner I stuck my head around: four patios with French doors faced a fenced garden; voices came from the open door of the second. I moved closer.

"… You killed her, you bastard!"

Unintelligible response—a man's voice.

"I gave you the information in good faith! I didn't know there would be killing involved."

"You didn't ask, either." Deep, raspy tones. "Besides, she came at me like a crazy woman, screaming and fighting for that paper. What did you expect me to do?"

"You didn't *have* to kill her, Yatz."

The curtains on the first unit were closed; I moved quickly past them.

"Maybe not. But why're you getting so worked up? You've got what you wanted, haven't you? We're going to be able to build your casino."

I risked a quick glance into the room. Junior Jakes stood with his back to the door pointing his rifle at a burly brown-haired man wearing shorts and a sport shirt. Yatz stood oddly at ease, arms loose at his sides, as if being held at gunpoint was nothing unusual. His eyes were a cold, unblinking blue.

Jakes's hands shook—with fury, I thought. He said, "I'm worked up because she was my daughter, that's why."

Yatz's expression didn't change. "You removed your own daughter from the tribal rolls?"

"My illegitimate daughter. Her mother was a white woman."

"You poor son of a bitch. Forced to kick out your own daughter and grandson." Yatz laughed.

Jakes raised his rifle. I leaped through the door and rammed into his back just as he pulled the trigger; the bullet clanged off the metal wall behind Yatz. Jakes struggled to maintain his footing, but I managed to trip him; he went down on his side, dropping the rifle.

I kicked it out of both men's reach, covering Yatz with the Magnum.

My ears were ringing from the blast, but I could hear cries and running feet. I backed up, called out, "The situation's under control. Will somebody get security, please?"

A man's voice said, "Will do."

I then shut the French doors against prying eyes. Said to Yatz, "You—go over and sit down on that chair."

He did as told, still calm and controlled. Even the close call with the rifle bullet didn't seem to faze him. He returned my gaze steadily.

Typical enforcer. He's here to keep an eye on the situation till the higher-ups arrive and take over.

Still on the floor, Jakes moaned.

"You all right?" I asked.

"Yeah, mostly."

"That rifle—Yatz jumped you, and it went off by accident."

"... Right."

"You brought it along only for protection."

"I get you."

"The rest of it you tell as it happened."

I glanced at Yatz. Still unconcerned; his firm could afford the best lawyers money can buy. But what he hadn't realized—yet—was that he'd been flying under the radar for many years, and a court case would destroy his anonymity. At the least it would put him out of work and possibly expose additional crimes for which he might be prosecuted. Maybe even make him the target of another well paid enforcer.

He'd pay for his crimes, one way or the other.

• • •

"Daughter? This is Elwood. I hear you found the man who killed Elise Fourwinds and that he is in custody."

I pushed hair off my face and looked at the illuminated numbers of the bedside clock in my room at the Best Western. It was nearly two in the morning.

"How did you ...?"

"Moccasin telegraph works round the clock. Sylvia Wilson, an

Ione who lives in Jackson, found out what happened and this afternoon she called her nephew, Rich Three Wings, who lives up near that ranch of yours in Mono County. I believe he knows you. Rich called a cousin of Junior Jakes in Jackson, who knew about the arrest but not where you were staying. The cousin couldn't reach Jakes, and your agency was already closed, so he called his stepdaughter in Oakland. She happens to know that office manager of yours—"

My God, now non-Indians are on the wire!

"Daughter? Are you listening?"

I yawned. "Yes, Elwood."

"The office manager didn't answer his phone, but the man he lives with did, and he gave the cousin's stepdaughter the number of one of your employees and ..."

Telegraphing.

• • •

A native of the Detroit area, **MARCIA MULLER'S** early literary aspirations were put on hold in her third year at the University of Michigan, when her creative writing instructor told her she would never be a writer because she had nothing to say. Instead she turned to journalism, earning a master's degree, but various editors for whom she freelanced noticed her unfortunate tendency to embellish the facts in order to make the pieces more interesting. In the early 1970s, Muller moved to California and began experimenting with mystery novels because they were what she liked to read. After three manuscripts and five years of rejection, *Edwin of the Iron Shoes*, the first novel featuring San Francisco private investigator Sharon McCone, was published by David McKay Company, who then cancelled their mystery list. Four years passed before St. Martin's Press accepted the second McCone novel, *Ask the Cards a Question*. In the ensuing thirty-some years, Muller has authored more than thirty-five novels—three of them in collaboration with husband Bill Pronzini—seven short-story collections, and numerous nonfiction articles. In 2005 Muller was named a Grand Master by Mystery Writers of America, the organization's highest award. The Mulzinis, as friends call them, live in Sonoma County, California, in yet another house full of books.

THE VALHALLA VERDICT

By Doug Allyn

The jury wouldn't look at us when they filed back in. Even the foreman, a rumpled old timer who'd offered my mother sympathetic glances during the course of the trial, was avoiding our eyes now.

A bad sign. But I wasn't really worried. The case was open and shut.

A rich playboy knocks up his girlfriend. He offered to pay for an abortion but she refused his money. She wanted the child whether he did or not. A week later, as she was walking home from work, my nineteen-year-old sister, Lisa Marie Canfield, was clipped by a hit and run driver who never even slowed down. Dead at the side of the road. Killed like a stray dog.

Police found traces of blood on the bumper of her boyfriend's Cadillac SUV. Lisa's blood. A simple, straightforward homicide. In Detroit. Or New York.

But Valhalla is a small, northern Michigan resort village and Lisa's boyfriend, Mel Bennett, is a hometown hero here. A football star at Michigan State and later for the Detroit Lions, Mel owns the biggest Cadillac/GMC dealership in five counties.

Lisa, on the other hand, was only a shopgirl, a wistful little retro-hippie who sold candles and incense in one of the tourist traps on Lake Street. She was too young to get involved with a player like Mel. If I'd known she was seeing him ... but I didn't know. I'd been too wrapped up in my teaching career to pay much attention to my little sister's life.

And now it was too late for brotherly advice. Or anything else. Only justice remained.

But Mel Bennett was a sympathetic figure on the witness stand. Tanned, tailored and charismatic, Mel sheepishly admitted that my sister wasn't his only girlfriend, he was dating several other women. And one of his lovers, Fawn Daniels, still had keys to his apartment. And to his car.

When Fawn took the stand, she refused to say where she was at the time of the killing. She took the Fifth Amendment instead, scowling at the jury, hard-eyed and defiant as a Mafia don.

And now the jury looked uneasy, even angry. Like they'd been arguing. Perhaps they'd settled on a charge less than murder. Manslaughter, maybe.

It never occurred to me they'd let the bastard walk.

But that's exactly what they did.

The foreman read the verdict aloud from the verdict slip. "On the sole charge of murder in the second degree, we find the defendant, Mel Bennett, not guilty." And the packed courtroom actually burst into applause.

Outside, on the courthouse steps, the foreman told a ring of reporters the jurors thought Mr. Bennett was credible when he swore he cared for Lisa Canfield and would never harm her. And when his mistress, Fawn Daniels, refused to answer, many of us felt there was reasonable doubt. Maybe she—"

But he was talking to the air. Mel and his entourage swept out of the courthouse and the reporters flocked around them like gulls at a fish market.

Smiling for the cameras, Mel said he had no idea who'd killed poor Lisa, but he was sure the authorities would find the person responsible. He offered his sincerest condolences to her family.

"How does it feel to be a free man?" a reporter shouted.

"I was never worried," Mel said solemnly. "I knew I could count on a Valhalla jury for a fair shake."

Scrambling into a gleaming red Escalade, Mel roared away, waving to the crowd, grinning like he'd just scored the biggest touchdown of his life. Or gotten away with murder.

When the prosecutor was interviewed, he griped that Mel Bennett got a Valhalla verdict. A reporter asked him to explain, but he just shrugged and stalked off. Implication? What do you expect from a hick town jury?

And he was right. Valhalla is a small town. By New York or even Detroit standards, most folks who live up north are hicks. More or less.

My extended family, Canfields and La Mottes, are redneck to the bone, and proud of it. My uncle Deke's clan, the La Mottes, are the roughest of our bunch, jack-pine savages who grow reefer and cook crystal meth in the trackless forests. The rest of us are solid, working class citizens. Blue collar, for the most part.

All but me. I'm Paul Canfield, the first of my family to earn a bachelor's degree. I teach Political Science at Valhalla High School. My relatives call me Professor. A compliment or an insult, depending on the tone.

After the trial, on a golden, autumn afternoon, our small clan gathered in my Uncle Deacon's garage, still stunned by the verdict. We'd intended to hold a delayed wake, in honor of my sister. Lisa

Marie was dead, but at least the monster had been punished. Or so we'd expected.

Instead it felt like Lisa had been slaughtered all over again. Along with her unborn child. A Canfield baby none of us would ever hold.

But there was beer on ice, hot dogs and potato salad already laid out. And folks have to eat.

So we gathered around the banquet table in somber silence, Canfields and La Mottes, in-laws and cousins. But with none of the usual good-natured banter. No one spoke at all. Until my mother, Mabel Canfield turned to me for an explanation.

"I just don't understand it, Paul," she said simply. "How could a thing like this happen? Where's the justice?"

"Justice is only a concept, Ma. An ideal."

"I still don't—"

"People go to court expecting to win because they're in the right. But the truth is, every trial is a contest, a debating match between lawyers. One side wins, one loses, and we call it justice. And it usually is."

"But not this time," my cousin Bo La Motte snorted. "The jurors were morons."

"No," I said, "they were just home folks. Like us. Mel Bennett's a professional salesman and that jury was just one more deal to close. He had a sharp lawyer and the prosecutor thought the case was a slam dunk—"

"It should have been!" Bo snapped. "Lisa's blood was splattered all over Bennett's damn car!"

"But the Daniels woman had keys to that car. When she took the fifth and refused to say where she was at the time of Lisa's death, the jury had reasonable doubts. And they gave Mel the benefit of those doubts."

"Is there any chance at all that Daniels woman could actually have done this thing?" my mother asked.

"No," Uncle Deke said quietly. "I had some people look into that. Word is she was shooting pool at the Sailor's Rest when Lisa was run down. She'll probably claim she bought dope or committed some other petty crime to justify taking the Fifth, but her alibi is rock solid. She didn't kill Lisa, Mel Bennett did. I expect Fawn collected a fat payoff to cover for him."

"Then I say we should pop that bastard today," Bo said. Burly and surly, my cousin Bo is the hothead of the family. He inherited his father's straight dark hair, obsidian eyes, and black temper. But in school, nobody ever picked on me when my cousin Bo was around.

"Popping Bennett is a great idea, Cousin," I said, "as long as you've got no plans for the rest of your natural life."

"Bull! No jury in the world would convict me! They'd—"

"You just saw firsthand what a small town jury can do! You're already a two-time loser for weed and grand theft auto, Bo. Nobody'd give you the benefit of a doubt."

"Then to hell with them! And to hell with you too, Professor!" Bo snapped. "If you got no belly for this, go back to school and leave the rat killin' to men who ain't afraid to—"

Whirling in her chair, my mother backhanded Bo across the mouth! Hard! Spilling him over backwards onto the garage floor.

He was up like a cat, fire in his eyes, his fist cocked—but of course he didn't swing.

Instead, he shook his head to clear it, then gingerly touched his split lip with his fingertips. They came away dripping blood.

"Damn, Aunt May," he groused, "most girls just slap my face."

"Not Canfield girls," my mother said. Uncle Deke chuckled, and gradually the rest of us joined in. It was a thin joke, but our family hadn't done much laughing lately.

Uncle Deke tossed Bo a paper towel to mop up the blood and we all resumed our seats.

"All right, Professor," the old man growled. "You're the closest thing we got to a legal expert in this family. What are our options now? Is there any way to get justice for Lisa? If we dig up more evidence—?"

"I don't think it wouldn't make any difference," I said. "Now that Mel's been found not guilty, he can't be tried again, period. He could confess to killing Lisa in a church full of witnesses and the worst he could get is a perjury charge. A year or two, no more."

"You're saying the law can't touch him?" Bo said dangerously. "Is that what you're telling us?"

"Look, I'm only a teacher, Bo, not a lawyer. But I don't believe there's anything we can do. Legally, it's over."

"Except it ain't," Bo said.

"It is for now," my mother said firmly, rising stiffly, looking up and down the banquet table. "Deacon, you're my older brother and I love you, but you've got an evil temper and your three boys are no better. Lisa was my daughter, not yours. You missed most of her growing years while you were in prison. I absolutely forbid you to throw any more of your life away in some mad dog quest for vengeance."

"You *forbid* me, Mabel?" Deke echoed, with a faint smile.

"I swear to God, Deacon La Motte, if you or Bo go after Mel Bennett, I'll cut you off. I'll never speak to either of you again as long as I live, nor will any of my family. Ever."

"That's too hard, Sis," Deke said, his smile fading. "That sonofabitch murdered your girl and her unborn child. I can't let it pass."

"I'm not asking you to. I'm only saying we should wait. In six months—"

"Six months!" Bo interjected. "No way!"

"In six months we'll all have cooler heads," Mabel continued firmly. "Maybe we'll feel differently. Maybe Bennett will get hit by a bus or someone else will settle his hash. If not, in six months, we'll look at this again. But for now, I want your word, Deke, yours too, Bo, that you'll stay away from him. We've already had a Valhalla verdict. We don't need a La Motte verdict added on top of it."

"That's bullshit, Aunt May!" Bo began—

"Watch your mouth!" Uncle Deke barked, slamming the table with his fist, making the beer bottles jump. "Mabel's right, as usual. If Mel Bennett gets struck by lightning or catches the flu, the police will be coming for us. Because they'll *know* damned well we were involved. We'd best lay back in the weeds awhile, and cool off. Think things through. If anybody's got a problem with that, he can step out back and talk it over. With me."

Deke was glaring at Bo, his oldest boy. Uncle Deke is rawboned with thick wrists and scarred knuckles, dark hair hanging in his eyes, lanky as Johnny Cash back in his wilder days. Pushing fifty, though.

Twenty years younger and forty pounds heavier, Bo has a serious rep as a bad-ass barroom brawler.

But when we were boys, my Uncle Deke shotgunned Bo's mother and her lover in a local tavern. Then ordered up a beer and sipped it while he waited for the law to come for him.

Fourteen years in Jackson Prison, he never backed down from anybody and had the battle scars to prove it. None of us had any doubt how a scrap between Bo and Uncle Deke would come out.

Not even Bo.

"Whatever," he muttered.

"Speak up, boy," Deke said. "I didn't hear you."

"Whatever ... you say. Sir," Bo added, glaring at his father. Then at me for good measure.

"It's settled then," Deke nodded. "We wait six months."

But he was dead wrong about that.

• • •

I called one of my old professors over the weekend, but she only confirmed what I already suspected. Simply put, double jeopardy means that once you're found innocent of a charge, you can never be tried for that crime again. Period. A civil lawsuit for damages might be possible, but it would be a long, expensive process with only a faint hope of success.

I told my mother what I'd learned over dinner that night. She took it as she did most things, with a wan smile. Determined to carry on in spite of everything. The bravest woman I've ever known. But even Canfield girls have their limits.

Nine days after the Valhalla verdict that freed Mel Bennett, my mother, Mabel La Motte Canfield, collapsed in her kitchen. And died on the floor.

A massive coronary thrombosis, the coroner said.

Medical terminology for a broken heart.

• • •

Making arrangements for my mother's funeral was the hardest thing I've ever done in my life. Coming so soon after Lisa's death and the botched trial, it felt like we'd suffered a double homicide. Like somebody'd ripped stitches out of a fresh wound with a lineman's pliers. And then it got worse.

Greeting folks at the funeral home, accepting and offering condolences, I was one of the final few in the viewing line. And as I gazed down at my mother's careworn face for the last time, my eye strayed to a showy wreath at the foot of the casket. With a condolence card.

From Melvin Bennett. And family.

• • •

After the viewing that evening, I stayed on, sitting alone in the empty parlor in numb silence. So lost in thought I scarcely noticed when my uncle Deacon eased down beside me. A familiar aroma of woodsmoke and whiskey.

"You all right, Paul?"

"Hell no. How could I be? And why would he do a thing like that? Send flowers, knowing how we'd feel."

"Remember back when Mel was playing football for the Lions? Every time he scored, he'd do a little dance around the end zone. Showing off. I think that's how he feels now. Like he just pulled off his biggest score ever. Sending the flowers is like dancing."

"Taunting us, you mean?"

"Nah, he doesn't give a damn about us. It's more like he's taunting the world. Look at me. I'm rich, I'm pretty. I can whack my hicktown girlfriend and the law can't touch me."

"And he's right," I said bitterly.

"Only half right," Deke countered. "The law can't touch him. That don't mean he can't be reached."

I turned slowly to face him. "Uncle Deke, if you go after Mel Bennett now, you'll die in prison. You know that."

"I've done hard time, Paul. I can do it again if I have to."

"My mother didn't want this."

"Maybe she's changed her mind," Deke said evenly. "Why don't you ask her? Or ask Lisa. Lemme know what they say."

"You know what they'd say."

"Dammit, when Mabel asked me to wait I went along for her sake, but I'm done waitin', Paulie, so save your breath."

"I'm not asking you to wait, Uncle Deke. You're right, we're way past that. But whatever you decide to do, I want in."

"You'd better think about that, boy. Your mother—

"I don't have a mother anymore! Mel Bennett saw to that! We've held two Canfield funerals and that sonofabitch doesn't have a mark on him. And now this?" I nodded at the flowers. "Enough already! I can't let this pass anymore than you can."

"Slow down, Paul. We ain't talking about some classroom problem here. Collecting a debt like this will be an ugly, dangerous business. And afterward, you'll have to live with what's done for the rest of your life. You really think you're up for that?"

"I'm in, Uncle Deke. All the way. If you tell me no I'll do it on my own!"

He eyed me in silence, reading my face like a stranger. Which wasn't a comfortable experience.

My uncle and I were never close. I was already a teenager when my uncle got out of prison. I heard he'd gotten mobbed up in Jackson and hadn't been straight since. Some people call him a gangster.

I call him sir.

He's my mother's brother. She loved him and he'd always been welcome in our home. And that was good enough for me. Especially now.

"Well?" I demanded.

"Maybe there's more La Motte blood in you than I thought, boy," he shrugged. "Take a look at this." He handed me a typewritten note. *Lisa, I heard about your situation. Maybe I can help. We should talk. I'll pick you up after work. F.* "It was on Lisa's office computer," he explained. "She got it the day she was killed."

"How did you get it?"

"Don't ask. My crew's got more connections in the north counties than Michigan Bell."

"All right then, who's *F*?"

"The police think *F* is Fawn Daniels, but it was e-mailed from a coffee shop so it can't be traced. The DA couldn't use it. It makes sense, though. Lisa was pregnant, who better to talk to about it than Mel's other girlfriend? Or so she thought."

"My god, that's why Lisa walked home alone that night. She was expecting a ride."

"I think the Daniels woman set Lisa up for Mel," Deke nodded. "Probably expected to be Mel's new lady, but he's banging some high school cheerleader now, seventeen years old. Fawn's history, in more ways than one. She goes first."

"I don't understand."

"It ain't complicated, boy. The Daniels woman and Bennett killed Lisa together. She's as guilty as he is. They're both going to pay for it, but she has to be first."

"Why?" I managed, swallowing hard.

"Your mother called it right. If anything happens to Bennett, the law will be all over me and my sons. But the Daniels woman is a different matter. They won't be expecting that, especially not from you. If I set it up right, you'll get away clean. And if not, well, you're a simple schoolteacher who lost his mother and sister. Maybe you'll get the benefit of the doubt. One of them Valhalla verdicts. Me and Bo definitely won't."

"But if I ..." I swallowed, hard.

"Kill her. Say it."

"If she dies first, won't that make Bennett even harder to get to?"

"For awhile. But he'll be scared spitless the whole time. Waiting for his number to come up. Could be he'll get nervous enough to make a mistake."

"What kind of a mistake?"

"Maybe he'll take a run at me or Bo. If he tries that, it'll be the last thing he ever does. Or maybe he'll confess, and take that perjury fall you mentioned."

"Why would he do that?"

"To a frightened man, a jail looks like a safe place. Stone walls surrounded by guards. Serve a few months, wait for things to cool down. But I've got contacts inside, guys who'll do Bennett for a carton of cigarettes. If he ever steps through a cell door, he won't come out."

"And if he doesn't confess?"

"Then I'll let him sweat awhile, then take care of him myself. Up close and personal."

"You can't possibly get away with it."

"I don't expect to," Deke said simply. "If I die in the joint over this, so be it. That's my problem. Fawn Daniels is yours, if you got the belly for it. I know it goes against your nature, Paul, but it's the only way. If you want out, say so now."

I looked away, avoiding his eyes. Found myself staring at my mother's casket instead. I knew what she'd say to this. But she couldn't talk me out of it. Nor could Lisa. Never again.

"I'm said I'm in, Uncle Deke. I meant it. What do you want me to do?"

"Nothing for a few days. If you change your mind—"

"I won't."

"Then go back to your life and stay cool til I contact you. Bo will come by with instructions. When that happens, you'll probably have to move fast. Understand?"

I nodded. I didn't trust myself to speak.

"Say it!" he snapped.

"I understand!"

But I didn't. Not really.

I stumbled through my mother's funeral service like a zombie, going through the motions. I read her eulogy, and laid a final rose on her coffin as they lowered it into the ground. And I didn't understand any of it.

She was laid to rest beside my father, who was killed long ago in Vietnam. And beside Lisa and her unborn child. Buried so recently the earth was still raw over the grave. As raw as the jagged wound in my heart.

Somehow I managed to teach classes over the next few days, but I must have asked myself a thousand times how it all happened. The two funerals, so close together, had shattered my life. Everything was spinning wildly out of control.

Our branch of the family was suddenly reduced to an army of one. Me. And I was waiting for my uncle's instructions to murder a woman I'd never met.

My god, how had it come to this?

Then I'd see Mel Bennett doing an interview on television, offering a million-dollar reward for the arrest of Lisa's killer. Smiling all the while.

And I'd get a quick memory flash of Lisa's smile. Or my mother's.

And I'd remember exactly how it all happened. And what I had to do now.

• • •

Ten days later, I was walking to my car after the day's classes, when a black Cadillac Escalade pulled up beside of me. Bo La Motte climbed out, glancing around to be sure we were alone.

"Put these on," he said, stripping off a pair of black leather gloves. "The Caddy's stolen so you'll have to move quick. Fawn

Daniels jogs along the lake shore after work. There's a hundred yard stretch near Michikewis where the shore road parallels the beach. Run her down there, just like Lisa. Put that bitch in the ground! You sure you're up for this?"

I nodded, too shaken to answer.

"Afterward, dump the Caddy in the supermarket lot downtown, then walk to Valhalla Park. We're having a family barbecue this afternoon. Twenty witnesses will swear you were there the whole time. Gimme your car keys. Move!"

As I fumbled them out of my jacket, he grabbed my arm.

"One last thing, cousin. You remember all the times I stood up for you in school?"

"I remember."

"Good. Because if anything goes wrong, if you get stopped, get stuck, whatever, you dummy up and take the weight, understand? If my dad does one day in prison because of you, Paulie, I'll make up for every beatin' you ever missed and then some!"

Scrambling into my Volvo, Bo sped off.

A moment later I was on the road too, heading for the lakeshore in a stolen Cadillac SUV. Taking deep breaths. Pumping myself up. For a killing.

I didn't question the justice of it. Fawn Daniels helped arrange my sister's death and by standing mute on the witness stand, she'd gotten Lisa's killer off scot-free. And put my mother in her grave.

Half the men in my family were army vets and my father died in Vietnam. If killing strangers on behalf of our government was honorable, how could I fail to retaliate against people who'd murdered members of my family?

The Daniels woman justly deserved a death sentence. But knowing that, and being able to carry it out are very different things.

I didn't know if I was capable of killing. I only knew that the law had utterly failed our clan. Justice had been left to me.

Turning onto the shore road, I headed toward Michikewis Beach. Half a mile ahead, I could see a blonde jogger running along the shore. Fawn Daniels, lithe and athletic, decked out in skin tight pink spandex. Enjoying a relaxing run in the warm autumn afternoon.

While my mother, my sister and her unborn baby lay cold in the moldering darkness.

Flooring the gas pedal, I rapidly closed the distance. There were a few tourists strolling along the beach, but none were close enough to interfere. All they could do was watch.

Not that they could see much. The stolen Escalade's windows were smoked glass. And in the split second before I whipped it off the road onto the beach, it occurred to me that my Uncle Deke had planned this killing extremely well on very short notice. A sobering thought.

Then it was too late for thinking! The big SUV slewed in the sand, and I was fighting the wheel to keep the unruly machine upright, wrestling it back on course. Forty yards ahead, I glimpsed Fawn Daniels' terrified face as she glanced over her shoulder to see the monster Cadillac hurtling toward her. It must have looked like a messenger of death. A roaring black juggernaut.

For a split second our eyes met through the windshield—and then I cranked the wheel over, veering away to avoid her! Too late!

I heard a thump, saw Fawn go sprawling into the shallows. But then she was up again, scrambling to her feet, sprinting out into deeper water, limping, but making pretty good time.

Matting the gas pedal, I nearly rolled the SUV in the loose sand as I swerved back toward the shore road. Running for my life.

Though I knew it was already too late.

She'd glimpsed my face, if only for a moment. And she'd seen me often enough during the trial to know who I was.

I'd destroyed myself. Thrown my life away. For nothing.

At the moment of truth, I simply couldn't do it.

I didn't hear police sirens yet, but they'd be coming soon enough. All I could do now was try to avoid dragging anyone else down with me.

As instructed, I abandoned the Escalade in the supermarket lot, but I didn't join my family in the park. I'd failed them. I'd take the weight for that failure alone.

I walked home instead. Not to my apartment. Home. To my mother's house. A small white clapboard on a quiet side street, shaded by maple trees.

It stood empty now. Locked, shades drawn, eyeless windows staring blindly at me as I trudged slowly up the porch steps. Utterly exhausted.

I still had a key, but didn't bother to use it. Sat on the front steps instead. Waiting for the police. Knowing they'd be on their way as soon as the Daniels woman got to a phone.

It was a good place to wait. I'd grown up in this house, roamed these streets as a boy. With my little sister tagging along after me. Closing my eyes, I could almost hear Lisa's voice calling me. The autumn sun warm on my face ...

I snapped awake, startled. Wasn't sure how long I'd been asleep but dusk was coming on now, shadows falling.

A car screeched to a halt at the curb.

Not a police car. My Volvo. With my Uncle Deacon at the wheel.

"What the hell are you doing here, Paul? You're supposed to be at the park."

"You'd better get out of here, Uncle Deke. I blew it completely. The police will be coming."

"They've already been. They arrested Mel Bennett twenty minutes ago. Seems he tried to run down Fawn Daniels. Half a dozen people saw his car at the beach. That big, ugly SUV was hard to miss."

"Mel's SUV?" I echoed stupidly.

"Whose did you think it was? He left it parked in front of his new girlfriend's place. She swore he was with her the whole time, but a star-struck kid isn't much of an alibi. Not with Fawn Daniels in the back of a prowl car, screaming that Mel tried to run her down. Positively identified him."

"I don't understand. She saw me! At the beach she—"

"Saw what she was most afraid of," Deke finished. "Mel's car coming straight at her. She'll swear on her mama's eyes he was at the wheel because she damn sure knows how he did his last girlfriend. I expect they're going at each other like rats in a box about now, throwing their own lives away."

"I still don't—" But suddenly I did understand. "My god. This was the plan all along, wasn't it? You knew I'd never go through with it. Why the hell did you ask me to do it?"

"It had to be you, Paul. Your mama was right, the law's been all over us since the trial. We couldn't make a move."

"Bo managed the car."

"I said they were watching us. I didn't say they were real good at it."

"And if I'd been caught, Uncle Deke? What then?"

"A poor, heartbroken schoolteacher who just lost his mom and sister? You'd get the benefit of the doubt, same as Mel Bennett did. What did the DA call it?"

"A Valhalla verdict," I said slowly.

"Exactly," Deke grinned. "Sometimes, livin' in a town where folks cut one another a break ain't such a bad thing, Professor. C'mon, the family's at the park and you need to be with your people. Damn it, Paul, we've won for once. And it was long overdue."

I couldn't argue with that. Trotting down the steps, I slid into the car beside my uncle. Breathing in the aroma of woodsmoke and whiskey. Reading his wolfish smile as he gunned away from the curb.

I knew he'd played me. All the way. Maybe he had the right to. Maybe it was the only way we could get justice.

Still, I couldn't help wondering ... About those flowers.

Did Mel Bennett really send that wreath to my mother's funeral?

But I didn't ask. Uncle Deke was my mother's brother. She loved him and that was good enough for me.

And it's best to give people you love the benefit of a doubt.

Even when you know better.

• • •

Award-winning author **DOUG ALLYN** has been published internationally in English, German, French, and Japanese and more than two dozen of his tales have been optioned for development as feature films and television. The author of eight novels and over a hundred short stories, his first story won the Robert L. Fish Award for Best First from Mystery Writers of America and subsequent critical response has been equally remarkable. He has won the coveted Edgar Allen Poe Award (plus six nominations), three Derringer Awards for novellas, and the Ellery Queen Readers Award an unprecedented nine times, including this year. He studied creative writing and criminal psychology at the University of Michigan while moonlighting as a guitarist in the rock group *Devil's Triangle* and reviewing books for the *Flint Journal.* Career highlights are sipping champagne with Mickey Spillane and waltzing with Mary Higgins Clark.

PURE PULP
By Bill Crider

One

I was pounding out the words so fast that the keys of my battered Underwood were almost smoking. I could practically smell the hot metal.

Ding went the bell, and I slapped the return lever. The carriage double-spaced, slid to the right, and stopped hard. When you're working for a quarter of a cent a word, some of the time, and half a cent a word at better times, you have to write fast. Either that or give up eating and drinking, and I wasn't ready to give up either one, especially drinking.

Which reminded me that I was thirsty. I stopped typing for just long enough to take a small sip of cheap bourbon from the squat, thick-bottomed glass that sat to my right. A quick swallow, and I was typing again.

The story was titled "Tommy-Gunner's Holiday." It was aimed at *Gun Molls*, and I'd just reached the big scene where a dangerous dame, a blonde, of course, had gunned down a bespectacled teller during a botched bank job when I heard a roscoe sneeze: KA-CHOW!

That's the way Dan Turner, Hollywood Detective, would have put it, anyway, though the sound was nothing at all like a sneeze. It was more of a sharp *crack*, as if someone had slapped a couple of flat boards together. Not that I'm criticizing Robert Leslie Bellem. His Dan Turner stories sold for a good bit more than any of mine ever did. Maybe it was the scantily clad babes that did it, but it could have been the roscoes. You never know.

At any rate, I didn't jump right up from my chair to see what was going on. I had a page to finish, and I couldn't stop, not when I was going so well, not even for gunshots. So the teller dropped twitching to the cold marble floor of the bank, the moll sneered and asked if anybody wanted some of what the teller had gotten, and then I reached the bottom of the page.

I took the paper out of the Underwood, separated the original from the carbon, and removed the carbon paper. I stacked each page one in the proper place. I put the carbon paper, which was getting pretty worn, between two fresh white sheets, and inserted them behind the typewriter roller. After I rolled the paper into place, I stepped out into the hall.

Two or three men were standing outside Ron Thane's door. Or Guy Dane's door. Or Frank Lane's. Or lots of other names. Thane, or whatever his real name was, had so many pseudonyms that it was next to impossible to keep up with them. The same was true of the three standing outside his door, and of me, too, for that matter.

We all lived in The Regis Arms, a shabby residence hotel not too far from Columbia University. Now and then we'd catch sight of a co-ed, which was about as close as any of us came to having any contact with the opposite sex. We were too busy hacking out hair-raising tales for that kind of thing. Well, I was. I couldn't really speak for the others though I was sure their situation was the same.

I walked down the hall, being careful not to soil the soles of my shoes on any of the unknown substances that spotted it or any of the vermin that roamed the shadows. When I got to Dane's door, I asked what was going on.

"I heard a gunshot," Tony Lomax said.

Tony was a short little gink with curly black hair, dark eyes, and five o'clock shadow that showed up by noon on the days he bothered to shave. His specialty was gimp detectives, but he also did mob stories, cop stories, and powder-burning Westerns.

"I heard it, too," Stan Burke said. He had a light, clear tenor, and on a good night in a bar, he'd sing "Danny Boy" sweet enough to put a tear in your eye. "A roscoe snarled in Ron's room. Maybe he shot himself."

Burke was a rail of man. He looked like Ichabod Crane on a bread-and-water diet, but his long, thin fingers could knock out a story in one sitting, usually a story about some guy fighting giant snakes on Venus or asteroids exploding or some other kind of ray-gun stuff.

Also, he wasn't above stealing from Bellem, at least in conversation.

"Like hell he shot himself," said Al Roberts.

Of the four of us, Roberts was the one who made the most money. He had three regular series in the detective pulps, two or three in the Western pulps, and the love pulps bought everything he could turn out, which was a lot. So Al ate a little better than we did, and it showed.

"He just sold a story to *Black Mask*," Roberts went on, "and Shaw said he'd take more. Would you kill yourself if you were selling to Cap Shaw?"

The answer to that for all of us was, *hell, no.*

"So what now?" Lomax said. "Break down the door?"

"You tried the knob?" I said.

Lomax nodded. "Locked. I tried it, and then I knocked. No answer."

"He's in there, though," Burke said. "I heard his typewriter when I went to the phone a while back."

A pay phone in an alcove at the end of the hall was the only one on the floor. None of us could afford a phone line, or if we could, we didn't want one.

"A locked room mystery," Roberts said. "Who writes those?"

Nobody admitted it.

"Move out of the way," Roberts said.

We did. Roberts moved up, took hold of the door knob, drew back to arm's length, and threw his beefy shoulder against the door. It popped right open. The Regis Arms didn't put a lot of money into buying sturdy bolts.

Roberts went into the room, and we all followed. I could smell gunpowder as soon as I got inside.

The light wasn't on, but Thane's typing desk was set up near the room's only window. Thane had fallen forward onto the desk, his head resting in a small pool of blood beside the Royal upright typewriter. One arm hooked over the typewriter as if protecting the sheet of paper he'd been typing on. The other arm dangled limp, the fingers near the gun that rested on the floor.

"Jesus Christ," Burke said, crossing himself. I hadn't thought of him as being religious. "He did shoot himself."

I walked over to the desk, careful not to touch anything. Several pulps were scattered beside the typewriter: *Amazing Stories, Fantastic Adventures, Weird Tales.* I thought that was odd since Thane, like me, wrote mostly for the crime and Western pulps. Maybe he was thinking about breaking into a new market. Not what I'd be thinking about if I'd just sold to *Black Mask,* but Thane wasn't me.

He wasn't anybody now.

"Jesus Christ," Burke said again, and I turned to see why.

Burke was looking out the window, as were Roberts and Lomax. I stared over their shoulders.

Standing in the twilight on the roof of the building next door, one floor below us, was a man. Not just any man, either. He was dressed all in black, including his slouch hat and mask. And his cape.

It definitely wasn't Jesus Christ.

"It's The Spider," Lomax said.

"Or The Shadow," Roberts said.

I didn't say anything. The man in black gave us an ironic salute, swirled his cape, and ran across the rooftop. He clambered over the low ledge on the other side and disappeared.

"Somebody better call the cops," Lomax said.

"I will," I said.

Two

Detective McCoy, in spite of his name, wasn't Irish, or not recently. He was pure New York, from his beady little eyes right down to the tops of his worn-out shoes.

He questioned me in my room, and I could tell he didn't believe a word of what I told him, not after he got a sniff of my breath. I wouldn't have believed me, either, even though the others must have told him essentially the same thing.

One problem was that the window was locked. From the inside.

"So there was a guy on the roof next door, all decked out like one of your crazy pulp heroes, and your pal was locked in the room, dead."

I lit a Camel, sucked in some smoke, and said, "Sounds a little funny, but that's the way it happened."

McCoy stuck out a hand. I tapped a Camel out of the pack, and he took it. I lit it for him.

"Want me to smoke it for you, too?" I said.

He didn't crack a smile. "You writers are all nuts," he said, brushing smoke away from his eyes with one hand. "Or liars. Maybe lying for a living's affected your brains. If you got any."

"You don't read?"

"Don't have time, and if I did, I wouldn't waste it on that crap you turn out."

I knew I wasn't any Hemingway, but I couldn't let that pass. "We don't write crap, McCoy. You might not like it, and the highbrows might not like it, but there are plenty of guys who do. They plunk down their money, and they get something that takes their minds off their troubles for a while. That might not seem like much to you, but it's a lot to them."

"So you think you're Shakespeare, so what?"

"I don't even think I'm Dash Hammett, but I write the best I can, every story, every line, every time. Nobody ever feels cheated by one of my stories. They're mine, and I'm proud of them. All the others would tell you the same. What we do means something to us."

I crushed my cigarette out in the overflowing ashtray on my desk. McCoy did the same. I didn't offer him another.

"Yeah," he said, "you're all proud of what you do, and I bet you're extra proud of that yarn about the man in the cape. The one that disappeared without a trace."

"That's not a story. That's the truth."

"Bull corn. What happened is this. Your friend shot himself. Simple as that. Maybe he wasn't selling anything, maybe he had love troubles, maybe anything at all. Case closed."

McCoy wanted it simple. In and out, no work for him, no suspects to chase, all neatly tied up in a swell little package. I wasn't going to let him off the hook, not yet.

"He was selling plenty," I said. "He didn't have any love troubles because he didn't go out. And there *was* a man on the roof."

"So you say. You find him, maybe I'll talk to him. But you won't find him, because he was never there. Suicide, that's what we have here."

"No note."

I'd looked at the page in Thane's typewriter. It wasn't a suicide note. It was a story of some kind.

"Not everybody who decides to take that way out leaves a note," McCoy said.

"Thane would have. He's a writer. That's what he did. He couldn't have resisted writing something if he'd planned to kill himself."

"Yeah, right. And the Spider was hanging out on the roof next door."

"Might have been the Shadow," I said.

McCoy just stared at me. "The door was locked, the window was locked. Nobody came in or out. Not even your masked man."

He had a point, I suppose. I asked if our conversation was over.

He nodded. "Damn right. And don't bother me again with stories about little men dressed in black."

McCoy left. I stared at the paper in my own typewriter. I needed to finish the story I'd been working on, but I couldn't concentrate on it, now with what had happened. Somehow a make-believe gun moll didn't interest me at the moment. I lit another Camel, smoked it down as far as I could without burning my fingers, then mashed it out. I had a few sips of my cheap bourbon, thought things over a little longer, then went down to Thane's room.

They'd already carted Thane off to the morgue, and the door was closed. Getting inside was no problem, however, since Roberts had broken the lock and the Regis Arms wasn't going to repair it until the room was rented again, if then. I slipped into the room and closed the door behind me.

The first thing I did after turning on the light was to look out the window. I don't know what I thought I'd see, but if I'd been expecting a masked man, I'd have been disappointed. It was getting late now, and the moonlight gave a white glow to the empty roof. I stood there a minute, watching, but nobody showed up. I hadn't expected anyone to.

I went to the typewriter. The paper had been removed, but it lay on the desk. I read what Thane had typed.

• • •

The dame was no good. She had a heart as cold as a banker's smile and a mouth as cruel as a cobra's. I didn't care. I pulled her to me and crushed her against me. I could feel the softness of her breasts, the beating of her heart.

"You're good, baby," I said. "You're really good."

"No, I'm not," she breathed. "I'm bad clean through."

"That's what I mean," I said.

• • •

Deathless prose, all right, and nothing about suicide in it. If there was a clue, I couldn't see it. What writer would kill himself in the middle of a story? Not me, not Thane. They'd put a bag over Thane's hand, but I didn't think they'd even try a paraffin test, not if McCoy could prevent it, and I was sure he could.

I looked at the magazines by the typewriter. I still couldn't figure out what they were doing there, but maybe Thane didn't like to read the same kind of stuff he wrote.

Most writers I knew did read occasionally. They *liked* to read, which is why they became writers in the first place. Then they found out that writing took up more and more of their time, and they didn't read much any more. But everybody found time to read something now and then.

I picked up the magazines and took them back to my room. Then I sat down and started to read. I don't know what I was looking for, maybe something that would explain how a guy standing on a rooftop could have gotten inside a locked room and killed a man.

I didn't find anything like that, of course.

But I did find something else.

Three

It was cold out on the roof. I could hear the cars in the street grinding along. There weren't many of them, and the noise was muted by the wind that swirled down the alley between the buildings and brought up the stink of garbage.

I walked over to where the man in the cape had stood. There was no sign of him, but then I hadn't thought there would be. McCoy might not have believed us about the man, but he'd sent a couple of uniforms to check, just to be sure he was right about us being nuts, or liars, or both. I didn't think the uniforms would have checked everywhere, though, and I didn't think they'd have been too careful.

I'd looked all along the stairway on the way to the roof, but I hadn't found a thing. The closet that held the doorway onto the roof had been bare as well.

On the other side of the room was a fire escape. The man in the cape had gone down it after saluting us, I was sure, so I swung over the ledge and clattered down the iron steps. When I hit the bottom, the counterweight swung me down into the alley. An overflowing wooden trash bin sat in heavy shadow against the wall opposite me when I stepped off.

A man wearing a mask, a cape, and a slouch hat in the early evening would be conspicuous even in New York, even near the university. Me, I'd have ditched part of the outfit before going out on the street, and I'd have bet my last check from *Dime Detective* that the cops hadn't thought of that.

So I went over and pawed through the trash. I jerked back my hand a time or two when it touched something wet and slimy I couldn't identify, but before long I grabbed hold of a thin piece of cloth and pulled it out. It was the mask, no doubt about that, and after another couple of grabs, I came up with the cape. I didn't find the hat. Maybe the guy had thought it was fashionable and kept it on. He was wrong, but nobody would pay much attention to a hat, and it would disguise his appearance.

It seemed to me that the mask and cape had been too easy to find, though. If I'd been the man who'd worn them, I'd have been more careful about where I'd but them, or I'd at least have hidden them deeper in the garbage.

I folded the mask and cape, tucked them under my arm, and went back to the Regis Arms.

• • •

There were six rooms on the hallway we writers lived on. I was on the end nearest the stairs, and Al Roberts lived opposite me. Roberts lived next door. Then came Lomax down at the end. The room opposite mine was empty. Some university prof, the kind who didn't mingle with writers, had moved out a couple of days earlier, probably to much better quarters. Thane lived, or had lived, next door, and Burke lived in the last room on that side. Roberts was the one I wanted to talk to, but first I stopped by my own room for one of the magazines that had been on Thane's desk. I took it with me and went next door.

If anybody was harder on typewriters than I am, Roberts was the one. I've mentioned that he was big, and he treated his typewriters like punching bags. He broke one down every five or six months and bought another one. Not a new one. He always bought his machines at pawnshops, his theory being that if he was going to tear them up so soon, he might as well get the cheapest ones he could find.

I stood outside the door and listened for a couple of seconds. He was giving the typewriter a real workout. All of us worked well into the night, most days, and I could hear him talking as he typed. That was a peculiarity of his. He'd talk to the typewriter, to his characters, to himself. He wasn't shy about it, either.

"Give it to him, sister," his muffled voice said. "Don't let him get away with making you look small. Atta girl! Slap him again!"

I knocked on the door.

"Come in!"

I opened the door. Roberts was at his desk, his thick fingers a blur as they danced over the clackety keys.

"What is it?" he said.

"Don't you ever lock your door?"

"Why the hell should I? I don't have anything worth stealing."

Good point.

"I've been thinking about Thane," I said.

"Yeah? Why? Don't you have any work to do?"

All the time he talked, Roberts' fingers kept moving. He could write and talk at the same time, a talent I lacked.

"I was wondering who killed him," I said.

"Didn't you talk to McCoy? Suicide, pure and simple."

"What about that man we saw?"

"We didn't see anybody. McCoy told me so."

The clickety-clack of the keys was starting to annoy me. I walked over and tossed the cape and mask on top of Roberts' Royal, stalling the keys.

"What the hell?" he said, and gave me a look. At least he'd stopped typing.

"Take a gander," I said.

He did, turning the cloth in his hands, and then he shook his head. "I'll be damned. Where'd you find 'em?"

"In the trash in the alley."

"That would explain the stains."

I wiped my hand on my pants without being conscious of why I was doing it.

"McCoy's not much for police work," Roberts continued. "The cops I write about do a better job."

"Except for the bent ones," I said.

"Yeah, except for those. He fingered the mask. "Pretty cheap material. What're you gonna do about it?"

"Nothing at the moment."

He pitched the mask down, and I handed him the magazine I'd picked up in my room.

"*Amazing Stories?*" he said. "I don't read this stuff. Nice cover, though."

I was fond of women in metal bathing suits, myself.

"Ever write any of it?" I said.

"Never tried."

"What about Thane?"

"Nope. He hadn't written any that he ever mentioned to me."

"Then what was he doing with those magazines?"

Roberts clearly hadn't thought about that. Now he took a couple of seconds to consider it.

"Seems to me he picked them up last week. He mentioned something about trying his hand at something different."

That had been my first thought. You couldn't blame a guy for wanting more markets, even if he'd just sold to *Black Mask*.

"Did he say anything else about it?"

"Don't remember. He might have mentioned that he'd come across something interesting, but he didn't say what it was. It didn't seem important at the time." He looked at me. "Still doesn't."

"It might be more important than you think," I said. "Take a look at the story on page thirty-two and see."

Roberts flipped the pages, the stopped. "'The Cult of the Eagle People'?"

"That's the one."

"By Jack MacLane? Whose he?"

I told him I didn't have any idea. He laid the magazine on his desk and put his finger on the line drawing that illustrated the tale.

"People with eagles' heads?"

I shrugged. "Either that or eagles with people's bodies."

"And why the hell would I be interested in a piece of crap like that?"

"Just read a little of it and see," I told him.

He groused some more, but he gave it up after a second or two started reading. I smoked a Camel and waited.

After a couple of minutes, he said, "Well, I'll be damned."

Four

"Does the story seem familiar?" I said.

"Damn right, it seems familiar. I wrote it."

"You did, huh?"

"Well, not this exact story, but one just like it, without the goofy stuff."

I nodded. The story he was reading took place on one of the moons of Jupiter, where the followers of the eagle cult had kidnapped the beautiful daughter of Earth's ambassador, who had hired a down-and-out spacer to penetrate the cult and find her.

In Roberts' story, which had been in *Thrilling Detective* a year or so ago, the beautiful daughter of the mayor of New York City had been kidnapped by the members of a cult of Satan worshipers, and the mayor had hired a down-and-out private dick to penetrate the cult and find her.

The only reason I knew about Roberts' tale was that a story of my own had appeared in the same issue of the magazine, right next to his, and I'd read it to pass the time one evening. "The Cult of the Eagle People" was almost word-for-word the same, except of course for the description of the characters and setting.

Roberts closed the magazine and tossed it on the desk, and I stuck my cigarette in his ashtray and ground it out.

"Did you get lazy, Al?" I said. "Did you figure it would be easy enough to sell the same story twice with just a few little changes? Is that what happened?"

For a second I thought he'd come out of the chair and flatten men. But he got control of himself and settled back.

"You know me better than that," he said.

I wasn't so sure I did. It seemed to me the gag would work. Double the money for the same story, with very little work other than retyping. An editor for one publisher wouldn't know what another one had bought, and the people who read *Thrilling Detective* weren't likely to be reading *Amazing Stories*. Most readers tended to stick to one kind of story or the other. They were loyal to what they liked.

"Not that it's a bad idea, now that I think about it," Roberts said. "I'd never do it, though. You might think it's dumb, but I believe in what I write." I must have looked a little surprised because he went on. "Oh, sure, I do it for the money. Who doesn't? But it's mine, and I'd never screw around with it."

I felt the same way. I said, "Somebody screwed around with it."

"Yeah, and I'd sure as hell like to know who."

"What if it was Thane?"

Roberts rubbed thick fingers across his balding head. "You mean he stole my story?"

"That would be one way to break into a new market."

"Yeah, but ... Wait a minute!"

I waited.

"You think I killed Thane because he stole my story?"

I didn't know what I thought. To tell the truth, Roberts seemed to me more likely to beat the hell out of Thane than to kill him.

"Thinking I'd kill Thane is just as crazy as thinking I'd kill him because he found out I'd sold the same story twice," Roberts said. "Which I didn't."

I believed him, but I didn't know where that left us.

"Besides," he said, picking up the cape and mask and clenching them in his hand, "what about this?"

"The classic red herring. Everybody's looking for the Shadow, or the Spider. Nobody's looking for the killer."

"If that's the case, it didn't work. McCoy doesn't even believe it was murder. The doors were locked, and Thane was inside the room. Suicide. And McCoy sure as hell doesn't believe in the man on the roof."

Roberts was right, but the locked door was easily explained.

"You know as well as I do that the lock on the door would click shut when the door was closed if you set it to do that. You don't lock your door. You just told me so, and it wasn't locked when I came in. I don't lock my door, either, not until I get ready to go to bed. I don't think Thane locked his, either, not while he was home."

"You know how those locked-room stories are," Roberts said. "Unnecessarily complicated."

"No, they're *necessarily* complicated. Only amateurs put in too many complications."

Almost as soon as I said that, things started to click into place. I didn't know the *why* of things, not exactly, but I thought I knew the *who*.

"You look funny," Roberts said.

"I blame heredity."

"Don't get cute. Tell me what you're thinking."

"Let's talk to Lomax," I said.

I picked up the cape and mask. Roberts got the magazines.

Five

"I wrote this one," Lomax said, holding up a magazine to show us. "Except when I wrote it, it was called 'Death Holds the Cards,' and it was in one of the Western pulps."

This time it was in *Fantastic Adventures,* and it was called "Ghosts Don't Bluff." By Steve Gargan. And it wasn't a Western. The red sands of Mars took the place of the American desert. The little mining town was pretty much the same, though, and so were the hard-bitten miners involved in the card game that was central to the plot.

"I don't get it," Lomax said. "This isn't my story, but it's the same thing. The setting and the names have changed, but that's all."

"Maybe you're double-dipping," Roberts said. "Selling the same story to two different markets."

"Just a damn minute," Lomax said, standing up.

Roberts laughed and held up a hand. "Don't get riled. I'm just saying to you what was said to me. I got just as mad as you did."

"Then what's the joke?" Lomax said.

"It's no joke," I said. "It's murder."

Lomax, like Roberts, went through McCoy's suicide explanation. I showed him the mask and cape.

"So we did see a man. I thought maybe we'd all had more to drink than usual and hallucinated him."

"He was real enough. He was a red herring, or maybe just an unnecessary complication, tossed in by an amateur."

"That's the second time you've used that word," Roberts said. "What kind of amateur are you talking about?"

"An amateur mystery writer. Someone who might be okay writing other stuff, but not a mystery. He had his plot all laid out, though, and maybe the complication was necessary after all. If McCoy hadn't taken the suicide bait, I have a feeling somebody would've found the mask and cape. They weren't hidden very well, hardly at all, really. If the cops hadn't found them, the killer would have."

"The killer?" Lomax said. "Why would he find them."

"To prove there was someone out on that roof and draw suspicion away from himself. Red herring."

Lomax and Roberts looked at each other, than at me.

"Burke?" they said together.

"That would be my guess. He knows all the editors of the scientifiction pulps. That's where he sells his stuff. What would be easier for him than to take one of our stories, make some changes, and sell it as his own work?"

"Pretty thin," Roberts said. "McCoy wouldn't buy it."

"Okay, then, who was the first one at Thane's door?"

"Burke," Lomax said. "He was there when I got there."

"He said he was out in the hall to use the telephone," I said. "I think he went into Thane's room, killed him, and came back into the hall to stand by the locked door, pretending he couldn't get inside."

"He couldn't," Lomax said. "The door was locked."

"Burke locked it," Roberts said, catching on. "And he was the one selling the suicide theory from the start."

"He's the one who went to the window and saw the guy on the roof, too," Lomax said. "He was leading us by the nose."

"That's the way I see it," I told them.

Lomax headed for the door. "Let's go talk to him.

Burke's door wasn't locked, and we didn't knock. We just barged right in.

Burke looked up from his typewriter in surprise, but he knew instantly that we were onto him. He reacted quickly. He grabbed manuscript pages and carbons from two different stacks and made a run for his window. Before we could get to him, he'd raised it and stepped out onto the fire escape.

I followed. He clanked down, his long legs taking two rungs at a time. I wasn't quite as fast, but I was persistent. When he dropped down to the alley, I was close behind him.

Then he surprised me. He stopped on a dime, turned sharply, and kicked me in the knee.

I went down, skidding a foot or so on the side of my face. I jumped back up, my face burning. Burke turned the corner of the alley and disappeared.

I realized that I still had the cap and mask in my hand. I swirled on the cape and snapped it at the neck. Then I slipped on the mask.

Just as I emerged from the alley, Burke looked back. He must have thought that the Spider was after him, or the Shadow. I wished I had the hat, but I was effective enough as it was.

"The Shadow knows!" I yelled, sounding nothing at all like Orson Welles.

It didn't matter. Burke stumbled in shock. His left foot slipped off the curb, and he joggled into the street, trying to regain his balance. He almost did, but it was too late. The lights of the on-coming taxicab turned him into a black silhouette just before it hit him.

He flew backward about ten feet. Manuscript pages sailed and swirled and then settled to the street. Some of them landed on Burke, as if trying to cover him up.

A couple of people stood on the edge of the sidewalk, staring. First at Burke and then at me.

"Better call the cops," I told them.

They took off, happy for an excuse to get away from me, I guess. I went out on the street and started gathering up pages. Just as I thought I had enough, I heard sirens. I took off the mask and cape. My work as a crime-fighter was done.

• • •

I explained things as I understood them to McCoy, who showed up for a visit a few days later. He'd talked to Burke in the hospital and got the whole story. Burke had been selling our stories as his own almost from the start. It started with the Westerns. He'd read a lot of scientifiction stories that he said were just Westerns in disguise, so it was easy to convert them. Then he'd moved on to the mysteries, which he'd found equally simple to change for his purposes.

"Why our stories, though?" I said.

"The answer was right there in your hands," McCoy said. "You guys never lock your doors. If you went out for a beer or a smoke, Burke'd slip in, go through your carbons, and pick out a story he liked. After he'd made it over, he'd find a chance to slip the carbon back."

"And Thane found out?"

"Right."

"Must have pissed him off."

"Not so much. According to Burke, Thane was blackmailing him. He was going to tell you and the others, and Burke was afraid you'd beat the hell out of him."

"We would have," I said, meaning Roberts would have. "We're proud of what we do. We don't want anybody stealing it."

"Yeah. Well, Burke wasn't getting rich, even by stealing from you, and Thane was going to bleed him. So Burke figured he'd just get rid of him. He says he thought it out just like he'd think out a story."

"He wasn't much of a mystery writer," I said.

"Nope."

"You planning to apologize about what you said when we told you about the man on the roof?"

"I still haven't seen any man."

"He was just some goof that Burke hired. You could find him if you wanted to."

"Don't need him. We got Burke cold."

"Thanks to me," I said.

McCoy admitted nothing. He didn't even thank me. He just nodded and left.

After he'd been gone a minute or so, I tried on the cape and mask. I don't know why I'd kept them. Maybe I thought a career as a masked crime-fighter might be an improvement.

Then I thought about the story I was writing, one with a private dick who'd been framed for the murder of his best friend. It was going to be damned good, maybe better than good.

I tossed the cape and mask into a chair and sat down at the Underwood.

Too bad about Thane being so greedy, I thought, and Burke being a thief. But I didn't think about them long. Things like that were for people like McCoy. I had other things to do. Pretty soon the keys of the Underwood were smoking. It was good to be back at work.

• • •

BILL CRIDER is the author of more than fifty published novels. He won the Anthony Award for best first mystery novel for *Too Late to Die* (1987) and he and his wife, Judy, won the best short story Anthony for "Chocolate Moose" (2002). His short story "Cranked" was nominated for an Edgar Award. His latest novels are *Mississippi Vivian* (Five Star) and *Murder in the Air* (St. Martin's). Check out his homepage at www.billcrider.com.

BLOOD SACRIFICES
AND THE
CATATONIC KID
By Tom Piccirilli

Two moves from mate Barry the chronic masturbator started pawing at the white bishop like he was choking his chicken and said, "Heya, hey, look there—" I turned in time to see the Catatonic Kid get up off his coma couch and cut Harding's throat with a shiv made from a shard of ceramic ashtray.

Harding the orderly stood six-three and went 230 of mostly muscle. He didn't go down easy. Arterial spray shot around the intensely white walls of the ward as Mary the Nictophobe started losing her shit. She screamed and sort of danced in place and couldn't even get herself out of the path of Harding's spurting carotid.

I didn't mind watching him go down. He was a rude, rotten son of a bitch who liked to intimidate and humiliate the patients. He had a habit of opening mail and stealing cash or candy bars or whatever appealed to him at the moment. Now he was scrambling on the floor trying to clamp one hand across his slashed throat. But he was so taken by the wondrous and terrifying sight of his own pouring blood that he kept pulling his hand away and staring at the frothing red puddling in his palm.

Harding checked around the room looking for mercy. Our eyes met and he saw I wasn't going to help. I mouthed, *Fuck you, prick.* He glanced up at Barry and, even as he bled out, an expression of disgust crimped Harding's features as he got a look at the unholy sight of what Barry was currently doing with my black rook.

The rest of the nuts, freaks, depressives, hysterics, deficients, and paranoids didn't seem to notice and just kept up with their muttering, hand-wringing, floor-licking, and carrot-waxing. Mary had crumpled trying to rub the blood out of her eyes.

The Catatonic Kid riffled Harding's pockets and snatched his wallet. He unclipped the huge key ring from Harding's belt, drew out Harding's smaller set of car keys from the orderly's back pocket, and even pulled the dripping watch from Harding's wrist. I thought that was going a little far.

Harding croaked, "Please—" and the Kid kicked him in the face.

Harding tried to lever himself to his feet one last time and toppled across the ping pong table. It collapsed under his weight and he lay unmoving atop the crushed net.

The Kid had been in a non-responsive fugue state for the three months we'd been here. He came in the same day I did and both of us were placed into the same group therapy. They tried to snap him out of his unresponsive state by pretending that he wasn't in one. They talked to him, asked questions, waited for answers. I thought the doctors were some ripe stupid assholes.

They finally wised up and dumped the Kid in the community lounge where he'd lay on his coma couch and stare at the ceiling. The other nuts kept clear of him. The doctors and nurses came in and flashed a light in his eyes every so often, tossed pills down his throat, and fed him. He'd eat slowly, hardly ever blinking. They'd wipe his chin and let him lie back down, and the rest of us would pass him by like he was a piece of furniture.

He'd been faking the entire time and I admired the amount of willpower it had taken. Not just to pretend, but to pretend for so long and then still manage to make it all the way back. I knew guys in prison who'd tried to fake insanity so they could get out of solitary or into the hospital wing. Some of them faked it so well for so long they just went crazy.

The Kid knew which key got him out of the ward. He'd been watching, aware, careful. He moved with a certain predator canniness, swift but cautious, with a restrained sense of power. During the nights he must've been exercising, keeping himself fit and sharp.

I followed along behind him, silent in my little baby booty slippers. When he got to the next security station, where Jenkins sat filling out his logbook and helping one of the nurses get medication ready for the patients, the Kid slid along the wall holding his shiv up like he was going to kill them both. I grabbed his wrist and pulled him into an alcove.

He tried to talk but his voice was inhuman, clogged with months of dust. I said, "Not through the front. There's a three-man team at the gate, two in a booth and one patrolling in a truck, and the administrative offices are between you and the door. Besides, Jenkins is a nice guy, not like that fucker Harding."

I let go of his wrist. I could see him thinking about stabbing me with his shard of ashtray. His eyes were red with bridled excitement. He was on the move for the first time in weeks and he wanted to cut loose. The taste of murder was in his teeth. I waited for him to try it.

But he wasn't just cunning, he was smart. He checked the halls and gracefully eased toward the east exit. It opened up onto the back grounds, the landscaper's shed, and the staff parking lot.

I followed him to the door and watched him unlock it and push through. I stayed behind. It was too chancy to shoulder my way into his escape more than I already had. He turned around. I waited. He rushed back.

His voice was returning. He tried a few more words. They didn't sound like English. He spoke again and I recognized what he was saying. "Come on, old man. Let's go."

"Hey," I told him, "I'm here for voluntary committal. I'm depressed, not nuts. Choose one of the other loons for your big breakout."

"Now or you'll get the same thing that bastard Harding did."

"What do you want me for?"

"I might need help along the way."

"How do you know I'll be any help?"

"Because I'll stab you in the heart if you're not."

I had been threatened with a lot of things in my time, but never a shiv made from a ceramic ashtray. I recognized the ashtray too. It was Barry's. I couldn't help picturing him working the clay, squeezing it, getting his hands slippery, and—Christ, I shook my head, I didn't want to think about it. He'd made it for his mother. On visitor's day she'd shown up with the family priest and tried a kind of impromptu exorcism to drive away what she called his "naughty touch demons." They'd given it a real go. The priest calling down the power of the holy spirit, Barry's mother wailing on about the power of Jesus, and Barry turning red and twitching, trying his damnedest to keep from tugging out his mushroom. The Kid must've filched the ashtray while everyone had been watching the show.

The Kid and I crept along the outer wall of the hospital. Jenkins and the nurse would be coming around in five minutes or so to hand out the meds. We didn't have long to get to Harding's car.

The Kid tried the remote unlock and an SUV tweeted. We rushed to it and the Kid tried to hop into the driver's seat. I told him, "Move over."

"What?"

"Let me drive."

"Why?"

It was a good question. I didn't have a good answer. I spun the smoothest lie I could. "Forty years without an accident or a speeding ticket."

"We've got to ram the gate and outrun the security trucks."

Point taken. "I live in town. I know this area. I can lose anyone who comes after us. Can you?"

I knew he couldn't. The Kid was new to the area. "If you fuck up," he said, "I'll kill you."

"I won't."

"Remember what I said."

I started it up and felt the thrum of the engine work into my chest, my hands, the back of my skull. There were only twenty-two thousand miles on it. She'd been well taken care of. I put it in drive and grooved on the feel of my foot on the pedal. Driving with the slippers was almost like driving barefoot. I hadn't been behind the wheel in three months, the longest period of time since I was fourteen years old, nearly a half century ago. I circled the lot once before heading for the gate. I wished to Christ I'd had time to put on some clothes. The pjs and robe just weren't proper attire for a crash-out.

I centered myself, tamped down my rage, agitation, and impatience and let the cool take me over. The problem wasn't getting through the gate. An SUV had more than enough muscle to break through. I could outmaneuver the security detail in his truck.

The trouble was the state trooper station about three miles up the highway. They'd radio our escape and the staties would catch us in a roadblock or just chase us all to hell until they ran us down.

If we floored it in the other direction we'd wind up in a state park that ran out to a spit of land surrounded by the bay. It would be impossible to hide. The Kid would get nervous and try to take someone hostage. Or he'd make a grab for a boat at the nearby marina, and the water patrol would nab us before we got around the point.

"What are we waiting for?" the Kid said. He held his shiv to my throat.

"I'm working out a plan."

"Just go!"

"That's not a plan."

There was really only one choice. I eased down on the pedal and headed for the gate. No other visitors or employees were heading out, so it was shut. The guards didn't have guns but they did have tasers. They stood in their little booth talking and watching a little television. There was a direct phone line to the staties in there. I didn't gun it. I drove slowly while the Kid got more and more anxious. He liked the throat, it called to him. His eyes were fixed on my jugular. He liked to make a mess and splash blood.

The rage started to climb to the surface again and I pushed it back, not so easily this time. I took deep breaths and pulled up to the booth.

When the two guards showed their faces I smiled and said, "Get the fuck out now."

I put Harding's SUV in reverse, got up some ramming speed, and then floored it.

The guards hung in there until the last second. Maybe they were trying the staties, maybe they were calling in the rest of security from the perimeter and the hospital. They weren't going to have time. I sped towards them. The assholes inside finally realized I was serious. They both dove out the door. I spun the wheel at the last second and hit the booth broadside. It wasn't a paragon of architecture and went over like a kid's tree house. I straightened the SUV out and smashed into the gate. It was thicker than it looked but not by much. The front end of the truck buckled a bit, but we only lost one headlight and the hood stayed clamped down.

The locking mechanism on the gate screeched and the mangled fencing exploded as we went through. I twisted the wheel in order to keep from rolling over, overcorrected and we went up on two tires. I rode it like that for forty feet and we came down on all fours again in the middle of the road. I headed for the highway.

They would call the other security guards first. Then radio the cops. The cops would call in their own cars before informing the staties. It would take an extra four or five minutes. That was enough time to burn right past the trooper station. I got to triple digits and kept punching the engine.

"Jesus, you can drive," the Kid said.

"I've had a lot of experience."

"Yeah? Where?"

"All over."

"You said you knew this area."

"I do. I've lived out this way for a long time."

"Where's a good place to lay low?"

I grinned at him. "I know the perfect spot."

"Where?"

"My granddaughter's place."

"And where's she?"

"Away."

I got off the highway and onto the parkway, heading for the safe house. Things were rolling the right way now. I turned on the radio and clicked in an oldies station. I expected the Kid to give me shit but he kept quiet. We listened to a few crooners, Frankie and Dino, with me humming along.

I jockeyed among the thickening traffic. I took Sunset Highway through Port Jackson. I felt good for the first time in twelve weeks.

"So what are you so depressed about?" he asked.

"I've got issues."

"And what would they be?"

"I've been having trouble enjoying life lately."

"Are you fucking with me?"

"No."

"You sound as if you're fucking with me."

"I'm not."

"You're smiling and singing. I guess you're on the upswing."

"I think maybe I am."

"You're never as full of life as when you're on the edge of death."

"That's as clichéd as they come."

"Maybe," he said, "maybe, but it's true. Don't you feel your heart racing like it wants to bang out of your chest?"

"No."

He got in close. He whispered in my ear. "You're not afraid of me? Of what you just saw back there?"

"No."

"Not afraid of dying either. The way you took out that security shack, we almost rolled, but you kept your head. You didn't panic. Not even when I was this close to cutting your throat."

"No."

He snorted. "You are a lunatic."

"That's a matter of opinion. Tell me something. Why did you take the watch?"

"What?"

"Harding's watch. Why'd you snag it?"

"It's a nice watch."

"But you can't even read the time, his dried blood covers the crystal."

"Who the hell wants to know what time it is?"

He let out a barking laugh. The entire time his voice had been getting stronger. He sounded confident, effectual, his words and laughter resonating. I laughed along with him. He was going to start recognizing sites soon. I circled Port Jackson and went by the supermarket, the high school, the bank, the homeless shelter, the police station, the post office, the jewelry store.

The Kid said, "Where are we?"

"Port Jackson."

"Slow down."

I slowed down. I hung a left and cut into a housing development.

"Go back," he said.

"Go back?"

"Around the block and onto the main road again."

"Why?"

"You do what I tell you, right?"

"Okay."

I drove around the block and let him get his bearings. He nodded to himself. His face broke into a self-satisfied grin. He flipped the oldies station and put on something loud and obnoxious and unbearable. It was just as well. The rage was welling up in me. He was going to cut me soon. It would be a small cut, just to get my attention. Just to prove that he had the capacity, that he was capable. I glanced at my face in the rearview mirror. I'd been cut and beaten before, plenty of times. One more scar wouldn't mean much.

"Thank you," he said.

"For what?"

"Taking me where I needed to go."

"Where's that?"

"Never mind." He looked at me and grinned. It was a warm and amiable smile, the kind that young girls would fall for. "How far is it to your granddaughter's place?"

"A couple miles. We're almost there."

"We have to stop somewhere first."

"Where?" I asked.

"The post office."

"Kid, we're dressed in hospital pajamas, robes, and slippers. Shouldn't we keep a lower profile?"

"Pull over."

"What?"

"Pull the fuck over."

I pulled over. I turned in my seat and said, "Kid, you should listen to me here. If you—"

He reached out and slashed me on the forehead with his little shiv. It was so sharp that I barely even felt it, but the blood immediately began to pour into my eyes. The cut was small but there are a lot of blood vessels close to the skin on your head and any wound will bleed like a bastard.

That's what he'd been counting on. He thought the blood would rattle me. It was an old trick. It was a bad bet. He already knew I kept calm under pressure, but it hadn't mattered. He fell back to type.

The Kid was growing edgy. The months of inactivity had worn down his composure. He was getting excited.

I tore the pocket off my pajama top, folded the cloth and held it to the cut. I tied it there with the belt of my robe. I looked at him through the blood dripping off my eyelashes. He was self-satisfied, his eyes alive and bright. Blood had leaked down my chin and smeared across the front of my shirt.

He said, "When I tell you to do something, you do it. You understand me?"

"Sure."

"Let's go."

With the wadded tail of my robe I wiped the blood off my face as best I could and drove over to the post office. He said, "Come on."

"You want me to come with you?"

"Quickly. We're in and out in under a minute. And I don't trust you."

"Take the keys. I'll wait."

"You're still arguing. Should I cut you again?"

"No."

"You'll come with me. Now."

I went with him. We walked in the front door. The employees and the folks buying stamps and mailing letters gasped and squeaked and backed away. I didn't look like a depressive who'd voluntarily committed himself. I looked like a maniac who'd probably killed somebody. The Kid pulled a key out of his pocket and walked confidently towards a PO box. He unlocked it and pulled out a satchel. He couldn't contain himself and let out a giggle.

I thought again of his innate willpower. To swallow the key before he went into the hatch, and then to shit it out and hide it on his person for months, lying there on his coma couch dreaming of the day when he'd get back here.

I glanced up at the cameras in the corners. My face was obscured by the bandage and the belt and the blood. The Kid turned and shoved me out the door. We got back in the SUV and I drove down towards the small house that Emily had rented right on the beach. It was a six-month lease, paid up front. She used to lay out in a bikini and sun herself while I jogged along the shoreline.

"What's in the satchel?" I asked.

"None of your fucking business, old man."

The wind was up and the ocean road was obscured with sand and sawgrass. I had to drive over a couple of drifts. The sand spun out from our tires. I pulled into the cracked driveway. The Kid said, "This is it?"

"Yeah."

"It's a total shithole! You let your granddaughter live in a junker like this?"

"It's a bungalow, tucked away on a private beach. A good cool-off spot. The cops will drop their search in a couple of weeks. They'll figure we made it out of state."

"Where's your grandkid again?"

"Away."

"She live here alone?"

"Yeah."

I climbed out and opened the garage door. Then I pulled in and parked. He was going to go for my throat soon. We walked into the bungalow through the inside garage door and the Kid said, "Thanks for the ride, old man, but—"

I spun on him reaching out with the shiv to slash me the same way he'd done Harding. I caught his wrist and wrenched it to the left. The snap was loud in the empty house. The opening note of his scream was even louder. I let it ring and ring, a nice tremolo. He dropped the shiv and I punched him in the Adam's apple. He gagged and went to his knees, tears leaking from his eyes. He huffed air. In agony he turned his eyes up toward me and I gripped the back of his head and drove my knee into his face. He flopped onto his back, out cold.

I checked the satchel. All the jewelry was there. It was worth just under a million on the market. Any good fence would take eighty percent off the top. There was no way to clean jewelry except get it out of the country or sell it to private collectors. That's why a professional crew almost never took down a jewelry shop. The return just wasn't worth it. But our team had been small and tight and the payoff was good enough to give it a go.

I showered and shaved and got my own clothes out of the closet. The cut on my forehead wasn't all that bad, it wouldn't even scar. I cleaned it with peroxide and put a tiny band-aid on.

I sat on the couch and looked at the Kid. His nose was pulped, his face mottled, and he was still sucking air through his teeth. He'd been smart and sharp and paranoid, but not paranoid enough. The jewelry score could've been a pretty sweet deal if only he hadn't gotten greedy.

I knew the Kid wouldn't recognize me.

We hadn't been formally introduced. He'd been chosen last minute by Cole as a replacement for Wellington who'd been picked up for flooring it through a yellow light, the prick. He'd had a shootout with the cops and been iced.

I'd wanted to call the score off, but funds were too low. Emily talked me into rolling the dice. Cole knew somebody who knew somebody who knew the Kid, who was fresh to the coast. Hershaw okayed the replacement.

We still should've moved the plan back a week or two and gotten a feel for the Kid. But there was no time. I'd picked him up and he'd climbed into the car and sat behind me. I'd caught his eyes once in the rearview. I hadn't suspected anything hinky. I'd done my job and driven to the shop and planned on getting us back to the safehouse without incident, where we'd wait a couple of weeks together until the heat was off. Emily and I would lounge around another month or two after that until the end of summer and then split.

I pulled up to the shop and Cole, Hershaw, and the Kid had gotten out. The three of them had entered the place while I kept an eye out for the cops.

My Blackberry rang almost immediately. It was Emily. She wasn't supposed to call. I answered and realized she was sending me video. I watched as the Kid's face filled the screen as he approached her. I could see Cole and Hershaw dead on the floor behind him. The Kid had popped them both in the back of the head with a pipsqueak .22. Up close it was an almost silent kill, I knew.

She had set her own Blackberry aside on the counter and it kept sending footage. I watched him reach out toward her and listened to her squeal in pain. That was him cutting Emily's forehead to get her attention and keep her from hitting any alarm. Then he asked about the jewels. She tried to explain that she was in on the score but he got antsy and slashed her throat. He was fast.

There was nothing I could do but drive away.

If I'd stayed, he would've popped me too. That was his plan all along.

I didn't carry a gun. No driver did.

Someone had hit an alarm. I pulled into the supermarket lot across the square and watched the door. He bolted through two minutes later, still on schedule. He looked around for the car and did a tiny dance of anguish. The police station was less than a minute away. They were already coming.

He'd been smart. He'd planned ahead for contingencies. He'd already taken out a P.O. box. He ran into the post office and hid the satchel of jewelry and then swallowed the key in case he got picked up. But he had no wheels. There was nowhere to run. He couldn't be caught on the street.

I had to give it to him, he stayed cool. He knew how to adapt and improvise. He took off his jacket and tore a hole in his T-shirt and kicked off his shoes on the way to the homeless shelter across the street. He stepped in the front door just as the cops came around the corner. It all seemed to have been perfectly rehearsed. I kept watch.

I found out the Kid played the crazy card and threw himself on the ground and pretended to be nuts. They shipped him off. I voluntarily committed myself the same day.

And I watched the Comatose Kid.

And I waited.

He rolled over on the floor, grunting in pain. "Aooww."

"You hear me, Kid?"

"Ooowww."

"I'll take that as a yes. Look at me."

He opened his eyes and touched his face and moaned again. "My nose—"

"Don't worry about it," I said. "I was your wheelman."

"What?"

"Your driver. I was your driver. Remember now?"

"You broke my nose."

I sighed. "Focus, Kid. You were a last-minute replacement. But we only met in the car. You sat behind me. You killed Cole and Hershaw. You killed the girl."

He cleared his throat. He tried to sit up and couldn't quite do it. "I didn't need partners."

"If you'd followed the plan, you wouldn't have been stuck pretending to be in a coma for three months."

"I didn't mind it."

"And you call me a lunatic. You popped your partners. You cut the girl. You cut her and then you killed her because you like feeling a knife chewing through cartilage."

"I did what I had to do."

"The girl was our inside player. She was the one who got us the alarm codes. She was my granddaughter."

"I didn't know."

"It wouldn't have mattered. You would've done her anyway. And me, if she hadn't sent me the video feed."

"That's why you drove off."

"Yeah."

"And you committed yourself? And waited? In the hospital?"

"Yeah."

"But. But you could've taken me at any time. Why? Why did you wait?"

"I had to make sure you had the key on you," I said. "I wanted the score. I'm a thief."

I kicked him in the face, then slung him over my shoulder and walked out the back door. He didn't have much struggle left in him but he squirmed around and mewled a bit. I marched down the path through the dunes out to the beach. I tossed him down. Emily's chaise lounge was still where it was the last time she'd laid on it, but it was almost completely covered by sand now. I dug it out and there was a pretty sizeable hole left over. I buried the Kid in it and smoothed the sand out and placed the lounge over the spot. I sat down for a while watching the waves roll in.

• • •

TOM PICCIRILLI is the author of more than twenty novels, including *The Cold Spot*, *The Midnight Road*, *Headstone City*, and *A Choir of Ill Children*. He's a four-time winner of the Stoker Award and has been nominated for the World Fantasy Award, the International Thriller Writers Award, and Le Grand Prix de L'Imaginaire. Learn more about him and his work at his website, www.tompiccirilli.com.

PATTERNS

By Richard A. Lupoff

Keweenaw Bay Gazette

Keweenaw Bay, Michigan

July 5, 1940

Mr. Zachary Grand

Editor-in-Chief

Grand Publications

143 West 43rd Street

New York, 16, New York

Dear Zach,

Well, you'll never guess who turned up here in Keweenaw Bay a couple of days ago. Tony LoPresto! What the heck was Tony doing in this little town? Bet you've never heard of it. But there he was.

I was on my lunch break, stopped into Helen's Café for a chicken salad sandwich and an iced coffee, and there he was sitting at the counter. You could have knocked me over with a feather.

Tony LoPresto! Carried me right back to the days of the Three Cheshire Cats. Remember the Three Cheshire Cats? Of course you do! Tony was as surprised to see me as I was to see him, but as soon as we both got over the shock we started exchanging biographies. It's been what, six, seven years, right, seven years since we said good-bye to North Cheshire Central College. Funny how three fellows who were roommates for four years, formed the best little swing trio that northwestern Massachusetts has seen, chased co-eds, shared homework, got into and out of trouble with the local law, and somehow managed to escape with bachelor's degrees, can disappear out of each other's lives as if they'd never known each other.

But I guess that's life.

Would you believe that Tony is police chief of Napoleonville, the flower city of Bayou Richelieu, Louisiana? He still loves bird-watching and he was up here on vacation, field glasses in one hand and notebook in the other, studying the local feathered wildlife. Stopped into Helen's for his ham and eggs and ran into me.

Two of the Three Cheshire Cats back together! Naturally we reminisced about good old North Cheshire Central College, good old President Lucas Smith, poor old Professor Percival Dunning, and all the great times we had together. And of course, the Three Cheshire Cats. I still play a little piano, although just for fun. Tony says he hasn't touched his trumpet in years. Do you still keep your old bull fiddle around, Izzy—or should I say Zach?

When your name came up, Tony told me that you went back to your old hometown and got a job in the publishing world. How things change, don't they? Good old Isaac Goldberg, editor of the *North Cheshire Literary Quarterly,* is now Zachary Grand, editor of *Grand Adventures, Grand Western, Grand Mystery,* and *Grand Ghost Stories.*

Did I leave anything out?

Those pulp magazines are a far cry from the *Literary Quarterly,* I guess, but everybody has to earn a living. Who would have thought

I'd become production manager of the Keweenaw Bay *Gazette*?

Tony says you're always looking for new talent, which is how he discovered you're "Zachary Grand." I'd like to try my own hand at something like that. Being over on the production side of the *Gazette* is okay, but I sometimes get an itch to try writing the stuff instead of printing it. Thought maybe the sad end of poor old Dunning might furnish the ingredients for a story. Might even find a place in your *Grand Mystery* pulp. Just let me know, old roomie.

It's been fun reminiscing about the old days anyway, please write back when you get a chance.

Meow, Cats, Meow!
Robert "Bobcat" O'Brien

• • •

Keweenaw Bay Gazette

Keweenaw Bay, Michigan
July 15, 1940

Mr. Zachary Grand
Editor-in-Chief
Grand Publications
143 West 43rd Street
New York, 16, New York

Dear Zach,

It was great to hear from you after all these years. I know you must be dreadfully busy there at Grand Publications, running all those magazines, and I'm actually flattered that you remembered me as you did. I'm also flattered that you asked about my job here at the Keweenaw Bay *Gazette*. A small-town weekly is a far cry from your line of big magazines.

Actually, what I do here at the *Gazette* is not so different from the work I did on the *North Cheshire Literary Quarterly* when you were the editor-in-chief. My title here is "production manager," but in fact I'm pretty nearly the whole production department. The owner is a fellow named Jack Miller. Editor-in-chief is Tim Holcomb, although in fact he's also our chief reporter, feature writer, and advertising salesman. I'll send along a half dozen recent issues so you can see what we're all about.

What passes for hard news in Keweenaw Bay is the opening of hunting season in the fall and fishing season in the summer, weddings, funerals, and births, and graduation at the local high school. Come out here for a visit and you'll think you're in an Andy Hardy movie.

My job—well, I set type, pull and read proofs, lay out pages, and even run the press. We set type on a second-hand Mergenthaler Linotype that we got at a bankruptcy sale at the Kearsarge Recorder when they went belly-up. Of course at the *Quarterly* we hand-set type and ran vellum on a letter press. Out here we run newsprint on a small rotary, a Goss Sextuple that's older than Methuselah but still runs okay. Not nearly as pretty as the *Quarterly*, but a whole lot cheaper.

You know, I've been thinking about the old gang at North Cheshire since Tony LoPresto was here. You and Tony and I were quite the trio, weren't we, and I mean that in more ways than one. I've been thinking about some of the young ladies we chased, too. Remember Carolyn Deering, Annie Mayfield, Jennie Lipton? I'll admit, I used to dream about Annie. What a girl! What a figure! I wonder what ever became of Annie and the others.

And the professors, oh, weren't there some characters in the faculty? Shakey Simmons, Henry von Eisen, Percival Dunning. Poor guy. Remember how he used to whisper his lectures? Well, not exactly whisper, but you remember that soft, breathy voice he always used. Remember how he got it?

Oh, you wouldn't, of course. He didn't like to talk about it, never mentioned it in class, I only remember him talking about it one time. It was at one of his Friday night soirees. He used to invite a few students in to his apartment there in Wellington Hall on Friday nights. He'd lay out sandwiches and serve brandy and put on music, and we'd talk about everything from the benzene ring to Schopenhauer to the history of the Hittites. Of course there was a certain amount of pairing off, too. Normally coeds wouldn't have been in a men's dorm but Dunning used to invite them to his parties and nobody complained.

I'm sure he would have invited you, Izzy. He always spoke highly of you. But you were over in Great Cheshire at the synagogue on Friday nights. I had a lot of respect for you, Izzy. I think you were the only Jew at Central Cheshire, and you didn't bother to deny it, you took whatever you had to and you stood up for who you were.

That rat von Eisen, Henry von Eisen, I remember he used to rag you every chance he got. I don't know why he hated Jews but he certainly did, and he never missed an opportunity to slam you, pal. Percival Dunning would never have done that, it just happened that he held his gab-fests on Friday nights and you couldn't attend.

Anyway, one Friday Percival must have had a little too much brandy. I remember he had his radio on. He used to play records most of the time, he was a big fan of Ralph Vaughan Williams and Frederick Delius and Gustav Holst, but once in a while he'd turn on the radio instead. The news came on and there was something about the election in Germany, this thug who was running against old President von Hindenberg. Dunning got pretty upset about it.

When the news went off somebody asked him why he was so agitated. Dunning said that the Great War was starting up again, this bum Hitler was worse than the Kaiser and the slaughter was going to happen all over again.

Everybody else said, Look, Hitler lost the election, there's nothing to worry about, but Dunning just sat there looking unhappy and drinking brandy. Finally a coed, I think it was actually Carolyn Deering, put her hand on Dunning's hand and asked him why he cared so much about Europe, it was three thousand miles away anyhow.

Dunning was English. Of course you knew that, Izzy, you could tell from the way he talked, right? Everybody knew he was English.

What he told us was that he'd been a Tommy in the Royal Fusiliers in the Great War. He'd been in the Battle of the Marne. There were Spads and Fokkers flying over and cannons going off and both sides were using poison gas. I thought they had gas masks but I guess they didn't work very well, and poor Dunning wound up gassed.

He said he was nearly dead. His comrades to the left and the right in the trench were dead. He was lying in the bottom of the trench, water and mud nearly a foot deep. He had no food. He was so weak he couldn't move, just lay there with his rifle at his side pointing up in the air, the bayonet fixed.

The Germans tried a charge, and a German soldier must have lost his footing. He fell into the British trench, landed on Percival's bayonet. It went right through his gut. The German landed on Percival and Percival was too weak even to crawl out from under him. The German was as good as dead, he would have been better off dead but he was alive. He was screaming in pain. Then he just moaned and cried.

Percival said it took the German a day and a night to die. Finally a German graves registration unit came through and pulled the corpse off Dunning and took it away, and one of the Germans noticed that

Dunning was alive. They pulled him out of there and sent him to a field hospital and he spent the rest of the war in a prison camp.

That was why he always whispered, Izzy. It was his lungs. They were ruined by that poison gas. It was a miracle that he didn't die. Didn't die then, I mean.

Say, I'm sorry to ramble on like this, Izz. I know you're a busy man and you have plenty of work to do. And I have to get back to setting type myself. You didn't say anything about my writing for your magazines in your last letter. What do you think? Do write when you get a chance, Izz. We old Cheshire Cats have to stick together!

Meow, Cats, Meow!

Robert "Bobcat" O'Brien

• • •

Keweenaw Bay Gazette
Keweenaw Bay, Michigan
July 20, 1940

Mr. Zachary Grand
Editor-in-Chief
Grand Publications
143 West 43rd Street
New York, 16, New York

Dear Izzy,

I'm glad you got a kick out of those copies of the Keweenaw Bay *Gazette* I sent you. The owner, Jack Miller, wanted to know if we might get a subscription out of you. When I told him I doubted it he made me pay for the copies and postage. What a cheapskate! Well, I guess he's a businessman and he has to watch expenses.

I hope you didn't mind my mentioning your being a Jew and all, and your attending synagogue in Great Cheshire. I wonder what Percival Dunning would think of the war in Europe if he were alive. He predicted it back in '31, I think it was, when Hitler ran for President of Germany against old Paul von Hindenburg. Was it '31? No, '32, I think. Of course Hitler lost but that was only a temporary setback for him, wasn't it?

And I wonder what Henry von Eisen thinks. He used to talk about Hitler and his theories of Aryan purity. I wonder what he thinks nowadays. Remember how he used to hate That Man in the White House, said he was secretly Jewish, his real name wasn't Roosevelt at all, it was really Rosenfeld and he was part of the International Zionist Movement and that we needed a Hitler in America to stop Rosenfeld from selling out the country to the Jews? And where is that rat von Eisen now?

Hey, I don't need to tell you about this, do I? Sorry, Izz.

I had a nice letter from Tony LoPresto this week. He's back in Louisiana, of course. Who would have thought our fellow Cheshire Cat would turn out to be the Sherlock Holmes of the Bayou Country? Back in our undergrad days it seemed as if Tony's only interests were the time he spent on the bandstand and the football field.

Man, could he play that horn! He could have given lessons to Ziggy Elman or Harry James. And when he put down his trumpet and put on a North Cheshire uniform, those pads and that leather helmet, he was something else! You wouldn't think a barrel-shaped guy like Tony, North Cheshire's own Two-Ton Tony, could move the way he did. But ...

Remember the big game in '32 against Willow Lakes Institute? The way Tony snagged that pass from the Willow Lakes quarterback in our own end zone, and dodged his way the length of the field to win the county championship for us? Beautiful! And then he turned around and batted .380 for our baseball team in the spring of '33.

But now he's running Bayou Richelieu like J. Edgar Hoover. Who would have guessed?

I've been thinking about your magazines, Izzy. Somebody like Tony LoPresto could make a great character, don't you think? I don't mean to make a pest of myself and I always enjoy hearing from the old gang, but you haven't responded to my questions about writing for your pulps. I hope I'll hear from you soon.

Meow, Cats, Meow!

Robert "Bobcat" O'Brien

• • •

Keweenaw Bay Gazette

Keweenaw Bay, Michigan

August 2, 1940

Mr. Zachary Grand

Editor-in-Chief

Grand Publications

143 West 43rd Street

New York, 16, New York

Dear Izz,

You are a prince of a fellow, Izzy! Not a word from you in a week and a half, and suddenly there's a package on my desk at the *Gazette*, all the way from New York City. Once Tim Holcomb, the editor-in-chief, saw the return address he couldn't wait for me to open it, and when he saw what was inside he didn't know what to make of it. I think he suspects you're trying to lure me away from the bright lights and fast action of Keweenaw Bay and get me to come to the big town to work for Grand Publications.

And I just might do it, too, if I got the right offer. (That isn't a hint, old roomie, I'm just pulling your leg.)

Still, copies of *Grand Adventures, Grand Western, Grand Mystery, and Grand Ghost Stories* all in one heavy bundle made quite a stir around the Gazette office.

I took *Grand Adventures* over to Helen's Café and spent my lunch hour poring over it. It's quite a magazine. I know you've got your competition, but they'll have to go a long ways to top *Grand Adventures*. That was some picture on the cover. That guy Saunders can sure paint up a storm! That native gal was really something. I hope you don't get into trouble with the censors over it.

And the story was every bit as good as the picture. Splash Shanahan is some hero! I thought the nasty Sea Lynx was going to put a knife between his ribs at any time. Good writing, good story-telling. I'll bet you never dreamed you'd be publishing yarns like this one when we were working together on the *North Cheshire Literary Quarterly.*

Some of the other stories were just as good, and of course there are all the other magazines you sent me. *Grand Ghost Stories* is next up on my nightstand. I don't mind a good scare every now and then. You are one heck of a pal, Izzy!

You know, thinking about the old days, recalling the times we all had together puts me in a funny mood. Remember the night you rolled that old Cole roadster on your way back to North Cheshire from Great Cheshire? You showed up at our digs in Warren Hall with your clothes ripped up and blood all over, but you were mainly worried about your car.

What a night that was! I didn't think you ought to make your weekly pilgrimage to your synagogue, but I'm not a very religious person and I can only stand back and respect people who are, like yourself. Still, pitch black out, temperature down around zero, sleet in the air, ice on the roads, and what had to be an out-of-season nor'easter blowing. You were lucky to get home alive, Izzy.

Tony and I got a few of the gang to hike out to the Cheshire Pike in the middle of the night. At least the storm clouds had blown over and the moon was as big as a wagon wheel. Still, there were ice crystals in the air and the roadway as slick as a mirror. Took every muscle in the gang to set that old Cole back on its wheels, but once we did the flivver started up and ran. And you were lucky at that not to crash into the landfill out there, roomie. If you had you'd never have made it back to campus and nobody would ever have found you, most likely. But after all of that, your Cole got you back to the dorm. What a car! They don't make 'em like they used to, I'll tell you that, Izzy.

That was the same night that poor old Percival Dunning disappeared, and Henry von Eisen had apparently had all he could take of small town, small college, campus life and lit out for parts unknown, deserting his classes in mid-semester. What a guy! If I hadn't disliked him before that, I surely would have then.

Meow, Cats, Meow!
Robert "Bobcat" O'Brien

• • •

Keweenaw Bay Gazette
Keweenaw Bay, Michigan
August 12, 1940

Mr. Zachary Grand
Editor-in-Chief

Grand Publications
143 West 43rd Street
New York, 16, New York

Dear Izz,

Don't know if I ever mentioned Charlie Potts to you. Nice kid, finished high school last June, always wanted to be a big-time news hound. Used to cover Keweenaw Bay High news for the *Gazette*. Sports mainly, but class elections, dances, amateur plays, whatever would fill space around the ads. Anyway, Tim Holcomb, our editor-in-chief, took him on as an office boy and cub reporter and he's working out fine.

Brought a little radio to work and set it up on the desk we let him use, and he turned on a Detroit Tigers ball game. They were playing the Philadelphia Athletics. Made me think of our old pal Tony and the North Cheshire baseball team, and all the trouble there was over Coach von Eisen.

Young Potts is not just a baseball fan, he's a real scholar, studies up the old records, can give you every player's batting average since the game got started. The Tigers had a new pitcher this season, young right-hander named Dickie Conger, and Potts up and says the kid reminded him of Heinie von Eisen.

That made me perk up my ears. "Heinie Who?" I said.

"Von Eisen. Pennsylvania farm kid named Heinrich von Eisen. Lefty. He was supposed to have the wickedest curve anybody ever saw. Was a star in the bush leagues. Came up to the Tigers in twenty-six. No, twenty-five."

As if anybody in the Gazette office was going to catch him on that!

Well, Charlie Potts told the story to anybody who would listen, which meant Jack Miller, Tim Holcomb, and yours truly, Izzy. Seems like this von Eisen kid was a drinker and a brawler and something of a womanizer. Made it all the way up through the minors, got his first start with the Tigers and beat the St. Louis Browns one to nothing. Threw a three-hitter. Phenomenal.

Went out to a bar that night and a young lady he spotted there caught his eye and he tried to pick her up. Seems she already had an escort who took exception to Heinie's remarks. They got into a brawl and somebody pulled a knife. There are different versions of the story. One of 'em, Potts said, is that this all happened in darktown. Anyhow, the knife man swings, Eisen puts up his hand to defend himself and the knife slices right across the palm of his hand. He wound up in the hospital and got his hand stitched back together, but he could never throw that curve again. Never made it back into the lineup. Before long he was out of baseball and he completely disappeared.

Izzy, do you think Heinie von Eisen is our Henry von Eisen? You think he was baseball coach when you and Tony and I were at North Cheshire Central College? It makes sense, doesn't it? He seemed to know so much about baseball, at least Tony said, and yet all the players hated him because they felt as if he hated them.

What do you think, Izzy?

Say, I don't mean to bother you with this rambling. I'd better close this letter and get some shut-eye, tomorrow it's back to the old salt mine for yours truly.

Oh, before I close, I do want to thank you again for the magazines. I'm lying here on my bed, my feet propped up, watching the moths bang against the glass and wondering if it's ever going to cool down again. I'll tell you something about this part of Michigan, it so cold in winter you'd think those New England freezes we used to have were days on the beach in Havana. But then it gets so hot in

July and August, you can't believe that you were ever cold. I swear, even the moths must be sweating on a night like this!

Going through the other magazines you sent, I find that a lot of stories seem to have continuing characters. I guess there's nothing new about that, Izzy, all the way back to the Three Musketeers and that Poe detective, what was his name, and then of course Sherlock Holmes. For that matter, didn't Mark Twain bring Tom Sawyer and Huck Finn back for a couple of encores?

You've got some good ones. I like that Crimson Wizard fellow that Arl Felton writes about, and the Golden Saint. And of course you've got those cowboys and detectives and that spook-busting crew in *Grand Ghost Stories.* Tell you what, I've scratched a few notes and if you don't mind I'll type 'em up on the old Blick Ninety down at the *Gazette* office and mail 'em off to you soon as I get a chance. I hope you'll find some ideas you like there. Let me know, hey, old roomie?

Meow, Cats, Meow!
Robert "Bobcat" O'Brien

• • •

Keweenaw Bay Gazette
Keweenaw Bay, Michigan
August 19, 1940

Mr. Zachary Grand
Editor-in-Chief
Grand Publications
143 West 43rd Street
New York, 16, New York

Dear Izzy,

That sure is exciting news, that you're starting up a comic book line there at Grand Publications. Of course I won't breathe a word about it, not that there's much of anybody to breathe it to here in Keweenaw Bay. But sometimes we stop in at the Tip Top Tavern for a couple of wee ones after we close up shop for the day and people do talk. "We" being Jack and Tim and myself. Charlie Potts keeps trying to invite himself along but Marty O'Hara runs a tight ship down at the Tip Top and he says he can't have any minors in there or he'd risk losing his liquor license.

Funny, Percival Dunning didn't worry about people being over twenty-one to join his Friday night soirees and nobody ever said a word. But then I think the whole campus, from Prexy on down, felt sorry for old Percival and wouldn't say boo at anything he did, so long as he was quiet about it.

Everybody except Henry von Eisen, that is. I'm not just saying this because I know there was bad blood between von Eisen and you, Izzy. The man was a brass-plated son of a sea cook, if you know what I mean. I think Charlie Potts had the key to von Eisen. If he really was the same Heinie von Eisen who pitched that game against St. Louis and then got his hand sliced open and lost his curveball, that would explain a lot about him and why he was always so sour and so ready to jump down anybody's throat.

I think he especially hated Percival Dunning because Dunning was English and had been in the King's Fusiliers during the Great War. Von Eisen was a few years younger than Dunning and he couldn't have been in the war himself, and besides, we were on the same side as the English, weren't we? But von Eisen was Pennsylvania Dutch, not really Dutch, you know, *Deutsch*, German, and there was a lot of pro-Kaiser sentiment out there in western Pennsylvania during the war.

Oh, you know this as well as I do. We used to sit in the same row in Professor Trowbridge's modern history class, just Carolyn Deering between us to help us not concentrate on Professor Trowbridge's lectures. Wasn't that girl something, with those sweaters of hers and those plaid skirts she used to wear! You'd think she'd freeze herself half to death in those Cheshire County winters, but I don't think she ever did.

Anyway, I never heard von Eisen say a kind word about Percival Dunning. Used to mock the way he walked, hunched over as if his chest was killing him, and talked, in that soft, almost whisper of his. Well, his chest was killing him. He never got over that gas attack in France. And as for the whisper, I just don't think he had the breath to do any more than that. But von Eisen loved to parade back and forth in his classroom, all hunched over like Dunning, and whispering so you couldn't make out what he was saying.

One sweet guy despite all his suffering, one brass-plated s.o.b. who brought his trouble on himself. I guess it takes all kinds.

Enough for now, Izzy. I hope you're well and happy. Take a look at those little ideas that I sent you last week and let me know if you think I could write for one of your magazines. It's getting a little bit dull here on the production side.

Meow, Cats, Meow!
Robert "Bobcat" O'Brien

• • •

Keweenaw Bay Gazette
Keweenaw Bay, Michigan
August 28, 1940

Mr. Zachary Grand
Editor-in-Chief
Grand Publications
143 West 43rd Street
New York, 16, New York

Dear Izzy,

Well of course I know about comic books. Jumping Jehosophat, old roomie, Keweenaw Bay isn't exactly New York or Boston but it's still on this planet. We even heard about that invasion from Mars a couple of years back, we have radios out here and running water and everything.

Hey, just pulling your leg, old friend. But you really don't need to explain comic books to me. The kids in this town are as addicted to the things as they are anywhere. The schoolteachers are outraged, the town librarian has banned 'em from her sacred precincts, but Bud Campbell, owner, manager, stock boy, cashier, and chief cook and bottle washer over at Pine Street News and Magazines, loves 'em. Says they've cut into his pulp magazine sales a little but more than made up for it by bringing every six- through twelve-year-old in town through his door day after day. Once school starts again in a few weeks that may cut down a little, but right now Bud is as happy as a clam.

Favorite scene these days: two kids standing outside Pine Street News and Magazines arguing to beat the band. Resolved: Superman could beat up Captain Marvel in a fair fight. Sometimes the kids get so carried away they decide to knuckle it out themselves. One of those muscle men wears red tights and the other one wears blue tights and I can never remember which is which, but I don't suppose

276 By Hook or By Crook

it matters, I'm a few years too old to get involved. But I've even seen young Charlie Potts sneaking a read along with a sandwich when it's his lunch time down at the *Gazette*. Says his favorite is a fellow who can set fire to himself, fly around, throw fireballs at his enemies, and then come home without so much as a blister on his nose. Okay with me.

Seems to me, Izzy, these comic book heroes aren't anything different from the good old pulp heroes we used to read about back in Warren Hall when we didn't have our noses buried in chemistry or calculus texts or Shakespeare. The rough preliminary for *Captain Grand Comics* looks good, I didn't mean to take any shots at it.

Let's see if I have this one right.

Gary Grant is exploring in Antarctica when he discovers a lost race of wizards from Atlantis. They decide to initiate him into their sacred rites, which include walking through the hot lava of an active volcano right there at the South Pole. They've given him a magical cloak that will protect him as long as he exercises total will power and concentration; otherwise, he's a toasted marshmallow.

After a couple of years of study and discipline, the chief wizard decides that Gary's ready to give it a try. So off he goes, he passes the test, and he emerges as Captain Grand, Master of Mysticism.

Okay, pal. I guess the kids will go for it. Not so different from some of the pulp stories we used to read. Or the ones you publish, if you don't mind my saying so. Tell you what. I know you want to keep *Captain Grand Comics* under the rose for now, but when you're ready I'll bounce this thing off Charlie Potts or maybe some of the town kids if I can pry 'em away from Superman and Captain Marvel for a few minutes. I'll let you know what they have to say.

We could have used somebody like Captain Grand, Master of Mysticism, back at Central Cheshire, couldn't we? Somebody like

Captain Grand could have saved poor old Percival Dunning's life. I'll never forget the way his disappearance hit the campus. Nobody knew where he'd gone or what had happened to him. Personally, I thought he'd gone back to England or at least up to Canada to try and enlist in the Army. Nobody on campus took this fellow Hitler seriously except for Dunning. You have to give him credit for that. Soon as Hitler announced he was going to run for President of Germany, Dunning predicted what was going to happen. And look at Europe now!

Then when his car turned up in Big Star Pond—Izzy, I still can't get over it. It must have been there since November of '32. Dunning must have driven that funny Pullman coupé of his onto the ice and it cracked under the car and the car sank with Dunning in it. Imagine being trapped in that little car, icy water coming in, and you can't get out.

And then we had our ice skating parties that winter, the annual Founder's Day Bonfire and all, and all that time poor old Percival Dunning's body lying there in his car on the bottom of the pond until the spring thaw. There were the Three Graces, Carolyn Deering, Annie Mayfield, and Jennie Lipton, out for a picnic by the pond and they spotted something in the water that scared the bejesus out of them.

Yep, it poor old Dunning, still trapped in that little car of his.

Did I say that Dunning was the only one who knew what Hitler was up to in the old days? I shouldn't have left out Henry von Eisen. You'd think von Eisen had a direct line to Berlin, the way he spouted the Hitler line every chance he got. Heck, Izzy, it was really annoying. I know nobody stood up to von Eisen. That was cowardly of us, and I apologize.

Tony LoPresto and Jack Remington and Roland Stephenson and some of the gang used to sit around in one of the Double You

Dorms—Warren or Winston or Watson or Wellington—and talk about it. We could all see what von Eisen was doing to you, Izz, but everybody was afraid of the son of a sea cook. We should have got together and made a petition to Prexy about it. We really should have.

But that's all past now. Percival Dunning is in his grave and Henry von Eisen is—wherever he is. You have to wonder, don't you, what ever became of von Eisen.

You know what I regret more than anything else that ever happened at Cheshire Central? It was dedicating our yearbook, the *Cheshire Cheese,* to von Eisen our senior year. How the heck did that ever happen, Izzy?

No, you don't have to tell me. That was just a rhetorical question. Von Eisen took over the job of faculty advisor for the yearbook when old what-was-his-name retired. Dr. Standish. That was the old gent's name, David Donald Standish, Ph.D. Must have been the head of the English Department from the day the college opened its doors. I've never seen anybody so old.

Dr. Standish must have been faculty advisor for the *Cheshire Cheese* as well as the *North Cheshire Literary Quarterly* since McKinley was shot. When he finally packed his bags and retired to sunny Florida, Hermione Zeller took on the job at the quarterly and von Eisen took it at the yearbook. Nobody was surprised that Miss Zeller got involved with the quarterly. She was already college librarian, she fit right in, and remember the fun we used to have with her? But nobody expected von Eisen to take on the yearbook.

Nobody except his personal toady, Gene Stullmeier.

I'm sorry, Izzy. I'm raking up too many old embers. And I'm going on too long anyway. You still haven't commented on the ideas I sent you. I could write those stories for *Grand Adventures* or some of the other pulps, or I suppose I could turn 'em into stories for some of your new comic books.

Let me know when it's okay to show the dummy *Captain Grand Comics* to Charlie Potts and the local urchin brigade and I'll send you back some comments. And let me know when you want me to start writing for you. I'm starting to get the itch.

Meow, Cats, Meow!
Robert "Bobcat" O'Brien

• • •

Keweenaw Bay Gazette
Keweenaw Bay, Michigan
August 31, 1940

Mr. Zachary Grand
Editor-in-Chief
Grand Publications
143 West 43rd Street
New York, 16, New York

Dear Izzy,

I couldn't believe my eyes when I got your wedding announcement. You and Carolyn Deering. I still don't believe it! Well, congratulations, roomie. Carolyn was one of the prettiest gals on campus, but of course you know that. And smart, and sweet. I envy you, Izzy. How the heck did you ever catch her? You must have been studying hypnosis.

Just kidding, Izz. Thinking about you and Carolyn makes me think about the six of us—you and Tony and me in the Three Cheshire Cats and Carolyn Deering and Annie Mayfield and Jennie Lipton, the Three Graces. Didn't we have great times together! And now Isaac Goldberg and Carolyn Deering are Mister and Missus Zachary Grand.

You know that Tony LoPresto and Jennie Lipton are married, don't you? Living there in Bayou Richelieu and raising a house full of bambinos, that's what Tony tells me. I never pictured Tony as a lawman or Jennie as a *mater familias* but that just goes to show you, doesn't it?

Where did Annie Mayfield go after graduation? Maybe I ought to look her up, see if the old spark is still smoldering. I'll tell you, Izz, there isn't much social life in a town like Keweenaw Bay. Not that I'm knocking this burg. I'm pretty comfortable here, I've got a decent job and I make a living. But I think I could use a dose of the bright lights every now and then.

Since you said it was all right to show the dummy *Captain Grand Comics* to Charlie Potts and some of the local kids, I've got some reactions to share with you. Everybody likes Captain Grand, but they think he needs a good enemy. A guy who can do all the things Captain Grand can do is wasted on kidnappers and bank robbers. One of the local kids suggested a mad scientist for an enemy. Another kid says he'd like to see a beautiful, evil woman in the strip. Charlie Potts says he's starting to outgrow some of these wild stories. He's getting very literary, thinks you should read Steinbeck or Hemingway for inspiration.

Ho, ho, ho.

I was thinking of another character myself. So many of these heroes are musclemen, what about somebody who uses his brains to fight crime? I was thinking of a strip called "The Scholar." Something like Sherlock Holmes. He tackles crimes that the police can't solve because they're just not smart enough.

What would you think of that, Izzy? Do let me know.

I've got to turn in now, roomie. Tomorrow's a school day down at the *Gazette* and I can't stay up all night the way I used to back at

North Cheshire Central, not if I'm going to be all full of pep and energy in the morning.

Oh, one more thing. Tony LoPresto says that he and Jennie are planning a trip back to Massachusetts for the big homecoming game next month. Going to bring all their youngsters with them, too. The old campus is in for a real treat! I wish I could make it but every time I look my budget in the eye and ask, How about it? the old budget looks right back at me and says, Not this year, old fellow!

So maybe next year, Izzy. I assume that you and Carolyn will attend, it can't be much of a trip from New York City. Say hello to Tony and Jennie for me, and congratulations again to yourself and Carolyn. You lucky dog—or should I say, Cheshire Cat!

Meow, Cats, Meow!
Robert "Bobcat" O'Brien

• • •

Keweenaw Bay Gazette
Keweenaw Bay, Michigan
September 20, 1940

Mr. Zachary Grand
Editor-in-Chief
Grand Publications
143 West 43rd Street
New York, 16, New York

Dear Izzy,

This is a letter I never expected to write, old roomie. You know, Keweenaw Bay may be isolated and all, but we do have radios and we get out of town newspapers even if we have to wait a few days to see what's happening in the rest of the world. But Tony LoPresto telephoned and gave me the lowdown on what happened during homecoming weekend, and then there were reports in the Boston and New York dailies.

Now we know what happened to Henry von Eisen.

Who would ever have expected an Atlantic hurricane to make it all the way to Massachusetts, and then to sweep inland as far as Cheshire County, setting off that waterspout from Big Star Pond and then turning into a tornado and ripping up the old landfill near the old Cheshire Pike? Mainly, everybody was upset that the big homecoming parade was cancelled, the football game against Billerica Tech was called off, and the gymnasium was flooded so the homecoming dance never happened.

At least, that's what Tony LoPresto said when he phoned me. I don't know if he paid for the call himself or found some way to get the city fathers in Bayou Richelieu to foot the bill, but one way or another all that gab must have cost plenty.

The kids at North Cheshire were disappointed by the mess the storm made of homecoming weekend, but Tony was more interested in what the storm pulled out of the old landfill. Tony told me that the human remains that turned up were identified as belonging to some old tramp who'd fallen into the landfill years before and died there. The local authorities gave Tony the run of the place. Professional courtesy, they call it.

But Tony knew better. He didn't say so, but he knew better.

We both knew who that corpse was, or what was left of it after almost eight years lying there in the landfill. There are raccoons and lynxes and even a few wolves in those woods. There wasn't much left of that fellow. But Tony told me there was one odd thing about the body. You know how freakish Old Ma Nature can be, and somehow, for all the scavengers who'd worked over that body and then the effects of lying in the earth all these years, the flesh was almost perfectly preserved on the left hand.

Isn't that odd, Izzy?

Tony told me that the left hand of the body showed a big scar running straight across the palm. As if the owner of that hand had got into a fight and his opponent came at him with a really nasty knife, and that fellow put up his hand to try and stop the knife and wound up with a terrible gash running right across the palm of his hand.

Looked as if the cut had healed up all right, Tony said, but the scar was something to behold. And Tony figured that whoever owned that hand would never be able to do very much with it ever again, even after the wound had healed.

Oh, it was Henry von Eisen all right. Tony has some wild theory about von Eisen getting into a scrape with poor old Percival Dunning that icy night back in the winter of '32–'33, and maybe beating old Percival into a helpless state and then putting him in his old Pullman coupé and sending it out onto the ice of Big Star Pond.

And then, Tony figures, somebody else comes along, somebody von Eisen doesn't like to start with, and now this other person has seen von Eisen practically murder poor old Percival Dunning. So von Eisen goes after this other person, too. You'd think von Eisen would win a fight, but who knows, under those conditions, anything could happen. Anything. Right, Izz?

Even though I'm not a religious person, I know a few Bible stories. I know about David and Goliath. Do you think Henry von Eisen might have been a kind of Goliath? And who would be David?

Who, Izzy?

Well, I guess I missed all the excitement of homecoming weekend, the hurricane, the waterspout, the tornado, the body in the landfill. Things are quiet here in Keweenaw Bay. Must be more exciting back East where you are, Izzy.

Congratulations again on your marriage. Give Carolyn my best wishes. You are one lucky son of a gun!

Meow, Cats, Meow!
Robert "Bobcat" O'Brien

• • •

RICHARD A. LUPOFF'S novels and short stories cover a spectrum from mysteries to mainstream, fantasy and horror to science fiction. Even his mysteries range from fair-play puzzle stories to hardboiled. He is best known for his tales of insurance investigator Hobart Lindsey and homicide detective Marvia Plum of the Berkeley Police Department. His most recent books are *Quintet: The Cases of Chase and Delacroix* (Crippen & Landru); *Killer's Dozen* (Wildside Press), a collection of criminous tales; and *The Emerald Cat Killer* (St. Martin's Press), the eighth novel in the Lindsey and Plum series. His nonfiction books include *The Great American Paperback* (Collectors Press), *Writer at Large* (Gryphon Books), and *Master of Adventure: The Worlds of Edgar Rice Burroughs* (University of Nebraska). He has taught at the University of California, Stanford University, the College of Marin, and other institutions.

THE TELL-TALE PURR

By Mary Higgins Clark

There comes a time when in the name of common decency grandmothers ought to die. I confess that in the early stages of my life I had a half-hearted affection for my grandmother but that time is long since past. She is now well up in her eighties and still exceedingly vain even though at night her teeth repose in a water glass by her bed. She has a constant struggle every morning to get her contact lenses popped into her myopic eyes and requires a cane to support her arthritic knees. The cane is a custom-made object affair designed to resemble the walking stick Fred Astaire used in some of his dances. Grandma's story is that she danced with him when she was young and the cane/walking stick is her good-luck charm.

Her mind is still very keen and seems to become keener even as her eccentricities grow. She, who always proudly considered herself frugal, is spending money like water. Thanks to several investments her husband, my grandfather, made, she is downright wealthy and it has been with great pleasure that I have observed her simple lifestyle. But now it is different. For example she just put in an elevator which cost forty thousand dollars in her modest home. She is sure she will live to be one hundred but is contemplating building a state-of-the-art gym in the backyard because in the *Harvard Medical Report,* she read that exercise is good for arthritis.

I submit to you that a better cure for her arthritis is to put an end to it forever. This I propose to do.

You must realize that I am her sole grandson and heir. Her only child, my mother, departed this earth shortly after I was graduated from college. In the twenty-six years since then I have married and divorced twice and been involved in many ill-fated ventures. It is time for me to stop wasting my time on useless enterprises and enjoy a life of comfort. I must help to make that possible.

Obviously her demise would need to seem natural. At her advanced age, it would not be unlikely to have her pass away in her sleep but if someone holding a pillow were to help that situation occur there is always the danger of a bruise that might make the police suspicious. Suspicious police look for motive and I would be a living, breathing motive. I am uncomfortable about the fact that when under the influence of wine I was heard to say that the only present I wanted from my grandmother for my next birthday was a ticket to her funeral.

How then was I to help my grandmother sail across the River Styx without arousing suspicion?

I was quite simply at a loss. I could push her down the stairs and claim she fell but if she survived the fall, she would know that I caused it.

I could try to disable her car but that ancient old Bentley, which she drives with the skill of Mario Andretti, would probably survive a crash.

Poison is easily detectable.

My problem was solved in a most unexpected way.

I had been invited to have dinner at the home of a successful friend, Clifford Winkle. I value Clifford's superb wines and gourmet table far more than I value Clifford. Also I find his wife, Belinda, insipid. But I was in the mood for a splendid dinner in comfortable circumstances and looked forward to the evening with pleasure.

I was seated with Clifford and his wife, enjoying a generous scotch on the rocks which I knew had been poured from a two-hundred dollar bottle of single malt reserve, when their little treasure, ten-year-old Perry, burst into the room.

"I've decided, I've decided," he shouted, spittle spraying from the space between his upper front teeth.

The parents smiled indulgently. "Perry has been reading the complete works of Edgar Allen Poe this week," Clifford told me.

The last time I was a guest I endured Perry's endless description of a book he had read about fly fishing, how by reading it, he could really, really understand all about baiting and casting and catching and why fly fish were really, really special. I wanted desperately to interrupt him and tell him I had already seen *A River Runs Through It*, Robert Redford's splendid film on the subject, but of course I did not.

Now Perry's all-consuming passion was obviously Edgar Allan Poe. "'The Tell-Tale Heart' is my favorite," he crowed, his short red hair spiking up on the crown of his skull, "but I could write a better ending, I know I could."

Barefoot Boy with Cheek out-Poes Poe, I thought. However I wanted to show some small degree of interest. I was down to my last sip of the two hundred dollar scotch and hoped that by directing attention to myself, Clifford might notice my empty glass and not neglect his duty as my host. "In high school I wrote a new ending to 'The Cask of Amontillado,'" I volunteered. "I got an A in my English class for it. I remember how it began." I cleared my throat. "'Yes. I killed him. I killed him a long fifty years ago ...'"

Perry ignored me. "You see, in 'The Tell-Tale Heart' the guy kills the old man because he can't stand looking at his eye. Then he buries the old man's heart but when the cops come he thinks he hears the heart beating and goes nuts and confesses. Right?"

"Right!" Clifford affirmed enthusiastically.

"Exactly. Um-hum," Belinda agreed, beaming at her quiz kid.

"In my book, the guy is going to kill the old man, but another guy watches him and helps him cut up the body and bury the heart under the floor. When the cops come in, the murderer laughs and jokes with them and think he's getting away with it. Then when the cops go, the friend comes back and as a joke says he can hear the old man's heart beating. Isn't that good?"

Fascinating, I thought. If only Poe had lived to meet Perry.

"But then the murderer, 'cause he doesn't know it's a joke, believes he really is hearing the heart and you know what?"

"What?" Clifford asked.

"I can't guess," Belinda gushed, her eyes wide, her hands clutching the arms of her chair.

"The murderer dies of fright because of the heart he thinks he's hearing."

Perry beamed at his own brilliance. Send for the Nobel Prize, I thought, not realizing there was more to come.

"And the twist is that his friend was going to split the money the old man had hidden somewhere in London and now he realizes he'll never know where to find it so he's punished for the crime too." Perry grinned triumphantly, an ear-splitting grin that made all the freckles on his cheeks bond together in a henna-tinted mass.

It was I who led the applause and my reaction was genuine. *The sound had scared the murderer to death.* My grandmother's fear of cats rushed into my mind. She shakes and trembles to the point of almost fainting at the sight or sound of one. It goes back, I am told, over eighty years when a rabid cat attacked her in the garden. She still bears a scar on her left cheek from that long-ago encounter.

My grandmother has a new elevator.

Suppose … just suppose, Grandma got stuck in her new elevator in the dark during a power failure. *And then she hears the sounds of cats yowling and hissing and howling and purring. She hears them scratching at the door of the elevator. She is sure they will break through. She cowers, shrieking against the back of the elevator, then crumbles onto the floor of the elevator, the memory of that long-ago attack overwhelming her. No, it is not a memory. It is happening. She is sure that the cat is poised to attack her again, not just one cat but all the cats in this hydrophobic pack, foaming at the mouth, teeth bared.*

There is only one way to escape the panic. She is frightened into heart failure and her death would be blamed on her being trapped, alone, at night in the new elevator.

I was so excited and thrilled at this solution to my problem that I hardly tasted the excellent dinner and was uncommonly responsive to Perry who, of course, dined with us and never shut up.

I planned my grandmother's death carefully. Nothing must arouse even the slightest suspicion. Fortunately in her area of northern Connecticut during a wind storm there are frequent power failures. She has talked of installing a home generator but so far that has not happened. Still, I knew I had to move swiftly.

Night after night for the next few weeks, I roamed through the nearby towns, slithering through dark alleys and around abandoned buildings, any place where wild cats gathered. I tossed pieces of meat and cheese to get them fighting with each other, their teeth bared, their ungodly yowls rumbling from their throats. One night I was attacked by a cat that sprung on me, frantic for the food in my hand, her front claw ripping my right cheek in the same spot my grandmother was scarred.

Undeterred I kept on my mission, even recording cats in animal shelters where I caught the plaintive meows of discarded felines bewildered at their fate. At the home of a neighbor I secretly caught on tape the contented purring of her treasured pet.

A cacophony of sound, a work of genius. That was the result of my labors.

As I was engaged in my nocturnal wanderings, by day I was also dancing attendance on my grandmother, visiting her at least three times a week, enduring at mealtime the vegetarian regime that was her latest quirk in her battle to stay alive til her hundredth birthday. Seen with such frequency, the annoying habits she was developing became increasingly hard to take. She began to avoid my eyes when I spoke to her, as though she was aware everything I said was a lie. She also took on a nervous mannerism of pursing then releasing her lips, which gave the impression she was always sucking on a straw.

Grandma lived alone. Her housekeeper, Ica, a kind Jamaican woman, arrived at 9:00 AM, prepared Grandma's breakfast and lunch, tidied the house, then went home and returned to prepare and serve dinner. Ica was very protective of Grandma. She had already confided to me her distress that Grandma might somehow get trapped in the elevator when she was alone. "You know how when it gets very windy, she gets power failures that can last for hours," Ica worried.

I assured Ica that I, too, was troubled by that possibility. Then, impatiently I waited for the weather to cooperate and a good wind storm to come along. It finally happened. The weather report was for heavy winds during the night. That evening I had dinner with Grandma, a particularly difficult dinner, what with the vegetarian menu, Grandma's averted eyes, her twitching mouth, and then the dismaying news that she was meeting an architect concerning her idea for building a personal gym. It was clearly time to act.

After dinner, I kissed Grandma goodnight, went into the kitchen where Ica was tidying up, and drove away. At that time, I lived only three blocks from Grandma. I parked my car and waved to my next-door neighbor who was just arriving home. I felt it was fortuitous that, if necessary, he could testify that he had seen me enter my own modest rental cottage. I waited an hour and then slipped out my back door. It was already dark and chillingly cold, and it was easy to hurry undetected back to Grandma's house. I arrived through the wooded area checking to be sure that Ica's car was surely gone. It was and I slipped across the lawn to the window of the den. As I expected I could see Grandma, hunched up on her recliner, an old fur lap robe wrapped around her, watching her favorite television show.

For the next ten minutes she stayed there, then, as I had expected, promptly at nine o'clock, the fur robe dragging behind her, she turned off the television and made her way to the front of the house. In a flash, key in hand, I was at the basement door and inside. As soon as I heard the rumble of the elevator, I threw the switch, plunging the house into silence and darkness.

My feet, noiseless in my sneakers, my flashlight a thin beam, I crept upstairs. From the sound of my grandmother's cries for help I could detect that the elevator was only a few feet off the floor.

Now for the tricky part. I placed my tape recorder on the vestibule table behind a book I had left for Grandma. I reasoned that Ica, if indeed she noticed it, would think nothing of it being there. I had developed the habit of bringing books and little gifts for Grandma.

And then I turned on the tape. The sound that thundered from it was a litany from cat hell, meowing, clawing, scratching, and howling, their shrieks interwoven against the suddenly incongruous rattle of purring contentment.

There was absolute silence from the elevator.

Had the recording done its job already? I wondered. It was possible but I wouldn't know for sure until the morning. The tape was twenty minutes long and would play repeatedly until midnight. I was sure that would be sufficient.

I let myself out of the house and walked home at a quick pace, bracing against the sharp wind that was now making tree branches bend and dance. Chilled to the bone, I went directly to bed. I confess I could not fall asleep. My mental image of my grandmother's stiffening body inside her elevator kept me from restful slumber. But then as I allowed myself to imagine finally getting my hands on all her money, my frame of mind improved and from dawn til eight o'clock I enjoyed a refreshing slumber.

But then as I began to prepare breakfast, several possibilities occurred to me. Suppose Grandma's face is frozen into a frightened mask? Would that make anyone suspicious? Worse yet, suppose for some reason the recording had not automatically turned off!

My original plan had been to await Ica's phone call, the one that would convey the sad news that Grandma had been trapped in the elevator and must have had a heart attack. At the frightening possibility that the recording just might be still playing, I leaped up from the breakfast table, threw on some clothes and rushed over, arriving as Ica was opening the front door. To my vast relief there was no sound from the recorder.

The morning was overcast, which meant that the vestibule was dark. As Ica greeted me she tried to turn on the light. Then she frowned. "My God, there must have been another power failure." She turned and made a beeline for the stairs to Grandma's bedroom. I, on the other hand, raced down to the basement and threw the master switch on the panel. The whirr of the elevator rewarded me. I rushed up the stairs and was there when Ica yanked open the elevator door.

Grandma was on the floor wrapped in her mink lap robe. She opened her eyes and blinked up at us. With the fur wrapped around her head, the strands of fur resting on her cheek, for all the world she had the face of a cat. Her mouth pursed in and out as though she was sipping milk.

"Grandma ..." My voice failed. With Ica's help, she was struggling to her feet, her hands on the floor, her back arched to help regain her balance.

"Eerr ... Eerr ...," she sighed. *Or was she saying "purrrr ... purrrr?"*

"Eerr, that's the best sleep I've had in years," Grandma said contentedly.

"Weren't you frightened trapped in there?" Ica asked incredulously.

"Oh, no, I was tired and I just made the best of it. I tried calling but there was no one to hear me. I decided not to waste my voice."

The record had been playing. I had heard it myself.

Grandma was eyeing me. "You look terrible," she said, "I don't want you worrying about me. Don't you know I'll live to be one hundred? That's my promise to you. So I was stuck in the elevator. The carpet is thick. I laid down and was nice and warm under the robe. In my dreams I was hearing this faint purring sound like water lapping against the shore."

Afraid I would give myself away, I stumbled downstairs and grabbed my recorder from the table, then realized that in my haste I had knocked a small object off the table. I bent down and picked it up. It was a hearing aid. I started to lay it down and saw there was another one on the table.

Ica was coming down the stairs. "How long has Grandma been wearing hearing aids?" I demanded.

"They're just what I'm coming for. She leaves them on that table every night. She's so vain that I guess she didn't tell you that her hearing has been going steadily down hill and she's practically deaf now. She's been studying lip reading and is quite good at it. Haven't you noticed the way she always looks at your lips when you're talking? She finally got the hearing aids but only uses them for television in the evening and always leaves them right here."

"She can't hear?" I asked, dumbfounded.

"Only a few sounds, deep ones, nothing shrill."

That happened five years ago. Of course I immediately destroyed the tape but in my sleep I hear it playing over and over. It doesn't frighten me. Instead it keeps me company. I don't know why. There's something else that's a little strange. I cannot look at my grandmother's face without seeing the face of a cat. That's because of those little whiskers on her cheeks and lips, the odd pursing movement of her mouth, the narrow intense eyes that are always focused on my lips. Also, her bedchamber of choice is now the elevator where, for naps and at night, she curls on the carpeted floor wrapped in her mink lap robe. Her breathing has even taken on a purring sound.

I can hardly keep my wits about me as I await my inheritance. I do not have the courage to try to precipitate its arrival again. I live with Grandma now and as time passes, I believe I am beginning to resemble her. The scar on her cheek is directly under her left eye; mine is in the same spot. I have a very light beard and shave infrequently. At times my beard looks just like her whiskers. We have those same narrow green eyes.

My grandmother loves very warm milk. But then, she pours it into a saucer to cool it before she laps it up. I tried it and now I like it that way too. It's purr-fect.

• • •

MARY HIGGINS CLARK'S books are world-wide bestsellers. In the U.S. alone, her books have sold over eighty million copies. She is the author of twenty-six suspense novels, three collections of short stories, a biographical novel about George Washington, and her memoir, *Kitchen Privileges*. She is the number one fiction bestselling author in France, where she received the Grand Prix de Literature Policière and The Literary Award at the 1998 Deauville Film Festival. In 2000, she was named by the French Minister of Culture "Chevalier of the Order of Arts and Letters." She was chosen by Mystery Writers of America as Grand Master of the 2000 Edgar Awards. An annual Mary Higgins Clark Award sponsored by Simon & Schuster, to be given to authors of suspense fiction writing in the Mary Higgins Clark tradition, was launched by Mystery Writers of America during Edgars week in April 2001. She was the 1987 president of Mystery Writers of America and, for many years, served on its board of directors. In May 1988, she was the Chairperson of the International Crime Congress. Her most recent novel is *The Shadow of Your Smile*.

THE BIG SWITCH
A MIKE HAMMER STORY
By Mickey Spillane and Max Allan Collins

They were going to kill Dopey Dilldocks at midnight the day
after tomorrow.

He had shot and wiped out a local narcotics pusher because the
guy had passed Dopey a packet of heroin that had been stepped on
so many times, it wouldn't take the pain out of a pinprick. The
pusher deserved it. Society said Dopey Dilldocks deserved it, too.
The jury agreed and the judge laid on the death sentence. All the
usual delays had been exhausted, and the law-and-order governor
sure as hell wouldn't reprieve a low-life druggie like Dopey, so the
little schmoe's time to fly out of this earthly coop was now.

Nobody was ever going to notice his passing. He was just another jailhouse number—five feet seven inches tall with seven digits
stamped on his shirt. On the records his name was Donald Dilbert,
but along the path laid out by snorting lines of the happy white stuff,
it had gotten shortened and twisted into Dopey Dilldocks.

A week ago his lawyer, a court-assigned one, had written me to
say that Mister Dilbert had requested that I be a witness to his execution. And it seemed Dopey also wondered if I might stop in, ASAP,
and have a final chat with him before the big switch got thrown.

In the inner office of my PI agency in downtown Manhattan, I handed the letter to Velda, my secretary and right-hand man, if a doll with all that raven hair and a mountain road's worth of curves, could be so described. I was sitting there playing with the envelope absently while she read its contents. When she was done, she frowned and passed the sheet back to me. "Donald Dilbert ... You mean that funny little guy who—"

"The same," I said. "The one they called Mr. Nobody, and worse."

She frowned in mild confusion. "Mike—he was only a messenger boy. He didn't even work for anybody important, did he?"

"Probably the biggest was Billy Whistler, that photographer over on Sixth Avenue. Hell, I got Dopey that job because the little guy didn't mind running errands at night."

"You know what he did over there?"

"Sure. Took proofs of the late-night photo shoots over to the magazine office."

Velda gave me an inquisitive glance.

I shook my head. "No dirty Gertie stuff—Whistler deals with advertising agencies handling big-ticket household items—freezers, stoves, air conditioners, that sort of thing. Not paparazzi crap."

"Big agencies—so little Dopey was getting large pay?"

"Hardly. You said it yourself. He's been around for decades and started a messenger boy and that's how he wound up."

She arched an eyebrow. "Not really, Mike."

"Huh?"

"He wound up a killer. He'll wind up sitting down at midnight."

"Yeah," I nodded. "And not getting up."

She was frowning again. "Messenger boy isn't exactly big bucks, Mike. How could he afford a narcotics habit?"

"They say if you're hooked," I said, "you'll find a way."

"Maybe by dealing yourself?"

"Naw. Dopey doesn't have the brains for it."

"What kind of pusher would give a guy like that credit?"

"Nobody I know," I admitted. "Something stinks about this."

"Coming off in waves. You going to the execution? You thinking of paying him a visit first?" Her voice had a strange tone to it.

My eyes drifted up from the envelope I was fidgeting with and met hers. We both stared and neither of us blinked. I started to say something and stopped. I reached out and took the letter from her fingertips and it read it again.

Very simple legalese. The lawyer was simply passing along a request. It was only a job to him. The state would reimburse him for his professional time, which couldn't have been very much.

Before I could say anything, Velda told me, "You haven't done a freebie in a long time."

"Kitten ..."

"You could make it a tax deduction, Mike."

"Going to an execution?"

"Giving this thing a quick look. Just a couple of days to you, but to Dopey Dilldocks, it's the rest of his life."

I shook my head. "I don't need a deduction. What's gotten into you? The poor slob has been through a trial, he was declared guilty of first-degree murder and now he's paying the penalty."

Very quietly Velda asked, "How do you know it really *was* first-degree?"

I shook my head again, this time in exasperation. "There was a squib in the paper."

"No," she said insistently. "Dopey didn't even rate a 'squib.' There was an article on narcotics and what strata of society uses them. It gave a range from high-priced movie stars to little nothings like Donald Dilbert, who'd just been found guilty in his murder trial."

"Wasn't a big article," I said lamely.

"No. And Dopey was just a footnote. Still ... you recognized his name, didn't you?"

I nodded.

"And what did you think?"

"That Dopey had finally come up in the world."

"Baloney. You were thinking, how the hell could Dopey Dill-docks plan and execute a first-degree murder—weren't you?"

She had me and she knew it. For the few times I had used the schlub to run messages, I had gotten to know him just enough to recognize his limitations. He knew the red light that meant stop was on the top and he wouldn't cross the street until the bottom one turned green, and that type of mentality didn't lay out a first-degree kill.

"So?" she asked.

The semblance of a grin was starting to twitch at her lips and she took a deep breath. The way she was built, deep breathing should have had a law against it.

I said, "Just tell me something, doll. You barely know Dopey. You haven't got the first idea of what this is all about. How come you're on his side suddenly?"

"Because I'd give him a couple of bucks to buy me a sandwich for lunch and he'd always bring the change back in the bag. He never stole a cent from me."

"What a recommendation," I said sourly.

"The best," she came back at me. "Besides, we need to get out of this office for a while. It's a beautiful Spring day, the bills are paid, there's money in the bank, nothing's on the platter at the moment and—"

"And we might pass one of those 'Medical Examination, Wedding Ceremony, One Day' places, right?"

"Could be," she said. "Anyway, we could use a day trip."

"A day trip where?"

"Someplace quiet upstate."

"A little hotel on the river, you mean?"

"That's right."

Sing Sing.

• • •

A looker like Velda could have caused a riot in places that didn't consist of concrete and cells, and anyway the court-appointed lawyer could only arrange for one visitor. So she sat in the car in a lot outside the massive stone facility, while I sat in a gray-brick room in one of several cubicles with phones and wire-reinforced glass.

Dopey was a forty-something character who might have been sixty. He had a gray pallor that had been his before he entered the big house, and his runny nose and rheumy eyes spoke of the weed and coke he'd consumed for decades. Smack was never his scene, as his fairly plump frame indicated. His hair, once blond and thick, was white and wispy now, and his face was a chinless, puffy thing.

"I think they musta framed me, Mike," he said. He had a mid-range voice with a hurt tone like a teenage boy who just got the car keys taken away.

My hat was on the little counter. I spoke into the phone, looking at his pitiful puss. "And you want me to pry if off of you, Dopey? You might have given me more notice."

"I know. I know." Phone to his ear, shaking his head, he had the demeanor of guy in a confessional. Too bad I wasn't in the sin-forgiving game.

"So why now, Dopey?"

"I just been thinking, Mike. I been going back through my whole life. They say it flashes through your brain, right before you die? But I been going through my life, one crummy photo at a time."

I sat forward. "Is that a figure of speech, Dopey? Or are you getting at something?"

Dopey swallowed thickly. "I never gave nobody no trouble, Mike. I never did crime, not even for my habit. I worked hard. Double shifts. Never made no enemies. I'm a nobody like they used to call me, just a damn inanity."

He meant nonentity, but I let it go.

"So you been thinking," I said. "What have you been thinking?"

"I think it all goes back to me sending that photo to LaSalle."

"LaSalle? You don't mean *Governor* LaSalle?"

The chinless head bobbed. "About six months ago, I ran across this undeveloped roll of film. It was in a yellow envelope marked Phi U 'April Fool's Party.'"

Where the hell was this going?

"I remembered that night. Up at Solby College? It was wild. Lots of kids partying—girls with their tops off. Crazy."

"When was this?"

"Twenty years ago—April 1, like I said. I was taking pictures all over the frat house. They was staging stuff—lots of fake murders and suicides and crazy stuff right out of a horror movie."

"And you got shots of some of that?"

Dopey's head bobbed again. "I was going around campus taking oddball pictures. I even got some 'peeper' type shots through a sorority house window, where this girl was undressing—then this guy pretends to strangle her. It was very real looking. Frankly, it scared me silly, it was so real looking."

"Is that why you didn't develop the film?"

"No, the frat guys never paid me, so I said screw it. But when I ran across that roll of film, I don't know why, I just remembered how pretty that girl was—the one that played at getting strangled? She had her top off and ... well, I can develop my own pics, you know."

"And you did?"

"I did, Mike. And the guy doing the pretend strangling? He looked just like a young version of Governor LaSalle! So I sent it to him."

I thought my eyes would pop out of my skull. "You *what?*"

"Just as a joke. I thought he might get a kick out of it, the resemblance."

I squinted at the goofy little guy. "Be straight with me, Dopey— you didn't try to blackmail him with that, did you?"

"No! I didn't think it was *really* him—just looked like him."

My stomach was tight. "What if it really was him, Dopey? And what if that wasn't an April Fool's stunt you snapped?"

Dopey swallowed again and nodded. "That was what started me thinking, Mike. That's why I hoped you might come see me."

"You told your lawyer about this?"

"No! How do I know I could trust him? He works for the state, too, don't he?"

But he trusted me. This pathetic little doper trusted me to get him out of a jam only an idiot could get into.

Well, maybe I was an idiot, too. Because I told him I'd look into it, and to keep his trap shut til he heard from me next.

"When will that be, Mike?"

"It won't be next week," I said, and got my hat and went.

• • •

Our jaunt upstate didn't last long. I called Captain Pat Chambers of Homicide from the road and he was waiting at our favorite little deli restaurant, down the block from the Hackard Building. Pat was in a back booth working on a soft drink and some fries. We slid in opposite him.

The NYPD's most decorated officer wore a lightweight gray suit that went with the gray eyes that had seen way too much—probably too much of me, if you asked him.

"Okay," he said, with no hellos, just a nod to Velda, "what are you getting me into now?"

"Nothing. You found something?"

Those weary eyes slitted, and this time his nod was for me. "Twenty years ago, April 2, a coed from Solby College was found strangled, dumped on a country road."

"And nobody got tagged for it?"

"No. There were some stranglings on college campuses back then—mostly in the Midwest—and this one got lumped in as one of the likely unsolved murders that went along with the rest."

"Didn't they catch that guy?"

"Yeah. He rode Old Sparky in Nebraska. But the Solby College murder, he never copped to."

"Interesting."

"Is it?" Pat sat forward. "Mike, do I have to tell you there's no statute of limitations on murder? That no murder case is truly ever closed til somebody falls? If you *have* something ..."

"I do have something."

"What, man?"

"A hunch."

The gray eyes closed. He loved me like a brother, but he could hate me the same way. "Mike ... do I have to give you the speech again?"

"No. I got it memorized. Tell me about Governor LaSalle."

The eyes snapped open. Pat looked at Velda for help and didn't get any. "You start with a twenty-year-old murder, chum, and then you ask about ... What do you *mean*, tell me about Governor LaSalle?"

"He got elected as a law-and-order guy. How's he doing?"

Pat waved that off. "I stay out of politics."

"Which is why you been on the force since Jesus was a baby and still aren't an inspector. What's the skinny on the Gov?"

His voice grew hushed. "You've the heard the stories."

"Have I?"

"I can't say anything more."

"Then you can't confirm that an Internal Affairs investigation into the Governor's relationship with a high-end prostitution ring got shut down because of political pressure?"

"No."

"Can you deny it?"

"No."

"What *can* you tell me, buddy?"

He stared at the soft drink like he was trying to will it into a beer. Then, very quietly, he said, "The word is, our esteemed governor is a sex addict. He uses State Patrol Officers as pimps. It's a lousy stinking disgrace, Mike, but it's not my bailiwick. Or yours."

"What about the rumors that he has a little sex shack upstate? A little cabin in the mountains where he meets with female constituents?"

Pat's grin was pretty sick. "That's impossible, Mike. Our governor's a happily married man."

Then Pat stopped a waitress and asked for a napkin. She gave him one, and Pat scribbled something on it, something fairly detailed. Then he folded the napkin, gave it to me, and slipped out of the booth.

"Get the check, Mike," he said, and was gone.

Velda frowned over at me curiously. "What is it?"

"Directions."

. . .

This time I took the drive upstate alone, much to Velda's displeasure. But she knew not to argue, when I said I had something to do that I didn't want her part of.

The shade-topped drive dead-ended at a gate, but I pulled over into the woods half a mile before I got there. I was in a black T-shirt and black jeans with the .45 on my hip, not in its usual shoulder sling. The night was cool, the moon was full and high, and ivory touched the leaves with a picture-book beauty. An idyllic spring night, if you weren't sitting on Death Row waiting for your last tomorrow.

It was a cabin, all right, logs and all, but probably bigger than what Old Abe grew up in—a single floor with maybe four or five rooms. Out front a lanky state trooper was having a smoke. Maybe I was reading in, but he seemed disgusted, whether with himself or his lot in life, who knows?

I spent half an hour making sure that trooper was alone. It seemed possible another trooper or two might be walking the perimeter, but security was limited to that one bored trooper. And that cruiser of his was the only vehicle. I had expected the Governor to have his own wheels, but I'd been wrong.

Positioned behind a nice big rock with trees at my back, I watched for maybe fifteen minutes—close enough that no binoculars were needed—before the Governor himself, in a purple smoking jacket and silk pajamas right out of Hefner's closet, exited with a petite young woman on his arm. He was tall and white-haired and handsome in a country club way. She was blonde and very curvy, in a blue halter top and matching hot pants. If she was eighteen, I was thirty.

At first I thought she had on a lot of garish make-up, then I got a better look and realized she had a bloody mouth and one of her eyes was puffy and black.

The bastard had been beating her!

She was carrying not a purse but a wallet—clutched in one hand like the life-line it was, a pro doing business with rough trade like the Gov—and her gracious host gave her a little peck on the check. Then he took her by the arm and passed her to the trooper like a beer they were sharing.

I could hear most of what LaSalle said to his trooper/pimp. "Take Miss So-and-So home, and come pick me up. I want to be back to the mansion by midnight."

The trooper nodded dutifully, opened the rear of the cruiser like the prostie was a suspect, not a colleague, and then they were off in a crunch of gravel and puff of dust.

There was a back door and opening it with burglar picks took all of twenty seconds. The Gov wasn't much on security. I came in through a small kitchen, where you could hear a shower on in a nearby bathroom.

That gave me the luxury of getting the lay of the land, but there wasn't much to see. The front room had a fireplace with a mounted fish over it and a couch and an area to watch TV and a little dining area. I spent most of my time poking around in his office, which had a desk and a few file cabinets, and a comfortable wood-and-cushions chair off by a window. That's where I was sitting, .45 in hand, when he came in only in his boxer shorts, toweling his white hair.

He looked pudgy and vaguely dissipated, and he didn't see me at first.

In fact, I had to chime in with, "Good evening, Governor. Got a moment for a taxpayer?"

He dropped the towel like it had turned to flame. He wheeled toward me, his ice-blue eyes wide, though his brow was furrowed.

"What the hell ... *who* the hell ...?"

"I'm Mike Hammer," I said. "Maybe you heard of me."

Now he recognized me.

"Good God, man," he said. "What are you doing here?"

"I was in the neighborhood. Go ahead. Sit at your desk. Make yourself comfortable. We need to talk."

His shower must have been hot, because his doughy flesh had a red cast. But the red in his face had nothing to do with needles of water.

"There's a trooper on his way back here right now," the Governor said.

"Yeah, but he has to drop your date off first. Tell me, was that shiner and bloody mouth all of it? Or would I find whip marks under that halter top?"

He had gone from startled to indignant in about a second. Now he made a similar trip from indignant to scared. I waved the gun, and he padded over to the desk and got settled in his leather chair.

"What is this," he said, "a shakedown?"

"You mean, low-life PI stakes out sex-addict governor and tries for a quick kill? Maybe. Your family has money. Your wife's family has more."

He sighed. The ice-blue eyes were more ice than blue. "You have a reputation as a hard-ass, Hammer. But I don't see you as a blackmailer. Who hired you? One of these little chippies? Some little tramp get a little more than she bargained for? Then she should've picked another trade."

"You know, they been talking about you running for president. You really think you can keep a lid on garbage like this?"

He gestured vaguely. "I can reach in my desk drawer and get a check book, and write you out a nice settlement for your client, and another for you, and we'll forget this happened. I just want your guarantee there will be no … future payments."

I shifted a little. The .45 was more casual in my hand now. "I have a client, all right, Gov. His name is Dopey Dilldocks."

He frowned. "Your *client* is a murderer."

"No, Gov. You are. My client is an imbecile who thought you might be amused by what he thought was a gag photo taken years ago, involving either you or more likely some college kid with a resemblance to you. But that was no gag—you really strangled that girl. You hadn't quite got a grip, let's say, on your habit, your sick little sex hobby."

The big bare-chested white-haired man leaned forward. "Hammer, that's nonsense. If this is true, where *are* these supposed photos?"

"Oh, hell. Your boys cleaned up on that front right after you framed Dopey. You've got underworld connections, like so many law-and-order frauds. You can't maintain a sadistic habit like yours without high friends in low places—you're tied in with the call girl racket on its uppermost levels, right?"

"You don't know what you're talking about, Hammer."

I stood. I was smiling. I wouldn't have wanted to be on the other end of that smile, but it was a smile.

"Look, Gov—I'm not after blackmail money. All I want is a phone call from the governor."

He frowned up at me. "What?"

"You've seen the old movies." I pointed at the fat phone on his desk. "You're going to call the warden over at Sing Sing, and you are going to tell him that you have reason to believe Donald Dilbert aka Dilldocks is innocent, and you are issuing the prisoner a full pardon."

"It's not that easy, Hammer …"

"It's just that easy. Then you're calling the Attorney General and inform her that you've made that call, and that the pardon is official."

And that's what he did. Under the barrel of my .45, but he did it. And he was a good actor, like so many politicians. He didn't tip it—sounded sincere as hell.

When he'd hung up after his conversation with the Attorney General, he said, "What now?"

I came around behind the desk and stood next to the seated LaSalle. "Now you get a piece of paper out of your desk drawer. I want this in writing."

His face seemed to relax. "All right, Hammer. If I pardon Dill-docks, this ends here?"

"It will end here."

He nodded, the ice-blues hooded, his silver hair catching moon-light through the window behind him. He reached in his bottom-right hand drawer and came back with the .22 revolver and he fired it right at me.

The click on the empty cylinder made him blink.

Then my .45 was in his face. "I took the liberty of removing that cartridge, when I had a look around in here. Lot of firearms acci-dents at home, you know."

My left hand came around, gripped his right hand clutching the .22, and swung the barrel around until he was looking cross-eyed at it.

"But there's another slug waiting, Gov," I said, "should the need arise."

And my hand over his hand, my finger over his finger, squeezed the trigger. A bullet went in through his open mouth and the inside of his head splattered the window behind him, blotting out the moon.

"Some sons of bitches," I said to the suicide, "just don't deserve a reprieve."

• • •

Co-author's note: *I expanded a fragment in Mickey's files of what might have been intended as a first chapter into this short story, utilizing his plot notes. M.A.C.*

• • •

MICKEY SPILLANE (1918–2006) and Max Allan Collins collaborated on numerous projects, including twelve anthologies, two films, and the Mike Danger comic book series. Spillane was the best-selling American mystery writer of the twentieth century. He introduced Mike Hammer in *I, the Jury* (1947), which sold in the millions, as did the six tough mysteries that soon followed. The controversial PI has been the subject of a radio show, comic strip, and two television series; numerous gritty movies have been made from Spillane novels, notably director Robert Aldrich's seminal film noir, *Kiss Me Deadly* (1955). Collins has earned an unprecedented fifteen Private Eye Writers of America Shamus nominations, winning twice. His graphic novel *Road to Perdition* is the basis of the Academy Award–winning film starring Tom Hanks and Paul Newman, directed by Sam Mendes. An independent filmmaker in the Midwest, he has had half a dozen feature screenplays produced. His other credits include the *New York Times* best sellers, *Saving Private Ryan* and *American Gangster*. Both Spillane and Collins received the Private Eye Writers life achievement award, the Eye.

CRAZY LARRY SMELLS BACON

By Greg Bardsley

"Honey," my mom whispers, "Larry's got a buck knife."

Our neighbor Larry lives across the street. On weekends, he tends to his cactus garden in flip-flops and a skin-colored Speedo. And cocoa butter—lots of cocoa butter.

My mom squints through our sheer curtains.

"Honey," she whispers harder. "Larry's lost his mind."

My dad flips through the *Chronicle*, bifocals on the tip his nose. When it comes to Larry, my dad has heard it all, except for maybe the buck knife.

Larry is heaving the buck knife into his garage door. Every ten seconds or so, a loud thud echoes throughout the deserted neighborhood.

We watch Larry.

He does look good in the Speedo.

My mom sighs. "That poor lady."

• • •

Crazy Larry lives with his three sons. His boys have big, giant brown eyes that never seem to blink—a trait they inherited from their mom, who moved across town with the girls about four years ago, right about when Larry started making adult comments to his daughters. Sometimes the boys stand over there and look at us with these giant brown eyes, these eyes that don't blink. They don't say much.

• • •

Crazy Larry has traveled around the world to design giant power plants. I don't think he does that anymore—my mom says they made him stop—but he has the memories. From each of his jobs he brought back mementos, including lots of wooden masks from Africa. They're on his walls, some of them looking angry, some of them with no expression at all. He likes masks, I figure. He's got so many them over there.

At night, Larry turns off the lights and sits on his covered porch facing our house, smoking and drinking. We can't see him, just the glowing red ember of his tobacco pipe.

I wonder what he's thinking about there in the dark.

• • •

My mom watches as Larry throws the knife.

"You think I could kill him, John?"

I roll my eyes. My mom loves *what-if* games.

My dad looks up from the paper. "You could kill him, maybe, but could you get away with it?"

My mom watches as Larry throws the knife again. "I'd get him at night. Just use a gun, then run back over here and hide it. No one would know."

My dad peers over the *Chronicle*, grinning. "Yeah? And what am I supposed to say when the cops start asking questions?"

My mom turns and mocks a frown, fists on her hips. "What are you supposed to say?" She pouts. "You're supposed to say I was with you the whole time."

My dad tosses the paper aside, beaming, and stands up. "Oh, I am, huh?"

My mom comes to him. "And that's exactly what you'll do." She wraps him up in her arms. "You're gonna tell them I was with you the whole time."

My dad kisses her. "You know I could never let Crazy Larry—his violent death or otherwise—get between us." He kisses her again, a little longer, and they laugh.

I hate it when they kiss in front of me. I roll my eyes, turn and peer through the sheers one last time. Larry has thrown his knife so hard he has to plant a foot on the garage door and yank it out with both hands.

• • •

I'm pretty sure Crazy Larry is sweet on my mom.

When I walk by, he'll say things like, "Say hi to that mom of yours, okay?"

His eyes twinkle when he talks about her.

My mom says Crazy Larry thinks he's God's gift to women, due to his power-plant smarts and Speedo body—and that he couldn't be more wrong. "They don't say 'tall, dark, and psychotic,' do they, sweetie? They say, 'tall, dark, and handsome,' like your dad."

One time, in the middle of a Tuesday, Larry trots over to help my mom unload groceries from our car. My mom won't even look at him. She just stares at the groceries and says, "Oh thank you, Larry, but we're fine."

Crazy Larry narrows his eyes as he backs away. "Any time, Judy."

He gives her a long look, from head to toe, like I'm not even there. "Any time … any place."

My mom never looks up.

• • •

My mom always ignores Crazy Larry. Sure, she'll gossip about him with my dad, and sure she'll guess what kind of bad things he's done, even wondering if he's got buried bodies behind his house. She'll walk into the kitchen and announce, "Larry's making flames with a can of WD40."

But to his face, she'll ignore him.

"Never reward attention from a crazyman," she explains.

"Do you think Larry likes you?"

She fails to hide an amused grin. "Maybe," she allows, "which is even more reason to act like he doesn't exist."

"Except when you're spying on him from the dining room."

She smiles to herself.

• • •

The next day my mom whispers, "Honey, you gotta see this."

From the other room, the newspaper shuffles.

Larry is wearing his skin-colored Speedo, army boots, and dark sunglasses. He's got a samurai sword in his hands, and he's studying his garage door. My mom and I glance at each other and grin.

He heaves the sword, and it sinks deep into the garage door with a loud crack, vibrating hard.

My mom yelps a little too loud.

Larry turns and squints at our house.

"Well," my mom whispers, and backs away, "time to get dinner going."

She leaves and I peer through the sheers again. Crazy Larry is staring at me.

• • •

A week later the "Check Engine" light flashes on the dashboard of my mom's Chevy.

At the dealership, the waiting room is cold, grimy and barren. We sit and wait as the mechanics take turns coming in from the garage to lean against the counter, page through catalogs and stare at my mom. The biggest mechanic, this man with a small forehead and a mouth that hangs open, doesn't even look at the catalogs; he just stands there and stares, snorting over and over, like he's trying to get her attention.

My mom never looks at him. She's paging through a *Sunset* magazine.

Finally he says, "Ma'am, you mind if I give your young'un a little tour of the back area?"

Slowly, she takes my wrist. "He needs to stay here."

He snorts, looks her up and down, and then glances at me. "I got Pong in my trailer out back."

My mom finally looks up at him and forces a smile. "He needs to stay with me."

"You like Pong, little fella?"

I look at my mom. "I better stay here."

Snort. "Maybe we'll get together some other time." He turns and lumbers back into the garage.

I look up at my mom. She rolls her eyes as she turns a page. "You think we need to find a new auto garage, kiddo?"

Inside, I feel weird. "Maybe."

"Your dad likes this place." She flips a page, hard. "Your dad's getting an earful tonight."

Finally, the manager comes back to the office with a crooked grin and a leer in his eyes, insisting the light is flashing because of an "intake valve alignment irregularity," which will cost almost three hundred dollars.

My mom sags her head. My parents always worry about money.

The big guy and another mechanic saunter in as the manager gives her the crooked smile. "You see, ma'am, the intake valves are crucial to the integrity of the engine; they maintain alignment with the fuel injection intake switches and their responsiveness to the sub panels."

The mechanics smile at each other.

My mom sighs again. "Alignment with the what?"

The manager, his hair like a golden helmet, suppresses a grin. "Fuel injection intake switches."

I inch closer to the mechanics.

After a pause, my mom says, "I just brought the car in two weeks ago."

"Well, sometimes these things come in waves."

My mom steps away, pulls her hair back and looks out the window. The men devour her, looking her up and down. When she returns to the counter, she pains, "Okay."

"You're making the right choice, ma'am." The manager leans forward, forcing a serious look. "It's important to get this fixed. That's why the engine light went on." He waits a second, bites his lip. "A pretty little sweetheart with young ones?" He nods to me. "You don't wanna end up broken down on a road ..." He pauses, studies her mouth. "... all alone."

My mom looks away.

I slip closer to the mechanics. The big one whispers, almost laughing, "Another score from the Sucker Light." He releases a quiet squeal and slaps a low-five with the other guy. "Sucker Light always delivers."

The engine light doesn't look like a sucker to me.

• • •

We leave our Chevy at the dealership, so the big mechanic drives us home in one of their cars. On the drive home, no one says a word—the mechanic is wheezing hard, and I find myself staring at his whiskery jowls. His name tag—"Ed"—is stitched into his baby-blue shop shirt, which is darkened by massive sweat stains around his pits. Tattooed on his right forearm is a reproduction of the name tag, and I realize he must really like his name. I wish I liked my name that much.

Ed keeps glancing at my mom, a gleam in his bloodshot eyes, and my mom keeps sliding closer to the passenger-side door. After a while, he snorts louder than I've ever heard anyone snort, and glances at my mom, an eyebrow arching. My mom looks out the window.

Ed pulls a hard left, and suddenly we're headed out of town, into the country.

"What are you doing?"

Snort. "You live this way, you said."

"No, we're in town. I told you—we're on Walnut."

Ed isn't turning around. "I know a faster way."

My mom tenses. "You need to turn us around now."

Ed forces a chuckle, keeps driving.

My mom stiffens, clutches her purse closer. "Ed," she warns, "you need to turn us around right now."

Ed ignores her, flips on the radio. The Eagles.

My stomach tightens, and suddenly I want my dad really bad.

"Ed." My mom reaches inside her purse. "Last warning."

He glances at her and lets off the gas. We coast onto the side of the road, the sound of gravel crunching under rubber. We're surrounded by hilly pastureland, and there is not another soul in sight. No one says a word as Ed gazes at my mom and my mom glares back.

"Ed, take us back into town."

Snort. "But I know a shortcut."

"No you don't, Ed. This is the opposite way, and you know it. You need to turn around right now."

They stare at each other for a real long time.

Finally, Ed pulls us onto the road and makes a U-turn. He's sighing. "Just wanted to show you my special place."

My mom seems like she's about to cry, but she doesn't.

I feel the same way, and I do.

• • •

When we finally pull up to our house, Larry is sitting on his porch. I can feel him watching us.

My mom bolts out of the car, opens my door and pulls me out. Ed looks at her one last time and pulls away.

Larry watches.

My mom has her back to me as she walks to our front door. "Why don't you play out front, sweetie? I need to call your dad."

I glance at Larry, and he's waving me over.

I wipe my nose and look to my mom, but she's already in the house.

• • •

"Hi, Larry."

He smells like cocoa butter and pipe tobacco. He nods to where the car was. "I know that individual. What's he doing with you and your mom?"

I sniffle. "He's from the dealership."

Larry gazes into space.

"Our engine light went on."

Slowly, he nods.

I make a long sigh. "It's gonna cost three hundred dollars." After a long pause, I add, "That guy called it the Sucker Light."

Larry squints into space. "Ed said that?"

I nod. "I'm not sure what that means, Sucker Light."

"Don't worry about that, Teddy."

"They didn't want my mom to hear them."

Larry examines his fingernails—they seem perfect. I stand there and watch him, wondering if he's really crazy or just different, or if that's the same thing.

"He tried driving us into the country," I say, my voice suddenly cracking. "My mom almost cried."

Larry squints into space for a long while, then forces a weird smile, his mouth just pretending to be happy, his eyebrows arching. Slowly he cocks his head to me.

"The scent of bacon frying in the wild." He widens his eyes, really trying to smile. "Does that affect you, Teddy?"

I look at him. "Affect me?"

"You see, Teddy, bacon scent in the woods drives me nuts." His arms and legs seem to tighten. "That scent is so arresting, so powerful, so mouth-watering, it just shuts off my frontal lobe, if you will, the evolved part of my brain." I look into his eyes, and I realize they're nice-looking eyes. "The animal takes over, and all I know is that I must eat that bacon." He pauses. "That I must have my way."

I don't know what to say. After a long weird silence, I offer, "I like bacon."

He nods. "Yes, well you see, Teddy, I think I smell bacon."

• • •

If Crazy Larry smells bacon, he sure has an odd way of showing it.

Larry spends the rest of the afternoon going back and forth to stores, each time unloading things like rebar, chicken wire, twine, propane canisters, foundation blocks, cotton balls, duct tape, several sealed buckets of dark liquid, two car batteries, three jumper cables, a roll of fabric, an ironing board, a hacksaw, and a case of Budweiser. In the garage, he stands at his workbench and pokes through a bunch of Walgreen's bags as Alvin and the Chipmunks sing "Pop Goes the Weasel" on his tape player—I love Alvin and the Chipmunks, and I decide that anyone who loves them, too, can't be that crazy.

I walk up his driveway as he pulls out a can of shaving cream, a jar of Vaseline, and two cans of WD-40. On the shelf above the workbench, I notice a black handgun placed beside a can of wood stain. On the other side of the can is one of his African masks—it has big angry eyes and long, sharp teeth.

My mouth falls open.

Larry notices me.

Finally I manage, "Are the boys around?"

He shakes his head no. "Larry needs some time to himself, Teddy."

I back away.

Alvin and the Chipmunks blare from Larry's garage.

Around around the mulberry bush,

The monkey chased the weasel

The monkey thought it was a joke,

Pop goes the weasel

• • •

I'm in the dining room, watching Larry.

My mom is on the phone.

Larry has crawled into the back of his station wagon.

"It was entirely inappropriate," my mom says.

Larry is measuring the windows with a tape measure.

"I was *very* concerned."

Larry sits there and stares into space.

"Well, to be quite honest, I don't care if you've known him for years. That has nothing to do with this."

Larry is now staring at his fingernails.

"No, the fact is, it was a few seconds away from becoming a kid-napping."

Larry scrambles out of the station wagon and bolts for the garage.

"Well, I appreciate that, but I *have* called my husband."

When my mom comes into the dining room, she pulls me to her, keeps me there and gazes at Larry's house. She forces a happy voice. "You doing some good Larry-watching, honey?"

I look up at her. "Larry smells bacon."

She frowns. "Bacon?"

Larry trots out of the house in tight jeans and a loose collar shirt. I don't think she realizes it, but my mom's eyes widen as she watches him jump into the station wagon.

I ask her, "Do you really think he's a crazyman?"

It looks like Larry has fallen into another trance.

"Well, maybe." She scratches my head, softly, like she's been doing since I was very small. "But maybe the thing is, we can consider Larry *our* crazyman."

• • •

Later that afternoon, I'm kicking the soccer ball against our garage door when Larry pulls up in his station wagon. I stop and watch as he backs the car into his driveway; the back windows are covered by cardboard. He gets out, glances at me and opens his garage door.

I keep watching.

Larry returns to the station wagon, lowers his head and glares at me.

Suddenly I want to go inside.

"Bye," I say.

"Yes, that's right," he says. "Bye-bye."

Inside, my mom is making meatloaf.

I stand in the dining room and watch as Larry backs the station wagon into his garage. A few seconds later, he stands under the garage door and looks around one last time before pulling it down behind him.

It takes hours before I have the guts to go back out there.

• • •

It's getting dark as I stand outside Larry's garage.

There's lot of noise in there. I hear hammering, metal rustling and heavy breathing. There's electronic buzzing and snapping, too.

And someone is moaning.

I step closer and hear a faint trace of Alvin and the Chipmunks. It's "The Witchdoctor," the one where the chipmunks dance in tribal masks. I inch closer to the door.

I told the witchdoctor, I was in love with you

And then the witchdoctor, he told me what to do

He said,

OO EE OO AH-AH ting-tang walla-walla bing-bang

OO EE OO AH-AH ting-tang walla-walla bing-bang

I creep closer to the side of the door, where a slice of light escapes from the garage. I hear something wet hitting the floor, then another moan.

I creep a little closer.

Another moan.

I step closer.

Alvin and the Chipmunks.

I creep closer to the light and peek in. From a weird angle, I see Larry dancing around in his tribal mask, his knees kicking high, his arms flailing, his mid-section swirling.

I can't see the other side of the garage, but I hear moaning.

I told the witchdoctor you didn't love me true

I told the witchdoctor you didn't love me nice

And then the witchdoctor, he gave me this advice

He said,

OO EE OO AH-AH ting-tang walla-wall bing-bang

I'm light-headed, and all I know is, I want to go home.

• • •

That night my mom and dad talk long and hard about everything. My dad looks at me, shakes his head and snaps at her, "Next time, just call me."

My mom tells me to go play out front.

It's completely dark. No one else is outside; they're probably all watching *Eight Is Enough*, which is what I'd be doing. I walk around in front of our house, kicking pebbles, when finally I can't resist looking across the street.

It's dark over there. On the porch, an ember fades.

I hear a muffled groan coming from his garage, followed by faint traces of Alvin and the Chipmunks.

Now, you've been keeping love from me just like you were a miser

And I'll admit I wasn't very smart

So I went out and found myself a guy that's so much wiser

And he taught me the way to win your heart

I bite my lip. I don't want to look that way.

"Teddy."

Another muffled moan from the garage, then an electronic buzz-snap.

"Yeah?"

The ember glows. "Come here." His voice is strong, like he's not asking.

Wet squishy noises echo from the garage.

The ember fades.

I walk across the street, but I still can't see him.

"Larry?" I step closer.

Still, nothing. Only darkness.

"Larry?"

The ember brightens, and finally I see Larry. He's sitting there on the porch wearing a baseball cap, and he's staring into space. Stitched neatly to the front of the cap is Ed's name-tag tattoo.

The ember fades, and Crazy Larry dissolves into the darkness.

• • •

GREG BARDSLEY has worked as a metro newspaper reporter, editor, ghostwriter, video producer and speechwriter, he has been to sweat lodges, shootouts, remote Chinese villages, gangbanger cribs, and Communist compounds. His crime fiction has appeared in the anthologies *Sex, Thugs, and Rock & Roll* (Kensington Books) and *Uncage Me* (Bleak House Books) and in *Plots with Guns, 3:AM Magazine, Thuglit, Out of the Gutter, Storyglossia, Pulp Pusher,* and *Demolition.* He lives with his family in the San Francisco Bay Area.

FEMME SOLE

By Dana Cameron

North End

"A moment of your time, Anna Hoyt."

Anna slowed and cursed to herself. She'd seen Adam Seaver as she crossed Prince Street, and for a terrible moment thought he was following her. She'd hoped to lose him amid the peddlers and shoppers at the busy market near Dock Square, but she couldn't ignore him after he called out. His brogue was no more than a low growl, but conversations around him tended to fade and die. He never raised his voice, but he never had a problem making himself heard, even over the loudest of Boston's boisterous hawkers. In fact, with anxious glances, the crowd melted back in retreat from around her. No one wanted to be between Seaver and whatever he was after.

Cowards, she thought. But her own mouth was dry as he approached.

She turned, swallowed, met his eyes, then lowered hers, hoping it looked like modesty or respect and not revulsion. His face was weathered and, in places, blurred with scars, marks of fights from which he'd walked away the winner; there was a nick above his ear where he'd had his head shaved. Seaver smiled; she could see two rows of sharp, ugly teeth like a mouthful of broken glass or like one of the bluefish the men sometimes caught in the harbor. Bluefish were so vicious they had to be clubbed when they were brought into the boat or they'd shear your finger off.

He didn't touch her, but she flinched when he gestured to a quiet space behind the stalls. It was blustery autumn, salt air and a hint of snow to come, but a sour milk smell nearly gagged her. Dried leaves skittered over discarded rotten vegetables, or was it that even the boldest rats fled when Seaver approached?

"How are you, Mr. Seaver?" she asked. She tried to imagine that she was safely behind her bar. She felt she could manage anything with the bar between her and the rest of the world.

"Fair enough. Yourself?"

"Fine." She wished he'd get on with it. "Thanks." His excessive manners worried her. He'd never spoken to her before, other than to order his rum and thank her.

When he didn't speak, Anna felt the sweat prickle along the hairline at the back of her neck. The wind blew a little colder, and the crowd and imagined safety of the market seemed remote. The upright brick structure of the Town House was impossibly far away, and the ships anchored groaning at the wharves could have been at sea.

He waited, searched her face, then looked down. "What very pretty shoes."

"Thank you. They're from Turner's." She shifted uncomfortably. She didn't believe he was interested in her shoes, but neither did she imagine he was trying to spare her feelings by not staring at the bruises that ran up the side of her head. These were almost hidden with an artfully draped shawl, but her lip was still visibly puffy. It was too easy to trace the line from that to the black and blue marks. One mark led to the next like a constellation.

One thing always led to another.

"What can I do for you, Mr. Seaver?" she said at last. Not knowing was too much.

"I may be in a way to do something for you."

Anna couldn't help it: she sighed. She heard the offer five times a night.

"Nothing like that," he said, showing that rank of teeth. "It's your husband."

"What about him?" Gambling debts, whores, petty theft? Another harebrained investment gone west? Her mind raced over the many ways Thomas could have offended Mr. Seaver.

"I saw him at Clark's law office this morning. I had business with Clark ... on behalf of my employer ..."

Anna barely stifled a shudder. Best to know nothing of Seaver or his employer's business, which had brought a fortune so quickly that it could only have come from some brutal trade in West Indian contraband. Thick Thomas Hoyt was well beneath the notice of Seaver's boss, praise God.

"... and your husband was still talking to Clark."

"Yes?" Anna refused to reveal surprise at Thomas visiting a lawyer. He had no use or regard for the law.

"He was asking how he could sell your establishment."

"He can't. It's mine," she said before thinking.

Seaver showed no surprise at her vehemence. "Much as I thought, and exactly what Clark told him. Apparently, Hook Miller wants the place."

"So he said last night. I thanked him, but I'm not selling. He was more than understanding."

Seaver tilted his head. "Because he thinks the way to acquire your tavern is through your husband."

The words went through Anna like a knife, and she understood. Her hand rose to her cheek. The beating had come only hours after Miller's offer and her refusal. Thomas had been blind drunk, and she could barely make out what had driven him this time.

"If I sell it, how will we live? The man's an idiot." She was shocked to realize that she'd actually said this, that she was having a conversation, *this* conversation, with Seaver.

"Perhaps Thomas thinks he can weasel a big enough price from Miller."

"The place is *mine*. No one can take it, not even my husband. My father said so. He showed me the papers." *Feme sole merchant* was what the lawyers called her, with their fancy Latin. The documents allowed her to conduct business almost as if she was a man. At first, it was only with her father's consent, but as she prospered— and he sickened—it was accepted that she was responsible, allowed to trade on her own. Very nearly independent, almost as good as a man, in the year of Our Lord 1745. And, though she could never say so aloud, better than most.

"I think Clark will be bound by the document," Seaver said. "At least until someone more persuasive than Thomas comes along."

The list of people more persuasive and smarter than her husband was lengthy.

"It's only a piece of paper." Seaver shrugged. "A fragile thing."

Anna nodded, trying not to shift from one foot to another. Eventually, Hook Miller would find a way. As long as she'd known him, he always had.

Anna swallowed. "Why are you telling me this?"

He shrugged. "I like to drink at your place."

She almost believed him. "And?"

She knew what was coming, was nearly willing to pay the price that Seaver would ask. Whatever would save her property and livelihood, the modicum of security and independence she'd struggled to achieve. What were her alternatives? Sew until she was blind, or follow behind some rich bitch and carry *her* purse, run *her* errands? Turn a sailor's whore?

"And?" she repeated.

"And." He leered. "I want to see what you will do."

• • •

The bad times were hard for everyone, but it was the good times that brought real trouble, she thought. A pretty young lass with no family and a thriving business on the waterfront. She might as well have hung out a sign.

Anna hurried back to the Queen's Arms, shopping forgotten. No one had ever paid the property any attention when her father ran the place. It was only after she'd taken over the tavern, within sight of the wharves that cut into Boston Harbor, that business grew and drew attention.

The Queen was a neighborhood place on Fleet Street. "The burying ground up behind you, and the deep, dark sea ahead," her father used to say, but in between was a place for a man to drink his beer after work—or before, as may be the case—the occasional whiskey, if he was feeling full and fat. Or three or five, if he was broke and buggered.

She stumbled over the cobbles in the street, but recovered and hurried along, needing to reassure herself the place was still there, that it hadn't vanished, hadn't been whisked away by magic from the crowd of buildings that lined the narrow streets above the harbor. Or been burned to the ground, more likely. She never doubted that her husband, stupid as he was, would find a way to rob her for Miller, if that's what Thomas imagined he wanted.

Had Thomas Hoyt been content with hot meals twice a day, too much to drink and ten minutes sweating over his wife on Saturday night, church and repentance Sunday morning, Anna could have managed him well enough. She wanted a more ambitious man, but Thomas had come with his mother's shop next door. When that allowed Anna to expand her tavern, she thought it a fair enough trade.

Until she discovered Thomas *was* ambitious, in his own way. While she poured ale, rum, and whiskey, he sat in the corner. Ready to change the barrels or quell the occasional rowdiness, he more often read his paper and smoked, playing the host. His eyes followed his pretty wife's movements and those of all the men around her.

There were two men he had watched with peculiar interest, and Anna now understood why. One was Hook, named Robert Miller by his mother, a ruffian with a finger in every pie and a hand in every pocket. Hook's gang were first to take advantage of all the trade on the waterfront, from loading and unloading ships to smuggling. But he did more for the local men than he took from them and was a kind of hero for it. Of course Hook appealed to Thomas: he was everything Thomas imagined he himself could be.

The other man he watched was Seaver, but even Thomas was smart enough to be circumspect when he did it. When one of Miller's men drunkenly pulled Seaver from his chair one night, claiming his looks were souring the beer, Seaver left without a word. But he came back the next night, and Miller's man never did. That man now drank at another house, where no one knew him. Three fingers from his right hand were broken and his nose bitten off.

The other men left Seaver alone after that. Anna smiled as she served his rum, but it stopped at her eyes. He was content to sit quietly, alone with who knew what thoughts.

• • •

Thomas was scrubbing the bar when she arrived. He looked up, smiled as though he remembered nothing of what had happened the night before. Maybe he didn't.

"There's my girl. Shopping done?"

"I forgot something."

"Well, find it and I'll walk you to the dressmaker's myself. It's getting dark."

He said it as though the dark brought devils instead of the tradesmen who came regularly to her place. Who worshipped her. She had married him a year before, after her father died, for protection. She ran her tongue along the inside of her cheek, felt the swelling there, felt a tooth wiggle, her lip tear a fraction.

"I won't have you be less than the best-dressed lady in the North End," he said expansively, as if he emptied his pockets onto the counter himself. Anna and Mr. Long, the tailor, had a deal: Anna borrowed the latest gowns; wearing them, she showed them to perfection, the ideal advertisement with her golden hair and slim waist. The men at her place either sent their wives to the dressmaker's so they'd look more like Anna, or spent more money at Anna's just to look at her, a fine, soft, pretty thing amid so much coarseness.

She pretended to locate some trifle under the bar, and Thomas wiped his hands on the seat of his britches. She forced a smile; her mouth still hurt. Better to have him think she was stupid or in love. Even better, afraid.

"The best news, Anna," he said, taking her arm as they went back onto the street. "Rob Miller has added another twenty pounds to his asking price. We were right to wait."

It was still less than half the value of the place. Under no circumstances would she consider selling to Hook Miller and give Thomas the money to invest and lose.

She nodded, as if her refusal to sell had been a joint decision.

"I think we'll wait until Friday, see if we can't drive the price a little higher," he said, patting her hand. His palm was heavy and rough. She saw the faint abrasions along the knuckles, remembered them intimately.

She nodded again, kept her eyes on her feet, shoes peeping out from under her skirt, as she moved briskly to keep up with Thomas. He raced across the cobbles, she a half-pace behind.

Friday, then. Three days. Between Miller's desire for her tavern and Thomas's wish to impress him, she was trapped.

• • •

Friday night came despite Anna's prayers for fire, a hurricane, a French invasion. But the place was as it always was: a wide, long room, stools and tables, two good chairs by a large, welcoming fire. The old windows were in good repair, the leads tight, and decent curtains kept out the drafts. The warm smells of good Barbadian rum and local ale kept the world at bay.

When Miller came into the tavern, Thomas got up immediately, offered him the best upholstered seat, nearest the fire. Miller dismissed him outright, said his business was with Anna. Anna tried with all her might to divert his attention back to Thomas, but Miller could not have made more of a show of favoring her in front of the entire room, who watched from behind raised mugs. Thomas glowered, his gaze never leaving Anna.

"Why won't you sell the place, Anna?" Miller's words and tone were filled with hurt; she was doing him unfairly.

Anna's eyes flicked around the room; the men sitting there drinking were curious. Why would Anna cross Miller? No profit in that, they all knew.

"And if I did, what would I live on then?" she asked gaily, as if Miller had been revisiting a long-standing joke.

"Go to the country, for all of me," he said, draining his glass. It might as well have been *Go to the Devil.*

As if she had a farm to retire to, a home somewhere other than over the barroom. "I promised my father I would not," she said, trying to maintain the tone of a joke, but the strain was audible in her voice, her desperation a tremor in her answer.

"Well, come find me—" he set his empty glass down. "When you're ready to be reasonable." He tipped his hat to her, ignored Thomas, and left.

After that, the other regulars filed out, one by one. None wanted to see what they all knew would come next. Anna tried to entice them to stay, even offering a round on the house on the flimsy excuse of someone's good haul of fish. But it couldn't last forever, and eventually even the boy who helped serve was sent home. Only Seaver was left.

It was late, past the time when Thomas generally retired. It was obvious he wasn't going to bed.

Seaver stood up. Anna looked at him with a wild hope. Perhaps he would come to her aid, somehow defuse the situation. He put a coin down on the counter and leaned toward her.

She glanced hastily at Thomas, who was scowling as he jabbed the fire with a poker. Anna's face was a mask of desperation. She leaned closer, and Seaver surreptitiously ran a finger along the back of her hand.

"Better if you don't argue with him," he breathed, his lips barely moving. "Don't fight back too much."

She watched his back as he left. The room was empty, quiet, save for the crackle of the fire, the beating of Anna's heart in her chest.

Thomas straightened, and turned. "I thought we had an agreement."

Anna looked around; there was no one to help her. The door ...

"I thought, any man comes in here looking for a piece, you send him up to that fancy cathouse on Salem Street. And yet I see you, a damned slut, making cow eyes at every man in here, right in front of me."

She ran, but just as her fingers touched the latch, she felt the poker slam across her shoulders. She cried out, fell against the door. The next blows landed on her back, but Thomas, tired of imprecision and mindful of leaving visible marks that would make the punters uneasy, dropped the poker and relied on the toe of his boot.

When his rage diminished, Thomas stormed out. Anna remained on the floor, too afraid and too hurt to get up. She measured the grain of the wood planks while she thought. Thomas would go to Miller, reassure him the sale was imminent. Soon she would have no choice.

She eventually forced herself up, pulling herself onto a stool. No bones broken, this time.

In her quest to find security, independence, she'd first tried the law, and when that wasn't enough, she'd put her faith in her husband's strength. Now ... she wasn't sure what would work, but knew she would be damned if she gave in. Not after all she'd done to make the place her own. Her father had taught her the value of a business, repeated it over and over, as she held his hand while he died. He said there were only two books she needed to mind, her Bible and her ledger, but now the latter had her in deep trouble. She moved stiffly to the bar, poured herself a large rum, drank it down neat, exchanging the burn of the liquor for the searing pain in her back.

• • •

Thomas didn't return in the morning, but Anna hadn't expected him to. He often stayed away after a beating, a chance for her to think over her sins, he'd told her once before. But never for more than a day or two.

She moved stiffly that day, easier the next, but late the third evening, when Anna was about to bar the door for the night, a man's hand shoved it open. Maybe Thomas had had a change of heart, had come home—

It was Hook Miller.

She didn't offer a drink. He didn't ask for one.

"Why not sell to me, Anna Hoyt?" he asked, warming his hands at the fire. "I want this place, so you might as well save yourself the trouble."

"I told you: my father said I should never sell. Property—it's the only sure thing in this world."

Miller didn't seem bothered, only a bit impatient. "There's nothing sure, Anna. Wood burns, casks break, and customers leave. And I've had the lawyer Clark make your rights over to Thomas. Take my money, leave here."

She said nothing. Felt the paper she kept in her shoe, the copy of the document that gave her the Queen's Arms, the property, the right to do business. Now they were, he was telling her, worthless. After all her work, all she'd done ...

Suddenly, Anna had a dreadful thought. "Where's Thomas? Have you seen him?"

"Indeed, I have just left him." Miller stood straight, smiled crookedly. He continued, mock-serious: "He's ... down by my wharf. He couldn't persuade you to sell, but he's still looking after your interests."

The blood froze inside her. Thomas was dead, she knew it.

Miller tilted his head and waited. When she couldn't bring herself to respond, he left, closing the door behind him.

The paralyzing cold spread over her, and, for a blessed moment, Anna felt nothing. Then the shivering started, brought her back to the tavern. Anna's first thought was that her knees would give way before she reached the chair by the fire. She clutched the back of it, her nails digging into the upholstery. When she felt one of them snap, she turned, took three steps, then vomited into the slops pot on the bar.

Better, Anna thought, wiping her mouth. *I must be better than this.*

Still trembling, but at least able to think, she climbed the stairs to her rooms. She saw Thomas's good shirt hanging from a peg, and buried her face in it, breathing deeply. She took it down, rubbing the thick linen between her fingers, and considered the length of the sleeves. She stared at the peg, high on the wall, and reluctantly made her decision.

• • •

Everything was different in her new shoes. Since she was used to her thin slippers, the cobbles felt oddly distant beneath the thick soles, and it took her awhile to master the clunkiness of the heels. She relied on a population used to drunken sailors to ignore her, relied on the long cloak to conceal most of her blunders. Thomas's clothes would have been impossible, but she still had a chest full of her father's things, and his boots were a better fit. Best not to think about the rest of her garb. She needed to confirm what Miller had hinted, and she couldn't be seen doing it. Anna was too familiar a figure to those whose lives were spent on the wharves, and most of them would be friendly faces. But not if she were caught. If they caught her, so scandalously dressed in britches, well ... losing the tavern would be the least of it.

Somehow, her need to know for sure was stronger than fear, than embarrassment, and the bell in the Old North Church chimed as she found her way to Miller's wharf. The reek of tar and wood fires made her eyes water, and a stiff breeze combined drying fish with the smells of spices in nearby warehouses, making her almost gag.

The moon broke through the clouds. She walked out to the harbor, feeling more and more exposed by the moment ...

Nothing on Miller's wharf that shouldn't be there. She stopped, struck by a realization. Hook would never lay the murder at his own doorstep.

The urge to move a short way down to the pier and wharf that belonged to Clark, Miller's detested rival in business, was nearly physical.

At first, Anna saw nothing but the boards of the pier itself. She climbed down the ladder to the water's edge, hooked one of the dinghies by its rope, and pulled it close. She boarded, cast off, and rowed, following the length of the pier. Though she preferred to be secret, there was no need to muffle the oarlocks; the waterfront's activity died down at night, but it was never completely silent along the water. Sweat trickled down her back even as thin ice crackled on the floor of the boat beneath her feet.

The half hour rang out, echoed by church bells across Boston and Charlestown, and Anna shivered in spite of her warm exercise.

Three-quarters of the way down the pier, Anna saw a glimpse of white on the water. She uncovered her lantern and held it up.

Among the pilings, beneath the pier, all manner of lost and discarded things floated, bobbing idly on top of the waves: broken crate wood, a dead seagull, an unmoored float. There was something else.

A body.

Even without seeing his face, she knew it was Thomas, his fair hair floating like kelp, the shirt she herself had patched billowing around him like sea foam. A wave broke against the piling of the pier and one of his hands was thrust momentarily to the surface, puffy and raw: the fish and harbor creatures had already been to feast.

Anna stared awhile, and then maneuvered the boat around. She rowed quietly back to the ladder, tied up the dinghy, and headed home.

She brought the bottle of rum to her room, drank until the cold was chased away and she could feel her fingers again. Then she drank a good deal more. She changed back into her own clothing and, keeping her father's advice in mind, opened her Bible. In an old habit, she let it fall open where it would, closing her eyes and placing a finger on the text. The candle burned low while she read, waiting for someone to come and tell her Thomas Hoyt was dead.

• • •

Hook Miller came to the burial on Copp's Hill. As he made his way up to where Anna stood, the crowd of neighbors—there were nearly fifty of them, for nothing beat a good funeral—doffed their hats out of respect to his standing. Miller's clothes were showy but ill-suited to him, Anna knew, and he pretended concern that was as foreign to him as a clean handkerchief. He even waited decently before he approached her, and those nearby heard a generous offer of aid to the widow, so that she could retreat to a quieter life elsewhere.

The offering price was still an affront. When she shook her head, he nodded sadly, said he'd be back when she was more composed. She knew it wasn't solicitousness but the eyes of the neighborhood that made him so nice. The next time Miller approached her, it would be in private. There would be no refusing that offer.

When Seaver came in for his drink later, she avoided his glance. She'd already made up her mind.

• • •

The next morning, she sent a note to Hook Miller. No reason to be seen going to him, when there was nothing more natural than for him to come to the tavern. And if his visit stood out among others, why, she was a propertied widow now, who had to keep an eye to the future.

He didn't bother knocking, came in as if he already owned the place, and barred the door behind him. She was standing behind a chair, waiting, a bottle of wine on the table, squat-bodied and long-necked, along with two of her best glasses, polished to gleaming. One was half-filled, half-drunk. The fire was low, and there were only two candles lit.

He bowed and sat without being asked. His breath was thick with harsh New England rum. "Well?"

"I can't sell the place. I'd be left with nothing."

Miller was silent at first, but his eyes narrowed. "And?"

Anna straightened. "Marry me. That way ... the place will be yours, and I'll be ... looked after."

"You didn't sign it over to Thomas."

"Thomas Hoyt was as thick as two short planks. I couldn't trust him to find his arse with both hands."

Thomas's absence now was not discussed.

Miller pondered. "If I do, you'll sign the Queen's Arms over to me."

"The day we wed." Her father had given her the hope and the means, but then slowly, painfully, she'd discovered she couldn't keep the place alone. She swallowed. "I can't do this by myself."

"And what benefit to me to marry you?"

Her hours of thought had prepared the answer. "You'll get a property you've always wanted, and with it, an eye and an ear to everything that happens all along the waterfront. More than that: respectability. This whole neighborhood is getting nothing but richer, and you'd be in the middle of it. What better way to advance than through deals with the merchant nobs themselves? To say nothing of window dressing for your other ... affairs."

Miller laughed, then stopped, considered what she was saying. "Sharp. And a clever wife to entertain my new friends? It makes sense."

"Those merchants, they're no more than a step above hustling themselves. We can be of use to each other," she said carefully. She'd almost said *need*, but that would have been fatal. "Wine?"

He looked at her, looked at the bottle, the one empty glass. "Thanks."

She poured, the ruby liquid turning blood-black in the green-tinged glasses, against the dark of the room.

He stared at the glass, his brow furrowing. "I've more of a mind for beer, if you don't mind."

She looked disappointed, but didn't press him. "You'll have to get a head for wine if you expect to move up in the world." She rose and slid a pewter mug from a peg on the wall, then filled it from the large barrel behind her bar.

Miller smiled, thanked her. She raised her glass to him, sipped. He saluted and drank too.

It was then he noticed the large Bible on the table next to them. He reached over, flipped through carelessly.

"Too much theater for one about to be so soon remarried, don't you think?" He flicked through the pages, as if looking for something he could make use of. "Devotion doesn't play. Not around here, anyway."

Anna suppressed her feelings at seeing him handle the book so roughly. She shut it firmly, moved it away. "My father said it was the only book besides my ledger to heed."

Miller shrugged. Piety was unexpected, especially after her reaction—or lack thereof—to her husband's murder, but who could pretend to understand a woman? Her reaction aroused him, however. Any resistance did. "Let me see what I'll be getting myself into. Lift your skirts."

Anna had known it would come to this; still, she hesitated. Only a moment. But before Hook had to say another word, she bunched up the silk, slippery in her sweaty palms, and raised her skirts to her thighs. Miller reached out, grabbed the ribbon of her garter, and pulled. It slithered out of its knot, draped itself over his fist. He leaned forward, slid a finger over the top of her stocking, then collapsed onto the table. His head hit hard, and he didn't say another word.

Repulsed, Anna unhooked his finger from her stocking, let his hand fall heavily, smack against the chair leg. She straightened her stocking, retied her garter, then picked up the heavy Bible. She hesitated, gulping air, then, remembering her father's words and the fourth chapter of Judges, nodded.

I must be better than this. I must manage.

She reached into the cracked binding of the Bible and withdrew a long steel needle. Its point picked up the light from the candle and glittered. Her breath held, she stood over the unconscious man, then, aiming carefully, she drove it deep into his ear.

Shortly, with a grunt, a shudder, a sigh, Miller stopped breathing.

• • •

She had been afraid she'd been too stingy, miscalculated the dose, unseen in the bottom of the pewter mug, not wanting to warn him with the smell of belladonna or have it spill as it waited on the peg. Her father had been frailer, older, and when she could stand his rasping, rattling breathing no longer, could wait no longer to begin her own plans for the Queen's Arms, she had mixed a smaller amount into his beer. No matter: either the poison or the needle had done its work on Hook Miller.

Anna threw the rest of the beer onto the floor, followed it with the last of the wine from the bottle. No sense in taking chances. She had a long night ahead of her. She could barely move Hook on her own. Slender though she was, she was strong from hauling water and kegs and wood from the time she could walk, but he was nearly two hundred pounds of dead meat. She'd planned this, though, with as much meticulousness as she planned everything in her life. Everything that could be anticipated, that is. Thomas's ill-conceived greediness she hadn't counted on, nor Miller's interest in her place. These were hard lessons and dearly bought.

She would be better. She would manage.

She went to the back, brought out the barrow used to move stock. With careful work, and a little luck, Anna tipped Miller from his chair into the barrow, and, struggling to keep her balance, wheeled him out of the public room into the back kitchen ell. She left him there, out of sight, and checked again that the back door was still barred. She twitched the curtain so that it hung completely over the small window.

Lighting a taper from the fireplace, she considered her plan. A change of clothes, from silk into something for scut work. She had hours of dirty business ahead of her, as bad and dirty as slaughtering season, but really, it was no different from butchering a hog.

A small price to pay for her freedom and the time to plan how better to keep it.

Holding the taper, she hurried up the narrow back stairs to the chamber over the public room. When she opened the door, her breath caught in her throat. There was a lit candle on the table across from her bed.

Adam Seaver was sitting in her best chair.

Anna felt her mouth parch. Although she'd half expected to be interrupted in her work, she hadn't thought it would be in her own chamber. But Seaver had wanted to see what she'd do—he'd said so himself. She swallowed two or three times before she could ask.

"How?"

"You should nail up that kitchen window. It's too easy to reach in and shove the bar from the door. Then up the stairs, just as you yourself came. But not before I watched you with Miller." He pulled an unopened bottle from his pocket, cut the red wax from the stopper, opened it. "I'll pour my own drinks, thanks. What is the verse? 'After she gave him drink, Jael went unto him with a peg of the tent and smote the nail into his temple'?"

"Near enough."

"A mistake teaching women to read. But then, if you couldn't read, you couldn't figure your books, and you wouldn't have such a brisk business as you do." He drank. "A double-edged sword. But as nice a bit of needlework as I've ever seen from a lady."

Keep breathing, Anna. You're not done yet. "What now?" She thought of the pistol in the trunk by the bed, the knife under her pillow. They might as well have been at the bottom of the harbor.

"A bargain. You're a widow with a tavern, I'm the agent of an important man. You also have a prime piece of real estate, and an eye on everything that happens along here. And, it seems, an eye to advancement. I think we can deal amiably enough, and to our mutual benefit."

At that moment, Anna almost wished Seaver would just cut her throat. She'd never be free of this succession of men, never able to manage by herself. The rage welled up in her, as it had never done before, and she thought she would choke on it. Then she remembered the paper hidden in her shoe, the document that made the tavern and its business wholly her own, and how she'd fought for it. She'd be damned before she handed it over to another man.

But she saw Seaver watching her carefully and it came to her. Perhaps like Miller not immediately grasping that the obvious next move for him was civil life and nearly legitimate trade—with all its fat skimming—she was not ambitious enough. Instead of mere survival, relying on the tavern, she could parlay it into more. Working with Seaver, who, after all, was only the errand boy of one of the most powerful—and dangerous—men in New England, she might do more than survive. She saw the beginning of a much wider, much richer future.

The whole world open to her, if she kept sharp. If she could be better than she was.

She went over to the mantel, took down a new bottle, opened it, poured herself a drink. Raised the glass.

She would pour her own drinks, and Seaver would pour his own. She would manage.

"To our mutual benefit," she toasted.

• • •

DANA CAMERON uses her archaeological training to explore the darker side of humanity—and the past—in fiction. Her "colonial noir" story, "Femme Sole," was honored with Edgar and Agatha nominations. She's not afraid of werewolves and vampires, either; her urban fantasy "The Night Things Changed" (Wolfsbane and Mistletoe, 2009) won an Agatha and a Macavity. More "Fangborn" stories are on the way, starting with "Swing Shift" in the MWA anthology

Crimes by Moonlight (2010). A member of the American Crime Writers League, The Femmes Fatales, Mystery Writers of America, and a past president of the New England chapter of Sisters in Crime, Dana lives in Massachusetts with her husband and feline overlords. Learn more at www.danacameron.com.

THE DARK ISLAND

By Brendan DuBois

Boston Harbor

She was waiting for me when I came back from the corner store and I stopped, giving her a quick scan. She had on a dark blue dress, black sensible shoes, and a small blue hat balanced on the back of thick brown hair. A small black leather purse was held in her hands, like she knew she was in a dangerous place and was frightened to lose it. On that last part, she was right, for it was evening and she was standing in Boston's Scollay Square, with its lights, horns, music, honky-tonks, burlesque houses, and hordes of people with a sharp taste who came here looking for trouble, and more often than not, finding it.

I brushed past a group of drunk sailors in their dress blues as I got up to my corner, the sailors no doubt happy that with the war over, they didn't have to worry about crazed kamikazes smashing into their gun turrets, burning to death out there in Pacific. They blew past me and went up to one of the nearby bars and ducked in. There were other guys out there as well, and I could always spot the recently discharged vets: they moved quickly, their eyes flicking around, and whenever there was a loud horn or a backfire from a passing truck, they would freeze in place.

And then, of course, they would unfreeze. There were years of drinking and raising hell to catch up on.

I shifted my paper grocery sack from one hand to another, and went up to the woman, touched the brim of my fedora with my free hand. "Are you waiting for me?" I asked.

Her face was pale and frightened, like a young mom, seeing blood on her child for the very first time. "Are you Billy Sullivan?"

"Yep."

"Yes, I'm here to see you."

I shrugged. "Then follow me, miss."

I went past her and opened the wooden door that led to a small foyer, and then upstairs, the wooden stairs creaking under our footfalls. At the top of the stairs a narrow hallway led off, three doors on each side, each door with a half-frame of frosted glass. Mine said B. SULLIVAN, INVESTIGATIONS, and two of the windows down the hallway were blank. The other three announced a watchmaker, a piano teacher, and a press agent.

I unlocked the door and flicked on the light and walked in. There was an old oak desk in the center with my chair, a Remington typewriter on a stand, and two solid filing cabinets with locks. In front of the desk were two wooden chairs, and I motioned my guest to the nearest one. A single window that hadn't been washed since Hoover was president overlooked the square and its flickering neon lights.

"Be right back," I said, ducking through a curtain off to the side. Beyond the curtain was a small room with a bed, radio, easy chair, table lamp, and icebox. A closed door led to a small bathroom that most days had plenty of hot water. I put a bottle of milk away, tossed the bread on a counter next to the toaster and hotplate, and then went back out to my office. I took my coat off and my hat, and hung both on a coat rack.

The woman sat there, leaning forward a bit, like she didn't want her back to be spoiled by whatever cooties resided in my office. She looked at me and tried to smile. "I thought all private detectives carried guns."

I shook my head. "Like the movies? Roscoes, heaters, gats, all that nonsense? Nah, I saw enough guns the last couple of years. I don't need one, not for what I do."

At my desk, I uncapped my Parker pen and grabbed a legal pad, and said, "You know my name, don't you think you should return the favor?"

She nodded quickly. "Of course. The name is Mandy Williams ... I'm from Seattle."

I looked up. "You're a long way from home."

Tears formed in the corner of her eyes. "I know, I know ... and it's all going to sound silly, but I hope you can help me find something."

"Something or someone?" I asked.

"Something," she said. "Something that means the world to me."

"Go on."

She said, "This is going to sound crazy, Mr. Sullivan, so please ... bear with me, all right?"

"Sure."

She took a deep breath. "My fiancé, Roger Thompson, he was in the Army and was stationed here in Boston, before he was shipped overseas."

I made a few notes on the pad, kept my eye on her. She said, "We kept in touch, almost every day, writing letters back and forth, sending each other mementoes. Photos, souvenirs, stuff like that ... and he told me he kept everything I sent to him in a shoebox, kept in his barracks. And I told him I did the same ... kept everything that he sent to me."

Now she opened her purse, took out a white tissue, which she dabbed at her eyes. "Silly, isn't it ... it's been nearly a year ... I know I'm not making sense, it's just that Roger didn't come back. He was killed a few months before the war was over."

My hand tightened on the pen. "Sorry to hear that."

"Oh, what can you do, you know? And ever since then, well, I've gone on, you know? Have even thought about dating again ... and then ..."

The tissue went back to work and I waited. So much of my working life is waiting, waiting for a phone call, waiting for someone to show up, waiting for a bill to be paid. She coughed and said, "Then, last month, I got a letter from a buddy of his. Name of Greg Fleming. Said they were bunkmates here in Boston. And they shipped out together, first to France and then to the frontlines. And Greg told me that Roger said that before he left, he hid that shoebox in his barracks. He was afraid the box would get lost or spoiled if he brought it overseas with him."

"I see," I said, though I was practically lying. "And why do you need me? Why not go to the base and sweet talk the duty officer, and find the barracks your fiancé was staying at?"

"Because ... because the place he was training at, it's been closed since the war was over. And it's not easy to get to."

"Where is it?"

Another dab of the tissue. "It's out on Boston Harbor. On one of the islands. Gallops Island. That's where Roger was stationed."

The place was familiar to me. "Yeah, I remember Gallops. It was used as a training facility. For cooks, radiomen and medics. What did your man train for?"

"Radioman," she said simply. "Later ... later I found out that being a radioman was so very dangerous. You were out in the open, and German snipers liked to shoot at a radioman and the officer standing next to him ... that's, that's what happened to Roger. There was some very fierce fighting and he was ... he was ... oh God, they blew his head off ..."

And then she bowed and started weeping in her tissue, and I sat there, feeling like my limbs were made of cement, for I didn't know what the hell to do, so I cleared my throat and said, "Sorry, miss ... look, can I get you something to drink?"

The tissue was up against her face and she shook her head. "No, no, I don't drink."

I pushed away from my desk. "I was thinking of something a bit less potent. I'll be right back."

• • •

About ten minutes later, after spending time in my private quarters and hovering over the hotplate, I came back with two chipped white china mugs, and passed one over to her. She took a sip and seemed surprised. "Tea?"

"Yeah," I said, sitting back down. "A bit of a secret, so please don't tell on me, okay? You know the reputation we guys like to maintain."

She smiled, and I felt like I had won a tiny victory. "How in the world did you ever start drinking tea?"

I shrugged. "Picked up the habit when I was stationed in England."

"You were in the Army?"

I nodded. "Yep."

"What did you do?"

I took a sip from my own mug. "Military police. Spent a lot of time guarding fences, ammo dumps or directing traffic. Pretty boring. Never really heard a shot fired in anger, though a couple of times, I did hear Kraut artillery as we were heading east when I got over to France."

"So you know war, then."

"I do."

"And I'm sure you know loss, as well."

Again, the tightening of my hand. "Yeah, I know loss."

And she must have sensed the change in my voice, for she stared at me and said, "Who was he?"

I couldn't speak for a moment, and then I said, "My older brother. Paul."

"What happened?"

I suppose I should have kept my mouth shut, but there was something about her teary eyes that just got to me. I cleared my throat. "He was 82nd Airborne. Wounded at the Battle of the Bulge. Mortar shrapnel. They were surrounded by the Krauts, and I guess it took a long time for him to die ..."

"So we both know, don't we."

"Yeah." I looked down at the pad of paper. "So. What do you need me for?"

She twisted the crumpled bit of tissue in her hands. "I ... I don't know how to get to that island. I've sent letters to everyone I can think of, in the Army and in Congress, and no one can help me out ... and I found out that the island is now restricted. There's some sort of new radar installation being built there ... no one can land on the island."

I knew where this was going but I wanted to hear it from her. "All right, but let me say again, Miss Williams, why do you need me?"

She waited, waited for what seemed to be a long time. She took a long sip from her tea. There were horns from outside, a siren, and I could hear music from the nearest burlesque hall. "Um ... well, I've been here for a week ... asking around ... at the local police station ... asking about a detective who might help me, one from around here, one who knows the harbor islands ..."

"And my name came up? Really? From who?"

"A ... a desk sergeant. Name of O'Connor."

I grimaced. Fat bastard, never got over the fact that my dad beat up his dad ten or fifteen years ago at some Irish tavern in Southie, and always gave me crap every time he saw me. "All right. What did he tell you?"

"That you used to work with your dad in the harbor, pulling in lobster pots, working after school and summers, and he said ... well, he said ..."

"Go on, Miss Williams. What did he say?"

"He said, 'if anyone could get me out to the islands and back, it'd be that thick-skulled mick Billy Sullivan.'"

I tried not to smile. "Yeah, that sounds like the good sergeant."

She looked at me and her voice softened, and she said, "Please, Mister Sullivan. I ... I don't know what else to do. I can't get out there without your help, and getting those memories from my man ... that would mean the world to me."

"If the island is off-limits during the day, it means we'll have to go out at night. Do you understand, Miss Williams?"

She seemed a bit surprised. "I ... I thought I could draw you a map, a description, something like that."

I shook my head. "Not going to work. I'm not going out to Gallops Island at night without you with me. If I find that box of mementoes for you, I want you right there, to check it out."

"But—"

"If that's going to be a problem, Miss Williams, then I'm afraid I can't help you."

My potential client sounded meek. "I ... I don't like boats ... but no, it won't be a problem."

"Good. My rates are fifty dollars a day, plus expenses ... but this should be relatively easy. And that fifty dollars has to be paid in advance."

She opened her purse, deftly pulled out three tens and a twenty, which I scooped up and put into my top desk drawer. I tore off a sheet of paper and wrote something down, and slid it over to her. "There. Address in South Boston. Little fishing and tackle shop, with a dock to the harbor. I'll see you there tomorrow at 6:00 PM. Weather permitting, it should be easy."

My new client folded up the piece of paper and put it in her purse, and then stood up, held out a hand with manicured red nails. "Oh, I can't thank you enough, Mister Sullivan. This means so much to me, and—"

I shook her hand and said, "It's too early to thank me, Miss Williams. If we get there and get your shoebox, then you can thank me then."

She smiled and then walked to the door, and I eyed her legs and the way she moved. "Tomorrow, then."

"Tomorrow," I said.

And then she shut the door.

I counted about fifteen seconds, and then, probably no doubt to the surprise of my new client if she knew, I immediately went to work.

. . .

I put on my hat and coat, and went out, locking the door behind me. I took the steps, two at a time, and then went out to the chaos that was Scollay Square, and then I spotted her, heading up Tremont Street. I dodged some more sailors and some loud red-faced businessmen, the kind who had leather cases full of samples and who decided to raise hell in big bad Boston before crawling back to their safe little homes in Maine or New Hampshire.

My client went around the corner, and then, when I made the corner, I had lost her.

Damn.

I looked up and down the street, saw some traffic, more guys moving around, but not my client. A few feet away was a man in a wheelchair, with a tartan blanket covering the stumps that used to be his legs. Tony Blawkowski, who was holding a cardboard sign: HELP AN INJURED VET. I went over to him and said, "Ski."

"Yeah."

He was staring out at the people going by, shaking a cardboard coffee cup filled with coins. "You see a young gal come this way?"

"Good lookin', small leather purse in her hands, hat on top of her pretty little head."

"That's the one."

"Nope, didn't see a damn thing," he said, smiling, showing off yellow teeth.

I reached into my pocket, tossed a quarter in his cup. "Well, that's nice, refreshin' my memory like that," Ski said. "Thing is, she came right by here, wigglin' that fine bottom of hers, gave me no money, the stuck-up broad, and then she got into a car and left."

Somehow the noise of the horns and the burlesque hall music seemed to drill into my head. "You sure?"

"Damn straight. A nice Packard, clean and shiny, was parked there for a while, and then she got in and left."

"You see who was in the Packard?"

"You got another quarter?"

I reached back into my pocket, and there was another clink as the coin went into his cup. He laughed. "Nope. Didn't see who was in there, or who was driving. They jus' left. That's all."

"All right, Ski," I said. "Tell you what, you see that Packard come back, you let me know, all right?"

Ski said, "What's in it for me?"

I smiled. "Keeping your secret, for one."

He shook his head. "Bastard. You do drive a hard bargain."

"Only kind I got tonight."

I walked away and then looked back, as a couple of out-of-towners dropped some coins in Ski's cup, and thought about the sign. It was true, for Ski was an injured vet. He had been in the Army and one night, on leave here in town a couple of years ago, he got drunk out of his mind, passed out in front of a bar, and was run over by an MTA trolley, severing both legs.

Nice little story, especially the lesson it gave, for never accepting what you see on the surface.

• • •

About a half hour later, I was at the local district headquarters of the Boston Police Department, where I found Sergeant Francis Xavier O'Connor, sitting behind a chest-high wooden desk, passing on whatever was considered justice in this part of Boston. In the lobby area, the tile floor yellow and stained, two women in bright red lipstick, hands cuffed together, shared a cigarette while sitting on a wooden bench. O'Connor had a folded-over copy of the *Boston*

American in his hands, his face red and flush, and he glanced up at me as I approached the desk.

"Ah, Beantown's biggest dick," he said, looking down at me over half-glasses.

"Nice to see you, too, sergeant. Thought you'd be spending some time up at your vacation spot, up at Conway Lake."

"Bah, the hell with you," O'Connor said. "What kind of trash are you lookin' for tonight?"

I leaned up against the desk, my wrists on the wooden edge. "What I'm looking for is right in front of me."

"Eh?"

"Quick question," I said. "Got a visit tonight from a young lady, mid-twenties, said she was from Seattle, looking for some help. She told me she came here, talked to you, and somehow, my name came up. Why's that?"

He grinned, bounced the edge of the folded-over newspaper against his chin. "Ah, I remember that little flower. Came sauntering in, sob story in one hand, a Greyhound bus ticket in the other, and she told me what kind of man she was lookin' for, and what the hell. I gave her your name and address. You should be grateful."

I said, "More curious than grateful. Come on, Francis, answer the question. Why me?"

He leaned over, close enough so I could smell old onions coming from his breath. "Figure it out. Young gal had some spending money, spent it for some info ... a name. And you know what? Her story sounded screwy enough so that it might fuck over whoever decided to take her on as a client, and your name was first, second, and third on my list. Any more questions, dick?"

I stepped away from the desk. "Yeah," I said. "Your dad's nose still look like a lumpy potato after my dad finished him off?"

His face grew more red and he said, "Asshole, get out of my station."

• • •

The next night I went into the Shamrock Fish & Tackle, off L Street in South Boston, near where I grew up, and in the crowded place, I went by the rows of fishing tackle, rods, other odds and ends. Out in the back, smoking a cigar and nursing a Narragansett Beer, Roddy Taylor looked up as I came in. He had on a sleeveless T-shirt that was probably white at one time, and khaki pants. He was mostly bald but tufts of hair grew from his thick ears.

"Corporal Sullivan, what are you up to tonight?"

"Looking to borrow an outboard skiff, if that's all right with you."

"Hell, of course."

"And stop calling me corporal."

He laughed and leaned back, snagged a key off a nail on the wall. He tossed it to me and I caught it with my right hand. "Number five."

"Okay, number five."

"How's your mom?" Roddy asked.

"Not good," I said. "She ... well, you know."

He took a puff from his cigar. "Yeah. Still thinking your brother's coming home. Am I right?"

I juggled the key in my hand. "I'll bring it back sometime tonight."

"Best to your mom."

"You got it."

• • •

Outside I went to my old Ford, went into the back seat and took out a canvas gym bag. From the dirt parking lot I went out to a dock and went down the line of skiffs and boats, found the one with a painted number four on the side, and undid the lock. I tossed my gym bag in the open skiff, near the small fuel tank and the drain plug at the stern. I stood up and stretched. Overhead lights had come on, illuminating the near empty parking lot and the dock and the line of moored boats.

She was standing at the edge of the dock. She still had her leather purse but the skirt had been replaced by slacks and flat shoes.

"Miss Williams," I said.

"Please," she said, coming down the dock. "Please call me Mandy."

"All right, Mandy it is," I said.

She came down the dock and looked down at the skiff. "It looks so small."

"It's big enough for where we're going," I said.

"Are you sure?"

"I grew up around here, Miss—"

"Mandy."

"Mandy, I've grown up around here." I looked about the harbor, at the lights coming on at the shoreline of Boston harbor and the islands scattered out there at the beginnings of the Atlantic Ocean. "I promise you, I'll get you out and back again in no time."

She seemed to think about that for just a bit, and then nodded. She came closer and gingerly put one foot into the boat, as I held her hand. Her hand felt good. "Up forward," I said. "Take the seat up forward."

My client clambered in and I followed. I undid the stern line and gently pushed us off, and then primed the engine by using a squeeze tube from the small fuel tank. A flick of the switch and a couple of tugs with the rope starter, and the small Mercury engine burbled into life. We made our way out of the docks and then were on the waters of Boston Harbor, motoring into the coming darkness, my right hand on the handle and throttle of the Mercury engine.

• • •

After about five minutes she turned and said, "Where are the life jackets?"

"You figuring on falling in?"

She had a brittle laugh. "No, not at all. I'd just like to know, that's all."

I motioned with my free hand. "Up forward. And nothing to worry, Mandy. I boated out here before I went to grade school, and haven't fallen in yet."

She turned into herself, the purse on her lap, and I looked over at the still waters of the harbor. It was early evening, the water pretty flat, the smell of the salt air pretty good after spending hours and hours on Scollay Square. Off to the left, the north, were the lights of Boston Airport, and out on the waters were the low shapes of the score or so more of the islands of Boston Harbor. Off to the right was Boston Harbor, and the lights of the moored freighters.

One of the islands was now off to starboard and Mandy said, "What island is that?"

"Thompson," I said.

"I see buildings there. A fort?"

I laughed. "Hardly. That's the home of the Boston Farm and Trade School."

"The what school?"

"Farm and trade. A fancy name for a school for boys who get into trouble. Like a reform school. One last chance before you get sent off to juvenile hall or an adult prison."

She turned and in the fading light I could make out her pretty smile. "Sounds like you know that place first-hand."

"Could have, if I hadn't been lucky."

Now we passed Thompson and up ahead was a low-slung island that had no lights, and the wind shifted and there was a sour smell, and Mandy said, "What in God's name is that?"

"That's Spectacle Island. That's where Boston dumps its trash. Lots of garbage up there, and probably the bodies of a few gangsters. Good place to lose something."

"You know your islands."

"Sure," I said. "They all have a story. All have legends. Indians, privateers, ghosts, pirates, buried treasure ... everything and anything."

Now we passed a lighthouse, and I said, "Long Island," but Mandy didn't seem to care. There was another, smaller island ahead, and I said, "That's Gallops. You ready?"

"Yes," she said, her voice strained. "Quite ready."

• • •

I ran the skiff aground on a bit of sandy beach, and waded in the water, dragging a bowline up, tying it off some scrub brush. There was a dock just down the way, with a path leading up to the island, and by now it was pretty dark. From my gym bag I took out a flashlight and cupped the beam with my hand, making sure only a bit of light escaped.

"I want to make this quick, okay?"

She nodded.

"I asked around," I said. "I know where the barracks are. Now, do you know where his bunk was located?"

"Next to a window overlooking the east, in the far corner," she said. "He always complained that the morning sun would hit his eyes and wake him up before reveille."

"All right," I said. "Let's go."

. . .

From the path near the dock, it was pretty easy going, much to my surprise. The place was deserted and there were no lights, but my own flashlight did a good job of illuminating the way. We went along a crushed stone path and halfway there, something small and furry burst out of the brush, scaring the crap out of me and making Mandy cry out. She grabbed my free hand and wouldn't let it go, and I didn't complain. It felt good, and she kept her hand in mine all the way up to the barracks.

A lot of the windows were smashed, and the door leading inside was hanging free from its hinges. We went up the wide steps and gingerly stepped in. I flashed the light around. The roof had leaked and there were puddles of water on the floor. We went to the left, where there was a great open room, stretching out into the distance. I slashed the light around again. Rusting frames for bunks were piled high in the corner, and there was an odd, musty smell to the place. Lots of old memories came roaring back, being in a building like this, smelling those old scents, of the soap and the cleaning and the gun oil ... and the smell of the men, of course.

I squeezed Mandy's hand and she squeezed back. Here we had all come, from all across the country, to train and to learn and to get ready to fight ... and no matter what crap the RKO movies showed you, we were all scared shitless. It was a terrible time and place, to come together, to know that so many of you would never come back ... torn up, blown up, shattered, burned, crushed, drowned. So many ways to die ... and now to come back to what was called peace and prosperity and hustle and bustle and try to keep ahead. What a time.

"Let's go," I whispered, not sure why I was whispering. "I want to get out of here before someone spots our light."

"Yes," she whispered back, and it was like we were in church or something. I led my client down the way, our footsteps echoing off the wood, and I kept the light low, until we came to the far corner, the place where the windows looked out to the east, where a certain man had been in his bunk, the sun hitting his face every morning.

"Here," she whispered. "Shine the light over here."

She knelt down at the corner of the room, her fingers prying at a section of baseboard, and even though I half-expected it, I was still surprised. The board came loose and Mandy cried out a bit, and I lowered the flashlight and illuminated a small cavity.

"Hold on," I said, "you don't know what—"

But she didn't listen to me. She pushed her right hand and arm and rummaged around, and she murmured, "Oh, Roger. Oh, my Roger,"

She pulled her hand back, holding a shoebox for Bass shoes, the damp cardboard held together with gray tape. She clasped the box against her chest and leaned over, silently weeping, I think, as her body shook and trembled.

I gave her a minute or two, and then touched her shoulder. "Mandy, come on, we've got to get out of here. And now."

And she got off her knees, wiped at her eyes, and with one hand, held the cardboard box and her small leather purse against her chest.

Her other hand took mine, and wouldn't let go, until we got back to the boat.

• • •

In the boat I pushed her off and started up the engine, and we started away from Gallops Island. The wind had come up some, nothing too serious, but there was a chop to the water that hadn't been there before. With the box in her lap, she turned and smiled at me, and then leaned forward to me. I returned the favor, and kissed her, and then kissed her again, and then our mouths opened and her hand squeezed my leg. "Oh, Billy ... I didn't think it would work ... I really didn't ... look, when we get back, we need to celebrate, okay?"

I liked her taste and her smell. "Sure. Celebrate. That sounds good."

But I kept on looking at the water.

I kicked up the throttle some more.

• • •

It didn't seem to take too long, and as we motored back to the docks of the Shamrock Fish & Tackle, Mandy turned to me and started talking, about her life in Seattle, about her Roger, and now that with this box in hand, she was ready to start a new life, and I tried to ignore her chatter as I got closer to the dock, and I looked up at the small parking lot, and there was an extra vehicle there.

A Packard, parked underneath a street lamp.

As I got closer to the docks, doors to the Packard opened up, and two men, with hats and topcoats and hands in their coats, got out.

Mandy was still chattering.

I worked the throttle, slipped the engine into neutral, and then reversed. The engine made a clunk-whine noise, as I backed out of the narrow channel leading into the docks, and Mandy was jostled, saying, "What the—"

"Hold on," I said, backing away even further, now going back into neutral, then forward, and then speeding away. I turned and saw the two guys climb back into the Packard and back out onto L Street. I turned and grabbed my flashlight and switched the engine off, and now we drifted, in the darkness, by all those dark islands. Mandy turned around, looked at me, and said, "Billy ... what the hell is going on?"

"You tell me," I said.

"I don't know what you mean."

"Mandy ... what's in the box?"

"I told you," she said, her voice rising. "Souvenirs! Letters! Photos! Stuff that means so much to me ..."

"And the guys in the Packard? Who are they? Friends of Roger who want to giggle over old photos of him in the Army?"

"I don't know what you mean, about—"

I pointed the flashlight at her face, flicked it on, startling her. I reached forward, snatched the damp box from her hands, sat back down. The boat rocked, a bit of spray hitting my arm. "Hey!" she called out, but now the box was in my lap.

I lowered the flashlight, seeing her face pursed and tight. "Let's go over a few things," I said. "You come into my office with a great tale, a great sob story. And you tell me you get hooked up with me because you just happened to run into one of the sleaziest, in-the-bag cops on the Boston force, a guy who can afford a pricey vacation home on a New Hampshire lake on a cop's salary. And right after you leave my office, a sweet girl, far, far away from home, you get into somebody's Packard. And now there's a Packard waiting for you, at dockside. Hell of a coincidence, eh? Not to mention the closer we got to shore, the more you blathered at me, trying to distract me."

She kept quiet, her hands now about her purse, firmly in her lap. "Anything to say?"

My client kept quiet. I held up the box. "What's in here, Mandy?"

Nothing.

"Mandy?"

I put the box in my lap, tore away at the tape and damp cardboard, and the top tore away easy enough. There was damp brown paper in the box, and the sound of smaller boxes moving against each other. I turned the box over a bit, shone the light in. Little yellow cardboard boxes, about the size of a small toothpaste container, all bundled together. There were scores of them. I shuddered, took a deep breath. I knew what they were. I looked up to her.

"Morphine," I said. "Morphine syrettes. Your guy ... if there was a guy there, he wasn't training as a radioman. He was training as a medic. And he was stealing this morphine, to sell later once the war was over. Am I right? Who the hell are you, anyway?"

My client said, "What difference does it make? Look, I had a job to do, to get that stuff off that island, easiest way possible, no fuss, no muss, and we did it. Okay? Get me to shore, you'll get ... a finder's fee, a percentage."

I shook the box, heard the other boxes rattle. "Worth a lot of money, isn't it."

She smiled. "You have no idea."

"But it was stolen. During war time."

"So what?" she said, her voice now showing a sharpness I had never heard before. "Guys went to war, some got killed, some figured out a way to score, to make some bucks ... and the guys I'm with, they figured it was time to look out for themselves, to set something up for later. So there you go. Nice deal all around. Don't you want part of it Billy? Hunh?"

I shook the box again, fought to keep my voice even. "Ever hear of Bastogne?"

"Maybe, who knows, who cares."

"I know, and I care," I said. "That's where my brother was, in December, 1944. Belgian town, surrounded by the Krauts. He took a chunk of shrapnel to the stomach. He was dying. Maybe he could have lived if he wasn't in so much pain ... but the medics, they were low on morphine. They could only use morphine on guys they thought they might live. So my brother ... no morphine ... he died in agony. Hours it took for him to die, because the medics were short on morphine."

Mandy said, "A great story, Billy. A very touching story. Look, you want a tissue or something?"

And moving quickly, she opened up her purse, and took out a small, nickel-plated semi-automatic pistol.

"Sorry, Billy, but this is how it's going to be. You're going to give me back my box, you're going to take me back to the dock, and if you're a good boy, I'll make sure only a leg or an arm gets broken. How's that for a deal?"

I thought for a moment, now staring at a face I didn't recognize, and I said, "I've heard better."

And I tossed the box and the morphine syrettes into the dark waters.

• • •

She screamed and shouted something, and I was moving quick, which was good, because she got off one shot that pounded over my head, as I ducked and grabbed something at the bottom of the boat, tugging it free, and then I fell overboard. The shock of the cold water almost made me open my mouth, but I was used to it, though never this cold. I came up, coughing, splashing, and my flashlight was still on the boat, still lit up, which made it easy for me to see what happened next.

The skiff was filling with water, as Mandy moved to the rear, the boat rocking, trying to get the engine started, I think, but with her added weight at the stern, the boat quickly swamped and flipped over, dumping her in. She screamed. She screamed again. "Billy! Please! I can't swim! Please!"

I held up my hand, holding the drainplug to the rear of the skiff, and let it go.

She floundered some more. Splashing. Yelling. Coughing. It would be easy enough to get over there, calm her down, put her in the approved life-saving mode, my arm about her, to get her safely to shore. So easy to do, for I could find her in the darkness, just by following the splashes and the yells.

The yells. I had heard later from someone in my brother's platoon, how much he had yelled, towards the end.

I moved some, was able to gauge where she was, out there in the darkness.

And then I turned and swam in the other direction.

• • •

BRENDAN DUBOIS is the award-winning author of eleven novels and more than one hundred short stories. His short fiction has appeared in *Playboy, Ellery Queen's Mystery Magazine, Alfred Hitchcock's Mystery Magazine,* and numerous other magazines and anthologies, including *The Best American Mystery Stories of the Century,* published in 2000 by Houghton-Mifflin. His short stories have twice won him the Shamus Award from the Private Eye Writers of America, and have also earned him three Edgar Award nominations from the Mystery Writers of America. Visit his website at www.BrendanDuBois.com.

THE CARETAKER

By Terence Faherty

One

"Jackson Hole is the name of the valley. Jackson is the town. Never call the town Jackson Hole, or people will think you're a flatlander."

To Anne Abbott's ear, the person offering this advice sounded like a flatlander himself—from Iowa, perhaps, or Kansas—but she didn't call him on it. She needed the job he'd offered her too badly. And she liked this real estate manager, Wayne Sedam. True, he spent more time on his hair and clothes than the men she'd grown up around, though in keeping with the local convention his current outfit—sheepskin coat, jeans, and cowboy boots—was elaborately casual. But he hadn't balked at the idea of hiring a female caretaker for one of the properties under his charge, Osprey House. The previous caretaker had left without notice to join a cowboy band, so Sedam was well motivated if not desperate. Still, Anne was grateful.

They were standing on the flagstone patio behind the house as they spoke. Anne was admiring the log home's many windows and gables. In one of the French doors, she caught her own reflection and appraised it: tall, broad shouldered, and plain. The sketch made her sigh, and she glanced quickly at Sedam to see if he'd noticed. He was examining the neighboring mansion.

"This part of the valley was all little ranches not many years ago," he said. "Now it's half ranches and half estates. Ten years from now, you'll have to drive down to Hoback Junction if you want to see a cow."

Anne, who'd lived all her life around cows, doubted she'd put forth the effort, but she nodded as though carefully making a mental note as Sedam went on.

"Neither Osprey House or that place over there is rented out when the owners are away, which is most of the year. In fact, I doubt the owners of Osprey House will ever be back. It was built by a dot com millionaire named Zollman as a vacation home for the skiing season. His wife took one look around Jackson and lit out for the coast. Wyoming was too far from Malibu for her. She'd like her husband to sell the place, but he's run off to sulk somewhere in the South Pacific and no one can get hold of him."

Thank God for that, Anne thought, *or I'd be waiting tables somewhere.* She'd come to Wyoming to work as a guide on the Snake River, but the short summer season wouldn't feed her all year. The caretaker's job was ideal, giving her a place to live as well as a steady income. Mrs. Zollman might not have cared for Jackson Hole, but to Anne it was close to heaven, even if it did snow in late May.

It was flurrying now. Sedam was holding the lapels of his beautiful coat tightly together with one hand, his attention still absorbed by the large house across the meadow. It was cedar-sided with chimneys and front porch pillars of stacked stone.

"What's that place called?" Anne asked.

"Millikan House, after the owners, a husband and wife team of New York cardiologists. They should have called the place Heart Disease House, after what paid for it. The Millikans come out for two weeks in the winter and five weeks in the summer. Those years we have a summer. Let's go inside."

Sedam showed her from room to room, starting in a large television and game room with fireplace and cathedral ceiling. The gourmet kitchen was open to a farmhouse style dining room, the long table of which could seat twelve. Anne pictured the Zollmans sitting at opposite ends of that table, glowering at each other. The master suite, its bathroom larger than any apartment Anne had ever rented, and a mechanical room completed the ground floor. The latter held duplicate hot water tanks and furnaces.

Sedam explained the redundancy. "Because of the log construction, there are no ducts in the house. Heating is by hot water. One system supplies the radiators, the other the sinks and showers. All running continuously, per the owner's last orders. You should see the bills. By the way, you will see the cleaning people. They come once a week, also according to orders. I don't know what they find to clean."

Upstairs there were four more bedrooms, each with its own bath. Throughout the house, the gray daylight was warmed by the honey color of the walls. The logs were so perfectly smooth that Anne ran her fingers along them to convince herself that they were really wood. Nowhere in the house did she see a personal touch, a family photograph or a book.

Her own quarters were in a small ranch house behind the four-car garage. Compared with Osprey House, it was Spartan, but Anne fell in love with it at first sight. She had to fight the temptation to seize its keys from Sedam when, at the end of their tour, he displayed his first reservations.

"I feel a little guilty about leaving you out here by yourself," he said, as he twirled the key ring maddeningly on one finger. "You're only a few miles from town, I know, but this is a lonely spot. Feel free to call my cell if you're ever uncomfortable."

Anne asked herself if this manicured man might be interested in her. But before she'd more than worded the thought, Sedam added, "Or you could call Gitry."

"Gitry?"

"He's the Millikans' caretaker." Sedam waved the keys in the direction of the cedar house. "It's not one of my properties—it's managed out of Cheyenne, a stupid arrangement—so I don't really know the man, except by his reputation. He's become a little bit of a recluse, from what I hear. And a man of mystery. Still, if some emergency comes up, I'm sure he'll help out. You caretakers have to stand by one another."

"It's part of your code," he added, laughing.

He handed Anne the keys, pressing them into her hand. "Good luck."

Two

One week later, Anne paused on her morning run to admire the beauty of her valley. To the north, beyond Jackson, the snow-covered and jagged Grand Tetons stood out against a deep blue, cloudless sky. To the east and nearer to hand were the foothills of the Wyoming Range, already clear of snow and very green. They'd be covered in wild flowers in a week or two if the weather would only hold. Anne resumed her run, climbing high enough into those hills to gain a panoramic view of the spur valley in which Osprey House stood.

That morning there was a low fog in the valley, so low that the taller trees and rooftops pierced it. Anne heard the cattle calling to one another on a nearby ranch and felt a delicious guilt. Those cows were someone else's responsibility, not hers. Then a pair of trumpeter swans flew past her just above the fog bank, honking to each other as they went, as though arguing about directions.

"The Zollmans," she thought, "reincarnated."

The swans' noisy flight took them directly over Millikan House.

"That'll wake you up, Mr. Gitry."

She'd yet to glimpse her fellow caretaker, though she'd spent most of her first week in the valley watching for him. There'd been little else for her to do. No snow had fallen, so she couldn't plow, and the grass wasn't growing yet, so she couldn't mow. She'd started the tractor and the ATV and changed the oil in each. She'd set out family photos and well-worn novels around the little ranch house, giving it something the log mansion lacked. And she'd watched for Gitry.

His failure to appear was intriguing to her, more intriguing even than Wayne Sedam's description of Gitry: a man of mystery. Her practical side told her to be patient, as it often did. Gitry was simply holed up like she was, waiting for the seasons to sort themselves out.

She lost what little warmth the recently risen sun was providing when she descended again into the valley proper. The fog that was holding off that sun reflected and amplified the very regular sound of her footfalls and the complaints of the magpies she disturbed as she followed an overgrown fence row.

It also shrouded Millikan House. Its doctor builders had flaunted their wealth with an overabundance of gables and dormers and chimneys. Seeing it now, almost in silhouette, Anne was reminded of an English manor from one of her favorite books. At least, she was reminded of her mental picture of such a place.

She was about to turn for the last sprint to breakfast when she saw a figure come around one corner of Millikan House. The form was no more distinct than the building, but Anne could tell it was a man of medium height and slight build who was walking with a limp. The elusive Mr. Gitry.

Without breaking stride, Anne raised an arm in greeting. The other turned abruptly and hobbled away.

Three

The next morning, Anne sat in a small, storefront coffee shop, the Elk Horn Café, a block from Jackson's town square. Across from her was the woman Anne considered her real boss, Mattie Koval, owner and head river guide of Snake River Explorers.

"We're starting to get some serious snow melt," Koval said. "From now until the Fourth of July, the Snake will be running so fast we'll be doing our four-hour float trip in two and a half. If you were on the river right now, you'd hear the rocks on the bottom clacking together like billiard balls. It's the worst time to train you or the best time, depending on how game you are."

"Bring it on," Anne said.

She'd been trying to guess Koval's age, without success. The weathered skin of the guide's face and neck suggested that she was in her forties. But the long blonde hair, secured in a loose pony tail, and toned body belonged to a much younger woman. Working the long sweeps of a raft loaded down with tourists kept you in shape, Anne decided.

Koval noticed Anne examining her arm. She held it up and flexed the biceps.

"Not much now, after a winter of flipping through catalogs, but nobody wants to arm wrestle me come Labor Day. You won't have any trouble handling a raft, either, not a big girl like you."

Anne unconsciously stooped in her chair, and Koval laughed. "Never be ashamed of being tall," she said. "You can't be too tall or too rich."

"You can so be too rich," the waitress busing the table behind Koval said.

"How's that Rachel?" Koval asked. As she did, she winked at Anne, as though to say, "Watch this."

The woman threw her rag down on the table she'd been cleaning and crossed to them. She was olive-skinned and as solid as Koval was spare. Anne was sure she wouldn't want to arm wrestle the waitress before or after Labor Day.

"I said you can so be too rich," Rachel repeated. "It isn't the rich who are ruining this valley. It's the too damned rich. The people so rich they don't need to rent their houses out when they're not in them. It's bad enough to lose the ranch land, but if we don't pick up tourists in exchange, we're sunk. We need rental properties turning over every week or two, new people buying groceries and T-shirts, eating out, booking raft trips. We don't need big places sitting empty, giving work to one layabout caretaker apiece. Present company excepted," she added to Anne.

Before Anne could ask how Rachel knew about her other job, Koval said, "I mentioned that you were looking after a house."

"Osprey House," Anne volunteered.

"Oh," Rachel said. "So you're out there in the boonies with Chaz Gitry."

She and Koval exchanged significant looks.

"Chaz is our local lothario," Koval explained. "Snowboard instructor in the winter, mountain guide in the summer, hound dog all year long."

"I've heard he's mysterious," Anne said.

"Heard that from a man, I'll bet," Koval said. "There isn't a man around here who can understand Chaz's success with the ladies. Shaggy and homely he may be, but the boy's got something."

"She's talking about the ex-wife," Rachel said to Koval. "She's what's so mysterious." Her attitude had softened somewhat at the mention of Gitry. Now it hardened all over again. "She sneaks in to see him about once a month. Chaz got plenty cagey after that started happening."

"It's a good story, though," Koval said. "Kind of romantic."

Again, Anne leaned unconsciously, this time forward in her seat.

"Nobody even knew Chaz had been married until she started showing up six months back," Koval said, "wearing dark glasses and a scarf over her hair. She lives in Idaho somewhere. Idaho Falls, maybe, right across the state line. Drives in through the pass at Victor. Wimp Dragoo saw her up there once buying gas."

"Can't get away with anything around here," Rachel said, her look so pointed that Anne felt she was being warned.

To cover an incipient blush, Anne said, "There's an airport in Idaho Falls. Maybe she flies in from somewhere."

Rachel waved a dismissive hand. "There's a better airport right here in Jackson."

Koval said, "After she'd snuck in three months in a row, Chaz admitted the truth. Seems years back he married his childhood sweetheart, Laura. They were happy for a few years skiing and bumming around. Then Laura decided she wanted more. Chaz wouldn't change, so they parted ways. Laura must have found the success she was after. The one time I saw her, she was all in fur."

"But she couldn't get Chaz out of her system," Rachel cut in. "So she keeps coming back."

"He must not have gotten over her, either," Koval countered. "He hasn't been the same old Chaz since she started visiting. No more chasing around after every loose ski bunny. Comes into town less and less."

"Hasn't come at all in the last two weeks," Rachel said, as though it was a personal affront.

"He's become a recluse," Anne said, quoting Wayne Sedam again.

The waitress nodded. "I heard that last week he quit his mountain guide job. Left Bill Granger flat just when the season's about to start. Sent him an e-mail about hurting his leg."

"He was limping when I saw him this morning," Anne said.

"He'd better heal fast, then," Koval said. "Laura is overdue for a visit. There's been snow up in the passes until this week."

"Here's hoping for an avalanche," Rachel said and stomped away.

Four

That night, Anne settled in with a book in the living room of the little ranch. The book was a dog-eared romance novel, *Love's Forbidden Memory.* She'd selected it from her cache of similar titles because its plot—lovers separated by fortune and class but unable to forget one another—was similar to the tale she'd been told about Chaz Gitry and his Laura.

All the books Anne had brought with her were a legacy from her mother, who had died when Anne was very young. When Anne had turned sixteen, her father, the honest, practical man who'd raised her, had given her a box of her mother's things. In the bottom of the box, Anne had found a dozen yellowed paperbacks, all romance novels.

She'd come to think of the books as a message in a bottle from her dead mother, a glimpse into an alien world of excitement and feeling totally unlike the workaday ranch where she'd grown up.

Anne dozed over the novel's familiar pages and awoke to the sound of an alarm coming from one corner of the small front room. The source was the computer that monitored the security cameras and systems in Osprey House. Anne had used it to spy on the cleaning crew as they'd watched a soap opera in the log home's great room. Now the computer's screen was alternately flashing red and yellow.

Anne clicked on the single message being displayed: heating alert. A second message came up, informing her that the temperature in the main house had dropped to fifty-seven degrees. It should have been seventy-two. Anne knew that because Wayne Sedam had mentioned the setting as yet another example of the Zollmans' disregard for money.

As Anne struggled to shake off the last of her sleep, the displayed temperature dropped to fifty-six. She checked the outside temperature. Thirty-one.

Without bothering to get her coat off its peg, she grabbed the keys to Osprey House and followed the asphalt path to the back door. She'd entered the house and begun to switch on lights before it occurred to her that the temperature drop might have been caused by a burglar who'd defeated the security system and left a window or door open. She'd also forgotten to put down the book she'd been reading. She placed it on the ornate hallway table, whose carved legs were rearing dragons.

The inside of the furnace room was the warmest place in the house. One of the two duplicate systems was humming away, the one that provided hot water to the showers and the taps. The other made only the odd ticking noise, like a cooling car engine. Anne could see no leaking water and smell no escaping gas. She turned to the system's control panel, feeling like a character in a movie who has to select the right button from dozens to prevent a meltdown or an explosion. A single instruction blinked at her from the panel's LCD screen: standby. Anne weighed the advice, decided it was worth following, and retreated to the kitchen.

Once there, she debated with herself over whether to call Sedam, hesitating because of the hour, one o'clock, and because she hated to ruin her record of independence. As she debated, she happened to look out the window. A light was burning in the upper story of Millikan House, over the garage, she thought. Chaz Gitry's room, she was willing to bet.

She went back to the ranch house long enough to grab her down jacket and the keys to the ATV. She could have walked the distance easily, but she'd remembered Gitry's hurt leg. And the four-wheeler's barely muffled engine would announce her better than any doorbell.

Nevertheless, she rang the doorbell when she arrived at Millikan House. The porch light snapped on immediately, and Anne stepped back so Gitry could look her over though the front door's peep hole. When the door opened a crack, Anne was surprised to see that the room beyond it was dark.

"What do you want?" a man's voice asked.

"Mr. Gitry, I'm the new caretaker at—"

"I've seen you." The curt response was a restatement of the original question.

"Something's gone wrong with the heat over there," Anne said. "I'm afraid the pipes might freeze."

"Not that cold tonight," the other said. "You should make it through to morning. Call the manager then."

"He said I should ask you if I needed help. Said it was part of the caretaker's code."

She'd hoped for a laugh from Gitry but got a grunt instead. And an excuse: "I hurt my leg."

"I know. I'll drive you over and bring you back."

This time Gitry sighed. "Wait a minute."

Five

Anne was seated on the idling ATV when he came out, pulling on a coat that seemed too big for him. Koval had called him a boy, and Anne wondered now whether a boyish quality was part of Gitry's mysterious appeal.

He climbed on behind Anne, grasping her shoulder with one hand. "Okay."

At the house, Gitry headed for the mechanical room without waiting to be shown the way.

Anne said, "You know the place."

She got her first good look at him then, in the light of the front hall. As Koval had said, he was shaggy, his ginger hair unkempt and his razor stubble approaching a beard. But the river guide had also called Gitry homely, and Anne considered that a slight if not a slur. She thought Gitry's narrow face and sharp features would have been handsome but for his eyes. They were so dark-rimmed they almost looked bruised. And they were haunted. By thoughts of the lost Laura, Anne told herself. The unworthy Laura, who had turned her back on love.

"I should know my way around," Gitry was saying. "Your predecessor could never figure out the boilers, either. What happened to him?"

"Joined a band," Anne said.

Gitry grunted again. "I noticed the guitar playing had stopped. Thought the coyotes had complained."

Once inside the mechanical room, he glanced briefly at the control panel of the dormant unit and then began pressing buttons. "Happen to know the date?" he asked over his shoulder.

"It's the last day of May."

"Before midnight it was. Now it's the first day of June. That's why the thing went to standby mode. The genius who set it back in January told it to expect new instructions in June. Guess he didn't know anything about the weather up here. Thought it'd be balmy by now. Serves them right for putting in a system that has more brains than it needs to do a simple job."

By then, the furnace was humming. Gitry showed Anne what he had done, had her repeat the instructions, and led her back into the hallway. There he noticed the paperback she'd left on the Chinese table.

"*Love's Forbidden Memory,*" he read. "All memories of that poison should be forbidden. Yours?"

Anne plucked the book from his hand.

Gitry considered her curiously. "This mausoleum have a coffee pot?"

"There's one in my place," Anne said. Before Gitry could jump to the wrong conclusion, she added, "We shouldn't use the Zollmans' stuff."

"Why not? They won't be using it again. And I'm pretty sure that caretaker's code of yours has a clause about grabbing whatever you can. Kitchen this way?"

He went off without waiting for an answer, limping more than ever. Following along, Anne asked, "How did you hurt your leg? Snowboarding?"

"Chopping wood. Hell of a thing for a caretaker to admit."

"Your mind must have been somewhere else," Anne almost said, biting it off at the last second. Instead she asked how he knew the Zollmans. "I heard they were only here once."

Gitry had located the coffee maker. He concentrated for a moment on filling the pot at the island sink. Then he said, "She was only here once. He came out regularly while this place was being built. It was his baby. Presented it to the missus like a proud cat presenting a dead mouse. Went over like a dead mouse, too. There's a moral there somewhere."

"Let your wife pick the house?" Anne asked.

"More like, if you've got to make payments on a wife, make damn sure your checks don't bounce."

He wasn't really speaking of the Zollmans now, Anne decided. He was speaking of Laura, the woman who had tired of Gitry's hand-to-mouth life.

Anne realized with a start that the caretaker was addressing her. "You awake? I asked where the coffee was. Never mind. I found it."

While it brewed, Gitry limped to the windows that faced the lights he'd left burning. He stared out for a long time without speaking.

Forget her, Anne thought, *She's no good.* Aloud, she said, "She won't come tonight. It's too late."

Gitry turned on her, his bruised eyes flashing. Then his gaze widened to take in the dark timbers around them, the steaming coffee maker, the neon-bordered clock that glowed above the sinks.

"It is late," he said. "Sorry. I haven't talked to anyone in a while. Didn't realize you could miss it so much. I'll drive myself back. You can pick up the ATV in the morning when you finish your run."

Six

Anne spent the next morning replacing a fence post on one corner of the Zollman property. It was the corner closest to Millikan House, but that was only a coincidence, as Anne told herself repeatedly. The fence post was certainly rotten or at least showing a tendency that way. The project took hours of what turned out to be her first warm day in Jackson, but Gitry never appeared.

She regretted the soreness in her shoulders later when she reported to the headquarters of Snake River Explorers for a training session. Leaving her cats to mind the ramshackle building, Mattie Koval loaded her entire staff—two experienced guides, two trainee guides, and a grizzled driver—into one of her two white vans and headed north out of Jackson on 191.

The route took them past the National Elk Refuge, a huge expanse of bottom land drained by the Snake's tributaries, where, according to Koval's running commentary, thousands of elk gathered to shelter and feed in the winter. On the other side of the highway was the Jackson airport. Anne watched an airliner on final approach, its wings rocking in the winds off the Tetons, and thought of Rachel, the stout waitress. The connection escaped Anne for a moment. Then she remembered Rachel's curt dismissal of the idea that Gitry's Laura might be flying in from distant parts because she would never have chosen Idaho Falls' airport over Jackson's. Something about that reasoning had bothered Anne at the time and bothered her again now.

She was still thinking about it when they arrived at Moose Junction and unloaded one of the big red rafts from the trailer behind the van. Anne then watched as Koval prepared herself, donning first a compact life vest, then fingerless gloves, then a broad-brimmed hat with a chin strap. Finally, the guide put on mirrored sunglasses that completely hid her eyes. They reminded Anne of Koval's description of Laura in dark glasses with a scarf over her hair. Anne felt she had the key to the airport mystery, but before she could work it out, Koval was calling them into the raft.

Jubal, the driver, pushed them down the slick ramp and into the swift brown current, then turned and walked away without a backward glance. Koval was at the sweeps, standing in the center of the raft between metal uprights that held the oarlocks at waist height. As she worked the long oars, she lectured on the best way to negotiate the Moose Junction Bridge, already looming above them. Once past it, she handed over the sweeps to Anne and the other trainee, Daniel, in alternating ten-minute shifts. Koval taught them to spin the raft and to move it left and right in the current, while the two experienced guides kept watch for "strainers," Koval's term for debris in the river.

Anne ended every session at the sweeps with aching shoulders and the conviction that the Snake was really the one in charge. During the last of her shifts, she was chased down the river by a monster strainer, a thirty-foot pine tree, stripped of its branches and bark but with a huge root ball that rose out of the water like a galleon's high stern. Or so it seemed to Anne as she struggled to stay clear of the skeleton ship that paced them without masts or sails.

By the time the strainer finally grounded on a bar, the Teton Village Bridge, which marked the end of the run, was in sight. Even at a distance, Anne could see the water roiling at the base of the bridge's midstream support like a continually crashing wave. Just short of the span was the landing area. Jubal stood there, hands in pockets.

Anne extended the handles of the sweeps in Koval's direction. The guide shook her head.

"You're doing fine. You can take us in. Just don't miss. The next chance is fourteen miles downstream. Start moving us over. Bow to the bank so you can see what you're doing. Push on those oars, girl. Push!"

Jubal's only sign of interest was the removal of his hands from his pockets when Koval tossed him a line. The raft was still moving downstream so fast that Anne was sure the little man would be pulled in after them. But he stood like a bollard, pivoting the raft shoreward when the line went taut.

"Ship your oars," Koval ordered. "Fred, Bob, give Jubal a hand."

The guides splashed into the shallows. By the time Anne had the sweeps secured, the raft was aground on the rocky bank.

"Good work, Anne. Good work, everybody. Jubal, show these newbies how to back the van down."

Seven

Back at their base, Anne volunteered to hose off the raft for the chance of a private word with Koval. It came when the guide emerged from the office carrying two sodas, her cats trotting behind her.

Anne thought she might be in for a performance evaluation. She wanted to discuss something else, the insight that had been inspired back at Moose Junction by Koval's sunglasses, so she spoke first.

"I think I know why Laura doesn't use the Jackson Airport."

"Gitry's Laura?" Koval handed her one of the sodas. "Have you seen her?"

"No," Anne said, "but I met him last night. Early this morning, I mean." She watched Koval's mouth draw down in the same lopsided grimace she'd used whenever Anne had dragged an oar. "Nothing happened."

"Sure of that?" Koval asked. "What's this about airports?"

"It's something that's been bothering me. Rachel thinks Laura must live in Idaho because she drives instead of flying into Jackson. It doesn't make sense to Rachel that someone would fly into Idaho Falls and drive over the mountains."

"To me either," Koval said.

"But you said Laura wears dark glasses and a scarf over her hair. In other words, she's wearing a disguise. A disguise wouldn't work if she flew in. To fly back out, she'd have to show a photo ID. I think she's remarried. That's how she found her better life. She doesn't want her new husband to know she can't give up her old one. Gitry is wasting himself on a woman who's cheating on two men at once."

"When he could be doing what?" Koval asked.

Anne didn't answer, and the two women stood side by side, Anne scattering the cats with the jerky movements of her hose, Koval waving occasionally to cars passing on the highway.

Finally, the guide said, "I hope I didn't make a mistake by telling you about Chaz Gitry. He's an interesting man, maybe even an exciting one, but he isn't a man I'd wish on a friend of mine.

"I probably should keep my mouth shut now, but if you're right about this airport thing, it opens up an even more sordid possibility. You should be ready for it. It's easier to deal with things you see coming."

"What is it?" Anne asked.

"That disguise business has always bothered me. I mean, why would Laura go to the trouble? It's not like anyone around here knows what Gitry's ex looks like. But you've got me thinking that maybe we'd know her after all."

"How could you? You didn't even know Chaz had been married until he told you."

"Exactly. We only know because he told us. Suppose that was a cover story. Suppose there is no Laura. This valley is the two-months-a-year address of a lot of wealthy wives. Maybe one of them got a taste of Chaz Gitry and ended up hooked.

"Like I said, if you see a rock ahead you can pull away from it. Any reasonable person would."

Eight

Koval's last words haunted Anne as the long day slipped into evening, both because she knew the warning was well-meant and because she knew she wouldn't heed it. Again and again she thought of the tree trunk that had chased her down the Snake that afternoon, sometimes grinding away at the bank, sometimes disappearing behind an island, but always coming back. The fascination of Chaz Gitry was exactly the same: nagging, powerful, and—Anne couldn't quite say how—dangerous.

She was less bothered by Koval's suggestion that Laura wasn't Gitry's ex at all, but only a trophy wife who wouldn't stay in her case. She had to admit it was the logical conclusion of the chain of reasoning she'd started herself. But that only made her more certain that Gitry was wasting his time with the wrong woman. What was more, Anne was sure that Gitry knew it, too. That was the only possible explanation for the desperation she'd seen in his eyes.

Or maybe not the only explanation. While she cooked a dinner she didn't want, Anne wondered if Koval hadn't been wrong in one particular at least. Maybe it was Gitry and not the straying wife who'd had a taste and gotten hooked. Maybe the local lothario had made the mistake of falling for a woman who only wanted a risky fling.

But who was this woman if she wasn't Laura? At first, Anne considered that a question she'd never be able to answer, new to the valley as she was. She could see Gitry's woman without sunglasses and scarf and never know her, unless she turned out to be Mattie Koval or Rachel. The only other Jackson women she knew were just names and last names at that: a Dr. Millikan and a Mrs. Zollman.

Anne, who had given up on dinner by then and was sitting with *Love's Forbidden Memory* unopened on her lap, asked herself if it could be Dr. Millikan, the woman who owned the house Gitry watched. That relationship would certainly have thrown them together. She pictured the place as she'd seen it the morning of the fog, a spectral house, imagined Gitry alone, walking through rooms filled with the doctor's things, week after week, waiting for her to slip back. That would more than account for those bruised, sleepless eyes.

Putting her book aside, Anne crossed to the computer and signed on to the Internet. She searched on "Dr. Millikan," adding "cardiologist" and "New York City" to narrow the field. She was hoping for a photograph but found instead a brief biography on a hospital's website. The bio proved to be enough. Dr. Millikan, first name Edith, was sixty-six years old.

Almost as an afterthought, Anne entered "Zollman." Wayne Sedam had mentioned only one other useable fact: Zollman's husband was a dot com millionaire. Anne added "Internet" to the search parameters and hit the enter key. If she could first identify the husband, maybe she could backtrack to the wife, perhaps finding a photo of her at some charity event in Malibu. The search returned an entry for a Johnathan Zollman, inventor of an Internet security system called Osprey.

"Bingo," Anne said aloud, clicking on the link for the site.

Its welcome page featured a color photograph of a smiling young man with ginger hair and sharp features, the man she'd met the night before when she'd shown up uninvited at Millikan House.

Nine

Anne sat staring at the photograph for a long time. Then the humming of the computer made her realize that she was in danger. Its owner might be monitoring her searches at that moment, might even have tapped into Osprey House's security cameras to watch her as she had watched the team of house cleaners.

She signed off and made a show of turning out all the lights in the little house before going into her bedroom. Once there, she bent down to look under her bed. She felt more than saw the box her mother's books had traveled in and pushed it aside. Behind it was another box her father had given her, this one when she'd left his house for good. It contained a few tools, a favorite fishing reel, and, wrapped in a well oiled rag, a Colt single-action .44.

Anne retrieved the gun and a box of shells. She tested the pistol's action and loaded it. Only then did she pause to listen for any sound of movement outside the ranch house. Hearing nothing, she opened a window and slipped out. She made a wide detour around the main house and its cameras, crossing the meadow that ran parallel to the road.

As she walked, she thought it all through. She understood now why Koval's description of Gitry had fit him no better than his coat, why he knew his way around Osprey House, why he hadn't been seen in town for weeks. Anne even knew why "Laura" had worn a disguise when she'd driven in from the airport at Idaho Falls. Mrs. Zollman had only been to Jackson once under her real name, when she'd somehow met Chaz Gitry, but that once might have been enough for some local to remember and place her.

When Anne arrived at Millikan House, she was thinking of the nickname Wayne Sedam had given it with uncanny insight: Heart

Disease House. This time the front door opened wide to her ring. The man she'd known as Gitry wore the same clothes he'd had on the night before. Anne decided that if he hadn't slept in them, it was only because he hadn't slept at all.

"I can't visit tonight," he said. "She's coming. I got an e-mail this afternoon."

"We'll wait for her together," Anne said. She'd been holding the big Colt behind her leg. She raised it now. "Back inside, Mr. Zollman."

"Mr. Zollman? I don't—"

"I found your picture on the Internet. Back on in. I have to call the police."

The man in the shadows licked his lips. "You haven't called them yet?"

"I couldn't risk your wife showing up while I was at it. You'd only need a minute to kill her."

Anne followed Zollman into the house, turning on lights as they went. Under the florescent ceiling of the very modern kitchen, he looked to Anne like a corpse prepared by a careless undertaker.

When she picked up the phone, she saw Zollman eye a rack of knives. Then he turned his back on it, limped to a chrome and steel breakfast nook, and sat down.

After she'd finished her call, Anne asked, "How'd you really hurt your leg?"

"Gitry threw a hatchet at me when he saw my gun. I think I only meant to scare him until he did that."

"Where's the gun?"

"Upstairs."

"And Gitry?"

"Under a pile of firewood. I didn't think it would be weeks until my wife came. If only it hadn't snowed up in the passes. If only that pothead caretaker at my place hadn't quit, bringing you around."

"If only you'd really gone to the South Pacific," Anne wanted to say. "If only you'd found someone else." She got as far as "if only." Then a siren sounded in the distance.

"Do something for me," Zollman said. "I really love that house. Would you look after it?"

"Always," Anne said.

• • •

TERENCE FAHERTY is the author of two mystery series, the Shamus-winning Scott Elliott private eye series, set in the golden age of Hollywood, and the Edgar-nominated Owen Keane series, which follows the adventures of a failed seminarian turned metaphysical detective. His short fiction, which appears regularly in mystery magazines and anthologies, has won the Macavity Award and been nominated for the Anthony and the Derringer. His work has been reissued in the United Kingdom, Japan, Italy, and Germany. Faherty's eleventh novel, Dance in the Dark, will be published by Five Star in 2011.

THE CASE OF COLONEL CROCKETT'S VIOLIN

By Gillian Linscott

"Admit it, Watson. Texas has not come up to your expectations."

My old friend lounged in a cane chair on our hotel balcony, the hint of a smile on his lips. Our days at sea had done wonders for his health and spirits. His face was lightly tanned, shaded by the brim of a Panama hat.

"It's not as I'd imagined," I agreed.

He laughed.

"You'd hoped for cowboys with lariats and six shooters, Indian chiefs in war bonnets."

Since that was pretty well the vision that had come to my mind when the unexpected invitation arrived on a drizzly day at Baker Street, I tried to hide my irritation.

"Certainly San Antonio seems peaceable enough," I said.

Two floors below, in the courtyard of the Menger Hotel, broad leaves of banana trees shifted gently in the breeze. Our suite, with its lounge, two bedrooms and bathroom, was as clean and comfortable as anything you might find in London, perhaps more so. From where I was standing I could glimpse a corner of the town's plaza, with men crossing from shade to sun and back, looking much like men of business anywhere, though moving at a leisurely pace in the heat. A neat landau, drawn by a grey pony and carrying a woman in a white dress, trotted briefly into sight and out again.

"We've come too late for the wild days, Watson. Seventy years ago we might have arrived in a covered wagon, pursued by as many braves or Mexicans as your warlike heart could wish. I confess my preference for the Mallory Line."

We'd travelled in comfort down the coast from New York to Galveston on Mallory's three-thousand-ton steamer, *S.S. Alamo*, then on by Pullman car. The letter of invitation had implored us to make all convenient speed and spare no expense—both admonitions quite wasted on Holmes, who would spend time and money exactly according to his opinion of what was necessary and nobody else's. He stood up and joined me at the rail of our balcony, looking down at the courtyard. A gentleman in a white suit and hat had appeared from the reception area and was walking towards the foot of our staircase. Holmes gave a chuckle of satisfaction.

"Unless I am mistaken, Watson, here comes our client now."

• • •

Benjamin Austin Barratt was a gentleman of fifty years or so, still vigorous, straight-backed and broad shouldered, with thick dark hair and a small moustache on an otherwise clean shaven face. His manners were courtly, asking after our health and our journey, as if his only purpose were to make us welcome in his native town. It was Holmes who cut short the preliminaries and brought us to business.

"You mentioned in your letter that you were writing on behalf of the Daughters of the Republic of Texas. Do we take it that you are their representative?"

"Indeed so, sir. You will surely be aware that before Texas became part of the United States of America it was an independent republic in its own right by virtue of ..."

"We are aware of it, yes."

Holmes spoke with some impatience. Almost everybody we'd met, from our fellow passengers on the voyage down, to the lad who'd carried our cases to our rooms on arrival, had offered this fact as soon as setting eyes on us. Barratt showed no annoyance and went on with his explanation.

"The ladies thought it preferable that you should be approached by a businessman with some standing in our community. Since I have the honour to be one of the benefactors of their Alamo project and have an interest in the matter under discussion, it was agreed that I should write to you. You will have gathered something of our dilemma from my letter."

"The case of Davy Crockett's superfluous fiddle," Holmes said.

His tone was light. He'd responded to the letter in something of a holiday spirit because it piqued his curiosity. Barratt's posture stiffened for a moment and there was a hint of reproach in his tone.

"Colonel Crockett's violin, yes indeed, Mr. Holmes. The most famous musical instrument in our country's history. That it should have survived the battle is miraculous. That there are two of it is a matter so embarrassing that the ladies decided it could only be settled by the greatest detective in the world, who also happens to be an amateur of the violin."

• • •

Holmes nodded at the tribute, as no more than his due.

"Your letter spoke of urgency."

"Yes, sir. This year the Daughters of the Republic of Texas took on responsibility for safeguarding what remains of the old Alamo mission building, where the battle took place sixty-nine years ago. They plan to open it as a national shrine and a museum. Naturally, the very violin that Colonel Crockett carried with him when he brought his men of the Tennessee Mounted Rifles to join the defenders in the Alamo, the violin he played to hearten them all during the siege, will be its most precious exhibit."

"It is a fact that Davy ... that is, Colonel Crockett had his violin with him in the Alamo," I said. "There was one evening when he had a competition with a man who played the bagpipes and ..."

I'd done some reading on the subject before we left London. All it brought me was an impatient look from Holmes.

"We can take that as established. But is there any explanation of how such a fragile thing as a violin escaped the destruction of everything else when the Mexicans stormed the Alamo?"

"One of the violins is in my possession," Barratt said. "I look forward to telling you its story when I hope you will do us the honour of taking dinner with us tomorrow night, but I believe its history is as well authenticated as anybody could wish."

"And the other violin?" Holmes asked.

"I'm sure Mrs. Legrange will tell you that hers has a well authenticated history too. I know she plans to meet you. One thing I should like to make clear."

For the first time in our conversation, his voice was hesitant. Holmes raised an eyebrow, inviting him to continue.

"There is no enmity between Mrs. Legrange and myself, none whatever," Barratt said. "She is a very charming and patriotic lady and we all admire her very much. We have both agreed that this business must be settled in a quiet and peaceable manner as soon as possible, and we shall both abide by your verdict. May I send my carriage for you two gentlemen at six o'clock tomorrow?"

Holmes told him that he might.

As Barratt crossed the courtyard, one of the hotel's messenger boys passed him in the opposite direction and came up the stairs to our suite carrying an envelope.

"I believe we are about to receive an invitation from the owner of the second fiddle," Holmes said.

A knock sounded at the door. I answered it and was handed an envelope by the messenger boy.

"Pray open it and read it aloud, Watson," Holmes said.

The signature was *Evangeline Legrange,* with as many curls and loops to it as a tangled trout line. I read:

> *My dear Mr. Holmes,*
>
> *I hope you will excuse this informality of approaching you without introduction, but I wonder whether you and Dr Watson would care to join us on a picnic luncheon outing to San Pedro springs tomorrow. If I may, I shall send a gig for you at eleven.*

Holmes told me to ask the boy to wait while he dashed off a polite line of acceptance on hotel notepaper.

"She gives no address," I objected.

"She has no need," he said. "If you look out of the other window, you'll see she's waiting outside in the landau with the grey pony."

And I thought he hadn't noticed.

• • •

I spent the rest of the day exploring San Antonio, while Holmes refused to be drawn from our shady balcony, smoking his pipe and reading a book that had nothing whatsoever to do with the subject under investigation. The town proved to be every bit as calm and prosperous as on first acquaintance. In whatever direction you might stroll, you were never far away from a river bank. Breezes rustled the groves of their strange twisted oak trees and freshened the southern heat. To my pleasure, I even saw several unmistakable cowboys in broad-brimmed hats and leather chaps, lounging on their raw-boned horses in saddles as large and deep as club armchairs. I climbed the hill to the barracks in the hour before sunset to watch the soldiers drilling, then walked back down to try to persuade my companion to take a stroll before dinner. There was no sign that he'd stirred all the time I'd been away and I might have failed in my purpose if his eye had not been caught by a flare of fire in a corner of the wide plaza.

"Good heavens, Holmes, has a building caught fire?" I cried.

"Nothing so calamitous. Shall we go and see?"

• • •

His keen senses had caught, as mine soon did, the smell of spices and the scent of charred meat. We strolled across the plaza in the dusk and found that part of it had been taken over by dozens of small stalls with charcoal braziers, tended by Mexicans. A band was playing jaunty music on accordions, violins and a kind of rattling object, a woman singing in a plaintive voice that cut across the music and gave it a touch of sadness and yearning. We were surrounded by brown smiling faces with teeth very white against the dusk, women with silver ornaments twined in their black hair and voices that spoke in murmuring Spanish. It was as if our few steps across the plaza had taken us all the way to the far side of the Rio Grande and were in Mexico itself. Holmes seemed delighted, as he always was by things unexpected. He even allowed a woman to sell him something that looked like a kind of rolled-up pancake.

"Good heavens, Holmes, what are you eating?"

"I've no idea, but it's really very good. Try some."

Its spiciness made me gasp and cough. As we were walking back towards the hotel, a Mexican man came towards us out of the shadows. He was perhaps thirty years old or so, a handsome fellow and respectable in his manner.

"Excuse me, *señor*, you are Sherlock Holmes?"

He spoke in English. Holmes nodded. The man passed him a piece of paper.

"My address. I should be grateful if you would call on me."

He wished us good evening and stepped back into the shadows as smoothly as he'd stepped out of them.

"So you've got yourself a new client," I said, laughing. "He probably wants to consult you about a missing mule."

"Very likely," Holmes said.

But he seemed thoughtful and I noticed he put the piece of paper carefully into his pocket.

• • •

Next morning the gig arrived to carry us a mile or so north of the town to San Pedro Springs. It was as pleasant a park as I've ever seen, with three clear springs trickling out of a rocky hill and running between grassy slopes and groves of pecan nut trees. Our hostess had established camp in one of the groves, surrounded by preparations for an elaborate picnic luncheon, with folding chairs and tables loaded with covered dishes and wine coolers. Four black and Mexican servants were in attendance, serving drinks to guests who had arrived before us. Evangeline Legrange was sitting on a bank of cushions, leaf shadows flickering over her pale blue dress and white hat with a blue ribbon that tied in a bow under the chin. She jumped up with a cry of pleasure and came tripping over the grass towards us.

"Mr. Holmes ... so kind ... I can hardly believe it. And you must be Dr Watson, such a pleasure."

Her small white-gloved hand was in mine, the scent of jasmine in the air around us. Her hair, worn loose under the hat, was the colour of dark heather honey and her skin white as alabaster. Close to, if one must be ungallant, she was older than she had looked under the shade of the tree, perhaps in her late thirties, but she moved and spoke with the freshness and impetuosity of a girl. She set her gentlemen guests to pile up cushions for us beside her, calling on one of the servants to bring us iced champagne. California champagne, as it turned out. Several people assured us that it was vastly superior to the French article. When we were settled, she clapped her hands at guests and servants alike.

"Now, leave us alone while I tell Mr. Holmes about my violin. You all know the story in any case."

They melted obediently away and this is the story she told us, in a voice as pleasant to hear as the stream flowing beside us.

• • •

"As everybody knows, the men in the Alamo were under siege with Santa Anna and his Mexicans camped outside. But for the local people, who knew the old building, there were secret ways in and out. Naturally, our brave defenders wouldn't use them. But people who were daring enough could get in to the fort, to bring food or nurse the wounded. Some of those daring people were women, and I'm proud to say that one of them was my grandmother on my mother's side, Marianne. She was only nineteen years old, and one of the defenders was her sweetheart. Five times that brave girl climbed out of her bedroom at night and carried food and water to him in the Alamo. The sixth time, they knew the end must be near. Colonel Crockett himself took Marianne aside and told her she must not come again. I can tell you the very words he said to her, as Marianne told them to my mother, and my mother told them to me. He said, 'I honor you for what you have done, but in future Texas will need its brave wives and mothers. Our duty is to die for Texas and yours is to live for Texas. Go and tell all the ladies that.'"

Mrs. Legrange's voice faltered. She wiped a tear from her cheek with her gloved finger.

"And the violin?" Holmes said brusquely.

He never did like to see tears. She smiled at him, disregarding his tone.

"Yes, his violin. That was when he gave it to Marianne. Again, I'll quote his exact words. 'I don't suppose there'll be much occasion for music in here from now on. This violin's been through a lot with me, but maybe it will enjoy a gentler touch.' So Marianne took it away with her and it's been the precious treasure of our family ever since. Here it is."

• • •

She reached into the cushions behind her and brought out a rectangular case, covered in white Morocco leather, tooled with gold. When she undid the gold clasp and opened the lid we saw a violin and bow nestled in blue velvet. She signaled with her eyes that Holmes was to pick up the violin. He turned it over in his long-fingered hands, care-

fully as one might handle any musical instrument, but with no particular reverence. It was the copper-red colour of cherrywood and
looked to me like the kind of country fiddle you'd expect a fron-
tiersman to possess.

"Nobody has played it since Colonel Crockett," she said.

When Holmes simply nodded and handed the violin back to
her, I caught a shadow of disappointment in her eyes. It was gone in
a moment. She put the instrument carefully away and became instantly the gracious hostess, necessarily so because more guests were
arriving. It seemed that most of the Daughters of the Republic of
Texas and their friends and families had been invited to the picnic to
meet Holmes and the grove was soon full of laughing and chattering
people. They included Benjamin Barratt and his family and I noticed that Mrs. Legrange paid them particular attention, as if to em-
phasize to the world that there was no quarrel between them. From
the way Belmont looked at her, I guessed there might have been
some feeling of *tendresse* between them a long time ago. If so, it
seemed to be replicated by Mr. Barratt's son Lee, a good-looking military cadet of twenty or so. He was always at Mrs. Legrange's side or
running errands for her. When we left, Lee Barratt was even allowed
to carry the precious violin to her landau.

• • •

That evening, we had the history of the other violin in the drawing
room of the Barratts' fine home, after dinner. In this case, the instrument was a deep mahogany colour, on display above the marble
fireplace in a glass case, with the Texas flag above it and swords with
tasseled hilts flanking it on either side. Benjamin Barratt stood on his
hearthrug, brandy glass in hand.

"I'm sure you gentlemen know the story. When he knew the case
was hopeless, the commanding officer of the defenders, Colonel

Travis, offered all his men a free choice: stay with him and die or leave without any reproach from him. One man only chose to leave. His name was Louis Rose. Travis kept his word and did not reproach him, but the other men were naturally contemptuous. Colonel Crockett could not express his contempt directly, in the face of what Travis had said, so he did it another way. He gave his violin to Rose, with these words: 'Well, Rose, it seems you're no soldier after all, so maybe you'd better get practicing so you can make your living with this.' Rose took the violin, but he knew that San Antonio would be no place for him. My father had a reputation as a charitable man. Rose came to him at dead of night, begging for a loan of money to get away, offering the violin as security. My father gave him the money, on condition that he wrote a statement of how the violin came into his possession. He did so, exactly as I have told it to you. I have the statement in my desk, signed by Rose and witnessed by my father's servant. I shall show it to you. My father knew the money would never be repaid. We have guarded Colonel Crockett's violin ever since."

• • •

While Holmes was reading the document, our hostess Mrs. Barratt did her best to make polite conversation with me, but she seemed uneasy and kept glancing at the clock on the mantelpiece.

"Please excuse me, but I'm anxious about Lee. Mrs. Legrange was going on after our picnic to visit some friends who have a ranch north of San Pedro Springs. Lee offered to ride with her, which was only right and proper, but he should have been home long ago."

I wondered whether she was concerned for her son's safety or the effect of the lady's charms on the lad. An unworthy thought, as it immediately proved, because a clamour broke out in the hall. We all dashed out, to see Lee, with a bloodied bandage round his head, being supported by two of Mrs. Legrange's servants. Behind them was Mrs. Legrange herself, tears streaming down her cheeks, trembling like a trapped sparrow.

"It's my fault, my fault entirely. How can you ever forgive me?"

Barratt took charge of events with efficiency and had a couch made up in the parlor. I offered my services but also suggested sending for the family doctor, as a matter of professional courtesy. He arrived in a short time and confirmed my diagnosis of concussion as a result of two blows to the head with a heavy object, the patient's life not in danger, but absolute quiet and rest prescribed.

• • •

I returned to the drawing room, where Mrs. Legrange was huddled deep in an armchair taking delicate sips of brandy, Holmes sitting opposite her.

"Here's a how d'you do, Watson. It appears that some villain has snatched Mrs. Legrange's violin."

"The lad Lee kept trying to talk about the violin," I said.

"It's all my fault," Mrs. Legrange said again. "I should never have left him to carry it up. But here at home on my very doorstep, how was I to know?"

Between sobs and sips, she repeated the account for me. The visit to the ranching friends had lasted longer than expected, so it was dusk before she returned to San Antonio, with Lee riding alongside her landau. She'd gone straight upstairs, leaving the coachman to stable both horses and Lee to follow her with the precious violin in its case. Startled by a cry from below, she'd gone back downstairs to find Lee semi-conscious on the pavement and the violin gone.

"The coward had come up behind him. He never even saw his face. Did you ever hear of such villainy? And if poor Lee dies ..."

I assured her that there was no fear of that, provided he was kept quiet.

With Barratt and his wife both occupied by their son, it fell to Holmes and myself to take Mrs. Legrange home in a hack and see her into the care of her housekeeper. Holmes behaved with unexpected courtliness, jumping ahead of me to hand her down from the hack, and even raising her gloved wrist to his lips as we left her in the hall. I smiled to myself, thinking that southern air and manners had made my old friend more susceptible than usual. We walked the short distance back to the hotel.

• • •

"If somebody went to such lengths to steal her violin, that must be because he believed it to be the authentic one," I ventured.

"A false conclusion, Watson. Might it not have been any sneak thief?"

"You surely don't believe that?"

"No, a thief bold enough to commit a violent robbery in a public place would choose some more disposable booty."

"So is Mrs. Legrange's the real Crockett violin? It surprises me, I must confess. I found Barratt's story far more convincing."

Instead of responding, he clapped his left hand to the pocket of his jacket.

"A one pipe problem. Now, which pocket did I put my pipe in?"

"Your right, surely."

At home, it always weighed down the right pocket of his dressing gown. He patted his other pocket, frowning.

"Not there."

"Surely it's not in your waistcoat pocket. Or did you somehow manage to slip it in my pocket by mistake?

I started slapping my own pockets. He laughed.

"My dear Watson, I may not have the polished manners of our Texans, but you surely don't think me barbarian enough to take my pipe to a dinner party with a lady present. It's where it should be, on the table back at the hotel."

"But ... ?"

I stared at him.

"Think about it, Watson. By the by, you mentioned that young Lee had suffered two blows to the head. As far as you could tell, was one more violent than the other?"

"Yes, but that's not unusual. We may suppose that the thief's first blow was not hard enough to fell the young man, so he struck again."

"We may suppose anything we like, Watson. It's still only supposing."

I could get no more out of him that night.

• • •

The next day Barratt had arranged to take us to lunch at his club, which occupied the same building as the opera house, opposite our hotel. The news of his son was encouraging: the young man had woken with a sore head but was rational and showing no signs of permanent damage. Holmes asked if he had any memory of his attacker.

"None whatsoever," Barratt said. "But at least we have the rascal in custody."

Holmes raised his eyebrows.

"Indeed. Has he confessed?"

"No, but he was actually seen half a mile away from Mrs. Legrange's home soon after the attack, carrying a violin."

"And he was arrested there and then?"

"No. The gentleman who saw him did not hear about the theft until this morning. Naturally he remembered what he'd seen and as it happened, he knew the fellow by sight, a Mexican tradesman. Our sheriff's officer went straight to the thief's home this morning and arrested him."

"And the violin?"

"Found in his house."

"What's the name of this Mexican?"

Barratt looked surprised, clearly thinking that such details could mean nothing to Holmes.

"His name's Juan Alvarez. He lives on South Flores Street, down by the stockyards."

By this time, we'd arrived at the club. While our host was turned away, Holmes slid a piece of paper from his pocket and quickly showed it to me, his finger to his lips. I had to suppress a gasp of surprise. It was the slip of paper the Mexican had given him the night before last and the name and address were those of the man under arrest. Over the soup Holmes asked if he might have a word with the prisoner. Barratt was surprised.

"I hardly think it's a case worthy of your attention, but if it amuses you, by all means."

• • •

An hour later, the three of us were sitting in a small room in the county jail, with Señor Alvarez handcuffed to a chair in front of us. In spite of his predicament, there was nothing hangdog about the man. He met Holmes' eye and nodded recognition as if meeting an old acquaintance. Barratt started saying something about a cowardly attack, but Holmes held up a hand to silence him and spoke directly to the prisoner.

"I'm sorry I was not in when you called at our hotel last night," he said. "It might have saved you some unpleasantness."

Alvarez replied in the same civil tone.

"You had not called on me, as I hoped, so I came to call on you."

"Bringing the violin?"

"Yes, *señor*, bringing the violin."

Barratt almost exploded.

"You rogue, I suppose you were trying to get a reward from Mr. Holmes for bringing back Mrs. Legrange's violin. The nerve of the man."

"Except it wasn't Mrs. Legrange's violin, was it?" Holmes said.

"Well, whose else would it be?"

"I suggest we take a look at it. I assume it was brought in as evidence."

Barely restraining his annoyance, Barratt went to the door and called for a sheriff's officer. The violin was brought, wrapped loosely in a table cloth, and handed to Holmes. He unwrapped it and held it up for us to see.

"You see, nothing like Mrs. Legrange's."

It was true. This was an entirely different fiddle, made of some pale wood and varnished the colour of light amber.

"Then what the thunder has happened to Mrs. Legrange's violin?" Barratt said. "And who attacked my son?"

Holmes stood up.

"If we may call on you this evening, I shall have an answer to both questions. Meanwhile, if you'll excuse us, Watson and I have work to do. I suggest that you tell them to release Señor Alvarez. Unless it's against the law to walk through the streets of San Antonio with a violin."

• • •

The hotel hired horses for us, and the cumbersome-looking saddles proved surprisingly comfortable. We rode past San Pedro springs where we had attended our picnic, northward on a dirt track between broad and dry pastures grazed by cattle with horns wider than the handlebars of a bicycle. Holmes kept glancing from left to right and seemed to be sniffing the air like a hunting dog. Two miles or so along the track he reined in his horse.

"Over there, in the trees."

We followed a narrower track to the left, towards a clump of live oaks. It was a lonely spot, not a barn or homestead to be seen. When we came nearer, we saw that the leaves of one of the oaks were scorched brown, with a small pile of ash on the ground beneath them. Holmes dismounted and kneeled down by the ashes.

"Cold, but still light and dry. This fire was lit yesterday afternoon or evening."

He picked up a stick and poked the ashes, then gave a sigh of satisfaction.

"Just as I thought. Do you recognise this?"

He was holding a piece of white Moroccan leather, singed at the edges.

"The case where Mrs. Legrange kept the violin," I said. "So where's the violin itself?"

He gave the ashes another stir.

"Here, Watson."

• • •

When we arrived at the Barratt house that evening, Holmes suggested to our host that we should first pay a visit to his son. Barratt took it as proper consideration for the invalid, but when we were shown into the parlor that was doing duty as a sick room, the look of alarm on the lad's face showed that he knew better.

"I'd be grateful if you'd leave us alone with Lee for a few minutes," Homes said.

Then the older man looked alarmed too, but he withdrew. Lee sat up against a bank of pillows, staring at us. His face was pale, with dark circles round the eyes. Holmes took a chair by the couch.

"Was it your idea, or Mrs. Legrange's?" Holmes said.

The lad said nothing.

"No matter," Holmes said. "I fancy the idea came from the lady. She stayed in the carriage and watched while you burned the violin. Then you returned home with her, as if you'd simply been on a visit, and carried out the next part of the plan. The harder part, I daresay. It must have taken some resolution on your part to kneel there and wait for the second blow."

Lee couldn't help wincing from the memory of it. Holmes smiled.

"You told Mrs. Legrange that she must hit harder to make it look convincing and the second time she managed it. A blow with a heavy brass poker is no laughing matter, even from a lady."

"So she told you."

Lee blurted it out, a flush on his pale cheeks. Holmes did not contradict him.

"Does my father know?" Lee said.

"Not yet, but he must learn of it," Holmes said. "It would come better from you than from me. Shall I send him in?"

Lee nodded, eyes downcast. We went out to the hall where Barratt was waiting anxiously and Holmes said his son had something to tell him.

• • •

When the parlor door had closed on him, I turned to Holmes.

"How in the world did you know it was a poker?"

He smiled.

"You may have observed that I kissed the lady's hand. I could see from your face that you thought I'd fallen victim to her charms. In fact, I wanted to smell her glove. I'd already observed ash on one of Lee's boots …"

"And then you smelled it on her glove. Admirable."

"No, I confess I expected to smell it. I should have known better. She'd leave such work to her male accomplice. The smell I caught was of something quite different: metal polish. Now, a lady of her standing would hardly polish her own household utensils, therefore she'd recently handled some metal object. In view of the young man's injuries, a poker seemed a near certainty, confirmed by his reaction."

"But why, Holmes?"

"Surely you can see. She knew I wasn't taken in for a minute by that romantic tale about the fiddle. Rather than have it lose the contest, she decided to destroy it—with the help of a besotted young man."

• • •

After a while, the parlor door opened. Barratt came out, stern-faced and led us through to the drawing room.

"Gentlemen, I must apologise to you for my son's deception."

"I believe it was Mrs. Legrange's deception," Holmes said.

"Lee would not stoop to putting the blame on a lady."

"Even a lady who deserved it?"

"I'm sure you cannot find it in your heart to blame her. She had believed in the authenticity of that violin."

"Just as you believe in yours?"

Holmes glanced at the instrument enshrined over the mantelpiece.

"That's one good thing to come out of it at any rate," I said, trying to lighten the atmosphere. "Mr. Barratt's violin is now the only one in the field."

Holmes and Barratt stared at each other. Barratt was the first to drop his gaze. Holmes settled himself in an armchair.

"Before we came here, Watson suggested that I should read the history of the Alamo." His tone was conversational. "As he knows, I dislike burdening my mind with useless detail. Nonetheless, there was one aspect that interested me. The person out of step is always more interesting than the ones in step, don't you find?"

I could not see where this was leading, but Barratt evidently did. "Rose?"

"Yes, Louis Rose. The coward of the Alamo. The man who supposedly brought your father Colonel Crockett's violin."

"Supposedly? You doubt my father's word, sir?"

"I do not doubt that your father acquired that violin under circumstances exactly as you described. Equally, I don't doubt that he believed the vagabond at his back door to be Louis Rose. But he wasn't."

I expected an outburst from Barratt but he said nothing.

"I've done a little reading about Rose," Holmes went on. "One detail interested me. The man was illiterate. He couldn't read or write. You're an intelligent man. You must have done your own research. I think you knew that he couldn't have written that statement."

Silence from Barratt.

"But why should any man impersonate a notorious coward?" I said.

"Because whoever the man was, he needed money and had a violin he could sell," Holmes said. "He must have been sharp enough to realise that a hero's violin from the Alamo would be worth much more than any old fiddle."

• • •

Holmes took his pipe from his pocket and asked Barratt's permission to smoke. It was given with an abstracted nod.

"I played a trick on Watson when we were walking home from your house the other night," Holmes said. "I asked him which pocket I'd put my pipe in. He gave the matter his close attention, ignoring the obvious fact—that I hadn't brought my pipe at all."

"Really, Holmes, I ..."

He ignored me, and went on speaking to Barratt.

"You take my point, I'm sure. The question you posed to me from the start was which one of two, hoping that little puzzle would distract me from other possibilities. As it happened, it was of small importance to you which I chose. The thing that mattered above all was that the violin which eventually went on display at the Alamo should be certified as genuine by none other than Sherlock Holmes. Who would question that? I believe you expected me to pick up that point about Rose and to be so pleased with myself that I would give the verdict in favour of Mrs. Legrange's instrument. Unfortunately, you neglected to inform Mrs. Legrange of your plan. Rather than have her violin slighted, she destroyed it—proving in the process that she'd never in her heart believed the family legend about it, or she couldn't have brought herself to do it."

"So neither of you believed in your violins?" I said to Barratt in astonishment.

He raised his eyes and gave me a long look.

"There are things you believe with your head and things you believe with your heart. My heart said that violin should have survived."

• • •

Holmes puffed at his pipe.

"You remember Señor Alvarez wished to see me?" he said.

Barratt nodded, his thoughts clearly elsewhere. Holmes slid a rough-looking piece of paper from his pocket.

"Do you read Spanish, Mr. Barratt?"

Barratt shook his head.

"It seemed more likely to me that if Crockett's violin had survived at all, it would be in Mexican hands," Holmes said. "You know the saying—to the victor, the spoils of war."

Barratt snapped out of his abstraction and stared at Holmes.

"You mean, the man Alvarez and his violin? Has he proof?"

Holmes said nothing, only smoothed out the piece of paper. I could see the struggle in Barratt's face.

"Crockett's violin, in a Mexican's possession?"

Still Holmes said nothing. Barratt paced the room, backwards and forwards.

"I put it in your hands," he said at last. "If you think the man's claim is authentic, then negotiate for us. I authorise you to go up to five hundred dollars if necessary."

"Thank you."

Holmes rose and thumbed out his pipe.

"You'll go tonight?" Barratt said.

"Certainly, if you wish. Come, Watson."

• • •

From my earlier wanderings, I knew my way to the stockyards area. The house of Señor Alvarez was a white painted cube of a dwelling, sandwiched between an ironmonger's and a baker's shop with a galaxy of brightly sugared pastries in its lamp-lit window. The house door was wide open, cheerful voices speaking Spanish coming from inside. When Holmes called, Juan Alvarez came out to meet us, like a prince welcoming an equal. We were led to seats by an open fireplace where something savoury was cooking in a pot, and introduced to his wife, children, and grandmother. After some minutes of this, Holmes brought us to business.

"You wished to talk to me about your violin."

"Yes, *señor*."

The violin, still wrapped in the tablecloth, was lying on a shelf. Alvarez took it down and placed it in Holmes' hands.

"Colonel Crockett's violin, rescued from destruction by my father's father, an officer in the Mexican army. He found it by Colonel Crockett's body and kept it in memory of a brave enemy. No man has played it since Colonel Crockett himself. I offer you that honour now, *señor*."

Holmes took the violin, nodded and rose to his feet. A bow was produced. Holmes tightened the bow, tuned the instrument to his satisfaction then began to play. The tune he chose was a simple melody that I had heard one of the cowboys singing, called *The Streets of Laredo*. The sight of his absorbed face in the firelight, the rapt expressions of Señor Alvarez and his family and the thought of all that this rustic fiddle stood for brought a tear to my eye. When he'd finished there was a little silence. He bowed and handed the instrument back to Alvarez.

"Mr. Barratt is offering you five hundred dollars for the violin," he said.

"To put in their museum?"

"Yes."

Alvarez stood for a while, deep in thought.

"It was our victory, not theirs," he said at last. "It was our country, not theirs."

Then he threw down the violin to the stone-flagged floor and stamped on it time and time again, like a man performing a Spanish dance, until he'd smashed it to smithereens.

• • •

"It is the greatest of pities," I said, still shaken, as we walked towards the hotel through the warm night. "To find Crockett's violin and then have it end like this."

Holmes laughed.

"My dear Watson, why should you think that fiddle was any more genuine than the other two? I'm sure Crockett was more likely to have died with his rifle beside him than his violin. No, Alvarez's family tale was as much a fiction as the others, though I think the man himself believed it."

"But the statement, Holmes, the paper in Spanish that you showed Barratt. Whatever it said seemed to be enough to convince you."

He laughed.

"Did I say so? I simply showed Barratt a paper and he chose to draw his own conclusion. I admit I took a small gamble. If he had happened to read Spanish, I should have had to do some quick thinking."

"Holmes, what is this? What was in the paper?"

"You remember that first night, when we walked in the Mexican market, I found one of the local delicacies suited my taste. This morning I descended to the kitchens of our hotel and was lucky enough to find a Mexican cook. She spoke few words of English but was obliging enough to understand what I wanted and write down the recipe. Tamales, I believe they're called."

"And you led Mr. Barratt to believe that this recipe was proof that ..."

"I led him nowhere, Watson. He led himself. He had tried, for reasons that doubtless seemed honorable and patriotic to him, to take advantage of my reputation. This is a small revenge."

"But what shall you tell him?"

"That the Alamo museum must, alas, do without Colonel Crockett's violin. Texas seems to be a resilient state. I hope it may learn to live with the disappointment."

• • •

GILLIAN LINSCOTT is the author of the Nell Bray crime series, featuring a militant suffragette detective in Britain in the early years of the twentieth century. One of the series, *Absent Friends,* won the CWA Ellis Peters Dagger for best historical crime novel and the Herodotus Award. She has worked as a news reporter for the *Guardian* and a political reporter for BBC local radio stations. She lives in a 350-year-old cottage in Herefordshire, England, and in addition to writing now works as a professional gardener. Interests include mountain walking and trampolining.

THE CASE
OF COLONEL
WARBURTON'S
MADNESS

By Lyndsay Faye

My friend Mr. Sherlock Holmes, while possessed of one of the most vigorous minds of our generation, and while capable of displaying tremendous feats of physical activity when the situation required it, could nevertheless remain in his armchair perfectly motionless longer than any human being I have ever encountered. This skill passed wholly unrecognized by its owner. I do not believe he held any intentions to impress me so, nor do I think the exercise was, for him, a strenuous one. Still I maintain the belief that when a man has held the same pose for a period exceeding three hours, and when that man is undoubtedly awake, that same man has accomplished an unnatural feat.

I turned away from my task of organizing a set of old journals that lead-grey afternoon to observe Holmes yet perched with one leg curled beneath him, firelight burnishing the edges of his dressing gown as he sat with his head in his hand, a long-abandoned book upon the carpet. The familiar sight had grown increasingly unnerving as the hours progressed. It was with a view to ascertain that my friend was still alive that I went so far against my habits as to interrupt his reverie.

"My dear chap, would you care to take a turn with me? I've an errand with the bootmaker down the road, and the weather has cleared somewhat."

I do not know if it was the still-ominous dark canopy that deterred him or his own pensive mood, but Holmes merely replied, "I require better distraction just now than an errand which is not my own and the capricious designs of a March rainstorm."

"What precise variety of distraction would be more to your liking?" I inquired, a trifle nettled at his dismissal.

He waved a slender hand, at last lifting his dark head from the upholstery where it had reclined for so long. "Nothing you can provide me. It is the old story—for these two days I have received not a shred of worthwhile correspondence, nor has any poor soul abused our front doorbell with an eye to engage my services. The world is weary, I am weary, and I grow weary with being weary of it. Thus, Watson, as you see I am entirely useless myself at the moment, my state cannot be bettered through frivolous occupations."

"I suppose I would be pleased no one is so disturbed in mind as to seek your aid, if I did not know what your work meant to you," I said with greater sympathy.

"Well, well, there is no use lamenting over it."

"No, but I should certainly help if I could."

"What could you possibly do?" he sniffed. "I hope you are not about to tell me your pocketwatch has been stolen, or your greataunt disappeared without trace."

"I am safe on those counts, thank you. But perhaps I can yet offer you a problem to vex your brain for half an hour."

"A problem? Oh, I'm terribly sorry—I had forgotten. If you want to know where the other key to the desk has wandered off to, I was given cause recently to test the pliancy of such objects. I'll have a new one made—"

"I had not noticed the key," I interrupted him with a smile, "but I could, if you like, relate a series of events which once befell me when I was in practice in San Francisco, the curious details of which have perplexed me for years. My work on these old diaries reminded me of them yet again, and the circumstances were quite in your line."

"I suppose I should be grateful you are at least not staring daggers at my undocketed case files," he remarked.

"You see? There are myriad advantages. It would be preferable to venturing out, for it is already raining again. And should you refuse, I will be every bit as unoccupied as you, which I would also prefer to avoid." I did not mention that if he remained a statue an instant longer, the sheer eeriness of the room would force me out of doors.

"You are to tell me a tale of your frontier days, and I am to solve it?" he asked blandly, but the subtle angle of one eyebrow told me he was intrigued.

"Yes, if you can."

"What if you haven't the data?"

"Then we shall proceed directly to the brandy and cigars."

"It's a formidable challenge." To my great relief, he lifted himself in the air by his hands and crossed his legs underneath him, reaching when he had done so for the pipe laying cold on the side table. "I cannot say I've any confidence it can be done, but as an experiment it has a certain flair."

"In that case, I shall tell you the story, and you may pose any questions that occur to you."

"From the beginning, mind, Watson," he admonished, settling himself into a comfortable air of resigned attention. "And with as many details as you can summon up."

"It is quite fresh in my mind again, for I'd set it down in the volumes I was just mulling over. As you know, my residence in America was relatively brief, but San Francisco lives in my memory quite as vividly as Sydney or Bombay—an impetuous, thriving little city nestled among the great hills, where the fogs are spun from ocean air and the sunlight refracts from Montgomery Street's countless glass windows. It is as if all the men and women of enterprise across the globe determined they should have a city of their own, for the Gold Rush built it and the Silver Lode built it again, and now that they have been linked by railroad with the eastern states, the populace believes nothing is impossible under the sun. You would love it there, Holmes. One sees quite as many nations and trades represented as in London, all jostling one another into a thousand bizarre coincidences, and you would not be surprised to find a Chinese apothecary wedged between a French milliner and an Italian wine merchant.

"My practice was based on Front Street in a small brick building, near a number of druggist establishments, and I readily received any patients who happened my way. Poor or well-off, genteel or ruffianly, it made no difference to a boy in the first flush of his career. I'd no long-established references, and for that reason no great clientele, but it was impossible to feel small in that city, for they so prized hard work and optimism that I felt sudden successes lay every moment round the next corner.

"One hazy afternoon, as I'd no appointments and I could see the sun lighting up the masts of the ships in the Bay, I decided I'd sat idle long enough, and set out for a bit of exercise. It is one of San Francisco's peculiar characteristics that no matter what direction one wanders, one must encounter a steep hill, for there are seven of them, and within half an hour of walking aimlessly away from the water, I found myself striding up Nob Hill, staring in awe at the array of houses.

"Houses, in fact, are rather a misnomer; they call it Nob Hill because it is populated by mining and railroad nabobs, and the residences are like something from the reign of Ludwig the Second or Marie Antoinette. Many are larger than our landed estates, but all built within ten years of the time I arrived. I ambled past a gothic near-castle and a Neo-Classicist mansion only to spy an Italianate villa across the street, each making an effort to best all others in stained glass, columns, and turrets. The neighborhood—"

"Was a wealthy one," Holmes sighed, hopping out of his chair to pour two glasses of claret.

"And you would doubtless have found that section of town appalling." I smiled at the thought of my Bohemian friend eyeing those pleasure domes with cool distaste as he handed me a wine glass. "There would have been others more to your liking, I think. Nevertheless it was a marvel of architecture, and as I neared the crest of the hill, I stopped to take in the view of the Pacific.

"Standing there watching the sun glow orange over the waves, I heard a door fly open, and turned to see an old man hobbling frantically down a manicured path leading to the street. The mansion he'd exited was built more discreetly than most, vaguely Grecian and painted white. He was very tall—quite as tall as you, my dear fellow—but with shoulders like an ox. He dressed in a decades-old military uniform, with a tattered blue coat over his grey trousers, and a broad red tie and cloth belt, his silvery hair standing out from his head as if he'd just stepped from the thick of battle.

"Although he cut an extraordinary figure, I would not have paid him much mind in that mad metropolis had not a young lady rushed after him in pursuit, crying out 'Uncle! Stop, please! You mustn't go, I beg of you!'

"The man she'd addressed as her uncle gained the kerb not ten feet from where I stood, and then all at once collapsed onto the pavement, his chest no longer heaving and the leg which had limped crumpled underneath him.

"I rushed to his side. He breathed, but shallowly. From my closer vantage point, I could see one of his limbs was false, and that it had come loose from its leather straps, causing his fall. The girl reached us not ten seconds later, gasping for breath even as she made a valiant effort to prevent her eyes from tearing.

"'Is he all right?' she asked me.

"'I think so,' I replied, 'but I prefer to be certain. I am a doctor, and would be happy to examine him more carefully indoors.'

"'I cannot tell you how grateful we would be. Jefferson!' she called to a tall black servant hurrying down the path. 'Please help us get the Colonel inside.'

"Between the three of us, we quickly established my patient on the sofa in a cheerful, glass-walled morning room, and I was able to make a more thorough diagnosis. Apart from the carefully crafted wooden leg, which I re-attached more securely, he seemed in perfect health, and if he were not such a large and apparently hale man I should have imagined that he had merely fainted.

"'Has he hurt himself, Doctor?' the young woman asked breathlessly.

"Despite her evident distress, I saw at once she was a beautiful woman, with a small-framed, feminine figure and yet a large measure of that grace which goes with greater stature. Her hair was light auburn, swept away from her creamy complexion in loose waves and wound in an elegant knot, and her eyes shone golden brown through her remaining tears. She wore a pale blue dress trimmed with silver, and her ungloved hand clutched at the folds in her apprehension. She—my dear fellow, are you all right?"

"Perfectly," Holmes replied with another cough which, had I been in an uncharitable humour, would have resembled a chuckle. "Do go on."

"'This man will be quite all right once he has rested,' I told her. 'My name is John Watson.'

"'Forgive me—I am Molly Warburton, and the man you've been tending is my uncle, Colonel Patrick Warburton. Oh, what a fright I have had! I cannot thank you enough.'

"'Miss Warburton, I wonder if I might speak with you in another room, so as not to disturb your uncle while he recovers.'

"She led me across the hall into another tastefully appointed parlour and fell exhaustedly into a chair. I hesitated to disturb her further, and yet I felt compelled to make my anxieties known.

"'Miss Warburton, I do not think your uncle would have collapsed in such a dramatic manner had he not been under serious mental strain. Has anything occurred recently which might have upset him?'

"'Dr. Watson, you have stumbled upon a family embarrassment,' she said softly. 'My uncle's mental state has been precarious for some time now, and I fear recently he—he has taken a great turn for the worse.'

"'I am sorry to hear it.'

"'The story takes some little time in telling,' she sighed, 'but I will ring for tea, and you will know all about it. First of all, Dr. Watson, I live here with my brother Charles and my uncle, the Colonel.

Apart from Uncle Patrick, Charles and I have no living relatives, and we are very grateful to him for his generosity, for Uncle made a great fortune in shipping during the early days of California statehood. My brother is making his start in the photography business, and I am unmarried, so living with the Colonel is for the moment a very comfortable situation.'

"'You must know that my uncle was a firebrand in his youth, and saw a great deal of war as a settler in Texas, before that region was counted among the United States. The pitched fighting between the Texians—that is, the Anglo settlers—and the Tejanos so moved him that he joined the Texas Army under Sam Houston, and was decorated several times for his valour on the field, notably at the Battle of San Jacinto. Later, when the War between the States began, he was a commander for the Union, and lost his leg during the Siege of Petersburg. Forgive me if I bore you. From your voice, I do not think you are a natural-born American,' she added with a smile.

"'Your story greatly interests me. Is that his old Texas uniform he is wearing today?' I asked.

"'Yes, it is,' she replied as a flicker of pain distorted her pretty face. 'He has been costuming himself like that with greater and greater frequency. The affliction, for I do not know what to call it, began several weeks ago. Indeed, I believe the first symptom took place when he changed his will.'

"'How so? Was it a material alteration?'

"'Charlie and I had been the sole benefactors,' she replied, gripping a handkerchief tightly. 'His entire fortune will now be distributed amongst various war charities. Texas War for Independence charities, Civil War charities. He is obsessed with war,' she choked, and then hid her face in her hands.

"I was already moved by her story, Holmes, but the oddity of the Colonel's condition intrigued me still further.

"'What are his other symptoms?' I queried when she had recovered herself.

"'After he changed his will, he began seeing the most terrible visions in the dark. Dr. Watson, he claims in the most passionate language that he is haunted. He swears he saw a fearsome Tejano threatening a white woman with a pistol and a whip, and on another occasion he witnessed the same apparition slaughtering one of Houston's men with a bayonet. That is what so upset him, for only this morning he insisted he saw a murderous band of them brandishing swords and torches, with the identical Tejano at their head. My brother believes that we have a duty as his family to remain and care for him, but I confess Uncle frightens me at times. If we abandoned him, he would have no one save his old manservant; Sam Jefferson served the Colonel for many years, as far back as Texas I believe, and when my uncle built this house, Jefferson became the head butler.'

"She was interrupted in her narrative as the door opened and the man I knew at once to be her brother stepped in. He had the same light brown eyes as she, and fine features, which twisted into a question at the sight of me.

"'Hello, Molly. Who is this gentleman?'

"'Charlie, it was horrible,' she cried, running to him. 'Uncle Patrick ran out of the house and collapsed. This is Dr. John Watson. He has been so helpful and sympathetic that I was telling him all about Uncle's condition.'

"Charles Warburton shook my hand readily. 'Very sorry to have troubled you, Doctor, but as you can see, we are in something of a mess. If Uncle Patrick grows any worse, I hate to think what—'

"Just then a great roar echoed from the morning room, followed by a shattering crash. The three of us rushed into the hallway and found Colonel Warburton staring wildly about him, a vase broken into shards at his feet.

"'I left this house once,' he swore, 'and by the devil I will do it again. It's full of vengeful spirits, and I will see you all in hell for keeping me here!'

"The niece and nephew did their utmost to calm the Colonel, but he grew even more enraged at the sight of them. In fact, he was so violently agitated that only Sam Jefferson could coax him, with my help, toward his bedroom, and once we had reached it, the Colonel slammed the door shut in the faces of his kinfolk.

"By sheer good fortune, I convinced him to take a sedative, and when he fell back in a daze on his bed, I stood up and looked about me. His room was quite Spartan, with hardly anything on the white walls, in the simple style I supposed was a relic of his days in Texas. I have told you that the rest of the house also reflected his disdain for frippery. The bed rested under a pleasant open window, and as it was on the ground floor, one could look directly out at the gardens.

"I turned to rejoin my hosts when Sam Jefferson cleared his throat behind me.

"'You believe he'll be all right, sir?'

He spoke with the slow, deep tones of a man born on the other side of the Mississippi. I had not noticed it before, but a thick knot of scarring ran across his dark temple, which led me to believe he had done quite as much fighting in his youth as his employer.

"'I hope so, but his family would do well to consult a specialist. He is on the brink of a nervous collapse. Was the Colonel so fanciful in his younger days?'

"'I don't rightly know about fanciful, sir. He's as superstitious a man as ever I knew, and more afeared of spirits than most. Always has been. But sir, I've a mind to tell you something else about these spells the Colonel been having.'

"'Yes?'

"'Only this, Doctor,' and his low voice sunk to a whisper. 'That first time as he had a vision, I set it down for a dream. Mister Patrick's always been more keen on the bogeymen than I have, sir, and I paid it no mind. But after the second bad spell—the one where he saw the Tejano stabbing the soldier—he went and showed me something that he didn't show the others.'

"'What was it?'

"He walked over to where the Colonel now slept and pointed at a gash in the old uniform's breast, where the garment had been carefully mended.

"'The day Mister Patrick told me about that dream was the same day I mended this here hole in his shirt. Thought himself crazy, he did, and I can't say as I blame him. Because this hole is in exactly the spot where he dreamed the Tejano stabbed the Texian the night before. What do you think of that, sir?'

"'I've no idea what to think of it,' I replied. 'It is most peculiar.'

"'Then there's this third vision,' he went on patiently. 'The one he had last night. Says he saw a band of 'em with torches, marching toward him like a pack of demons. I don't know about that. But I sure know that yesterday morning, when I went to light a fire in the library, half our kindling was missing. Clean gone, sir. Didn't make much of it at the time, but this puts it in another light."

Sherlock Holmes, who had changed postures a gratifying number of times during my account, rubbed his long hands together avidly before clapping them once.

"It's splendid, my dear fellow. Positively first-class. The room was very bare indeed, you say?"

"Yes. Even in the midst of wealth, he lived like a soldier."

"I don't suppose you can tell me what you saw outside the window?"

I hesitated, reflecting as best I could.

"There was nothing outside the window, for I made certain to look. Jefferson assured me that he examined the grounds near the house after he discovered the missing firewood, and found no sign of unusual traffic. When I asked after an odd hole, he mentioned a tall lilac had been torn out from under the window weeks previous because it blocked the light, but that cannot have had any bearing. As I said, the bed faced the wall, not the window."

Holmes tilted his head back with a light laugh. "Yes, you did say that, and I assure you I am coming to a greater appreciation of your skills as an investigator. What happened next?"

"I quit the house soon afterward. The younger Warburtons were anxious to know what had transpired in the sick room, and I comforted them that their uncle was asleep, and unlikely to suffer another such outburst that day. But I assured them all, including Jefferson, that I would return the following afternoon to check on my patient.

"As I departed, I could not help but notice another man walking up the side path leading to the back door. He was very bronzed, with a long handlebar moustache, unkempt black hair, and he dressed in simple trousers and a rough linen shirt of the kind the Mexican laborers wore. This swarthy fellow paid me no mind, but walked straight ahead, and I seized the opportunity to memorize his looks in case he should come to have any bearing on the matter. I did not know what to make of the Colonel's ghostly affliction, or Jefferson's bizarre account of its physical manifestation, but I thought it an odd enough coincidence to note.

"The next day, I saw a patient or two in the afternoon and then locked my practice, hailing a hack to take me up Nob Hill. Jefferson greeted me at the door and led me into a study of sorts, shelves stacked with gold-lettered military volumes and historical works. Colonel Warburton stood there dressed quite normally, in a grey summer suit, and he seemed bewildered by his own behavior the day before.

"'It's a bona fide curse, I can't help but think, and I'm suffering to end it,' he said to me. 'There are times I know I'm not in my right senses, and other times when I can see those wretched visions before me as clear as your face is now.'

"'Is there anything else you can tell me which might help in my diagnosis?'

"'Not that won't make me out to be cracked in the head, Dr. Watson. After every one of these living nightmares, I've awakened with the same pain in my head, and I can't for the life of me decide whether I've imagined the whole thing, or I really am haunted by one of the men I killed during the war in Texas. Affairs were that muddled—I've no doubt I came out on one or more of the wrong Tejanos. So much bloodshed in those days, no man has the luxury of knowing he was always in the right.'

"'I am no expert in disorders of the mind,' I warned him, 'although I will do all I can for you. You ought to consult a specialist if your symptoms persist or worsen. May I have your permission, however, to ask a seemingly unrelated question?'

"'By all means.'

"'Have you in your employ, or do any of your servants or gardeners occasionally hire, Mexican workers?'

"He seemed quite puzzled by the question. 'I don't happen to have any Hispanos on my payroll. And when the staff need day labour, they almost always engage Chinese. They're quick and honest, and they come cheap. Why do you ask?'

"I convinced him that my question had been purely clinical, congratulated him on his recovery, and made my way to the foyer, mulling several new ideas over in my brain. Jefferson appeared to see me out, handing me my hat and stick.

"'Where are the other members of the household today?' I inquired.

"'Miss Molly is out paying calls, and Mister Charles is working in his darkroom.'

"'Jefferson, I saw a rather mysterious fellow yesterday as I was leaving. To your knowledge, are any men of Mexican or Chileno descent ever hired by the groundskeeper?'

"I would swear to you, Holmes, that a strange glow lit his eyes when I posed that question, but he merely shook his head. 'Anyone does any hiring, Dr. Watson, I know all about it. And no one of that type been asking after work here for six months and more.'

"'I was merely curious whether the sight of such a man had upset the Colonel,' I explained, 'but as you know, he is much better today. I am no closer to tracing the source of his affliction, but I hope that if anything new occurs, or if you are ever in doubt, you will contact me.'

"'These spells, they come and they go, Dr. Watson,' Jefferson replied, 'but if I discover anything, I'll surely let you know of it.'

"When I quit the house, I set myself a brisk pace, for I thought to walk down the hill as evening fell. But just as I began my descent, and the wind picked up from the west, I saw not twenty yards ahead of me the same sun-burnished labourer I'd spied the day before, attired in the same fashion, and clearly having emerged from some part of the Warburton residence moments previous. The very sight of him roused my blood; I had not yet met you, of course, and thus knew nothing whatever of detective work, but some instinct told me to follow him to determine whether the Colonel was the victim of a malignant design."

"You followed him?" Holmes interjected, with a startled expression. "Whatever for?"

"I felt I had no choice—the parallels between his presence and Colonel Warburton's nightmares had to be explained."

"Ever the man of action," my friend shook his head. "Where did he lead you?"

"When he reached Broadway, where the land flattened and the mansions gave way to grocers, butcheries, and cigar shops, he stopped to alight a streetcar. By a lucky chance, I hailed a passing hack and ordered the driver to follow the streetcar until I called for him to stop.

"My quarry went nearly as far as the waterfront before he descended, and in a trice I paid my driver and set off in pursuit toward the base of Telegraph Hill. During the Gold Rush days, the ocean-facing slope had been a tent colony of Chilenos and Peruanos. That colony intermixed with the lowest hell of them all on its eastern flank: Sydney-Town, where the escaped Australian convicts and ticket-of-leave men ran the vilest public houses imaginable. It is a matter of historical record that the Fierce Grizzly employed a live bear chained outside its door."

"I have heard of that district," Holmes declared keenly. "The whole of it is known as the Barbary Coast, is it not? I confess I should have liked to see it in its prime, although there are any number of streets in London I can visit should I wish to take my life in my hands. You did not yourself encounter any wild beasts?"

"Not in the strictest sense; but inside of ten minutes, I found myself passing gin palaces that could have rivaled St. Giles for depravity. The gaslights appeared sickly and meagre, and riotous men stumbled from one red-curtained den of thieves to the next, either losing their money willingly by gambling it away, or drinking from the wrong glass only to find themselves propped insensate in an alley the next morning without a cent to their name.

"At one point I thought I had lost sight of him, for a drayman's cart came between us and at the same moment he ducked into one of the deadfalls. I soon ascertained where he had gone, however, and after a moment's hesitation entered the place myself.

"The light shone from cheap tallow candles, and ancient kerosene lamps with dark purple shades. Losing no time, I approached the man and asked if I could speak with him.

"He stared at me silently, his dark eyes narrowed into slits. At last, he signaled the barman for a second drink, and handed me a small glass of clear liquor.

"I thanked him, but he remained dumb. 'Do you speak English?' I inquired finally.

"He grinned, and with an easy motion of his wrist flicked back his drink and set the empty glass on the bar. 'I speak it as well as you, *señor*. My name is Juan Portillo. What do you want?'

"'I want to know why you visited the Warburton residence yesterday, and again this afternoon.'

"His smile broadened even further. 'Ah, now I understand. You follow me?'

"'There have been suspicious events at that house, ones which I have reason to believe may concern you.'

"'I know nothing of suspicious events. They hire me to do a job, and to be quiet. So I am quiet.'

"'I must warn you that if you attempt to harm the Colonel in any way, you will answer for it to me.'

"He nodded at me coldly, still smiling. 'Finish your drink, *señor*. And then I will show you something.'

"I had seen the saloon keeper pour my liquor from the same bottle as his, and thus could not object to drinking it. The stuff was strong as gin, but warmer, and left a fiery burn in the throat. I had barely finished it when Portillo drew out of some hidden pocket a very long, mother-of-pearl–handled knife.

"'I never harm the Colonel. I never even see this Colonel. But I tell you something anyway. Men who follow me, they answer to this,' he said, lifting the knife.

"He snarled something in Spanish. Three men, who had been sitting at a round table several yards away, stood up and strode towards us. Two carried pistols in their belts, and one tapped a short, stout cudgel in his hand. I was evaluating whether to make do with the bowie knife I kept on my person, or cut my losses and attempt an escape, when one of the men stopped short.

"'Es el Doctor! Dr. Watson, yes?' he said eagerly.

"'After a moment's astonishment, I recognized a patient I had treated not two weeks before even though he could not pay me, a man who had gashed his leg so badly in a fight on the wharf, his friends had carried him to the nearest physician. He was profoundly happy to see me, a torrent of Spanish flowing from his lips, and before two minutes had passed of him gesturing proudly at his wound and pointing at me, Portillo's dispute had been forgotten. I did not press my luck, but joined them for another glass of that wretched substance and bid them farewell, Portillo's unblinking black eyes upon me until I was out of the bar and making for Front Street with all speed.

"The next day I determined to report Portillo's presence to the Colonel, for as little as I understood, I now believed him an even more sinister character. To my dismay, however, I found the house in a terrible uproar."

"I am not surprised," Holmes nodded. "What had happened?"

"Sam Jefferson stood accused of breaking into Charles Warburton's darkroom with the intent to steal his photographic apparatus.

The servant who opened the door to me was hardly lucid for her tears, and I heard cruel vituperations even from outside the house. Apparently, or so the downstairs maid said in her state of near-hysterics, Charles had already sacked Jefferson, but the Colonel was livid his nephew had acted without his approval, theft or no theft, and at the very moment I knocked they were locked in a violent quarrel. From where I stood, I could hear Colonel Warburton screaming that Jefferson be recalled, and Charles shouting back that he had already suffered enough indignities in that house to last him a lifetime. Come now, Holmes, admit to me that the tale is entirely unique," I could not help but add, for the flush of colour in my friend's face told me precisely how deeply he was interested.

"It is not the ideal word," he demurred. "I have not yet heard all, but there were cases in Lisbon and Salzburg within the last fifty years which may possibly have some bearing. Please, finish your story. You left, of course, for what gentleman could remain in such circumstances, and you called the next day upon the Colonel."

"I did not, as a matter of fact, call upon the Colonel."

"No? Your natural curiosity did not get the better of you?"

"When I arrived the following morning, Colonel Warburton as well as Sam Jefferson had vanished into thin air."

I had expected this revelation to strike like a bolt from the firmament, but was destined for disappointment.

"Ha," Holmes said with the trace of a smile. "Had they indeed?"

"Molly and Charles Warburton were beside themselves with worry. The safe had been opened and many deeds and securities, not to mention paper currency, were missing. There was no sign of force, so they theorized that their uncle had been compelled or convinced to provide the combination.

"A search party set out at once, of course, and descriptions of Warburton and Jefferson circulated, but to no avail. The mad Colonel and his servant, either together or separately, against their wills or voluntarily, left the city without leaving a single clue behind them. Upon my evidence the police brought Portillo in for questioning, but he proved a conclusive alibi and could not be charged. And so Colonel Warburton's obsession with war, as well as the inscrutable designs of his manservant, remain to this day unexplained.

"What do you think of it?" I finished triumphantly, for Holmes by this time leaned forward in his chair, entirely engrossed.

"I think that Sam Jefferson—apart from you and your noble intentions, my dear fellow—was quite the hero of this tale."

"How can you mean?" I asked, puzzled. "Surely the darkroom incident casts him in an extremely suspicious light. All we know is that he disappeared, probably with the Colonel, and the rumour in San Francisco told that they were both stolen away by the Tejano ghost who possessed the house. That is rubbish, of course, but even now I cannot think where they went, or why."

"It impossible to know where they vanished," Holmes replied, his grey eyes sparkling, "but I can certainly tell you why."

"Dear God, you have solved it?" I exclaimed in delight. "You cannot be in earnest—I've wracked my brain over it all these years to no avail. What the devil happened?"

"First of all, Watson, I fear I must relieve you of a misapprehension. I believe Molly and Charles Warburton were the authors of a nefarious and subtle plot which, if not for your intervention and Sam Jefferson's, might well have succeeded."

"How could you know that?"

"Because you have told me, my dear fellow, and a very workmanlike job you did in posting me up. Ask yourself when the Colonel's mental illness first began. What was his initial symptom?"

"He changed his will."

"It is, you will own, a very telling starting. So telling, in fact, that we must pay it the most stringent attention." Holmes jumped to his feet and commenced pacing the carpet like a mathematician expounding over a theorem. "Now, there are very few steps—criminal or otherwise—one can take when one is disinherited. Forgery is a viable option, and the most common. Murder is out, unless your victim has yet to sign his intentions into effect. The Warburtons hit upon a scheme as cunning as it is rare: they undertook to prove a sane man mad."

"But Holmes, that can scarcely be possible."

"I admit that fortune was undoubtedly in their favour. The Colonel already suffered from an irrational preoccupation with the supernatural. Additionally, his bedroom lacked any sort of ornament, and young Charles Warburton specialized in photographic technique."

"My dear chap, you know I've the utmost respect for your remarkable faculty, but I cannot fathom a word of what you just said," I confessed.

"I shall do better, then," he laughed. "Have we any reason to think Jefferson lied when he told you of the ghost's earthly manifestations?"

"He could have meant anything by it. He could have slit that hole and stolen that firewood himself."

"Granted. But it was after you told him of Portillo's presence that he broke into the photography studio."

"You see a connection between Portillo and Charles Warburton's photographs?"

"Decidedly so, as well as a connection between the photographs, the blank wall, and the torn out lilac bush."

"Holmes, that doesn't even—"

I stopped myself as an idea dawned on me. Finally, after the passage of many years, I was beginning to understand.

"You are talking about a magic lantern," I said slowly. "By God, I have been so blind."

"You were remarkably astute, my boy, for you took note of every essential detail. As a matter of fact, I believe you can take it from here," he added with more than his usual grace.

"The Colonel disinherited his niece and nephew, possibly because he abhorred their mercenary natures, in favour of war charities," I stated hesitantly. "In a stroke of brilliance, they decided to make it seem war was his mania and he could not be allowed to so slight his kin. Charles hired Juan Portillo to appear in a series of photographs as a Tejano soldier, and promised that he would be paid handsomely if he kept the sessions dead secret. The nephew developed the images onto glass slides and projected them through a magic lantern device outside the window in the dead of night. His victim was so terrified by the apparition on his wall, he never thought to look for its source behind him. The first picture, threatening the white woman, likely featured Molly Warburton. But for the second plate ..."

"That of the knife plunging into the Texian's chest, they borrowed the Colonel's old garb and probably placed it on a dummy. The firewood disappeared when a number of men assembled, further off on the grounds, to portray rebels with torches. The lilac, as is obvious—"

"Stood in the way of the magic lantern apparatus," I cried. "What could be simpler?"

"And the headaches the Colonel experienced afterwards?" my friend prodded me.

"Likely an aftereffect of an opiate or narcotic his family added to his meal in order to heighten the experience of the vision in his bedchamber."

"And Sam Jefferson?"

"A deeply underestimated opponent who saw the Warburtons for what they were and kept a constant watch. The only thing he stole was a look at the plates in Charles's studio as his final piece of evidence. When they sent him packing, he told the Colonel all he knew and they—"

"Were never heard from again," Holmes finished with a poetic flourish.

"In fact, it was the perfect revenge," I laughed. "Colonel Warburton had no interest in his own wealth, and he took more than enough to live from the safe. And after all, when he was finally declared dead, his estate was distributed just as he wished it."

"Yes, a number of lucky events occurred. I am grateful, as I confess I have been at other times, that you are an utterly decent fellow, my dear Doctor."

"I don't understand," I said in some confusion.

"I see the world in terms of cause and effect. If you had not been the sort of man willing to treat a rogue wounded in a knife fight who had no means of paying you, it is possible you would not have had the opportunity to tell me this story."

"It wasn't so simple as all that," I muttered, rather abashed, "but thank—"

"And an admirable story it was, too. You know, Watson," Holmes continued, extinguishing his pipe, "from all I have heard of America, it must be an exceedingly fertile ground for men of mettle. The place lives almost mythically in the estimations of most Englishmen. I myself have scarcely met an American, ethically inclined or otherwise, whose did not possess a certain audacity of mind."

"It's the pioneer in them, I suppose. Still, I cannot help but think that you are more than a match for anyone, American or otherwise," I assured him.

"I would not presume to contradict you, but that vast expanse boasts more than its share of crime as well as of imagination, and for that reason commands some respect. I am not a complete stranger to the American criminal," he said with a smile.

"I should be delighted to hear you expound on that subject," I exclaimed, glancing longingly at my notebook and pen.

"Another time, perhaps." My friend paused, his long fingers drumming along with the drops as he stared out our front window, eyes glittering brighter than the rain-soaked street below. "Perhaps one day we may both find occasion to test ourselves further on their soil." He glanced back at me abruptly. "I should have liked to have met this Sam Jefferson, for instance. He had a decided talent."

"Talent or no, he was there to witness the events; you solved them based on a secondhand account by a man who'd never so much as heard of the Science of Deduction at the time."

"There are precious few crimes in this world, merely a hundred million variations," he shrugged. "It was a fetching little problem, however, no matter it was not matchless. The use of the magic lantern, although I will never prove it, I believe to have been absolutely inspired. Now," he finished, striding to his violin and picking it up, "if you would be so kind as to locate the brandy and cigars you mentioned earlier, I will show my appreciation by entertaining you in turn. You've come round to my liking for Kreutzer, I think? Capital. I must thank you for bringing your very interesting case to my attention; I shall lose no time informing my brother I solved it without moving a muscle. And now, friend Watson, we shall continue our efforts to enliven a dreary afternoon."

• • •

LYNDSAY FAYE is the author of the historical thriller *Dust and Shadow: an Account of the Ripper Killings by Dr. John H. Watson*, in which the Great Detective must trace the infamous serial killer in a pre-Freudian world, amidst the hostile censure of the gutter press, and at the risk of his own life. She spent many years in the San Francisco Bay Area, working as a professional actress. Lyndsay and her husband, Gabriel Lehner, now live in Manhattan with their cat, Grendel; she is a proud member of Actor's Equity Association and the Adventuresses of Sherlock Holmes.

TIME
WILL TELL

By Twist Phelan

Lauren Winslow swept into my office a half hour after my secretary left, twenty minutes before Security came on duty downstairs. As slim as a fading hope, she wore a long sapphire sheath that was sexy but modest at the same time. She hung her wet umbrella on the coat tree next to the door and collapsed into her favorite chair, the one closest to my desk.

I turned over the spreadsheet I'd been reviewing and put on a welcoming smile. "You're looking lovely this evening, Madame Prosecutor. What's the occasion?"

"Annual judges' dinner at the Downtown Club. If I'd known the weather was going to be this bad, I would have rented a tux." She brushed off the raindrops that spangled her hem, revealing a pair of satin slingbacks with vicious heels. "They're roasting Galletti, so I have to be there. Would you please just kill me now?"

Laura going to an event for Glamour Boy Galletti? "An evening of lawyers in white ties telling white lies—you'll be in your element, Counselor."

She chuckled; a low sound of genuine mirth. She had deep-set brown eyes, wavy chestnut hair, and a dusting of freckles so fine I often wondered if I'd imagined them. "I think you'd hold your own, Tommy."

Lauren headed up the Complex Crimes Unit for the regional office of the Department of Justice. A dozen attorneys under Galletti were on a crusade against "sophisticated" criminals—corporate fraudsters, identity thieves, computer hackers, pay-for-play politicos, big-time polluters. "We're not interested in ordinary crooks," Lauren had told me when we first met. "We go after the smart people who've gone bad, the ones who screw over widows and orphans."

I held up an almost-empty tumbler of whiskey. "Care to get a head start on the festivities?"

She declined, as she always did during her impromptu visits. Instead, she stood up and walked to the window, all fine-boned elegance and height. What began as an afternoon shower had turned into leaden rain. It was an ugly day, exactly as forecast.

I wondered why Lauren was here. Usually she dropped by to regale me with some courtroom triumph—the defeat of a defendant's motion to suppress evidence, a unanimous Guilty verdict, a plea that sent somebody away for twenty-five years. Her stories hinted at rules she had to bend, witnesses she had to bully into fatal admissions.

Tonight, though, she was different. There was something about her I hadn't seen before; she was wired, so electric she nearly set the air vibrating. I swallowed a mouthful of scotch, felt the warmth spread through my belly, and waited.

"Have I ever told you what brought me to Seattle?" she asked, gazing out at the city. Her skin was pale against the darkness on the other side of the glass.

"No." Although Lauren was familiar with my background, she had always been closed-mouthed about hers. I took another sip of my drink. In less than a week, I'd be downing mojitos instead of single malt.

She turned, and her dress pulled tight against her thigh. I glimpsed the outline of lace through the thin fabric and sucked in my breath. Lauren was the only woman I knew who wore a garter belt. Her legs were great, and outside the courtroom she preferred short skirts to pants. During our first meeting she had leaned across a table to hand a document to Nick, exposing a thin strip of smooth flesh at the top of her stocking. Nearly a minute had passed before I'd been able to focus on her questions again.

"It was four years ago," she said, turning away from the window to reclaim her chair. I could smell her perfume. She always wore the same scent—subtle but crisp, not too flowery. I imagined her touching the glass stopper to the hollow of her neck, dabbing it between her breasts ...

I felt the heft of my new watch as I lifted the whiskey bottle from the desk drawer and replenished my tumbler. Audemars Piguet—the only brand Arnold Schwarzenegger wore. With its gold face and thirty-two diamonds rimming the bezel, the thing weighed almost a pound. The black rubber wristband made it popular among the yachties in Boca.

Lauren noticed my new hardware. "Check out the bling. I could hire another paralegal for what that cost."

More like two, I didn't say. Eighty thousand dollars, no discount for cash.

"What happened to the Rolex?" she asked. "Or was that a Patek Philippe in your briefcase?"

I put the bottle back into the drawer, next to the mini digital recorder. I touched the square red button and left the drawer open. "I still can't believe you snooped."

"Your driver shouldn't have left the backseat door open. And briefcases come with locks for a reason."

I was tempted to ask what part of *no unreasonable searches and seizures* she didn't understand. "Next you'll be telling me, if I carry cash, I deserve to have my pocket picked. You're lucky I didn't think you were a carjacker."

Lauren looked at me through her eyelashes. "What if you had, Tommy? Would you have shot me?"

"Jesus, how can you—"

"I never figured you for one of those big-watch guys," she interrupted. "Bonus from a grateful client?"

"If you're gonna keep asking questions, Madame Prosecutor, I want my lawyer." I said it automatically. Not a big-watch guy. I turned my wrist so the diamonds wouldn't show so much.

Lauren made a face. "Very funny, Tommy."

As hilarious as the Fourth Amendment, Lauren. Bad guys aren't the only ones who think the end justifies the means. I pulled at my drink. *Galletti knows it, too.*

Outside, headlights were yellow smears in the downpour and a foghorn mooed. I knew I shouldn't spill the beans, but I couldn't resist.

"As a matter of fact, the watch is a going-away present to myself. Good-bye, perpetual rain; hello, eternal sunshine."

Lauren tilted her head. "You're moving? Where?"

I picked up the Prada sunglasses from my desk—another recent purchase—and put them on.

"Next week I'll be sitting on the private beach of one of the ritziest golf communities in Florida." Harbour View or Vista or something like that. Harbour with a *u* of course, and a gated entrance even more pretentious than the name.

Gated, alarmed, rent-a-copped. Drop-ins at the office were one thing, but I've never been keen on clients—or anyone else—showing up at my house. "And I won't be back," I added in my best Ahnuld imitation.

A small crease appeared between Lauren's brows. A big reaction, if you knew her. I took off the glasses, prepared to launch into my sun, beach, and golf riff. None of these things actually mattered to me, but the explanation had satisfied everyone else.

Few people ever surprised me like Lauren.

"So you're walking away before things are finished," she said.

"What do you mean? The practice is all wrapped up. Not that there was much to do. After what happened to Nick, things went into the crapper pretty fast."

When my partner got shot in our parking garage, the local news feasted on it for a week. There was a lot of speculation—fueled by an anonymous source—that it was a mob hit. That was enough to scare off old clients and keep away new ones. I regarded Lauren. And with my other reason to stay in Seattle leaving too.

"I'm not talking about your accounting firm," she said.

I looked at my watch, no longer giving a damn what she thought of it. "Aren't you supposed to be at Galletti's roast?"

Lauren tossed back her prodigal curls. Usually she wore her hair in a ponytail. I decided I preferred it loose around her face.

"I want to arrive late." Her tone turned coy. "Besides, don't you want to hear why I came to Seattle?"

It was impossible to stay annoyed with her. Besides; this could be our last evening together before I left. "Go ahead."

"Ever play Monopoly when you were a kid?"

You could get whiplash trying to follow her train of thought. "Sure."

"Did you know it's the only game where going to jail is an accepted risk?"

I put on an Uncle Sam scowl and pointed at her. "Do not pass Go, do not collect two hundred dollars."

Her eyes sparkled. "I used to really rub it in when my brother pulled that card. Sometimes I made him so mad, he'd kick me out of the game."

You're still pissing off the other players, Lauren. "All I cared about was collecting rent," I said.

"Spoken like a true accountant. So, Tommy, did Monopoly make us what we are today?"

I wasn't exactly sure what she was getting at, so I sipped my whiskey and stayed quiet. The rain increased its patter on the windows. It sounded impatient, like a dealer's fingers drumming on the felt.

Lauren broke the silence. "Private placement offerings put together by Merrill Bache—coal-mining deals. That's what brought me here."

She was talking about PPOs. If the investment banks won't touch you, they're a way to raise capital without jumping through too many government hoops. Lawyers and accountants vet you and your numbers, then brokers sell the deal to "accredited" investors, rich people who've been around the financial block a few times.

I always thought private placements were small-time. Give me a REIT any day. You pool investor funds to buy commercial rental properties or mortgages—that's serious money.

"I don't remember hearing anything about coal."

Since meeting Lauren, I'd made a point of keeping up with local financial and legal news. The deals must have gone down before I moved to Seattle.

"It was a pretty standard fraud. The geology was faked—there wasn't any coal. The investors got stuck with worthless holes in the ground."

I shrugged. "So a few of the privileged class spent the summer at their lawyer's offices instead of the beach."

"Not so privileged," Lauren said, her voice like ice. "The brokers sold units to anyone who walked in the door, even if they weren't accredited. Retirement savings, college finds, cushions against medical emergencies—they took in millions, tens of millions."

Although we'd never talked about it, I sensed that Lauren took investors' losses personally. I wondered if there was a private history.

"The money was gone, of course." I tried to sound sympathetic.

"I followed the funds through three banks before the trail went cold. As usual, nothing was left stateside. Rich crooks don't need walking-around money."

"Promoter disappear too?"

"As soon as the deal went south, he followed it."

I swirled the scotch in my glass. "So you were left with the professionals. I assume you picked the obvious target."

She nodded. "The brokers who peddled the deal. You know how I hate white-collar types who think the rules don't apply to them. When these guys tried to play games during discovery, it really ticked me off. I wasn't going to settle for a fine after that. I wanted them in prison."

"Any defense?"

"The usual." Her voice became singsong. "Each investor received documents describing the risks, the brokers had no way to know the attorneys hadn't done the due diligence or that the accountants had inflated the numbers, it wasn't their fault unqualified investors bought into the deal, blah blah blah blah."

"Did the jury buy any of it?"

"Not after it took the head broker a full five minutes to locate where the lawyers had buried the risk disclosures in the offering memorandum. The printing was so small, he couldn't read it without borrowing the judge's glasses. Meanwhile, the projected returns were smack dab in the middle of the first page, in typeface as big as the top line on an eye chart."

"I take it you won."

"Don't I always?"

That had been true for as long as I'd known her. Lauren was a real buccaneer. She tried cases other prosecutors would have passed on, and she was willing to do whatever it took to win, even if it meant sailing to the edge of legal boundaries, or beyond. *I get the message, Lauren.*

I took a long pull from my tumbler. "A criminal conviction makes a civil suit practically a slam-dunk. I bet some class-action attorney had a complaint on file the same day your jury came back." I could feel my neck getting red.

She plucked at a thread on her sleeve and looked bored. "Probably."

"What did the investors finally end up with? Ninety, ninety-five cents on the dollar?" I heard the edge in my voice, so I gulped some of my drink. I had to choke back a cough as the whiskey scorched my throat.

Lauren hitched up her dress so she could cross her legs. "A little more than a hundred, actually. The jury was generous with punitive damages.

I forced myself to look away from her slender ankles. "I bet you went after the attorneys and accountants, too." I set the tumbler down hard on my desk. Amber liquid sloshed over my hand.

"The law allows—"

"To hell with the law! The investors got back more than they put up. And they're no less greedy than the professionals you're so hot to put in prison. Most people wouldn't go near these deals if they didn't think they'd get a big tax write-off, plus beat the market. Why not be reasonable? Dial it back after things are more or less even again, go after real bad guys."

"I do! Lawyers and accountants are supposed to be the watchdogs who make sure offerings are legit. And the ones in these deals did more than look the other way. The promoter was smart, but not that smart. He couldn't have put the fraud together without professional help."

I made a calming motion with my hands. I was determined not to argue with her. Besides, it was an old debate. "Okay, okay, these lawyers and these accountants were dirtbags. You have my blessing to prosecute them."

She grimaced. "Easier said than done. I barely had enough evidence for a search warrant. By the time it was executed, they had shredded all the documents. I needed the promoter's testimony that the attorneys and accountants were in on the scam from the get-go."

I rubbed a thumb against the rubberized band of my watch. "Those guys can be hard to find once they're in the wind."

"The coal mines were in Kentucky, so I started there. I went to the town, talked to the guy's landlord, the people who leased him office equipment, even the waitresses at his favorite diner. Wasn't hard—I was raised in a place like that. Turns out the guy's Norwegian, grew up working on a family fishing boat. He emigrated to the States about ten years ago with plans to make it big."

"Let's hear it for the American dream!" I took a mouthful of scotch and let it sizzle on my tongue. I was feeling good again. "He must have played Monopoly when he was a kid."

Lauren glared at me. "I expected him to go back to Europe. But Immigration didn't have a record of him leaving."

"How about Canada?"

"They said he wasn't there either. So that left Seattle."

"Seattle? What made you think—"

"When we went through his office in Kentucky, we found a bunch of blank Seattle postcards and some country-western CDs in the back of a desk drawer. Apparently he missed them when he cleaned out the place."

"You thought he came here because of some postcards?"

"Don't give me a hard time, Tommy. It was all I had to go on. The databases—"

"I was wondering when you'd get to those." I heard that edge in my voice again. "Do you feds even bother with warrants anymore? Or do you just whisper the word 'terrorist' and wait for the sysop to hand over the master password?"

Lauren's expression told me she wasn't in the mood for my privacy-rights rant. "Oh, we got the password all right, but the databases were a bust. There was nothing in the computers—no driver's license, no address, no credit cards."

I was impressed by Lauren's quarry. Despite disposable cell phones, false identities for sale on the Internet, and banks that were more interested in fees than references, it was harder than ever to live off the grid. "So what did you do?"

She flashed that luminous smile. "Drove around in the rain, hyped on caffeine. I went to bars, hotels, used-car lots—anywhere he might have gone or done business. Nada. It was as though he'd never been here."

Despite myself I was getting interested. "Why not give up?"

"I almost did. I was running out of places to look. But I knew— I just knew—he was here. The local Norwegian community, the climate, the fishing, the postcards—" she ticked each one off on a finger, "—made Seattle the most logical place for him to go to ground." She shook her head. "Thank goodness for clams."

"What do clams have to do with this?"

"I was eating lunch at this tiny joint downtown—"

"The one next to the bridge? You ever have the chowder?"

"Every Tuesday. White, with extra crackers." She ducked behind a grin. "And an Elysian Fields Pale Ale, no glass."

A noontime beer should be the least of your worries, Lauren. For half a second, I wondered if she would go to lunch with me. Maybe if I called it a bon voyage thing ...

"Anyway, I was eating on the patio when the ferry came in from Bainbridge Island. That's when it hit me."

"A boat," I said.

"A boat," she repeated, clearly relishing the memory. "And I had five days to find it before I had to start working another case."

"The State of Washington must have a hundred thousand registered vessels. How did you think you were going to come up with the right one in time?"

"Make that three hundred thousand, plus transients." Lauren flicked invisible lint from her dress. "Still, it was no problem."

"Okay, I'll bite. How did you find the needle in a third of a million boats?"

"Did you know the DMV is in charge of maritime registrations? It handles them just like cars. I sat in a back office and scrolled through the listings for vessels over thirty feet—the DMV guy said that would be the minimum size for someone to live on. I found it the second day." Her tone was only slightly smug.

"He couldn't have been stupid enough to put his name down as the owner."

Lauren looked offended. "Of course not. Besides, I didn't look at the owner registry. I figured title would be held by some offshore corporation. I went through the list of boat names instead."

"Boat names? Why would you do that?"

"Because men aren't sentimental, except when they are." She looked at my watch. "They can't hide the things that matter to them."

I tugged my cuff over the gold dial. "So did he go for a name from the old country? Or something dumb, like *Other People's Money* or *Sucker Bet*?"

"Wrong, and wrong. But I knew I'd found the right one as soon as I saw it." She grinned, and I half-expected to see canary feathers sticking out of her mouth. "The *Loretta Lynn*."

"Isn't that a country-western singer?"

"You got it. Born and raised in Butcher Hollow, Kentucky."

"Why would this guy name his boat after her? He's Swedish."

"Norwegian." Lauren hugged herself happily. "Remember when I told you the coal mines were in Kentucky? Well, guess what town they're in."

"You've got to be kidding. I still don't see how the hell you made the connection with Loretta Lynn. I didn't think you were a country-western buff."

"I'm not. But the CDs he'd left in his office were all hers, except for—here's the good part—the soundtrack from *Coal Miner's Daughter*, the movie they made about her life."

The pride in her voice was beginning to grate. "So then what did you do?"

"The records said the *Loretta Lynn* was a converted trawler. The DMV guy said that meant it ran on diesel. I called around to the fuel docks until I found the one that knew the boat. The gas jockey ID'd an e-mail photo of my guy, and the Harbor Patrol took me out there. Two days later, I was waiting when he showed up with empty tanks and a grocery list."

"I suppose you called the media for the perp walk," I said into my glass. The tumbler was almost empty again, and I considered re-filling it.

"Of course." She almost purred the words. "You know I love the look of a man in a monogrammed shirt and handcuffs."

"Yeah, those initials come in real handy when it's time to sort prison laundry."

The corner of her mouth twitched. "Always the clever one, Tommy."

Looking out the window, I could see the interior of my office reflected endlessly across the skyline, illuminated boxes filled with bland furniture, screen-savered computers, and generic wall art. As I scanned the warren of other buildings, I half-expected to see someone like me looking back. It made me uncomfortable, and I pulled my gaze back to. Lauren.

"So why did you stay?" I fiddled with the thick clasp on my watch—opening it, snapping it shut, opening it again. The diamonds winked at me. "In Seattle, I mean."

Her reply was quiet, measured. "I met you, Tommy."

I stopped playing with my watch.

Lauren got up from her chair.

"Assuming that ridiculous sundial on your wrist is correct, I better get going," she said. "One of the secretaries let slip that part of tonight's program includes a small celebration in my honor."

The words jumped out before I could stop them. "A celebration?"

Her eyes drilled into mine. Anticipation shimmered off her.

"I'm leaving Seattle too."

I felt something flutter in my chest, forced my eyebrows up in feigned surprise.

"You're looking at the new DOJ liaison with the local SEC office." Lauren leaned forward and placed her hands flat on the desktop. Her fingers were long and tapered, the nails filed into perfect ovals. "In Boca Raton."

The change in her demeanor was subtle but unmistakable. Damn. Sooner or later, we always came to this point in the conversation.

"You may be clever, Tommy, but you're not clever enough." Her voice was as soft as cashmere, but underneath I could feel the chill of steel. "I'm going to get you. Three years left on the securities fraud SOL. And, of course, there's Nick. There's no statute of limitations on murder."

Even when I held the winning hand, she still made me feel like I was chasing the pot. Had I refilled my glass twice or three times? I passed a damp palm over my face.

"This isn't one of your coal deals." My tongue felt slightly too big for my mouth. "For starters, the REIT investors' lawsuit was tossed."

Lauren blew out a dismissive breath. "Plaintiff's lawyer jumped the gun. Doesn't affect the criminal prosecution."

"*Lack of evidence*—that's what the judge said when he granted my lawyer's motion to dismiss. If the plaintiffs didn't have enough proof to get past more likely than not, how are you going to make it all the way to *beyond a reasonable doubt*?"

The determination was plain on her face. "I'll find the evidence."

By any means necessary. I tapped my watch. "You know as well as I do, the more, time that passes, the more memories fade, the more documents are lost, the more people decide to put all this behind them and move on. As for what happened to my partner—" I put on the sad expression I'd used for the reporters, "—carjacking gone wrong. Real tragedy."

"Four thousand investors lost everything in your REIT, Tommy. *Four thousand.* Already there have been two suicides, plus God knows what other damage—divorce, derailed retirements, ruined careers ..." Lauren paused, bit down on her lip.

But it wasn't my fault, I wanted to tell her. I'd been in hock up to my eyeballs to those deranged Russian bookies. They "let me" pay off my marker by washing their gambling profits through the REIT. I didn't know they were going to rip off the investors too.

"And we both know Nick wasn't killed by any carjacker." Her voice had dropped to a whisper, and I had to lean forward to hear her. Our faces were so close, I could see the pulse beating at her temple and smell her perfume. *Definitely grapefruit. Maybe a little cypress?*

"He's dead because he decided to take the immunity offer and testify." She nearly spat the words. "Against you."

Also not my fault. Since when did my partner the schmoozer ever bother to look into the mechanics of a deal? Nick's job was to bring in the business, not run it. When he stumbled onto the money laundering, I had no choice. Otherwise the Russians would have left me lying on that cold concrete floor.

Lauren pushed herself off the desk. "Run to Florida, run halfway around the world. It won't make a bit of difference. You'll never be able to put enough distance—or time—between us. More search warrants, new witnesses—I'll plant the damn evidence if I need to— I'll get the proof I need. Then it'll be like that hideous watch of yours was turned back to yesterday."

Her look of distaste stung. I dropped my eyes to the digital recorder in the drawer. I imagined I could hear its motor humming. *Everybody's on the run from something, Lauren. Or should be.*

"I'll see you in Florida, Tommy. Don't get too comfortable in your new place. Before you know it, you'll be moving to another gated community—the kind where Security carries pump shotguns instead of cell phones and the bars on the windows aren't just for show."

With a rustle of blue silk, she was gone.

I'll see you in Florida, Tommy.

The black October rain beat against the window. I checked my watch, drained the last of the scotch, and pushed back my chair. I picked up the recorder from the drawer, turned it off, and dropped it into my pocket.

The irony of where I was headed hit me in the hallway and kept me laughing all the way to the elevator. I punched the Down button. Galletti wouldn't have offered a talk-and-walk on the Russian thing if he suspected anything about Nick. Lauren must have been keeping her cards close. Made it sweet for me. Once her overeager—or dumb—boss put blanket immunity on the table, I had my get-out-of-jail-free card. If I took his deal, I'd be untouchable for the murder.

As the elevator doors slid open on the parking garage, I thought back to that night. I hadn't expected Nick to struggle, let alone rip the watch from my wrist. The Rolex had fallen into a crack in the cement floor beside one of the support beams, wedged out of reach. I averted my eyes as I walked past the spot. What the hell had possessed me to engrave the damn thing?

My DNA, Nick's blood—the feds had already been over the scene. But Lauren was talking about a new search warrant. If she found the watch before I disappeared into witness protection, my deal with her boss would evaporate. I'd be facing the needle instead of twenty years.

The gray Buick was parked next to the exit ramp, its engine running, in one of the spaces with a good view of the main, entrance. The air was thick with the stink of exhaust. I could hear tires swishing through the puddles at street level.

I slid into the backseat and rested my head against the plump leather. Galletti eagerly twisted around in the driver's seat. No doubt he'd seen Lauren leave. Jesus, the guy had it in for her so bad, he was going to be late to his own roast.

Our last meeting had not gone well. He'd moaned about my coming up empty-handed again. I'd dropped the bomb about my Florida move.

"We both know witness protection is gonna stick me in someplace like Oshfart, North Dakota," I'd told him when he finished squawking. "I want to see sun and beach and girls in bikinis one last time. Besides, isn't this all moot, like you lawyers say? If Lauren's moving to Florida, she's not your problem anymore, right?"

He hadn't been able to hide the ambition and spite in his hooded eyes. Galletti wasn't gunning for Lauren because she crossed the line. He wanted to take her down because every month she won more cases, more headlines, more fans. She wouldn't be the first prosecutor to parlay those into a glory ride. But it was a trip her boss wanted to take himself.

I let my eyelids close as his voice once again bore into my skull, more excruciating than the hangover I knew I'd have in the morning.

He asked me the question.

How many had it been this time? Two—no, three counts of prosecutorial misconduct, any one of which was enough to deliver Lauren's head—and career—to Galletti on a silver platter.

"Nothing." I shifted in the seat. The recorder jabbed me in the rib. "Didn't even get a chance to turn it on."

I got out of the car and went back to my office. I sat down at my desk, took the whiskey bottle out of the drawer, and poured slowly until my glass was full again. I thumbed the Rewind button on the recorder and turned up the volume so I could hear her voice over the rain.

I'll see you in Florida, Tommy.

• • •

A Stanford graduate and former plaintiff's trial lawyer (her specialty was suing middle-aged white guys who stole other people's money), **TWIST PHELAN** is the author of the critically acclaimed and award-winning Pinnacle Peak mystery series (Poisoned Pen Press) and short stories for various anthologies and *Ellery Queen's Mystery Magazine.* "Time Will Tell" was a finalist for the 2010 Crime Writers of Canada Arthur Ellis Award for Best Crime Short Story.

Twist is currently at work on a financial thriller. Find out more about Twist and her work at www.twistphelan.com.

BY HOOK
OR BY CROOK

By Charlie Drees

I set the compact tape recorder on the scarred table and watch
Dexter Bass pace back and forth in the cramped tooth. He's six-
three—give or take an inch—with a sinewy build and long, sun-
bleached blond hair. The police file indicates he's been a guest of the
state on two prior occasions, but his muscles appear to come from
hard manual labor rather than from pumping iron on a prison workbench. Watching Bass, I feel more like an audience than his court-
appointed attorney. He catches me glancing at my watch and slides
into the chair on the other side of the table.

"Am I boring you?"

"Mr. Bass, I've been appointed—"

"I've had lawyers like you before," he says, fixing me with his
charcoal-colored eyes. "Just going through the motions—and I did
the time."

I settle back in my chair. Due to a shortage of public defenders
in our jurisdiction, judges pick from a rotating pool of defense attorneys and assign them to defendants who can't afford legal counsel.

And they frown on attorneys who do a less than stellar job with the assignment. As luck would have it, I'm at the top of the list this week. I can't afford to annoy the judge, so I swallow my pride. I haven't had much practice, and the words stick in my throat.

"Mr. Bass, I apologize. I'm not bored. I'm just eager to get started."

Bass studies my face, checking for any sign of deceit. It's hard to fool an ex-con, but he's overmatched and he looks away after a few seconds. Hey, I'm a lawyer. I've had plenty of practice looking sincere.

Bass brushes his blond hair off his forehead. "What do you want to know?"

I click on the tape recorder and grab his file. "Let me go over what's in the police report, then you can tell me your version, okay?"

"Sure." He glances at my briefcase. "You got any cigarettes?"

"Sorry. It's a no-smoking facility."

Bass snorts. "Figures. They want me healthy so they can stick a needle in my arm."

Like most cons, Bass knows the law. I open the case folder. "You were arrested early this morning at the Shamrock Bar following a fight with Cletus Rupp. Rupp died from injuries he sustained during this fight. Witnesses claim you two had been arguing." I peer at Bass over the top of the file. He's busy scrutinizing something trapped underneath his fingernails.

"After your arrest, the police discovered a gym bag in your car containing $10,300 in cash. They also found a hammer covered with blood and strands of hair, a man's Rolex watch, and a wallet containing $63. The driver's license and credit cards were issued to Steven Toscar."

Everyone knows who Steven Toscar is. Was. Toscar made tons of money in real estate. Two years ago, he shut me out of one of his projects, costing me a chance for a big score. It upset me at the time, but I got over it. It appears not everyone is as forgiving as I am.

"Toscar's wife called 911 at eleven 11:38 PM." I rustle the pages until Bass looks at me. "The police are checking to see if your fingerprints match the ones found on the hammer. So what's your story?"

"Rupp was self-defense. He attacked me. But I swear I didn't kill Toscar."

"The evidence suggests you did."

"Cops plant evidence all the time."

"Are you saying that's what happened here?"

All I'm saying is I didn't kill Toscar. Somebody must've planted that evidence."

A con's typical defense. I lean back in my chair. "Why don't you tell me what happened."

Bass rests his hands on the tabletop. They're large hands, tanned and callused as though they're used to hard manual labor. Like swinging a hammer.

"Two months ago," he begins, "I'm sitting in a bar, having a few drinks, minding my own business, when this guy grabs the stool next to me and orders a beer. I don't pay any attention until he pays for it. That's when I see the hook."

"A hook?"

"Yeah, a hook."

I arch an eyebrow. "Like a pirate's hook?"

"Not exactly," Bass says. "It had these pinchers that were curved on the end. He didn't have any problem digging the money outta his wallet." Bass pinches his fingers together. "He was really ..."

"Adroit?"

Bass frowns. "Huh?"

I dumb it down a notch. "Skillful?"

"Yeah, skillful. I never met anyone with a hook. We had a few beers, got to talking. He said his name was Cletus Rupp and he owned a swimming pool business. He asked if I wanted a job."

"Rupp offered you a job?"

Bass nods. "I told him I was an ex-con. He didn't care. There aren't that many jobs for ex-cons, so I said sure. The first contract he gave me was the Toscars' pool. That's how I met Eve."

I recall a picture from the society pages of a young, attractive woman thirty years younger than Toscar. "You got involved with Toscar's wife?"

Bass's dark eyes look haunted. "Mr. Cleary, I didn't stand a chance."

I watch the tape spin for a few moments. "What happened?"

"I worked on the pool twice a week," Bass says. "At first, Eve acted like I wasn't there. Then one day she asked if I wanted a drink. I told her I wasn't supposed to drink on the job. She said it was just lemonade—and she wouldn't tell anyone."

"Were you nervous?"

"Hell yes," Bass says. "I'm not stupid. I figured she had something on her mind."

"And did she?"

"Yeah. She wanted to know if I'd kill her husband."

The tape runs out. I fumble the little plastic cassette out of the tape recorder, flip it over, and shove it back in. Before I start the tape, Bass asks for something to drink. I step outside, talk to the guard, and he brings us two Pepsis. After he leaves, I push the Record button.

"Mrs. Toscar asked you to kill her husband?"

Bass unscrews the top on his drink. "Not in so many words. First, she told me she knew I was an ex-con. I asked if that mattered. She said no. And that's when she told me to call her Eve." Bass faces me. "Mr. Cleary, I've been in some nasty prison fights, but when she said that, she scared the hell outta me."

"What happened?"

Bass sips some Pepsi before replying. "She told me how her husband didn't pay any attention to her. How a woman like her had needs." He takes a deep breath. "One thing led to another, and we ended up in bed."

My heart ratchets up a notch. "Go on."

"Afterward," Bass says, "she kept telling me how much she hated her husband." He rakes his fingers through his hair. "This went on for a month. Eve would say she wished we didn't have to sneak around. I'd laugh and tell her she'd never settle for an ex-con. She'd pout until I'd say I was sorry. It was weird, but it felt kinda good too. It made me feel … special."

"So when did she ask you to kill her husband?"

"Last week," Bass says. "I showed up for work, and Eve was crying, said her husband accused her of having an affair. She denied it, but it didn't matter. He wanted a divorce."

I lean forward. "So what's the problem? In this state, she'd get half in a settlement."

Bass nods. "That's what I told her. But Eve said there was a prenup and she wouldn't get a dime. She said she deserved something for all she put up with over the years. She wanted him dead and asked if I'd do it. She told me he kept money in a safe in their bedroom. She said I could make it look like a robbery gone bad."

"What'd you tell her?"

"That I had to think about it. That's when she mentioned the life insurance policy."

This just gets better and better. "How much?"

"Five million dollars."

I tent my fingers. "So once Toscar's out of the picture, Eve's a rich lady. And she wants you to come along for the ride. Sounds like a sweet deal."

Bass scans the cramped room. "You think?"

I shrug. "A fortune and a fine-looking woman to share it with. What's not to like?"

"Murder, for one thing," Bass says. "Look, I've made my share of mistakes, but I never killed anyone."

"What about the evidence?"

"I told you. It was planted."

"You don't seriously believe the cops planted it, do you?"

"Doesn't have to be the cops."

That gets my attention. "What do you mean?"

"I think Eve got tired of waiting for me to make up my mind and found someone else. Cletus Rupp."

"Are you serious?"

Bass nods. "When I saw Eve yesterday afternoon, she was hysterical. Her cheek was bruised. She said her husband hit her. She said if I loved her, I'd kill him, so we could get his money and be together." Bass picks at a callus on his palm, avoiding my eyes. "I told her okay."

I sit up. "Wait a minute. I thought you said—"

"I was just gonna scare him," he explains. "Get him to reconsider. Eve said she was going to stay with a friend, so Toscar would be home alone. She gave me the combination to his safe and said she'd unlock the patio doors. I got to their place around ten thirty. There was a light on in the study. That's where I found him. He was already dead. I got the hell outta there."

"Why didn't you call the police?"

"With my record?"

I nod. "I understand. Then what happened?"

Bass drains the rest of his Pepsi. "I drove home. Around midnight, Rupp called and told me to meet him at the Shamrock. He said it was important, life or death. I got there about a quarter to one, but Rupp didn't show up until one fifteen. The minute he got there, he said he'd followed me to Toscar's place and he'd seen the body. He wanted ten grand to keep his mouth shut."

"The amount the cops found in the bag."

"Yeah," Bass says. "I told him I didn't know what he was talking about. He went ballistic. Said to pay up or he'd go to the cops. He wouldn't shut up, so I left."

"But he followed you outside," I say, imagining the events in my mind.

Bass nods. "He pushed me. I told him to leave me alone, but he just wouldn't back off. He swung at my head with his hook. I ducked and shoved him hard as I could. He slammed up against a pickup and dropped to the ground. He started jerking. I rolled him over and saw the hook stuck in his throat.

"The cops showed up, and I told them it was self-defense," Bass adds. "They arrested me anyway. They didn't charge me with Toscar's murder until later." He leans back in his chair. "And here we are."

"What if they find your fingerprints on the hammer?"

Bass shrugs. "It means I used that hammer for some reason, and Cletus took it. With his hook, he wouldn't leave any prints." Bass must notice the doubt on my face. "If I was gonna kill Toscar, don't you think I'd be smart enough to wear gloves?"

I sip some of my Pepsi. "Then explain how the gym bag got in your car."

Bass's leg starts bouncing. "Cletus must've planted it there while I was waiting for him. That's why he wanted me at the Shamrock by one. He would've had enough time to kill Toscar, clean up, and dump the bag in my car."

"But if he already had the money; why argue with you about it?"

"I don't know. I haven't figured that out yet."

"So you think Mrs. Toscar and Rupp set you up?"

Bass stares into my eyes. "Mr. Cleary, I know they did, but I can't prove it. With Cletus dead, it's my word against hers. Who do you think a jury'll believe?"

My silence tells him all he needs to know.

Bass slumps back in his chair. "That's why you gotta help me. Look, I'm a two-time loser. If I'm convicted, I'm looking at a death sentence. I need you to fight for my life."

I stare into his dark eyes. "Mr. Bass, I'll do all I can."

The guard pokes his head inside the room and tells me my time's up. I shake hands with Bass and promise him I'll be in touch. I exit the building into the early-afternoon heat and smile when I see the vanity license plate on my silver BMW: SHARK. Who says lawyers don't have a sense of humor? I toss my suit coat in the backseat and sink into the soft leather seats. After loosening my tie, I crank up the air-conditioning. The interior is cool by the time I leave the parking lot.

I turn on the radio. My fingers tap a rhythm on the steering wheel while I ponder Bass's story. All in all, he has a good grasp of how he's been set up. Just not of who set him up. But that's the beauty of this plan. After all, why would he suspect his court-appointed lawyer?

I take the exit for Channel Drive. A few cars pass me, but I'm not in any hurry. I know where I'm going and I know who'll be there when I arrive.

• • •

Eve Toscar stands in the front doorway clipping on a pearl earring. It matches the necklace around her neck. They contrast vividly with the sleeveless black dress she wears. The dress is demure enough for grieving, but it clings here and there, hinting at the lush body beneath it. Eve looks good. It's something she takes for granted. Like breathing.

I step inside and close the door. "Where's Inez?"

"I sent her home. She's a wreck. She worked for Steven for a long time." Eve brushes past me and heads toward the kitchen, leaving a hint of her perfume in the air. "What did Bass say?"

"About what we figured." I watch the way her hips twitch beneath the dress. Her jet-black hair is piled on top of her head, and a few loose wisps graze her neck. Her cheek is bruised from where I hit her, but her makeup hides most of it. "He knows he was set up—and that no jury will believe him."

"He's right." Eve fills a glass with ice from the dispenser on the refrigerator door. She adds a splash of vodka from the open bottle sitting on the granite-topped counter and takes a sip. She peers at me over the rim of her glass, her dark blue eyes locked onto mine. "Want one?"

I drop my briefcase on the floor, pry the glass from her fingers, and set it on the counter. "I had something else in mind."

Eve turns her head, and my kiss lands awkwardly on her cheek. A tiny ember of worry sparks deep in my gut. "What's wrong?"

She smooths the front of her dress. "We don't have time. The funeral director is coming by to talk about the memorial service." She avoids my gaze. "Besides, I've been thinking maybe we should cool things for a while, at least until after the funeral."

The ember flares into a full-fledged blaze. When Eve showed up in my office six months ago, I confirmed the details of her husband's will: she would never see a dime of his money if they divorced. She profited only if he died. When I didn't hear from her, I thought that was the end of it. But two weeks later she called. During our follow-up appointment, I found myself plotting Steven Toscar's death. In my defense, it should be noted that my trousers were bunched around my ankles at the time. Since then, I'd come to think of Eve as my personal 401(k).

So I don't like the idea of my retirement plans going up in smoke. I put on my sincere face—the one I used on Bass. "Don't worry, everything's under control."

She sips some of her drink. "That's easy for you to say. You didn't have to talk to the police."

"What'd you tell them?"

Eve fidgets with the strand of pearls. "What we talked about. I was with my friend Anne. I came home and found Steven dead."

"Anne will back you up?"

She nods. "Of course."

"Good. Stick with your story and the cops can't touch you."

"They want to talk again. You said once they arrested Bass we'd be in the clear."

I brush a stray hair off her cheek. "And we are. Look, with Rupp dead, there's no way the cops can link him to us. As for Bass, it's his word against yours. And with his history, you'll win every time. Just stick to our plan and you'll be spending Steven's money in no time."

She smiles. "I'm going to be rich. And I have you to thank for it."

The burning in my gut fades. "Glad I could help."

Eve inches closer. "You were so smart to use Rupp to find a loser like Bass."

I shrug. "He owed me a favor."

"Don't be so modest," she coos, molding herself against me.

Eve's good looks distract a lot of people—you'd have to be blind to be immune—but her matchless gift is how special she makes you feel. Bass nailed that right on the head. Pretty soon, you do whatever you can to hoard her for yourself. By then it's too late. You're hooked, and you'll promise her anything. Addiction is an ugly thing.

I smile. "It was clever."

Eve nips my earlobe. "Very clever. And making sure you were assigned as Dexter's lawyer was pure genius."

My heart hammers against my ribs. We both know I'm going to give in, but my ego wants her to work for it. I untangle myself and step back. "You know, you may be right. Maybe we should cool it for a while. I don't want to jinx anything."

She unbuckles my belt. "In that case, we should make this memorable."

I grip the countertop. "I thought you said we didn't have time."

"Shhh," she says, placing a finger over my lips. "This won't take long."

• • •

From the moment we hatched our scheme, I planned to help Eve spend her fortune. That's the main reason I sweated the details plotting Toscar's murder. Sure, love entered into it—the love of money. So I'm not a romantic. Sue me. Now with Rupp dead and Bass in jail, all the pieces have fallen into place.

So I'm stunned when a herd of cops shows up at my house three days after my meeting with Dexter Bass. The one in front is wearing an off-the-rack navy blazer and wrinkled khaki slacks, spotted with the remnants of his lunch. His thick-soled black shoes tell me he spends a lot of time on his feet, and the bags under his bloodshot brown eyes tell me he isn't getting much sleep. He shows me his gold badge.

"Jack Cleary?"

"Yeah?"

"I'm Detective Frank Hall. We have a warrant for your arrest."

"Wait a second," I say, backpedaling as several cops crowd past me. "What's this about?"

He hands me the warrant. "It's all in there, but I'll make it easy for you. You're under arrest for the murder of Steven Toscar."

• • •

Before Hall begins the interrogation, I look at the one-way mirror built into the wall. "I want to talk to whoever's back there."

Hall shakes his head. "You aren't in any position to make demands."

"Then we're finished here."

Hall gives me his best tough-cop stare. When I yawn, he glances at the mirror. After a moment, the door opens. Assistant DA Lois Stone strolls in and deposits her briefcase on the table.

"I'll take it from here, Detective," she says. After Hall vacates his chair, she sits down. "Hello, Jack. Fancy meeting you here."

Lois Stone is the best prosecutor in the DA's office. Defense attorneys call her "Stone Cold" because she shows no mercy in court. But she's no ice queen. Cinnamon-colored, shoulder-length hair frames a face that is more striking than beautiful, and the bookish, tortoise-shell frames she wears complement a pair of jade-green eyes a Mayan would covet. We met years ago when I worked in the DA's office and she had just passed the bar. I took her under my wing and taught her everything she knows about prosecuting the bad guys. Now I'll find out if 1 did a good job.

Stone adjusts the glasses on her nose. "Did they read you your rights?"

"Yes."

"And you're consenting to this interview without a lawyer present?"

"I'm a lawyer, remember?" I always respected Lois Stone, but the look on her face suggests the feeling isn't mutual. It'll be a pleasure to wipe that smirk off her face.

"How could I forget?" She points to the built-in video camera on the wall. "Okay if we tape this?"

"Sure. I've got nothing to hide."

"Okay, then let's get started."

"I didn't kill Steven Toscar. I'm innocent. I'm being framed." Stone tilts her head. "Really?" She opens her briefcase and pulls out a folder but doesn't open it—a ploy I taught her to make a suspect sweat. "You sound a lot like Dexter Bass," she says. "Except I'm starting to believe him."

"That would be a mistake." I stare at the folder. My heart speeds up. It's a whole other world on this side of the table.

"Didn't you defend Cletus Rupp?" Stone asks. "Something about him stalking his ex-wife?"

I meet her gaze. "The woman was imagining things. She needed therapy."

Stone shrugs as if conceding the point. "Had you seen Rupp recently?"

"I hadn't spoken to him since his trial." Rupp and I met face-to-face. There won't be a telltale message on his answering machine for the cops to find.

"No chance encounter?"

"None."

Stone locks her green eyes on me. They're still as hypnotic as I remember. "Where were you last Monday evening between 9:00 PM and one?"

Thank God for TiVo. "I was home watching TV."

She looks skeptical. "Anybody there with you?"

"No."

Stone lifts a corner of the file. "Did you make any calls, or did anyone call you?"

"No." I try to peek inside the folder, but she closes it. It's another tactic I taught her, but my chest tightens anyway.

"Did you go anywhere? Have a pizza delivered?"

"No, I stayed home all night. Look, I'm sorry no one can vouch for me, but I didn't think I'd need an alibi."

Stone ignores my tone. "So what you're saying is that you didn't kill Steven Toscar and frame Dexter Bass."

I lean close enough to smell her perfume—a hint of lilac. "Yes, that's exactly what I'm saying."

Stone twists the ends of her hair around her fingertips. "Well, Jack, I guess that makes you a liar and a murderer."

I jerk forward in my chair. "Now just—"

"Save it," Stone snaps. She stares at me and flips open the folder. It's full of pictures—eight-by-ten blow-ups—and she hands me the top one.

"This is a photo of you and Cletus Rupp. That is your Beemer, right? The one with SHARK on the plates?" She doesn't wait for my reply. "You notice the date in the bottom right-hand corner? It was taken two months ago."

"You can program a camera to any date."

"Is that your defense, Jack? That someone faked the date?"

I stare at the photo. "I'm just saying it's possible. So, where did you get this?"

"We found it in Rupp's office. You want to tell me about this, Jack?"

My brain kicks into overdrive, trying to come up with an explanation Stone will buy. I snap my fingers. "I remember now. Rupp wanted to borrow some money. I told him no, and that was that. It must've slipped my mind."

Stone leans back in her chair. "I wonder why Rupp felt the need to photograph your meet."

"You'd have to ask him."

"Too bad we can't." Stone pauses. "I'd be worried if I were you, Jack. You're too young to have Alzheimer's."

Beads of sweat snake down my ribs. "We met one time. That's the truth."

Stone nods. "The truth is good. Who knows? Maybe it'll set you free."

My mouth goes dry. I glance at Hall, and he smirks. I drop my gaze and stare at the scarred tabletop. Stone rattled me with the picture. The pupil has learned some things on her own.

"So you met just once with Rupp?"

I look up. Maybe she's tossing me a lifeline. "Yeah, just the one time."

She takes a deep breath and shakes her head, a look of disappointment on her face. She pulls more photos from the file and lines them up in front of me. The dates and locations differ, but each of them shows the same thing: Rupp and me sitting in my car.

"You know what I think? I think you hired Rupp to murder Steven Toscar and frame Bass. Why? I'm not sure."

"That's crazy."

She shrugs. "Maybe, but right now I feel sorry for Dexter Bass."

I hold up my hand. "Wait a minute. Maybe Rupp did this on his own. Maybe after I turned him down, he asked Toscar for money. Rupp had the service contract for Toscar's pool, and Bass did the work on it."

"Bass worked for Rupp?"

I nod. "For the past two or three months."

Stone grabs the file and heads toward the door. "I'll be right back."

After she leaves, Hall count ceiling tiles while I try to figure a way out of the jam I'm in. Neither of us speaks. Stone returns in a few minutes and hands me a Pepsi.

"I didn't know Bass worked for Rupp. Thanks for the tip."

I take a sip to ease the dryness in my throat. "Anything to help clear me."

Stone places the folder on the table and hooks one arm over the back of her chair. "So how do you think the evidence got in Bass's car?"

I lean forward. "Rupp must've found out Toscar kept a lot of money in his safe. He knew Bass had done time for burglary. Maybe he offered Bass a cut to pull off the job. Maybe Toscar surprised Bass during the robbery and things got out of hand. My guess is, Bass threw the hammer in his car and planned to ditch it later. But he and Rupp got into a fight at the Shamrock and he never had the chance. That's why it was in his car."

I sit back in my chair and feel some of the tightness leave my chest. I've always done my best thinking under pressure. It's why I've done well in court. I've given Stone a scenario that fits the facts—and she's got to know my version offers a jury enough room for reasonable doubt.

But she won't let it go. "You're saying you didn't have anything to do with the gym bag found in Bass's car?"

"How could I? I was home all night."

Stone reaches into the folder once again, pulls out more photos, and spreads them in front of me. Seconds later, I realize I'm facing the death penalty.

"Last year," she says, "after being robbed three times in two months, the pawnshop across the street from the Shamrock installed state-of-the-art surveillance cameras." She pauses and picks up one of the photos, then places it back in front of me. "As you can see, they offer a pretty good view of the Shamrock's parking lot."

Stone taps the photo farthest on my left. "In this one, you've just arrived in the parking lot. I can even make out the writing on the baseball cap you're wearing." She squints at the photo. "What do you know? We listen to the same radio station."

I stare at the photos, unable to avert my eyes.

"See how clear your face is in the one where you're putting the gym bag in Bass's car?" She leans closer to me. "And guess what? We found your prints on the hammer used to kill Steven Toscar."

My head snaps up. I know I didn't leave any fingerprints. I wrapped the handle in plastic and wore gloves. The latex made my hands sweat. I rack my brain, searching for an explanation.

All at once, I know who set me up, and the realization leaves me lightheaded. I bend over and suck air into my lungs.

"What's wrong?" she asks, her green eyes sparkling. "Cat got your tongue?"

I look into her eyes. "Why'd you keep looking when you already had Bass in custody?"

Stone scoops up the photographs and slips them into the folder. "The fingerprints on the hammer didn't match his. We expanded our search and got a hit on yours. You remember getting printed when you worked in the DA's office? After we got the photos of you and Rupp—plus the ones from the pawnshop—all the pieces fell into place."

The walls seem to close in on me. "I'll tell you who set this up, but I want a deal."

She considers this for a moment. "I'll have to talk to my boss."

I slowly nod. "I'm not going anywhere."

Stone pauses in the doorway. "There's one more thing." "What's that?"

"You're slipping, Jack. I'd call another lawyer if I were you."

• • •

I follow Stone's advice and call Curt Beyer. Beyer is the best defense attorney I know. He's expensive, but from what I've seen in court, he's worth every penny. I make the call, and forty-five minutes later he shows up. After two hours of hurried meetings with, me and the DA, he hammers out a deal: I testify for the state and the DA won't seek the death penalty. There's even the slim possibility of parole in the distant future. When Stone returns, I agree to the deal.

She leans back in her chair and peers at me through her lenses. "So, what've you got?"

With my lawyer's blessing, I spill my guts, from my initial meeting with Eve Toscar to the night of the murder. Stone listens quietly. She doesn't look impressed.

"This is your big expose? That Toscar's wife wanted him dead?"

I didn't expect high-fives or pats on the back, but I thought she'd be more excited. "That's right. Eve wanted his money, but due to the prenup, she couldn't get it any other way."

"Jack, do I look stupid?" Stone's voice drips with scorn. "Don't you think we'd check her out?"

"Of course, but—"

"We put her under a microscope," she says. "She came off smelling like a rose. Everyone we talked to—including Toscar's friends—said the marriage was rock-solid. Hell, Jack, Toscar recently changed his will to dissolve their prenup."

The news hits me like a sledgehammer. "What?"

Stone smirks. "Didn't know that, huh? Here's something else I bet you didn't know. When we asked if her husband had any enemies, she gave us your name. She swore Toscar told you threatened him when he cut you out of a business deal."

"That's a lie!" I shout.

"So you say. She also denied knowing Dexter Bass, and he confirms that."

"No way. I've got him on tape telling how Eve asked him to kill her husband."

Beyer grabs my arm. "Shut up, Jack. You can't divulge anything Bass told you in confidence."

I jerk my arm free and look at Stone. "You want to hear it?"

Lois Stone sits back in her chair and taps her lush lips with her index finger. "Curt's right. Whatever Bass told you is covered by attorney-client privilege. It's not admissible."

"Screw privilege," I say. "The tape's in my briefcase at home."

Hall clears his throat. He's been so quiet, I forgot he's in the room. "His briefcase is in the evidence lab."

Stone's eyes narrow. "You're kidding, right?"

Hall can't meet her gaze. "We, uh, brought it just in case."

Stone looks at me and shrugs. "I guess I can't stop you from playing the tape."

Ten minutes later, over Beyer's repeated objections, I pop open the locks on my briefcase and pull out my tape recorder. After I met with Bass, I never listened to the tape. Why bother? But now, with my life on the line, I'm glad I taped it. My hand shakes as I press the Play button. The tape spins. Nothing.

"Are you sure it's the right tape?" Stone asks.

I paw through my briefcase, searching for other tapes, but the rest are still in their cellophane wrappers. I fast-forward the tape, hoping to hear Bass's voice, but all I get is faint static. Then it hits me.

"I had the tape when I went to Eve's house after meeting with Bass," I explain. "She would've had plenty of time to grab the tape while I was in the shower."

"You have anything else to back up your story?" Stone asks.

I scour my memory but come up empty. My meetings with Eve

took place after office hours, after everyone had gone home. She wanted to keep our meetings hush-hush, so I never logged them in my appointment book. And I never billed her, since she paid me in her own special way.

"No," I mutter. "Nothing else."

The door opens and a uniformed officer hands Stone several sheets of paper. She studies them, then looks at me.

"While we've been talking, the police checked Rupp's employee records. There's no record that Bass worked for him. No job application, no W-2, nothing. We even checked the service records for Toscar's pool. All the forms were signed by Dan Dorsey." She hands me the sheets of paper. "See for yourself."

I glance through the pages. "Maybe Bass used that name as an alias."

Stone shakes her head. "Rupp's secretary said Dorsey has worked there for years. We talked to Dorsey, and he confirmed that he did all the work on Toscar's pool."

The pages slip from my hands and flutter to the floor. Stone stands up and walks to the door. "Jack," she says, then waits until I look at her. "You've got zilch. No deal." She looks at Hall. "See that Mr. Cleary gets back to his cell."

• • •

At my arraignment, Beyer works his magic and gets me out on bail. It's a miracle, but that's why I'm paying him the big bucks. I have to wear a tracking bracelet on my ankle, but it beats sitting in jail. Stone objects, but the judge cuts her off and calls for the next case. After. I'm released, I go home, make a couple of phone calls, and wait.

Three hours later, I stroll into the Shamrock Bar. At this time of day, even the hard-core drinkers have other places to be, so it's easy to spot Dexter Bass waiting in the booth in the far corner. With my arrest, his claim of self-defense rang true. His new attorney didn't have any problem getting the charges dropped. Bass raises his glass when he notices me.

"I didn't think you'd come," I tell him.

"I'm a curious guy," he says, a sly grin creasing his face. It quickly fades. "So, what'd you wanna talk about?"

"How did you do it?"

Bass sits up straighter. "Hold on there, Counselor. How'd I do what?"

"Cut the crap," I hiss. "I'm looking at life, maybe even the needle. The least you can do is tell me how you and Eve set me up."

"I don't know what you're talking about." Bass finishes his drink and starts to leave. I grab his wrist, stalling his exit. I need to hear the truth, and to get it I'm gambling that his ego is bigger than mine.

"C'mon, you can tell me. I'm pretty bright, but I know when I've been outsmarted. It was your idea, wasn't it?"

Bass jerks his hand free. "You wearing a wire?" I tell him no, but he isn't convinced. "Follow me."

We head to the bathroom and Bass motions me inside. The smell stings my nose, and I watch where I step. Must be the maid's day off. Bass locks the door.

"Unbutton your shirt."

I undo the buttons and show him my bare chest. He spins me around and shoves me against the wall. He frisks me, leaving no place unchecked. I've had less thorough exams at my doctor's office. Bass seems satisfied.

"It was Eve's idea," he says.

My stomach churns as Bass guides me through the double-cross. He and Eve worked a few scams in Vegas until he went to prison and she reinvented herself. When he got out, they hooked up again and looked for a patsy. I fit the bill. After I contacted Rupp, Eve had Bass take the photos of my meetings with him. Then Bass "bumped" into Rupp in the bar. Once everything was in place, he and Eve waited for me to murder her husband. And while I was busy killing Toscar, Eve snuck into Rupp's office and planted the photographs.

"How did my fingerprints get on the hammer? I wore gloves that night."

He gives me a smug grin. "It's your hammer."

"I don't understand."

"Eve took the hammer from your garage," Bass explains. "She gave you your own hammer and said it was one I'd used. But I never touched it."

My cheeks burn. "What about Dan Dorsey?"

Bass smirks. "What about him? I never met the guy. I visited Eve on the days Dorsey wasn't scheduled to be there."

I step toward him. "Was it worth it?"

Bass jabs his fingers in my chest. "Don't go righteous on me, Counselor. You tried to frame me too."

"Aren't you worried she'll set you up?"

"No. Lucky for me, Eve likes outlaws better than lawyers." There isn't much to say after that. Bass looks at his watch and tells me he has a plane to catch. He unlocks the bathroom door and walks out.

The bartender is clearing the table where Bass was sitting. As I walk by, he puts his hand on my chest. I recognize him as one of the cops who searched my house.

"Stone's waiting for you across the street," he says.

I push through the back exit and cross the street to the pawn-shop's parking lot. I knock on the side door of the gray cargo van parked in the shadows. Lois Stone opens the sliding door and steps out into the afternoon heat. She's wearing a dark green pantsuit that complements her auburn hair. There's something on her lips—lipstick or gloss—that leaves them shiny. I'd like to think she did it for me, but that's wishful thinking.

"Did you get it?"

"Loud and clear. There's enough for arrest warrants. Eve Toscar and Dexter Bass won't be spending her money anytime soon."

"How'd you know he wouldn't find the bug?"

Stone grabs the van's door handle. "Jack, guys like you and Bass always think you're smarter than the rest of us. That's your downfall. Once he frisked you and didn't find anything, I knew he'd stop looking. There was no way he'd suspect we bugged the john."

I know she's right. "So is our deal back on?"

"Yeah, it's back on. You've got until Monday to get your affairs in order."

I shake my head. "I'm gonna die an old man in prison."

Stone's face softens for a moment. "Cheer up, Jack. With good behavior, you could get paroled in fifteen, twenty years. You'll still have plenty of life left."

"Not quite what I had in mind."

She shrugs. "A word of advice?"

"Sure, what've I got to lose?"

Her eyes sparkle. "When you're in the shower, don't drop the soap."

• • •

CHARLES DREES admits that when it comes to his literary preferences, he's a mystery-genre snob. "Chances are, if someone doesn't die, I won't read it," he says. "By Hook or By Crook," first story accepted for publication, appeared in the Mystery Writers of America anthology *The Prosecution Rests*, edited by Linda Fairstein. A licensed psychotherapist with more than twenty years experience, he lives with his wife in Manhattan, Kansas—the Little Apple.

THE FINAL NAIL:
A VAL O'FARRELL STORY
By Robert J. Randisi

ONE

When Val O'Farrell entered Muldoon's, he immediately spotted his friend, Sam McKeever, sitting at the bar. It was early and the basement Bowery speakeasy was pretty empty. Even the regulars didn't start drinking in earnest until after noon. Of course, at one corner of the bar was Eddie Doherty, who started drinking the minute his eyes opened and didn't stop until they closed.

O'Farrell approached the bar and shook his head at Lars, the Swedish bartender, indicating he did not want a drink. When Lars picked up the coffee pot and raised his eyebrows, O'Farrell nodded. A steaming mug was on the bar by the time he seated himself next to McKeever.

His friend was staring morosely into a shot glass of what O'Farrell had no doubt was Irish whiskey.

"Kind of early for that, don't you think, Sam?" O'Farrell asked. "Especially when you have to go in to work."

Without looking at the private detective, the cop said, "No, it ain't early, and no, I don't have to go to work."

O'Farrell picked up his mug of coffee and asked, "You takin' a day off?"

"A career off," McKeever said, raising his glass. "I've been suspended."

"A disciplinary thing?" O'Farrell asked. "They'll make you stew and then reinstate you."

"I don't think so," McKeever said. "I'm finished."

"Why, Sam?"

"They say I've been taking payoffs."

"It's 1924," O'Farrell said. "We're in the midst of Prohibition. Who isn't taking payoffs?"

"Well," McKeever said, "I guess I'm gettin' roasted for it. That's the difference."

"Let 'em go to hell, then, Sam," O'Farrell said. "Come in with me."

For the first time, the cop looked at the shamus.

"Me? A private dick? Don't make me laugh. I'm a cop. My father was a cop. He'd turn over in his grave."

"Then don't just sit here and take it," O'Farrell said.

"What am I supposed to do?"

"Fight them."

McKeever laughed and turned his attention back to his Irish whiskey. "With what?"

O'Farrell grinned and said, "Me."

O'Farrell got McKeever off the stool and told him to go home to his wife. He'd been up all night and hadn't seen her since the previous night when he went to work.

"I can't go home, Val."

"Isn't she going to be worried when you don't show up?"

"She's used to me not coming home," McKeever said. "What she's not used to is me coming home without my gun and badge, suspended pending a payola investigation."

"Okay," O'Farrell said, digging into his pocket. "Go to my place, get some sleep. I'll clear this up today so you don't have to tell her."

• • •

As O'Farrell installed the police detective behind the wheel of his roadster, the cop asked, "How'd you know where to find me?"

"Lars called when you started drinking Irish whiskey at 6:00 AM," O'Farrell told him.

"Snitch."

"He's a good friend," O'Farrell corrected, "and an even better bartender."

Luckily, he'd gotten to McKeever before he could have a third drink, so he was fine to drive home.

With McKeever on his way home, O'Farrell went to his own car—a yellow Pierce Arrow Roadster—and drove to police head-quarters.

TWO

Police Headquarters had been located on Mulberry Street until 1909 when it moved to 240 Centre Street. O'Farrell spent his last ten years on the job working out of that building so he knew his way around. He also knew a lot of the men who still worked there, some by name, others on sight.

It was surprisingly easy for him to get in to see Captain Mike Turico, even though he'd sent his name in ahead. Turico was not only

McKeever's commanding officer, but O'Farrell's old C.O. as well. They never got along when they were peers and since O'Farrell left the department and made a name for himself as a private detective, their relationship had not gotten any better.

"Whataya want, Val?" Captain Turico demanded as O'Farrell walked in. "I'm busy."

"Putting the final nail in Sam McKeever's coffin?" O'Farrell asked.

Turico looked up from his desk and locked eyes with O'Farrell. They were both in their forties; had joined the police force at the same time. O'Farrell knew Turico resented him, not so much for leaving the force as for becoming so successful as a private ticket.

"Your buddy McKeever supplied all the nails himself, O'Farrell."

"Is that a fact?" O'Farrell asked. "You mind if I take a look at the file then?"

"Why? Is he askin' for your help? That figures."

"What figures?"

"That he'd go outside the force to get help—and from you."

"I guess if he thought he could get help from inside the force— like from his boss—he'd be here instead of me."

"So he did hire you?"

"Let's just say I'm here on my own," O'Farrell said, "to satisfy my curiosity."

"You wonderin' if your boy could be guilty?" Turico asked.

"I'm wondering why, if he got caught with his hand in the till, you're persecuting him for it. It's not like he's the only boy in blue on the take." O'Farrell gave Turico a long, knowing look. "I know a few pads with your name on them, Mike."

Turico's face clouded. He pointed his pen at O'Farrell, but the look on his face said he wished it was a gun.

"That's old news, O'Farrell," he said. "The days of you and me linin' our pockets is gone. I'm clean."

"If you're clean, then you should be able to recognize it when you see it, Mike," O'Farrell said. "Sam McKeever's the straightest arrow we know."

"That's what I thought, too," Turico said. "Maybe that's why he's such a disappointment."

"What are you talking about?"

"Here." Turico opened his top drawer, pulled out a file and dropped it on his desk. "Take a look for yourself."

O'Farrell reached for the file, but Turico slapped a ham hand down on it.

"You look at it right here," he said. "It don't leave this office."

"Fine by me, Mike."

• • •

It didn't take long for O'Farrell to read through the file and take some notes. He closed it and tossed it back on the captain's desk. He hadn't bothered to hear McKeever's side of it because he knew the man was innocent. He wanted to see the evidence against him and it didn't look so cut and dried to him.

"This is bullshit."

"Which part?"

"All of it," O'Farrell said. "The money, the girl—"

"The dead girl, you mean."

O'Farrell sat forward.

"You don't mean to tell me he might be charged for that?"

"Just because he's a cop don't mean he can't be charged with murder."

"You don't believe that."

"The hell I don't," Turico said. "I'm the one who took his gun and badge from him."

O'Farrell rubbed his jaw, thought a moment, then got it. "You don't think he did it."

"What makes you say that?"

O'Farrell tapped the file with his forefinger. "There's no way you'd let me look at this file unless you wanted me to work on this," O'Farrell said. "You hate my guts and you'd eat nails before you'd help me ... normally."

"That's true enough."

"So then why did you let me look at it?"

"You wanna help your buddy, O'Farrell?"

"You know I do."

"Then why are you lookin' a gift horse in the mouth?" Turico said. "Get out of here, Val."

O'Farrell stared at Turico and decided there was nothing worth arguing about. Turico obviously thought McKeever was innocent, but had to act on the evidence and suspend him. The Captain didn't particularly like McKeever any more than he liked O'Farrell, but McKeever was the best detective he had. Every time McKeever closed a case, it made Turico look good. With McKeever off the job or in jail, who was going to take his place?

"I'm going to clear Sam," O'Farrell said. "You can count on it."

"Sure," Turico said, "you clear your squeaky clean friend, Val, and I'll give him his badge back."

O'Farrell stood up, headed for the door and said, "You better polish it up then."

THREE

O'Farrell left the Police Headquarters building at 240 Centre Street, walked two blocks to Crosby Street and entered the speak he knew many off-duty cops frequented. He'd asked for McKeever's partner before leaving and had been told the man, Ed Melky, was out.

As he looked around the speak, he realized he didn't know Ed Melky, didn't even know what he looked like. He must have been a newly assigned partner to McKeever, who went through partners faster than some men went through women. He did, however, recognize several cops in the place which—like Muldoon's—had not started to do a brisk business yet.

He went to the bar, got a coffee, and walked over to a trio of cops who were drinking illegal hooch.

"Hello, boys."

They looked up at him and while two of them looked away, the third man said, "Hey, Val. How's it goin'?"

"Pretty good for me, Dooley," he said, "not so good for McKeever, I hear."

"Yeah," Dooley said, "I heard about that."

Dooley was a detective O'Farrell had worked with a few times while he was still on the job. He knew the other men on sight, but not their names.

"What do you know about it, Kevin?" O'Farrell asked.

Kevin Dooley frowned, then stood up and said, "Over here, Val."

They walked away from the other two men and sat at a small table together. O'Farrell took off his fedora and set it on the table. The hat had cost more than the suit the police detective was wearing. He knew Dooley didn't hold his success against him like a lot of cops did.

"Why you interested, Val?"

"I'm going to clear Sam."

"I don't know how you're gonna do that," Dooley said. "The evidence is pretty damning."

"You know McKeever," O'Farrell said. "You know he's married and loves his wife, so he wouldn't be messing with a two-bit whore, and you know he doesn't take money. Never has, never will."

"I do know that," Dooley said. "McKeever's always been clean, but you know as well as I do it's the clean ones who fall hard."

"Not Sam."

"I don't know what to tell you, Val," Dooley said. "I don't know that much about it."

"Where's his partner?" O'Farrell asked. "This fella, Ed Melky. Do you know him?"

"I know Ed," Dooley said, nodding. "He's only been partnered with McKeever for about a month since he transferred from Brooklyn. Might be why he's not catchin' any fallout from this. He and McKeever really don't know each other that well."

"I read the file, Kevin," O'Farrell said. "It didn't have the name of the detective assigned. Who's working the case?"

Dooley hesitated, then said, "Ed Melky."

"Sam's own partner is making the case against him? Why would he do that?"

"Maybe because he's also the main witness."

"The file said some madam named Sadie fingered McKeever for killing one of her girls."

"Melky ain't about to appear in the file as a witness."

"You know anything about this place where the girl was killed?"

"It's over on Varick Street," Dooley said. "It's a speak downstairs, a whorehouse upstairs. Owned by a guy named Jay Watson."

"And Watson pays off?"

"Oh, yeah."

"So why was McKeever supposed to be there collecting?" O'Farrell asked. "He's no bag man."

"Supposedly, he was just makin' some extra dough," Dooley said.

"And then he goes upstairs with one of the whores and kills her? This stinks."

"Don't I know it."

"Do you know anything else, Kevin?"

"You saw the file, that means you know more than me," Dooley said. He looked over at his buddies, who were eyeing him. "I gotta get back."

"Is anybody on McKeever's side in this?" O'Farrell asked.

"You are, Val," the other man said. "You are."

FOUR

O'Farrell drove to the Varick Street building, knocked on the door of the speak downstairs. A slot opened and two beady eyes regarded him.

"Yeah?"

"I'm here to see Jay Watson."

"What's your business?"

"Police."

"You ain't no cop."

"I used to be, but I'm here on police business anyway."

"You mean that cop who killed Lulu?"

"Yeah."

"What's your name?"

"Val O'Farrell."

"I know you. Hold on." The slot closed, a bolt was thrown and the door was opened. A small man appeared, kicking aside a stool he'd used in order to look out the slot. "I hearda you."

"What did you hear?" O'Farrell asked.

"That yer all right. You was friends with Bat Masterson, right?"

"That's right." Masterson had died at his typewriter recently, in his office at *The Morning Telegraph.* "Is Watson in?"

"He is."

"What's your name?"

"Canto."

"Take me to him, Canto."

"Okay. Follow me."

O'Farrell followed Canto across the floor, half a dozen sets of eyes following him. When they reached a door, Canto knocked.

"Come in," a voice called.

Canto opened the door, said, "Somebody to see you, Jay."

"Who—?"

O'Farrell moved past Canto and into the room, then turned and told the little man, "Shut it."

Canto closed the door.

Jay Watson stood up from a rickety-looking desk, an alarmed look on his heavily lined face. The deep lines made it hard to guess his age.

"Who are you?" he demanded. "Whataya want?"

"My name's O'Farrell. I'm here because you claim Sam McKeever took a payoff from you and killed one of your girls."

"You a cop?"

"Private," O'Farrell said, "but I'm working this."

"I don't hafta talk to you—"

"Yeah, you do, Jay," O'Farrell said. "And so does Sadie. Get her down here."

"Sadie? She's workin' upstairs—"

"Send Canto to get her. I want to talk to both of you at the same time."

"Why should I do that?"

O'Farrell opened his jacket to show the man the gun in his shoulder rig.

"Canto!" Watson yelled.

• • •

Sadie was a worn out, faded forty, thinner than she used to be. O'Farrell could tell because she no longer filled out her dress. When she entered the room, she looked at Watson with frightened eyes— one of them still yellowish from a recent shiner.

"Now I'm going to tell the two of you something," he said. "Sam McKeever never took a payoff in his life and he wouldn't mess with any whores—especially not the diseased lot you likely have upstairs."

"My girls are clean—" Sadie started to object.

"Shut up, sister," O'Farrell said. "Who gave you that shiner? And don't tell me it was McKeever."

Her hand instinctively went to her eye. "Um—" she said.

"I give it to her," Watson said. "Gotta keep her in line. Also, she let one of my girls get killed."

"You?" O'Farrell said. "I don't think you can hit that hard, Jay."

"I … I had somebody do it."

"Who? Canto? Or maybe Ed Melky did it for you."

At the mention of Melky's name, both of them stiffened. It was pretty clear to O'Farrell what had happened. It was Melky who was taking payoffs from Watson and using the girls upstairs. It had to be, for the simple reason that Sam McKeever was clean—cleaner than any cop O'Farrell ever knew, including himself. That was why nobody was on his side. By not taking payoffs, he made all the others look bad. O'Farrell didn't even know why McKeever wanted to keep his badge.

"Sit down, both of you," O'Farrell said. "We're going to go over this until I get the truth."

"But—" Watson said.

"Sit!"

FIVE

O'Farrell decided not to search the city for Ed Melky. Instead, he went back to headquarters because sooner or later the man would have to show up there.

Melky didn't have an office, just a desk opposite Sam McKeever's. That meant O'Farrell was going to be able to brace him in front of his colleagues. He was sitting in McKeever's chair when Melky finally appeared. In fact, he'd just hung up the phone on McKeever's desk.

O'Farrell could see why Jay Watson and Sadie were afraid of the man. He was a bull, well over six feet with bulging biceps, broad shoulders, and a thick waist. Even seasoned detectives moved out of his way as he crossed the floor to his desk.

He stopped short when he saw O'Farrell. He had a jaw like granite, covered with stubble, and a fat cigar right in the middle of his mouth, which he removed.

"I'm not a replacement, if that's what you're thinking," O'Farrell said.

"I know who you are, O'Farrell," Melky said. "What are ya doin' here? This place is for cops. You ain't a cop no more."

"I'm here on behalf of Sam McKeever."

"Jesus," Melky said, seating himself behind his desk, "he hired you to clear him? That's rich."

"Well," O'Farrell said, "he couldn't count on his partner, could he?"

"Hey," Melky said, "I ain't gotta back no murderer." He pointed at O'Farrell with the soggy end of the cigar. "He shoulda thought of that before he beat that girl to death."

"He didn't beat her to death, Melky," O'Farrell said. "You did. And he wasn't making Jay Watson pay extra money to stay open, you were. And he wasn't beating up on Watson's girls regularly, you were. And it all started happening just about last month, when you got here."

"That what he told you?"

"I didn't bother hearing what McKeever had to say, Melky," O'Farrell said.

"That how you run an investigation?"

"It is when I know a man is innocent."

"Figures you'd try to clear your buddy by puttin' the blame on me. What about the witness?"

"The witness? Oh, you mean Sadie? You sure put a scare into her, blackening her eye right after you killed that girl, Lulu. I had a talk with Sadie. Jay Watson, too. They're changing their stories. Sadie says you like to play rough with her girls and you finally killed one. I also spoke to a couple of other girls you brutalized. They couldn't work for a while after you finished with them. I sort of assured them you wouldn't be coming by anymore. And no more payoffs from Jay Watson. You're through."

The other detectives in the room had stopped what they were doing by now and were watching and listening. Mike Turico had come out of his office to watch as well.

"You're a liar," Melky said. "You got nothin'."

"I just got off the telephone with your old boss in Brooklyn," O'Farrell said. "Great invention, the telephone. I was able to sit right here and listen to him complain about you. Seems you got in some trouble in Brooklyn, too, only they couldn't prove anything. They shipped you here so you'd be somebody else's problem. And once you got here, you couldn't wait to start up again, so you found the house on Varick Street and started working it."

"McKeever killed that girl," Melky said with a sneer. "And he was takin' money."

"That's where you made your mistake, Melky," O'Farrell said. "I would have believed that of any other detective in this room." He looked around. "No offense, boys." Then back at Melky. "But not McKeever. See, you might as well have tried to frame a priest. Mike would cut his hands off before he'd take a payoff and he'd cut off his dick before he'd stick it in a whore."

O'Farrell stood up and Melky quickly got to his feet. He had a gun in a holster on his belt, but O'Farrell had removed his jacket and the cop could see the gun in the shoulder rig.

"Want to shoot it out here, Melky?" O'Farrell asked. "This isn't the Old West."

"Yer lyin' about the washed-out bitch," Melky said. "She's too scared—" He stopped short, but not short enough.

"Too scared to finger you?" O'Farrell asked. "Too scared to testify against you? Not anymore. I guaranteed her safety, personally. Jay's, too. You're through."

Melky went for his gun. O'Farrell didn't move, but suddenly the room was filled with the sound of hammers being cocked. More than half a dozen guns were trained on Ed Melky, including Mike Turico's.

"Take his gun, Owens," Turico said to one of the other detectives. "You're done, Melky. Going for your gun, you might as well have confessed."

"This is bullshit," Melky said as detective Owens took his gun. "Them two would never testify against me! They're too scared!"

"You're right," O'Farrell said. "I lied."

He had, indeed. No matter how much he interrogated Jay Watson and Sadie, they were just too afraid of Ed Melky to say a word. The only way they'd say anything was if Melky was behind bars.

"I made it all up, but now that you went ahead and fingered yourself, I think they'll come forward and testify. You can't hurt them anymore."

Turico approached Melky and said to Owens, "Take him downstairs and put him in a cell."

"I'll, uh, need help," Owens said.

"Take as many men as you need."

Four detectives ended up escorting Ed Melky down to the cell block.

Turico holstered his gun and looked at O'Farrell.

"You're pretty slick, bracing him here in front of all of us."

"By all accounts," O'Farrell said, "he has a pretty bad temper. I figured he'd finger himself."

"So everything you said about Melky was true of him?"

"Yes, everything."

"Your buddy owes you big for this."

"You just have that badge nice and shiny for when detective Sam McKeever comes walking back through that door, Mike. And you can forget about that final nail."

• • •

ROBERT J. RANDISI is the author of 540 mystery and Western novels and over fifty short stories. His novels include the Rat Pack and Joe Keough Mysteries. Some of his recent titles are *The Bottom of Every Bottle* (Perfect Crime Books, 2011) and the *I'm a Fool to Kill You* (Severn House, 2011). Randisi is the co-founder of the American Crime Writers League and *Mystery Scene* magazine, as well as founder of the Private Eye Writers of America, and creator of the Shamus Award. He is a four-time nominee of the Shamus and has received the Lifetime Achievement Award from PWA. He has also edited thirty mystery anthologies, including *Hollywood and Crime* (Pegasus, 2007). His latest mystery novel is *You're Nobody 'Til Somebody Kills You* (Minotaur, 2009).

AMAPOLA

By Luis Alberto Urrea

PARADISE VALLEY

Here's the thing—I never took drugs in my life. Yes, all right, I was the champion of my share of keggers. Me and the Pope. We were like, Bring on the Corona and the Jäger! Who wasn't? But I never even smoked the chronic, much less used the hard stuff. Until I met Pope's little sister. And when I met her, she was the drug, and I took her and I took her, and when I took her, I didn't care about anything. All the blood and all the bullets in the world could not penetrate that high.

The irony of Amapola and me was that I never would have gotten close to her if her family hadn't believed I was gay. It was easy for them to think a gringo kid with emo hair and eyeliner was *un joto*. By the time they found out the truth, it was too late to do much about it. All they could do was put me to the test to see if I was a stand-up boy. It was either that or kill me.

You think I'm kidding.

• • •

At first, I didn't even know she existed. I was friends with Popo. We met in my senior year at Camelback High. Alice Cooper's old school back in prehistory—our big claim to fame, though the freshmen had no idea who Alice Cooper was. VH1 was for grandmothers. Maybe Alice was a president's wife or something.

You'd think the freak factor would remain high, right? But it was another hot space full of Arizona Republicans and future CEOs and the struggling underworld of auto mechanics and hopeless football jocks not yet aware they were going to be fat and bald and living in a duplex on the far side drinking too much and paying alimony to the cheerleaders they thought could never weigh 298 pounds and smoke like a coal plant.

Not Popo. The Pope. For one thing, he had more money than God. Well, his dad and his Aunt Cuca had all the money, but it drizzled upon him like the first rains of Christmas. He was always buying the beer, paying for gas and movie tickets and midnight runs to Taco Bell. "Good American food," he called it.

He'd transferred in during my senior year. He called it his exile. I spied him for the first time in English. We were struggling to stay awake during the endless literary conversations about *A Separate Peace*. He didn't say much about it. Just sat over there making sly eyes at the girls and laughing at the teacher's jokes. I'd never seen a Beaner kid with such long hair. He looked like some kind of Apache warrior, to tell you the truth. He had double-loops in his left ear. He got drogy sometimes and wore eyeliner under one eye. Those little Born Again chicks went crazy for him when he was in his devil-boy mode.

And the day we connected, he was wearing a Cradle of Filth T-shirt. He was staring at me. We locked eyes for a second and he nodded once and we both started to laugh. I was wearing a Fields of the

Nephilim shirt. We were the Pentagram Brothers that day, for sure. Everybody else must have been thinking we were goth school shooters. I guess it was a good thing Phoenix was too friggin' hot for black trenchcoats.

Later, I was sitting outside the vice principal's office. Ray Hulsebus, the nickelback on the football team, had called me "faggot" and we'd duked it out in the lunch court. Popo was sitting on the wooden bench in the hall.

"Good fight," he said, nodding once.

I sat beside him.

"Wha'd you get busted for?" I asked.

He gestured at his shirt. It was originally black, but it had been laundered so often it was gray. In a circle were the purple letters, *VU*. Above them, in stark white, one word: *HEROIN*.

"Cool," I said. "Velvet Underground."

"My favorite song."

We slapped hands.

"The admin's not into classic rock," he noted. "Think I'm … advocating substance abuse."

We laughed.

"You like *Berlin*?" he asked.

"Berlin? Like, the old VH1 band?"

"Hell no! Lou Reed's best album, dude!"

They summoned him.

"I'll play it for ya," he said, and walked into the office.

And so it began.

Tía Cuca's house was the bomb. She was hooked up with some kind of Lebanese merchant. Out in Paradise Valley. The whole place was cool floor tiles and suede couches. Their pool looked out on the city lights, and you could watch roadrunners on the deck cruising for rattlers at dusk. Honestly, I didn't know why Pope wasn't in some rich private school like Brophy or Phoenix Country Day, but apparently his scholastic history was "spotty," as they say. I still don't know how he ended up at poor ol' Camelback, but I do know it must have taken a lot of maneuvering by his family. By the time we'd graduated, we were inseparable. He went to ASU. I didn't have that kind of money. I went to community college.

Pope's room was the coolest thing I'd ever seen. Tía Cuca had given him a detached single-car garage at the far end of the house. They'd put in a bathroom and made a bed loft on top of it. Pope had a king-size mattress up there, and a wall of CDs and a Bose iPod port, and everything was Wi-Fi'd to his laptop. There was a huge Bowie poster on the wall beside the door—in full Aladdin Sane glory, complete with the little shiny splash of come on his collarbone. It was so retro. My boy had satellite on a flat screen, and piles of DVDs around the slumpy little couch on the ground floor. I didn't know why he was so crazy for the criminal stuff—*Scarface* and *The Godfather*. I was sick of Tony Montana and Michael Corleone! Elvis clock—you know the one, with the King's legs dancing back and forth in place of a pendulum.

"Welcome," Pope said on that first visit, "to Disgraceland."

He was comical like that when you got to know him.

He turned me on to all that good classic stuff: Iggy, T. Rex, Roxy Music. He wasn't really fond of new music, except for the darkwave guys. Anyway, there we'd be, blasting that glam as loud as possible, and it would get late and I'd just fall asleep on his big bed with him. No wonder they thought I was gay! Ha. We were drinking Buds and reading *Hustler* mags we'd stolen from his Uncle Abdullah or whatever his name was. Aunt Cuca once said, "Don't you ever go home?" not mean like. Friendly banter, I'd say. But I told her, "Nah—since the divorce, my mom's too busy to worry about it." And in among all those excellent boys' days and nights, I was puttering around his desk, looking at the *Alien* figures and the Godzillas, scoping out the new copy of *El Topo* he'd gotten by mail, checking his big crystals and his antique dagger, when I saw the picture of Amapola behind his stack of textbooks. Yes, she was a kid. But what a kid.

"Who's this?" I said.

He took the framed picture out of my hand and put it back.

"Don't worry about who that is," he said.

• • •

Thanksgiving. Pope had planned a great big fiesta for all his homies and henchmen. Oh, yes. He took the goth-gangsta thing seriously, and he had actual "hit men" (he called them that) who did errands for him, carried out security at his concerts. He played guitar for the New Nouveau Nuevos—you might remember them. One of his "soldiers" was a big Irish kid who'd been booted off the football team, Andy the Tank. Andy appeared at our apartment with an invitation to the fiesta—we were to celebrate the Nuevos' upcoming year, and chart the course of the future. I was writing lyrics for Pope, cribbed from Roxy Music and Bowie's *The Man Who Sold the World* album. The invite was printed out on rolled parchment and tied with a red ribbon. Pope had style.

I went over to Tía Cuca's early, and there she was—Amapola. She'd come up from Nogales for the fiesta, since Pope was by now refusing to go home for any reason. He wanted nothing to do with his dad, who had declared that only gay boys wore long hair or makeup or played in a band that wore feather boas and silver pants. Sang in English.

I was turning eighteen, and she was fifteen, almost sixteen. She was more pale than Popo. She had a frosting of freckles on her nose and cheeks, and her eyes were light brown, almost gold. Her hair was thick and straight and shone like some liquid. She was kind of quiet too, blushing when I talked to her, shying away from all us males.

The meal was righteous. They'd fixed a turkey in the Mexican style. It was stuffed not with bread or oysters, but with nuts, dried pineapple, dried papaya and mango slices, and raisins. Cuca and Amapola wore traditional Mexican dresses and, along with Cuca's cook, served us the courses as we sat like members of the Corleone family around the long dining room table. Pope had seated Andy the Tank beside Fuckin' Franc, the Nuevos' drummer. Some guy I didn't know but who apparently owned a Nine Inch Nails–type synth studio in his garage sat beside Franc. I was granted the seat at the end of the table, across its length from Pope. Down the left side were the rest of the Nuevos—losers all.

I was trying to keep my roving eye hidden from the Pope. I didn't even have to guess what he'd do if he caught me checking her out. But she was so fine. It wasn't even my perpetual state of horniness. Yes it was. But it was more. She was like a song. Her small smiles, her graciousness. The way she swung her hair over her shoulder. The way she lowered her eyes and spoke softly … then gave you a wry look that cut sideways and made savage fun of everyone there. You just wanted to be a part of everything she was doing.

"Thank you," I said every time she refilled my water glass or dropped fresh tortillas by my plate. Not much, it's true, but compared to the Tank or Fuckin' Franc, I was as suave as Cary Grant.

"You are so welcome," she'd say.

It started to feel like a dance. It's in the way you say it, not what you say. We were saying more to each other than Cuca or Pope could hear.

And then, I was hit by a jolt that made me jump a little in my chair.

She stood behind me, resting her hands on the top of the chair. We were down to the cinnamon coffee and the red grape juice toasts. And Amapola put out one finger, where they couldn't see it, and ran her fingernail up and down between my shoulder blades.

Suddenly, supper was over, and we were all saying goodnight, and she had disappeared somewhere in the big house and never came back out.

Soon, Christmas came, and Pope again refused to go home. I don't know how Cuca took it, having the sullen King Nouveau lurking in her converted garage. He had a kitsch aluminum tree in there. Blue ornaments. "*Très* Warhol," he sighed.

My mom had given me some cool stuff—a vintage Who T-shirt, things like that. Pope's dad had sent presents—running shoes, French sunglasses, a .22 target pistol. We snickered. I was way cooler than Poppa Popo. I had been over to Zia Records and bought him some obscure '70s CDs: Captain Beyond, Curved Air, Amon Duul II, the Groundhogs. Things that looked cool, not that I'd ever heard them. Pope got me a vintage turntable and the first four Frank Zappa LPs; I couldn't listen to that shit. But still. How cool is that?

Pope wasn't a fool. He wasn't blind either. He'd arranged a better gift for me than all that. He'd arranged for Amapola to come visit for a week. I found out later she had begged him.

"Keep it in your pants," he warned me. "I'm watching you."

Oh my God. I was flying. We went everywhere for those six days. The three of us, unfortunately. Pope took us to that fancy art deco hotel downtown—the Clarendon. That one with the crazy neon lights on the walls outside and the dark gourmet eatery on the ground-floor front corner. We went to movie matinees, never night movies. It took two movies to wrangle a spot sitting next to her, getting Pope to relinquish the middle seat to keep us apart. But he knew it was a powerful movement between us, like continental drift. She kept leaning over to watch me instead of the movies. She'd laugh at everything I said. She lagged when we walked so I would walk near her. I was trying to keep my cool, not set off the Hermano Grande alarms. And suddenly he let me sit beside her, and I could smell her. She was all clean hair and sweet skin. Our arms brushed on the armrest, and we let them linger, sweat against each other. Our skin forming a thin layer of wet between us, a little of her and a little of me mixing into something made of both of us. I was aching. I could have pole-vaulted right out of the theater.

She turned sixteen that week. At a three o'clock showing of *The Dark Knight*, she slipped her hand over the edge of the armrest and tangled her fingers in mine.

This time, when she left, Pope allowed us one minute alone in his garage room. I kissed her. It was awkward. Delicious. Her hand went to my face and held it. She got in Cuca's car and cried as they drove away.

"You fucker," Popo said.

• • •

I couldn't believe she didn't Facebook. Amapola didn't even e-mail. She lived across the border, in Nogales, Mexico. So the phone was out of the question, even though her dad could have afforded it. When I asked Pope about his father's business, he told me they ran a duty-free import/export company based on each side of the border, in the two Nogaleses. Whatever. I just wanted to talk to Amapola. So I got stamps and envelopes. I was thinking, what is this, like, 1980 or something? But I wrote to her, and she wrote to me. I never even thought about the fact that instant messages or e-mail couldn't hold perfume, or have lip prints on the paper. You could Skype naked images to each other all night long, but Amapola had me hooked through the lips with each new scent in the envelope. She put her hair in the envelopes. It was more powerful than anything I'd experienced before. Maybe it was voodoo.

At Easter, Cuca and her Lebanese hubby flew to St. Thomas for a holiday. Somehow, Pope managed to get Amapola there at the house for a few days. He was gigging a lot, and he was seeing three or four strippers. I'll admit, he was hitting the sauce too much—he'd come home wasted and ricochet around the bathroom, banging into the fixtures like a pinball. I thought he'd break his neck on the toilet or the bathtub. The old man had been putting pressure on him— I had no idea how or what he wanted of Pope. He wanted the rock 'n' roll foolishness to end, that's for sure.

"You have no idea!" Pope would say, tequila stink on his breath. "If you only knew what they were really like. You can't begin to guess." But, you know, all boys who wear eyeliner and pay for full-sleeve tats say the same thing. Don't nobody understand the troubles they've seen. I just thought Pope was caught up in being our Nikki Sixx. We were heading for fame, world tours. I thought.

And there she was, all smiles. Dressed in black. Looking witchy and magical. Pope had a date with a girl named Demitasse. Can you believe that? Because she had small breasts or something. She danced at a high-end club that catered to men who knew words like "demitasse." She had little silver vials full of "stardust," that's all I really knew. It all left Pope staggering and blind, and that was what I needed to find time alone with my beloved.

We watched a couple of DVDs, and we held hands and then kissed. I freed her nipple from the lace—it was pink and swollen, like a little candy. I thought it would be brown. What did I know about Mexican girls? She pushed me away when I got on top of her, and she moved my hand back gently when it slipped up her thigh.

Pope came home walking sideways. I had no idea what time it was. I don't know how he got home. My pants were wet all down my left leg from hours of writhing with her. When Pope slurred, "My dad's in town," I didn't even pay attention. He went to Cuca's piano in the living room and tried to play some arrangement he'd cobbled together of *Tommy*. Then there was a silence that grew long. We looked in there and he was asleep in the floor, under the piano.

"Shh," Amapola said. And, "Wait here for me." She kissed my mouth, bit my lip.

When she came back down, she wore a nightgown that drifted around her legs and belly like fog. I knelt at her feet and ran my palms up her legs. She turned aside just as my hands crossed the midpoint of her thighs, and my palms slid up over her hip bones. She had taken off her panties. I put my mouth to her navel. I could smell her through the thin material.

"Do you love me?" she whispered, fingers tangled in my hair.

"Anything. You and me." I wasn't even thinking. "Us."

She yanked my hair.

"Do," she said. "You. Love me?"

Yank. It hurt.

"Yes!" I said. "Okay! Jesus! Love you!"

We went upstairs.

• • •

"Get up! Get up! Get the fuck up!" Popo was saying, ripping off the sheets. "Now! Now! Now!"

Amapola covered herself and rolled away with a small cry. Light was blasting through the windows. I thought he was going to beat my ass for sleeping with her. But he was in a panic.

"Get dressed. Dude—get dressed now!"

"What? What?"

"My dad."

He put his fists to his head.

"Oh shit. My dad!"

She started to cry.

I was in my white boxers in the middle of the room.

"Guys," I said. "Guys! Is there some trouble here?"

Amapola dragged the sheet off the bed and ran, wrapped, into the bathroom.

"You got no idea," Pope said. "Get dressed."

We were in the car in ten minutes. We sped out of the foothills and across town. Phoenix always looks empty to me when it's hot, like one of those sci-fi movies where all the people are dead and gone and some vampires or zombies are hiding in the vacant condos, waiting for night. The streets are too wide, and they reflect the heat like a Teflon cooking pan. Pigeons might explode into flame just flying across the street to escape the melting city bus.

Pope was saying, "Just don't say nothing. Just show respect. It'll be okay. Right, sis?"

She was in the backseat.

"Don't talk back," she said. "Just listen. You can take it."

"Yeah," Pope said. "You can take it. You better take it. That's the only way he'll respect you."

My head was spinning.

Apparently, the old man had come to town to see Pope and meet me, but Pope, that asshole, had been so wasted he forgot. But it was worse than that. The old man had waited at a fancy restaurant. For both of us. You didn't keep Big Pop waiting.

You see, he had found my letters. He had rushed north to try to avert the inevitable. And now he was seething, they said, because Pope's *maricón* best friend wasn't queer at all, and was working his mojo on the sweet pea. My scalp still hurt from her savage hair-pulling. I looked back at her. Man, she was as fresh as a sea breeze. I started to smile.

"Ain't no joke," Pope announced.

We fretted in silence.

"Look," he said. "It won't seem like it at first, but Pops will do anything for my sister. Anything. She controls him, man. So keep cool."

When we got there, Pope said, "The bistro." I had never seen it before, not really traveling in circles that ate French food or ate at "bistros." Pops was standing outside. He was a slender man, balding. Clean-shaven. Only about five-seven. He wore aviator glasses, that kind that turn dark in the sun. They were deep gray over his eyes. He was standing with a Mexican in a uniform. The other guy was over six feet tall and had a good gut on him. What Pope called a "food baby" from that funny movie everybody liked.

The old man and the soldier stared at me. I wanted to laugh. That's it? I mean, really? A little skinny bald guy? I was invincible with love.

Poppa turned and entered the bistro without a word. Pope and Amapola followed, holding hands. The stout soldier dude just eye-balled me and walked in. I was left alone on the sidewalk. I followed.

They were already sitting. It was ice cold. The way I liked it. I tried not to see Amapola's nipples. But I noticed her pops looking at them. And then the soldier. Pops told her, "*Tápate, cabrona.*" She had brought a little sweater with her, and now I knew why. She primly draped herself.

"Dad ..." said Pope.

"Shut it," his father said.

The eyeglasses had only become half-dark. You could almost see his eyes.

A waiter delivered a clear drink.

"Martini, sir," he said.

It was only about eleven in the morning.

Big Poppa said, "I came to town last night to see you." He sipped his drink. "I come here, to this restaurant. Is my favorite. Is *comida Frances*, understand? Quality." Another sip. He looked at the soldier—the soldier nodded. "I invite you." He pointed at Pope. Then at her. Then at me. "You, you, and you. Right here. Berry expensive." He drained the martini and snapped his fingers at the waiter. "An' I sit here an' wait." The waiter hurried over and took the glass and scurried away.

"Me an' my brother, Arnulfo."

He put his hand on the soldier's arm.

"We wait for you."

Popo said, "Dad ..."

"*Callate el osico, chingado*," his father breathed. He turned his head to me and smiled. He looked like a moray eel in a tank. Another martini landed before him.

"You," he said. "Why you dress like a girl?" He sipped. "I wait for you, but you don't care. No! Don't say nothing. Listen. I wait, and you no show up here to my fancy dinner. Is okay. I don't care." He waved his hand. "I have my li'l drink, and I don't care." He toasted me. He seemed like he was coiled, steel springs inside his gut. My skin was crawling and I didn't even know why.

"I wait for you," he said. "Captain Arnulfo, he wait. You don't care, right? Is okay! I'm happy. I got my martinis, I don't give a shit."

He smiled.

He pulled a long cigar out of his inner pocket. He bit the end off and spit it on the table. He put the cigar in his mouth. Arnulfo took out a gold lighter and struck a blue flame.

The waiter rushed over and murmured, "I'm sorry, sir, but this is a nonsmoking bistro. You'll have to take it outside."

The old man didn't even look at him—just stared at me through those gray lenses.

"Is hot outside," he said. "Right, gringo? Too hot?" I nodded—I didn't know what to do. "You see?" the old man said.

"I must insist," the waiter said.

"Bring the chef," the old man said.

"Excuse me?"

"Get the chef out here for me. Now."

The waiter brought out the chef, who bent down to the old man. Whispers. No drama. But the two men hurried away and the waiter came back with an ashtray. Arnulfo lit Poppa's cigar.

He blew smoke at me and said, "Why you do this violence to me?"

"I ..." I said.

"Shut up."

He snapped his fingers again, and food and more martinis arrived. I stared at my plate. Snails in garlic butter. I couldn't eat, couldn't even sip the water. Smoke drifted to me. I could feel the gray lenses focused on me. Pope, that chickenshit, just ate and never looked up. Amapola sipped iced coffee and stared out the window.

After forty minutes of this nightmare, Poppa pushed his plate away.

"*Oye*," he said, "*tú.*"

I looked up.

"Why you wan' fock my baby daughter?"

• • •

Sure, I trembled for a while after that. I got it, I really did. But did good sense overtake me? What do you think? I was full-on into the Romeo and Juliet thing, and she was even worse. Parents—you want to ensure your daughters marry young? Forbid them from seeing their boyfriends. Just try it.

"Uncle Arnie," as big dark Captain Arnulfo was called in Cuca's house, started hanging around. A lot. I wasn't, like, stupid. I could tell what was what—he was sussing me out (that's a word Pope taught me). He brought Bass Pale Ale all the time. He sidled up to me and said dumb things like, "You like the sexy?" Pope and I laughed all night after Uncle Arnie made his appearances. "You make the sexy-sexy in cars?" What a dork, we thought.

My beloved showered me with letters. I had no way of knowing if my own letters got to her or not, but she soon found an Internet café in Nogales and sent me cyber-love. Popo was drying up a little, not quite what you'd call sober, but occasionally back on the earth, and he started calling me "McLovin." I think it was his way of try-ing to tone it down. "Bring it down a notch, homeboy," he'd say when I waxed overly poetic about his sister.

It was a Saturday when it happened. I was IM-ing Amapola. That's all I did on Saturday afternoons. No TV, no cruising in the car, no movies or pool time. I fixed a huge vat of sun tea and hit my lap-top and talked to her. Mom was at work—she was always at work or out doing lame shit like bowling. It was just me, the computer, my distant girlie, and the cat rubbing against my leg. I'll confess to you—don't laugh—I cried at night thinking about her.

Does this explain things a little? Pope said I was whipped. I'd be like, that's no way to talk about your sister. She's better than all of you people! He'd just look at me out of those squinty Apache eyes. "Maybe," he'd drawl. "Maybe …" And I was just thinking about all that on Saturday, going crazier and crazier with the desire to see her sweet face every morning, her hair on my skin every night, mad in love with her, and I was IM-ing her that she should just book. Run away. She was almost seventeen already. She could catch a bus and be in Phoenix in a few hours and we'd jump on I-10 and drive to Cali. I didn't know what I imagined—just us, in love, on a beach. And suddenly the laptop crashed. Just gone—black screen before Amapola could answer me. That was weird, I thought. I cursed and kicked stuff, then I grabbed a shower and rolled.

When I cruised over to Aunt Cuca's, she was gone. So was Pope. Uncle Arnie was sitting in the living room in his uniform, sipping coffee.

"They all go on vacation," he said. "Just you and me."

Vacation? Pope hadn't said anything about vacations. Not that he was what my English profs would call a reliable narrator.

Arnie gestured for me to sit. I stood there.

"Coffee?" he offered.

"No, thanks."

"Sit!"

I sat.

I can't relate the conversation very clearly, since I never knew what the F Arnie was mumbling, to tell you the truth. His accent was all bandido. I often just nodded and smiled, hoping not to offend the dude, lest he freak out and bust caps in me. That's a joke. Kind of. But then I'd wonder what I'd just agreed to.

"You love Amapola," he said. It wasn't a question. He smiled sadly, put his hand on my knee.

"Yes, sir," I said.

He nodded. Sighed. "Love," he said. "Is good, love."

"Yes, sir."

"You not going away, right?"

I shook my head. "No way."

"So. What this means? You marry the girl?"

Whoa. Marry? I … guess … I was going to marry her. Someday. Sure, you think about it. But to say it out loud. That was hard. Yet I felt like some kind of breakthrough was happening here. The older generation had sent an emissary.

"I believe," I said, mustering some balls, "yes. I will marry Amapola. Someday. You know."

He shrugged, sadly. I thought that was a little odd, frankly. He held up a finger and busted out a cell phone, hit the speed button, and muttered in Spanish. Snapped it shut. Sipped his coffee.

"We have big family reunion tomorrow. You come. Okay? I'll fix up all with Amapola's papá. You see. Yes?"

I smiled at him, not believing this turn of events.

"Big Mexican rancho. Horses. Good food. Mariachis." He laughed. "And love! Two kids in love!"

We slapped hands. We smiled and chuckled. I had some coffee.

"I pick you up here at seven in the morning," he said. "Don't be late."

• • •

The morning desert was purple and orange. The air was almost cool. Arnie had a Styrofoam cooler loaded with Dr. Peppers and Cokes. He drove a bitchin' S-Class Benz. It smelled like leather and aftershave. He kept the satellite tuned to BBC Radio 1. "You like the crazy *maricón* music, right?" he asked.

"… Ah … right."

It was more like flying than driving, and when he sped past Arivaca, I wasn't all that concerned. I figured we were going to Nogales,

Arizona. But we slid through that little dry town like a shark and crossed into Mex without slowing down. He just raised a finger off the steering wheel and motored along, saying, "You going to like this."

And then we were through Nogales, Mexico, too. Black and tan desert. Saguaros and freaky burned-looking cactuses. I don't know what that stuff was. It was spiky.

We took a long dirt side road. I was craning around, looking at the bad black mountains around us.

"Suspension makes this road feel like butter," Arnie noted.

We came out in a big valley. There was an airfield of some sort there. Mexican army stuff—trucks, Humvees. Three or four hangars or warehouses. Some shiny Cadillacs and SUVs scattered around.

"You going to like this," Arnie said. "It's a surprise."

There was Big Poppa Popo, the old man himself. He was standing with his hands on his hips. With a tall American. Those dark gray lenses turned toward us. We parked. We got out.

"What's going on?" I asked.

"Shut up," said Arnie.

"Where's the rancho?" I asked.

The American burst out laughing.

"Jesus, kid!" he shouted. He turned to the old man. "He really is a dumbshit."

He walked away and got in a white SUV. He slammed the door and drove into the desert, back the way we had come. We stood there watching him go. I'm not going to lie—I was getting scared.

"You marry Amapola?" the old man said.

"One day. Look, I don't know what you guys are doing here, but—"

"Look at that," he interrupted, turning from me and gesturing toward a helicopter sitting on the field. "Huey. Old stuff, from your

Vietnam. Now the Mexican air force use it to fight *las drogas*." He turned to me. "You use *las drogas*?"

"No! Never."

They laughed.

"Sure, sure," the old man said.

"Ask Amapola!" I cried. "She'll tell you!"

"She already tell me everything," he said.

Arnie put his arm around my shoulders. "Come," he said, and started walking toward the helicopter. I resisted for a moment, but the various Mexican soldiers standing around were suddenly really focused and not slouching and were walking along all around us.

"What is this?" I said.

"You know what I do?" the old man asked.

"Business?" I said. My mind was blanking out, I was so scared.

"Business." He nodded. "Good answer."

We came under the blades of the big helicopter. I'd never been near one in my life. It scared the crap out of me. The Mexican pilots looked out their side windows at me. The old man patted the machine.

"President Bush!" he said. "DEA!"

I looked at Arnie. He smiled, nodded at me. "Fight the *drogas*," he said.

The engines whined and chuffed and the rotor started to turn.

"Is very secret what we do," said the old man. "But you take a ride and see. Is my special treat. You go with Arnulfo."

"Come with me," Arnie said.

"You go up and see, then we talk about love."

The old man hurried away, and it was just me and Arnie and the soldiers with their black M16s.

"After you," Arnie said.

• • •

He pulled on a helmet. Then we took off. It was rough as hell. I felt like I was being pummeled in the ass and lower back when the engines really kicked in. And when we rose, my guts dropped out through my feet. I closed my eyes and gripped the webbing Arnie had fastened around my waist. "Holy God!" I shouted. It was worse when we banked—the side doors were wide open, and I screamed like a girl, sure I was falling out. The Mexicans laughed and shook their heads, but I didn't care.

Arnie was standing in the door. He unhooked a big gun from the stanchion where it had been strapped with its barrel pointed up. He dangled it in the door on cords. He leaned toward me and shouted, "Sixty caliber! Hung on double bungees!" He slammed a magazine into the thing and pulled levers and snapped snappers. He leaned down to me again and shouted, "Feel the vibration? You lay on the floor, it makes you come!"

I thought I heard him wrong.

We were beating out of the desert and into low hills. I could see our shadow below us, fluttering like a giant bug on the ground and over the bushes. The seat kicked up and we were rising.

Arnulfo took a pistol from his belt and showed me.

"Amapola," he said.

I looked around for her, stupidly. But then I saw what was below us, in a watered valley. Orange flowers. Amapola. Poppies.

"This is what we do," Arnulfo said.

He raised his pistol and shot three rounds out the door and laughed. I put my hands over my ears.

"You're DEA?" I cried.

He popped off another round.

"Is competition," he said. "We do business."

Oh my God.

He fell against me and was shouting in my ear and there was nowhere I could go. "You want Amapola? You want to marry my *so-brina*? Just like that? Really? *Pendejo*." He grabbed my shirt. "Can you fly, gringo? Can you fly?" I was shaking. I was trying to shrink away from him, but I could not. I was trapped in my seat. His breath stank, and his lips were at my ear like hers might have been, and he was screaming, "Can you fly, *chingado*? Because you got a choice! You fly, or you do what we do."

I kept shouting, "What? What?" It was like one of those dreams where nothing makes sense. "What?"

"You do what we do, I let you live, *cabrón*."

"What?"

"I let you live. Or you fly. Decide."

"I don't want to die!" I yelled. I was close to wetting my pants. The Huey was nose-down and sweeping in a circle. I could see people below us, running. A few small huts. Horses or mules. A pickup started to speed out of the big poppy field. Arnulfo talked into his mike and the helicopter heaved after it. Oh no, oh no. He took up the .60 caliber and braced himself. I put my fingers in my ears. And he ripped a long stream of bullets out the door. It was the loudest thing I'd ever heard. Louder than the loudest thing you can imagine. So loud your insides jump, but it all becomes an endless rip of noise, like thunder cracking inside your bladder and your teeth hurt from gritting against it.

The truck just tattered, if metal can tatter. The roof of the cab blew apart and the smoking ruin of the vehicle spun away below us and vanished in dust and smoke and steam.

I was crying.

"Be a man!" Arnulfo yelled.

We were hovering. The crew members were all turned toward me, staring.

Arnie unsnapped my seat webbing.

"Choose," he said.

"I want to live."

"Choose."

You know how it goes in *Die Hard* movies. How the hero kicks the bad guy out the door and sprays the Mexican crew with the .60 and survives a crash landing. But that's not what happened. That didn't even cross my mind. Not even close. No, I got up on terribly shaky legs, so shaky I might have pitched out the open door all by myself to discover that I could not, in fact, fly. I said, "What do I do?" And the door gunner grabbed me and shoved me up to the hot gun. The ground was wobbling far below us, and I could see the Indian workers down there. Six men and a woman. And they were running. I was praying and begging God to get me out of this somehow and I was thinking of my beautiful lover and I told myself I didn't know how I got there and the door gunner came up behind me now, he slammed himself against my ass, and he said, "Hold it, lean into it. It's gonna kick, okay? Finger on the trigger. I got you." And I braced the .60 and I tried to close my eyes and prayed I'd miss them and I was saying, *Amapola, Amapola,* over and over in my mind, and the gunner was hard against me, he was erect and pressing it into my buttocks and he shouted, "For love!" and I squeezed the trigger.

• • •

Winner of the 2010 Edgar Award for short fiction for "Amapola,"
LUIS ALBERTO URREA is a prolific and acclaimed writer who uses
his dual-culture life experiences to explore greater themes of love,
loss, and triumph. Born in Tijuana, Mexico, to a Mexican father and
an American mother, he is the critically acclaimed author of eleven
books, as well as an award-winning poet and essayist. *The Devil's
Highway*, his 2004 non-fiction account of a group of Mexican im-
migrants lost in the Arizona desert, was a national bestseller, and
named a best book of the year by the *Los Angeles Times*, the *Miami
Herald*, the *Chicago Tribune*, the *Kansas City Star,* and many other
publications. It has been optioned for a film by CDI Producciones.
His most recent book, *The Hummingbird's Daughter* (Little, Brown,
2005), is the culmination of twenty years of research and writing.
The historical novel tells the story of Teresa Urrea, sometimes known
as The Saint of Cabora and the Mexican Joan of Arc. Urrea's other
titles include *By the Lake of Sleeping Children, In Search of Snow,
Ghost Sickness,* and *Wandering Time.* His writing has won an American Book Award, Western States Book Award, Colorado Center for
the Book Award, and Christopher Award. Urrea lives with his family in Naperville, Illinois, where he is a professor of creative writing
at the University of Illinois-Chicago.

COUGAR

By Laura Lippman

"Sorry," said the young man who bumped into her, although he didn't sound particularly sorry. Almost the opposite, as if he were muffling a laugh at her expense. At least it was water, and she could change into her other blouse, the one she had worn on the walk here, assuming Mr. Lee didn't object. Surely, Mr. Lee wouldn't make her work the rest of the shift in a soaked white blouse that was now all-but-transparent.

"Sean!" his girlfriend chided without conviction.

"Hey," said he-who-must-be-Sean. "It was an accident. I didn't even see her."

Of course, Lenore thought, going to the back to change. *A five-foot-ten blonde in a sushi bar is hard to spot.* Yet she knew he wasn't lying. He hadn't seen her. No one ever saw her. She was here every Friday and Saturday night—seating them at their tables, bringing them their drink orders when the wait staff got backed up. But even the regulars didn't seem to recognize her from week to week. For young people who came here, the sushi dinner they gulped down was just preamble, preparation for the long night of bar-hopping ahead. If she wasn't their mother's age, she was close enough, forty-two. And, fact was, she had her own twenty-one-year-old son at home, living in the basement with his nineteen-year-old girlfriend, and she was invisible to them, too.

Still, at least one young man seemed to register her presence as she walked to the back room to get her shirt. Well, he noticed her tits, given that the thin white blouse was now plastered to her front. "Nice," he said to his friend, not even bothering to lower his voice. "Check out the cougar."

So now she was presumed to be deaf as well as invisible. Deaf, or in some strange category where she was expected to tolerate whatever others said about her. Was it the job? Her age? But then, it was the same at home. Worse, actually.

• • •

"A kid at work called me a cougar last night," she said over breakfast the next morning, a Sunday. Not hers. Lenore had eaten breakfast at 10:00 AM, a respectable time for a woman whose shift ended at midnight. Now it was almost 1:00 PM, but her son and the girlfriend had just roused themselves a few minutes ago and were nodding over bowls of cereal, their heads hanging so low that their chins almost grazed the milky ponds of Trix.

"Was he nearsighted? I can't imagine anyone thinking you was hot." That was Marie, the girlfriend, and the insult was so automatic that it carried no sting. As far as she could tell, it was the reason that Frankie kept Marie around, to insult Lenore. Otherwise, he would have to do it himself and that was too much effort.

"I think it's because my shirt was soaked through. Another kid bammed into me when I was carrying a tray of water glasses."

"Big thrill," Marie said.

"Well," Lenore said, "pretty big." She had a showgirl's figure and she didn't care what the magazines deemed fashionable—an hourglass figure would always be in style. Marie, meanwhile, was flat-chested and soft with baby fat. Which made sense, because Marie was still a baby—lolling in bed all day, watching cartoons, eating all the sugar she could find.

"Shut up," Frankie said tonelessly. They did as he said. They always did what he said.

If Marie was a baby, then Frankie was a six-foot-two toddler, perpetually on the edge of a tantrum. He had returned home quite unexpectedly six months ago, with no explanation for where he had been or what he had been doing in the two years since Lenore had last seen him. She had offered him his childhood room, but he sneered at that, claiming the basement that she had just renovated into a television room. She had planned the room as a retreat, a place to watch television late at night, maybe work on her various craft projects. But now it belonged to Frankie and she had to knock if she wanted to enter, even if it was to do his laundry in the utility room in the back. Once, just once, she had walked in without knocking and she wasn't sure what scared her more—the drugs on the coffee table or the look on Frankie's face.

I could lose my house, she thought as she backed out of the room, laundry basket clutched to her middle. Until that moment, she had—what was it called?—plausible deniability. She had suspected but not known what went on in her basement. But now she knew and if Frankie got caught, the government could take her house. That very thing had happened to Mrs. Bitterman up on Jackson, and there were rumors that it was why the house on Byrd Street was going to auction at the end of the month. Lenore lived every day torn between wishing her son would get busted, and knowing that his arrest would probably destroy her life instead of saving it.

Kicking him out wasn't an option. She was scared of Frankie. *She was scared of her son.* It was such an awful thought, she hadn't dared to let it form, not for a long time. She had even daydreamed that the man in her basement wasn't Frankie at all, just some audacious imposter. Certainly, he bore no resemblance to the boy she remembered, a serious but sweet child, who never quite stopped puzzling over his father's disappearance when he was still such a little thing. And he was so much bigger than the fourteen-year-old they had taken away from her, put in the Hickey school, then that weird place out in western Maryland, where they taught them to cut down trees or something. He didn't even resemble the nineteen-year-old who had moved out in disgust two years ago, when she had said he had to live by her rules if he wanted to stay under her roof. She had been shocked when he actually went because she had no idea how to make him do anything—pick up his clothes, rinse a plate. If he had refused to leave, she would have been powerless.

In the two years since then, Frankie must have figured out that out. And now he was in her basement, dealing drugs, running up her electricity bills, leaving crusty bowls strewn about, eating everything in sight and contributing nothing. Once, she had steeled herself to ask him if he might kick in for food or utilities. "Marie don't eat much," was all he said. His meaning was clear. She owed him room and board for the rest of his life, however long that might be. She owed him everything he wanted to take from her. She owed him for the big mistakes—not being able to hold onto his father—and the small ones, such as not getting him the right kind of sneakers when he was at Thomas Heath Elementary. Sometimes, late at night, when she heard police cars hurtling down Fort Avenue, she wondered where Frankie was, if he was dead, and she wouldn't have minded too much if that were so.

And then she thought how unnatural she was, how a mother should always love her child no matter what.

• • •

Frankie had come home in March and now it was August, the end of a miserable, fretful summer. Working two jobs—the sushi place on weekends, Sparkle-and-Shine cleaning service on Monday through Thursdays—she should have been able to save on her AC bill, but Frankie and Marie ran it full force, forgetting to turn it down when they headed out, which was usually about four in the afternoon. Every day, Lenore came home to a chilled catastrophe of a house. She tried to remind herself how lonely she had been, over the past two years, how empty her free evenings had seemed. That's when she had taken up various crafts, in the first place teaching herself crocheting and knitting, figuring out what her computer could do, where it could take her. But the computer was in the basement, along with the television, and it made her heart sore to see what that once-pretty room had become since Frankie took it over. She was stuck in the kitchen, listening to the Orioles on the radio, or sitting out in the living room with the newspaper, which she never had time to read in the mornings.

Only on this particular August afternoon, there was a man on her sofa. A young man, Frankie's age, dressed like Frankie—T-shirt, baseball cap, jogging pants as Lenore still thought of them, although Frankie insisted that she say *track suit*. Dozing, he looked harmless, but Frankie probably looked smooth and sweet, too, when he was sleeping.

She cleared her throat. The stranger jumped, and his feet—huge, puppy-ish feet, as if he hadn't gotten his full growth yet, although he was already pretty big—just missed the porcelain lamp on the end table. As it was, he had already left vague scuff marks on the peach leather.

"Who are you?" he asked.

"Frankie's mother," she said. It took her a second to remember that she had a right to know who he was.

"Aaron," he said. "Frankie said I could crash here for a while."

Beaten down as she was, she had to ask: "Here, as in the house? Or here, as on my sofa? Because that's a nice piece, and your shoes have already—"

Aaron jumped to his feet and Lenore thought, *This is it, this is where I get hit for standing up for myself in my own home.* Until that moment, she had never allowed that thought to form, had never admitted to herself what it was that made her fear Frankie. Not just the drugs and the consequences of his business being discovered. And not just the physicality of a slap or a punch, but the meaning of such a blow. She hadn't been a good mother, or a good-enough mother, and Frankie, ruined as he was, had returned home to remind her of that fact for every day of the rest of her life and maybe his, depending on how things worked.

But this boy, this Aaron, actually felt bad. He kneeled to examine the mark. "That was stupid of me," he said. "But I know a trick my aunt taught me. She had six boys, so believe you me, she knew how to get any kind of stain out of anything. You got any talcum powder?"

She did, a rose-scented talc that she hadn't thought to use for months, years. He sprinkled it on the arm of the sofa, his fingers light and gentle as the priest who had baptized Frankie, then said: "Now we let it sit overnight. The powder will draw out the grease."

"Like salt on a red wine stain," she said.

"Exactly. The main thing is you don't want to use water, this being leather and all. It's an awfully nice sofa. I feel bad about not taking my shoes off. But Frankie and Marie were downstairs and wanted to be alone—" he actually blushed, as if Frankie's mother might not know why her son and his girlfriend preferred to be alone in the basement. "He told me to come up here, and I got so sleepy. I coulda gone upstairs, I guess, but that seemed forward."

He looked at her strangely and then Lenore realized the only thing strange about the look was that it was direct. He felt bad, he cared what she thought of him, at least for this moment. If he hung around, he would soon absorb Frankie's attitude toward her. But, for now, he was the kind of boy that she always wished Frankie would bring home. She cast around in her memory. What did you do with your son's friends when they came to visit?

"Hey," she said. "You want a snack? Or a beer?"

• • •

Unlike Marie, Aaron didn't move in, but he was there more nights than not and Frankie offered him the guest room on the second floor. "Is that okay?" Aaron asked Lenore. Frankie didn't give her a chance to answer. "Of course it's okay."

She was the one who offered Aaron a key, however. It was over breakfast. Although he came in at 3:00 or 4:00 AM with Frankie and Marie, he would get up when she rose at seven for her cleaning job and share a cup of coffee with her. He said he couldn't sleep once he heard her moving about and she believed him because she had found she couldn't really fall asleep until she heard the trio come home.

"You don't have to—" he began.

"It's no big deal," she said. "And this way, if you want to come home earlier than the others, you don't have to wait around with them." Then, after a moment's hesitation, she asked what she had never dared to ask Frankie. "Where do you go? I mean, all the places close down at two, don't they?"

"Most of them. But there are some. And—well, the corner, there's usually some late-night business. Although ..." Now it was his turn to hesitate. He got up, rinsed his coffee cup out in the sink, placed it in the dishwasher. He was considerate that way. Sometimes, he even brought Frankie and Marie's dirty dishes up from the basement and rinsed them.

"What, Aaron? Is he taking chances? You can tell me. You know I don't judge."

"There've been some ... disputes. Guys moving in. But meth isn't as territorial as crack, so you don't have to worry."

Meth. Right, she had nothing to worry about. If Frankie didn't get her arrested, he would blow her sky high. "So he is—?"

"Yeah," Aaron admitted.

So not only selling it and storing it, but making it in her house.

"I don't like it," she said, catching Aaron's eye. "I wish I could make him stop."

"It's hard for anyone to tell Frankie anything."

"Yeah. I'm scared of him, you know." She had never said that out loud to anyone. It didn't sound so bad.

"He wouldn't hurt you."

"He might."

"No, I wouldn't let him."

And that was as far as she let it go, that time. Lenore resolved not to discuss Frankie again with Aaron, not unless Aaron brought the subject up.

• • •

She started taking a little more care with her appearance. Small things, like lipstick in the morning, before she came downstairs to put the coffee on. A new peach robe, modest in cut, but silkier and more close-fitting than the old terry cloth one, and with a matching nightie. She got a pedicure, although now fall was coming on and the kitchen floor was cool beneath her feet as she padded about. Marie asked Lenore why she had bothered. "Pink toenails on an old lady like you? Who cares? Who sees your feet?"

"I'm only forty-two," Lenore said. "I'm not on the shelf. Some women have babies at my age."

"Gross," Marie said, and Frankie nodded. Aaron didn't say anything. Lenore poured him a glass of juice and passed him the plate of muffins—from a box mix, but still fresh and hot. "What about me?" Frankie asked and she slid the plate across the table to him—but only after Aaron had made his choice.

• • •

And this was how the days went by, fall fading into winter, Aaron sleeping in the spare bedrooms more often than not, Lenore taking ever more care with her appearance—looking younger day by day, even as she behaved far more maternally than she ever had. She cut back on drinking and joined the local Curves. She splurged on lotions and moisturizers, choosing those with the most luxurious smells. Alone with Aaron, she confided in him, but always in a maternal way. How she worried about Frankie, how she wished he would just say no to drugs, how she was nervous about him getting busted. How she wished she could save him from himself, but wasn't sure that anything would work for Frankie, even the forced sobriety of prison.

The only problem was Marie, who was turning out to have sharp eyes in that pudgy little face.

"Flirting with a boy your son's age," she said one night, peeved because Lenore had forgotten to buy Lucky Charms, Marie and Frankie's new favorite, although she had remembered Aaron's Mueslix. "You're pathetic."

"I'm just being nice," Lenore said. "Besides, a young kid like that could never be interested in an old broad like me."

"Got that right," Marie said, stomping downstairs to the basement. Soon, Lenore heard her laughing with Frankie, and their laughter was as ugly and acrid as the smells that rose from the floor below. Aaron was down there, too, but he wasn't laughing with them. Lenore was sure of that much. She was also sure that she was going to have to sleep with him, eventually. The only question in her mind was whether it would be before or after.

• • •

It turned out to be after, and it was Frankie, in his way, who made it happen. The four of them had been sharing another late breakfast—this one with cinnamon rolls, the kind that you baked at home, then coated with sticky white frosting. There were eight in a carton, two apiece, but Lenore had decided she wanted only one and passed her extra to Aaron.

"I wanted that," Frankie objected.

"I'm sorry," Lenore said, not the least bit sorry.

"You act as if *he* were your son," Frankie said. "Or your boyfriend. Just like when I was younger."

"I never had boyfriends when you were a boy," Lenore said, upset at the unfairness of it all. She might not have been a good mother to Frankie, but she had never been a slutty one. "I was strict about that."

"Oh, you didn't let guys move in or have breakfast with us, but you still brought them home sometimes, did them up in your room and sent them on their way before I woke up. If I didn't have a step-daddy, it wasn't for the lack of free samples. You just never could seal the deal."

"Who wants the cow when you already have the milk," said Marie, clearly unaware of how much milk she had given away in her young life.

"I wasn't that way." Lenore realized her voice was trembling. "I did the best I could, under the circumstances."

"You were a shit mom. You chased away Dad, then you just sat back and let them take me to juvie, didn't even spring for a decent lawyer when I got into trouble."

"I did the best—"

"You didn't do shit." Frankie banged his fists on the table. "You were a shitty mom and now you're a stupid cunt, mooning over some young guy. It's disgusting."

He stomped out of the kitchen, followed by Marie. Lenore began to clear the kitchen table, only to drop the dishes in the sink, her shoulders shaking with sobs that she didn't really have to fake.

"He didn't mean that." Aaron came over and started patting her shoulder awkwardly.

"He did," she said. "And he was right. I wasn't a very good mother. I should have found him a stepfather when his own father left, or at least put him in some program. Like Big Brother, or whatever it's called. I failed Frankie. I failed him over and over again."

"It will be okay," Aaron said, but it was more a question than a statement.

"How? He's either going to get arrested or killed. If he gets arrested—well, that'll be even worse for me, once he tells the police he was dealing here. They take your house for that, Aaron. Even if you can prove you didn't know, or couldn't stop it, they take your house."

"Frankie's pretty careful—"

"You said there was some quarrel over his territory?"

"Not so much now." She turned then, and the hand that was patting her shoulder passed briefly over her breast, then dropped in embarrassment. "A little."

"He could be killed. Some guys who want his corner could just open fire one night, and the police wouldn't even care. You know how they do. You *know*."

"Naw—" He met her gaze. "I guess so. Maybe."

"Killed, and no one would care. No one."

Two nights later, Aaron woke her at 3:00 AM to tell her that Frankie had been shot on the corner, gunned down. He was dead.

"Were you there?" she asked.

"I had gone to the 7-Eleven to buy smokes," he said, very convincingly. "When I started back, I saw all the cop cars, the lights, and decided not to get too close. Marie was shot, too."

"So she's a witness."

"Maybe. I don't know. What should we do?"

"What should we do?" She hugged him in a perfectly appropriate way, a maternal way. Her son was dead, his friend was dead. It made sense to hold him, to comfort one another. It also made sense when he kissed her, and when he reached under the peach gown that matched her silky robe. It made even more sense to crawl on top of him and stay there most of the night. Lenore had not been with a man for a long time, but that had only increased her stamina, and her longing. And, besides, she was very grateful to this young man, who had done what she needed him to do, and without her ever having to ask straight out.

In the morning, after the police called to ask if they could swing by before she went to work—Frankie didn't have current ID on him, so it had taken them awhile to sort out where he lived, if he had next-of-kin—she told Aaron that he should probably move on, go somewhere else, maybe back home to Colorado.

"Marie is conscious," she told him. "And saying she thinks it was a white guy who fired the shots at them."

She could see Aaron thinking about that.

"She's also saying it was a robbery, that she and Frankie were just walking home from a club. Still …"

"I've got a friend in New Mexico," he said.

"That's supposed to be nice."

"But not much saved up," he said, a little sheepish. "Even with you giving me a free place to stay, I never did put much away."

"That's okay," she said, reaching deep into a cupboard, behind layers of pots and pans, one place Frankie and Marie would never have meddled. "I have some."

She gave him the amount she had stashed away without admitting why she was saving it, a thousand dollars in all.

"I didn't—" he said.

"I know."

"I even thought—"

"Me, too. But I want you to be safe."

"I could come back. If things cool down."

"But they probably won't."

He looked confused, hurt even, but Lenore would knew he would get over that. Perhaps he felt used, but he would get over that, too.

The police were on their way. She would have to get ready for that, be prepared to cry for the loss of her boy. She would think about Frankie as a child, the boy she had in fact lost all those years ago. She would think about the boy she was losing now. Somehow, she would manage to cry.

And then, when the police were gone, leaving her to the business of burying her own boy—she would go down in the basement and begin the business of reclaiming her own house, washing sheets and throwing open the tiny windows in spite of the wintry chill. Her house was hers again, and no one would ever take it from her.

• • •

LAURA LIPPMAN has written fifteen novels, including ten in the award-winning Tess Monaghan series and a collection of short stories, *Hardly Knew Her.* Her latest book is *I'd Know You Anywhere.* She has won many prizes for her work, including the Edgar, Anthony, Agatha, Nero Wolfe, Quill, Macavity, and Barry awards. She lives in Baltimore.

DIGBY,
ATTORNEY AT LAW

By Jim Fusilli

After seven years of night study, Francis Michael Digby was graduated from the Rutgers School of Law, Newark, and some time thereafter, admitted to the New Jersey Bar. His modest ambition already spent, he hung his shingle outside a storefront below the cold-water flat in which he was born in 1927, some thirty-five years ago, and settled into the agreeable life of a small-town lawyer.

With his family providing references, Digby became the attorney of choice among the Narrows Gate Irish who hadn't escaped when the piers and factories began to shutter. Often, he was asked to represent both parties to a grievance. Thus it was with the Rooneys.

"A cross I need not bear," Mary Catherine Rooney summarized with a terse nod.

"Seeing as I'm pushed beyond the brink of dignity ..." Leaky Rooney explained when he turned up at day's end, surprisingly sober and equally resolute.

Though Leaky and Mary Catherine seemed opposites—he gray, wiry and devilish, she blonde, stout and considerate—they were of a like mind on the issue at hand: Divorce was the only solution. Both parties instructed Digby to draw up papers.

Twice he nodded his compliance, pausing each time to wipe clean his wire bifocals. Eight years with Mary Catherine at St. Matty's Elementary told him she wouldn't budge while angry. Though drink could render him sentimental, Leaky, an émigré from Hell's Kitchen across the Hudson, had a notorious and unpredictable temper. When Artie Meehan backed his Buick into Mary Catherine's cart at the A&P, Rooney took a baby sledgehammer to his collarbone. His arm and shoulder in a cast that made it appear he'd sprouted a plaster wing, Meehan came to Digby demanding redress. A civil suit would prove worthless, the attorney advised. What would you gain but his lasting enmity? Subsequently, Meehan moved down the shore, precise address unknown.

Now, their meeting at its end, Digby dropped his hands on his desk and hoisted out of his chair. "However regrettable, it is as you wish, Mr. Rooney," he intoned, offering him a dark cloud of finality. Then, claiming a late meeting at City Hall, he headed to Franziska's, intent on a steak sandwich dripping with buttery au jus and a mound of crisp onion rings.

Over seconds on side orders of roasted mushrooms and red cabbage, Digby deliberated. In matters such as Rooney v. Rooney, neither party actually wanted to nullify the marriage—he couldn't site precedent for divorce among the Narrows Gate Irish—and so a visit to his office was provocation, escalation and, *ipso facto,* part of the dance toward forgiveness. Digby understood his role was to bring them together, compelling dialogue. Inevitably, if only by the play of chance, a kindness would ensue and a spark would rise from the ashes. Then Digby would withdraw, returning to his role as public defender in minor criminal matters, filing Worker's Compensation claims against the mighty Jerusalem Steel and cozying deeper into the silky embrace of his undemanding life.

As he took the Buchanan Avenue jitney down to the eight o'clock showing of *Taras Bulba* at the Avalon, Digby decided he'd talk first to Mary Catherine, hoping her indignation had wavered. She'd once been a hazel-eyed beauty, and he remembered how she'd cried in class the day Roosevelt died. He assumed that somewhere beneath her now-matronly bosom remained a kind heart. He was confident she'd see her Leaky was pitiable in the first degree.

Digby bought a box of Good & Plenty at the concession stand, nestled under a heating duct in the balcony and, as the Coming Attractions began to blare, fell into a deep, satisfied sleep.

• • •

While Digby dozed, Leaky Rooney was invited to leave the Shamrock. Throwing back another shot of Four Roses, he'd fallen off his stool and, arms windmilling, landed squarely on O'Boyle's dog, a fourteen-year-old named Rat Catcher.

Her yelping echoing in his ears, Rooney drifted into the quiet alley behind the bar. As he ruffled sawdust out of his hair, the silence was broken, and he spun in dread, fearing he'd just heard his late mother's cackle. Often, she'd told him he'd end up drunk and alone.

Groping his way to a stoop in the shadows, he brushed aside a broken bottle with his shoe and sat, dropping his head in his hands.

Then, as a glimpse of a desperate future took hold, he stood, hitching his drooping slacks. Mewling cats watched curiously as he wobbled over cobblestone, failing to avoid overstuffed garbage cans.

He knew she wouldn't take the safety chain off the first door so he came around back and started up the fire escape.

"Mary Catherine!" he bellowed when he reached the second floor. His hands were covered in rust.

Third floor and Rooney tried to pry open Emmy Ahern's kitchen window.

"Up one more, you idiot," the widow Ahern instructed.

Mary Catherine sighed in resignation. "Go get your father," she told Kevin and Robert, age eleven and ten, respectively.

"I thought you gave him the boot," said Anna, the little one. "For good."

Twelve-year-old Katie toed the yellowed linoleum, peeling it from the floorboards. "I'll wager you don't remember what it's about. The fight," she said.

Mary Catherine shrugged sadly while kneading a dishtowel. "No, I suppose I don't."

"He forgot your Lucky Strikes," recalled Anna, who, though only seven years old, was an experienced busybody. "Remembered his L&Ms, and a six pack of Piels, but he forgot your Lucky Strikes."

Robert opened the kitchen window to begin his descent.

"Mary Catherine! It's me. Your loving husband. Your breadwinner."

Since the layoff at National Can, he'd been trying his hand at roofing, with little success. Hence, his new nickname.

"I forgive you!" he added. "As God is my witness, I forgive you!"

Katie headed to the icebox. "I'll reheat the stew, Ma," she said.

Hours later, as they lay in bed, the children down and drowsing, Leaky Rooney said, "And to think I wasted my good and precious time with Digby."

"Digby?" Mary Catherine turned toward him. "You saw Francis Michael Digby?"

"Indeed," he replied, hands folded on his stomach.

"*My* Francis Michael Digby?"

"The same."

She said, "I saw Digby."

Rooney wriggled to sit. "That louse. Playing us against each other."

Not so, she thought. He seemed quietly proper, as he was in grammar school. A good boy, a keen student, the nuns often said. Mary Catherine was proud her classmate had done well.

"You know," Rooney said, "he was pushing those damned papers hard at me, then rushing to City Hall, him thinking who he is—"

"I suppose he was doing what we asked."

"—pulling the wool, pressing on. Like I don't know the game."

"Means nothing now," Mary Catherine tried.

Rooney was building toward a full head of steam. "Attorneys. Cocks of the walk ..."

"Come on," she said as she dropped a hand amid the tufts of prickly hair on his shoulder. "What's the use of it?"

Moonlight peeked through the blinds. "You know what he wants?" Rooney said, "He wants you."

"Oh my goodness." She raised to her elbows. "That's ridiculous."

"Ah. I'm ridiculous, am I?"

"I didn't say—"

Though still dizzy from drink, he spun and bent over to search for his shoes.

"Where are you going?" she asked.

"Like you'd care."

"For heaven's sake—"

"Don't you be bringing the Almighty into this," he snapped. "This is between me and you and your boyfriend Francis."

"My boyfriend?" Mary Catherine was out of bed now too. Mounds of freckled skin wiggled before settling under her nightgown. "Have you lost your mind?"

He hurried to the corridor and reached down into the closet. Old paint cans and roller skates rattled.

"You'll wake the whole house."

"To the devil with the whole house."

She said, "Would you use the brain—"

There stood Leaky Rooney, his baby sledgehammer in his fist. "No one makes a fool of me," he announced.

"Except you," Mary Catherine muttered as he began his bumble down four flights of stairs.

• • •

The following day, Rooney caught a day's work helping to tar the roof at Narrows Gate High School, other men walking away when it started to rain. So he postponed his search for Digby, who in his mind had grown devil's horns and a pig's snout, and was all set to slip an arm around Mary Catherine's waist, serenading her with oink-oinks, sweeping her off her feet with his silver-tongued attorney talk. Last night, Rooney sobered as he waited between the fins of cars parked nose in outside Digby's office. Soon, midnight came, but Digby had not.

Walking his beat, Malatesta the cop saw Rooney once, twice, and the third time told him to go home, his family was waiting.

"That'll be the day I need advice from the likes of you."

"How's that, Rooney?" Malatesta said, cupping his ear.

A man had to reclaim his wife. It was natural law, for which no degree was required.

Malatesta smacked his open palm with his nightstick. "Home, Leaky," he repeated.

While Rooney melted and applied tar, his wife toiled diligently at the small, storefront Bell Telephone office on Sixth and Buchanan. The working life was still new to Mary Catherine, but she'd taken commercial courses in high school and knew how to do what she was told. Her boss was easygoing: though Mrs. Leibowitz wore a bun that brought her head to a point, she allowed the day shift to correspond to school hours. At three o'clock, the mothers were succeeded by single women who called themselves the Night Owls.

Knowing this, Digby arranged to find himself walking the avenue as Mary Catherine headed home. What a coincidence, he'd say when they met, offering to share his umbrella. Then, lowering his voice, he'd add that he had the papers ready for her to sign. In the course of their stroll, he would refer calmly to the finality of her actions, how such a thing done couldn't be easily undone. As the wiser of the two, she was likely to express some reservation. Then why not sleep on it? Digby would propose. Then, several hours later, he'd drop in the Shamrock and who should he see but Leaky. Mr. Rooney, what a coincidence, he'd say, and buy him a round, whispering discreetly that he had papers in his office. Should we go now? he'd asked, knowing Leaky wouldn't leave the stool until he toppled off it. He'd propose—

Digby was shaken from his reverie by a small voice from behind.

"Hey, Digby." The little girl wore a St. Matty's uniform, its white blouse dislodged from a checkered skirt. Polish failed to hide the wear on her saddle shoes.

"Hi there ..."

"Anna. Anna Rooney."

"Anna, yes." Exhibit A as to why the Rooneys should remain united. A pinprick to tranquility's balloon, the freckly kid needed guidance. "How are you?"

"Me, I'm always good."

He looked at her. She was more Leaky than Mary Catherine, the glint of wicked mischief in the eyes, blunt chin high in defiance.

"Digby. My dad is looking for you."

"OK. I'll be in my office—" here Digby looked at his wristwatch "—in about an hour."

"No Digby, you don't want to do that," Anna told him. "My dad's not too happy with you."

"Now why would you say something like that? Your father—"

"You went to St. Matty's with my mother, right?"

"Yes, but—"

"Was she pretty?"

"I suppose," Digby replied. "Well, yes. Yes, she was. But why—"

"My father's going to take his hammer to your head, Digby." She was tapping her foot at the edge of a puddle, causing ripples in the murky water.

"Anna—"

"Don't say I didn't warn you."

• • •

Digby hurried home, aware a law degree was no match for a lunatic with his sledgehammer. He locked the door, and went to the refrigerator to retrieve a cold drink, his throat parched from his rapid retreat up Rogers Point. But all he found was a jar of mayonnaise and a soggy carton of chow fun. Tap water sufficed.

Apparently, in the splish-splash of his alcohol-addled mind, Leaky Rooney had concluded Digby was engineering their divorce so he could step in on Mary Catherine. If Rooney had caved in Meehan's shoulder for bumping her shopping cart ...

Digby couldn't remember the last time he faced violence. He was a peaceable man, as his thoughtful manner and plump frame suggested, and not at all quick on his feet.

Hmmm.

Digby loosened his tie, took out a yellow pad and began to develop a strategy, standing now and then to pace. He sat, scribbled, paced. Stroked his chin. Yes, he thought finally, maybe so. He removed the pages and transcribed them, his handwriting neat, the flow of logic impeccable.

For safety's sake, he decided to bypass dinner at a Buchanan Avenue restaurant. Warm buttered popcorn would have to do as *Taras Bulba* unfolded and until his nap began. There was an all-night diner by the Erie-Lackawanna Terminal that had a fine grilled ham steak, or maybe the Grotto would still be serving its famous *zuppa di vongole* when the late movie let out. Digby would make do until he could implement his plan.

As he slipped back into his coat, he looked around his apartment, his bachelor's nest. Shutting the lights, Digby said goodbye to solitude and headed into the chilly Narrows Gate evening.

• • •

"And so what does he do, this Digby? This Michael Francis Digby? This *attorney at law?* He ..."

Rooney paused to order another bullet, and Finnerty limped over with the Four Roses bottle, its spigot reflecting the Shamrock's dull lighting. The jukebox was silent, the pool table abandoned save for the cue ball and bridge.

As Finnerty lifted a dollar, Rooney raged on.

"Not as a man would. No. Not. Hiding behind the law. Digby, this ... Digby. Trying to—And a working man at that. Me." Rooney tapped his chest. "I'm earning and he's ... O'Boyle, what's the word? He's ... He's conspiring. That's it. Conspiring!"

Staring at the rows of bottles stretched before him, seventy-two-year-old O'Boyle nodded, though he was hardly listening. His beloved Rat Catcher slept on sawdust under her master's feet.

Rooney burped. He'd put a sizable dent in the money he'd earned today, the short stack of singles all but flat now. Immediately after leaving the job site, he'd marched through the rain to Digby's storefront office, which he found empty again, but with its lights aglow. Short of ideas on where to look next, he repaired to the bar, sledgehammer looped in his belt.

"Rooney, it's none of my business, but I got to say I know Digby since we was in kindergarten at St. Matty's and I never seen him steal so much as a piece of penny candy," Finnerty said.

O'Boyle nodded.

"Ah. So I'm a liar, am I?"

Finnerty leaned his hands on the bar. "What I'm saying is maybe you're mistaken."

"Mistaken," Rooney grumbled.

"And Mary Catherine—"

"Mrs. Rooney to you," he said, his eyelids bobbing.

"Mary Catherine wouldn't spit at you and say it's raining, Rooney. That I know."

"I see as she's under his spell," he replied. "The web he spins with the big words, his education ..."

As he wiped his hands on his apron, Finnerty rolled his eyes.

"Digby's spell," O'Boyle chuckled.

"That's enough from you," Rooney said, jabbing O'Boyle's bony shoulder with a finger.

Rat Catcher stood, fixing Rooney in her sights, ready to bare her remaining teeth.

"Why don't you talk to him?" Finnerty said. "Digby don't lie."

"I would but for his hiding. As for his lying—"

"Digby's not hiding," O'Boyle said as he reached for the beer nuts. "He's at the movies."

Finnerty grimaced.

"The movies ..." Rooney said. Draining the last of his bourbon and the foamy Rheingold, he slid carefully off the stool, avoiding

Rat Catcher, who sneered at him nonetheless. Bending to peer at the mirror behind the liquor bottles, he matted down his hair, centered the shoulders of his work coat and gathered up his change, leaving a dime for Finnerty. Without a word, he staggered toward the door, red neon reflecting in his pinwheeling eyes.

When Rooney left, Finnerty stared at O'Boyle. "Now why did you do that, putting Digby in his sights? You know full well Digby can't—"

O'Boyle slowly raised his fist, which held Rooney's baby sledgehammer.

• • •

Finnerty called from the bar.

"All right, Thomas," Mary Catherine groaned. "I thank you. Give my regards to Lucy, and to your mother too."

Anna's sharp tongue and sinister logic made her unbearable to her siblings, so Mary Catherine had to drag her along. As they took their seats on the jitney, she turned to her daughter, who was pinned against the sidewall and rain-streak window by her mother's heft.

"Anna, if you say one word out of turn, I swear I'll send you to Grandma before the night is through."

"I don't mind Grandma McIlwaine," Anna replied.

"I wasn't talking about Grandma McIlwaine."

"Well, Grandma Rooney is dead."

"Exactly so." She stared ahead toward the driver.

Twelve blocks later, they hurried through the rain to under the sputtering lights of the Avalon's marquee, late for the sunset matinee and early for the eight o'clock show. They paid full price—one adult, one child—and took the faded red carpet on the sweeping staircase to the balcony where, as long-time Narrows Gate's residents knew, Francis Michael Digby napped. As furious Cossacks stormed into battle on screen, horses stampeding in rhythm to the glorious orchestral score, Mary Catherine ducked beneath the flickering projection. Hand above her brow, she located Digby nuzzled against a chipped wall, his chin cupped in his hand.

Dragging Anna behind her, she approached.

"Digby," she whispered, in order not to disturb the other patrons sprinkled throughout the musty balcony. "Digby."

The sound of gunfire ricocheted around the theater.

"Whack him," Anna suggested.

A cannon exploded. But Digby continued to purr.

Mary Catherine hesitated, then jostled his shoulder. "Digby. Francis." She sat in the seat next to his. "Francis, wake up ..."

Suddenly, there was a ruckus down below. Patrons hissed, and then shouted over the picture as it blared. When Mary Catherine looked beyond the tarnished brass rail, she saw her husband climbing onto the stage, his shadow on the screen.

"Digby!" he wailed, as the battle raged behind him. "Digby, I'm here to kill you, I am. Where in God's name are you?"

"They're up here, Dad," Anna screamed. She pointed an accusing finger at her mother and Digby, who now sat side by side.

• • •

Leaky Rooney raced up the stairs, an usher giving chase.

Fists on her hips, Mary Catherine stood before Digby, who was rousting himself from the grip of a deep sleep. She glared at her husband.

"Mary Catherine ..." Rooney warned as he skidded to a stop. "So help me God."

Almost alert, Digby peered over her shoulder. As quickly as he could, he silently recounted the strategy he crafted in his apartment.

The balcony patrons gathered above the exit.

"Step aside, Mary Catherine," Rooney said as he slowly padded toward them. "I have no taste for harming you. But that ... That ... That *attorney*," he sputtered. "Death is too good for his likes, believe me."

"Where's your hammer, Dad?" Anna said.

Staring at Digby, Rooney patted his empty belt.

Peering over his former classmate's shoulder, Digby saw his opening. "I love Mary Catherine," he blurted. "Always have."

Rooney recoiled. *Sweet mother of Jesus, it isn't only in my head,* he thought.

Mary Catherine turned. "Digby ... ?"

"He's right, Mary Catherine. Your husband is right. I've tried to free you for my own gain ..."

"Holy moley," Anna said.

Digby recited his speech from memory. "Mary Catherine, I remember like it was yesterday the tears in your eyes when Sister Dolores told us President Roosevelt had died. Your beautiful face as you led us in prayer. Your hazel eyes ... From that moment on—"

"That'll be enough of that, Digby," Rooney barked. "Step over here so I can kill you proper."

The exit was now filled with patrons from downstairs, the picture continuing without an audience.

Digby took Mary Catherine's hands. "You deserve the best, my dear," he said as sweetly as he could manage.

"That's it!" Rooney announced, raising an empty fist. "Say your prayers, Digby!" Charging in, he pushed his wife directly into Digby's embrace.

Stunned, Digby tried to retreat, but he was blocked by a row of seats.

Mary Catherine held tight as she brought her lips to his ear. "Thank you, Francis Michael Digby," she whispered.

"Dad, look! She's saying she loves him. She said it!"

Rooney clapped his daughter on the back of the head. But then he said, "Is it so, Mary Catherine?"

In the eternity it took to turn, Mary Catherine had a fleeting vision of what might've been. She blinked to shake from its satisfying grip, though not before remembering that, yes, she had been beautiful and once had dreams. "And what if it is?" she said.

Rooney quaked. He could not believe his life was at its end. Mary Catherine, who he loved from the moment he saw her in her cheerleader's uniform—pleated skirt, dimpled knees, socks drooping over her saddle shoes. Her face shone like a thousand suns and, as God is my witness, it still does.

"I— " Speechless, Rooney dropped into a padded seat. His sow of a mother was right: he was ending up drunk and alone.

Digby gave Mary Catherine a gentle shove. "Go on ..."

Sighing, she stepped forward and held out her hand.

"Come on," she said to her hapless husband.

Rooney looked up. "Me?" he said in amazement.

"Yes. You."

Rooney raised slowly, his head bowed in shame. Then he looked up and stared in his wife's eyes.

"I'm a dope," he said.

"Indeed," replied Mary Catherine.

"Congratulations, Rooney," Digby said cheerfully. "You're a lucky man."

Digby waved as the Rooneys, the usher and the downstairs patrons retreated, leaving much of the balcony empty.

On the screen, the battle had ended. Smoke had begun to clear, the cannons now silent. The remaining horses grazed somewhere far off and unseen.

Digby returned to his seat, wriggling until he reclaimed his warm spot. Contented, he nestled in, ready to resume a life of simple pleasures.

Soon, he was fast asleep.

•   •   •

JIM FUSILLI is the author of five novels. In 2010, his short story, "Digby, Attorney At Law," was nominated for an Edgar Award by the Mystery Writers of America. His story "Chellini's Solution," appeared in the 2007 edition of *The Best American Mystery Stories,* and his story "The Guardians" was selected for *A Prisoner of Memory,* a 2008 anthology of the year's finest mystery short fiction. Jim is the rock and pop critic of *The Wall Street Journal. Pet Sounds,* his book on Brian Wilson and the Beach Boys' album *Pet Sounds,* was published in 2006 by Continuum and in 2009 by Audible. He lives in New York City.

THE WAY THEY LIMP

By Clark Howard

Angus Doyle was having a late breakfast on the east patio of his gated, guarded estate home, when his attorney, Solomon Silverstein, arrived.

"You eat yet?" Doyle asked by way of greeting.

"No. And I probably won't all day," the lawyer snapped. "I've lost my appetite. And my ulcer is going crazy. It'll probably perforate."

"Oh? What's bothering your ulcer, Sol?"

Silverstein sat and drew over an extra chair on which to place and open his briefcase. From it he extracted four documents folded in blue legal covering. "These are what's bothering me," he said, placing them directly in front of Angus Doyle's breakfast plate.

"What are they?" Doyle asked, not touching them.

"Subpoenas, Gus. Federal grand jury subpoenas. For Quinn, Foley, Dwyer, and Connor."

"But not for me?"

"Not yet."

Doyle grunted quietly. "What's the grand jury looking at? RICO again?"

RICO. Racketeering Influenced Corrupt Organizations. An all-purpose federal crime designed to bring down organized crime operations.

"No, not RICO. Not this time, Gus." The lawyer's expression turned grim. "This time it's income tax evasion."

"What!" Doyle was taken aback. "I pay my taxes!" he declared indignantly.

"Of course you do," Sol said. "On your legitimate businesses. On your up-front operations: the bowling alleys and bars, the laundry and dry cleaning services, the limo and escort services, the convenience store franchises, all the rest. But you don't pay income tax on the other stuff: the gambling, hijacking, prostitution—"

"How the hell can I?" Doyle demanded. "Those things are *illegal*!"

"Exactly. And that's what they're now trying to get you for. Income is income, whether it's legal or illegal. Remember a fellow named Al Capone?" The attorney leaned forward urgently. "Can't you see what they're doing? Quinn, Foley, Dwyer, and Connor. Your four top men. Between them, they know *everything* about your operation. Everything you run, all the front businesses, the payoffs, where the money comes from, where the bodies are buried—"

"Sol, please. I'm eating," Doyle said.

"Do you see my point?"

"No."

"Look, they're going to bring in each of your men separately to be questioned by department of justice attorneys in front of a secret grand jury. No defense lawyers are allowed, there's no transcript, no rules of evidence apply because the purpose is not to *convict* anyone, merely to indict." Silverstein took a deep breath. "Do you suppose I can get a glass of cold milk?"

Doyle rang a small silver bell on the table. In seconds a white-coated attendant appeared and the milk was ordered. "Sure you wouldn't like something to eat, Sol? Eggs, bacon, O'Brien potatoes?"

"Good god, no! Do you want to kill me?"

There was a twinkle of mischief in Angus Doyle's eyes, with just a hint of malice attached to it. Doyle was a stout, almost brutish, ruddy-faced man who could eat anything, and who could, and had, killed enemies with his bare hands. He was Black Irish to the core, and while he valued Solomon Silverstein to a large degree, he had never really been fond of him. In his entire life, Angus Doyle had never really been fond of anyone who was not Irish.

Sol fidgeted with a corner of the starched white cloth of Angus Doyle's breakfast table. A thin, hyper, dedicated worrier of a man, he was nevertheless a brilliant litigator and appellant attorney who had kept Angus Doyle out of legal harm's way for two decades, and whom Doyle had made very wealthy in return. When his glass of cold milk arrived, the lawyer gulped it down in several swallows, then rubbed his stomach as if to spread around its soothing effect.

"Tell me in plain language what's bothering you, Sol," Doyle said, continuing to devour the O'Brien potatoes laced with onions and green peppers.

"Quinn, Foley, Dwyer, and Connor. They will be questioned individually, in secret, and no one except the justice department attorney and the anonymous grand jury members will ever know what they say. *But*—everything they say can be used to find evidence against anyone they give testimony about."

Doyle belched. "So?"

"So, Gus, suppose one of them cuts a deal with the government?"

"One of *my* men? Sol, please."

"It could happen, Gus. One of them gives enough information for the government to find cause to indict you, and you'd never know which one did it. Even *they* wouldn't know which one did it. You go down. Your entire organization is wiped out. And the government gives immunity to Quinn, Foley, Dwyer, and Connor—so nobody ever knows who the informer was."

"None of my men would ever do that," Doyle said confidently.

"What makes you so sure? How do you know how much the government has compiled on each one of them over the years? How do you know how much pressure can be put on one of them? Immunity, Gus, can be an orchid in a field of weeds."

Doyle stopped eating. His expression grew thoughtful. "All right," he said quietly, "for the sake of argument, suppose one of them *does* cut a deal. What happens next?"

"The government indicts you on numerous counts of income tax evasion over the years. They prove that you could not possibly have maintained the life style you've established on the legitimate income you claimed on your tax returns."

"How the hell can they prove something like that?"

"Paper trail, Gus. The cars you've bought over the years. The Canali suits and shirts you've had made. The Salvatore Ferragamo Python shoes you wear. That Girard

Perregaus wristwatch you're wearing that cost five hundred thousand dollars. The yacht you've got docked in Florida. The homes you own in Vail, Barbados, Costa Rica. Vera's jewelry. Doreen's private school in Switzerland—"

"Okay, okay," Doyle raised a hand to stop the lawyer's soliloquy, "I get the picture." He pushed his plate away in disgust. "A man can't even buy gifts for his wife and see that his daughter gets a proper education without the goddamned government sticking its nose into it," he muttered irritably. After a few moments, he sighed wearily and said, "Assuming you're right, what exactly happens then?"

"A caravan of federal agents will show up at daybreak some morning, put you under arrest, declare this place a crime scene, evict Vera, Doreen, and all the servants—"

"How can they do that? This is my *home*, for god's sake! What right do they have to declare it a crime scene!"

"Your vault, Gus," the lawyer said quietly. "Whoever blows the whistle on you will tell them about your vault."

Doyle's eyes widened to the point of bulging. Beneath his mansion was a lower level that housed an extensive wine cellar, a mammoth gun collection, and a floor-to-ceiling bank-style vault that was one of his most prized possessions.

"My vault," he said to Sol Silverstein in a flat, dangerous tone, "is *private* property. It's where I keep my rare stamp collection, my movie memorabilia collection, my ancient coin collection, my gem collection, my early American post card collection, and my baseball card collection." Now his voice faltered a bit. "Those things are *personal*, Sol. They mean a great deal to me. The government has no right to meddle with my *hobbies!*"

"That vault," Sol quietly reminded him, "is also where you hoard money, Gus. I've seen sheaves of currency stacked to the ceiling in a back corner. The government will seize that money and everything else of value in that vault. I advised you not to have it installed, remember? Just as I advised you to have Quinn, Foley, Dwyer, and Connor retain private individual attorneys of their own, instead of having me representing them *and* you."

"I like to have everything under one roof, Sol," Doyle fretted. "Easier to keep track of things."

"Yes, well in this case it just made it *easier* to subpoena everyone with one stop."

Doyle rose and walked to one end of the patio, from which he could see across meticulously manicured, flower-lined grounds to an eight-car garage behind and detached from the main house. In front of an open port was parked one of his wife Vera's cars, a silver Bentley Arnage sedan. It was being wiped down with a chamois cloth by Harry Sullivan, a quiet but deceptively tough young man who was employed as a driver and bodyguard for Doyle's second wife, Vera Kenny Doyle. Sullivan, known more commonly as Sully, also drove and bodyguarded Doreen, Doyle's twenty-one-year-old daughter by his first wife, Edna Callahan Doyle, whom Doyle had lost to lymphoma when Doreen was only ten. Three years later, with Doreen approaching adolescence, Doyle had seen the need of a stepmother for her; there were, after all, many things of a sensitive, female nature with which even the most devoted single father was ill prepared to deal.

For his second wife, Angus Doyle had chosen and courted twenty-eight-year-old Vera Kenny, who managed Doyle's escort service, and who was the daughter of a late friend of the younger Angus Doyle, at that time just making his mark in the Irish mob known as The Clan. Doyle, at forty when he took his second wife, was twelve years older than Vera Kenny, but the two made a good fit and young Doreen took to her stepmother at once, thus removing a good deal of worry from Doyle's mind. In all, Gus Doyle would have been a man of continuing contentment had it not been for the goddamned Department of Justice.

"All right, Sol," Doyle said, turning his attention away from the eight-car garage, "what do we do now?"

"We have to get you as clean as possible before Quinn, Foley, Dwyer, and Connor are questioned at the grand jury. That means divesting yourself of as much liquid assets as possible. The other assets—real property, cars, the boat—we can put under protective mortgages so that the government can't say that you bought them outright, therefore they can't be used as evidence against you in a tax evasion case. You see, it's *cash*—that's what they need. Cash in bank accounts, safe deposit boxes, certificates of deposit, cash in that vault of yours—how much do you have stacked up down there anyway?"

"I don't know," Doyle shrugged self-consciously. "Maybe seven or eight."

"Seven or eight hundred thousand?"

"Million."

"Seven or eight *million*? For god's sake, Gus."

"It's money I put away for a rainy day." Doyle pointed an accusing finger at the lawyer. "You don't know what it's like to grow up dirt poor, Sol. If you did, you'd understand."

Silverstein stared at his client in astonishment. From an inside coat pocket, he removed a handkerchief and blotted his forehead. He did not want to hear Angus Doyle's poverty-in-the-Chicago-slums story again. "Gus," he said firmly, "I want to know—*exactly*—how much money you have—*anywhere,* Gus—that can be traced to you. How much?"

Doyle sat back down and drummed his thick fingertips silently on the tablecloth. After a long moment of staring at his attorney with pursed lips, he said, "Twenty-five million."

"How long will it take to pull it all together—close all the accounts, empty all the safe deposit boxes, cash in all the certificates of deposit?"

Another shrug from Doyle. "Three, four days, I guess. But what the hell am I supposed to do with that much cash?"

"Convert it to bearer bonds, Gus. Convert all of it, along with your 'rainy day' cash in that vault of yours."

"What the hell are bearer bonds?"

"They are unregistered negotiable bonds payable to the holder regardless of who they were issued to. They're as good as cash at any bank in the world."

"So what do we do with these bearer bonds then?"

"Get them out of the country. Move them to a Swiss bank in the Cayman Islands, where U.S. officials won't have access to them."

"How do we do that?"

"Someone you trust has to take them there. Who do you trust?"

"You."

"Me! I'm your *attorney*, Gus. I can't do anything like that. It wouldn't be ethical. I could be disbarred." Sol blotted his forehead again. "Who else do you trust?"

"Quinn, Foley, Dwyer, and Connor."

"For god's sake, Gus! They're the ones I'm trying to protect you against! You can't ask any of them to *help* you, because you don't know which one to ask. They're all suspect at the moment. What about Vera? Or Doreen?"

"Not Doreen," Doyle shook his head vehemently. "I don't want any of my business touching Doreen. I want her kept out of this completely. Do you understand that, Sol?"

"Yes, of course," the attorney said quickly. He recognized Angus Doyle's cold, hard, warning tone, his deadly tone. "I understand. Doreen will be kept out of it entirely, I assure you. That leaves Vera."

"Yes," Doyle said, rubbing his chin thoughtfully. "That leaves Vera."

After Solomon Silverstein departed, Doyle went inside to his richly appointed, soundproof, and surveillance-protected office and pushed the intercom button for his garage. After three rings it was answered by Harry Sullivan.

"Sully, will you come up to my office, please."

"Yessir, Mr. Doyle, be right there," Harry Sullivan said.

By the time Doyle had opened a cold bottle of root beer from an executive refrigerator and was back at his desk drinking it, Harry Sullivan was there.

"Sit down, Sully."

"Thank you, sir."

Doyle smiled a slight, pleased smile. "How long have you worked for me now, Sully?"

"Two years and eight months, sir."

"Do you know what the first thing was that I liked about you, Sully?"

"No, sir."

"You always addressed me as 'sir.' Nobody ever did that before—except, of course waiters and clerks, servants, people like that. But nobody *close.*" He tilted his head slightly. "Why did you do it, Sully? From the very beginning, I mean."

"I don't know, sir," the younger man replied. "It just seemed like the natural thing to do. The respectful thing, I guess I mean to say."

Doyle fell silent for a long moment, studying Harry Sullivan. The driver-bodyguard was more common looking than handsome, with light brown hair and brooding deep blue eyes. He had, Doyle thought, a dependable look about him, a *steadiness.* He could, Doyle already knew, be dangerous when necessary, as he had proved two years earlier when a drunken college boy at a house party had gone a little too far in his advances toward Doreen, had in fact torn open her blouse in the shadows of a porch, causing Doreen to yell for Sully, who was parked nearby waiting for her. Sully had broken the young man's right eye socket with brass knuckles and ruptured his testicles. Doyle, of course, had paid all the medical bills, and *reasoned* with the parents to convince them not to file criminal charges against Sully, whom he promised to seriously punish himself. Sully's punishment came in the form of a thousand dollar bonus.

"Do you like your job here, Sully?" Doyle asked.

"Yessir. Very much."

"Tell me what you like about it."

"Well, sir, you pay me very good wages. I have nice living quarters over the garage. The work is easy. Mrs. Vera and Miss Doreen treat me very well; they give me Christmas presents—"

"I give you Christmas presents too, Sully. Two thousand dollars it was last year, I think."

"Yessir, I know that, and it was very generous of you. But what I meant was, Mrs. Vera and Miss Doreen give me *personal* Christmas presents."

Doyle frowned slightly. This was something he didn't know. "Personal presents like what, Sully?"

"Well, sir, last Christmas Mrs. Vera gave me a really nice sweater, cashmere. And Miss Doreen gave me a wallet with my initials on it. Here, I'll show you—"

Sully drew a wallet from his hip pocket and stood to hold it over the desk for Doyle to see.

"Very nice," Doyle complimented.

"That's what I meant by personal, sir. They just treat me real nice, both of them."

"Good. That's good." Leaning forward, Doyle clasped his hands on the desk. "Sully, I want to ask you a few questions and I don't want you to be embarrassed by them, or afraid to give me honest answers. You drive for my wife and daughter, but you work for me. You do understand that, don't you?"

"Definitely, yessir."

"Good. Very good." Doyle's icy gray eyes fixed steadily on Sully. "Do you think my daughter is attractive, Sully?"

"Yessir, very much. She's one of the prettiest girls I've ever seen."

"You'd never get too, ah—friendly with my daughter, would you, Sully?"

"Never, Mr. Doyle! I know my place, sir. Miss Doreen is way out of my league. If I have any personal feelings about her at all, it's like she was a little sister to me."

"Little sister?" Doyle sat back and began drumming his fingers on the desk top while deciding whether he liked that analogy or not. He finally decided that it was all right. "I like that, Sully," he said, giving the younger man a genuine smile. "You're doing fine, boyo, fine. Now let me ask you a few things about Mrs. Vera. And remember," he pointed a finger, "be honest with me."

"I will be, sir."

"Tell me about the places she has you drive her to."

"Ah, let's see, sir. There's the hair salon, the manicure shop, her doctor now and again, the dentist, that big book store on Michigan Avenue, a lot of those—what are they called—bow something—?"

"Boutique shops?"

"Yessir, that's it."

"Does she ever have you take any place you think is unusual?"

"No, sir. Mostly the same places all the time."

"And what do you and my wife talk about when you're driving her?"

"Not much at all, sir. Mrs. Vera is usually on her cell phone."

"Who's she mostly talking to?"

Sully looked down. "I couldn't say, sir. I try not to listen."

"Well, if you had to venture a guess, would you say she was talking to men or women?"

"Women, definitely, sir. I can't help picking up snatches of her end of the conversation, and it sounds like they're talking about clothes and shoe sizes and styles and spa treatments, things like that."

"I see. Does she ever meet anyone for lunch?"

"Yessir. Two or three times a week."

"Any men?"

"No, sir. Always ladies."

"Always? Without exception?"

"Without exception, sir. I've never seen Mrs. Vera even speak to a man anywhere I've ever taken her—"

Just then there was a brief knock on the office door and Doyle's daughter Doreen stuck her head in. "Daddy, do you know where Sully is? I want to go—oh, he's in here with you. Sorry, Daddy." She started to back out but Doyle stopped her.

"No, no, it's all right, dear, come in. Sully was just reporting on the condition of our cars. Where is it you want to go?"

"Miranda's Fashions, downtown. Some dresses I ordered came in and I want to try them on."

Doyle and Sully were both standing now, and Doreen's father came around the desk to give her a kiss on the cheek. Doreen was what most people would describe as cute rather than pretty. She looked younger than her age and had a fleshy figure without exactly being plump. By the look on her father's face, she clearly was adored by him.

"Sully can run you down right now," Doyle said. "We were finished anyhow."

"I'll bring the car right up, Miss Doreen," Sully said.

"No, I'll walk down to the garage with you," Doreen said. "I need the exercise."

"Do you know where Vera is?" Doyle asked his daughter as they were leaving.

"Out by the pool, last I saw."

After they left, Doyle watched them through a big picture window as they walked side by side across the manicured lawn. Little sister, he thought. Good. Very good.

Grinning to himself, Doyle returned to his desk and called Sol Silverstein on the lawyer's cell phone.

"I'm going to take your advice, Sol. I'll make up some lists today, then tomorrow I'll have some security people take Vera around to pick up all the cash I have locally. They'll have a backup car follow them for protection. The outside money, bonds and stuff, I'll have one of my brokers wire transfer to a central bank. I'll have that same bank pick up what I've got in the vault and what Vera collects tomorrow. Then I'll have the bank convert everything to bearer bonds, like you said. I've decided to have Vera take it all by charter jet to the Caymans on Saturday. You make the arrangements down there."

When he finished the call, Doyle went outside and strolled around the west grounds of his estate to the pool to look for Vera.

• • •

A mile down the road from the Doyle estate, Sully pulled over and stopped to allow Doreen Doyle to move from the rear seat of the Mercedes-Benz McLaren to the front seat with him.

"What was the big pow-wow with Daddy all about?" she asked, lighting a forbidden cigarette.

"He wanted to make sure I wasn't making any moves on you," Sully said. They leaned together and kissed briefly on the lips.

"If he had any idea the moves you've *already* made," she declared lightly, squeezing the inside of his thigh, "he'd kill us both."

"Me, anyway," Sully agreed. "I sure he'd find a way to forgive his little princess.

Is everything all right between him and Vera?"

"Far as I know. Why?"

"He asked me a lot of questions today about where I drove her, who she talked to on her cell phone, whether she ever met any men for lunch."

"Really! You don't think he thinks she's cheating on him, do you?"

"I don't know what to think."

"I wonder. You know Sol Silverstein was up to see him this morning."

"Yeah, I saw his car."

"They had a kind of intense talk out on the east patio while Daddy was having breakfast. I watched them from my bedroom window. Sol tossed some papers of some kind onto the table. They both seemed very serious. Daddy got up and paced. And he drummed his fingers on the table, you know how he does sometimes. Could he be thinking about divorcing Vera?"

"I doubt it. Not for cheating anyway. He knows if she was cheating on him, I'd be suspicious. And he knows I'd tell him."

"You would?"

"Sure. I *work* for him, Dorry."

"That doesn't keep you from sleeping with his daughter."

"That's different. I couldn't help myself. You seduced me."

"*I* seduced *you!*" Doreen reached to his thigh again, this time pinching it smartly. "You practically *raped* me the first time we did it after the party that night when you put poor Freddie Carter in the hospital. God, I will *never* forget that night!"

"Me neither. I think we probably raped each other."

Now she rubbed his thigh a little higher. "Step on it, baby. Let's pick up those damned dresses and get out to the room."

Sully kept a small kitchenette that he rented by the month at a long-term executive motel in a nearby suburb. Feeling warm from Doreen's touch, he eased down on the accelerator.

• • •

Back at the mansion, Vera Doyle was sitting up on the chaise lounge where her husband had found her, staring at him in uncertainty.

"This was all Sol's idea?" she asked.

"Yeah. He said it was the only thing to do. To be on the safe side, you know."

Doyle had drawn up a deck chair beside Vera's chaise lounge, and was drinking another root beer.

"What do you think of his theory about Quinn and the others?"

"I don't know. I've known the four of them since we were all kids together on the lower West Side. We were all in the West End Dukes together. We were like brothers."

"People change," Vera said pragmatically. "Then too, Sol is only guessing. He doesn't *know* what the justice department is planning."

"Well, Sol is usually right about those things."

Vera nodded. "I can't argue that." She took the root beer bottle from him and had a sip for herself. "It's the money thing that really bothers me, Gus. That's a lot of money to be moving at one time. And why me? Can't somebody else do it?"

"Like who?" Doyle shrugged. "Those four guys are the only ones in the whole of my outfit that I've *ever* trusted. If I only knew which one was about to rat me out, maybe I could have one of the others move the bearer bonds. But that's the snag: I *don't* know."

"You've no idea at all who it might be? Not even a suspicion?"

"None. Ed Quinn and Tom Foley and me grew up together down around Halsted and Van Buren. Mike Dwyer and Dan Connor

I met in the reform school out in St. Charles. Charleytown, we called the place." He grunted quietly. "I can't imagine any one of them betraying me. If only one of them limped."

"What do you mean?"

"There's an old Irish prayer. My granddad Padric taught it to me when I was a boy. Goes like this:

"May those that love me, love me.
And those that don't love me,
May God turn their hearts.
And if He doesn't turn their hearts,
May He turn their ankles,
So's I'll know them by the way they limp."

"If only that were true," Vera said.

Doyle took her hand. "Look, sweetheart, the money isn't going to be that big a deal. After Sol has it all converted into bearer bonds, they'll be packed neatly in a suitcase. You'll fly to the Cayman Islands on a chartered plane. I'll have Sully go with you—"

"Sully? Why Sully? He's only a driver."

"And a bodyguard. He's dependable and very loyal to you. Naturally he won't know about the bearer bonds; it'll just be another suitcase. There are several Swiss bank branches in the Caymans; Sol will tell you which one to use. Sully will accompany you to the bank, where a large safe deposit drawer will be already be arranged. Have him wait outside the safe deposit vault; he won't ask any questions. You'll put the bonds in the drawer, get the key, and that will be that. Sully will fly back the next day with the key and leave you to have a nice carefree vacation. I'll set you up with a suite at the Casuarina; that's the place you like, remember? As soon as I can, I'll join you."

Doyle lifted her hand and sucked on her forefinger. "Say you'll do this for me, Vera."

She took her finger out of his mouth and kissed it. "You know I will, Gus. I'd do anything for you, love."

• • •

It took four days to accumulate all the cash into a central downtown bank, and another day for it to be tallied by auditors and bearer bonds converted for the total. The bonds were then moved by a private security firm to Doyle's mansion, where they were put into his underground vault.

In the interim, Doyle took Sully down to a line of expensive shops on Michigan Avenue and bought him a wardrobe of fashionable vacation wear: sport coats, slacks, shirts—everything he needed to look good with the always elegantly attired Vera.

When they got back from their shopping trip. Doyle himself driving his prized Rolls Royce Phantom, Doreen came out to meet them in the *porte-cochere*. As Doyle got out and Sully came around to put the car away, Doreen said, "Sully, did you happen to see my yellow-tinted sunglasses in the Mercedes? I can't find them anywhere."

"No, but I'll look for them, Miss Doreen," Sully said.

"I'll ride down to the garage with you in case they're there." She kissed her father on the cheek. "Vera wants to talk to you, Daddy. Something about her trip, I think."

With Doreen in the front seat beside him, Sully guided the big luxury car around a drive that circled the grounds back to the garage building.

"What's all this about you going somewhere with Vera?" Doreen asked, a little crossly.

"Beats me," Sully said. "I was hoping you might know. We're going to the Caymans."

"For how long?"

"Not long for me. I'm coming back the next day. Vera's staying on."

"Something very weird is going on. Sol has been in and out of the house for two days now. And Daddy didn't hold his usual Tuesday morning meeting with Mr. Quinn and Mr. Foley and the others."

"I noticed that too. Very unusual."

Doreen slapped his knee. "I'm not wild about you flying off to some romantic island with Vera."

"Come on, Dorry. She's your stepmother."

"So? She's not that much older than you. And more than easy to look at, as I'm sure you've noticed."

"You're talking crazy. This is all business of some kind."

"It'd better be," she warned, not a little sternly.

Sully reached over and ran a hand up her skirt.

"Relax, baby. I'm all yours."

• • •

The flight from O'Hare to Grand Cayman was non-stop, six hours, in a luxurious chartered Gulfstream V-SP jet. Sully personally handled all the luggage, including a new Hartmann leather bag Doyle had bought for Sully's own clothes. In flight, Vera and Sully were served drinks and a three-course gourmet meal pre-ordered by Vera. A limousine met them at Owen Roberts International Airport in Grand Cayman and drove them to the ultra-deluxe Casuarina Resort and Spa, where a two bedroom beachfront suite had been reserved for Vera. As soon as they had checked in, Vera went into her bedroom and called her husband on one of a dozen disposable, untraceable cell phones she carried.

"We're here, Gus," she reported. "No problems. I asked at the desk and was told that the bank is open for another three hours. We're going there now."

"Good girl. How's Sully doing?"

"Like a fish out of water, but he's okay. I have to admit, it was a good idea sending him. I feel safer with him along. But it'll be a relief to get this stuff into a bank drawer."

"To me as well. Let me know when it's done."

After the call, Vera gave the cell phone to Sully and watched as he put it under his heel on the patio and crushed it to pieces. Gus, Vera knew, had done the same with a disposable phone on which he had taken her call.

The Cayman Island branch of the Private Bank of Switzerland was on Sheddon Road in George Town. "It's very easy to find," Sol Silverstein had told Vera when preparing her for the trip. "Just down from the American Express offices. You'll ask for a Mr. Unterman. He'll be expecting you. There'll be a safe deposit drawer already rented and waiting for you in one of the private cubicles in their vault. Have Sully take the suitcase in and then wait outside for you. Just put the packets of bearer bonds into the drawer, close it up, and ring for Mr. Unterman. He will lock the closed drawer back into its niche and give you one of the two keys to the niche door; the bank retains the other key—the two keys are different, you see, and it takes both of them to open the door. You send the key he gives you back with Sully the next day. It's all very simple, really." Sol had given her a brief hug around the shoulders. "Don't be nervous, dear. We'll have this grand jury mess cleared up for Gus in a couple of weeks at the most. In the meantime, just relax and enjoy yourself."

"I'll try," Vera said.

• • •

The federal grand jury testimony of Edward Quinn, Thomas Foley, Michael Dwyer, and Daniel Connor took place one week later, and consumed only two court days. None of the four gave any testimony that could in any way incriminate Angus Doyle.

But on the third day, a surprise witness did.

"State your name, please," said the federal prosecutor after the witness had been sworn.

"Vera Kenny."

"Were you previously Vera Doyle?"

"I was."

"You were married to Angus Doyle, the subject of this inquiry?"

"I was."

"Are you now divorced from Angus Doyle?"

"I am."

"When were you divorced?"

"Five days ago."

"And where were you divorced?"

"In the Dominican Republic."

"Your honor," the prosecutor said to the presiding federal judge, "at this time we offer the grand jury a certified copy of the Dominican Republic divorce of the witness, along with a ruling from the U.S. Department of State confirming that one-party Dominican Republic divorces are recognized as legal in the United States." He then turned back to the witness. "Miss Kenny, were you recently in the Cayman Islands?"

"I was."

"What was the purpose of your trip there?"

"To deposit a quantity of bearer bonds into a safe deposit drawer."

"What was the value of those bearer bonds?"

"Ten million dollars."

"Did you deposit them into the safe deposit drawer?"

"No."

"What *did* you do with them?"

"I brought them back to Chicago after my divorce in the Dominican Republic and turned them over to the Department of Justice."

Again the prosecutor addressed the judge. "Your honor, we would now offer the grand jury a receipt from the Department of Justice for ten million dollars in bearer bonds received from Miss Kenny." Facing his witness again, he asked, "From whom did you get the bearer bonds in question?"

"From my former husband, Angus Doyle."

"The same Angus Doyle who is the subject of this grand jury inquiry?"

"Yes."

"Now then, Miss Kenny, in return for turning over the bearer bonds to the government, and for your testimony before this grand jury, have you been promised anything in return?"

"Yes. The Department of Justice has guaranteed me full immunity from any federal prosecution, and the Department of State has promised me a permanent residence visa in a foreign country. I am also being given protective custody until I am safely out of the U.S."

"That concludes the testimony of this witness," the federal prosecutor said.

Two hours later, the grand jury voted a true bill against Angus Doyle and indicted

him for on twenty-one counts of federal income tax evasion, each count being a separate criminal felony.

• • •

Later that day, a federal strike force surrounded and closed off the estate and grounds of Angus Doyle, and Doyle himself was arrested, handcuffed, and taken away.

Doreen Doyle, in a daze bordering on shock, watched as federal agents began swarming into the house. She was standing out front when Sully and several agents walked up from the garage. Hanging around Sully's neck was a Department of Justice photo ID credential identifying him as federal agent Harry Sullivan O'Keefe.

"You son of a bitch," Doreen said.

"Give me a minute with her," Sully instructed the other agents, gesturing them into the house.

"You dirty, low-life, lying bastard." No longer in a daze, Doreen was glaring coldly at him.

"What is it that you're angriest about?" Sully asked. "The arrest of your father? Or the fact that we had sex?"

"Forget about the sex," she snapped. "I enjoyed it as much as you did. But without my father, I have nothing. I'll be all alone—no family, no money—"

"Not true," Sully told her. "Check with Sol Silverstein. You'll find that you have a five-million-dollar trust that your father set up for you shortly after your mother passed away. The government can't touch it. You are very well off, Dorry. You can make a good life for yourself."

"What about Vera? Do you know where she is?"

"She's on her way to a foreign country where she will be under the protection of the U.S. Embassy. You'll never see her again."

"What will happen to my father?"

"He'll probably receive a fifteen-year sentence on the criminal tax evasion charges, and new racketeering violations will be brought against him while he's in prison. Your father is a major crime figure; he'll probably never be a free man again. Get use to that, Dorry."

"Stop calling me 'Dorry.'"

"All right. Miss Doyle, then. I'll give you an hour to pack your things, then you'll have to leave the premises."

She smiled wryly. "I don't suppose you'll be driving me away, will you, Sully?"

"I'll have another agent give you a lift to a downtown hotel."

She started into the house. At the doorway, she stopped and turned back. "About the sex. I suppose that was just part of your job."

"No. That was real."

"Thanks for that much," Doreen said. She continued inside.

• • •

The senior Department of Justice agent in charge of Operation Gus, as it was called, smiled broadly across his desk at Agent Harry Sullivan O'Keefe.

"One hell of a job, Sully," he praised. "With all the other bits and pieces of intelligence you provided during your undercover assignment, we'll be able to get Quinn, Foley, Dwyer, and Connor too. We may even be able to nail Solomon Silverstein on something. I think we can at least get him disbarred."

"You'll leave Doreen Doyle's trust alone, right?" asked Sully.

"Absolutely. You kind of liked her, didn't you? No, we don't need it for our case. But we'll attach everything else. And about a year from now, after we get everybody else, they can all have a big reunion at the federal Supermax prison in Colorado. And *you*, my friend," he pointed a finger at Sully, "will get a nice commendation from the department."

"That's nice," said Sully, "but I'm more interested in my thirty-two months accumulated salary—*and* the six months paid leave I was promised when I went under."

"That money has already been credited to your personal bank account, as will your monthly salary while you're on leave," said the senior agent. "And that paid leave officially begins right now. Incidentally,

I meant to ask you: When you returned from the Caymans, did Angus Doyle or Sol Silverstein ever seem suspicious about the safe deposit key you brought back?"

"Not a bit. There was no way they could tell that it came from a Chicago bank. It was just a key with a number on it, like any other safe deposit key."

"That was a clever plan you worked up with Vera Doyle, switching keys so that they thought the ten million in bearer bonds that she took down there were still in the Caymans bank, instead of being turned over to us." The senior agent whistled. "Ten million, Sully. A lot of money."

"Yes, a lot of money."

And even more, he thought, *was the other fifteen million.*

The two men shook hands and Sully left the office.

• • •

A week later, in the Air Emirates travel office in Manhattan, a lovely Arab woman dressed in the airline's stylish ground employee's uniform, smiled at Sully and said, "Your visa to the United Arab Emirates is valid for six months, Mr. O'Keefe, but is renewable every six months thereafter. You'll find that the U.A.R.'s visa restrictions are very flexible; our small federation is actively encouraging Western tourism and retirement considerations."

"That's good to know," Sully said.

"Now then, for your flight over, Air Emirates offers a variety of fares. The most comfortable accommodation, of course, are our new private suites which can be closed off from the rest of the cabin, and which are equipped with individual storage space, a coat closet, vanity desk, and personal mini-bar. Their extra-large seats recline to become a fully flat bed, and the front wall is a wide-screen LCD monitor featuring six hundred channels of entertainment in all languages. Gourmet food service is available on call at any time. The flight time is twelve hours forty-five minutes, and you will be met in Dubai by a chauffeured Bentley sedan. The ticket price is 12,322 U.S. dollars, plus sixty-three U.S. dollars tax. Shall I book a suite for you?"

"Please do," Sully said, handing her an American Express Platinum card. Vera had wire-transferred fifty thousand dollars to him and he was standing there in a Canali suit, Hathaway shirt, Gianfranco Ferre necktie, and Ferragamo shoes. *Might as well get use to going first class all the way,* he thought.

As he waited for his ticket to be processed, Sully took from his pocket and reread the letter Vera had sent to him.

You'll love Dubai, darling. I've already leased an absolutely gorgeous apartment for us at the Jemeirah Beach Residence Hotel, with a terrace overlooking the Arabian Gulf where we can sit and have cocktails while the sun goes down. This city is fantastic, restaurants, clubs, entertainment, shopping like I've never imagined. We'll have a wonderful life here, Sully. Hurry over to me. I'm hungry for you ...

Ticket in hand, Sully left the Air Emirates travel office and walked down 59th Street in the direction of his hotel to pack for the midnight departure of his flight.

Vera was right, he thought. They could have a wonderful life together in Dubai. Fifteen million U.S. dollars would buy a lot of good living.

As long as Vera never found out about Doreen.

• • •

CLARK HOWARD has been a prolific short story writer since selling his first story on July 5, 1955. Although he has ventured into the fields of Westerns and war stories, the main body of his work has been in the crime and mystery genres, where he has won the Edgar and five Ellery Queen Readers awards, and garnered nominations for Shamus, Spur, Anthony, and Barry awards. Most recently he received the first Edward D. Hoch Memorial Golden Dagger Award for Lifetime Achievement in the field of mystery writing. He has also received Edgar nominations for books in the true crime genre. His work has appeared in anthologies worldwide.

O'NELLIGAN'S GLORY

By Michael Nethercott

One

It began with a phone call for my dead father.

"Plunkett and Son Investigators," I answered.

"Buster! How ya doing, you dirty old—"

"No, this is his son Lee."

"Really? Cripes, kid, you sound just like your old man."

At thirty-one, my claim to being a "kid" was somewhat tenuous. And as for sounding like my father, I guarantee he had more gravel in his gullet then I could ever muster.

"Buster's deceased," I informed the caller. "About a year now."

"Aw, no! I can't believe it! Buster was a bull ..." Then the voice softened. "I should have stayed in touch. This is Jojo Groom. Remember me, kid?"

My father's life seemed to revolve around guys with names like Jojo and Slick and Lefty. His own moniker, Buster, had replaced the unfortunate Leander, his birth name, which for some reason he decided to pass on to me. My rough and tumble sire—World War I doughboy, city cop, private gumshoe—was every inch a Buster; whereas I, with my large round spectacles, slight frame and 4F classification, seemed tailor-made to be a Leander Plunkett. I'd shortened things to Lee to ease my burden.

"Sure, I remember you, Jojo." He was an old police buddy of my father's. "Dad always spoke kindly of you. I tried to call you for the funeral, but ..."

"Don't sweat it, Lee. I've moved around. Not so easy to track down. I'm up in Massachusetts now. But listen, I've got a case for you. I was thinking it was Buster I'd be tossing it to, but anyway ... It's right up your alley. Murder."

I should go on record as saying that a murder case was nowhere even remotely near my particular alley. Sure, back when Buster was at the helm, that caliber of job might have meant a nice paycheck for Plunkett and Son; but in my tenure, it was a struggle just to handle the infidelity and missing object cases. Dad had taken me on to give direction to my drifting life, but, within sixteen months, had died over a bowl of stew, leaving me to fumble on. Truth be told, in the year since my father's death, I hadn't done much to champion the family business.

"Murder's a little out of my league," I told Jojo.

"Look, kid, I'll level with you. If I'd known your pop wasn't around to take this on, I maybe wouldn't have called. But listen, you're Buster's boy, right? Your pop was a damned bloodhound. A bloodhound! And you got his fixings."

Jojo hadn't seen me since I was about seventeen, so his appraisal of my "fixings" didn't carry much weight.

He hurried on, "The expired gent was one Clarence Browley, age thirty-five, well-to-do, bludgeoned. That happened nearly a month ago and the local cops have pretty much crapped out on solving this thing. I was kind of pally with Browley and his wife, and she's looking to hire her own investigator. I told her, you want the best, get Plunkett and Son."

I sighed. "Unfortunately, only the 'son' part of that is still available. Why don't you follow up on this yourself?"

"Me?" Jojo snorted. "I've been out of the business since '37. Almost two decades, we're talking. Still got a bullet in my leg as a reminder. I just hawk insurance now. For this mess, a pro's needed. And I'll take a Plunkett, junior or senior, any day of the week. Here's the info ..."

Jojo offered a few more details before I interrupted and told him I'd have to think things over. I took his number and rang off, then spent a half hour polishing my glasses.

• • •

That evening, while slurping linguini with my fiancée Audrey at a local restaurant, I laid out the deal and sought her council.

"Are you nuts, Lee?" She tossed down her fork. "You didn't snap that case up? A rich man's widow wants to hire you and you don't leap at the offer?"

"But it's a murder."

"A wealthy murder! This is what we've been hoping for, isn't it? This kind of break? With a nice chunk of money, we could finally just do it. Get married, find some swell little place. We could—" She stopped herself abruptly and stared down at the mound of pasta. "Oh God, I'm sorry. I sound like a ..."

"Gold-digger?" The word just leapt out.

Audrey smiled without mirth. "Not the word I would have chosen, but, sure, gold-digger will do. Thanks, Lee, for identifying me so succinctly."

"I didn't mean ... I only meant ..." Oh, it was no use.

She sighed. "It's just that we've waited so long."

Undeniably, our engagement seemed to be a long-term proposition. We'd pledged ourselves to wed in the spring of '54, just after I'd joined Dad's business and things were looking rosy. Now here it was early autumn 1956 and the deed was yet undone. There always seemed to be one obstacle or another to keep us from walking the aisle, be it money, timing or bickering. Audrey was twenty-eight now, understandably eager to get the show on the road.

I took her hand. "I'm not my father. He was born for tackling murder and mayhem. I was born to take notes."

"Your dad always said you took a mean note."

"Yes, it was a real source of pride to him, I'm sure. Anyway, without him, I just don't think I have the tools to take on a murder."

"What if ... you had a cohort?"

"Cohort?"

"Someone to accompany you and bounce ideas off of."

"You mean you?"

Audrey laughed. "Lord no! I'm quite content selling doorknobs and undergarments at the five-and-dime. I was thinking, actually, of someone we both know. Someone bearded with a brogue and stacks of old books."

"Not Mr. O'Nelligan."

She squeezed my hand. "Yes. Mr. O'Nelligan."

Two

In Thelmont, our modest Connecticut town, in a little pine-crowded house three doors down from Audrey's parents, dwelt one Mr. O'Nelligan.

Now in his sixties, he'd emigrated from Ireland to New York with his wife twelve years before. His colorfully muddled history featured a string of professions including train conductor, schoolteacher, bricklayer, actor, and door-to-door salesman. Also, Mr. O'Nelligan had fought in his homeland's civil war back in the '20s, though this seemed to be an episode he preferred to forget. When his wife died two years back, he left New York for Thelmont and retired himself into a life of books and conversation. Audrey and he became fast friends. I, on the other hand, on the three or four times that I'd met him, always found him kind of an odd duck.

"He's a man of action," my fiancé insisted as we approached Mr. O'Nelligan's door the morning after our linguini dialogue. "Remember I told you about that scar?"

I did. Once, when Audrey had asked him why he wore a beard in these modern times, the old Irishman had muttered something about a knife scar and changed the subject.

"Maybe in his youth he was a man of action," I said. "These days, he's a man of musty books."

Audrey rang the doorbell. "Be open-minded, Lee."

"Aren't I always?"

She didn't have to answer that, because just then a muffled voice within called out to us, "Enter, ye early revelers!"

This was exactly the sort of weird flourish that always made me uneasy with the old guy. I whispered to Audrey, "This is my cohort?"

We entered into Mr. O'Nelligan's book-jammed front room. These early days of autumn were brisk ones, and the fireplace blazed lively. Close to the hearth, sunk in a massive armchair, sat our slender host, a book on his lap and a calm smile on his lips. I had never seen him when he was not decked out in a vest and tie; today was no exception.

"Many welcomes, Audrey," he said in his Irish lilt. "And so good to see your young man again."

His face was admittedly a pleasant one, with deep soft eyes and a high balding forehead. I made a quick study of his beard for any sign of old blade wounds, but the trimmed gray camouflage hid all.

We were gestured into chairs. A teapot and cups had been arranged on the coffee table, and Mr. O'Nelligan set his book aside and began to serve us.

"What are you reading today?" asked Audrey.

"*Moby Dick.* I'm facing the perils of the open main."

"You're so well-read, I would have thought you'd have already chalked that one up."

Mr. O'Nelligan finished pouring. "Oh, but I have, Audrey. Thrice! This is my forth voyage upon the Pequod, and Captain Ahab is as feisty as ever. A good book always yields new riches. Now then, when you rang up, you said something about a proposition, yes?"

"I did," Audrey said. "It's a situation Lee has been asked to look into."

"A situation?"

"Yes, a problem ..." She was easing into this.

Mr. O'Nelligan took up his teacup. "And what style of problem are we speaking of?"

"Murder!" I spit the word out, surprised at my own vigor. "Murder and bludgeoning."

Mr. O'Nelligan paused mid-sip. "Well now, that's an honest answer."

"A man was killed a month ago," I said. "Up in Greenley, Massachusetts. His wife thinks that someone among their houseguests did it, but the facts don't line up. That's all I know so far."

"He was a wealthy man," Audrey added. "So there would certainly be compensation if you helped Lee."

"I'm beyond compensation, my dear. But help Lee how?"

"You have a good mind on you, Mr. O'Nelligan," Audrey said. "You could go and assist Lee in his investigation."

Our host's eyes widened and he turned towards me. "You favor such an arrangement, young sir?"

"Yes," I said, not sure that I meant it.

Mr. O'Nelligan sipped his tea for a while before continuing. "By way of reply, I'll quote, as I oft do, William Butler Yeats, the greatest of Irish bards."

He closed his eyes and recited, as if in a trance,

"I will arise and go now, for always night and day
I hear the lake water lapping with low sounds by the shore;
While I stand on the roadway, or on the pavements gray,
I hear it in the deep heart's core."

I raised an eyebrow. "And that means ...?"

"It means that one must heed the call of life." Mr. O'Nelligan placed down his cup and met my eyes. "Command me as you will."

• • •

Mr. O'Nelligan and I sat silently for the first twenty miles of the two hour drive to Greenley, in mutual awkwardness, before he broke the ice.

"This man we're to meet, he's an old comrade of your da's, you say?"

"Jojo and my father were police detectives together in Hartford. Dad was a bit older than him. More experience and more exploits."

"Ah yes," Mr. O'Nelligan said. "Audrey's told me a little about your da's shenanigans. Nabbed a few villains in his day, I understand."

"He helped haul in the Reeper Brothers. And Ugly Joe Hully."

"They sound fierce."

"And he almost got King Carroway. Jojo and my father were part of the team on Carroway's trail. They'd staked out his wife at a boarding house for nearly a week. On the day they ambushed the gang, Dad was out with a flu. It turned out to be an old-time, no-holds-barred shootout. When the smoke cleared, Jojo was badly wounded, Carroway and two other crooks were dead, and the wife had escaped on a bicycle in the nude."

Mr. O'Nelligan took note. "A bicycle in the nude?"

"Yeah. Obviously quite the headline grabber. It was also the biggest regret of my father's life—the fact that he missed out on all that."

"Although, had he been there, he might have shared his friend's fate."

"That's right," I said. "For Jojo, it was the end of his career. A few years later, a heart attack led Dad to leave the force and move us to Thelmont to set himself up as a PI. He figured it was a good location, partway between Hartford and New York."

"And he figured being a private investigator would be a healthier lot?"

"I suppose," I said. "Though another heart attack finally took him down."

"And then you stepped into your father's shoes."

Not by a long shot, I thought to myself.

We lapsed into silence again. Eventually, I turned on the radio and "Heartbreak Hotel" filled the car.

Mr. O'Nelligan came alive. "Ah, I know this singer! It's Emmet Presley."

"Elvis," I corrected. "Elvis Presley."

"Yes, that's it. I saw him on the *Ed Sullivan Show* last week. The lad is teeming with energy. Just teeming."

"That music doesn't do much for me. Too twitchy."

"Twitchy? A young man like yourself should be open to such twitchiness."

"I'm thirty-one," I felt compelled to explain.

"Exactly. A young man poised on the pulse of life. By all means, twitch!"

We continued northward as Elvis moaned on about losing his baby and finding a place called Lonely Street.

• • •

As planned, Jojo Groom met us at a little diner on the edge of Greenley. He was pretty much as I remembered him—slim and tall, with dark, slicked-back hair (now winged with gray) and a narrow mustache. He was somewhere in his mid-fifties. Leaning on a walking cane, he limped over to our booth. The hobbled leg served as an unsettling testament to the dangers of detective work—and of facing down murderers.

"Lee, how's it going, kid?" He shook my hand, then Mr. O'Nelligan's. "And this must be the partner you mentioned."

Mr. O'Nelligan smiled. "I am actually more of an adjutant. Sancho Panza to Mr. Plunkett's Quixote, if you will."

"That's swell," said Groom without comprehension. He slid in next to my "Sancho" and stared across at me for a few long seconds. I assumed I was being measured against his robust memory of Buster … and coming up yards short.

After reminding me once again what a bull my pop was, Jojo kicked things off. "Okay, not that I know the whole beanhill here, but I'll give you what I got. Our boy Clarence Browley was plenty well off …"

"Hold on." I pulled out my notepad and started scribbling.

"Stocks and bonds, that kind of action. One of his spare homes is here in Greenley. Nothing too lavish, but fancy enough. He and his wife would spend most of the summer here. Browley liked to throw these dinner parties—small, special-invite deals—and bring in certain types. Tough guys, y'know?"

"Thugs?" I asked.

"Nah. Manly guys. Daring guys. You know, guys who were ..." Groom searched for a word, "Accomplished. For example, at one party, I ended up breaking bread with a mountain climber, a big game hunter and a matador. Adventurous guys, see?"

I nodded. "So Browley chose you as one of his 'manly types'?"

Jojo suddenly looked shy. "Oh, you know, on account of my earlier escapades."

"Well, you did take a bullet from King Carroway."

"Four bullets, and one's still in me." He glanced down at his leg. "Anyway, Browley finally figured out I'm less of a lawman and more of an insurance hawker these days, 'cause after a couple invites he stopped having me over. But still, his wife Nina's a nice, fun dame and when I ran into her recently, I said I'd try to round up some help. That's where you come in."

I looked up from my notes. "So, Browley was killed at one of these dinner parties?"

"Yeah, well, outside the house," Jojo said. "Apparently, someone brained him with something heavy. But look, like I told you, I've been out of that circuit for a while now. I'm going to put you onto Nina Browley herself. That's who's Hancocking your paycheck, and she knows all the lowdown. I'll introduce you, then get out of your hair. "

Mr. O'Nelligan now joined in. "Would it be advantageous for us to contact the local constabulary?"

"You mean talk to the cops?" Jojo shook his head. "I'll give it to you straight, the local boys aren't too delighted about Nina bringing in hired guns."

"Wait. We don't—" I wanted to declare that Mr. O'Nelligan and I carried no guns, but Groom cut me off.

"And stay clear of Handleman, their chief snooper. Nina says he's particularly nasty." Jojo clapped his hands. "Okay, gents, ready to rocket?"

Can't say that I was.

Three

Nina Browley met us at the door in a Japanese kimono, a large cocktail in one hand and a machete in the other. Some people certainly know how to make a first impression.

"My detective!" she cried out tipsily. She looked to be halfway through her thirties, blond, with a nice face presently distorted by alcohol. "You are my detective aren't you?"

Without waiting for an answer, she put the drink and the weapon down on a hallway table and pulled Mr. O'Nelligan inside.

"Sorry for the machete," she raced on. "It belonged to my husband. I was out back in the garden attacking the weeds. You need to be thorough, don't you? Weeds are evil. Evil! Clarence always said so. I'm an idiot with gardens, but Clarence was clever and now you're here to avenge him."

"Begging your pardon, madam," said Mr. O'Nelligan, "but I'm not the detective. Mr. Plunkett here is your man."

I entered the hallway with Jojo Groom. Nina looked me over and turned to Jojo. "But the other one is much more distinguished. And he's English like Sherlock Holmes."

"Irish!" said Mr. O'Nelligan. "I'm solidly Irish, madam."

Groom, true to his word, made brief introductions and promptly left. We stood alone now with the swaying Mrs. Browley.

"This is the last chance for Clarence, don't you see?" She began to cry. "The police have given up. Somebody killed my husband and is getting away with it ..."

She gave way now to trembling sobs. I was completely at a loss on how to proceed when another woman entered the hallway and put her arms around Mrs. Browley. This one was younger, probably in her twenties, very petit with wavy brown hair.

"There now, Nina," she comforted. "I know it's hard. Everyone knows it's terribly hard."

Her presence had a calming effect and Nina, after several deep sighs, stifled her crying.

"Let's all go sit in the living room," Nina said softly. "And I'll tell you everything."

I was hesitant. "Well, perhaps now's not the most convenient—"

"No, I'll be fine. You're thinking I'm too blitzed, but I'll fix myself, you'll see. Paige, bring them inside. I'm going to order up one of my soothers. It's a special concoction—orange juice, paprika and coffee. It always straightens me out."

Nina moved off in one direction as the girl called Paige led us in another. The living room we settled into was, like the exterior of the house, pretty much as Jojo had described it—not too lavish, but fancy enough. An Oriental rug, plush sofas, and shelves filled with crystal ornaments gave the space style.

The young woman sat across from us. "Please don't judge Nina too harshly. After all, she's been through so much."

"Without question," agreed Mr. O'Nelligan. "To have her husband so cruelly slain must be a great hardship."

Paige nodded. "All month I've tried to get her to stay down in the city, but she keeps coming back up here. She says she needs to find answers. Of course, I understand. Clarence died in her arms, you know."

No, we didn't know. There was little, in fact, that we did know about this case. I got out my notepad.

"You're a friend of Mrs. Browley's?" I asked.

"I am. My name's Paige Simmons, since you're taking notes."

"Were you here the night Mr. Browley died?'

"Yes. I was staying over. We all were, but I think Nina would be the first to tell you that I'd make a lousy suspect."

"These are just preliminary notes."

She smiled gently. "I don't mean to be defensive. It's just that the police detectives before you were so harsh. Anyway, I guess I'm what they call an 'aspiring actress.' More aspiring than actress, I'm afraid. I know the Browleys in Manhattan. They come here to Greenley in the summer and have people up on the weekends."

Nina Browley now entered, a cup in her hand, and seated herself besides Paige. "This is my second dose. I downed the first one, and I'm already feeling steadier."

I had to admit she seemed a bit more sedate.

"I'm so glad you're here," she went on. "I told everyone that I was going to pay for the best investigator out there. The absolute very best. I had some prospects lined up, but then Jojo told me, Get Plunkett. Plunkett's the one."

Swell. "Mrs. Browley, please tell us about that night."

She took a long sip of soother and began. "It was about a month ago, August 18, a Saturday. Clarence liked to have these dinner gatherings. He called them his 'glory tables' where men of a certain ilk would be invited."

"Men of daring, you might say?"

"Yes, well put. We had three 'men of daring' that night: a fighter pilot, a boxing champ, and a gunslinger."

"A gunslinger?"

"I'm being cavalier. It was Tom Durker, the film actor."

"The one from the Westerns?"

"Yes. Of course, Tom's brand of daring exists chiefly on the movie screen. Still, he does personify American ruggedness. And he's passably handsome."

"Very handsome!" Paige amended. "And such steely eyes."

"They're not steely, Paige dear, just narrow," Nina said.

I pushed on. "And the other men?"

"There's Captain Webster Sands. He was a pilot in the big war, leading missions over Berlin and such. Quite the ace. And then there's Polecat Pobenski."

"What's a Polecat Pobenski?"

"David Pobenski, up-and-coming middleweight fighter. Or was, I should say. He was slated to go to the Olympics in Australia as part of the U.S. boxing team, but he injured his hand. The doctors don't think it will ever mend right."

"No spouses accompanied any of them?"

"David's not married. Captain Sands is divorced, and Tom Durker has a nice little wife who he left back home."

"Any other guests?"

"Just those three," Nina said. "And Paige here to help keep me from sinking in all that maleness. Right now, Durker's off in Hollywood, tied up making a new movie, but I've asked the other two to meet you tomorrow. Pobenski's taking the train up from New Jersey and Captain Sands will be flying in from Philadelphia."

"So only you six were in the house that evening?"

"Well, of course, we had our cook, Mrs. Leroy, who we bring up from the city. And two local girls, the Daley Sisters, to help serve."

"So, that evening ..."

"We had cocktails, followed by dinner around nine thirty. Then everyone split up into smaller groups for cards and conversation. At about twenty minutes of twelve, several of us saw Clarence leave the house, carrying one of his swords. He was in an agitated state, but no one knew why."

"His swords?"

"Yes, my husband was a great one for swords. And battle axes. And paintings of warriors and Vikings. Most of that stuff is back in Manhattan, but some of it has found its way here." Nina indicated a pair of crossed daggers on the wall behind me. "So, as Clarence was heading out, he called for Ajax, but Ajax was sleeping somewhere."

My pages were filling up fast. "Ajax?"

"Our German Shepherd. I left him home this trip"

Mr. O'Nelligan perked up. "Aha! Ajax! Named for the hero of The Iliad. Homer describes him as being of colossal stature."

Nina shrugged. "Well, he is a big dog."

A woman in an apron entered the room, carrying a coffeepot. She was firmly into her fifties, slim but solid, with a no-nonsense air. "More soother, Mrs. Browley?"

"Yes, it's doing wonders." Nina extended her mug for a refill. "Mrs. Leroy, this is Mr. Plunkett. He's come to solve things. Isn't that comforting?"

The cook appraised me with one glance. "Yes, ma'am. Comforting." She clearly was not dazzled by my potential.

"Oh, and that's Mr. O'Nelligan," Nina said. "He's a Scotsman."

"Please, it's Irish!" the wronged Hibernian pleaded. "I'm an Irishman from scalp to soles."

Our hostess smiled innocently. "Would anyone else like some soother? You don't have to be pickled to enjoy it."

We all declined, and the cook exited.

"Anyway, Clarence went out alone," Nina said. "At twelve, I led everyone in a raid on the refrigerator. Midnight snacks, you know. It was then, just after we entered the kitchen, that Tom Durker saw my husband outside the window. Clarence was tapping with his sword, though as soon as he was seen, he hurried away. Tom asked if we should go find him, but I said 'don't bother.' I figured if Clarence wanted to play games, then let him. About ten minutes later, I changed my mind, grabbed a flashlight and went by myself to look for him."

"No one offered to join you?" I asked.

"Some nice Merlot had just been opened, so everyone was distracted. And, of course, I never would have imagined anything dangerous ..." She trailed off and lowered her eyes.

"Please, go on," I coached.

She continued in a more subdued manner. "I walked down to the Roost, Clarence's getaway place, thinking that's where he'd probably gone. It's the little building on our property just over the hill. It's not so far, but you can't see it from the house. I found him there sprawled on his back, just outside the open door. His sword lay under him, just useless. His forehead was all blood." She touched her own forehead in a gesture that I frankly found chilling. "And, though I didn't know it at the time, the back of his head was ... well, the blow had ..."

Paige reached over and took her friend's hand. "She's had to tell this so many times, over and over again, for the police."

"But Mr. Plunkett needs to hear it," Nina said. "Clarence had been struck twice on the head. Once in front, once in back. Hard.

The weapon was never found. I knelt down and tried to cradle him. I asked who did this to him, but I couldn't make out what he said. Then he raised his hand and pointed up here. You have to understand, it took his last spark of life to do it. He pointed and I asked if it was someone from the house. Then he said it. Clearly. He said, 'Yes.' A minute later, he was gone. I cried out for help and people came soon after."

Her narrative conveyed, Nina Browley now seemed to deflate. The alcohol and the emotion—and perhaps the paprika-laced soother—had combined to bring her to a state of exhaustion.

"That's the gist of it, Mr. Plunkett," she said heavily. "If there's anything else, perhaps tomorrow ..."

"Certainly. We'll be staying for the next few days at the Greenley Inn. We'll come by to see you again tomorrow morning, say ten o'clock?"

Nina waved a hand at us, presumably in assent. Her eyes slid closed and she spoke as if to herself, "The police say it was just some unknown robber. That no one from the house could have done it. But Clarence said yes. He said yes."

Paige led us back to the front door. "Nina's a fun, energetic person, but she can be pretty up-and-down, even at the best of times. This ordeal has just pushed her to the brink. She's been wound up all afternoon about your coming and, unfortunately, got herself snockered."

"We understand," Mr. O'Nelligan said. "Just one more question before we part, Miss Simmons. Why do the police believe it's impossible for someone from the house to have killed Mr. Browley?"

"Because we were all together in the kitchen during that fifteen-minute period when he was attacked."

"Fifteen minutes?" I asked.

"Yes," Paige said. "The time between when Clarence was seen at the kitchen window up to when Nina found him by the Roost. It was only fifteen minutes. But I suppose that's enough time to kill somebody, isn't it?"

Four

On the drive to the inn, we talked things over.

"What do you make of our Mrs. Browley?" Mr. O'Nelligan asked.

"Seems like a living rolling coaster."

"Ah! You do have a touch of the poet in you, Lee. Of course, what we observed must be seen in the light of her situation. The murder of one's spouse would be a devastating thing. And, too, she was in the grip of strong drink."

"Sure, but Paige said it was par for the course, didn't she?"

"And what do you make of Miss Paige Simmons?"

"She seems like a nice sincere girl."

"But an actress."

"Can't an actress be a nice girl?" I asked.

"Certainly. I have known several virtuous ingénues from my own time before the footlights."

"That's right, you were an actor yourself."

"For a short spell. But, unfortunately, my parts in New York were mostly of the 'stage Irish' variety. Deplorable caricatures dripping whiskey and sentimentality. I had to utter the phrase "saints preserve us' so many times, I nearly choked."

I laughed. "Well, you're safe from the footlights now."

"I am. But what I meant to convey is that Miss Simmons is by vocation an actress and, thus, presumably capable of putting on a façade."

"So you think she isn't so nice and sincere?"

"I don't mean that. I was merely saying that we should be nimble in our interpretations."

I decided to come clean. "You see, Mr. O'Nelligan, that's my problem—I'm not all that nimble. The deduction part of things is where I fall flat. I can take down the facts, all neat and legible, but as far as interpreting them, well ... I'm no Buster."

"Nor should you be! You're your own man, Lee Plunkett. And 'neat and legible' is a fine place to start things out. By all means, herd in those facts. Then peer at them in the light of reason and see what rises to the surface. But may I make a suggestion?" Mr. O'Nelligan smoothed his beard. "It's about your notebook ..."

"What? I told you, note taking is my one discernable skill."

"Of course, but the way you bury your face in it ..."

"So, no notebook?"

"I'm not saying that, boyo. You just might want to pop your head up from it occasionally. Don't let it separate you from the humanity of those you're interviewing. As the expression goes, you want to see what 'makes them tick.'"

"Duly noted."

"Aha! Clever."

"And may I make a suggestion? I noticed you didn't ask many questions back there."

"I didn't think it was my place to. My instructions were to 'assist.' I don't wish to be treading on your toes."

"My toes can take it. Anyway, I'd be happy if you were to ask these people whatever you think needs asking."

"As you wish, Lee. From here on out, my queries will gallop free."

• • •

We checked into the Greenley Inn and went upstairs to find our rooms. There, blocking the hallway, stood a behemoth in a crumpled trench coat, with no love for us in his eyes.

"Which of you is Plunkett?"

"He is," Mr. O'Nelligan was quick to say.

"I'm Handleman." He had a good half foot on me and used every inch of it to intimidate. "I'm heading up the Browley investigation. Or at least I was. Seems like you're the new golden boy who's here to crack the case."

"I'm not golden," I said stupidly.

Beneath the low brim of his hat, Handleman's eyes turned to bullets. "Don't screw with me. You ask around. Anyone'll tell you, don't screw with Handleman. I was born a little crazy, and I like it that way. Here, take this ..."

His hand darted into his coat pocket, and I fairly leapt back, bracing for the sight of a gun muzzle.

"Jumpy little bastard. What's your problem?" The hand slid out and pushed an envelope in my face. "My chief told me I had to give you this. Goddamn typical. The Browley woman squawks to the mayor, so he leans on the department to pass our info to some punk private dick."

"You're sharing your files with us?"

"Fat chance," Handleman said. "I only coughed up what I had to, but you should be kissing my size fourteens for even giving you this much. If you've got half a brain, you'll realize this was a robbery gone ugly, nothing more. Browley stumbles on the thief or thieves, they get spooked, crack open his skull and vamoose with the shield. Plain as vanilla."

"Shield? What shield?"

"Beautiful! Golden boy hasn't done his homework. The gem-studded shield that Browley kept in his 'roost,' that outbuilding of his. When his wife gets there, Browley's sprawled at the door and the shield is missing—a heist, plain as goddamn vanilla. The wife thinks the theft was just a cover-up for something else, but she's nutty as they come. The thieves will foul up eventually, leave a trail, and I'll collar them. That's how it works. Get it, nimrod?"

Mr. O'Nelligan stepped forward. "There's no need for animosity here, sir. Can we not consider ourselves colleagues in this venture?"

"Who the hell are you? His goddamned leprechaun?" Handleman shoved past us and pounded down the stairs.

Mr. O'Nelligan shook his head. "A sour man, that one. A pitifully sour man."

• • •

Over supper in the inn's near-empty dining room, we perused Handleman's notes. As promised, they were minimal, mostly confirming the timeline that Nina had already given us—including the significant quarter hour between 12:05 and 12:20 when the victim was unaccounted for. During that interval, all the other persons of the house were gathered together in the kitchen; the exception being the two young serving girls, who had left just before eleven thirty and were immediately picked up by a carload of relatives.

The only gap in timing concerned Pobenski, the boxer. He had come to the kitchen like the others, but about five minutes later. That is, five minutes after Browley had been seen at the window. Was that enough time to hurry down to the Roost, dispatch Browley, steal the shield, and make it back to the kitchen? The police thought it unlikely, and it was hard to argue otherwise.

We were just finishing up some homey cherry pie, when a man in a brown leather jacket strode into the room and made a beeline for our table. "Which of you is Lee Plunkett?"

Not again. This time I offered myself directly, "I'm Plunkett."

"All right." He dragged a chair over and dropped into it. "I'm Sands."

"Captain Webster Sands?"

"My reputation precedes me." He pulled out a cigar and fired it up. His lean, lined face marked him as a man of roughly forty, but his blond curls suggested the word boyish.

"Mrs. Browley told us you were due tomorrow."

He spoke briskly, "Yes, well, I finished some business I had and flew myself up early. I like making a landing at sunset. It's peaceable. Just caught a cab here from the air field."

"Have you contacted Mrs. Browley yet?" Mr. O'Nelligan asked.

"Who's this?" Sands wanted to know. Thankfully, this time there was no mention of leprechauns.

I introduced my companion and repeated his question.

"I'll call Nina tomorrow," Sands said. "I grabbed a room here, and I just want to settle in. I'm bushed."

"You're not staying at the Browley residence?" I asked.

Captain Sands blew out a stream of smoke. "Hell, no. Nina doesn't want anyone who was at that party lurking in her house at night."

"Why not?"

"Hasn't she told you? She thinks one of us beat Clarence to death."

"What would make her believe—"

Sands shoved back his chair and shot to his feet. "That's it for tonight. I told you I'm bushed. Just stopped over to let you know I'm around."

"We'll need to speak soon," I said.

"Listen, I'll tell you straight up, I'm only here as a courtesy to Nina. I answered all the cops' questions last month and didn't much like it. Those goons were pretty damned arrogant. We can talk tomorrow, but on my terms. Take Route 2 west out of town for about seven miles. Little yellow building on your left." He turned and marched off, calling over his shoulder, "Be there at 1:00 PM."

"Abrupt fellow," Mr. O'Nelligan observed.

"And one used to getting his way, I suspect."

"Our dramatis personae are proving to be quite piquant, wouldn't you say?"

I took a last bite of cherry pie. "If I knew what that meant, I'd probably say yes."

Five

That next morning, we drove onto the Browley grounds at ten o'clock, ascending, as we had the day before, the long, winding driveway to the house. We were greeted at the door by Mrs. Leroy, though greet might be too strong a word.

"Is Mrs. Browley up?" I asked.

"Up and out," the cook said brusquely. "She took Miss Simmons off to town an hour ago for breakfast. Why she did that, I couldn't say. My breakfasts are always hardy."

"That goes without saying, madam." Mr. O'Nelligan trotted out his best Irish lilt. "You have the air of a woman who runs a formidable kitchen."

The effect of this compliment was immediate. Mrs. Leroy's face softened into something akin to handsomeness, and a thin, but welcoming smile touched her lips. "Well, do come in and sit."

Mr. O'Nelligan proffered his own charming smile. "Actually, good lady, may we, by chance, see your work domain?"

"Why, of course."

We were led through the dining room with its long oak banquet table—no doubt the gloried one—into a large kitchen, immaculate and well-organized.

I sized up the space. "So, this is where Mrs. Browley and her guests were when her husband appeared at the window?"

"It is, indeed," the cook said.

"And you were here, as well?"

"Yes. I was finishing my clean-up when Mrs. Browley burst in with the others. She was coming to raid the icebox ... as she sometimes does." Obviously, the woman did not approve of such frolics in her realm. "Then, almost immediately, Mr. Browley was spotted at the window by Mr. Durker, the actor. He was the only one close enough."

Mr. O'Nelligan moved to the one window that looked out onto the front lawn. "This one, yes? But tell me, Mrs. Leroy, it seems that at night it would have been hard to truly see anything outside."

"There's an outdoor light that was on then. Also, the moon was just a couple days shy of full. It was actually quite illuminated out there. And Mr. Durker's face was only inches from the glass."

"I see," Mr. O'Nelligan said. "Had Mr. Durker imbibed much at that point in time?"

"As it turns out, Mr. Durker is a teetotaler. Quite rare, I imagine, for those Hollywood people. So, he wasn't impaired, if that's what you're wondering."

"Very good. Now, I believe Mr. Browley tapped his sword on the pane. Did you hear him?"

"No. It was terribly noisy in here. Mrs. Browley and her guests were rather ..." The cook made a diplomatic choice, "Rambunctious."

"I see," said Mr. O'Nelligan. "And where was everyone situated at that moment?"

"Well, I myself was bustling about dispensing food, and the others were all clustered around the table there."

Given the room's layout, it seemed unlikely that someone at the kitchen table would have had a view of anything out the window.

"And Tom Durker?"

"As I've said, Mr. O'Nelligan, he was over near the window, right where you're standing now. He told us he saw Mr. Browley just outside, but Mr. Browley had already darted off."

"Though no one else can verify that."

"No, but Mr. Durker seems like an honest man. I can't say I care much for his motion pictures—too much gunplay and fistfighting—but the man appears trustworthy."

"And what do you base that on?" Mr. O'Nelligan asked.

The cook gave a little shrug. "Just the cut of the man, I suppose."

"Ah, I understand you, madam," said Mr. O'Nelligan, gazing out the window. "Sometimes one just knows the worth of a being. Back in County Kerry, I had a neighbor who could judge a cow's milk capacity just by pinching its ear. Downright infallible he was, don't ask me how."

A phone rang in another room. Mrs. Leroy excused herself and left to answer it.

I turned to my cohort. "I have to agree with the police. It had to be an outsider. Everyone from the house is accounted for during the time of the attack, right here making merry. By the way, good job working your Irish wiles with the cook lady. Not a bad-looking woman, really, in a severe sort of way. I believe you noticed."

The old widower blushed so vividly that I regretted my ribbing. "Enough with your nonsense. Now, back to the facts. Yes, it does seem to be a closed equation. But since your client feels differently, I think we owe it to her to proceed in our inquiries."

The cook returned. "Mrs. Browley phoned to say she's running a little late. Feel free to explore the grounds if you wish."

"We were hoping to see the Roost," I said.

"When you step outside, it's a little walk over the hill. You'll have to wait for Mrs. Browley, though, if you want to get inside. There's only one set of keys and she has them. It used to be that Mr. Browley kept them on his person at all times, but now ..."

According to Handleman's notes, those keys were found in Browley's pocket after his death, the assumption being that the thieves never possessed them and had, instead, somehow picked the locks.

"Have you been in the Roost much yourself, Mrs. Leroy?" Mr. O'Nelligan asked.

"Heavens, no. It was Mr. Browley's special place. He had it built when he bought the place three years ago. I don't think that even Mrs. Browley has been inside more than a few times."

"What do you suppose he did there?" I asked.

"He slept there at night," the cook said. "Not when guests were staying over, during his glory tables, but all the other evenings."

That grabbed my attention. "How do you know this?"

"Because I'm always here. I have my own little room just off the kitchen. I'd see him go out and return in the morning."

"So he didn't sleep with his wife most nights. Is that how it was back in New York, as well? I mean, were there matrimonial concerns?"

Her voice tightened. "I'm sure I wouldn't know. I don't bother with what others do in their privacy."

Mr. O'Nelligan caught me by the arm, like a stage manager giving the hook to a failing vaudevillian. "We'll go explore now," he said. "Thank you, Mrs. Leroy, you've been kind beyond belief. When Mrs. Browley returns, have her bring us down the keys, will you?" He bustled me out of the house.

"What's our hurry?" I asked.

"I'm saving you from a thrashing! Didn't you see the fire in the woman's eyes? After all, you're probing the bed chamber of those who pay her wages." Mr. O'Nelligan was clearly displeased with me.

"But I'm obtaining useful information. And, did you notice, I never once brought out my notebook."

"Yes, admirable restraint on that front. But, listen, lad, when you go brandishing about terms like 'matrimonial concerns' you're likely to rile up proper folks. That wasn't a showgirl you were talking to back there."

I had to laugh. "You're coming off a bit prudish, Mr. O'Nelligan."

"Propriety and prudishness are two different beasts, I assure you. Now, in regard to the Browleys sleeping separately, it may not signify much. I knew an old farmer named Finnerty who slept in his barn while his wife kept to the house. He swore it wasn't out of animosity, but kindness, for he snored like a freight train. They were married sixty-odd years and still held hands when strolling."

A several-minute walk brought us in sight of the Roost. It proved to be an unusual building, round and made of stone, with several barred windows, one facing in the direction of the main house. As we came up to the small citadel, a tall figure in a long dark coat and fedora appeared from behind it. For a fleeting, illogical moment, I imagined it to be Clarence Browley himself, returned to the scene of his death.

"Sorry, didn't mean to jump out at you." He was a young man with a good face, if you discounted the somewhat flattened nose. "The train station's not far from here, and I decided to walk. I'm David Pobenski."

"Polecat." The word leapt to my lips.

His smile had a touch of sadness to it. "Sure. At least, I used to be Polecat." He held up his left hand to display three of the fingers curled in upon themselves. "Not much call for a one-fisted boxer. A few months back, I severed a couple tendons on a table saw. Pretty stupid of me. I was making a gift for my nephew, and ended up trading the Olympics for a wooden toy truck."

I told him who we were and that we'd like to ask him a few things.

"That's why I came up," he said. "But I have to be honest with you, I think Nina's just grasping at straws. I mean, I know this thing has thrown her for a loop, but the police called it a robbery, and that's seems to fit the bill."

"A second look never hurts," I said. "Can you tell us your view of that night?"

"Sure. I got to the house by about seven. I was the last to arrive. Paige and the Browleys had come up the night before, and Tom Durker and Captain Sands had made it in about an hour before me."

"Together?"

"Yeah. Sands had picked Durker up at New York International and flown him the rest of the way in his own plane. We all hung out for a while, had cocktails and sat down to dinner around nine thirty."

"You three were all members of Clarence Browley's glory table, were you not?'" Mr. O'Nelligan asked.

Pobenski grinned. "You make it sound like an official club, with rules and uniforms. It was more like Clarence surrounding himself with sports guys and adventurers and such."

"No other purpose?"

"He just enjoyed having people like that around, to hear their stories and live a little through them, I guess."

"You were a frequent guest at these gatherings?" I asked.

"I guess I was in the rotation. Captain Sands, too. I think for Tom Durker, that was his first time. Anyway, it was a long dinner, and afterwards we sort of scattered through the house. I ended up in the living room, playing cards with Nina and Paige."

I snuck out my notebook for an inoffensive jot or two. "How long did you play for?"

"Maybe forty-five minutes. At one point, Clarence stopped in looking for his dog, and he seemed upset. The dog wasn't there, so Clarence hurried off down the hallway. We heard the front door slam."

"And this was at 11:40, yes?"

"Sounds right. After Clarence left, we played some more. Then, just when the midnight clock chimed, Nina tossed all the cards in the air and said we should go on a food raid. She rounded up everybody and headed to the kitchen."

"But you didn't join them immediately?"

"I'd stopped to pick up the cards off the floor. I'm told I got there about five minutes after they did."

"So you weren't in the kitchen when Browley was seen at the window?"

"No, but people were talking about it. Tom Durker said Clarence was acting strange, that he hopped away when Tom saw him. A little after I got to the kitchen, Nina went out to find Clarence. Then we heard her scream for help, and all three of us guys ran outside. Paige, too. When we got to the Roost, Clarence was bloodied up, already dead, and Nina was holding him in her arms. Right there." Pobenski pointed to the earth just before the door. "It wasn't a nice thing to see."

"So here he expired," Mr. O'Nelligan said as we gazed down at the spot. "There is always something somber about a place where the soul has fled the body."

He closed his eyes and I noticed his lips slightly moving. It took me a moment to realize that he was reciting a prayer.

Six

"Hello!" a voice called from up the hill. We turned to see Paige Simmons approaching us.

"Nina sent me down with the keys. She can't bear to come near this building anymore." Paige passed me a ring of keys, then extended her hand to Pobenski, who accepted it with a shy smile. "Good to see you again, David."

After a bit of figuring, I managed to undo the three door locks. If robbers had indeed picked their way in, they must have done it skillfully, for none of the locks seemed damaged.

I pulled open the heavy oak door, and we stepped inside. The room was sparsely furnished: a single bed, night stand, table and chair. All basic, all oak. A burgundy rug covered the floor. The curved walls, also paneled in oak, contained two paintings, one of a medieval battlefield, the other of a man with a knife fighting a tiger. A kind of bolted metal bracket, slightly bent, was positioned just above the bed.

Pobenski pointed to this last feature. "That must be where the shield used to be."

"So you knew about the shield?" I asked.

"No. I mean, I only heard about it after Clarence was dead."

"I knew about the shield," Paige said. "Nina told me about it once. Clarence had it specially made and edged with real rubies and emeralds. He brought it with him to whichever of his three homes he was staying at. I think he considered it some kind of power thing."

"Power thing?" I asked.

"Perhaps like a totem," Mr. O'Nelligan said. "A sacred object such as your American Indians kept."

"Could be," Paige said. "Clarence certainly had an inclination towards old weapons. I think he fancied himself a kind of knight."

"A knight of stocks and bonds," Mr. O'Nelligan mused. "Were either of you aware that Mr. Browley slept here on those nights when he was not hosting his glory tables?" What? Hadn't the old nagger just reprimanded me for that very line of inquiry?

As Pobenski shook his head, Paige said, "Yes, I knew. He spent most of his evenings here whenever he was in Greenley. Clarence had a solitary side to him."

"In addition," Mr. O'Nelligan noted, "he might have been reluctant to leave such a valuable object as the shield unwatched at night, even in a locked building. Though, of course, on those nights when he slept in the house, there would have been no one here to see to its safekeeping."

"But on those nights he'd always release his guard dog," Paige said. "Right at midnight like clockwork. I was at quite a few of the glory tables, and that's what always happened. Clarence had trained Ajax to stay right around the Roost."

I led the others back outside and relocked the door.

"'At midnight like clockwork ...'" Mr. O'Nelligan repeated the line. "But on the night of his death, Clarence Browley summoned Ajax, albeit unsuccessfully, at around 11:40, a good twenty minutes before midnight. This was not the norm, was it?"

"No, it wasn't," the young woman agreed. "But, remember, Clarence seemed tense when he left the house. Something was wrong."

"Maybe he saw the robbers down here," Pobenski said.

Paige shook her head. "That couldn't be. You can't see the Roost from the house." We looked up towards the hill. Only the peak of the house was visible.

Pobenski retrieved a travel bag from next to the stone building. "I'd like to say hello to Nina. You know, I haven't seen her since that weekend."

We made our way back towards the house and found Nina Browley seated on a stool in a small side garden. A few last rugged flowers held their color against the coming autumn, and Nina studied them as if in a deep meditation. At our approach, her head jolted up and her eyes narrowed.

"David," she said flatly.

"Hello, Nina." Pobenski made no effort to move closer to her. "Just caught the train up."

"Thank you for coming. Have you been talking with Mr. Plunkett?"

"He has," I said. "He's been very obliging."

Several long moments passed before Nina spoke again. "Paige, perhaps you can run David down to the inn. I had Mrs. Leroy call ahead to book him a room. Unless you've already made accommodations, David?"

"I haven't, well, that is ..." the young boxer fumbled. "I wasn't sure where ..."

"I'm sure you'll have a pleasant stay there," Nina said. "And you'll be close to Mr. Plunkett if he needs to further interview you."

With nods of farewell, Pobenski and Paige headed off. In a minute, we heard the rumble of a car winding down the driveway. Mr. O'Nelligan pulled over an empty stool and sat close to Nina, all but knee to knee. As they spoke together quietly, almost intimately, I took it as my part to just stand aside and listen.

"It seems to pain you to see that young gentleman," Mr. O'Nelligan said.

Nina continued to appraise the flowers. "Not just him. Any of those men. When I talked to them on the phone, to ask them to come up, it somehow felt different. But now, seeing David here ..."

"Yes?"

"One of them killed Clarence. Vicious! Such a vicious thing. If you had seen all the blood ..."

"Of course, Mrs. Browley, of course. It must have been staggering."

"I have to tell you, Mr. O'Nelligan, I've never been a very good wife. I like to cast myself around and make everything a party. I like men. But as Clarence was dying and our eyes locked together, it felt almost like the day we married. I know that's bizarre to say, but it was like making a vow. A vow that I'd find out who did that to him. And even though I'd failed Clarence in life, maybe I wouldn't fail him now." Her voice broke. "But I have been failing him, same as always."

Mr. O'Nelligan patted her shoulder. "You have not, madam. You brought us in to take up the hunt, didn't you? It shows grand wisdom to know when one must summon aid."

"I hope so," Nina said almost inaudibly.

"You know, when my Eileen passed away, I took it powerful hard." Mr. O'Nelligan turned his own eyes to the fading garden. "Like yours, my heart was weighed down by all the kindnesses I had left undone, all the gentle words I might have bestowed upon that good woman, but somehow never made the time to." After a brief pause, he half-spoke, half-sung a verse,

"In a field by the river my love and I did stand,
And on my leaning shoulder she laid her snow-white hand.
She bid me take life easy, as the grass grows on the weirs;
But I was young and foolish, and now am full of tears."

"Byron?" Nina guessed.

"Yeats," Mr. O'Nelligan said. "Or, more accurately, an old peasant woman of Sligo, who Yeats once heard singing in the street. From a few lines, imperfectly remembered, he carved out a whole splendid poem. It just goes to show that there is gold to be found in the humblest places." He stood. "Like in our battered hearts."

Nina looked up at him. "You're a good little Irishman."

"Exactly!" said Mr. O'Nelligan.

• • •

As we drove to our meeting with Captain Sands, I wondered aloud if we shouldn't have spent more time at the Browley home.

"We can always return there," Mr. O'Nelligan said. "I think we did well in treading lightly with the woman."

It was Mr. O'Nelligan, and not I, who had done all the light treading. I had to admit, the old eccentric had the common touch.

"We're doing well, Lee. Thus far, we have made contact with all the principals of the case, excepting our Western star, Mr. Durker."

"Who's unfortunately on a whole other coast," I said. "So, tell me, from the trio of male guests that night, how many do you imagine Nina Browley slept with?"

"Come now! Must you wallow in coarse words?"

"What words would you want me to use?"

"Well, dalliance, for one. You could have referred to her dalliances."

"For God's sake, just yesterday you advised me to twitch like a rock-and-roller, and now you're badgering me with your Celtic decorum. You've got me reeling."

"Life's not always a steady deck," Mr. O'Nelligan counseled. "In answer to your crudely wrought question, it could be that any, all, or none of those three men have known Nina Browley's affections. But if one had, it might well have led to conflict between that man and Mr. Browley."

"Perhaps a fatal conflict," I added. "But the piece that confuses me is why would Browley have kept beckoning males to his home if he knew of his wife's appetites."

"Perchance he was blithely unaware. Or, conversely, he might have been very aware, but chose not to let that derail his dinner gatherings. Seen in that light, his uncustomary sleeping in the main house during those nights might have been to ensure his wife's fidelity. Or, yet another theory, he might have been that particular brand of man who takes pleasure in his wife's unfaithfulness."

Now it was I who was a little shocked. "A cuckold by choice?"

"Merely one explanation. Another being that Browley preferred the company of men, in the style of Oscar Wilde, and that he cared little if his wife strayed—as long as it wasn't under his own roof. These are cosmopolitan people we're dealing with, and we must be cosmopolitan in our speculations."

"Cosmopolitan, but not coarse. Got it."

My companion chuckled. "Now you're learning, Lee Plunkett! We'll have you finely polished in no time."

Seven

I had no idea that an hour later I'd be plunging through the wild blue yonder. Struggling to control my heaving stomach, I gripped the cockpit of Captain Sands' plane and made every effort to blaspheme our pilot. Unfortunately, no words could free themselves from my gritted teeth.

As it turned out, the little yellow building where we rendezvoused stood on the edge of a landing field where Sands' Apache twin-engined aircraft waited to deliver us skyward. This, then, was what Sands meant when he stated that he would only talk to us on his terms. Soon after we were in the air, he began amusing himself by putting us through a series of sharp swoops and spins. If these maneuvers were meant to separate the men from the boys, well, then I was more than willing to trade in my trousers for knee britches and call it a day. From behind me, Mr. O'Nelligan, who seemed less affected by these acrobatics, came to my defense. "Captain Sands!" He raised his voice over the din of the plane. "You've put Mr. Plunkett in some distress. Please ease up."

"Just trying to give you gentlemen a little excitement."

"So we see," Mr. O'Nelligan said. "But a murder case is all the excitement we presently require."

Sands leveled the plane, and my heart dislodged itself from my throat.

I turned on the smug aviator. "What the hell do you—"

"Ah, Captain." Mr. O'Nelligan jumped in to avert a fracas. "I see you are an admirer of President Eisenhower." He had taken note of the half dozen *I Like Ike* pins that ornamented the cockpit.

"Sure am. No question he'll win reelection come November." Sands smiled to himself. "The way I see it, it was pretty much Ike and I who beat the Nazis."

Just how conceited was this guy? Wanting to hasten our time together, I got down to business. "What happened the night Clarence Browley died?"

"I'll make it short and sweet. I picked up Tom Durker in New York and flew him here. I'd been at a few of Browley's dinners before, but it was Durker's first time."

"But you knew Durker?"

"Never met him before. I just flew him up as a favor to the Browleys. So, we get to the house. Drinks. Talk. Polecat shows up at some point. More drinks. Eat. After dinner, I end up with Browley and Durker in the den shooting the bull. Durker's telling about some picture where he portrayed an Indian scout. Browley says, hey, he has a genuine Comanche war lance up in the attic, so he goes to fetch it."

"There's an attic?" Mr. O'Nelligan asked.

"Apparently. Durker and I wait in the den. After a few minutes, we hear Browley calling for the dog. I step out in the hall and see Browley just as he's opening the front door. Seems he gave up on the war lance, but he grabs a sword, a rapier, out of the umbrella stand—there were always weapons just lying about—and he heads outside. I go back and joke to Durker that Browley has a blade and is probably off hunting dragons. Anyway, that's the last time I saw Clarence Browley alive."

I asked Sands about Browley.

"Clarence wasn't too bad. Hail-well-met sort, though somewhat strange."

"How so?"

"Tried a little too hard to impress. Made a bunch of cash fairly quickly and wanted to be a big man and flaunt things around. Like the swords and spears. And like that shield of his. Never saw it myself, but I heard about it. On the other hand, he kept his cards pretty close to the vest. I didn't really know what to make of him."

"And Mrs. Browley?" I asked. "What do you think of her?"

He adjusted something on the control panel before answering. "Nice lady," was all he said.

We began our descent and soon found ourselves again on terra firma, which did my mind and body much good.

After we'd all climbed out of the plane, Sands gave us an ingenuous grin. "Pleasant flying with you both. Hope you track down whoever used Browley's head for batting practice."

Mr. O'Nelligan stepped close to the pilot. "Captain, a man has been slain. Your flippancy is out of line."

Sands pulled off his flying gloves, his smile still fixed. "No offense meant. But I've been in war, you see. Death is a different creature when you've been in war."

"I've been in war," Mr. O'Nelligan said, a mix of fierceness and pain in his eyes. "Terrible war. And I tell you, a butchered man is a dark thing to behold."

Not waiting for a response, my friend turned abruptly and walked away. I followed.

• • •

Our drive back was conducted in near silence due to my post-flight queasiness and Mr. O'Nelligan's pensiveness. I wondered to what black field of memory his thoughts had summoned him. On returning to the inn, Mr. O'Nelligan opted for a late lunch with *Moby Dick,* while I went up to our room to lie down, just for a minute, to allow my innards to settle.

When I awoke, I discovered I'd been asleep for almost two hours; I vowed right there and then to remain earthbound for the rest of my natural days. I went downstairs in search of Mr. O'Nelligan. The desk clerk passed me a note that had been left not long before. It read:

> *Dear Lee,*
> *Gone for a little stroll to respire and reflect. Meet me at the Browley house after sunset.*
>
> *Yours, O'N*

I calculated that the walk from the inn to the house would take him a good two and a half hours. A little stroll? Well, more power to the man. I made some inquiries and found that Sands had been checked out since morning, but that Pobenski still had a room, right across from mine as it turned out.

Deciding I'd track him down later, I seated myself in the empty dining room and ordered black coffee. Normally, I took mine well sugared and glutted with cream, but at this moment I needed something more Spartan. Black and neat is the way Buster Plunkett always liked it, and if I possessed even a drop of his sleuthing blood, maybe unvarnished java would help bring it to the surface. I pulled out my notebook—with no O'Nelligans in sight to chastise me—and reviewed what I'd written down. Yes, a number of possibly pertinent facts had been logged, but none strong enough to pierce that impenetrable quarter hour of murder where all suspects dwelt together in cheerful innocence.

The tangle of potential dalliances did seem worth unraveling. Was Nina's unease at seeing Pobenski based purely on her general suspicion of the guests, or did a history exist between those two that caused shame? Was Sands' description of Nina as simply "a nice lady" just a little too terse to take at face value? And what about our unseen cowpoke, Tom Durker? True, we could always place a call to Hollywood, but that seemed a poor substitute for going face-to-face. Finally, at the heart of the mystery, stood the quirky Clarence Browley, hoarder of swords and shields, who slept in a stone circle and surrounded himself with valorous men.

I spent half an hour mulling things over, then pocketed my notes and ordered an early dinner. Later, as I stood in the lobby, David Pobenski entered from outside.

"Mr. Plunkett. Oh, right ..." He seemed distracted.

"Mr. Pobenski, I was hoping to talk some more, but I'm expected now at the Browley home. Later then?"

"Fine," he said softly. "I'll be here if you want me."

"Thanks." As I reached out to shake his hand, I was thinking that he seemed too gentle for a man so skilled at pummeling others. But as he gripped me with his right hand, the undamaged one, it felt like my knuckles would splinter. The guy was made of granite.

Eight

Daylight had just quit the sky when I pulled up to the house. This time it was Paige who answered the door, looking more tired than she had earlier. She led me inside to a small den where Nina sat intently watching television.

"I do love Lucy," Nina said without looking up. "But do you know who I love even more? Fred Mertz! His voice reminds one of rumbling thunder, and he possesses a certain gruff sex appeal."

I had absolutely nothing to offer on the subject of Fred's virility. "I'm looking for Mr. O'Nelligan."

"Check in the kitchen," Nina instructed, then let out a wild laugh in appreciation of Lucy's latest high jinks. She never once glanced my way.

Paige and I stepped back out into the hall.

"You never know which Nina you'll get, do you?" the young woman said, a note of apology in her voice. "That's just her nature."

"You're a faithful friend to her, it seems."

"I try. She's always been very good to me. Always introducing me to nice people ..." She trailed off.

I left her and made my way to the kitchen. Hesitating in the doorway, I stood for a while unobserved and watched my dignified old Irishman brazenly flirt with the cook.

"Ah, Mrs. Leroy," he said. "A woman who can produce a fine chicken cordon bleu is worthy of all praise. Mrs. Browley is lucky to have someone like yourself who respects French cuisine—which I myself hold in high esteem. Even, I must admit, beyond my own Irish cuisine."

"Irish?" Mrs. Leroy, who had been pounding chicken cutlets, paused and gave a wry smile. "Irish cuisine amounts to little more than boiled cabbage and a splash of whiskey."

"Madam!" Mr. O'Nelligan feigned outrage. "You overlook the potato." There was a glint in his eye that I'd have preferred to miss.

"French is good," the cook said simply and firmly. "It's the food of passion and the language of love."

Dear God, this was going too far. I was about to break things up with a theatric cough, when Mr. O'Nelligan reached across the kitchen counter for a waylaid slice of ham. Down slammed Mrs. Leroy's meat pounder the merest inch from Mr. O'Nelligan's fingers. "None of that," she said coquettishly. "This isn't a buffet."

At this point, the Irish Lothario noticed me. "Oh, Lee. Yes, well ..." Thrown by my presence, he took a deep breath to compose himself. "Come. I have a task for us."

He moved past me, and as I turned to follow, I swapped glances with Mrs. Leroy. Her face hardened and she resumed her pounding. Clearly, she was none too pleased with me for interrupting their tête-à-tête.

Through a circuitous route that he must have scouted out earlier, Mr. O'Nelligan led me upwards into a low, peaked attic. He switched on a light to reveal a clutter of boxes, trunks, and old chairs, as well as several swords leaning in a corner. But what stood out most was a full-sized suit of armor, missing one arm. As I examined this wounded knight, I felt a jab in my back and spun about to face my companion, a long feathered spear in his hands.

"It's as Captain Sands told us," he said. "A Comanche war lance in the attic. Now, look out that little window behind you. What do you see?"

I peered through the darkness to make out a round structure just beyond the hill. "The Roost ..."

"Exactly! We were told that it couldn't be seen from the house, and that's true—except from this one vantage point. When we were standing at the Roost earlier today, we could see the top of the house. Remember? I didn't perceive a window from that distance, but once Sands mentioned an attic, I guessed there might be one."

"So, Browley came up to get the lance, happened to glance out the window, and saw what? Even with a full moon, it would be pretty hard to see anything at night from up here. Unless someone below turned on the light in the Roost."

"Or was wielding an electric torch. You have one in your automobile, I believe."

"A flashlight? Yeah."

"Then retrieve it, if you will." Mr. O'Nelligan reached into his pocket and handed me a familiar set of keys. "I asked Mrs. Browley for these. Now, go position yourself in the Roost and flick on the wall switch. Then, after a bit, turn it off and use only your flashlight. We'll conduct ourselves a little experiment."

Minutes later, I had stationed myself inside the stone outbuilding and flipped on the light. As instructed, I soon turned it off and switched on my flashlight. I played the yellow beam around the room, pausing on the metal brace from which Clarence Browley's shield of power had been torn. Next, I lingered on the man wrestling the tiger, then on the medieval battlefield. After some time, I doused my light and stood there in the pitch blackness, which felt cold and clingy like a strange second skin.

I thought of ghosts. The unavenged ghost of the man who had been murdered just outside this door. The ghosts of fallen warriors, real men from real wars, not the romanticized figures on Browley's walls. I thought of the ghosts of Mr. O'Nelligan's youth—men he himself had perhaps killed in his own faraway war. And I thought of the ghost of my father, whose legacy now rested in my untested hands. In deep darkness, ghosts are easy to assemble and I was surely finding them all.

The door opened abruptly, shrilly, and a spectral form filled the threshold. I fumbled to turn on my flashlight, then aimed its beam forward to discover Mr. O'Nelligan.

"Our experiment worked," he said.

"How did you find your way here in the dark?"

"As a boy, I worked with a gamekeeper who taught me the trick. It's all about trusting your feet. As I say, our experiment worked. From the attic, I perceived a light in this window here, the one facing the house."

"When I flicked the wall switch on?"

"Yes, but this I expected. More telling is the fact that even when you used only your flashlight, I could still tell someone was down here. Fainter light, of course, but still visible from the attic."

"So, Browley saw somebody in the Roost and came out to face them."

"And, alas, never returned ..."

• • •

When we returned to the inn later that evening, Mr. O'Nelligan went to petition the night clerk for an after-hours cup of tea. Wishing him success, I headed upstairs. As I approached my door, a pair of small shiny objects on the carpet caught my eye. They lay directly below the doorknob of the opposite room, the one belonging to David Pobenski. I bent and retrieved them. For a very long time, I stood there transfixed by the two gleaming stones nestled in my palm. Unless I was mistaken, the green one was an emerald; the red one, a ruby.

Nine

They had Pobenski in custody by midnight.

As soon as I could pull my eyes away from the gems, I'd showed them to Mr. O'Nelligan, then phoned Handleman. The jumbo detective had rushed over with a number of policemen and promptly entered Pobenski's room. The boxer was absent, but another emerald and another ruby were discovered in his nightstand drawer. A protracted hunt eventually found Pobenski perched on a stool in a downtown bar, sloppy drunk.

We didn't learn of this last piece until the next morning, when Handleman showed up again at the inn to loom above our breakfast table and gloat. He bragged about Pobenski's arrest, adding that he'd just phoned Nina Browley to tell her everything was wrapped up.

"We're sitting pretty," he said. "It's like I explained it to you. Sooner or later, the thief screws up and I'm there waiting to reel him in."

Mr. O'Nelligan lowered his teacup. "Was it not, in fact, Mr. Plunkett here who discovered the evidence?"

"Dumb luck. Not that I don't appreciate his ability to step on jewelry." Handleman chuckled nastily. "The truth is, Pobenski's probably been feeling the heat from my investigation for a while. He gets nervous, gets careless, and makes a bonehead mistake like dropping the rocks outside his door. No question they came from

Browley's shield. That links poor little Polecat to the robbery and therefore to the murder. Case closed."

"But what about the timeline?" Mr. O'Nelligan asked. "David Pobenski was only unaccounted for during a five-minute interval. How could he have made his way to the Roost, conferred the death blows, purloined the shield and returned calmly to rejoin the others—all within five minutes?"

"The guy's an Olympic-class athlete," said Handleman. "He's young, he's strong, he's fast. That's how he does it."

"But in your earlier notes, you argued that such a feat was implausible."

Handleman snarled. "Listen, Shamrock, I said case goddamned closed. Now, if it's the money you two are worried about, I'm sure the Browley woman will settle up nicely for whatever hours you've clocked. But, face it, you're done here. Hang out for another day, just on the off chance I have any follow-up questions, then hit the ol' highway." He snagged a piece of bacon off my plate and popped it into his big mouth. "Enjoy your meal, boys."

After Handleman left, I pushed aside my violated breakfast. "It's over then. So, why do I feel like things are unresolved?"

"Because perhaps they are," Mr. O'Nelligan said, dabbing his lips with a napkin. Since the moment I'd showed him the gems, he had offered little by way of advice or reflection, preferring, it seemed, to keep his own counsel.

"What do you mean, 'perhaps they are'?"

"Oh, probably nothing." He folded the napkin primly and set it aside. "I would just like to ponder some more."

"Ponder away. You have all day to do it."

Later I joined Mr. O'Nelligan in a short walk to a nearby newsstand. We'd just purchased the morning papers, when someone from behind called my name. I turned and saw Jojo Groom limping up the sidewalk.

"Hey, Lee! You did it, kid!" He grabbed my hand and shook it briskly. "I just heard the lowdown. You nailed that punch jockey dead-to-rights. Emeralds, rubies ... everything on him but gold doubloons. See, this is what I was saying—always trust a Plunkett. Was I on the money or what?"

My face reddened under the glare of undeserved praise. "Well, to be honest, Jojo, I really didn't—"

He slapped my shoulder. "Don't second guess yourself, kid! And don't be modest. God knows your old man wasn't. And I'll tell you this—Buster would be proud as a peacock of you. Proud as a big stinking peacock." Here his voice got low and solemn. "Y'know, when I heard your pop had died, they'd just renominated Eisenhower. Seemed fitting somehow. So, right there and then, I toasted the two of 'em—Ike and Buster—'cause they don't make 'em like those guys anymore ..." He punctuated this by tapping my chest with his walking cane. "Guys like you, neither."

"Thanks, Jojo," I had to say.

"So, you gents heading back to Connecticut?"

"Tomorrow."

"Okay then. Job well done, kid." He now acknowledged Mr. O'Nelligan. "You too, buddy."

My cohort merely smiled.

Jojo started away, but not before saying again, "Proud as a stinking peacock!" Just in case I didn't get it the first time.

• • •

Soon after, Mr. O'Nelligan and I parted ways for the bulk of the day. He seemed to be either satisfied with the outcome of things, or indifferent, and, as best I could tell, planned to divide his time between strolling the town and visiting Captain Ahab. As for myself, I eventually drove out to talk to Nina Browley about the latest turn of events. Instead of Nina, I found Paige Simmons sitting outside under a willow tree, her natural good looks spoiled by recent tears.

"Nina's gone shopping with the cook," she said. "She won't be home for a while."

"I can come back later."

"They say it was David. He's in jail now. But he's not the type. Not the type at all."

"The police have evidence."

"They told Nina some of the shield gems were found in his room."

"It's true."

"If David really did do it, why would he still be carrying them around a month later?"

"I'm not sure," I said. "Maybe he was letting things die down a little before trying to sell them."

"This is all wrong. David couldn't kill a man."

I thought, *Well, he has been known to beat them up.*

"What about you, Mr. Plunkett?" she asked. "Do you think David murdered Clarence?"

"The evidence is hard to overlook. And when I saw Pobenski last evening, he did seem distracted about something."

"It was about me!" She stood and looked me in the eyes. "David and I have been fond of each other ever since we met last year. He's a quiet, shy boy, not like the other men who come here. Yesterday afternoon, when I drove him to the inn, he told me that for him it was love. But he was worried that Nina's suspicions about him would make me afraid to trust him."

"And what did you say?" I asked, feeling immensely intrusive.

"I really didn't know what to say just then. I told him I had to get back to Nina, but we could talk by phone later if he liked. That evening he called the house and we spoke for a few minutes."

"When was this?"

"Sometime after Mr. O'Nelligan came, but a while before you showed up. I told David then that I thought I loved him, too, but that Nina's suspicions did make me hold back from him. This really upset him, saddened him. He said he was going back to his room, and that's when you must have seen him looking so distracted. Afterwards, I guess he went out to a bar and drank too much. And that's when the police came and ... and ..."

She couldn't bring herself to finish. Unsure of what solace I could give, I blathered something inane about it all working out and took my leave.

• • •

Hours later, when Mr. O'Nelligan and I regrouped, he informed me that we were going to the movies. What's more, we had to drive two whole towns away to enjoy the diversions of the silver screen. Then, to top it all off, he refused to say what film he intended us to see. He just treated me to an infuriating little smile and suggested I have faith.

The ride there found Mr. O'Nelligan back in his patented pondering mode. He stroked his beard, listened to the radio and kept largely silent. At one point, perhaps feeling the need to explain his aloofness, he offered a brief tale.

"I once knew a seamstress who barely spoke to her customers. She'd listen to your needs and accept your garments, but shunned all verbosity. Cleverest seamstress in the town, but quiet as a chapel. One night, the local postmistress pried her with a pint or three of stout and asked about the silence. The seamstress then confessed her belief that if she were to give herself to chatter, her needles would lose their sense of direction. So there you have it."

Yes, there I had it, whatever it was.

The movie, I soon learned, was a Western called *Sagebrush Ambush* and starred none other than Tom Durker.

"This was the nearest theater showing one of his pictures," Mr. O'Nelligan explained as the houselights dimmed.

The sagebrush looked authentic and the ambush was daring enough, but the acting lay flat as a prairie. Tom Durker obviously hadn't achieved B-picture stardom due to any thespian abilities. What he did have going for him was a deep voice, strong jaw, and moody eyes that seemed always half shut.

The nighttime drive back to Greenley resembled the earlier ride, except that my passenger seemed even more intensely lost in thought. When we pulled into town, he requested that I bring us once more to the Browley home. I didn't even bother to ask why. I'd barely parked the car when my companion pushed himself out and hurried to the door, a man on a mission. Nina Browley appeared, again in the kimono, and ushered us into the hallway.

Her present demeanor was fairly reserved. "Everyone else has retired, and I'm really not up for entertainment. Though I do appreciate you helping to bring the situation to a close."

"You're satisfied with Detective Handleman's conclusions?" asked Mr. O'Nelligan.

Nina tossed up her hands. "I suppose I must be. After all, David was caught with the goods. Isn't that how you put it—'caught with the goods'?"

"It occurs to me that we've never seen a picture of your husband," Mr. O'Nelligan said. "Could you possibly produce one?"

Nina left briefly and returned with a small framed photograph. In it, a slender, handsome man with a Clark Gable mustache smiled out at the world.

For good measure, he sported one of his beloved swords.

Mr. O'Nelligan thanked her, then turned to me. "Lee, I'd like you to walk around the building to the kitchen window. Mrs. Browley, is the outside light there on? The one that was on the night of your husband's passing?'

"It is. But why do you—"

"All in good time, Madam. Now, Lee, I'll go place myself inside the kitchen. When you arrive at the window, tap on it, then run off in the direction of the Roost. Go about partway, then come back. We don't have a full moon like that night, but we'll just have to make do. Oh wait! Take this with you." He reached down to an umbrella stand near the door, and slid from it a long, narrow sword that I hadn't before noticed. "Mrs. Browley, would this be the very weapon that Mr. Browley bore on that night?"

Nina looked a little pale. "Yes, it's the rapier. The police returned it awhile ago. I just placed it back there."

"Very well." Mr. O'Nelligan said, passing me the blade. "Now onwards, man, onwards."

I stepped out into the autumn night. An aggressive wind had come up and made itself known in the treetops beyond the lawn. I eased my way along the side of the house, feeling the heft of the sword in my hand. I found myself very aware that, in this manner, Clarence Browley had spent the final minutes of his life. Reaching the kitchen window, I raised the blade and tapped. Mr. O'Nelligan's face appeared immediately, just inches from the pane. Unexpectedly, this sent a shiver through me. As instructed, I then turned and ran towards the hill, soon leaving the influence of the outside light.

Though my assignment only required me to go partway to the Roost, something compelled me to continue on. Pressing forward into the darkness, my run slowed to an urgent walk, and I tried to trust my feet like Mr. O'Nelligan. As I drew closer to the outbuilding, I, in a sense, became Browley, being pulled seductively towards violence and death. Fear pressed on my chest, and I tightened my hold on the sword. The wind around me had become enraged, filling the world with a high, lamenting moan. I reached the Roost and placed my free hand against the cold stone of the outer wall.

Then someone, something, appeared next to me. I cried out and raised the sword, as what felt like a knot of iron slammed into my jaw. Through the power of the blow, my head bounced back against the stone wall, and the sword fell from my hand. I crumpled to the ground. Lying where Clarence Browley once had, I rolled over on my back. Somehow, my glasses had remained on, but, as I attempted to focus my vision, a strong light blinded me. I heard someone curse, and, seconds later, the light shifted slightly away. For one passing moment, just before my eyes rolled back in my head, I caught a glimpse of my attacker staring down at me. It was Polecat Pobenski.

Ten

I didn't regain consciousness until sometime the next morning, when I opened my eyes to find that Pobenski's face had been replaced by a far more welcomed one—Audrey's. She stroked my hair and told me that everything would be fine; I smiled, believing it would be. Then I passed out again. Over the next few hours, I'd slip in and out of my senses, occasionally noting my surroundings. I gathered that I was in a hospital room as various humans came and went: here a nurse; there a doctor; here a Mr. O'Nelligan. Once, Handleman even showed up, looking down at me in either pity or disdain. Throughout it all, Audrey seemed to be the one constant, and I found that greatly comforting.

Finally, a thick, dark cloud lifted, and I came back for good. I felt weak, but my brain appeared to have regained its standing in the world.

"I love you, Audrey," was the first thing I remember saying.

"Me, too," was her answer. She squeezed my hand and her eyes teared up. Darned if mine didn't, too.

The next thing I said was, "Pobenski hit me."

"We know." Mr. O'Nelligan now came into my line of vision. "You told me when I found you. It was all you said before you blinked away again."

"Pobenski was supposed to be in custody."

"He was, but he escaped last night due to an inefficient jailor. But rest up, Lee. There's much a'brewing right now. I've taken the liberty of pursuing matters in your absence, and tonight we've a little get-together that should be memorable. If the doctors think it practical, you'll be there in person, like Lazarus yanked triumphantly from the grave."

"I don't feel triumphant. Just glad to not be comatose."

"I'll see you tonight then, lad. Seven o'clock at Mrs. Browley's."

Mr. O'Nelligan hurried off and I turned back to Audrey. "I'm hungry."

"That's a good sign."

"Got a bit of a headache, too." I gingerly touched my skull and found it to be bandaged.

"You're lucky to be alive, Lee, after being hit so hard. When Mr. O'Nelligan called me, well … I don't want to think about it."

"Thanks for coming."

"What? You think I'd stay home and twiddle my thumbs while my fiancé's lying unconscious?"

"No, I guess not." I made a mental note to finally marry this girl.

• • •

That night's gathering commenced in the Browley kitchen where Mr. O'Nelligan had asked us to convene. Audrey and I sat at the table with Nina and Paige Simmons (who couldn't seem to look me in the eye.) Webster Sands leaned against a counter, puffing on a thick cigar, while Mrs. Leroy passed among us offering snacks. Most surprisingly, over near the window, stood a man I recognized as Tom Durker.

Like a maestro stepping before his orchestra, Mr. O'Nelligan entered the room and started things off. "Thank you all for your indulgence. I especially wish to acknowledge Mr. Durker for flying all the way from California on such short notice. A long trek, to be sure."

"A very long one," Durker concurred.

"And it goes without saying, that everyone is pleased to see Mr. Lee Plunkett here safely among us after his encounter last evening."

All eyes turned to me, and I did feel a little like a revived corpse.

Mr. O'Nelligan continued. "As Lee has been hindered by his injuries, I will, with his permission, speak on behalf of our investigation." He looked to me for confirmation; I gave a little nod. "Very well then. I'll try to present the facts of the case as delicately as possible, but with the understanding that the search for truth must be unflinching."

The man's time upon the stage had obviously served him well. He proceeded with poise and flourish. "Presently, I've been enjoying a rereading of *Moby Dick* and have found parallels between that superb tome and our investigation. In Melville's novel, as Ahab pursues the white whale, the narrative offers many side trips—forays into biology, philosophy, etymology, et cetera—before arriving at the climax. But all these diversions ultimately serve the narrative. Likewise, as we sought the truth of Clarence Browley's murder, we've had to take various side trips, which, while not directly leading to the resolution, nonetheless helped us see the grander picture."

Captain Sands discharged a hefty smoke ring. "We didn't come for a literature lecture. Can't we keep this brief?"

Nonplussed, Mr. O'Nelligan pressed on. "In Ahab's tale, it is his nemesis who finally prevails. Hopefully, our outcome here will turn out differently. Now, the kitchen in which we presently congregate is, in many ways, the heart of our story. It is here that Clarence Browley was viewed at the window, an event of great significance to our case. Let us lay out three assumed facts. Fact one: Tom Durker saw Clarence at the window at roughly five minutes after midnight."

Durker spoke up. "Saw him and heard him. He was tapping with that sword of his, and then scooted off when he caught sight of me."

"Yes, that has always been your testimony," said Mr. O'Nelligan. "Fact two: when Mrs. Browley discovered her dying husband at 12:20, he indicated to her that someone in the house was his assailant. These first two facts combine to limit the possible attack time to a fifteen minute interval. And fact three: during those fifteen minutes, everyone who'd been at the house that night was assembled here in the kitchen. Everyone, that is, except for three people—two being the Daley Sisters, who left by eleven thirty in a car filled with relations—and one other, who had arrived five minutes late to the kitchen. The same man who last night struck down Lee Plunkett."

Paige Simmons let out a pitiful groan. "David can't have done these things. It's just not in him."

"I disagree," Mr. O'Nelligan said. "And, yet, I also agree."

I now threw in my two cents. "It was Pobenski! No question it was Pobenski who hit me."

"That part is undeniably true," my cohort conceded. "But it was the action not of a murderer returning to the scene of his crime, but, rather, of a fugitive, desperate and falsely accused, who was startled in the darkness."

Paige nearly jumped out of her seat. "Yes! You believe he's innocent."

"I do not believe," Mr. O'Nelligan said. "I know. Pobenski is innocent. Innocent, but foolish, for had he simply remained in custody, the probings of Plunkett and Son would have inevitably freed him. Am I wrong in surmising, Miss Simmons, that you know young Polecat's present whereabouts?"

Paige lowered her eyes. "I ... I do. He left a note in my car."

"I'm not shocked to learn that. No doubt, he came here last night in an attempt to assure you of his blamelessness. When we are done here, you may contact him and tell him to present himself. Of course, he'll still have to clear things with the authorities—and with the man he knocked out."

Again, all eyes enwrapped me, most imploringly, Paige's. I said, "If he's innocent, I'll let things slide."

"But, wait now." Nina Browley seemed confused (and she was not alone.) "What about the gemstones? David had them in his room."

"They were placed there by another party." Mr. O'Nelligan said. "Someone found the opportunity to enter the inn, pick Pobenski's lock and scatter the gems. Someone who wished to bring this investigation to a premature end. But, let us return to our trio of facts. I say that all three cannot be mutually true. The third fact—that everyone had gathered in the kitchen—is undeniably true. Everyone is everyone else's alibi, so to speak. I will also insist that, despite police assertions, not even an athletic youth like David Pobenski could have raced to and from the Roost and committed murder in those few minutes before he joined the others. Thus, for all practical purposes, we can place him fully with his companions during that quarter hour."

"Yes!" Paige cried out again, clearly pleased with David's ongoing exoneration.

Our maestro played on. "Since we know the household was gathered together, then one of our two remaining facts must be wrong. Let us first examine Nina Browley's statement. She claims that Clarence indicated someone from the house was his killer, but could she be lying? And if so, why? One reason would be self-protection, if it was, in reality, Mrs. Browley herself who had felled her husband."

"How could you!" Nina leapt to her feet. Her face became a mask of rage, and I thought she might jump the aged Irishman.

Paige was at her side in a heartbeat, embracing her friend like the first time I'd seen them. "How can you even say that, Mr. O'Nelligan? Nina would never—"

"Never!" Nina echoed. "Why, I'm the one who paid you to come! Why would I do that if—"

"Madam, madam ..." Mr. O'Nelligan reached out and gently placed a hand on Nina's cheek. The unexpected gesture seemed to calm her. "Please, take ease and allow me to proceed."

The two women returned to their seats and Mr. O'Nelligan continued. "Mrs. Browley makes a compelling point. If she was the guilty party why then would she bring in investigators? As a courtesy to our client, we shall assume, for the time being, that she's telling the truth."

"I would hope so," Nina mumbled.

"As we journey across the landscape of this case, we must constantly ford rivers of doubt to get from one point of understanding to the next. Sometimes, we find solid bridges—solid information—

by which we can progress. Other times we must simply gird our loins and leap for the farther side. Leaps of faith, as the saying goes. We then trek on until such time as our faith seems ill-founded. When that happens, we must turn back, leap again the previous river, and find a new place to cross."

"Listen, old man," Captain Sands grumbled. "What the blazes are—"

"Hear me out, sir!" demanded Mr. O'Nelligan, cutting off any potential complaint about philosophy lectures. "Let us presume, until compelled not to, that Mrs. Browley is without guilt here and that she spoke the truth regarding someone from the house being the assassin. We are now forced to conclude that our remaining fact is the false one. Tom Durker cannot have seen Clarence at the window."

Durker huffed. "Are you saying I'm lying?"

"Why would one lie about seeing Clarence alive?" Mr. O'Nelligan mused. "Well, perhaps to cover up the fact that he himself was the assailant and had already left Clarence for dead."

Durker puffed up his chest. "I didn't fly all the way here to take this kind of bull. I've got a barrelful of L.A. lawyers I can sic on you."

Mr. O'Nelligan held up a hand. "Don't rush to conclusions, Mr. Durker. The truth is, I believe you were honestly mistaken about seeing Clarence. Yesterday, Mr. Plunkett and I took in one of your Westerns. *Sagebrush Ambush,* it was called. An admirable piece of film making."

Pride replaced anger in keeping the actor's chest swelled. "That's my latest. I sure raise hell in that one."

"Unquestionably. I did have a motivation, besides my love of cinema, in wanting to see one of your movies. It was something mentioned by Mrs. Browley and Miss Simmons regarding your eyes."

"Well, women do say I've got commanding eyes."

"One would argue that at his own peril." Mr. O'Nelligan stepped over to the window, looked out and gave a gesture of beckoning, apparently to someone near the front of the house. "Ah, Detective Handleman has arrived."

Nina scrunched up her face. "Handleman? What's that Neanderthal doing here?"

Mr. O'Nelligan turned away from the window. "Actually, he's come per my request. So, as I was saying, the women were disagreeing on how best to describe Tom Durker's eyes. One saw them as steely; the other called them narrow. After seeing you on the screen, the word I would hold out for is squinty. Mr. Durker, are you, by chance, nearsighted?"

The cowboy hero's face dropped. "Well, I ... I mean ..."

"That's it!" Nina Browley cried out. "I thought there was something about his stare. I couldn't put my finger on it, but it's obvious now. Do you wear glasses, Tom?"

"Sometimes," he said quietly. "Look, don't tell anybody. No one wants a half-blind gunfighter. But, I swear, I did see Clarence outside this window. I saw his face ... his sword ... Even with my lousy eyes, I couldn't just see someone who wasn't there."

Mr. O'Nelligan nodded in agreement. "That's exactly what I said to myself. With the outside light on and a full moon in the sky, it seemed impossible that even myopic eyes could perceive a nonexistent man. Then, on the ride back from the film, something occurred to me. What if the man Tom Durker saw was not Clarence Browley at all, but someone who generally resembled him? So, I asked Nina to see a photo of her husband."

Heavy footsteps could now be heard approaching us.

Mr. O'Nelligan did not pause. "The photo revealed a slender, dark-haired man with a thin mustache. I asked myself, does this image bring to mind anyone else involved in the case? Someone who was known to carry not a sword, but an object that could be mistaken for one? Then the answer came to me ..."

Handleman stomped into the kitchen, followed by three uniformed officers and, in handcuffs, Jojo Groom.

Eleven

"Jojo?" Nina Browley was on her feet again. "It was Jojo?"

"He does sort of resemble Clarence," Paige said.

My father's old buddy and I met eyes for a second or two. He looked quickly away. Nina started towards him, but Mr. O'Nelligan led her gently, yet firmly, back to her seat.

"Okay, Shamrock," Handleman said. "It's like you told us. When we ransacked Groom's place, we found a bunch more of the gems, maybe the complete lot."

Mr. O'Nelligan met the news matter-of-factly. "Yes, I speculated that Groom might have retained the gems. Presumably, to be cautious, he was waiting for more time to pass before attempting to sell them."

"Plus, we found these ..." Handleman produced a ring of three keys.

Mr. O'Nelligan smiled. "I think you'll find that those are a copy of the set that Mrs. Browley possesses."

"They're the keys to the Roost," Nina said. "But how did he get them? There was only one set."

"All shall be explained," promised the Irishman. "Jojo Groom does, you will admit, bear a basic resemblance to Clarence Browley. Mr. Durker knew that Clarence was outside with a sword, so it's understandable that he might mistake one man for the other, especially when peering with unreliable eyes through a glass pane. Although only inches separated Durker's face from Groom's, for someone with strong myopia, even such proximity may be a problem. What was actually a cane in Groom's hand, Durker saw as a sword in Browley's. What Durker perceived as Browley hopping away was, in reality, Groom limping off.

"Once I was aware of the resemblance between the two men, I reviewed a moment of note which occurred yesterday morning when Groom met us at the newsstand. He mentioned that on the day he first heard Buster Plunkett had died, Eisenhower had just secured the presidential nomination."

"Re-nomination," Webster Sands had to put in. "We're going for term number two, remember?"

Mr. O'Nelligan turned to the aviator. "Ah, Captain Sands, as an ardent supporter of the president, please tell me, when was his party's national convention held?"

"About a month ago, just after Browley's murder."

"That's right. August twentieth to the twenty-second, to be exact. I looked it up. I knew the conventions were generally held in the summer, so something did not sit right with me when Groom said he'd just heard then that Plunkett Sr. had died. Why, you might ask?"

"I know!" I finally had something to add. "Because when Groom called me five days ago with this case, he acted as if he was just that moment learning of my father's death. Not back in August." I don't know why I hadn't thought of this before.

Mr. O'Nelligan looked at me with what seemed awfully like paternal fondness. "Behold him, good people! Maimed as he is, Lee Plunkett still contributes to the investigation." Nice compliment, but I don't think he fooled anyone in regard to my deductive abilities.

"Hold on now," Nina said. "Why would Jojo pretend to not know that the older Plunkett was dead? And why would he talk me into getting Plunkett and Son in the first place? I was planning to hire someone else, but he insisted they were the best."

Suddenly, I understood a lot. Groom had heard that Nina was going to buy the finest private eye her considerable bankroll could afford, someone who might well succeed where the inept Handleman had not. To prevent this, Groom cajoled Nina into hiring someone with virtually no chance of solving the case—namely me. Through the grapevine, he'd no doubt heard that Buster's kid was definitely no Buster. When he called me last week, had he revealed that he knew Dad was dead, it would have meant that he was seeking the unproven Lee Plunkett for a top-drawer murder case. Would I have really believed that anyone of sound mind would do such a thing? Probably not.

"Well? Why would Jojo bring in Mr. Plunkett?" Nina still wanted an answer. Groom himself was staring at his shoes. He wasn't going to field any questions.

I met Mr. O'Nelligan's eyes and saw that he knew what I knew. To spare me embarrassment he simply said, "Groom probably believed that the devil you know beats the devil you don't."

"So, it was all just about stealing the shield," Paige said.

Handleman sniffed. "Hell, that's what I kept telling—"

"Please, Detective." Mr. O'Nelligan let him get no further. "You promised to observe in silence while I concluded my presentation here. Was that not our agreement?"

"Yeah, yeah," Handleman did not look joyful. "Get on with it then."

Once more, Mr. O'Nelligan took center stage. "This case has proved to be one of seeming contradictions. Yes, it was a straight robbery, as the police insisted, but, also, it was something more. For a time, the social aspects of Clarence Browley's life seemed to overtake the investigation. His need to surround himself with adventurous men, his relationship with his wife, his wife's relationship with others ... these things attracted our attention, but, in the end, did not provide a solution."

"Thank God," Nina said sotto voce.

Mr. O'Nelligan went on. "We realized two nights ago that Clarence, from the vantage point of the attic, could have observed someone moving about the Roost with a flashlight. This gave credence to the scenario in which Clarence rushes out to surprise a thief at his game. We are indeed looking at a robbery, and Jojo Groom is the thief, seeking the bejeweled shield. Poor Clarence was bludgeoned before he could apprehend Groom or summon help."

"But how could it be Jojo?" Nina asked. "I keep telling everyone, Clarence let me know it was someone from the house, but Jojo hadn't been here for a couple weeks. He can't be Clarence's killer."

"I never said he was," said Mr. O'Nelligan. "I only said that he was the thief."

He let that sink in.

"Wow!" This came from Audrey, who was obviously impressed by her friend's gala performance.

"Here we go, then ..." It felt as if Mr. O'Nelligan was ushering us onto a fast-moving carnival ride. "Since we now know the man at the window was Groom, it means that Clarence may have already been dead by then. Thus, the possible timeframe of the attack now expands to include the interval after Clarence left the house up until the window incident. Of course, everything may still point to Groom—he himself could have struck down Clarence when caught in the act of thievery. Except that he wasn't 'someone from the house,' as Mrs. Browley points out, at least not that night."

"Exactly! Exactly!" Nina cheered him on.

"Yes, Groom committed the robbery—we have the gems to prove this—but did he necessarily commit the murder? We must ask ourselves, why did he tap at the window in the first place? Remember, he could not have known the kitchen would be filled with Mrs. Browley and her guests. In fact, when he saw one of them staring back at him, he fled. So, who would he have expected to see? I'll tell you. It was someone who I believe orchestrated the theft, and, when it appeared the plan was about to be thwarted, followed Clarence Browley outside and brutally ended his life. Now, who here among us would we naturally expect to find in the kitchen?"

He paused for effect, as, one by one, all heads turned towards the same person. Mrs. Leroy the cook.

Twelve

Standing by the sink, Mrs. Leroy said nothing. For a fleeting moment, she fixed a cold eye on her accuser, then stared away.

He did not let up. "In that period between Clarence exiting the house and Nina finding him, three members of the party were playing cards, while two others were together in the den. We have, in fact, only one person unaccounted for ..."

"Mrs. Leroy." Nina finished for him. "Right, she was alone in the kitchen."

"Using my method of bridges and leaps, here is how I believe the events played out." Mr. O'Nelligan took a deep breath to fill his sails, then voyaged on. "Mrs. Leroy had, at some earlier point, procured, by stealth, Mr. Browley's key ring. A copy was made and the original replaced. Knowing that Browley did not sleep in the Roost when he hosted his glory tables, the cook instructed her confederate,

Groom, that such a night would be best for the purpose of stealing the shield. Since the canine would be released at midnight, the robbery needed to be accomplished before that hour."

I looked over at Mrs. Leroy. She stared blankly ahead, not reacting at all to the unfolding account.

"And so, we arrive at the night of August the eighteenth," Mr. O'Nelligan said. "Groom has snuck onto the grounds, probably leaving his car below, and uses the copied keys to enter the Roost. He begins to unfasten the shield from the wall. Meanwhile, Clarence Browley, in the attic of the house, notices Groom's flashlight below and decides to confront the intruder. A minute later, Mrs. Leroy, like the others, sees an agitated, sword-wielding Browley leave the house. She correctly surmises that her employer has seen something in the Roost. Fearing that Groom will be discovered, and her own complicity in the robbery revealed, she grabs something from the kitchen to use as a weapon."

Mr. O'Nelligan walked over to a rack on the wall and removed the meat pounder. "Although I don't know for certain, I have a feeling this tool would serve as a sufficient bludgeon. Detective, I believe there are determining tests that might be applied?"

As he handed over the pounder to Handleman, I thought, *I'll never eat chicken cordon bleu again.*

"Now, Mrs. Leroy has a room just off the kitchen." Mr. O'Nelligan pointed to a door near the refrigerator. "Right through there. I took note today that her room possesses its own exit. She can pass to and fro, unnoticed by the rest of the household. And that is what she does on that night, as, meat pounder in hand, she follows Browley down to the Roost. He is standing at the entrance of the building. Perhaps he has already confronted Groom, or is just about to. Mrs. Leroy creeps up behind him and strikes hard to the back of his head. Browley falls to the ground, then rolls over on his back and sees that it is his cook who has assaulted him. Mrs. Leroy then viciously delivers what she believes to be the death blow to the front of his skull."

Nina let out a low groan.

"Forgive me, madam." Mr. O'Nelligan allowed a long moment to pass before resuming. "Though appearing dead, Browley will linger more than a half hour, long enough to indicate to his wife that his killer came from the house. The fact that Browley was found facing upwards suggests that, of the two blows, the one from behind was delivered first. This leads me to believe that it was not Groom who waged the attack. He would probably have been confronted face-to-face by Browley and would not have had the opportunity to strike from behind. Am I correct, Mr. Groom?"

Jojo broke his silence. "Yeah! You got it, mister. You got everything right. I'm a thief, sure, but I'm not a murderer. I don't have the ice in my veins for that. But she does!" Here he pointed his hand-cuffed hands towards Mrs. Leroy. "Believe me, that one's cold as goddamned Alaska!"

The cook merely smoothed her apron and stared away.

"And so, the crime is done," Mr. O'Nelligan continued. "In the aftermath, Groom, shaken by the turn of events, remains at the Roost to complete the robbery. Mrs. Leroy, a steadier hand, returns directly to her room, changing any blood-splattered garments, then enters the kitchen. Here, she perhaps even washes her weapon, for when Mrs. Browley and her guests barge in, the cook is observed 'cleaning up.' Soon, Groom, expecting only Mrs. Leroy to be attendant, taps on the kitchen window to inform her that his task is complete. The rest we've covered ..."

"You sure know your racket!" Groom seemed so taken by Mr. O'Nelligan's account, I thought he might applaud. "Especially the part about me being shaken up. This murder stuff isn't my line, y'know? But, that one over there, she's goddamned Alaska. You know who she is, don't you? Who she used to be?"

"I was getting to that. Earlier today, I made some calls and accessed some pertinent records. I discovered that 'Dorothy Leroy,' while legally this woman's current appellation, is neither her original nor her married name. Born Dorothy Ritz, she became Mrs. George Carroway upon her marriage to a man better known as ..."

"King Carroway!" I stole my cohort's punch line.

"Precisely. The storied bank robber who died in a hail of gunfire some nineteen years ago." He indicated the unflinching Mrs. Leroy. "Yes, this woman was his wife. Captured shortly after her husband's death, she turned state's evidence against several of his associates in exchange for an abolished sentence. Later, to avoid notoriety, she took a name which, while inconspicuous, still cryptically honored Carroway. Having learned of her inclination towards French, I've been able to decode her little riddle. The name Leroy is derived from the French *le roi,* meaning the king. Mrs. Leroy is literally 'king's wife.'"

I looked at the aging cook with new eyes. In her younger days, this woman had escaped a gun battle perched naked on a bicycle.

"A last question remains," Mr. O'Nelligan said. "How did Mrs. Leroy and Groom become partners in crime? Here I have no solid bridge, but I will make a leap. At an earlier glory table this summer, the ex-police detective encounters the Browleys' cook, whom he recognizes from years before. This is, after all, the wife of the man who put four bullets in him. At some juncture, Groom perhaps threatens to reveal her unsavory past unless she pays him a certain fee. Perhaps she then makes an offer—why settle for a handful of cash when something as precious as a gem-studded shield can be obtained with her help and guidance? In this way, Mrs. Leroy turns her would-be blackmailer into her accomplice."

"You pretty much got it," Groom admitted. "I tell ya, that witch can make a guy jump through hoops. You wouldn't know it to look at her."

Mr. O'Nelligan now walked over to Mrs. Leroy and locked eyes with her. I wondered what was going through his mind. Only days ago, these two had been trading flirtations; now he was accusing her of murder. "Tell, madam, what do you say to all that I have laid at your door?"

Mrs. Leroy never said a word, but her eyes turned to fire. Then it all happened. She let out a high, animal scream, and a butcher's knife appeared in her hand. It flashed across the Irishman's chest, dropping him to the floor.

"Mr. O'Nelligan!" I knelt beside him, quickly joined by Audrey.

Mrs. Leroy ran into her adjacent room, and we heard a lock click. Handleman slammed his sizable girth against the door, splintering it open on the third try. Guns drawn, he and his men rushed in.

Audrey undid the top buttons of Mr. O'Nelligan's shirt to reveal a thin red line across his chest. "She barely marked me," he told us. "I'm all right." We helped him to his feet.

I heard Handleman curse. Moments later, he stepped back into the kitchen. "We found her on the bed. She drove the blade through her own heart. One cool customer."

We all just stood there, saying nothing. Then Mr. O'Nelligan walked over to the doorway of Mrs. Leroy's room and looked in. After a moment, he recited something no doubt by Yeats:

"I balanced all, brought all to mind,
The years to come seemed waste of breath,
A waste of breath the years behind
In balance with this life, this death."

Thirteen

The next morning, I felt well enough that Audrey agreed to leave me and return home for work. I would drive back later that day. After tying up a few loose ends with Handleman, who grumbled something at us that may have been a thanks, Mr. O'Nelligan and I stopped by Nina Browley's one last time. We found her outside at a little table with Paige and Pobenski, who, I noticed sat together with their fingers intertwined.

Polecat nearly fell over himself with his apologies for hitting me. I accepted them rather graciously, I thought, considering he darn near decapitated me. Nina presented me with a wildly generous check, then walked us to my car.

"This is my last day here," she said. "I'm selling the place directly."

I nodded. "I can understand why."

"And, of course, I'll need to find another cook. Who would ever have believed ... Well, thank you both for all you've done. We did avenge Clarence, didn't we?" She spun away from us and headed back towards the house, whistling cheerfully.

"A rare creature, indeed," observed Mr. O'Nelligan.

We drove home through a light, windy drizzle, the chatter of the radio in the background as we talked.

"We never actually learned what made Browley tick," I noted. "What did his glory tables really meant to him? What did he and Nina mean to each other?"

"No, we never learned. But then, in the end, we did not need to. Let him rest with his secrets. The hearts of other men are oft a mystery."

As is yours, Mr. O'Nelligan. I wondered how the heart of this old scholar-warrior was faring in the wake of what it had just passed through. I wanted to ask at what moment he began to suspect Mrs.

Leroy. And had that moment overlapped with their playful banter? I wanted to ask, but I didn't.

Mr. O'Nelligan continued. "We were here to solve a crime, not judge a man. As he would have wanted it, Clarence Browley perished like a knight, sword in hand. Ironically, he was slain by a king's wife while defending his own castle. Still ... to each man his glory.

"Well, you certainly earned yours," I said. "I owe you everything. All our success there was because of O'Nelligan, not Plunkett."

"What are you saying, Lee?" He looked aghast. "Are you not the man who took the blow of a middleweight boxer and lived to tell? Are you not the man who put pen to paper to chronicle this case so undauntedly? Are you not the very man who dragged me from my melancholic life into this grandest of adventures? It is I, dear friend, who owe you."

To Mr. O'Nelligan's delight, a familiar voice rose again from the radio.

This time Elvis informed us that we were nothing but hound dogs. Hound dogs ... aren't they trackers? Well, then, damned if I didn't agree.

• • •

MICHAEL NETHERCOTT is a writer of mystery and supernatural tales whose work has appeared in *Alfred Hitchcock's Mystery Magazine: Crimestalkers Casebook; The Magazine of Fantasy and Science Fiction; Plays, the Drama Magazine for Young People;* the anthologies *Dead Promises, Gods and Monsters and Damned Nation;* and various other periodicals. *O'Nelligan's Glory* received the Black Orchid Novella Award, and Nethercott has written a novel featuring the O'Nelligan/ Plunkett detective team from the novella. He lives in southern Vermont with his wife, daughter, and son. Visit his website is www.michaelnethercott.com.

BETWEEN SINS

By Robert S. Levinson

"A lot of people would like to see me dead," Judge Gillian Armstrong said. "I have no interest whatsoever in satisfying their desire."

"Walter Farnum in particular."

"Currently, yes, Detective. Farnum's the latest in a long line of criminals that started forming even before I graduated from the DA's office to Superior Court, but this is the first time I'm bothered. Enough to call on our police department's new Priority Protection Squad."

"The squad's not so new anymore," Detective Jack Reno said, adding a half smile that seemed to apologize to the judge for correcting her. "It's been a year-plus and so far, so good. Haven't dropped the ball and lost a VIP yet."

"Would that statistic have the law of averages working against me?"

"Not when the law is working for you, Your Honor."

Reno watched while Judge Armstrong absorbed his latest grain of logic, her stylishly maintained fingernails tapping out a nervous melody on the highly polished redwood surface of her desk. Her ocean blue eyes wandering the office walls; periodically stopping to examine his face. Pry inside his mind. Satisfy herself that his words reflected his true feelings about the situation.

He recognized he was seeing a side of the judge that wasn't part of any public record and added to what he did know: she was among the most popular jurists occupying the bench in Los Angeles Superior Court, especially with the law-and-order crowd that routinely hailed Judge Armstrong as one tough cookie, who meted out tough justice exclusively. Prosecutors and defense attorneys understood that the only way a convicted defendant might get a break in her courtroom was to trip and fracture a bone.

"You're staring at me," she said, abruptly putting an end to her finger-tapping, pushing her chair back from the desk and adjusting herself into a more judicial pose. "Tell me, why is that, Detective."

Reno considered the consequences of an honest answer before deciding to—what the hell—give it to her; some of it, anyway. It wasn't a punishable offense. For now, don't let on he saw the frightened little girl inside the steel-plated woman.

He said, "Only confirming what I always saw and thought back two months ago when I was testifying in the Keating murder trial, Your Honor, how your pictures in the newspapers and on television, they never once did you justice." He laughed. His pun, if that's what it was, had not been intentional.

The curiosity on Judge Armstrong's face briefly crossed over into concern, her sleek eyebrows drawn together at the rise of her perfectly sculpted nose, her sensual lips pulling tight, giving greater accent to her high cheekbones, then fell into a frown, as if flattery was not the kind of testimony she encouraged.

Reno knew instinctively the judge was playacting.

He'd never known a woman who didn't appreciate a kind word, from the lowest of the street hooks pumping their wares on Sunset Boulevard, back when he was working vice with Scotty Brinkman, to his ex, especially when she got to moaning and groaning about some new wrinkle signaling to the world how she was about to turn forty, making even worse noise than that in those last weeks before Jackie Junior and then Jenny were born.

After a moment, staring at the ceiling as if it were a memory screen, Judge Armstrong said, "Yes, I'm reminded now of how you spent much of your time on the witness stand with your eyes trained on me. I admonished you several times to address your answers to the jury or the district attorney' "

"The DA wasn't as pretty as you, Your Honor." She swatted away his words. Reno grinned. "Besides, I was only returning the favor," he said. "You did your own fair share of undressing me with those big baby blues of yours."

"Your ego is misinforming you, Detective. Any looks you received from me were of absolute and utter disdain for your testimony in Keating's trial for murder. You permitted the defense to break you down on the stand and single-handedly turned a certain conviction into a not guilty verdict."

"The truth did that, not me. It was a weak case going in, strictly circumstantial. All I did was tell the truth, especially when the DA tried to steer my testimony his way. Perjury wasn't a game I was prepared to play, Judge. Would ever play."

"And because of that, the jury sent that killer back on the street to kill again, as he did last month. Is it any wonder then that I consider you and people like you disrupters of justice whom I can not dismiss from my mind and my life fast enough?"

"That and worse you said about me to the media hounds after

the trial. Yet, here I am. Here we are. So, why's that, Your Honor? You have some explaining to do, don't you think?" He aimed a finger at her. "Nice necklace by the way."

She reached up and covered the necklace's centerpiece, a carved ivory lion in repose that seemed to be using as its den the gulf between her oversized breasts, erect as pyramids inside a midnight black cashmere sweater a size too small for her athletic frame. She was in her early fifties, a decade older than him, but not to look at her now, free of the staid judicial robes that hid a sensuous woman. She smelled good, too; not any perfume she'd ever worn in court, or he would have remembered.

She seemed to welcome his lingering gaze for another moment or two, then abruptly turned her back on Reno, saying, "Any explaining I have to do I've already done, to Assistant Chief Grace, before him to the chairman of the Board of Police Commissioners, Tommy Dix. I told them about the threats on my life. Both agreed Walter Farnum was the likely source and insisted on involving the Priority Protection Squad. And you, Detective, convincing me Jack Reno was the best man to supervise my safety and well-being, so—" whirling around to face him again, motioning a finger like an arrow aimed at his heart "—here you are, Detective, over my strong personal feelings."

"And my own," he said.

She leaned forward, palms on the desk surface, using it as a pulpit while declaring in words dripping with sarcasm, "At least we have that in common, Detective."

That look in her eyes suggested to Reno it was more than that—like a spider sizing up a fly. He said, "If we're going to be hanging together for the duration, please call me 'Jack.'"

"Call me 'Judge Armstrong.' Or 'Judge.' Or 'Your Honor' … Any one of those will do, Detective Reno."

• • •

Judge Armstrong lived in Beachwood Canyon, about a mile up from Franklin Avenue, in a modest bungalow sandwiched between a lavish Craftsman cottage and another of those ultra-glitzy three-story condominiums that were sucking the history out of the hills below the HOLLYWOOD sign.

Reno's original protection blueprint called for exterior surveillance on a 24/7 basis, with a pair of uniforms on-site even when the judge was not around, guarding against unlawful entry by persons unknown in an area given to high incidents of burglaries and break-ins.

He put himself on the day shift, glued to the judge's side from the time he met her at her front door to whatever time he dropped her off and said goodnight; always discreetly out of sight but within shooting range, if it came to that.

The blueprint worked for three days, until the morning Judge Armstrong didn't answer the doorbell.

Or his hammering on the door after a couple minutes.

Or Reno calling out her name after he broke open a window and climbed inside, his calls growing from a cautious question into an anxious shout as he methodically hunted after the judge, a two-handed grip on his Glock 23, using the weapon like a divining rod.

She had to be in here somewhere, damn it.

Reno had escorted her safely into the bungalow shortly after nine last night, after she'd hoisted more than a few at a retirement party for the Honorable Thurston Hale, stepping down from the Superior Court bench after forty-seven years because he was no longer able to stay reasonably awake or control his bladder during a trial.

Judge Armstrong had imbibed one bubbly too many, or two or three or four, and was rubber-legged. No way she as going to make it past the front door without Reno's help. He propped her up, one arm around her waist, the other supporting her elbow, and guided her one careful step at a time down the central hallway to her bedroom, smiling at the discovery it was furnished and decorated like a little girl's room.

Lots of pink and powder puff blue.

Stuffed teddy bears all over the place.

Display shelves on two of the walls full of Barbie dolls and other types he could not put a name to in a variety of sizes and shapes, all elegantly costumed.

Nothing he could reconcile with the tough-minded judge he was trying to maneuver onto the floral-patterned bedspread, only—

She wasn't making the job easy.

Crooning an incoherent song, Judge Armstrong locked her hands behind Reno's neck and pulled him down. He landed on his knees alongside the bed, but her tugging brought his face close enough for her to reach his lips with hers.

"Um," she said, a kittenish purr emanating from the base of her throat. She found his tongue. A growl replaced the purr and quickly was overshadowed by a moan.

Reno realized the moan was his.

"You bit my damn lower lip," he shouted at her. "I'm tasting blood."

"Mm, yummy. Me, too," she said.

He broke free of the judge, turned and fled the room, ignoring her mush-mouth calls for him to come back, help her get ready for beddy-bye, share her goodnight prayers, tuck her in, but the name she was signaling him with sounded nothing like "Jack" or "Reno." Nowhere close. Not that it made a difference. He knew to get the hell out of there, knew better than to get caught up in her emerging demons. He was attracted to her, yeah, but years of experience had taught him never to mix business with pleasure. Not an easy lesson to learn.

The first time he did, it had cost him his marriage.

The second time, a promotion.

The time after that—

Oh, hell.

He'd take his chances.

Reno wheeled around and headed back into the bedroom.

Judge Armstrong was dead to the world.

Snoring loud enough to bring in the hogs.

He threw a blanket over her and retreated, this time for keeps, quietly inching the door shut.

Now, this morning, at the bedroom again, Reno assumed the usual cop-cautious, gun-ready approach to entering, flat against the wall to the side of the closed door. He called for her and after several seconds of silence angled around and kicked the door open. Overnight, the room had become a disaster area. The bears and the dolls were scattered. Dresser drawers had been pulled open and their contents tossed. There was a diagonal crack in the vanity table mirror, Her clothing had been moved from the closet and piled bonfire style in the middle of the room, and Judge Armstrong—

Reno discovered her after busting through the connecting door to the bathroom. She was sitting in the tub, still in the outfit she'd worn last night at the Hale retirement party, her face set in an indifferent expression that suggested neither fear nor relief.

"What the hell happened?" he said, holstering his Glock and offering her his hand.

She looked up like she was seeing him for the first time and waved him away. "You'll find a tall bottle of aspirin in the medicine cabinet," she said. "Get me three."

That was it for conversation until they were settled at the kitchen table over coffees he'd had a uniform bring in from the Beachwood Village Coffee Shop.

"You asked what happened," she said. "Middle of the night, a noise startled me awake. Not sure what had caused it, not sure where I was or how I had gotten here, only certain I was not alone. I grasped the likelihood it was one or more of Walter Farnum's killer minions come after me and somehow—" turning especially sarcastic "—had penetrated your impenetrable system for ensuring my safety. I knew better than to inspire a confrontation. I hurried to the bathroom and locked the door and strangled on my breath while hearing my bedroom being torn apart. That's what happened to me, Detective. Now you tell me what happened that made it possible for this attack on my person to happen."

"It wasn't necessarily Farnum's people, Judge Armstrong. Maybe a burglar. Wouldn't be the first burglary in this neighborhood."

"Don't go dumb-ass on me, Detective. Nobody was supposed to get inside, past your eagle-eyed Priority Protection Squad, but last night somebody did. It happened, and I don't propose allowing it to happen again. Can you take care of it or must I go over your head?"

"I don't respond well to threats, Judge Armstrong."

"A threat? I'd call it a statement of fact, Detective. Can you or must I?"

He held his temper. "Matt Rubio's my second in command, too many sharp-shooting medals to fit on his chest the same time. I'll put him outside your bedroom door nights, with my personal guarantee no one will get to you through him. Good enough, Your Honor?"

The judge didn't even think about it, her head at once dancing left and right. "No. Not good enough. This Matt Rubio can join your friends standing guard outside if he's as good as you say, day or night, I don't care which. It's you I want protecting me in here, under my roof, your trigger finger on the gun nearest me, should Farnum again come after me in the middle of the night."

Reno wondered if he was imagining the judge's expression said she wanted more than his trigger finger near her. Or was it thoughts of playing humpety-hump with her ratcheting up again, although she wasn't his type? He'd been pretty much off women since the divorce and the period immediately afterward, when he was mixing his booze and his broads in equal proportion. That was a long time ago. There hadn't been many women since, except for the occasional hook picked off the boulevard to help him confirm he could still get it up and a fling that got too serious too soon with Liza Marie, who looked and sounded a lot like his ex, what attracted him to her originally, until he realized that was all they had in common, helped her pack and went back to sharing his blues with a bottle.

"Your Honor, I don't think that's a good idea," Reno said.

"I don't recall asking for your opinion," Judge Armstrong said. "You can bunk in my home office for the duration. The sofa opens into a bed." She pointed a direction. "Through there. The office connects to my bedroom through the bathroom, keeping you seconds away from me in any emergency." Making it sound like she wouldn't mind having him closer than that. Or was it only his mind stoking his imagination again?

"Anything else I should know?"

A sly smile inched up one side of her face. "The closer you are the safer I feel, but you know that by now if you're any detective at all." She reached across the table and touched the spot on his lower lip where she had bitten him last night. "Nasty, that," she said. "Cut yourself shaving?"

• • •

Reno called in Matt Rubio to look after her while he headed home to throw together a couple changes of clothes and a Dopp kit, but that's not all he had in mind for the two or three hours he'd be gone. First on the travel agenda was a quick trip downtown to County Jail and a visit with Walter Farnum, whose cuffs, leg irons and striped orange jump suit marked him as an inmate unlikely to become a trustee while waiting out the weeks before his murder trial in Judge Armstrong's courtroom.

To look at Farnum was to see a supermarket clerk or an accountant, an impression fortified by a shy demeanor and a speaking voice that rarely climbed above a smoker's hoarse whisper. He was small of stature, maybe five-two or five-three, with a ferret-shaped face half-hidden inside a neatly trimmed salt and pepper beard, but carried a giant reputation. Reading his jacket revealed a killer-for-hire who'd murdered his way to the top of the crime syndicate running the drug, sex, and protection rackets in L.A. twenty-something years ago, before his fortieth birthday.

Nothing ever proven, however.

Dozens of court appearances and a few trials that ended in a hung jury.

The difference this time was evidence tying Farnum directly to three mob murders dating back to the early nineties. The evidence turned up out of nowhere after he reportedly tried to partner himself in for a chunk of Indian reservation gambling revenues.

He laughed when Reno raised the rumor with him in one of the jail's private meeting rooms meant for lawyers consulting with their clients, instantly comfortable with someone he remembered from their encounters in the days Reno was working vice detail.

"Heard the same thing myself, Jack, that cockamamie Injuns on the warpath story," Farnum said. "For it to be true, you'd first have to believe I had any interest in their damn casinos. Not so, any more than it's true I was behind those old hits I'm now accused of, on Big Sid, Polish Joe, or Artie G."

"Not how the DA is reading the evidence he'll be presenting to a jury, Walter."

"When and if it ever gets that far, Jack. I have a streak going, or don't you remember?"

"This third time might be the charm for the DA."

"Don't bet on it, my friend. A lot can happen between now and whenever."

"As long as it doesn't happen to Judge Armstrong, Walter."

Farnum's easy smile dropped off his face. "Judge Armstrong, huh? I was wondering why this sudden interest, what brought you over here."

"Seems someone got by my Priority Protection Squad guys last night, broke into her home bent on killing her. Made a real mess of the place, but she managed to turn hiding into an art form."

"And I'm the designated big bad wolf."

"You're the one who threatened her with bodily harm after she denied your lawyer's bail motion."

"Like I ever thought it would be granted? Give me a friggin' break, Jack. When have you ever known me not to shoot off threats in the courtroom? You've seen it happen before. It's me blowing off steam, plain and simple."

"I'm thinking about some other judges you've crossed swords with in the past. Broken kneecaps for two or three of them. One lucky to escape a car bomb. A sniper's bullet that put another judge in the hospital in critical condition and hanging on by a heartbeat … How do you explain any of that?"

"Coincidence? Life's funny that way."

"I don't want it to be funny for Judge Armstrong, Walter."

Farnum thought about it. His smile eased back. "I liked seeing how I made her shake and bake in her courtroom, given the holier-than-thou act she's always put on, even when she was just starting out in the DA's office, making her reputation on more than her good looks. A saint she ain't, my friend. A saint she ain't."

"A saint she ain't. What's that supposed to mean?"

Farnum shrugged. "Just making small talk."

"Why do I sense it's more than that?"

"You're a cop, why else? The last cop who ever believed me, I was five years old and swiping apples and oranges off old man Bernstein's pushcarts in the Heights. No, Mr. Officer, sir, they fell off Mr. Bernstein's cart and I was picking them up from the street for him. You nosey enough, put it to the judge. Six'll get you sixty if she doesn't tell you the same. Small talk, Jack. Just making small talk."

• • •

Reno caught up with Judge Armstrong at the courthouse and watched her mete out her usual brand of hard-nosed jurisprudence as if last night's supposed attack on her life had never happened, except for the several times here eyes sought him out and seemed to offer appreciation for his protective presence. She turned his estimate into action later, after they were back at her place, and by morning she had him calling her "Gilly-girl," and he was the judge's "Jackie-boy."

It was a seduction that began with calculated subtlety, the judge cooing over the bottle of Château Latour she served with a meal she'd pulled together like a French chef overseeing a three-star Michelin restaurant—a perfectly cooked steak, sculpted fries, baby asparagus in a rich cream sauce, a mixed green salad, a vanilla custard topped with a caramel sauce to die for—expounding on the history of the wines like she was reciting legal precedents.

He was a beer can kind of guy, but every swallow tasted like he was robbing the U.S. Mint, and Reno didn't resist when she proffered a second bottle, then another.

Judge Armstrong matched him glass for glass, often pushing up from her chair to toast him for making her feel safe from harm, increasingly with an outsized gesture that dramatized her voluptuousness, always held in suspended animation until she was certain he had noticed.

Halfway through the third bottle, her words lost their sheen, tumbling beyond comprehension one into the next, her mushmouth English as undecipherable as the French expressions she'd been dropping all over the dining room table during the meal.

When the judge rose this time, it was to take a long swallow from the bottle and sing to the beamed ceiling, "Adieu, mon cher. Beddy-bye time." Hugging the bottle to her bosom, she twirled around and marched an unsteady line out of the room.

In that moment Reno found her curiously endearing.

She was human after all, he decided, or—

—was it his own one too many?

Reno cleared the table, helped himself to a brew from a half-gone six-pack in the fridge and headed for the home office she had designated as his bedroom, a mirror to the judge's professional life. Along with her desk and filing cabinets, there were shelves heavy with law books and orderly stacks of legal-size manila folders encased in blue plastic.

The walls were loaded with meticulously arranged framed diplomas, certificates of appreciation, commendation and awards citations; photographs that cataloged her years in law school, the district attorney's office and superior court, often paired with recognizable faces from the worlds of politics, show business and big business, tracking her as she aged with an angel's grace, growing increasingly attractive with the passage of time.

One color photo gave Reno pause, a young Gillian Armstrong on a boat deck, wearing a string bikini that left little to the imagination and a smile as broad as the sky. With her were a similarly clad young woman of exceptional dimensions and an older guy sporting a mop-top hairpiece that made him look more like Moe of the Three Stooges than one of the Beatles. He stood between them, wearing swim trunks disguised as a jock strap, arms around their waists and pulling them nearer to him while they toasted the camera lens with their martini glasses.

Although the photo was a bit blurred, maybe caused by shifting waters as the shutter snapped, something familiar about the guy made Reno move in for closer study. After a few minutes, he had mentally subtracted the mop-top, added a beard to the ferret-shaped face, and had convinced himself he was looking an early edition of Walter Farnum.

What was it Farnum had said about a holier-than-thou act when she was starting out in the DA's office and making her rep on more than her good looks?

A saint she ain't, Farnum had said.

Was the photo evidence to his declaration?

If so—

—would the judge give it this kind of display if there were something, anything about it that could ever come back to bite her on her well-toned ass, or—

—did the photo hold some other significance?

Reno tossed the beer can in the round file for two points and headed for the bathroom and the shower, where he always did some of his best thinking. He was working the questions when the stall door clicked open behind him. He turned and confirmed he'd been joined by the judge. She let him study her nakedness long enough for him to appreciate—it was as appetizing as the gourmet meal she'd made for them tonight—then took the bar of soap from him, ran her arms behind him and began a gentle scrubbing across his shoulder blades and up and down his spine.

"Tell me, Detective, you have anything against older women?" she said, not sounding as drunk as she had made herself out to be earlier.

"Not until now, Your Honor."

"Yes, your Gilly-girl can tell," she said.

• • •

A week passed before Reno put the question to her.

By now, he was sharing her bed on a nightly basis, the sex fantastic, ranging from the missionary sweetness he preferred to the roughhouse madness where she shouted commands and demands that by morning left him a jungle of aches, bruises, bites, and claw marks.

He freed himself from her wrestler's grip, rolled into a sitting position on the edge of the bed and, rubbing his arm where she'd last imprinted her teeth, said, "Do you plan to ever tell me the whole story about you and Walter Farnum?"

"Come back to bed," she said, tugging at his shoulder. "I'm not through yet with my Jackie-boy." He shrugged her off, answered her growl and hiss with silence. "You know all there is to know," she said. "Walter Farnum is why you're here protecting me, damn it. Come on back. I need more of your protecting."

"I don't know about the photo in your office."

"There are many photographs in my office."

"The one on the boat. You and some other gal and Farnum. I don't know about that photograph. It is Farnum under that stupid hairpiece, right?"

She sighed, pushed herself into a sitting position, reached for a teddy bear, and hugged it to her chest. "Do you know what I would give to have that marvelous bikini body again?" Reno didn't answer. She feigned a pout. "You're supposed to tell me I'm doing just fine with the body I have now."

She was.

Oh, was she ever.

But that's not why Reno had fallen for this damned overbearing boss of a woman he was certain was playing him for reasons he was yet to figure. He didn't know why, only that he had. Maybe because love is blind? Also deaf? And dumb? And so what?

What he did know: He was desperate to hear the truth about Gilly and Walter Farnum. The whole truth and nothing but.

Why?

Jealousy, maybe?

Jealousy, definitely.

And something else.

He turned and answered her impatient eyes, saying, "I hear tell you're no saint, Your Honor."

"Who told you that?"

"Walter Farnum. When I visited him in County Jail."

"You visited him in County Jail?"

"Put him on notice about you. A saint she ain't, that's what he said. His exact words."

She thought about it. "Between sins, I am. Everybody is. Even you, Jackie-boy."

"Even Walter Farnum?"

She flashed him a melancholy smile. "What else did he have to say about me?" Reno shook his head. "All right then, it's time for you to know the rest anyway. The photograph. I could have taken it down, hidden it in a drawer, but I left it on the wall because I wanted you to discover it. I was certain you'd recognize him, Walter. I needed you to challenge me about him, knowing I could never volunteer the story behind the picture because of where it might lead."

"That being?"

She eluded his stare, focusing her attention on the teddy bear, finger-combing its plush brown synthetic fur for several moments before attacking his eyes again and asking, "Are you sure you want to know?" Reno motioned for her to continue. "First come on back into Mama's arms, Jackie-boy. Then we'll talk." Her smile fired the room.

Reno said, "First we talk, then we fuck."

"Ooh, I love it when you talk dirty," she said, licking her lips.

• • •

Gilly made the bedroom a courtroom, the bed her witness stand, calmly giving quiet, well-articulated testimony to a jury of one, him, her memory pitch perfect on a train of events going back to when she was a freshman jockeying for position and prominence in the district attorney's office.

"The other girl in the picture, Kim, was my best friend from high school, and we were sharing an apartment in the mid-Wilshire district," she said. "Kim was your typical struggling actress, who had me believing she earned her share of the rent working as a waitress, when in fact it was with the tip money from her job pole dancing at a strip joint in the Marina. That's where Walter Farnum scored her, passing himself off as somebody who could help further her career. A few weeks into the relationship, she mentioned her gorgeous roomie worked for the DA, and Walter suggested we both join him for a day's outing on his yacht."

"The day the photograph was taken."

"Taken while it was still all sunshine and smiles, before the three of us got drunk, got high on quality grass and Colombian and Lord knows what else, got down and dirty, and—I passed out. Kim screaming startled me awake. She slapped Walter across the face, once, then again, before she turned and stumbled up the stairs and out of the bedroom suite. He chased after her, calling her a two-bit whore, worse, saying Kim had to be punished—he would show her—for daring to lay a hand on him. I was frightened out of my wits for her. I managed onto my feet and struggled upstairs after them, and—"

Gilly's voice failed her.

Her eyes moistened, then froze on empty space.

"It's okay, take your time," Reno said. He reached over and stroked her check, allowed her to capture his hand long enough to plant kisses on his knuckles.

Finally, she began again, "When I reached the deck, only Walter was there. No sign of Kim. Not then, not ever again. Walter propped my chin between his thumb and forefinger and told me in a voice as murderous as the act itself, 'not one word about today to anybody, like it never happened. You don't know me. I don't know you. Tell me you understand. Do you? Do you understand?'" Her labored breathing evolved into a whine as she grabbed after Reno and showered his back with her tears, confessing, "I understood, yes. Nothing was going to bring Kim back, but I could stay alive by keeping my mouth shut about what had happened on the yacht. I suppose it's what made me so tough as a judge, the need to make up for the biggest crime of all, my own sin in not going to the police."

"You never thought about blowing the whistle on Farnum?"

"Of course. For days and weeks. Often. Even after I'd learned who and what Walter Farnum really was, a killer without a conscience. Even after one of his minions delivered the photograph to me in that expensive sterling silver frame, telling me it was a gift from Walter, a reminder that silence was golden and to keep on doing the smart thing. The smart thing …" Her voice had sunk to a sad whisper.

"Yet here you are spilling your guts," Reno said. "Why? Why now, when you could have hidden the photograph instead of dragging it out for me to notice?"

"Because I'm tired of living the lie, Jack. When Walter showed up as a defendant in my courtroom, my first thought was to recuse myself, take myself out of harm's way, but the way he seemed to mock me with his every expression, his eyes daring me to do anything that upset him or worked against his favor, it was enough. It was too much. I denied his lawyer's motion for dismissal and motions to suppress evidence. I denied his lawyer's motion for bail. Walter exploded and made his open threats on my life. The rest you know. Why you're here. The one good thing to come of this so far. You and me, Jackie-boy." She reached for Reno, sandpaper noises like a bitch in heat rising from the base of her throat. Toyed with his chest hair, saying, "You're everything I suspected the first time I set eyes on you in my courtroom."

"And what was that?" Her hands were on the move and driving him nuts.

"You don't know by now, you're not as smart as I gave you credit for being. Help me, Jackie-boy? Help your Gilly-girl get Walter Farnum out of our life forever?"

"Forever? How?"

"You tell me, lover. I know you'll figure out something, but first—I'm desperate for you to satisfy something else."

● ● ●

Sunrise was illuminating the bedroom curtains when Reno pulled her closer to him, pampered her awake, and whispered, "I need you to put Farnum back on the street, Gilly-girl."

She unlocked herself from his arms, scrambled out of bed and toured the room panic-stricken by the idea, demanding reasons he wasn't anxious to share with her.

He said, "You want him out of your life forever, that's what I need you to do if my plan's going to work. Let it go at that."

"Plan? What plan? Turn that animal free and make it easier for him to come after me? Is that your plan?"

"You're better off not knowing."

"Why do I have to go on faith alone?"

"And love," he said. "Faith and love. Beyond that, you don't want to know. Trust me on this."

She drained the room of air and pushed it back in.

"With my life," she said, making it a declaration.

"As I trust you with mine," he said, matching her sincerity.

"But can either of us trust Walter Farnum?"

"It won't make any difference," Reno said, and told her as much as she had to know.

Farnum was out on bail three days later, based on what Judge Armstrong explained was a reevaluation of his lawyer's request once Farnum apologized in court for his malicious earlier outburst, which he did with all the sincerity of a snake. In fact, she had taken direction from Reno, whose idea it also was to set Farnum's bail high enough—a cool million dollars—to reinforce her reputation as a no-nonsense judge from the School of Guilty Until Proven Innocent.

Next, with the judge's nervous approval, Reno called off the Priority Protection Squad and spirited her away for a lust-satisfying weekend at the Hotel Del Coronado in San Diego, where they tracked after landmarks left behind by Marilyn Monroe when she filmed *Some Like it Hot* there when they weren't creating their own heat in an oceanfront suite.

• • •

Farnum was settled in her den watching a Laker game when they returned from San Diego. "Good evening!" he called to them, clicking off the set. "Expected you here an hour ago, Jack. Was beginning to get worried."

"Traffic, Walter. Murder on any Sunday."

"Murder on any Sunday, the man says. Good one, Jack. Good one. Hey, Judge, how they hanging?"

The judge broke away from Reno's hold around her waist. "You knew he was going to be here? What's going on, Jack?" Her voice was demanding, but her eyes betrayed her alarm.

Reno sent Farnum a hand gesture that invited him to speak.

"Come to set the record straight now that I'm breathing free air again and there's none of Jack's buddies in blue blocking the way," Farnum said.

Her eyes narrowed, causing a series of ridges and furrows to form across her forehead, eyeing Jack as she put the question to both of them. "The record straight?"

"The way you said what happened that time to your girlfriend, Kim, not like that at all, sweetheart." Farnum tucked himself into a corner of the sofa, hands in a schoolboy lock on his lap, and flicked a smile at the judge. "You were my girl back then, from the night we ignited at that strip joint where you hustled for bikini bucks all through your turning high-end tricks for me with selected VIPs who could, incidentally, further your daytime gig with the DA You brought Kim onto the yacht for a road test by me, but she balked when she figured out what I had in mind for her future and scrammed topside. You took it personally. Chased after her screaming and threatening. I dragged my drugged-out sorry ass after you, got there in time to see you give Kim a slap and a shove that sailed her over the railing and into the drink, where we left her to drown, locked into the fog halfway to Catalina."

"No, Jack, no. The bastard is lying. It was him," she said, spitting out the words like a personal declaration of innocence.

Farnum pitched his eyes to the ceiling. "I owned her after that, y'know? She did favors for me, I did favors for her. Her favors worked for me and any member of my crew whenever they stepped in it. When she decided she wanted to be a judge, I helped out there, too, money and cashing in on favors owed me by certain people who know how to swing an election. We could have gone on like this forever, except for the stupid thing she did in court, refusing me bail, leaving me no choice but to make good on my threat. Anything else and my guys would see it as a sign of weakness and maybe get some nasty ideas of their own, y'know? Ambition trumps loyalty every time."

"Not true, Jack. Not any of it," she said, as if delivering a verdict from the bench.

Reno held out a palm to quiet her. "Tell Judge Armstrong the rest, Walter."

Farnum smiled agreeably. He got up from the sofa, adjusted his camel's hair sports coat and strutted across the room like a bantam cock who owned the barnyard. Settled on a stool at the bar counter and threw open his arms. "Here's the rest of the deal your boy toy cooked up for us the last time he came calling on me, Gilly-girl. Our next court date, my shyster moves that all the charges against me get tossed. You go into your usual holier-than-thou dance, then grant the motion. I walk out a free man and you can quit looking over your shoulder. I'm out of your life for good, and it's happily ever after time for you and Jack here, y'know?"

Gilly stopped patrolling the den and sank into an armchair.

What color hadn't drained from her face when she first saw Farnum was gone now.

She picked at her nails, scraped off polish while buried in thought.

After two or three minutes, she said, "And if I refuse?"

Farnum smiled. "Just like a lawyer, right, Gilly-girl? Don't ever ask a question where you don't already know the answer." He withdrew a .38 caliber automatic from the shoulder holster under his jacket and held it up for inspection. "Our deal goes south—I gotta keep my crew's respect, y'know what I mean?"

"Jack, you'd let that happen?"

His eyes roamed between the two of them and settled on her. "Walter called you Gilly-girl."

"What?"

"Twice," Reno said. "He called you Gilly-girl, and I know first-hand what that means. It means him … you … him and you. It means he, not you, was talking truth about you and how Kim died, Your Honor. What other lies did you feed me after you steered me into falling hard for you, steered me into believing you were in love with me, steered me to the idea of getting Walter out of your life forever, you said, but killing him is what you really meant?"

She averted his hard stare and searched the room indiscriminately, nervously pushing back her hair and exposing gray roots under the bottle red, the sweat beads lining her forehead toning the scent of her perfume with fear. "Leading you to fall for me, maybe it was my idea at first, Jack, and about Walter, but—"

Farnum cackled. "I told you she was some piece of work, Jack."

They were his last words before Reno marched at him demanding, "Oh, shut up, damn you," firing the Glock he had pulled from his belt holster.

The bullet caught Farnum in the chest, flung him backward into the bar counter, arms flailing madly, then forward onto the floor face down.

Reno twisted around and straight-armed the Glock at the judge.

This time she answered his eyes with a look that begged understanding.

"I did fall in love with you, Jack. I do love you. Please. I need you to believe that, no matter what else. So help me God."

"God help me, even if I wanted to, it's too late for me to believe anything else," Reno said, lowering his weapon.

Her shoulders relaxed. She smiled approvingly. "I recognize now what you did, your plan … You needed Farnum out on bail so you could get him here on some pretext, kill him in a way that made it look like you got him before he could make good his courtroom threat and shoot me, am I right, Detective Reno of the Priority Protection Squad?"

"He's dead. You're not. He's where you wanted him, out of your life forever."

She embraced Reno, smothered his mouth with a lingering kiss that promised more and better to come and stepped over to Farnum. She kneeled and tested his neck for a pulse, as if the pool of blood inching out from under him wasn't proof enough Farnum was dead.

She said, "Two problems, Jack." Her declaration caught Reno off guard. "First, as an officer of the court and a strict advocate of law-and-order, I would be uncomfortable knowing I let you get away with murder."

"Very funny," he said, tossing off a laugh.

"Second, I have a problem with you knowing about Kim and me, something you might decide one day to hold over my head the way Walter did."

"You're not joking, are you?"

"I'm not," she said, rising, revealing her hold on Farnum's .38. She said, "Thank you and goodbye, Jackie-boy," and got off two quick shots before he could raise the Glock again. Her first shot caught Reno in the neck, the second in the chest.

He fought to sustain the light, watching Gilly catch her breath, bent forward with her hands on her knees, like a runner after a race. She looked down at him, nodded satisfaction, then nonchalantly fixed Farnum's .38 back in his grip, found her handbag and dug out her cell phone. She was saying, "Yes, this is an emergency," as her voice blurred and the smell of her perfume evaporated and Reno stopped hurting so much.

• • •

ROBERT S. LEVINSON is making his sixth consecutive appearance in a "year's best" mystery anthology. He is the bestselling author of eight novels, *The Traitor in Us All, In the Key of Death, Where the Lies Begin, Ask a Dead Man, Hot Paint, The James Dean Affair, The John Lennon Affair*, and *The Elvis and Marilyn Affair*, with his ninth, *A Rhumba in Waltz Time*, scheduled for publication in 2011. Bob is a regular contributor to *Alfred Hitchcock Mystery Magazine* and *Ellery Queen Mystery Magazine*, whose readers cited him in the annual EQMM Award poll three years running. His short story in Hitchcock, "*The Quick Brown Fox*," was a Derringer Award winner. He wrote, produced and emceed three Mystery Writers of American Edgar Awards shows, as well as two International Thriller Writers Thriller Awards shows. His website is www.robertslevinson.com.

ABOUT THE EDITORS

ED GORMAN has been called "one of suspense fiction's best story-tellers" by *Ellery Queen's Mystery Magazine*, and "one of the most original voices in today's crime fiction" by the *San Diego Union*. He's been published in many magazines, including *Redbook, Ellery Queen's Mystery Magazine, The Magazine of Fantasy & Science Fiction*, and *Poetry Today*. He has won numerous prizes for his work, including the Shamus, the Spur, and the International Fiction Writer's awards, as well as being nominated for the Edgar, Anthony, Golden Dagger, and Stoker awards. His work has been featured by the Literary Guild, the Mystery Guild, the Doubleday Book Club, and the Science Fiction Book Club. He lives with his wife, author Carol Gorman, in Cedar Rapids, Iowa.

MARTIN H. GREENBERG is the CEP of Tekno Books and its predecessor companies, now the largest book developer of commercial fiction and nonfiction in the world, with over 2,300 published books that have been translated into thirty-three languages. He is the recipient of an unprecedented three Lifetime Achievement awards in the Science Fiction, Mystery, and Supernatural Horror genres—the Milford Award in Science Fiction, the Bram Stoker award in Horror, and the Ellery Queen Award in Mystery—the only person in publishing history to have received all three awards.